Lady of Monza

The Scandalous True Story of the Nun of Monza
A Forbidden Convent Affair and the Murders That Followed

Copyright

History and Women Press
Lady of Monza
First Edition

http://www.mirellapatzer.com

This is a publication of History and Women Press
http://www.historyandwomen.com
http://www.mirellapatzer.com

This is a work of fiction inspired by the life of a noblewoman during the renaissance. I have endeavored to include the facts as accurately as possible. However, the passing of the centuries makes total accuracy impossible to achieve therefore this should not be read as a factual account.

Also by Mirella Patzer

The Emerald Conspiracy

The Prophetic Queen

Her Secret Legacy

Black Petals

Orphan of the Olive Tree

The Novice

About the Book

Italy, 1590. Behind the iron gates of the Convent of Santa Margherita, Virginia Maria de Leyva—daughter of Spanish nobility, cloistered against her will—is not praying.

When Gian Paolo Osio scales the convent wall in darkness, their forbidden affair ignites a chain of sins that will scandalize Renaissance Italy: passion, betrayal, murder. As ecclesiastical corruption festers and bodies disappear into unmarked graves, Virginia becomes both conspirator and victim in a web of deception that threatens to destroy everyone she has ever trusted.

But when the Cardinal's inquisitors arrive, Virginia must decide: confess the truth and face immurement, or blame sorcery and witchcraft for desires she chose freely.

Based on the true 17th-century scandal that inspired Manzoni's *The Betrothed*, this biographical historical fiction unveils the untold story of the Nun of Monza—a woman who defied her vows, murdered to protect her secrets, and paid the ultimate price for choosing love over salvation.

Dedication

For Judy Walters whose quiet strength and unshakable kindness carried me through the storm.

For Debbie Middleton-Hope who never let me walk alone when the path grew uncertain.

Canonical Hours

Vigil and Matins
2:00 to 3:00 a.m.

Lauds
5:00 a.m. to Dawn

Prime
6:00 a.m. to Sunrise

Terce
9:00 a.m. to Mid-morning

Sext
12:00 p.m. to Noon

None
3:00 p.m. to Mid-afternoon

Vespers
6:00 p.m. to Sunset

Compline
7:00 p.m. to 8:00 p.m.
Before bed

Church bells are tolled at the fixed times at these canonical hours

Chapter One
1589

The 25th of March
City of Monza

HE HAS ALREADY buried me.

The carriage jolted over Milan's cobblestones, each rut jarring through Marianna's spine. Her palazzo home receded with each turn of the wheels. The cathedral spires, the market square where merchants had once bowed, all of it fell away, the distance stretching like years.

Her father, Don Martino de Leyva, Count of Monza, sat across from her, face as impassive as the convent walls awaiting her. The money she had inherited from her mother, seized for his debts and Spanish ambitions, was nearly spent. Only enough remained for the convent dowry. Since they had departed, he had not spoken once. At thirteen, she would vanish behind the convent enclosure. Last month she had knelt at his feet in their palazzo library and begged. He had stepped around her as though she was furniture.

The carriage turned toward open countryside. Her fingers pressed against the door latch. Cold metal bit into her palm. She could run. Now.

"Sit still." Don Martino's voice cut like a blade.

Her hand dropped to her lap. He was the Count of Monza. Every soul in this province answered to him. There was nowhere to run.

Soon, the high walls of Santa Margherita appeared ahead, gray limestone stained with winter ivy. Their driver reined the horses to a stop in front of the iron gates, stepped down, and pulled the bell rope. The small bell tolled, each ring reverberating through Marianna's bones.

A nun appeared from inside the convent. Bright blue eyes peered out from beneath a white wimple, a nun in her forties with a tentative smile. "Who seeks entrance into the House of God?"

"The Most Illustrious Count of Monza and his daughter, Donna Marianna de Leyva."

"I am Sister Costanza, the portress. Our Reverend Prioress awaits you. Enter in peace."

The gates swung open. Don Martino stepped down, the hilt of his jeweled sword catching sunlight. Marianna followed, legs unsteady.

Stone walls rose around them, centuries pressed into mortar and limestone. The air smelled of damp earth and old prayers.

Sister Costanza led them to the parlatory, its vaulted ceiling shadowed by age-darkened beams. Beeswax and wilting flowers scented the chamber. Beyond the black iron lattice bisecting the room, nuns knelt in prayer in the chapel, their whispered Latin a soft hum.

"Please, be seated." Sister Costanza gestured to a bench before disappearing.

Marianna perched on the dense wood, hands clenched upon her embroidered silk gown. Don Martino paced beside her, hand on his sword hilt. The convent's wealth would now include what remained of her inheritance. She was a pawn in this transaction. Nothing more.

The Prioress emerged across the grille, austere features holding intelligence and authority. The silver cross and brass keys at her belt clinked softly.

"I am Reverend Mother Imbersaga. You are most welcome here." Her voice filled the chamber. She inclined her head to Don Martino with the exact deference his rank commanded, then her gaze moved to Marianna, cataloguing silk, embroidery, jewels. Nothing escaped that inspection.

"Don Martino de Leyva, Count of Monza. I present my daughter, Donna Marianna, as postulant to your holy order."

"She has reached the required age of twelve years?"

"Thirteen, Reverend Mother. She turns fourteen this December."

"And does Donna Marianna come of her own free will, without coercion?"

The question struck like icy water against bare skin. No one had asked what she wanted. Her father had decided, as he decided all things.

The Prioress's eyes bored into hers through the grille, demanding truth. *Tell her. Tell her he forces you.*

Don Martino's hand tightened on his sword hilt. Leather creaked.

Marianna's pulse drummed at her wrists, her throat.

Behind the grille, the whispered prayers stopped.

She dragged in a breath that scraped her lungs.

Her father's shadow fell across her shoulders.

"Yes, Reverend Mother." Each syllable tore itself free. "It is my dearest wish to dedicate myself to Christ as a nun of Santa Margherita." The lie coated her tongue like ash.

The Prioress studied her. A long breath escaped through the older woman's nostrils, her mouth tightening. "Provided the dowry arrangements are satisfactory, we would be honored to accept such a well-born postulant."

Don Martino produced a rolled parchment. The wax seal cracked. "Six thousand imperial lire held by my agent Giuseppe Molteno, dispensed upon her solemn profession. Two hundred twelve lire per annum until then, three hundred after perpetual vows. All notarized."

Her future, sold for silver and parchment.

Reverend Mother Imbersaga examined the document with a merchant's eye. "All appears in order." She handed it to Sister Costanza. "Have the procurator file this with the accounts."

Don Martino turned to Marianna, eyes flat and distant as winter sky. "Comport yourself with dignity. Bring honor to our name." His breath smelled of wine. "This is your life now. Embrace it, for you shall have no other."

No warmth. No affection.

"Farewell, daughter." He pivoted and strode from the parlatory without a backward glance. The door thudded shut.

The sound pressed against Marianna's ribs, final as a tomb sealing. She sat rigid. The air pressed heavy against her ribs.

"Approach, my daughter." The Prioress's voice softened.

Marianna forced herself forward on trembling legs until she stood at the iron lattice.

The Prioress's eyes were deep brown, flecked with gold. Age lined the woman's face, furrows at mouth and brow, loose skin at the jaw, but intelligence burned beneath.

"Tell me truthfully, Marianna. Do you wish to take religious vows? You may speak freely here."

The gentleness nearly undid her. Marianna gripped the rough grille, rust staining her fingers. "I am here by my father's command, not my own will. He means to be rid of me."

"I suspected as much." The furrows deepened. "Many girls arrive in similar circumstances. You are very young to face such a fate."

"I pleaded with him. To send me to our villa or my aunt in Pavia. He refused. Is there no other way?"

"No. With your arrival, his purpose cannot be altered. You stand within the enclosure now. The contract is signed."

The last thread of hope snapped.

The Prioress reached through the lattice to clasp her hand, dry skin, callused palms, surprising warmth. "I will not lie. The path ahead is not easy. But within these walls, no man will control your fate. You need never suffer an unwanted marriage or childbirth's dangers. We will teach you Latin, rhetoric, mathematics, natural philosophy; subjects most women never explore."

"My education would not end?"

"Quite the contrary. It begins in earnest here. With diligence, you could become a scholar, a teacher, perhaps rise to authority, as I did."

"You were sent here against your will?"

"I was. And I will not pretend it was not painful. But I discovered fulfillment in service to God and our community. In time, you may as well."

"I will try." Marianna lifted her chin, though it trembled.

"Sister Costanza has prepared a cell for you. Tomorrow you will be clothed in the postulant's habit and begin your journey with us."

Sister Costanza reappeared. "Come, Marianna."

Marianna dropped into a deep curtsy. "Thank you, Reverend Mother."

"Go in Christ's peace. Tomorrow, we begin again." The door closed behind her, iron meeting iron, the sound reverberating in her chest.

They climbed a narrow staircase, its steps worn concave from generations of feet. Through high windows, the cloister garden stretched below, vaulted arches, herb beds laid out in geometric precision, the tranquil courtyard denied her in the outer world. Only now, having surrendered everything, could she enter.

Sister Costanza paused outside a door. "Your cell."

Inside was a narrow bed with linen coverlet, a prie-dieu bearing a silver crucifix, a plain writing table with quill and inkpot, and an empty wardrobe. On the bed lay a pile of coarse black wool. "Your first habit, to wear until the Investiture Ceremony."

Marianna touched the rough fabric, so different from silk and velvet. This would clothe her now. This and nothing else.

"I can manage. Thank you, Sister."

Sister Costanza hesitated. "I know how difficult this is. My own entry was not so different. But you will find kindness here. Purpose. In time, even joy."

"I pray you are right."

"Rest. I will return to guide you to Vespers." She closed the door softly.

Silence rushed in. Marianna turned slowly, taking in the room that would frame her life. The bed for sleep and tears. The table where she would pour out her heart. The window connecting her to a world both lost and unknown. She crossed to the narrow casement. Beyond the walls, past bare trees, the gray ribbon of road wound back toward Milan. Back to her palazzo. Back to the only home she had known. But I am still Marianna de Leyva. Daughter of the Count of Monza. Whatever becomes of me, that remains.

A door slammed below. Voices rose, low, urgent. A woman's voice in protest or command before cutting off abruptly. Footsteps hurried past in the corridor, rapid and uneven, then faded.

Marianna turned from the window. Tomorrow, she would put on the rough wool habit. Tomorrow she would become someone else. But tonight, alone with strange voices echoing through stone walls, she remained herself. Still Marianna.

Still afraid. And something in this place, beyond the Prioress's gentle words and Sister Costanza's kind smiles, stirred like a current beneath still water. Something she could not yet name but already sensed would change everything.

* * *

The 26th of March

DAWN'S LIGHT STRETCHED across the stone floor. Marianna had passed her first night listening to unfamiliar sounds; timber settling, distant footsteps, whispered prayers. She stood at the window. A young woman emerged from the baker's shop across the street, turned left toward the market. A simple choice that would never again be hers.

Behind her, the oak door opened. Reverend Mother Imbersaga entered, a sealed letter bearing her father's crest in her hands, its wax already broken. "Your transformation begins now, child."

The Prioress unfolded the letter. Parchment crackled between her fingers. "Your father provided detailed instructions regarding your spiritual development."

Marianna's fingers curled against the window glass, cool and unyielding. "What manner of instructions?"

The Prioress's eyes moved down the document. The lines around her mouth deepened. "Your maintenance allowance, the funds for meals beyond basic provisions, warmer clothing, writing materials, candles, may be suspended at his or my discretion."

She set the letter down with deliberate care. "Your father believes simplicity of circumstance encourages spiritual focus."

Starvation cloaked in prayer.

"Additionally, should reports reach him of inappropriate curiosity about convent affairs, questioning of authority, or unsuitable associations, you are to be moved to the penitential cells for solitary prayer. Your father considers isolation essential for correcting prideful tendencies."

The punishment cells.

"Furthermore, any correspondence between you and family members will pass through my review. Don Martino wishes to monitor your spiritual progress. Letters expressing discontent will not be dispatched."

Even her thoughts would be censored.

"These methods trouble me greatly." The Prioress folded the documents, movements sharp and precise. "Understanding and guidance serve better than restrictions. But a father's authority cannot be questioned, and your family's position..." She let the words hang in the stale air. The de Leyva name carried too much influence to defy.

"I pray such measures will prove unnecessary. Perhaps you will find in your new companions the peace your father believes you lack."

She moved to the bundle of fabric Sister Costanza had left the day before. "Now we must complete your transformation."

Marianna shed her silk night rail. The rough wool habit scraped against her skin when she pulled it over her head. Coarse fibers against her skin. This texture would become as familiar as her father's threats. A plain white cap concealed her dark hair, pressing against her temples.

The Prioress nodded once. "Now you appear as a postulant, as you will remain until your investiture. Let me take you to your assigned cell. This chamber was only temporary."

Through narrow corridors they walked in silence, their footsteps echoing against stone. Up winding stairs where the air grew colder. At a heavy oak door, the Prioress paused. "Two other postulants share this chamber." Her pale eyes met Marianna's. "Your father trusts their example will provide encouragement. I pray you will find in them the sisters you need, rather than the observers he expects."

The Prioress turned the latch. Metal scraped against metal. The first young woman bounded forward.

"Welcome! I'm Caterina Ricci!" Her voice carried musical joy undercut by a tremor. "What blessed happiness, another soul called to serve Our Lord!" But her hands twisted together, knuckles white, her smile stretched too wide. This girl grasped the cost of her vows even as she dressed them in devotion.

The second stood with rigid posture. Sharp features, high cheekbones, eyes that assessed everything and offered nothing. "Giulia Homati. May God grant you wisdom in your new vocation." The words carried formal courtesy without warmth.

Marianna's fingers stilled on her sleeve. "Homati? Your family holds lands in Borgo San Donnino."

A flicker passed across Giulia's controlled expression. "Yes. I am of that family. Or should I say, was."

The words acknowledged everything while admitting nothing.

"But isn't it wonderful?" Caterina clasped her hands to her chest. "To dedicate our entire lives to prayer and contemplation."

Wonderful. A bitter retort rose in Marianna's throat, but she caught Giulia's gaze, cool and appraising. A test. Marianna swallowed the truth. "It is... a great deal to comprehend."

"Being worthy comes from following the Holy Rule every day," Giulia said, each word measured and precise. Her dark eyes lingered on Marianna's face. "Daily discipline helps the soul become devoted."

Every conversation in this chamber would be a test. Every admission potentially reported.

The hours stretched into afternoon, then evening. Nuns delivered their midday meal in the refectory where sunlight slanted through high windows—thin vegetable broth, dense gray bread, water tasting of iron. The air smelled of boiled turnips and tallow candles. They ate in silence, spoons scraping against wooden bowls.

Afterward, Caterina chattered about saints' lives while mending, her needle darting with frantic energy. Giulia read from a prayer book, posture rigid as a post. Shadows lengthened across the floor. Marianna's fingers worked thread through cloth, the repetitive motion steadying her breathing.

When the bell signaled Compline, Marianna knelt with the others in the chapel. Latin prayers rose and fell around her. Smoke from the candles stung her eyes, and incense hung thick in the chapel air.

As she lay in bed, through the walls came soft footsteps in corridors that should be empty. Whispered voices too low to understand. This was the Great Silence when no one was to move without grave cause.

"Should there be movement at this hour?"

Giulia's spine straightened. "Be silent. A sick sister is being tended to."

But her eyes showed no concern. Only watchfulness, calculation.

Marianna's fingers tightened on her rosary beads, the wood pressing into her palm. If the Prioress learned she'd noticed irregular activities, would that constitute 'inappropriate curiosity' worthy of punishment? "Of course."

Caterina's shoulders dropped. "I shall pray for the ill sister's recovery."

One wrong move, one reported conversation, and Marianna would find herself in a dark cell with its iron-banded door. Her correspondence monitored. Her every word weighed for rebellion. Her companions represented two paths: Caterina's anxious devotion masking fear, and Giulia's watchful compliance concealing ambition. One would report her from terror of punishment, the other to curry favor. They were not sisters. They were sentries. Her father had not merely imprisoned her. He had armed her jailers with her own vulnerability.

And as sleep finally came, one truth cut through the darkness like a blade: she had to learn the rules of this place not just to survive, but to win.

* * *

August

THE ARCHBISHOP BLESSED the white linen veils. Ancient Latin fell from his lips, cold and irretrievable.

Marianna knelt between Caterina Ricci and Giulia Homati on the altar steps, knees pressed against marble. Incense curled through late August light, acrid in her throat.

Five months behind these walls as a postulant, learning prayers and silences, rules that would govern every waking hour. Her father had brought her in March, when spring was softening the Lombard winter. Now came the investiture, when she and the others would formally become novices and receive new habits, white veils, and religious names.

The shears appeared, metal glinting. Cold blades kissed her scalp, and the first lock fell with a whisper against the silver salver. Thirteen years of her life surrendered in an instant. Another cut, closer to the skin. Another. The Prioress's hands moved in swift, sure strokes, and Marianna kept her eyes fixed on the marble floor's gray veins threading through white like paths leading nowhere. She would not look at her father in the congregation.

The lightness crept over her scalp, then rushed over her all at once. Her head. Naked. Exposed. Cool air touched skin that had never known daylight.

The archbishop's voice droned through Latin she had learned but never loved. Renunciation. Dedication. Easy words for a man who would leave this church and return to his palazzo, his servants, his supper.

In the sacristy, Marianna exchanged her postulant's dress for the new black wool habit that scraped her wrists raw. Camphor and old incense clung to the new fabric. Dust motes swirled in the narrow shaft of light from the high window.

When she returned to the chapel, the Prioress waited with white linen veils folded in her arms. "Caterina Ricci. You shall be known henceforth as Sister Ottavia."

Caterina bowed, lips moving silently. Testing the weight of her new name.

"Giulia Homati. You shall be known henceforth as Sister Benedetta."

Then Marianna. The Prioress's fingers positioned the veil over what remained of her hair. A yoke settling on her shoulders. "Marianna de Leyva. You shall be known henceforth as Sister Virginia Maria."

The name stopped her breath. Her mother's name. She pressed her lips together. A daily reminder of how she had become her father's inconvenient daughter after her mother's passing.

The Prioress placed the cincture around her waist and pulled. Coarse rope where silk should have been. The knot settled at her hip, tight enough to bind.

"Rise, Sisters." Three postulants had knelt. Three novices rose.

Virginia's fingers found the cincture, rough fiber chafing through thin wool.

Don Martino de Leyva stood behind the iron grille among the witnesses. His chin lifted slightly. One corner of his mouth settled into satisfaction, his duty complete, his inconvenient daughter consigned to God, her inheritance preserved for her brothers or already spent. They flanked him in expensive doublets, faces blank as marble saints. She searched their expressions for recognition, kinship. Nothing. Perhaps there had never been anything.

The heavy doors that led back into the convent stood open. Beyond lay two years of training that would lead to her final vows. The cloister. The chamber she now shared with Ottavia and Benedetta. Canonical hours measuring out days in increments of prayer. And at the end, solemn profession. The black veil. The permanent binding.

The Prioress gestured. Ottavia went first, then Benedetta. Virginia's legs trembled beneath the heavy wool. She did not stumble. Let her father see what his will created. Not a penitent daughter, but a prisoner walking into her cage with open eyes. Let him see she would not weep.

The doors closed with a hollow boom that reverberated through her chest, through the stone beneath her feet. Sister Virginia Maria. The name echoed with each step into the cloister. Each breath she drew. Thirteen years old. A novice. Marianna de Leyva had ceased to exist.

Chapter Two
1591

The 26th of September

TWO YEARS HAD passed since the investiture. Two years of rising before dawn for Matins, body stiff with cold. Two years of silent meals where only wooden spoons scraping clay bowls broke the quiet. Two years of copying manuscripts until her fingers cramped, ink staining her skin black.

The novice mistress had been thorough. A sharp rap across the knuckles for slouching. Hours of solitary prayer for speaking out of turn. Virginia had learned obedience, or at least its appearance.

But in the space between punishments and prayers, she had learned other things. She remembered copying Saint Augustine's Confessions, his cry: Grant me chastity and continence, but not yet. As her quill formed each letter, Virginia understood that Augustine had learned to perform devotion while protecting his true self. That survival required not surrender but careful theater.

She remembered another manuscript assigned by the novice mistress—a theoretical text on women's bodies, written in Latin so complex it was deemed safe for young minds. But between the philosophical discussions of conception and generation, Virginia had found passing references to herbs. And remembered.

Now, at fifteen, she stood on the threshold of final vows. The solemn profession that would transform her from novice to nun. No possibility of return. The black veil awaited, and with it, a binding that would last until death.

Unlike the investiture where three had knelt together, Virginia would take her vows alone. Benedetta and Ottavia had already professed months earlier.

Virginia stood in the dim sacristy as Mother Imbersaga and Sister Candida entered bearing the garments that would mark her final transformation. Only the sisters who would witness this private vesting.

The full-length black tunic came first, heavy and coarse, erasing the last traces of her novitiate.

The white linen wimple followed, starched so stiff she could barely turn her head.

The scapular hung to her ankles.

The leather cincture bore three knots—poverty, chastity, obedience—and Mother Imbersaga pulled it tight.

But the veil commanded her attention. Midnight black.

Sister Candida lifted the white novice's veil from her head. The girl who had worn white existed only in dreams now. The black veil fell over her head, heavy as judgment. "Sister Virginia Maria. Come. Your bridegroom calls."

Rosary beads pressed into her hands. In the other, a blessed candle, flame dancing.

The community assembled beyond the chapel, faces solemn in candlelight. Virginia took her place among them.

Bronze bells began their tolling as the procession wound toward the inner choir, announcing that another daughter of nobility was about to vanish behind convent walls forever. They entered through the narrow door. Beyond the grille dividing choir from visitors, the chapel overflowed.

The Trivulzio family in the front pews, beside them the Serbelloni, then the Marliani. The scent of perfumes, rose water, orange blossom, musk, drifted through the barrier, foreign after years of plain soap and incense. But Virginia could see them only dimly through the metalwork. Shapes. Colors. The gleam of jewels and silk.

Young girls sat scattered throughout, ten, twelve, fourteen years old, eyes wide. Future novices learning their fates. Virginia recognized Caterina Sfondrati, the youngest Visconti daughter, and another young girl, whose family had already negotiated her entrance for next spring. How many would follow her path?

Her father, Don Martino, occupied the place of honor. Cold. Distant. Beside him sat his second wife, Doña Anna, in deep blue silk. Through the grille's patterns, Virginia studied her stepmother's features. Only glacial satisfaction. Someone glad to be rid of her.

"Dearly beloved in Christ." The priest's voice filled the church. "We gather to witness our sister's eternal consecration to Almighty God."

Virginia knelt before the altar. Marble bit through wool to bone.

"What do you seek, my daughter?"

"God's mercy and perseverance in this community." Her voice steady.

"Are you resolved to remain until death, observing perfect fidelity to your sacred vows?"

The moment crystallized. One word would seal her fate. But something had shifted during the midnight hours she had spent praying last night. The scared girl was dead, replaced by someone who understood that even chains might contain weak links. "I am so resolved." Resolved to survive. Resolved to discover what possibilities might exist within impossibility.

The Litany of Saints began. Virginia prostrated herself, arms spread, face pressed to cold stone. "*Sancta Maria... Ora pro nobis.*" Each saint's name bound her deeper. Some had found ways to honor vows while claiming portions of life rightfully theirs.

When the litany ended, Virginia rose and approached her profession charter, inscribed in her finest hand. "I, Sister Virginia Maria de Leyva, promise stability, conversion of life, and obedience according to Benedict's Rule, in this monastery of Santa Margherita."

"Receive your eternal bridegroom's crown." The priest placed a silver circlet upon her veiled head. "Reign with Him in heaven's kingdom." The blessed ring followed, inscribed: "My beloved is mine and I am his." As it slid onto her finger, Virginia contemplated possibilities that might await someone with sufficient imagination.

"*Veni, Sposa Christi.*" Voices rose from both sides of the grille. "Come, Bride of Christ, receive the crown prepared from eternity."

Through the barriers, Virginia watched young noble girls mouthing Latin for identical futures. Some eager. Others calculating. A few frightened.

Then she saw him.

He stood near the back of the nave, apart from the others. Through the latticed ironwork, she found him watching her. Eyes of the darkest brown. An intensity that penetrated the metal barrier, that made her breath catch. Young, perhaps in his early twenties. Dressed in deep crimson and black. His doublet cut perfectly to broad shoulders. Even at this distance, even through the grille, his features commanded attention. Aristocratic. Perfect. Beautiful. Heat spread through her chest, pooling low in her belly. His gaze never wavered. While others shifted, whispered, looked away, he simply watched. Something dangerous lived in that stare. Something thrilling. Recognition. Challenge.

Virginia's throat went dry. The vows she had just spoken meant nothing. This immediate, dangerous pull toward a stranger was the only truth in the room. She forced her eyes away, back to the ritual. But her pulse betrayed her, quick and insistent beneath the heavy wool, pounding in her ears. Nearly sixteen. Newly professed. Supposedly a bride of Christ. And transfixed by a man whose name she didn't know.

At Communion, Virginia received the host. It dissolved, tasteless. But even then, her consciousness divided. Part moved by ancient beauty. Part calculating possibilities having nothing to do with spiritual marriage. And beneath both, those eyes still watching, burning into her.

When the ceremony concluded, noble families approached the grille, offering congratulations to shadows beyond.

Don Martino's face materialized through the ironwork. "You honor our name, daughter. May religious life provide peace worldly existence never could."

No warmth. Only satisfaction with completed business.

Doña Anna proved even more formal. "Sister Virginia Maria, may this day begin true fulfillment that worldly vanities can never bring." The woman spat the religious name with disdain.

Virginia's gaze betrayed her one final time, sliding back to that spot near the rear. He hadn't moved. Hadn't looked away. One corner of his mouth curved, as if he knew exactly what turmoil he'd caused. As if pleased by it.

As the observers dispersed, Virginia remained at the barrier, watching the nave empty.

The ceremony was complete. The heavy door to the choir closed with a final thud. Final separation from the world beyond.

Yet rather than crushing imprisonment, Virginia registered something different. Positioning for goals she was only beginning to glimpse. But beneath those thoughts ran another current, dangerous and insistent. Who was he?

* * *

THE EVENING BELL tolled for Vespers. Virginia adjusted her veil and moved toward the door. Behind her, Ottavia and Benedetta rose to follow. But Virginia's mind worked through questions she shouldn't be asking. Who was he? And why couldn't she stop thinking about him?

In the chapel, Latin prayers washed over her, but the words felt distant. Her thoughts kept returning to crimson and black, to eyes that had held hers.

When they returned to their chamber after Vespers, darkness had settled. The three women prepared for bed in quiet efficiency.

Benedetta moved with deliberate care, crossing to Virginia's cot. "The man at the back of the church today. The one in crimson and black. I saw your face when you looked at him."

Virginia's hands stilled on her profession charter. "I don't remember."

"Don't lie." Sharp. "I stood three sisters away. I watched you lose focus during the Litany. I saw the way your eyes kept returning to him."

Heat climbed Virginia's throat.

Benedetta moved to the window. "Gian Paolo Osio. Son of one of Milan's oldest families. Manages estates whose boundaries touch this convent's land." She turned, observing eyes missing nothing. "I asked after the ceremony. Discreetly."

"How did you know?"

"Because when I see a newly professed sister distracted by a man during her own profession, I want to know who poses that kind of danger."

Virginia lifted her chin. "I've done nothing wrong."

"No. You haven't." Benedetta settled in the chamber's single chair, spine straight. "But what I witnessed concerns me. Canonical law binds you now as completely as stone walls. You are Sister Virginia Maria de Leyva until death." She leaned forward. "I watched you speak those vows correctly, but without surrender. And then, during your consecration to Christ, you became transfixed by a man in the congregation."

"I spoke every word I was required to speak."

"You did. Which is why I'm here now, while this is still only a moment of distraction." Benedetta's gaze penetrated. "Whatever you felt today, put it aside. Forget his face. Forget his name."

Virginia forced herself to meet Benedetta's stare without flinching.

"You're newly professed. That moment can remain only what it was, a fleeting distraction." Benedetta stood. "But if you allow it to become more, the consequences will be catastrophic. Not only for you, but for everyone close to you. Sister Ottavia. Me. Every woman in this community."

"You assume much."

"I assume nothing. I observed, and as your friend, I'm concerned." She moved to her cot. "Your father stripped your wealth. The Church claims your obedience. You have taken vows that bind you until death. There is no path forward that doesn't lead to destruction." Her gaze held Virginia motionless. "So let it go. Today. Now. Before curiosity becomes something more dangerous."

The words hung between them, unspoken but heavy. Benedetta began unlacing her shoes. She paused, glancing toward the window. "I tend the herb gardens near the outer wall most afternoons. Solitary work. Private. Should you need a friend to talk about... difficulties with our vocation, those gardens offer space for conversations the chapel cannot accommodate." She hesitated. "And if you wish not to speak, the solitude itself is gift enough." Then she returned to her preparations for bed, her message delivered.

Virginia remained on her cot, Benedetta's words echoing.

Across the chamber, Ottavia sat on her bed, fingers working her rosary, the clicking audible in the quiet.

The black veil felt suddenly heavier. The profession ring caught moonlight, Solomon's inscription mocking her. She rose and moved to the window, looking toward the streets where a few lights still burned. Somewhere out there, Gian Paolo Osio lived his life, unaware that a newly professed nun had noticed him and could not stop thinking about what that moment had awakened.

She pressed her palm against the cold glass and remembered. The exact angle of his head. The precise curve of his mouth when he'd smiled—knowing, dangerous. The way his gaze had never wavered. Was he standing at a window now, in his palazzo in this dark city? Was he thinking of her?

The profession ring felt suddenly tight with its inscription inside, *My beloved is mine and I am his*. But which beloved? Put it aside, Benedetta had said. Forget his face. Forget his name. But Virginia knew, with a certainty that both thrilled and terrified her, that she would do neither. She couldn't. Not when she could still feel the heat of his gaze on her skin. Not when every rational thought dissolved beneath the memory of crimson and black, of eyes that saw through iron and veil and discovered something in her she hadn't known existed.

Gian Paolo Osio.

Even his name felt dangerous on her tongue.

Chapter Three
1597

September

THE APPLE STRUCK the stone wall inches from Virginia's face, exploding in a shower of juice that spattered her white wimple. She spun toward masculine laughter.

Dark eyes met hers. They swept over her nun's habit with such bold appreciation that heat flooded through her, unfamiliar and unwelcome.

Her breath caught. Not just from attraction, but from recognition.

She knew who he was instantly—the man who had watched from the shadows during her profession, two years ago. She had not seen him since, but his face had remained lodged in her memory like a splinter.

Now twenty-two, Sister Virginia Maria had spent eight years behind these walls, long enough to learn the names whispered in market gossip. Gian Paolo Osio. Younger son of old money, heir to a reputation that made mothers lock daughters away when he rode through town. And now he sat brazenly near the cloister itself, as if Church law meant nothing.

He perched in the apple tree straddling the courtyard's wall, one booted foot braced against bark, the other swinging free on the convent side where no man should set foot. September sunlight filtered through leaves touched with autumn gold, warming the stones beneath her feet. Those eyes remained fixed on her, unrelenting.

"My apologies, Sister." His voice carried the smoothness of a man accustomed to having his way. "My aim requires practice, it seems."

Liar. The apple had been thrown with perfect precision.

Virginia absorbed his casual arrogance, boots dangling over consecrated ground where his presence could bring destruction upon them all. Dark hair tousled, linen shirt open at the collar. The confidence of a man who believed his noble blood would protect him from consequences.

But Virginia knew better. She had heard what happened to men who breached convent walls. Imprisonment. Sometimes death. And for the nuns involved, expulsion. Charges of sacrilege. Stricter enclosure for the entire community.

"You're trespassing." Her voice held steady despite the chaos beneath her ribs. "This is holy ground."

"Holy?" His smile was pure mischief. "I'm merely sitting in a tree whose roots lie within my family's property." His gaze traveled deliberately from her flushed face to her hands clutching the sides of her rough wool habit.

"Do you understand the risk you bring?" she whispered. "If anyone discovers you here, what will happen?"

Delighted laughter interrupted her. Virginia spun to find Isabella degli Hortensi, a postulant and one of her charges, emerging from behind the chicken coop, arms laden with perfect red apples.

"Such marksmanship, Signor Osio!" The girl's voice rang with admiration. "You could join the Spanish arquebusiers!"

Virginia's chest tightened. One witness was perilous enough, but Isabella's enthusiasm could bring the entire community running.

But the girl's upturned face, the eager way her gaze sought Osio's attention. Something sharp twisted beneath Virginia's ribs.

Isabella was young, barely fifteen, with fresh beauty that made men forget propriety. And the way she gazed at him...

Virginia caught a movement at the courtyard's edge. Sister Benedetta stood in the garden doorway, a basket of herbs on her hip. How long had she been there? Those observant eyes tracked from Isabella to Osio to Virginia's flushed face.

Their gazes met. Benedetta made no move to intervene, simply stood in stillness.

Understanding struck. Isabella had been here before. The girl's comfort, her easy familiarity, this was established pattern, not first discovery.

"Isabella." Virginia's voice came harsh. "How long has this been happening?"

The girl's face crumpled, apples shifting in her arms. "He was only being kind, Sister Virginia."

"Answer me. How many times have you come here to let yourself be seen by him?"

Isabella's silence was confession enough.

Virginia looked up at Gian Paolo. That proprietary smile, those eyes fixed not on her but on the schoolgirl. Something dark and primitive surged through her blood.

From the corner of her eye, Benedetta shifted her weight. Still silent. Still observing. But now her head tilted slightly, filing away information for future use.

"Signor Osio. How dare you show such disrespect to this convent!" The words exploded with violence she hadn't intended. "This girl is in my charge!"

Osio raised an eyebrow, lounging with casual insolence. He plucked another fruit. "Surely there's no harm in bringing a little sweetness to these gray walls?" He made as if to toss it to Isabella again, dark eyes glittering with defiance.

Something snapped inside Virginia. Years of managing unruly noble daughters flooded out in a torrent of righteous anger.

"Leave at once!" Her voice cracked like a whip, echoing off stone. "Or I shall report this behavior to the authorities!"

She gave him a rebuke, such as he had likely never heard, each word chosen to cut, to humiliate. "You think your noble blood protects you? That your family name gives you the right to corrupt girls in holy care? I am still a de Leyva. You are the son of a lesser house, entertaining yourself with games that could destroy lives that aren't yours to risk!"

Benedetta's basket lowered slowly, herbs spilling onto flagstones. Her eyes never left Virginia's face.

Osio's confident mask slipped. Something cold flickered across his features, wounded pride and anger that sent a chill down Virginia's spine despite the heat of her fury.

He slid from his perch with fluid grace, but there was nothing playful now. He brushed dust from his clothes with exaggerated care. A muscle jumped in his jaw.

"A de Leyva." He smiled, slow and deliberate. "How fortunate. Then you understand the obligations of noble blood better than most. Perhaps we should discuss that... at length."

The words struck home with devastating accuracy. He knew. Somehow, he had seen straight through her fury to what lay beneath.

With a mocking bow that was pure insult, he walked away. But at the garden's edge, he paused, looking back not at Isabella, but directly at Virginia. The look of a man who intended to pursue what he'd found.

Men like Gian Paolo Osio did not forgive such wounds easily.

"Return to your lessons, Isabella." Virginia forced her voice level. "Speak of this to no one."

"But Sister."

"Now."

Isabella fled, apples cascading in a crimson shower across the stones.

Virginia turned. Benedetta remained by the garden door, herbs forgotten at her feet.

"Sister Benedetta." Virginia's voice came out defensive.

Benedetta bent to retrieve her basket with unhurried efficiency. "I came to gather rosemary. Instead, I witnessed quite the performance."

Heat climbed Virginia's throat. "The girl needed protection."

"From him? Or from you?"

The question landed like a physical blow.

"I observed your face when Isabella appeared," Benedetta said, voice pitched low. "I observed what crossed it when she smiled at him. That wasn't righteous fury."

"You're mistaken."

"Am I?" Benedetta stopped an arm's length away. "Your hands clenched when she laughed. Your breathing changed when his gaze followed her. And when you stepped between them..."

She left the implication unspoken.

"That's ridiculous."

"I've been observing you. Since you started positioning yourself near windows that overlook the Osio property. Since you began finding reasons to supervise the garden more frequently." Her mouth tightened. "I hoped I was wrong. This morning confirmed I'm not."

The words hung between them, impossible to deny. Something crumbled in Virginia's chest.

"What are you going to do?" she whispered. "Report me?"

"Report what? That you experienced inappropriate emotion many years ago over a man you've never spoken to?" Benedetta shook her head. "Mother Imbersaga would call it absurd."

"Then why?"

"Because emotion doesn't end with a single confrontation. Because wounded male pride seeks revenge. Because you've made yourself visible to him in precisely the way I warned against." She stepped closer. "You've given him reason to notice you specifically. To think about you. To wonder why a nun showed such personal investment in driving him away."

The truth settled over Virginia like ice water. In her fury, she had done exactly what she'd told herself she wouldn't do. She had made herself remarkable to Gian Paolo Osio.

"He'll return," Benedetta said. "Men like him always do. The question is what you'll do when he comes looking not for Isabella, but for the nun who dared to humiliate him."

Virginia pressed trembling hands against her habit, rough wool scratching her palms. "I didn't mean..."

"What you meant doesn't matter. What matters is what happens next." Benedetta's voice softened fractionally. "If he approaches you, will you have the strength to refuse?"

The question hung between them, unanswerable.

"I observed your face before Isabella appeared. That wasn't just attraction." She adjusted her basket. "And that makes what comes next far more perilous than if he'd simply been flirting with a schoolgirl."

Virginia wanted to deny it, but the denial died unspoken because Benedetta was right. She had looked at him and seen not just danger, but possibility. Escape from the cage her father had locked her in.

"What should I do?"

Benedetta was silent for a long moment. "Report the incident to the Prioress. Make it formal, documented. Let Isabella's family act to protect their honor." She paused. "And pray that when Osio returns, because he will return, you've found the strength to remember that some doors, once opened, can never be closed again."

She turned and walked away, footsteps echoing, leaving Virginia alone with apples scattered like blood across the flagstones.

The trembling didn't stop. Virginia made her way to the Prioress's door, standing open as it always did. Reverend Mother Imbersaga looked up from her accounts, expression sharpening with concern.

"Sister Virginia. You look unwell."

"Reverend Mother, I must report... I discovered Gian Paolo Osio throwing fruit to Isabella degli Hortensi from his tree. The girl has been deliberately positioning herself to catch his attention."

She did not mention the emotion that had surged through her. Did not speak of how her heart had fluttered when Osio's gaze met hers. Did not mention Benedetta's observations.

"I gave him a stern rebuke for showing so little respect for the convent. He departed, chastened."

That last part was a lie.

Mother Imbersaga's expression darkened. "Osio. I have been warned that he sometimes spies on the girls. It seems he's getting bolder."

"The Hortensi must be informed at once."

The Prioress rose, already reaching for paper. "This is a matter of family honor."

Virginia nodded, but unease coiled in her stomach. She wanted Isabella gone, but not for the girl's protection. She wanted her gone so those dark eyes would have no reason to return to the garden. No reason to look at him. She couldn't bring herself to regret the possibility.

The Hortensi family did not hesitate. Within days, Isabella was withdrawn and hastily married off to a suitable Milanese bridegroom before rumor could fasten her name to Osio's.

* * *

THREE WEEKS HAD passed. Three weeks of watching the apple tree, of Benedetta's observation sharp as broken glass.

Evening shadows stretched across the chamber Virginia still shared with Benedetta and Ottavia. Virginia attempted to focus on correspondence, Benedetta mended with precise stitches, and Ottavia worked her rosary beads, each click audible in the quiet. The smell of tallow candles mixed with the mustiness of old wool and parchment.

The silence pressed down tonight, heavier than usual. As though the very air knew something terrible approached.

Virginia went about her duties by rote, teaching, supervising, keeping routines. But beneath the surface, something had shifted. She caught herself studying the trees, listening for sounds beyond the walls. Waiting.

And she caught Benedetta observing her, cataloging every glance toward the Osio property.

Benedetta's posture grew more rigid in the days that followed, her words shorter, more cautious. Virginia observed her friend retreat into calculation, preparing for something, mapping potential disasters.

And Virginia knew it in the darkness before dawn as she lay in her narrow cot, while Benedetta and Ottavia slept, a sick certainty coiling in her chest.

She had started something. Whatever came next, she could not stop it.

* * *

October

IN THE SEWING room, Virginia was instructing the younger girls when loud voices drifted through the open windows. She rose and crossed to the window overlooking the main entrance, needle still clasped between her fingers.

Through the arched gateway, a small crowd had gathered. Two students pressed close to the iron bars, faces flushed with excitement. Sister Ottavia stood nearby, wringing her hands. Sister Constanza stood rigid, arms crossed.

At the center stood the man who had invaded her thoughts for four weeks.

Even from this distance, Virginia recognized him. The dark head bent attentively toward the girls, the midnight blue doublet, the casual hand on his sword hilt. The perfect nobleman.

Heat rushed over her skin, followed by something colder. Her fingers gripped the windowsill, knuckles white against gray stone.

He was speaking to her students again. One girl laughed and pressed closer to the bars. Gian Paolo's smile widened with effortless charm.

The thread snapped between her clenched fingers.

How dare he return? How dare he show himself to these innocent girls as if nothing had happened? The rules forbade any contact with the outside world unless sanctioned by the Prioress. His brazenness.

But beneath her anger, something else bloomed in her chest. Something shameful and intoxicating that made her breath come faster.

He had come back.

Not to the market square or church. Here. To her convent. To the gates of her domain.

And he was using these girls to provoke her.

Virginia's hands tightened. This entire performance, the public flirtation, the deliberate positioning where she might see him was all calculated to draw her out.

He wanted her angry and possessive and unable to stay away.

The knowledge should have kept her rooted in place. A wise woman would have sent Sister Benedetta to dismiss him. A true nun would have turned away.

But power coursed through her, intoxicating as wine. If he wanted a confrontation, she would give him one.

"Keep working," she told her students, setting down her needle. "I'll return in a moment."

She crossed the courtyard with measured steps, though everything in her wanted to sprint. The October sun warmed the stones beneath her shoes. Dust motes swirled in shafts of afternoon light. This time would be different. This time, she would show him exactly what happened to men who dared trifle with her peace.

Through the iron gates, she could see him more clearly. The midnight blue doublet with silver thread catching sunlight. The sword at his hip. His dark head still bent toward the girls.

He looked every inch the nobleman—comfortable, confident, utterly in control.

Her hands clenched inside her sleeves.

"Signor Osio." Her voice cut through the conversation so sharp that one of the girls gasped.

Every head turned. She watched Gian Paolo's easy confidence flicker. The charming smile stayed fixed, but his dark eyes sharpened with caution.

"Sister Virginia." His voice was carefully controlled. His hands clenched at his sides, knuckles white. "How... fortunate to encounter you here."

"Is it?" Virginia stepped closer to the iron bars, close enough to see his pulse beating at his throat, to smell leather and wine that made her head spin even as fury blazed through her. "I'm amazed to find you near convent property again, after our previous discussion about... proper boundaries."

Color climbed his neck. Around them, the students pressed closer. Fabric rustled. Sister Ottavia's face paled.

"I was simply offering to help these young ladies with their... religious readings."

"Religious readings?" Virginia's laugh was brittle. "How curious. Tell me, what qualifies you to guide young women in their religious studies?"

The question struck home. A dangerous flash crossed his dark eyes. For a moment, he looked almost feral, and Virginia's pulse quickened with shameful excitement.

But each sharp exchange drew more attention, created more witnesses. She was destroying both their reputations. Yet the words kept coming.

"I simply offered to share what little knowledge I have of Latin texts," he said through gritted teeth.

"Latin texts." Virginia tilted her head with mock curiosity. "And which particular works were you discussing? Perhaps some passages about how unmarried women should behave? Or Saint Paul's letters about feminine virtue?"

Sister Ottavia's hands twisted together. The girls looked between them with horrified fascination.

People walking past had stopped to listen. A small crowd formed beyond the gates.

Movement at the edge of the archway revealed Benedetta, standing in shadow, observing with that sharp, clinical gaze. Not intervening. Simply documenting.

"I was merely answering their questions about—" he began.

"About what, exactly?" Virginia cut him off. "About how to interpret scripture? About developing spiritual discipline? Or perhaps about matters that have nothing to do with their education and everything to do with your own... diversions?"

But as he struggled for a response, something changed in his expression. Beneath the humiliation and anger, she glimpsed something far more unsettling.

Amusement. Recognition. The look one would give a worthy opponent.

When he spoke again, his voice was soft, almost conversational. "Your concern for these young ladies is... remarkable, Sister Virginia. Such passionate devotion to their welfare suggests either extensive experience with the corruption you describe so vividly... or an active imagination about the forms such corruption might take."

The words struck like a sword thrust. Around them, the audience stirred, sensing undercurrents they couldn't understand but recognizing the shift in power.

He was turning her own weapons against her, using her passionate attack to suggest personal experience with the sins she claimed to condemn.

"I speak from the knowledge of my duty to protect those in my care," she managed, but her voice wavered.

"Indeed." His smile was sharp as a blade. "And such extensive knowledge suggests either careful study... or more intimate familiarity with the subjects in question."

Her cheeks burned. He had reversed their positions, transformed her righteous anger into something that resembled the very corruption she claimed to fear.

When had she lost control so completely?

A woman approached the gate, her head bowed over a heavy wicker basket. She stopped behind Gian Paolo, hesitating.

"Signor?" Her voice was barely audible.

Gian Paolo turned, irritation clear. "What is it, Apollonia?"

Virginia's breath caught. Apollonia. The laundry woman who came twice weekly, wife of Gioseffo Pesseno, Osio's chief bravo.

Virginia studied her more closely now. Young, perhaps only a few years older than the novices, face drawn and pale. A darkening bruise bloomed high on her cheekbone, stark purple against pallid skin. Fresh enough that the surrounding flesh remained swollen. She flinched as Gian Paolo spoke, knuckles white where she gripped the basket.

How many times had Virginia accepted linens from those trembling hands without truly seeing?

"The... the laundry, Signore. For the convent. The wicket gate is locked."

Gian Paolo stepped aside, dismissive. "Then ask the good Sister to open it. She seems to be the keeper of all gates today." He turned back to Virginia, eyes hard. "Well, Sister? Will you let your servant in, or are you too occupied lecturing me to attend to your duties?"

Virginia's gaze moved between the arrogant nobleman and the cowering woman. The bruise seemed to throb in the sunlight, a silent testament to life in the Osio household. This was the world Gian Paolo ruled. A world where women were beaten, silenced, made to carry heavy burdens while men played games.

Cold sickness doused her anger.

"Come, Apollonia," Virginia said, her voice softer now. Sister Constanza unlocked the small side gate. Hinges creaked, metal scraping against metal.

Apollonia hurried through, eyes fixed on the cobblestones. "Thank you, Sister."

As she passed, Virginia caught the scent of lye soap and fear. "Are you... are you well, Apollonia?"

The woman paused, glancing up with wide, terrified eyes. She touched her bruised cheek. "I am well, Sister. It is nothing. My husband... the heat affects his temper. And when the master is unhappy..." She trailed off, casting a frightened glance at Gian Paolo's back before hurrying toward the laundry rooms.

Virginia watched her go. Her stomach clenched. Her righteous war with Osio wasn't private. It spilled over. Her insults to the master became bruises on the servant.

She turned back to Gian Paolo. He was observing her, mockery back in his eyes.

"I trust you will find peace in your prayers tonight, Sister Virginia," he said. "And perhaps in that holy solitude you might reflect on the knowledge that troubles you so deeply."

Then he was gone, walking away with unhurried dignity, leaving Virginia alone with the echoing silence of her hollow victory and the image of a bruised woman hurrying into the shadows.

She had humiliated him, yes, but revealed far too much of herself. Worse still, she had shown him exactly how much power he held over her emotions.

And now she knew the cost. It wasn't just her reputation at stake. It was the safety of everyone caught between them.

As Virginia made her way back on trembling legs, one thought echoed: *This is only the beginning.*

* * *

GIAN PAOLO SAT in his palazzo's finest room, wine untouched on the carved table beside him. Virginia's reproaches still rang in his ears. The humiliation burned like acid. Not just that she had berated him, but that she had seen through his facade to the wounded pride beneath.

Candles flickered in silver sconces. The velvet cushion pressed against his back. Outside, footsteps echoed through the courtyard. Servants moving about their evening duties.

When Isabella degli Hortensi was snatched from his grasp, it was already intolerable. He was not a man given to half-measures. He did not forgive insults, did not forget humiliations. And Sister Virginia de Leyva had delivered the same indignity again, this time in front of witnesses, the girls, another nun observing from shadows, Sister Constanza. And even Apollonia. His own servant had seen him rebuked by a woman.

Bitter thoughts circled his mind like vultures. She had to learn that he was not some common boy to be tongue-lashed and dismissed. That his noble blood demanded respect, especially from a woman who had renounced the world but clearly hadn't renounced its passions.

Because he had seen it. That flash of jealousy when she'd looked at Isabella, the way her hands trembled with more than righteous anger. Sister Virginia wanted to pretend she was above such emotions, but Osio knew better.

And knowing that made his revenge all the sweeter to contemplate.

He needed to strike at something she valued, something she relied upon. Not another girl. That strategy had lost its effectiveness. No, something that would make her understand the cost of her insults.

He needed to know who she trusted. Who she depended upon. Who mattered enough that their loss would wound her deeply.

He summoned Pesseno. The red-haired bravo appeared, wiping grease from his mouth.

"Tell me," Osio said quietly. "The de Leyva family's financial administrator. Who manages the nun's affairs in Milan?"

Pesseno scratched his beard. "Molteno. Gioseffo Molteno. He handles all their accounts, their properties, their dowries."

Osio's smile was cold. Molteno, who handled Sister Virginia's business affairs. Molteno, whose death would send a very clear message about the price of humiliating Gian Paolo Osio.

"Thank you. You may leave."

For a moment, Osio hesitated. Killing Molteno would cross a line into genuine crime. The Church might shelter him, but even sanctuary could not protect him indefinitely if authorities decided to press charges. The Spanish governor himself might take notice of a nobleman murdering a functionary.

But then he remembered her voice, sharp as broken glass, echoing through the courtyard. The way her eyes had flashed with contempt, speaking to him as though he were a child before servants and nuns. The humiliation of standing at those gates, powerful and noble and utterly undermined by a woman in a black veil.

His jaw clenched. The muscle jumped beneath his skin. This was not impulsive rage. This was calculation. The cold logic of a man accustomed to having his will enforced through violence.

It would be legitimate redress, he told himself, pouring wine with steady hands. The dark liquid caught candlelight as it filled the silver cup. A point of honor, not merely a crime. She had insulted him publicly. He would answer publicly. Let her mourn her fiscal agent and know that every tear was payment for her sharp tongue.

The decision made, the burning rage settled into cold purpose. He would not hide from the consequences. He would kill Molteno and claim it openly as his right. The legitimate response of a nobleman to intolerable insult.

And if the authorities came for him, he would simply retreat to his house, from which he could slip into San Maurizio's Church through a secret passage and claim sanctuary. The Church would have to shelter him. His family's donations had purchased that privilege generations ago.

Sister Virginia de Leyva would learn that men like him did not forgive. And by the time she understood the full cost of her jealous fury, it would be far too late to take back the words that had set everything in motion.

The wine tasted sweeter now. Osio raised his glass to the darkness beyond his windows, to the convent walls where she slept, unknowing of the storm about to break.

"To honor," he murmured. "And to the lesson you are about to learn."

* * *

THE LATIN WORDS swam before Virginia's eyes. Autumn light slanted through the scriptorium windows, warming the worn tables. The smell of ink and vellum hung thick in the close air. Her students' voices droned on, *amo, amas, amat,* but the conjugations slid past without meaning. Virginia read the same line of Cicero three times, her finger tracing script that refused to make sense.

Each breath took deliberate effort.

The door crashed open. Books tumbled. Sister Ottavia stood frozen in the doorway, face drained of all color. Her rosary shook. Wooden beads rattled like teeth chattering in winter wind.

Virginia had spent eight years behind these walls. She had never seen Ottavia's composure crumble like this.

"Sister Virginia." The words barely escaped Ottavia's tight throat. "Come. Now."

The youngest student began to whimper.

Virginia rose. "Girls, continue your copying. Sister Ottavia, what is it?"

"The Prioress. Immediately." Ottavia's voice fractured.

Virginia followed through corridors that seemed to stretch endlessly. Each footstep echoed off stone. The scent of candle smoke and the sound of old prayers hung heavy. Her fingers trailed along the cold wall, stone rough beneath her palm.

But underneath lurked something else, metallic and sharp. Virginia's chest tightened.

Prioress Imbersaga stood rigid at her study window. Morning light carved harsh shadows across her face, aging her a decade. The smell of candle wax intensified in the small space.

"Close the door, Sister Virginia."

Virginia's fingers fumbled with the heavy iron latch. The sound was final.

"Reverend Mother, what's happened?"

The Prioress turned slowly. When their eyes met, Virginia saw something that made her grip the door handle until iron bit into her palm.

Pity. And beneath it, barely controlled fury.

"Gioseffo Molteno is dead."

The words struck like a blow. Virginia's legs buckled. She grabbed for the carved chair back, forced herself to remain upright. Her breath came in short, sharp gasps.

"Dead?" The word came out as a whisper. "But he was just here. How?"

Sweet, patient Molteno. The man who'd managed her family's affairs for fifteen years. He had five children and a wife who baked the finest bread in Monza.

"Murdered." The Prioress moved closer, her footsteps deliberate on the wooden floor. "Signor Molteno was ambushed on the road between Milan and this convent. They say his blood soaked the dirt. The murderer buried him in a field outside the city gate. A pair of mule-drivers heard a cry, glimpsed two or three armed men in the dim light. They reported it. The body has been recovered."

Virginia's stomach twisted. Bile rose in her throat, copper-tasting. She swallowed hard.

"Who would dare? Molteno never harmed a soul."

"Gian Paolo Osio."

The name dropped like a stone into still water. Shock rippled through Virginia's entire body. Her fingers went numb.

"That's impossible. He wouldn't..."

"He made no attempt to hide his crime. He proclaimed it openly in the town square before fleeing Monza. He told anyone who would listen that it was justice. Honor's demand for insults received at this very convent."

The memory crashed over Virginia. The garden scene. Her furious words. The angry encounter at the gates. With witnesses watching.

But surely those events couldn't justify this. Not gentle Molteno's murder.

"Molteno was innocent," she whispered. "He was only doing his duty to me and my family."

"Don't you understand?" The Prioress stepped closer. "He told half of Monza that you spoke demeaning words in front of witnesses. Words that demanded blood. Faithful Molteno, whom everyone knew served the de Leyva family with devotion, was the perfect target. The perfect way to demonstrate what happens to those who cross Gian Paolo Osio."

The truth struck. A knife between her ribs. Osio hadn't killed a random man. He'd killed the one person most visibly connected to her. He had selected Molteno with precision, understanding that his death would wound Virginia far more than any threat to herself.

She had unleashed this. Her pride. Her sharp tongue. Innocent Molteno lay dead because she had failed to control her temper. His blood stained her hands.

"His poor wife," she whispered. "His children."

But even as grief and guilt crashed over her, something else stirred beneath. Something that made her hate herself. It bloomed. Beautiful and deadly.

Gian Paolo had killed because of her. Her words had held such power that a man lay dead. A nobleman had stained his hands with blood to answer her pride.

Warmth spread through her chest at the thought. Shameful, unforgivable warmth.

What manner of woman experienced anything but pure horror? What manner of woman recognized this dark thrill threading through the grief?

The Prioress moved to her writing table and withdrew a formal document. "The magistrate of Monza, Judge Pirovano, knows what happened. He knows Osio is responsible. But Osio is a nobleman, and this was a crime of honor. Under our laws, the magistrate cannot arrest a man of his station for avenging an insult unless the offended family formally demands it."

She gestured to the document. "You are the Lady of Monza, Sister Virginia. The only representative of the de Leyva family in Lombardy. Judge Pirovano requires your formal complaint to issue the warrant. Without your signature, he cannot touch Osio. With it, the full weight of Spanish law will hunt him down."

The Prioress paused, her gaze holding Virginia motionless.

"You must choose. Do we let this murder pass as a quarrel? Or do you demand justice, knowing that doing so will tie your name to his in every court in Milan?"

Virginia pressed her fingertips to her temples. A sick throbbing pulsed behind her eyes. The room seemed to contract around her.

Poor Molteno's family would be preparing his body even now. His wife would need money. Protection. She would have to write to her father at once.

But when she closed her eyes, another image intruded. Gian Paolo at the convent gates. Magnificent in his fury. Dangerous as a drawn blade. His dark eyes burning with something that might have been admiration.

God forgive her. Part of her, some wicked, buried part that eight years of discipline hadn't killed, thrilled at the knowledge. Her words could drive a man to murder.

She held Gian Paolo Osio's life in her hands. She, who had been powerless for eight years, could now crush the arrogant man who had dared to mock her.

It was not just justice she wanted. It was submission.

"Sister Virginia?" The Prioress's voice drifted from far away. "What do you say?"

The words tore from Virginia's throat. "Molteno deserves justice. I will sign the complaint. I want him hunted down."

"Be very certain. I am wary of the consequences and the troubles this will bring upon our convent. Once the warrant is sworn, it cannot be unsworn without great cost."

"I am certain."

Virginia moved to the writing table. The quill was heavy in her hand, the feather smooth against her fingers. She dipped it in the inkwell and signed her name, Sister Virginia Maria de Leyva, across the bottom. Her hand barely trembled.

The scratch of the nib was loud in the silence. The sound of a trap snapping shut.

She had done it. With her signature, she had set the machinery of justice in motion. And beneath the righteous certainty, that dark thrill coursed through her veins.

The Prioress took the parchment and studied it. "This will be delivered to Judge Pirovano before nightfall."

"Yes, Reverend Mother."

The older woman set the document aside. "A good man is dead because of your pride, Sister Virginia. Because of your behavior. His blood cries out for vengeance. And whether you choose to answer that cry or silence it, the consequences will fall on all our heads."

Virginia met her gaze. The weight of what she had just done settled onto her shoulders, heavy and suffocating. Impossible to cast off.

Beneath the grief, something dangerous stirred where her heart should be. Fascination warred with genuine sorrow. Her hands trembled. She pressed them flat against her habit. Shame battled with terrible secret satisfaction that she couldn't suppress.

She should weep. Should throw herself at the Prioress's feet and beg forgiveness. Should fast and pray until her body was nothing but bones and repentance.

Instead, as she stood in that chamber thick with the scent of fear and wax, Virginia understood the truth. One that would damn her soul.

Every nerve in her body had awakened. Eight years of deliberate numbness, shattered in an instant.

She wanted to weep for the wickedness of it.

And couldn't.

And God help her, she didn't want that feeling to end.

Virginia stumbled from the Prioress's study, mind reeling. The heavy door closed behind her with a thud that echoed through the empty corridor.

She pressed her back to the cool stone wall, trying to steady her breathing, to slow her racing pulse. The stone was cold against her shoulders, grounding her.

Molteno. Dead. Murdered. Because of her.

She needed to reach the chamber she shared with Benedetta and Ottavia. Needed to process the horror of what she'd learned.

But as she pushed away from the wall and began to walk, footsteps echoing in the silence, one thought echoed with each step: Gian Paolo Osio had selected his victim with precision, knowing exactly which death would wound her most deeply.

He understood her.

And in understanding her, he had bound them together.

Yet she had just set out to destroy him.

The irony was exquisite and damning in equal measure.

* * *

November

THE LETTER LAY ON MOTHER Imbersaga's fingertips as if it were evidence, not correspondence. Afternoon light picked out the Prioress's rigid jaw, the throb of a vein at her temple.

"Read," she said, turning the sheet outward.

Virginia stepped closer. The script was controlled, deliberate. The hand of a man who had time to craft his words carefully while in hiding.

> *To the Most Revered Mother Prioress of Santa Margherita and to Sister Virginia Maria de Leyva.*
>
> *I am hunted because Sister Virginia swore a complaint against me for an act any man of honor would have committed. Sister Virginia insulted me in front of witnesses. The law calls this*

murder. I call it justice. Many nobles have petitioned Judge Pirovano on my behalf. All have been refused. Yet I am told the magistrate will grant mercy if Sister Virginia herself requests it. She alone holds my life in her hands.

I am a desperate man. Desperation drives men to speak truths better left silent. If I am to hang, I will not hang alone. I will tell the magistrate, the Bishop, and anyone who will listen exactly why Sister Virginia swore this warrant, because I dared to look at her too boldly at your gate.

Withdraw the complaint, and I disappear into exile. My family will ensure I trouble Monza no more. Refuse, and I will make certain that when they drag me to the scaffold, every man in Lombardy knows that a nun of Santa Margherita sent me there.

The ink had bled slightly at the signature, as though written in haste or anger.

"He threatens the convent," the Prioress said. "And you."

She set the letter down with deliberate care. "Whatever exists between you and Signor Osio, it ends now. I recommend you withdraw your petition. If you do not, I will have no choice but to remove you from this convent."

Virginia understood. Not merely that she could be expelled, but that such an expulsion would stain Santa Margherita for years.

"Do you understand me?" Mother Imbersaga asked quietly.

"Yes, Reverend Mother."

The Prioress extended the letter across the writing table. "Take it. Read it as many times as you need to understand what he's truly threatening. Then decide whether your pride is worth the cost."

Virginia's hand trembled as she took the parchment.

"You are dismissed. Do not wait too long to give me your answer."

* * *

THAT NIGHT, BENEDETTA read the letter in silence. When she finished, her dark eyes lifted to Virginia's.

"He's forcing your hand. Either you withdraw the warrant and accept his mercy, or he makes good on the threat."

"It's not a threat to me," Virginia whispered. "It's a threat to all of us."

"Yes. Which makes it far more effective than any threat to you alone. He understands what matters to you. And he's using it as leverage."

Virginia pressed the heels of her hands against her eyes until she saw sparks.

"He knows I will protect our convent."

"And he is counting on that." Benedetta handed the letter back. "This is his reply."

* * *

THE SIEGE INTENSIFIED. The Osio family sent three emissaries in quick succession: a bishop's secretary with veiled allusions to 'the Cardinal's displeasure'; a wealthy widow with ties to the Spanish governor; a notary bearing documents so generous they would have secured Molteno's family for generations.

Virginia received them in the parlatory with Mother Imbersaga present, the iron grille between them a reminder of enclosure that felt increasingly theoretical. She listened, answered with formal courtesy, and refused them all.

On the eighth day, Donna Sofia Osio came.

Gian Paolo's mother was an elegant woman in her fifties whose widow's clothes were immaculate. She entered with the bearing of someone long accustomed to deference. Yet when she knelt on the outer side of the grille, dignity crumpled beneath grief.

Her gloved hands pressed together in supplication; tears streaked the powder on her cheeks.

"Sister Virginia, I beg you. As a mother, surely you can imagine my love for Gian Paolo. My son is rash. Foolish. Proud beyond reason. But he is my son. My only living son."

Something twisted in Virginia's chest. This was not a bishop's secretary speaking the language of influence. This was a mother begging for her child's life.

"Signora, please rise. You dishonor yourself by kneeling."

"I will kneel until you grant mercy." Donna Sofia's voice grew stronger even as tears continued. "My Gian Paolo acted in madness. Hot blood and wounded pride drove him to this terrible sin. But must he die for it? Must I lose my son as Signora Molteno lost her husband?"

The comparison struck like a slap.

"Your son took an innocent life, Signora. The law must answer."

"The law?" Donna Sofia's tears ceased; something flinty kindled in her eyes. "The law that serves the powerful and crushes the weak? Surely you can show mercy."

"Mercy without justice is meaningless." Virginia rose, folding her hands so Donna Sofia would not see them shake. "I grieve for your pain. Truly. But I cannot grant what you ask. Signor Molteno's blood cries out for justice, and I will not silence that cry."

She inclined her head in dismissal and turned away.

Behind her, Donna Sofia's composure shattered. The older woman fled from the parlatory, muffled sobs echoing long after her footsteps faded.

That night, Virginia wept in her cell.

For Molteno. For his wife and children. For Donna Sofia on her knees. For the impossible choice that offered no right answer.

But beneath the tears ran another current, darker and more shameful.

Lying awake, staring into darkness, Virginia understood that every day she kept her refusal, she was choosing the convent's destruction as the price of her own righteousness.

* * *

THREE WEEKS BECAME four. The pressure mounted.

Letters arrived from Milan. The Governor's chancery sent an inquiry, the language smooth and polite even as it hinted at scrutiny. Influential families wrote stiff notes about their 'concern' with thinly veiled threats to withdraw their daughters. Word reached Virginia that even her father, in distant Madrid, had received letters describing his daughter's obstinacy.

Through it all, Judge Pirovano continued his investigation. But Virginia noticed they came less frequently now, stayed fewer hours, questioned with less vigor. The manhunt was losing momentum.

Sister Benedetta noticed too. "They're waiting for you to break," she said one evening. "The Osios. The Governor. Even Pirovano. They know if they apply enough pressure, eventually something will give way."

"I won't break," Virginia said.

Her own voice sounded thin.

"Everyone breaks eventually." Benedetta tied off her thread with neat precision. "The question is what breaks first. Your resolve, or the convent's ability to withstand this storm."

* * *

THE SUMMONS CAME after dawn. Sister Costanza's knock was sharper than usual.

"Mother Imbersaga requests your presence. Immediately."

Virginia dressed in gray half-light. Beside her, Benedetta pushed herself upright, instantly awake.

"Be careful," Benedetta murmured. "The Prioress met with the procurator and legal counsel yesterday."

Mother Imbersaga stood at her window when Virginia entered, a dark figure against a sky beginning to pale. She did not turn.

"Close the door, Sister Virginia."

The click of the latch sounded unnervingly final.

"Do you know what I have been doing these past three days? Meeting with our procurator. With our legal counsel. With representatives from the Archbishop's office. All attempting to assess the damage your vendetta against Signor Osio is causing this community."

"It is not a vendetta, Reverend Mother. It is justice."

"Is it?" Imbersaga turned. Exhaustion had etched itself deep into her face. "Because from where I stand, it looks less like justice and more like pride. Like a de Leyva unable to forgive an insult."

"He murdered a man. Molteno was innocent."

"And the law will make him answer for that. But you seem determined to make yourself the instrument of that answer."

She crossed to the writing table. Parchments lay in ordered stacks, their edges worn.

"Do you know what these are? Letters. Dozens of them. From families threatening to withdraw their daughters. From benefactors suspending endowments. From Church officials questioning our adherence to cloister. All because one nun has made herself the center of a political scandal that threatens to destroy what we have built over two centuries."

The words struck like blows. Virginia's hand caught the back of a chair.

"I have watched you since you arrived," Imbersaga continued. "I have seen your intelligence, your capability. I had hoped you might one day serve this community in leadership. But I have also seen your pride. Your need to assert your will against any who dare cross you. And now that pride threatens to consume us all."

"What would you have me do? Let a murderer go free?"

"I would have you remember your vows." Mother Imbersaga's voice rose. "You are not the Lady of Monza here. You are Sister Virginia Maria, bound by obedience to God and to me. Your father placed you in my care. I will not allow your stubborn pride to destroy what I have spent my life protecting."

Silence fell. Outside, the first bell for None began to toll.

When the Prioress spoke again, her voice had returned to terrible calm.

"You will write to Judge Pirovano. You will instruct him to grant Signor Osio respite and forgiveness. Or I will write to your father and request your transfer to a stricter house. One where your noble blood will grant you no privileges. Where discipline is enforced through means you cannot imagine."

She leaned forward, hands flat on the writing table.

"Do you understand me, Sister Virginia?"

Virginia's nails bit into her palms.

"Yes, Reverend Mother."

"Good. You have until Vespers to compose that letter. I will review it before it is sent. You are dismissed."

Virginia turned toward the door.

"Sister Virginia."

She looked back.

"I do not make this decision lightly. But I will protect this community. Even from its own members. Remember that."

* * *

TWO DAYS LATER, Mother Imbersaga summoned Virginia again.

"You have not written the letter as I requested. You will write to Judge Pirovano today. Now."

Virginia's heart lurched. "Reverend Mother..."

"Your father has written." The Prioress held up a letter sealed with the de Leyva arms. "He has arranged a generous pension for Signora Molteno and her children. They will not want. The debt to Molteno's family has been paid."

"That does not erase the crime."

"No. But it removes your justification for prolonging this feud. The widow is provided for. The children secured. Justice for the dead cannot return him to life. And your insistence on vengeance threatens to destroy the living."

"It is not a vendetta."

"Isn't it?" The Prioress's voice softened dangerously. "Four weeks, Sister Virginia. Four weeks of refusing every petition, every plea, every offer of reconciliation. You have refused them all. Why?"

Because Gian Paolo had killed for her. Because holding his life in her hands had felt like power, and power was the one thing she had been denied since childhood. None of that could be spoken.

"Because justice demands it," she said instead.

"Justice." Imbersaga lifted another bundle of letters. "The Governor of Milan informs me that if this matter is not resolved within the week, he will open an investigation into our convent. Into whether we have properly observed cloister. Into our financial arrangements. Into every private dealing and hidden corner of this community."

Virginia's breath caught. "He cannot."

"He can. And he will. The Osio family has mobilized half of Milan's nobility against us. Three families are withdrawing their daughters. Two major benefactors have suspended their endowments. The Bishop's office has begun asking questions."

She laid the letters down.

"We are a convent, Sister Virginia. We have no army, no weapons, no protection beyond the goodwill of the powerful. And you are stripping even that from us. This is no longer about you and your wounded pride. This is about every sister here. Every servant who depends on us. Every girl whose parents trust us with her soul. The world is unfair. The rich, like Osio, reap every benefit, even avoiding justice."

"So, I should simply forgive a murderer?"

"You should obey your Prioress." Steel entered Imbersaga's voice. "I am commanding you, under pain of disobedience to your vows, to write that letter. Today. Now."

The words landed like a blow. Disobedience to the Prioress was disobedience to God Himself, grounds for severe penance, imprisonment. Or expulsion.

Every fiber of Virginia's being rebelled. But she had no choice.

"I will write the letter."

"Now." Mother Imbersaga gestured to the writing table. "I will have it sent before Vespers."

Virginia moved like a woman walking to the scaffold. Fresh parchment, ink, and quill awaited. The instruments of her surrender.

Her hand shook only once as she wrote.

To Judge Pirovano, I write to inform you that I no longer wish to pursue charges against Signor Gian Paolo Osio for the death of Gioseffo Molteno. The matter has been resolved to my satisfaction through private arrangements. I request that you withdraw the warrant for his arrest and grant him full respite and forgiveness under the law.
Sister Virginia Maria de Leyva, Convent of Santa Margherita, Monza

She set the quill down before she could tear the sheet to shreds.

The Prioress read the letter, nodded once, folded it, and sealed it with the convent's wax.

"It will be delivered within the hour."

* * *

JUDGE PIROVANO'S REPLY arrived two days later. Virginia broke the seal and read.

Reverend Sister Virginia de Leyva,
I acknowledge receipt of your petition for mercy regarding Signor Gian Paolo Osio. Though many cavaliers and nobles have begged me to grant this pardon, I refused them all. But for love of you, and in recognition of your family's honor, I gladly consent. The warrant for Signor Osio's arrest has been withdrawn. He is free to resume his lawful life and business in Monza.
Your humble servant, Judge Pirovano

The words blurred. *For love of you.* As though she had chosen this.

She had ordered his arrest with one signature. Now she had saved his life with another. But neither act had been entirely hers. The Prioress had commanded.

Her father had paid. The magistrate had yielded to chains of obligation older than either of them.

Her supposed authority over Gian Paolo Osio's fate was revealed as illusion. She had no real power. She never had.

Virginia folded the letter carefully. By tomorrow, the whispers would start about the nun who condemned a man and then saved him. About what that might mean.

* * *

THE REQUEST ARRIVED the next morning.

"From Signor Osio," Ottavia said, offering the folded parchment.

Virginia broke the seal.

> *Signor Gian Paolo Osio respectfully requests an audience with Sister Virginia de Leyva in the convent parlatory, at her convenience, to express his gratitude for the mercy shown him.*

He wanted to thank her. In person. With iron bars between them.

Every instinct screamed to refuse.

"What will you say?" Ottavia asked.

Virginia looked up. She should refuse. She knew she should refuse.

"Tell him I will meet him this afternoon. After None."

* * *

THE LIGHT IN the parlatory was thin and cold. On the convent side of the iron grille, Virginia stood with hands folded within her sleeves. Sister Ottavia waited in the shadows, close enough to fulfill the requirement of a chaperone, far enough to grant the illusion of privacy.

On the outer side, Gian Paolo stood with his head slightly bowed, fine cloak draped over one arm.

"Sister Virginia." His voice was quiet, respectful. "I am grateful you agreed to see me."

"The Reverend Mother deemed it proper. You wished to express your gratitude for the pardon."

"More than gratitude." He lifted his gaze to her through the bars. Hiding had carved new angles into his face, sharpened what had once been only handsome into something harder. "I wished to beg your forgiveness directly. For Molteno. For the pain my rashness caused you."

"You were pardoned by the magistrate. There is no need."

"There is every need. I took a man's life over words spoken in anger. Words about you. I cannot restore what I destroyed. But I can stand before you and acknowledge the sin. And beg that you might grant me what the law cannot, your personal forgiveness."

Something in his humility caught her off guard. This was not the laughing nobleman in the apple tree. This was a man stripped of pretense, offering naked remorse. Or a perfect performance of it.

"I have already forgiven you," she said softly. "When I wrote to Judge Pirovano, it was not merely to satisfy your family's petitions. It was because I could not bear the thought of your suffering for a crime born of... of misunderstanding."

"Of my pride," he corrected gently. "And my inability to master my own passions."

The word hung between them. *Passions.*

Heat rose to her cheeks. She glanced toward Ottavia, but her friend had turned her head, granting them what modesty allowed.

"You have your freedom now," Virginia said, steadying her voice. "You may leave Monza, resume your life elsewhere. There is nothing more to be said."

"Is that what you wish? That I leave?"

She should say yes. She should send him away with a blessing and never allow his name to be spoken in these walls again.

Instead, she found herself stepping closer to the grille, as if the iron itself exerted some magnetic pull.

"What I wish is irrelevant," she whispered. "I am bound by vows. You are free. We cannot—"

"Cannot what?" His eyes searched hers through the bars. "Cannot speak? Cannot acknowledge what exists between us?"

"Nothing exists between us."

The denial came out too quickly.

"Then why do you tremble?"

Her hands rose without her bidding, pressing flat against the iron. He mirrored her, palms to bars. The metal between them was perhaps two fingers' breadth, close enough that she could feel the warmth of his skin, yet impossible to touch.

"You must go," she breathed. "This meeting was to give you peace. To let you leave Monza with a clear conscience."

"I will go, if you command it. But know this, Sister Virginia: I did not come only to beg forgiveness for Molteno's death. I came because I had to see you. To know if what I feel... if it is mine alone, or if you feel it too."

"Don't." She tore her hands from the grille as though burned. "Do not speak such things."

"Then I will not say them. But I will not leave Monza unless you order me to go. If there is any part of you that wishes me to remain, I will stay. As your servant. Nothing more."

Your servant. Coming from Gian Paolo's lips, the phrase meant something else altogether.

At the inner doorway, Ottavia cleared her throat softly. A reminder their time had long since passed.

"I must go," Virginia said, barely audible.

"Until we meet again, Sister Virginia."

"We cannot meet again."

Even as she said it, she knew it was another lie.

He bowed, then turned toward the outer door. The sound of it closing reverberated in her bones.

Ottavia came to her side. "Are you well?"

Virginia stared at the empty space beyond the iron grille. "No. I am not well at all."

But as they walked through the cold stone corridors, Virginia understood that the safety of these walls was now an illusion. Something had been set in motion that could not be stopped. She had saved his life. He had sworn himself to her service. And the iron grating between them felt, for the first time, like a promise rather than a barrier.

* * *

THAT EVENING, MOTHER Imbersaga sent for her once more. The Prioress stood at her window, looking out at the dark courtyard where fine snow had begun to drift. She did not turn when Virginia entered.

"Sister Costanza reports that Signor Osio's visit this afternoon lasted considerably longer than is customary. Nearly half an hour."

Virginia's heart stumbled. "We spoke of forgiveness, Reverend Mother. Of his contrition."

"You spoke for half an hour. For a man to thank you for saving his life, five minutes suffice."

"He wished to explain."

"What I wish," Imbersaga said, turning, her voice sharp as broken glass, "is to understand why you seem determined to entangle yourself with this man. First you demand his arrest. Then you refuse every petition for mercy. And now you grant him audiences that extend well beyond propriety."

"Sister Ottavia was present the entire time. As chaperone."

"Yes. As chaperone. Who reports that you and Signor Osio stood very close to the grating. That your hands... touched the iron where his touched it."

Virginia's face burned. "We did not touch."

"No. You were separated by two inches of blessed metal. How fortunate for your vows."

Silence settled between them, heavy and airless.

"I am watching you, Sister Virginia," the Prioress said at last. "I am watching you very carefully. If I see any further impropriety, any letters, any gifts, any communications whatsoever with Signor Osio, I will act. Do you understand me?"

"Yes, Reverend Mother."

"You are dismissed."

Virginia left with the sensation of eyes between her shoulder blades all the way down the corridor.

In the cell that night, Benedetta was waiting.

"The Prioress suspects," she said without preamble. "Sister Costanza has been reporting your movements. Sister Ottavia's discretion can only go so far when the Prioress demands answers. You need to be more careful, Virginia. Much more careful."

Virginia said nothing. Her fingers found the stiff edge of Judge Pirovano's letter in her pocket.

For love of you.

The game had begun.

And Virginia knew, with a certainty that both thrilled and terrified her, that she would not, could not, stop playing. Even if it destroyed them all.

Chapter Four
1598

January

VIRGINIA'S BREATH MISTED in the narrow stairwell as she climbed to the scriptorium. Seven days since the parlatory meeting with Gian Paolo. Seven nights staring at darkness while sleep refused to come.

The scriptorium occupied the convent's highest floor, positioned to capture precious light through windows facing the garden. She pushed open the heavy oak door.

Sister Candida sat hunched over her writing table, soft features illuminated by light streaming through diamond-paned glass. Ink stains marked her delicate fingers.

"Sister Virginia." Candida glanced up, startled. "I did not expect you this morning."

The window had called to her, that opening where she might glimpse the world beyond these walls. Her fingers found the sill.

"The Prioress suggested I assist you." The lie came smoothly. "The illuminated texts require careful attention."

Candida's face brightened. "Indeed, the Gospel of Matthew needs completion before Advent. Your calligraphy is excellent."

The world stopped.

Through the window, among trees silvered with morning light, Gian Paolo walked in his garden. Burgundy wool lined with fur caught the winter sun. A pardoned man strolling through pale shadows while Molteno's children wept over fresh earth.

He turned. Met her stare across the distance.

The window tilted. Virginia gripped the sill to steady herself. Those dark eyes found hers, and he smiled, the same mocking curve of lips that had poisoned her dreams. Slowly, with exaggerated precision, he swept the identical bow he'd offered that day when she'd challenged him at the gates. A nobleman's homage wrapped around naked insolence.

His smile spoke volumes.

She had saved his life. She had written the letter that freed him. And now he stood in his garden, untouchable and mocking, wearing his freedom like a crown.

The realization struck her chest like a fist. He had not appeared by chance. He had arranged to be visible, knowing she would see him from this window. Knowing exactly where she would be. Knowing she would want to see him.

"Sister Virginia?" Candida's voice seemed to come from far away. "Are you well? Your face has gone quite pale."

"I—" Virginia couldn't complete the sentence. The window pulled at her. His gaze held her across the distance, a taut line between them.

She turned from the window and fled.

Down the stairs that pounded beneath her feet. Past sisters who flattened themselves against walls, alarmed at her wild passage. Her wimple loosened, breath tearing in ragged gasps that echoed off stone.

The chapel lay ahead, shadowed and cool. She slipped through the heavy oak doors and found herself alone. The altar stood distant, candles casting dancing shadows. The faint smell of incense clung to the air.

She sank onto a pew near the back, in darkness, where no one would see her.

What kind of woman felt her pulse race at the sight of a murderer? What kind of nun found joy in the knowledge that a man marked by violence thought of her, watched for her, arranged moments for her to see him?

She had pardoned him. But at that moment through the window, she understood the terrible truth: she had not freed him from anything. She had bound herself to him instead.

He had wanted her to see him, and she had wanted to be seen.

"I thought I might find you here."

Virginia's head snapped up. Benedetta stood at the end of the pew, silhouetted against the candlelight. She did not ask permission. She simply sat down, her black habit merging with the shadows.

"You saw him." Not a question. "Sister Candida told me."

Virginia could not answer.

"In the garden. You were at the scriptorium window. He arranged to be visible. And you... you wanted to see him."

"Don't."

"I will. Because if you do not name it now, you will spend the rest of your life pretending it is something other than what it is. And that will make you very dangerous to yourself and everyone around you."

Virginia's hands clenched in her lap.

"He is a murderer," Benedetta continued. "That has not changed. He killed a man. But when you saw him through the window, that fact ceased to matter to you."

"You're wrong."

"Then name what you felt. Describe it to me. Tell me what happened when your eyes met his across the distance."

Virginia closed her eyes. He remained there, the burgundy cloak, the mocking smile, the deliberate precision of that bow. The pull of him, hooks in her chest.

"He wanted me to know he was free," Virginia said finally, barely audible. "He wanted me to know that I had freed him. That I held the power of his life in my hands, and I chose to save it."

"Yes."

"And he wanted me to understand that by saving his life, I had bound myself to him instead."

Benedetta said nothing. In her silence lay confirmation.

"What kind of woman realizes all of this," Virginia whispered, "and still does not look away?"

"The kind of woman who is honest about what she feels." Benedetta remained motionless. "You are not the first woman in a convent to desire a man she should condemn. But most of them live with the lie. They convince themselves it is spiritual love, or misguided charity, or Christian pity." Benedetta turned to face Virginia. "You, at least, have the courage to know what it is."

"Courage? This is not courage. This is sin."

"Yes," Benedetta said flatly. "It is. And you knew that the moment you saw him smile at you. You knew it, and you wanted it anyway."

The chapel seemed to close in around them. Virginia's chest tightened.

"What happens now?" Virginia asked.

"Now," Benedetta said quietly, "you accept that you have already made your choice. You made it the moment you went to the scriptorium window and looked toward the garden instead of your work."

* * *

SOFT FOOTSTEPS IN the corridor pulled Virginia from restless sleep. Too light for the Prioress. Too purposeful for sisters returning from Compline.

Benedetta and Ottavia had both fallen asleep.

She counted three breaths in the silence.

"Sister Virginia." The whisper barely stirred the air. "It's Silvia."

Virginia slipped from her cot and cracked open the door.

Sister Silvia stood in the dim corridor, her young face pale as candle wax. Barely eighteen, one of the newer postulants. Her merchant father had died drowning in debts, leaving his daughter with no choice but the convent or the streets.

"What is it?" Virginia kept her voice low.

Silvia glanced nervously along the corridor, then leaned close and pressed something small and warm into Virginia's palm. Her fingers trembled.

"Apollonia gave it to me. She came with the laundry delivery this evening and hid until she could find me alone. By the scullery door. I waited for everyone to be asleep before I brought it to you."

Virginia's breath caught. "Apollonia?"

"She was crying, Sister." Silvia's eyes were wide with distress. "She said the master, Osio, made her bring it. She begged me to give it to you. Said she was afraid to come because... because of her face."

Virginia's stomach clenched. She remembered the bruise on Apollonia's cheek. The violence of the Osio household had breached the convent walls again, carried by a terrified woman forced to serve a murderer.

Virginia's fingers closed around the object. Smooth limestone. Still warm from a man's pocket or palm. In the corridor's dim light, she turned it carefully.

Ordinary gray stone, the kind that littered the roads around Monza. But carved into its surface with a knife point, precise and deliberate, was a single initial: ***V***.

Her initial. His message.

"Did she say anything else?" Virginia's voice came out as a croak.

"Only that he is watching. And that he waits."

Behind Virginia, bedclothes rustled.

Benedetta's voice cut through the darkness, sharp and alert. "Close the door, Sister Virginia. Now."

Virginia obeyed as Silvia's footsteps retreated. She turned to find Benedetta sitting upright on her cot, fully awake. Ottavia stirred but didn't wake.

"What did she give you?" Benedetta asked quietly.

Virginia crossed to her bed and sank onto the edge. She opened her palm, letting moonlight illuminate the token.

Benedetta rose and moved closer. She studied the limestone without touching it.

"A message," she said flatly. "A claim. A promise." She met Virginia's gaze. "Do you understand what accepting this means?"

"I didn't ask for it."

"That's not what I asked. I asked if you understand what it means that you're still holding it. That you haven't thrown it out the window or handed it to the Prioress. That you're sitting here, clutching it like something precious."

Virginia's fingers tightened around the stone. "What would you have me do?"

"Either destroy that token and report this contact to the Prioress." Benedetta returned to her cot and sat. "Or keep it and accept that you've just taken the first step toward complicity in everything that follows."

"You make it sound simple."

"It is simple. Not easy, but simple." Benedetta pulled her blanket over her lap. "What's complicated is that you want two things—justice for Molteno and connection to his murderer. You want to be the righteous nun and the desired woman. You want safety and danger. You cannot have both. Choose."

Virginia looked down at the carved *V* in her palm. The stone felt warm now, heated by her own skin. Or perhaps by the touch of the man who'd carved it.

"I don't know what I want," she whispered.

"Yes, you do." Benedetta's voice held no judgment, only observation. "You've known since the moment you saw him in that apple tree. The question is whether you're brave enough, or foolish enough, to admit it."

Silence settled over the chamber. Ottavia continued sleeping peacefully. Benedetta lay back down, her breathing evening out.

But Virginia remained sitting on the edge of her cot, the limestone token clutched in her fist. Warm against her palm. Smooth as skin. Heavy as all the choices she hadn't yet made.

Outside their window, night deepened over Monza. Somewhere in that darkness, a murderer waited. For her response. For her choice. For whatever came next.

Virginia lay back on her cot, slipping the carved stone beneath her pillow. Her fingers lingered on the rough fabric of the pillowcase, on the weight of what lay hidden beneath. She should burn it. Should give it to the Prioress. Should report the contact and save herself from what would come next.

But she didn't move.

Somewhere beyond the convent walls, Gian Paolo Osio waited. For her response. For her choice. For whatever came next. And in the darkness before dawn, Virginia understood with terrible clarity: she had already made her decision the moment she kept the stone.

Everything that followed would be consequence.

* * *

THE SABBATH BELLS of Santa Margherita echoed, but Virginia heard only the rhythm of her own transgression. Three days had passed since she'd pressed her palm to the scriptorium window. Three nights staring at darkness while sleep refused to come.

She knelt in the choir stall. Latin chanting rose and fell, a meaningless hum. Her fingers worked the worn beads of her rosary, but her mind wandered corridors and gardens.

At the front of the church, among the patricians, Gian Paolo Osio bowed his head with practiced devotion. For a moment, she saw only the back of his dark head in the candlelight.

Then he shifted, as though by chance, and his profile came into view. His gaze flicked toward the grille. Their eyes met for the briefest instant. His lips moved, forming a single silent word.

Garden.

The service continued around her. Bells chimed. Congregants rose and knelt. Wax and incense thickened the air. But the word reverberated through her body like a touch. He wanted her to meet him.

She would not go to him.

After the service ended, she walked with the other sisters to the refectory. Sat at her place. Took her portion. Listened to the reading. Her hands followed the motions of grace and bread and cup while her mind replayed that one word over and over.

Garden.

The next two days dragged in small failures. She misplaced lines in the psalter. Spilled water at table. Found her gaze drifting toward the garden wall whenever footsteps sounded outside.

* * *

ON THE THIRD afternoon, Virginia climbed toward the scriptorium. The narrow stairwell carried the smell of stone dust and damp wool. Her hand skimmed the wall as she climbed.

At the highest level, the scriptorium windows glowed with winter light as she slipped inside.

Sister Candida sat hunched over her writing table, soft features illuminated by light streaming through diamond-paned glass. Ink stains marked her delicate fingers. The scratch of her quill whispered across parchment.

"Sister Virginia." Candida glanced up, startled. "I did not expect you this afternoon."

The window called to her, that opening where she might glimpse the world beyond these walls. Her fingers found the sill, glass cold beneath her skin.

"I thought I might assist you." The lie came smoothly. "The illuminated texts you've been working on require careful attention."

Candida's face brightened. "Indeed, these antiphons for Advent still need copying. Your hand is steady enough for the small script."

Virginia made some answer she did not remember. Her gaze slid past Candida's shoulder to the world beyond the glass.

Among the winter-bare trees, near the dividing wall, Gian Paolo stood. No pacing this time. No restlessness. He simply waited, his cloak dark against the pale trunks.

When she stepped into the window's full light, his head lifted. He saw her at once. The distance between them filled.

He did not bow. That courtesy had been spent already. Instead, he stood bareheaded in the cold, looking up at her as though she alone occupied his world.

Candida bent over her work again, oblivious. The scratch of her quill and the faint crackle of the fire in the brazier were the only sounds.

Virginia rested her palm against the glass. The cold bit her skin.

She stayed only a heartbeat longer than she should have. Then she stepped back from the light.

* * *

BY THE TIME Benedetta found her in the chapel that evening, Virginia knelt in the half-dark, fingers locked so tightly around her rosary that the beads dug into her skin.

"I thought I might find you here."

Virginia's head lifted. Benedetta stood at the end of the pew, silhouette edged with candlelight. She did not ask permission. She simply sat down, her black habit folding into the shadows.

"You went to the scriptorium," Benedetta said. "Candida told me you helped but spent a great deal of time at the window."

Virginia said nothing.

"He was there," Benedetta continued. "In the garden. Waiting." Not a question.

"You tell me," Virginia said, voice low. "Did I go to work? Or did I go to look?"

"Does it matter?" Benedetta's tone stayed quiet. "You went."

Virginia's hands tightened in her lap, knuckles whitening.

"He is a murderer," Benedetta said. "That has not changed. He killed a man. But when you stood at that window, that truth did not send you away."

"I know what he is." The words came out raw. "I know what he has done."

"And still." Benedetta turned her head, studying Virginia's profile. "You rested your hand on the glass. You let him see you. You let yourself be seen."

Virginia closed her eyes. The cold of the pane remained in her palm. So did the heat that had flared beneath it.

"What happens now?" she whispered.

"Now," Benedetta said quietly, "you stop pretending this is happening to you. It is happening because of you. You have begun answering him."

Virginia flinched.

"You are not the first woman in a convent to desire a man she should condemn," Benedetta continued. "But most of them soothe themselves with holy words. They call it charity or pity. You do not have that comfort. You know what it is."

"Sin," Virginia said.

"Yes. And choice." Benedetta's voice remained level. "Every time you go to that window, every time you let him see you, you choose."

The chapel closed in around them. The air thinned beneath Virginia's veil.

"If you mean to stop," Benedetta said, "stop now. Before there is anything more between you than looks through glass."

Virginia's fingers loosened around the rosary beads, then tightened again.

"I do not know if I can," she said.

"Then you know more than enough about what comes next," Benedetta answered. She rose. "And so do I."

She left Virginia in the dimness, kneeling in a pew that felt more like a prison bench with every passing breath.

* * *

February

CRISP MORNING AIR chilled Gian Paolo as he crossed the piazza toward the church of San Maurizio. The priest of that church, Father Arrigone, understood the delicate architecture of influence and favor. More importantly, Santa Margherita fell under his parish jurisdiction. That made Arrigone precisely the ally Gian Paolo needed.

He found the priest in his study, bent over correspondence. Morning light slanted through diamond-paned windows, illuminating dust motes above scattered papers. The room smelled of ink and dusty books and old vellum.

When Gian Paolo revealed his plan, the priest's quill paused mid-stroke. Silence stretched until it became a living thing between them. Arrigone set the quill aside with unhurried care, one eyebrow lifting.

"So," he said at last, "the lion has found his prey." A thin smile touched his lips. "Though I wonder if you understand which of you is truly the hunter."

"You disapprove?" Gian Paolo asked.

"Disapproval?" Arrigone leaned back in his chair. "My dear friend, I am a priest, not a saint. Disapproval is a luxury I cannot afford."

His fingers drummed once against the writing table. "But I counsel patience. Such a fortress cannot be taken by storm. You must appear to surrender even as you advance."

Gian Paolo's jaw tightened. "I have no interest in surrender."

"Exactly." Arrigone's eyes gleamed. "Leave the first approach to me. Your passion burns too bright, too transparent. It will frighten her. She must believe herself safe, even as the ground shifts beneath her feet."

"And you think you can accomplish what I cannot?"

"I think," Arrigone said softly, "that I can make her believe the corruption springs from her own heart rather than your design." His smile held no warmth. "Once she accepts that, you will not need to conquer her. She will walk toward you of her own accord."

Arrigone began crafting the first letter for Gian Paolo. His quill scratched against parchment in measured rhythm while Gian Paolo paced the length of the study, unable to settle. The words that emerged breathed devotion wrapped in spiritual longing so artfully woven that even Gian Paolo found himself moved by the apparent sincerity. Arrigone wrote of Gian Paolo's admiration for Virginia's piety, his desperate desire to walk a more righteous path through her example.

"Read it," Arrigone commanded, extending the parchment.

Gian Paolo scanned the lines, eyebrows rising. "You make me sound like a penitent seeking absolution."

"Precisely." Arrigone reached for the sand to blot the ink. "The last thing she expects from you is humility. It will intrigue her far more than bold declarations ever could."

He shook sand over the wet strokes and blew it away. "She expects arrogance. Perhaps crude advances. Instead, she will receive gentle contrition and promises of spiritual fellowship." Satisfaction settled across his features. "Pride is the first sin, yes, but curiosity runs a very close second."

Gian Paolo frowned. "She will guess it was not written by me. This hand is too neat. Too controlled."

"That is precisely the point." Arrigone folded the parchment. "Let her think your feelings are guided by a pious purpose, that wiser hands shape your words. Time enough for truth later."

Gian Paolo returned to his palazzo with the letter hidden inside his doublet. He turned toward the servants' entrance. Apollonia would be in the kitchen at this hour.

He sent a servant to fetch her, then waited in his study.

She appeared moments later, her face carefully blank. The fading bruise on her cheek had turned from purple to sickly yellow-green, a watercolor of old violence on fragile skin. Her husband's work. His, too.

"You summoned me, signore?" she asked, eyes on the floor.

He withdrew the parchment. "For Sister Virginia Maria. As you delivered the token before, you will deliver this."

He pressed it into her palm along with two silver coins, twice what he had paid before. Metal clinked softly against her skin.

Apollonia's eyes widened before she schooled her features. "The sisters are watching more carefully now, signore. After the token... Sister Silvia was nervous." Her fingers tightened around her apron. "If we are discovered..."

"You will not be discovered if you are careful." His voice hardened just enough to remind her of the limits of her choices. "You deliver laundry to the convent daily. Surely you can manage to pass a simple parchment to young Sister Silvia?"

"Yes, signore."

"Tell Sister Silvia it bears words of spiritual guidance for Sister Virginia. Nothing more." He paused. "Your husband has been most useful to me in certain... matters. I would hate for his position in my household to become uncertain."

The unspoken threat settled heavily between them. Apollonia's face went pale.

"I understand, signore." She curtseyed, the movement jerky. "The parchment will be delivered today."

She fled, the door closing softly behind her.

* * *

THE LETTER APPEARED three days later.

Virginia found it when she returned to her cell after None. Folded paper, sealed with dark blue wax, lay just inside the door like a fallen shadow.

She stared at it, pulse racing. She should carry it directly to Mother Imbersaga or drop it into the brazier. Should not touch it at all.

Instead, she knelt and lifted the parchment. The paper was heavy, expensive, smelling faintly of sandalwood and beeswax.

Her fingers trembled as she broke the seal.

The handwriting inside was unfamiliar, elegant, disciplined script. Not the hurried scrawl she imagined from a man whose temper ran hot, but the measured hand of a scholar.

> *To the Most Revered Sister Virginia Maria,*
> *I write this in trembling humility, seeking not your favor but your forgiveness. Since our brief encounter, my soul has known no peace. I came to you in passion, driven by worldly desires, but I left transformed by the radiance of your virtue.*

Virginia sank onto her cot, eyes devouring the words. This was not the arrogant nobleman who had mocked her from the garden. This was something else. A man speaking of spiritual awakening.

> *You have awakened in me a hunger for righteousness I had thought long dead. If I dare to write to you now, it is only to ask: how does one walk the path you have chosen? How does one find silence amidst the noise of the world?*

She read it twice, then a third time. He was not asking for her love. He was asking for her guidance. He was placing his soul in her hands.

Relief washed through her so sharply it left her dizzy. She had braced herself for demands, for raw passion, for the danger of his physical desire. Instead, he offered her a role she understood, one that felt safe, even holy. Teacher. Guide. The one who knew the path.

He wanted her to be his spiritual guide.

Surely there could be no sin in helping a lost soul find its way. In answering questions about prayer and discipline? In pointing a wicked man toward God?

She pushed down the prick of unease that rose with the thought and went to her small writing table. The quill felt heavier than it should when she dipped it into ink.

* * *

THE SECOND PIECE of correspondence required even greater delicacy.

Late the next afternoon, in the priest's chambers, Gian Paolo's wounded pride bristled against every word of apology Arrigone penned.

"This makes me sound like a schoolboy caught stealing apples," he protested, pacing.

"Exactly." Arrigone did not pause. "Nothing is more disarming than unexpected humility from a man of your reputation. She expects you to batter the gates. Instead, you kneel outside them."

"You transform me into something I am not."

Arrigone sealed the new parchment with firm pressure of his ring. "I transform you into something she needs you to be. The rest will follow naturally."

With the folded letter in hand, Gian Paolo returned to his palazzo and summoned Apollonia once more.

"Another," he said simply, handing her the sealed document and three silver coins this time. "Same method. Same discretion."

"When shall I deliver it, signore?" She did not look at the extra coin.

"Tomorrow evening." He considered a moment. "Let the first work on her while she prays. This second must arrive when she has already begun to question her resistance."

"As you wish, signore."

The next afternoon, Gian Paolo positioned himself in the winter-bare orchard beyond the convent's outer wall. He dressed plainly, no embroidery or jewels to catch an idle observer's eye and kept to the shadows where the scriptorium window could see him, but casual passersby could not.

His pulse quickened each time he caught movement. A white wimple, black wool, the flutter of a habit in the evening wind.

Then, there. A figure in the scriptorium window.

Virginia appeared behind the glass, her silhouette unmistakable. She stood motionless, looking down toward where he waited.

She had received his correspondence. Had read the words Arrigone had put forth. And now she had come to this window.

Slowly, deliberately, he removed his cap. The gesture was reverent, almost worshipful. He pressed it to his chest and offered a deep, courtly bow.

Virginia did not move at once. Then, with a movement so slight it might have been missed, she inclined her head.

With his free hand, he touched his heart, then extended his palm toward her. The motion was subtle, easily mistaken for a devotional gesture should any other eyes be watching, yet intimate enough to suggest deeper currents.

Behind the glass, her form shifted. A pale flash as she raised her hands, perhaps to touch the cold pane that separated their worlds.

Then she stepped back from the window and disappeared into the shadows of the room.

Gian Paolo replaced his cap. She had not fled or closed the shutters. Instead, she had acknowledged him, like a noblewoman accepting a courtier's homage.

As he walked back toward his palazzo, satisfaction settled into his chest. Virginia believed herself safe in spiritual correspondence, unaware that each exchange drew her deeper into waters where her pride would eventually drown her resolve.

Yet when he reached his own door and turned for one last look at the convent's dark silhouette against the star-pricked sky, Arrigone's earlier question echoed: which of you is truly the hunter?

* * *

THE SYSTEM, ONCE established, moved with terrifying efficiency.

Each evening at dusk, Osio slipped a folded parchment and a silver coin into Apollonia's hand. By the time darkness settled, Apollonia had pressed the letter into Sister Silvia's palm under cover of laundry and routine. Silvia slid it under Virginia's door with the practiced stealth of a girl who had learned quickly how secrets traveled through stone corridors.

By candlelight, Virginia wrote her replies, pouring her thoughts onto paper with a freedom she had never known. She wrote of prayer, yes, but also of her loneliness, her doubts, the suffocating sameness of the days. She described the discipline that had once sustained her and now felt like a noose. She wrote of saints and of silence, of the way the chapel's cool air sometimes felt like a hand on her throat.

In the morning, she slipped the folded parchments into the pillowcase when she made her bed. During cell inspections, Silvia collected them and carried them to Apollonia with the soiled linens. By noon, Osio held Virginia's soul in his ink-stained hands.

It was perfect. It was secret.

And like all secrets in a convent, it could not last.

Sister Benedetta moved through the lower corridor one chilly morning, her mind on account books she had been reviewing for Mother Imbersaga. Columns of numbers still marched behind her eyes, neat and unforgiving.

As she passed the receiving room near the main gate, a hushed exchange drew her attention. The door stood half open. Through the gap she saw Apollonia with her basket of folded linens glance nervously toward the corridor, then reached into her apron. A white packet appeared in her hand.

Young Sister Silvia stood before her, face pale.

"Please, Sister," Apollonia whispered. "He says it must reach her today."

Silvia took the parchment and tucked it into her habit. Two small silver coins followed, vanishing into the same fold of cloth. Payment for complicity.

Benedetta's hands tightened on the doorframe. She had arranged the first letter delivery; one controlled exchange to satisfy Virginia's curiosity and, she had hoped, to end the matter. But this was clearly not the first exchange. This was a system now: ongoing, regular, unsanctioned.

"Sister Silvia."

Both women froze. Silvia's face drained of color as Benedetta stepped into the room.

"Sister Benedetta. I was just—"

"Collecting laundry?" Benedetta's voice was quiet, almost gentle. All the more dangerous for it. She turned to Apollonia. "Leave your basket and go."

Apollonia fled, head bowed.

Benedetta closed the door and faced the trembling novice. "Show me what she gave you."

"I don't have anything."

"Do not lie to me." Benedetta's tone sharpened. "I saw it pass. Show me now, or I will take you directly to the Prioress."

Silvia's hands shook as she produced the parchment. Heavy paper. Blue wax seal. The coins slipped from her fingers and fell to the floor with a soft clink.

Benedetta picked up the parchment. She did not break the seal. She weighed it in her hand. Heavy. Substantial. Dangerous.

"How long has this been happening?" she asked.

"After you arranged the first delivery, Sister..." Silvia swallowed. "Apollonia came back two days later with another. And then another yesterday. This is the third."

"Three letters." Benedetta closed her eyes for a heartbeat, calculating the damage. She had authorized one. Instead of a single controlled spark, she had fed a fire. Three letters meant Virginia had likely written three replies. Three confessions of the heart already in Osio's possession.

"And I assume Sister Virginia has been replying?" she said.

Silvia nodded miserably. "She leaves them in her pillowcase when she makes her bed. I collect them during morning cell inspections and pass them to Apollonia with the linens."

"Does anyone else know?"

"No, Sister. I swear it. Only Apollonia and me."

Benedetta opened her eyes. The sum of it lay before her with brutal clarity. She could end it here, carry this parchment straight to Mother Imbersaga, confess her own part, and let justice fall where it might. It would likely save her soul.

It would destroy Virginia.

"Listen to me carefully, Sister Silvia." Benedetta's voice lost all softness. "This system will continue, but under new terms."

The girl blinked. "Sister?"

"From this moment on, you bring every parchment to me first. Every single one. Before you take it to Sister Virginia's door. And any reply she gives you, you bring to me before you give it to Apollonia. Do you understand?"

"Yes, Sister."

"If you fail in this, if you deliver even one scrap of paper without my knowledge, I will go to the Prioress myself. I will tell her everything. And you know what happens to novices who facilitate sin."

Silvia nodded frantically, tears spilling. "I swear, Sister. I swear on the Blessed Virgin."

"Go. Deliver this one. And wipe your face." Benedetta bent, picked up the silver coins, and pressed them back into Silvia's palm. "Hide these better. If anyone sees them, we are all lost."

She watched the girl hurry away toward the dormitory wing, habit swishing against stone. When the corridor was empty again, she looked down at her own empty hands, feeling the phantom weight of the parchment she had not opened.

She had lost control. She had thought she could manage this affair by granting Virginia one carefully monitored exchange. Instead, the correspondence had taken on a life of its own, continuing, accelerating, becoming something far more dangerous than she had intended.

She could still go to the Prioress. Could shift the burden upward where it belonged. But the image of Virginia's face, proud, hungry, already too exposed, rose before her.

The choice had been made long ago, in the silence of their shared cell, in the unspoken bond of years. Benedetta would not betray Virginia.

But she would not let her walk blindfolded into ruin, either.

* * *

THAT NIGHT, AFTER Compline, the atmosphere in the cell was brittle with tension. Shadows pooled in the corners. The candle on the small table burned low.

Virginia sat on her cot, reading by that unsteady light. The parchment, the third one, lay open in her lap. Her face was soft, unguarded, illuminated by private joy that made Benedetta's stomach knot.

"It is a dangerous game you are playing, Sister," Benedetta said from the shadows.

Virginia looked up, startled. She folded the parchment quickly, covering it with her hand. "I don't know what you mean."

"Do not insult my intelligence." Benedetta stepped into the candlelight. "I saw Apollonia today. I know about the correspondence."

Virginia went very still. Then, slowly, she lifted her chin. "They are spiritual," she said. "He asks for guidance. I provide it."

"Spiritual guidance?" Benedetta laughed once, a harsh, dry sound. "Do you truly believe that? Do you think a man like Osio writes to you because he cares for his soul?"

"You don't know him," Virginia said hotly. "You see only his reputation. In these words..." She touched the folded parchment with her fingertips. "He is different. He is seeking God."

"He is seeking you," Benedetta snapped. "And he is using the one lure he knows you cannot resist—your own need to matter. He makes you feel holy so you will forget to be careful."

"That is not true."

“Is it not?” Benedetta moved closer. “Look at yourself, Virginia. You are glowing. Is that the glow of religious fervor? Or the flush of a woman who knows she is desired?”

Virginia flinched as though struck. She looked down at the parchment in her lap, at the elegant script that had promised her she was saving a soul.

“It doesn’t matter,” she whispered. “It is the only thing I have. The only thing that is mine.”

The raw honesty silenced Benedetta. For a moment she saw not the reckless conspirator, but the girl who had arrived at thirteen with silk still clinging to her and found the gates closing behind her forever. A woman who had spent nine years starving for any connection not mandated by obedience.

“I cannot stop you,” Benedetta said at last, voice weary. “I know that now. You will write to him whether I encourage you to stop or not.”

“I must,” Virginia said simply.

“Then at least be smart about it.” Benedetta sat on the edge of her own cot. “Burn them after you read them. All of them. Never use names in your replies. And for the love of God, Virginia, do not believe everything he writes.”

Virginia looked at the parchment again. “He says he wants to change. He says I am his only hope.”

“He says what works,” Benedetta said. “Remember that.”

Virginia nodded, but her eyes had already returned to the page. She traced the signature with her fingertip. *Your devoted servant in Christ.*

Later, when the candle had been extinguished and the convent slept, Virginia lay awake in darkness. Benedetta’s even breathing filled one side of the small room; Ottavia’s soft murmured prayers filled the other.

Virginia knew Benedetta was right. She knew it was dangerous, perhaps even built on lies.

But in the darkness, she pressed the folded parchment to her heart. It was a bridge across the void. A lifeline thrown into the deep water where she had been drowning for nine years.

She would write back tomorrow. She would tell him about Saint Teresa and the discipline of prayer. She would guide his soul.

And if, in doing so, she lost her own?

Virginia closed her eyes and let the darkness rise around her. It was a price she had already begun to pay.

* * *

Early Spring

THE PACKAGE ARRIVED on Tuesday morning, just as the last notes of the convent bells died after their call to Terce. Virginia was lost in her breviary when Ottavia appeared, cheeks flushed and eyes bright.

"Virginia," she whispered, glancing down the hall before slipping inside. "There's a man at the gate, asking for you. He brings a gift from a devoted friend."

The breviary slipped in Virginia's hands. "What kind of gift?"

"He wouldn't say. Only that he must give it directly to you." Ottavia's excitement trembled in her voice. "Shall I say you're at prayer?"

Virginia almost refused. She'd spent the last week in penance, trying to wash Gian Paolo from her thoughts. She forced herself to focus on duties instead of staring through the window into his garden, where spring light now danced through new leaves. Yet curiosity gnawed at her resolve.

"Bring him to the parlatory," she said, closing her book. "I'll speak with him there."

When the man stepped in, she recognized Giuseppe Pesseno, Apollonia's husband, a burly man with cold eyes.

"Sister Virginia Maria," he began, removing his cap. "My master, Signor Osio, sends his most respectful greetings and begs you to accept this token of his devotion."

He placed a small package on the grille's ledge, wrapped in silk the color of fresh cream. The fabric was exquisite. Virginia stared at it as though it might devour her carefully constructed restraint.

"What does your master expect in return?" Her voice carried the chill of morning rain.

Pesseno shifted his weight. "Nothing, Sister. He says you'll understand his meaning when you see what's inside."

Virginia did not reach for the package. "And if I refuse?"

"I will return it unopened and carry your regrets. But he hopes most fervently you will not."

After a silence that stretched longer than prayer, Virginia reached for the package. The cream silk felt impossibly soft as she unwrapped it, exposing a smaller bundle tied with thread that gleamed like spun gold. When she opened this inner wrapping, air rushed from her lungs.

The gloves were white silk, so pure they seemed to glow. Gold embroidery traced delicate patterns across palms and fingers, vines and flowers worked with such skill they appeared to breathe. Each tiny stitch spoke of hours of patient labor. Tucked beneath them lay a letter sealed with red wax bearing Gian Paolo's signet.

"They're beautiful," she murmured before wisdom could catch the words. To Pesseno, she added with forced formality, "Please convey my thanks to your master."

"And shall I tell him you'll read his letter?"

"Tell him I'll consider it," she whispered.

After Pesseno departed, Virginia remained in the parlatory, turning the gloves over in her hands. The workmanship was extraordinary. They must have cost more than some families spent in a year, more than her father had ever spent on any single gift for her.

She slipped one glove onto her left hand, marveling at how it fit as though crafted for her fingers alone. The silk caressed her skin, and for one dangerous moment she allowed herself to imagine wearing them not in a stark convent cell but in a grand palazzo, reaching out to take the hand of a man who looked at her with hunger rather than duty.

The fantasy shattered when footsteps echoed beyond. Quickly, she stripped off the glove and tucked both deep into the pocket beneath her habit, along with the silk wrappings and unopened letter. But as she walked back to her cell, she sensed their presence against her thigh like a second heartbeat, warm, insistent, utterly forbidden.

She had barely reached her cell when she heard distinctive measured footsteps. Sister Benedetta appeared behind her, sharp eyes taking in Virginia's flushed face.

"Let's go inside and close the door," Benedetta said quietly, her tone brooking no argument.

Virginia obeyed, pulse jumping. "Sister Benedetta..."

"Show me what he gave you."

It wasn't a request. Virginia's hands trembled as she extracted the gloves and silk wrappings, laying them on the narrow bed like evidence at a trial. Benedetta moved closer, examining the items.

She picked up one glove, holding it to the window light. Her expression didn't change, but Virginia watched her jaw tighten.

"White silk. Gold thread embroidery. These cost more than most families earn in a year or two." She set the glove down with deliberate care. "Pesseno delivered them?"

"Yes. How did you know?"

"I make it my business to know who enters and leaves this convent. Especially when they're servants of men you're conspiring with."

Virginia's face burned. "I didn't ask him to send gifts."

"No. You merely accept them." Benedetta moved to the window. "Do you understand what accepting this gift means?"

"It's a token of spiritual friendship."

"It's a declaration of intent," Benedetta said, her voice sharp. "Gloves this expensive aren't given as tokens of spiritual friendship. They're given as courtship gifts. As promises. And by accepting them, you've signaled your willingness to receive such promises."

"I can return them," Virginia said, though the thought made her chest ache.

"You could. But you won't. Because you want them. Not for their beauty, not for their value, but for what they represent—his attention, his desire."

The brutal accuracy stole Virginia's words.

"There's also a letter," Virginia admitted, pulling the sealed parchment from her habit.

Benedetta's eyes narrowed. "Unopened?"

"Yes."

"Then don't open it. Not yet. Not until we've discussed what accepting expensive gifts means." Benedetta's posture radiated controlled tension. "These gloves create witnesses. Pesseno knows he delivered them. The artisan who made them knows they were commissioned. The merchant who sold the materials knows their value and destination. Every one of these people can provide evidence."

Virginia hadn't considered the trail of witnesses spreading outward like ripples in water.

"What do I do?" she whispered.

Benedetta was silent for a long moment, her calculating mind working through options. "You keep them hidden. Tell no one else about them, not even Sister Ottavia. They stay in this cell, wrapped in that silk, hidden where no casual search would find them." Her sharp gaze fixed on Virginia. "And you read his letter carefully. Not for the romantic sentiments, but for what he's proposing. What he expects in return for gifts this expensive."

"He expects nothing," Virginia protested.

"He expects everything," Benedetta corrected. "Men don't spend a year's worth of wages on gloves for women they have no hope of possessing. This gift is an investment, Sister Virginia. And investments always demand returns."

She moved toward the door, then paused. "One more thing. These gloves prove that Osio has substantial resources and is willing to spend them on you. That makes him more dangerous, not less. A man with resources can bribe servants, buy silence, create opportunities." Her gaze held Virginia motionless. "As your friend, and if you want my help, I need to know immediately if he sends more gifts, makes new requests, or changes his pattern. Do you understand?"

"Yes," Virginia whispered.

"Good." Benedetta opened the door, checked the corridor, then looked back. "And Sister Virginia? Whatever his letter says, whatever promises he makes, remember this: you're not in control of this correspondence anymore. He is. These gloves prove it."

Then she was gone, leaving Virginia alone with the beautiful, damning evidence of how thoroughly she'd been ensnared.

* * *

THAT EVENING, ALONE in her chamber with the door barred and a single candle casting wavering shadows, Virginia finally broke the seal on Gian Paolo's letter. His handwriting was elegant, each word carefully formed:

> *Most revered Sister Virginia Maria,*
> *I send these poor gloves as a symbol of the purity and devotion with which I wish to serve you. Their whiteness cannot compare to the radiance of your soul, yet I hope they may remind you that my intentions toward you are as unstained as the silk from which they are woven. I ask nothing but to be your faithful servant in all things honorable and holy. If my previous words offended your noble spirit, I beg your forgiveness with a contrite heart. I desire only to be guided by your wisdom and to find in your friendship the path toward a better understanding of virtue.*
> *Your devoted and humble servant, Gian Paolo Osio*

Virginia read the letter three times, searching for hidden meanings like a scholar parsing sacred text. The words were everything she had hoped for and feared, humble, penitent, proper in every sense. Yet something in their perfection made unease flutter in her chest, an echo of Benedetta's warning about investments and expected returns. They sounded rehearsed, as though crafted by someone else's more experienced hand rather than flowing from genuine feeling.

Still, they offered her what she desperately needed: justification. If Gian Paolo sought spiritual guidance, if his intentions were as pure as the silk of his gift, then surely there could be no sin in correspondence. She was meant to be a teacher and an example to others. Perhaps the Almighty intended her to guide this wayward soul toward redemption.

She took up her pen and wrote with careful deliberation:

Signor Osio,

I thank you for your thoughtful gift and the sentiments expressed in your letter. The gloves are beautiful beyond my humble deserving, and I accept them in the spirit of Christian charity in which they were offered. I am willing to accept your service, but only in the manner you have described, as a spiritual friendship aimed at your moral improvement. If you seek guidance in matters of virtue and faith, I am prepared to offer what counsel I can, provided our correspondence remains within the bounds of propriety. Your correspondence must be conducted with discretion, and your visits to our grounds kept to proper hours and locations. Any deviation from these conditions will result in the immediate cessation of our communication. May God bless your sincere efforts toward spiritual betterment.

Sister Virginia Maria de Leyva

She folded the letter with movements as precise as ritual, then held it for a long moment, sensing its weight like that of a stone about to be cast into still water. Tomorrow she would find a way to deliver it.

As she prepared for sleep, Virginia slipped the gloves beneath her pillow, where their silk whispered against rough convent linen. She told herself they were merely a gift between spiritual friends, a symbol of pure intentions and holy purpose.

But Benedetta's words echoed in her mind: *You're not in control of this correspondence anymore. He is.*

When she finally drifted into sleep, her dreams bloomed with golden thread and gentle hands, with whispered promises and stolen moments bathed in candlelight. In her dreams, the gloves belonged not to a nun seeking to guide a penitent soul but to a woman discovering the dangerous, intoxicating pleasure of being desired.

She woke before dawn, pulse racing and her hand pressed against the hidden silk, wondering with cold clarity if she had taken the first step toward salvation or damnation.

* * *

VIRGINIA WENT TO the scriptorium window more often than she meant to. The excuse was always plausible—better light for a folio, a sheet that needed drying in the draft, a passage to verify—but the truth was the view. From the third floor, the Osio garden lay open like a panel in an altarpiece: dark soil still damp from morning watering, young leaves bright as new cloth, and Gian Paolo moving through it as if every path had been laid for his feet.

"He speaks with that priest daily now," Sister Ottavia said one afternoon.

They stood in the deep stone embrasure, half hidden by shadow. Below, Gian Paolo sat on a marble bench beside a man in clerical robes. Their heads were bent together, close enough that the conversation felt private even at a distance. The priest was older, perhaps forty, square in the shoulders, with the settled bearing of someone used to being obeyed.

"The priest must be someone of considerable importance," Virginia murmured. Gian Paolo's usual insolence seemed checked in the man's presence; he listened as if the words carried weight. "Look how respectfully he listens."

"Perhaps he's Gian Paolo's confessor," Ottavia said. "Maybe the young man truly seeks spiritual guidance."

Virginia took the thought like a small mercy. If it was true, then all of this, her watching, her hoping, could still mean something other than weakness. Yet her gaze slid, disloyal, to the wrong details: sunlight caught in Gian Paolo's hair;

the ease of his hands; the way he leaned in, then sat back, as if he controlled the air between them.

"Try to discover who the priest is," Virginia said. Her voice barely carried in the stone throat of the alcove.

Ottavia's nod was quick. Too eager for piety, too bright for mere curiosity.

Virginia stored Gian Paolo's details the way others stored scripture. Not only his face, but his patterns—when he came, where he lingered, how long he stayed. The knowledge pricked at her conscience and still she kept it, as if she could build a fence out of facts.

"Could one see anything more beautiful?" The words slipped out, soft and unguarded.

Ottavia's head snapped toward her. "Sister Virginia?"

Warmth rose beneath Virginia's veil. "I meant... the garden. The way the light falls across the trees."

Ottavia's expression did not soften.

Day after day, Virginia returned. Sometimes alone, sometimes with Ottavia, always with a reason prepared. The reasons sounded thinner each time she spoke them. The truth sat in her throat like a swallowed pin.

* * *

IN THE REFECTORY, Sister Candida had mentioned seeing Osio in his garden. Virginia's spoon scraped the bowl, loud in her ears. A tightness drew under her ribs, as if her habit had shrunk. The room tilted, the long table, the bench legs, the faces turning, then sound and stone fell away.

She awoke on her bed with Ottavia pressing a damp cloth on her forehead. Vinegar stung Virginia's nose. The coolness should have steadied her. It only sharpened the shame: the body confessing what the mouth denied.

Before Virginia could speak, Sister Benedetta filled the doorway. Her eyes took in everything—Virginia's pallor, Ottavia's hovering hands, the loosened veil at Virginia's temple.

"Sister Ottavia, fetch some wine from the kitchen," Benedetta said quietly.

Ottavia fled. Her sandals hurried down the corridor; the sound thinned and vanished into the convent's thick walls.

Benedetta remained. Her gaze held Virginia in place better than any hand.

"You fainted at the mention of his presence in the garden," Benedetta said. No comfort, no cushion. "This is growing beyond what our conspiracy can contain."

"I just haven't been eating."

"You're obsessed with him." Benedetta's words landed clean, without heat, which made them worse. "You spend hours at the scriptorium window. You count his patterns. Now your body answers to his name. This is no longer manageable risk. This is loss of control."

Tears burned behind Virginia's eyes. She blinked hard. "I don't know how to stop."

"You can't stop. Not alone." Benedetta stepped closer, voice low, steady. "Two fears drive you now. The first that he'll come closer, and the second that he'll marry someone else. Either way, he fills your mind. And that fullness is beginning to show."

The accuracy stripped Virginia raw. "How did you know?"

"I've watched you for weeks." Benedetta did not look away. "And if I can see it, others will too. One sister has already remarked on how often you visit the scriptorium. Another noticed you barely eat. The Prioress asked me yesterday if you seemed... distracted."

Cold spread through Virginia's hands. "What did you tell her?"

"That you were engaged in intense spiritual study," Benedetta said. Her tone stayed level. "But I can't keep turning questions aside if you continue to sway at the mention of his name or spend every afternoon staring at his garden."

"What do I do?" Virginia whispered.

Benedetta let the silence press, then spoke. "You need to satisfy your curiosity. This priest he meets—you need to speak with him directly. Judge whether Osio's reformation is genuine or merely performance." Her eyes pinned Virginia. "If it's genuine, you'll seize it as justification. If it's an act, you'll know what you're facing."

"You want me to meet with this priest?"

"I want you to stop unraveling in ways that expose all of us." Benedetta's voice did not change. "Speaking with Osio's spiritual advisor serves two purposes. It answers your need to understand his intentions, and it gives you cover. You are concerned about a penitent's progress. Nothing scandalous in that."

She turned toward the door as Ottavia's returning footsteps echoed. "I'll arrange the meeting. Be ready."

* * *

TWO DAYS LATER, Ottavia brought news. They knelt together in the chapel after Vespers, the air still heavy with wax and extinguished wick, the last note of chant fading into the stone.

"We learned the priest's name," Ottavia said softly. "Father Arrigone recently assigned to San Maurizio. He's confessor to several noble families in Monza."

Virginia's fingers tightened around her rosary until the beads pressed crescents into her skin. Confessor to noble families: respectability, influence, a man whose reputation could not afford cheap games. Hope rose, thin, cautious, and sharp enough to cut.

"I need to speak with him," Virginia said. "If he's truly guiding Gian Paolo's spiritual development, then perhaps he can answer questions about the young man's progress."

Benedetta arranged the meeting with her usual efficiency. Within two days, Virginia stood in the parlatory facing the priest she had watched from above so often.

Up close, Father Arrigone looked more composed than he had in the garden. His features were refined; his hands rested neatly, as if order began at the fingertips. The room smelled of old wood and cool plaster. The grille between them made the rules visible—forced distance turned into architecture. His dark eyes held hers a beat too long, measuring rather than greeting.

"Sister Virginia Maria," he said, bowing his head. "I'm deeply honored to meet the nun whose spiritual guidance has so benefited young Gian Paolo. He speaks of you with the greatest reverence."

Warmth crept under Virginia's veil. "Father, I asked to speak with you because I'm concerned about certain… practical matters regarding Signor Osio's reformation."

"Of course. How may I be of service?"

She chose her words like steps on ice. "In your counseling of the young man, have you discussed his future plans? His family obligations?"

Arrigone's mouth moved, not quite a smile. "You're asking whether he intends to marry."

The bluntness left Virginia exposed. Her palms dampened against the ledge. "I merely wondered if his family was negotiating arrangements that might interfere with his spiritual development."

"No," Arrigone said, as if the matter were already settled. "There are no marriage negotiations currently under consideration. His affections appear to be entirely engaged… elsewhere."

The word 'elsewhere' rang in Virginia's head. Terror and relief braided together until she could not tell one from the other. "Elsewhere?"

Arrigone leaned forward slightly, lowering his voice. The parlatory seemed to tighten around the ledge and the barrier. "Sister Virginia, I know precisely why you ask these questions. I know you're interested in Gian Paolo."

The accusation did not need force. It landed and stayed. Virginia's fingers clenched.

"Don't say that," she whispered.

Denial tasted thin. Her visits, her vigilance, her fainting, everything had spoken.

"There's no shame in human feeling," Arrigone said, gentle now, almost tender. "Even for those who have taken the most sacred vows. The question is not whether we feel, but what we choose to do with such feelings."

Virginia wanted to rise and leave. Her knees did not obey. Shame held her, and need, sharp as thirst: the need for a door that opened without damnation behind it.

"What would you advise?" she whispered.

Arrigone smiled, and something colder flashed beneath the kindness—calculation, quickly covered.

"I would advise," he said, "that you continue to guide Gian Paolo's spiritual development as you have been. Your correspondence has already worked wonders on his soul. He speaks of little else but his desire to become worthy of your esteem."

Virginia swallowed. "You think the correspondence should continue?"

"I think it would be a grave disservice to abandon a penitent soul at such a crucial moment in his reformation." Arrigone leaned back, at ease in the argument. "However, letters alone may not suffice. A man of Gian Paolo's temperament requires more tangible guidance. Perhaps occasional meetings, carefully chaperoned, of course, where you might offer counsel on specific spiritual matters."

"Meetings?" The word snagged, as if barbed.

"In the parlatory, naturally. With proper supervision." His eyes stayed steady on hers. "There is no sin in spiritual friendship, Sister Virginia. The Church herself encourages the virtuous to guide those who have strayed. You would simply be fulfilling your calling as a bride of Christ, to bring lost souls back to the fold."

Everything he said was proper. That was the danger. His tone carried disguised pressure, a gentle hand that still pushed.

"And you believe his reformation is genuine?" Virginia asked. She needed the reassurance like air.

"I have heard his confessions. I have witnessed his anguish." Arrigone lowered his voice. "Sister Virginia, that young man is consumed with devotion to you. Whether you call it spiritual admiration or something else matters less than what you choose to do with such devotion. You can either nurture it toward holy purposes, or you can abandon him to return to his former wickedness."

Refusal began to look like cruelty. He had made it so. Virginia's stomach turned, not with disbelief but with recognition: a trap lined in velvet.

"I would need to consider this carefully," she said, though her mind had already followed the path he laid down.

"Of course. Prayer and contemplation are always wise." Arrigone rose. His robes whispered as he moved. "But do not wait too long. A soul in crisis cannot remain suspended indefinitely. It will either rise toward God or fall toward darkness. The question is which direction you will help him travel."

He blessed her with a gesture that should have soothed. It did not. It felt like a seal pressed into wax, an impression meant to hold.

After he departed, Virginia remained at the ledge. Her hands stayed clamped to the grille until her fingers ached. A respected priest had confirmed Gian Paolo's reformation and sanctioned their correspondence. Peace should have followed. Instead, she stood as if on a bridge spun from spider silk: delicate, shining, and one misstep from ruin.

Back in her cell, Benedetta waited.

"Well?" Benedetta asked.

"He said Gian Paolo's reformation is genuine. That I should continue to guide him." Virginia heard the thinness in her own voice. "He even suggested occasional meetings in the parlatory might be beneficial."

Benedetta's eyes narrowed. "Meetings."

"Carefully chaperoned. For spiritual counsel only."

"And you believed him?"

Virginia sank onto her cot. The straw mattress sighed. Exhaustion came down. Not the clean fatigue of work, but the dull fatigue of being pulled apart. "I don't know what I believe anymore. He said all the right things. Everything he suggested was technically proper. But..."

"But?"

"It felt like being maneuvered rather than advised. Like he was telling me what I wanted to hear, not what I needed to know."

Benedetta said nothing. She moved to the window, turning her back, as if the stones outside could answer what she would not.

"You're going to continue the correspondence," she said. It was not a question.

"Yes."

"And you'll agree to these parlatory meetings he suggested."

"Probably."

Benedetta turned. Her face looked carved from the same stone as the walls, stone that held secrets and did not soften. "Then we need rules. Protocols. Ways to contain this before it consumes us all." Her gaze held Virginia still. "Because that priest just gave you permission to walk deeper into the trap, Sister Virginia. And you're going to take every step he suggested, aren't you?"

Virginia wanted to deny it. A cautious virtuous answer arose, but it would not form.

"Yes," she whispered. "God help me, yes."

Benedetta's expression did not change, but resignation lived in her eyes, and something like calculation beside it. "Then we'd better make sure you survive it."

Outside, the spring afternoon thinned into evening. In the garden next door, Gian Paolo Osio stood at his window, watching the convent walls with the patience of a hunter who knew his prey was already ensnared.

* * *

June

VIRGINIA STOOD IN the corridor outside the parlatory with her hand on the iron latch, aware that lifting it would tilt her life onto a different track. Months of letters had brought her to this moment. First his crude propositions, which had scalded her with shock. Then his pious apologies, which had sounded so carefully sincere. Then the devotional verses, line after line, until resistance did not break but thin, like cloth rubbed too often between the fingers. Months of watching him from windows, learning the cadence of his stride in the garden. Months of telling herself she wanted only proof, only clarity, only safety.

Sister Benedetta stood beside her. "You have until the bell rings for Vespers," she whispered. "I've told the portress you're receiving a visitor for spiritual counsel. If the Prioress asks, you were advising a penitent nobleman. Nothing improper about that."

Virginia managed to make a nod. Her throat had closed around every useful word.

"If you're caught, we're all destroyed," Benedetta continued, flat and merciless. "Not just you. Every sister who helped you. Every servant who looked the other way. The entire convent will be investigated, and we will all pay the price for your choices."

"I know," Virginia whispered.

"Then go. Before I change my mind about helping you."

Virginia tightened her grip on the latch. The iron was cool beneath her palm. She turned it, pushed, and the door swung inward.

Sunlight poured through the window in a warm shaft of illumination.

He stood in the center of that light.

Gian Paolo Osio wore dark silk damask rich enough to announce him before he spoke. He held his cap in both hands and turned it slowly. Small, deliberate movements that did not fit the man she had watched below when he walked in his garden. The gesture unsettled her more than swagger would have.

For a long moment, neither of them moved.

He was elegant, sharp-featured, alive with a dangerous kind of vitality. Yet today there was no flourish. His head was bowed, his shoulders slumped in what might have been humility, or fatigue worn thin by weeks of pretending.

"*Donna* Marianna," he whispered.

Her worldly name struck like a slap. Habit and vows and nine years of enforced piety slid, for an instant, off her skin. Thirteen again with silk on her sleeves, her father's palazzo, a life with doors that opened outward instead of locking behind her. Then the convent gate, then the new name, then the long lesson of obedience.

"Sister Virginia," she corrected, though the steel she meant to use dissolved as soon as she touched it. "You should not be here."

"I know." He took a single step forward, then stopped when she flinched. "I know I have no right to ask this of you. To invade this holy place. To put you at such risk."

"Then why did you come?"

"Because I had to speak the truth." He lifted his gaze, and the sunlight caught his eyes—dark, tormented, bright with restless intensity. "I could not let you believe I am a monster."

Virginia pressed her back against the chair, needing the solid wood, the certainty of it, to keep her upright.

"But I did not come here to speak of the past," he said quietly. "I came because I am leaving."

The words hung in the dusty air between them, final and devastating.

Leaving.

For a beat, her body forgot its own rhythm. Then it returned, too fast, too loud in her ears.

"Where will you go?"

"Milan, perhaps. Or Rome. Does it truly matter?" He shrugged, careless in the shoulders, misery in the eyes. "I cannot stay here any longer, watching you from behind walls I can never breach, sending letters that pass through other hands, living on glimpses and shadows. It has become a torment I can no longer endure."

He moved closer to the grille. He was near enough now that the world beyond the convent came with him: leather and horses, sandalwood and summer air. The scent of streets and open sky. Freedom, carried on a man's skin, pressed into her breath.

"I came to say goodbye," he said softly. "And to offer you one final service before I go. If there is anything you need, anything at all, name it. I will see it done."

Virginia looked at him, truly looked at him, for perhaps the first time since he had entered. Not through a window and distance. Not through ink and a careful hand. Face to face, in a small room where the only witnesses were sunlight and shadow.

If he left, the silence would return. Days would stretch long and identical again, measured by bells and obedience. She would be safe. She would be good. She would keep the vows her father had forced into her mouth. She would go on breathing and feel nothing of it.

"Do not go," she said.

The silence that followed held hard and complete, broken only by the rough pull of breath from two throats that would not steady.

Gian Paolo went utterly still, his whole body tightening as though struck.

"Virginia."

"Do not go," she repeated. The words came stronger now, as if something inside her had finally stopped bargaining. "If you leave... if you leave, I will have nothing. Do you understand? Nothing."

"You have your God. Your sisters. Your vocation."

"I have a cage," she said, and the bitterness she had swallowed for nine years broke through at last. "I have stone walls and enforced silence and a life I never chose. I have prayers I mouth without meaning and vows I took under duress. You are the only thing in this world that is mine. The only choice I have made freely since I was thirteen years old."

His hand rose as if pulled by strings he could not cut, hovering near her face without quite touching. His fingers trembled as they traced the air beside her cheek, following the line of her jaw in a reverent gesture that shook her more deeply than any contact would have dared.

"If I stay," he said, his voice rough with what he fought to hold down, "I cannot promise to keep my distance. I cannot promise to be satisfied with letters and glimpses through windows. I cannot promise to remain the humble, pious servant I have tried to be."

"I know."

"I will want more. I will want everything you have to give and things you don't yet know you possess."

"I know."

From the corridor beyond, the bell for Vespers began to toll. The sound cut through the moment like metal on stone, summoning them back to rule and consequence.

Gian Paolo's hand dropped to his side. The spell that had held them both lasted one heartbeat longer, then cracked.

He stepped back, retreating into the afternoon light, his face turning again into a mask of shadow and gold.

"I must go," he said, though he did not yet move toward the door. "The visiting hour is ending."

"Will you return?"

He looked at her with an expression that held triumph and desire, and something she could not quite name, as if he, too, was startled by what she had just admitted.

"Try to stop me," he whispered.

Then he turned and moved through the outer door with the unhurried confidence of a legitimate visitor, leaving Virginia alone in the parlatory with her own breath coming fast and uneven.

She remained there for several long moments, forcing steadiness back into her chest, gathering her composure as one gathers dropped beads—one by one, with shaking fingers. Her hands would not keep still. She pressed her palms flat against the door and closed her eyes, feeling the rough grain of the wood bite into her skin.

Finally, she turned.

Benedetta waited in the corridor, her face tight with barely suppressed calculation. Behind her, Ottavia's round features drawn with worry.

"Well?" Benedetta demanded, sharp. "Is he gone?"

"Yes," Virginia said. The word came out steady, convincing. "He is gone."

"Good." Benedetta let out a long breath, rigid shoulders loosening by a fraction. "Then it is finished. You have said your farewells. The door is secured. This chapter is closed."

Virginia looked at her friend, at the sharp, intelligent eyes that catalogued the flush on her face, the unevenness of her breath, the way her hands still sought the door as if it were an anchor.

"Yes," Virginia said, and the lie tasted sweet on her tongue. "It is finished."

Benedetta held her gaze for one beat longer than necessary. Then she nodded and turned toward the stairs.

They made their way back through the silent convent, climbing the worn steps to their shared chamber. Ottavia led the way, quick and anxious. Benedetta followed at the rear, a silent watch. Virginia walked between them, feeling the weight of what she had done settle onto her shoulders. Not all at once, but in layers, like cloth laid over cloth until movement became difficult.

In their room, the three narrow beds waited in their familiar arrangement. Three lives contained in one small space, three women bound together by proximity and shared secrets.

They settled onto their cots without speaking. Ottavia lifted her mending; her needle moved by habit while her eyes stayed distant and troubled. Benedetta sat upright with her breviary open, though the pages did not turn.

Virginia lay down on her narrow bed and stared at the ceiling. The parlatory returned to her again and again: the shaft of light, the smell of summer on his skin, the words she had spoken that could not be taken back.

Do not go.

She had asked him to stay. She had claimed him as her own. She had chosen him over safety, over duty, over vows forced into her mouth. And she knew he would come back. Not to say goodbye this time, but to take what she had offered.

The thought should have driven her to confession, to punishment, to protection from herself and from him. Instead, a strange, terrible calm settled over her, as if the struggle itself had finally become exhausted and fallen quiet.

Outside the window, late afternoon sunlight slanted gold across the convent walls. Inside, in this brief suspension, Virginia let herself lie still, listening to the convent breathe around her, to the distant life beyond it, and to the new, dangerous quiet inside her own chest.

She remained Sister Virginia Maria, bride of Christ, bound by sacred vows. But beneath the layers of enforced piety, something else had stirred to life: a woman who had spoken and been answered.

* * *

Mid-June
Milan

GIAN PAOLO STOOD at his mother's window and watched rain turn the street to mud. Three days, and every conversation had circled around what he'd come to say—estate business, introductions to potential matches, his father's will, the tedious architecture of inheritance. Everything except Virginia.

The rain drummed harder. Afternoon light thinned toward evening. If he waited any longer, the moment would slip past and he'd have to manufacture another visit, another excuse.

He turned from the window. "Mama, I need to speak with you about Sister Virginia de Leyva."

Donna Sofia's hands stilled on her embroidery. The room tightened around the silence.

When she looked up, her face was stone. "No."

"You haven't heard what I have to say."

"No." She set down her embroidery with precise, controlled movements, each gesture a small act of restraint. "I don't care what you're about to propose. The answer is no. That woman humiliated me, Paolo. Forced me to my knees like a common beggar. Made me weep while she sat there, unmoved as stone. I will not help you with anything involving her."

The venom in her voice was sharper than he'd anticipated, but not unexpected. He'd prepared for this.

"She also saved my life," he said quietly.

"Under duress. Because the governor threatened her convent. Because your family mobilized half of Milan's nobility against her." Donna Sofia rose, black silk rustling. "Don't romanticize her actions, Paolo. Sister Virginia de Leyva is not some merciful saint. She's a proud, cold woman who only relented when she had no choice."

"Perhaps that's true." Gian Paolo moved closer. This had to be handled carefully. Every word mattered. "But the fact remains that I'm alive because she signed that pardon. Regardless of her motivations, our family owes her a debt."

"We owe her nothing."

"Honor would suggest otherwise." He let the word settle, watched his mother's expression shift by a fraction. "I was taught that nobility requires *magnanimità*. If we can extend grace to Sister Virginia, it demonstrates the strength of our family's character. Shows that the Osios are above petty vengeance."

His mother's eyes narrowed. "This isn't about honor. Tell me what you really want."

The directness forced his hand. Gian Paolo drew a slow breath, let it out with measured control.

"I want to send her gifts. Tokens of gratitude for the mercy she showed." He raised a hand before she could protest. "Through you, Mama. Charitable gifts from a noblewoman to a young religious, the kind of patronage you extend to convents all over Milan. Nothing improper. Nothing that would cause scandal."

"Why?" The single word cut. "Why do you care what that cold-hearted nun thinks of our family?"

Because she wasn't cold. Because when she'd told him not to leave, her voice had cracked with need. Because he woke every night with the memory of her pressed against that door, and the scent of her—beeswax and linen and something beneath it that was hers alone—stayed in his throat like hunger.

None of these truths could be spoken aloud.

"Because I'm tired of being known as the man who murdered Giuseppe Molteno," he said instead. "That scandal has followed me for months, damaged our family's reputation. If the Osios can demonstrate reconciliation with the woman at the center of that affair, it begins to repair our standing."

Donna Sofia studied him. Gian Paolo held her gaze, let her see what she needed to see: a son concerned with family honor, with reputation, with navigating the complex web of Milanese politics.

Not a man obsessed. Not a man who would manipulate his own mother to reach the woman he craved.

"What sort of gifts?" she asked finally, her voice still edged.

His shoulders eased, but he was careful not to let relief show in his face. "Simple things. Silk flowers. Scented balls. A beautiful prayer book. Items that demonstrate thoughtfulness without appearing too personal."

"Simple?" Donna Sofia's voice sharpened. "Paolo, silk flowers from Milan's best artisan cost more than a farmer earns in a year."

"Which suggests maternal concern. A noblewoman taking interest in a young religious woman's welfare." He softened his voice, made it pleading. "Mama, please. I'm not asking you to forgive her. I'm asking you to help me restore our family's reputation. That's all."

The lie sat bitter on his tongue, but it worked.

She moved to her writing table, pulled out parchment and quill. When she spoke, her voice had lost its edge, replaced by weary resignation.

"Fine. I'll send gifts to Sister Virginia de Leyva. As an act of Christian charity and family duty." She began making notes, each stroke of the pen deliberate. "But Paolo, understand this. I do it for our family's honor. Not because I've forgiven her. Not because I feel any warmth toward her. If this backfires, if she uses these gestures against you in any way, the consequences are yours to bear."

"Understood." Gian Paolo moved to stand beside her writing table. "Thank you, Mama."

"Don't thank me yet." She looked up, and something in her eyes made his chest tighten. "I'm not a fool, Paolo. I know when you're hiding something. I don't know what it is, but I can see it in your face. The same expression you wore as a boy when you'd done something you knew would disappoint me." She held his gaze. "Whatever game you're playing, be careful. Very careful. Because if I discover you've used me for something shameful, no amount of family loyalty will protect you from my wrath."

The threat hung between them, solid as the writing table, as the rain still drumming against the window.

Gian Paolo forced a smile. "There's no game, Mama. Only gratitude and honor."

She didn't look convinced. But she returned to her list, and Gian Paolo allowed himself to breathe again.

* * *

OVER THE FOLLOWING days, they visited Milan's finest craftsmen. Donna Sofia approached each shop with grim efficiency, treating the task like penance owed.

At the silk flower maker's studio, she examined roses with a critical eye. The air smelled of dyed silk and beeswax. "These are too ornate. For a nun, we need something simpler. Beautiful but modest."

She selected red and white roses, classic and appropriate. "Red for Christ's passion," she said to no one in particular. "White for purity. Let her meditate on both."

The words carried an edge that made Gian Paolo wonder how much she suspected.

At the perfumer's shop, she chose scents with deliberate symbolism. Glass vials lined the shelves; sunlight turned their contents amber and rose. "Lavender for devotion. Rose for prayer. And rosemary." Her voice hardened. "For remembrance. Let her remember what passed between us. Every time she smells these, let her remember the day she forced me to my knees."

Gian Paolo said nothing. Let his mother interpret the gifts through her own lens of resentment. Let her believe she was sending barbs wrapped in silk.

He understood what Virginia would read beneath it: *I haven't forgotten. I'm still here. You are mine.*

* * *

ON HIS FINAL evening in Milan, as Donna Sofia finalized arrangements for the first delivery, she turned to him with an unreadable expression.

"This woman," she said quietly. "Sister Virginia. Is she worth all this effort?"

The question came without warning. For a moment, he weighed deflection, the safety of another lie. But something in his mother's face—resignation, perhaps, or recognition—stopped him.

"Yes," he said simply. "She is."

Donna Sofia's eyes searched his face. Whatever she saw there made her mouth compress into a thin line. She turned back to her parchment, dipped her quill, and wrote in silence.

When she spoke again, her voice was low. "Then you're already lost."

She didn't look up. The scratch of the quill continued, steady and certain, sealing what had been set in motion.

* * *

Late June

THE WOODEN BOX arrived during the midday meal. Virginia sat in the refectory with her spoon halfway to her mouth when Sister Constanza entered carrying a package. The sound of fifty nuns eating, spoons scraping pottery, the shuffle of habits, Sister Francesca's voice reading from the lives of saints, stopped.

The portress crossed the long room. Every head turned to track her progress. She stopped directly before Virginia's place at the junior sisters' table.

"A delivery for Sister Virginia," she announced. "From Milan."

Virginia's spoon clattered against her bowl. She set it down with a hand that shook so badly the handle rattled against clay.

Every eye in the refectory fixed on her. Mother Imbersaga at the head table. Sister Bianca beside her, those faded eyes sharp as new blades. Benedetta three places down, her angular face carved into stillness. And Ottavia beside her, close enough that Virginia heard her sharp intake of breath.

"From Milan?" Mother Imbersaga's voice carried through the silence. "Who sends packages to Sister Virginia from Milan?"

The portress held up a card, white parchment that seemed to glow. "Donna Sofia Osio, Mother Prioress."

The name landed like a stone in still water.

Virginia's vision closed to a narrow point. Her breath came shallow and too fast, the sound a wounded animal makes when the hunter is near.

Donna Sofia. Gian Paolo's mother. The woman who had knelt in the parlatory and begged for her son's life while Virginia sat unmoved. The woman whose tears Virginia had watched without mercy.

The woman who had every reason to want Virginia destroyed.

"Sister Virginia." Mother Imbersaga's voice sharpened. "Come forward."

Virginia's legs turned to water. She had to walk past fifty sisters, all watching, all judging.

Behind her, Benedetta's sharp hiss: "Compose yourself."

Virginia reached the head table where Mother Imbersaga sat like a judge at tribunal. Sister Bianca leaned forward, watching every flicker of Virginia's expression.

"Donna Sofia Osio," Mother Imbersaga said slowly, as though tasting each syllable. "The mother of the man who murdered your family's agent. The woman you forced to her knees in the parlatory last year. That Donna Sofia Osio?"

"Yes, Mother Prioress." Virginia's voice barely carried.

"How... extraordinary." Mother Imbersaga gestured to Sister Constanza. "Give Sister Virginia her package. Let us all see what prompts such remarkable generosity."

The portress pressed the box into Virginia's hands. Fine-grained walnut, polished to a sheen. Brass hinges gleamed. Even from inches away, beeswax and something floral, roses, perhaps, or lavender, rose through the air.

"Open it," Mother Imbersaga commanded.

Not a request. An order.

Virginia's fingers fumbled with the brass clasp. Too clumsy, trembling where everyone could see.

The clasp released with a soft click.

Inside, nestled in white tissue paper, silk roses bloomed. Red and white, their petals so perfect they seemed to breathe. The craftsmanship was extraordinary. Not simple tokens, but the work of a master artisan, the kind of luxury that cost more than most families earned in a year.

A collective gasp rippled through the refectory.

Virginia lifted one. The silk whispered against her skin, impossibly soft.

He had chosen these. Had stood in some Milan shop and selected each flower, thinking of her. The roses would never wilt. Never fade. Never die.

Beneath the flowers lay six scented balls wrapped in gauze. Their perfume rose in a wave—lavender and rose and something else. Rosemary.

For remembrance.

The room tilted. Virginia's knees buckled.

She caught herself on the edge of the head table, fingers digging into wood, nails bending back. Sound rushed in her ears.

"Sister Virginia!" Sister Candida's hands were on her shoulders, supporting her weight. "Mother Prioress, she's ill—"

"I'm well." Virginia forced the words out. "Only... the shock. Forgive me. The shock of such unexpected kindness after..." She let her voice break slightly. "After the way I treated Donna Sofia."

"Sit." Mother Imbersaga's voice left no room for argument. A chair appeared and Virginia collapsed into it, still clutching one silk rose.

The refectory had erupted in whispers. Mother Imbersaga raised one hand, and silence fell.

"Sisters. We have witnessed an extraordinary act of Christian charity. Donna Sofia Osio, despite having every earthly reason for resentment, has extended grace to Sister Virginia. This is what our faith demands—forgiveness of enemies, generosity toward those who have wronged us."

She paused. "However. Such gifts, while generous, create... complications. Sister Virginia, you will write an immediate letter of thanks to Donna Sofia. Sister Benedetta will assist you. The letter will be reviewed by Sister Bianca before it is sent."

"Yes, Mother Prioress."

"Furthermore. There will be no gossip about this matter. No speculation. Donna Sofia has demonstrated Christian virtue. We will accept it as such and move forward. Is that understood?"

A murmur of assent rippled through the room.

But Virginia saw the looks that passed between sisters. Saw Sister Bianca's mouth compress. Saw Benedetta's white-knuckled grip on her spoon. They didn't believe it. Not any of it.

"Sister Virginia, you're excused from the remainder of the meal," Mother Imbersaga said. "Go to your cell. Rest. You're clearly overwhelmed."

Virginia rose on unsteady legs. The box weighed like stone in her hands. She crossed the refectory in silence, each footstep echoing.

Just before she reached the door, Sister Bianca's voice, pitched low but carrying: "Extraordinary indeed. One might think she was expecting them."

Virginia didn't turn around. Just kept walking, the silk roses clutched against her chest like something precious.

Or damning.

Benedetta and Ottavia followed her to their cell. Virginia set the roses and scented balls on the small night table like evidence awaiting judgment.

Benedetta stood rigid, arms crossed. Ottavia hovered near the door, wringing her hands.

"Tell me he didn't send those," Benedetta said.

Virginia opened her mouth then closed it.

"God in heaven." Benedetta's voice stayed barely above a whisper, but it carried the force of a shout. "He used his own mother. Convinced her to send gifts to the woman who humiliated her. Virginia, do you understand what this means?"

"That he's clever."

"That he's dangerous." Benedetta grabbed Virginia's arm, fingers digging in hard enough to bruise. "This isn't courtship. This isn't romance. This is a man willing to manipulate his own mother to reach you. What do you think he'll do when simple gifts aren't enough? When he wants more?"

Virginia pulled free. "He hasn't done anything wrong. His mother sent gifts. I'll write a polite thank you. That's all."

"That's all?" Benedetta laughed, a sound like glass striking stone. "Sister Bianca already suspects. Mother Imbersaga saw you nearly collapse in front of the entire community. How long do you think you can maintain this pretense before someone discovers the truth?"

"What truth?" Virginia's voice rose despite herself. "That a nobleman's mother sent me gifts? That's not a crime."

"The truth that you're in love with him." Benedetta's words cut through Virginia's protest. "The truth that he killed for you, and you've been watching his house ever since. The truth that something passed between you in that parlatory—I don't know what, but I can see it on your face every time his name is mentioned. That truth, Virginia. The one that will destroy all of us."

The silence stretched between them.

Finally, Virginia spoke, her voice very quiet. "What do you want?"

"Want?" Benedetta's smile held no warmth. "I want to survive this. Which means controlling every interaction between you and anyone connected to the Osio family. Every letter you write passes through me. Every gift you receive, I examine first. And if I determine the risk has become too great..."

"You'll tell Mother Imbersaga."

"I'll do what's necessary to protect this community." Benedetta's eyes held no compromise. "You've made your choice, Sister Virginia. Now you live with the consequences. But you don't get to drag the rest of us down with you."

Virginia sat at the writing table, blank parchment before her, while Benedetta stood at her shoulder like a guard.

"Write," Benedetta commanded.

Virginia picked up the quill. Set it down. Her hands shook too badly. "I can't."

"You must." Benedetta's voice held no sympathy. "A gift of this magnitude demands immediate acknowledgment. Every hour you delay raises more questions."

Virginia's hand found the quill again. She dipped it in ink.

Most Honored Donna Sofia Osio,

Your generous gifts surprised me with their arrival today, bringing beauty and grace to our humble convent. I confess myself moved by such kindness, given the unfortunate circumstances of our last meeting. Your forgiveness speaks to a nobility of spirit that humbles me. The silk flowers are exquisite works of artistry and will serve as lasting reminders that even behind these walls, God's beauty finds expression. The scented balls perfume our chapel with fragrances that lift the soul to prayer. Please know that your mercy, and that of your entire family, is remembered in our daily prayers. I ask God's blessing on the House of Osio, and on your son Gian Paolo in particular, that he may live a long and peaceful life.

Virginia paused before adding, in letters so small they were barely visible:

The roses will never wilt.

She set down the quill before Benedetta could see.

Benedetta read it twice. Finally, she nodded. "It will serve. Grateful but not effusive. The mention of her son is appropriate. Any nun would pray for the family of her benefactress." She folded the letter. "I'll bring it to Sister Bianca who will likely approve it and send it on the next courier to Milan."

After Benedetta left, Virginia remained at the table. Through the window, afternoon light slanted across the convent garden. Somewhere beyond those walls, Gian Paolo was waiting for her response.

* * *

THE SUMMONS CAME the next day. Sister Candida at her door, face grave. "Sister Virginia, Mother Imbersaga requests your presence in her study. Immediately."

The study was dim, shutters half closed. Mother Imbersaga sat behind her writing table, and beside her stood Sister Bianca, wrinkled face stern.

"Sister Virginia." Mother Imbersaga's voice stayed controlled, but something dangerous lurked beneath it. "Sit."

Virginia sat. Her hands shook again, hidden in her lap.

"Sister Bianca has brought concerns to my attention. Concerns regarding your recent behavior and the... unexpected delivery we all witnessed in the refectory."

"Mother Prioress, I assure you—"

"Let me speak." The command cut through Virginia's protest. "Sister reports that you have been distracted during Office for weeks. Staring out windows. Startling at sounds from the gate. And yesterday, you nearly fainted when you received gifts from Donna Sofia Osio. A woman you publicly humiliated last year."

Mother Imbersaga leaned forward. "I want to know why. And I want the truth, Sister Virginia. Not some convenient fiction. The truth."

Virginia's mind raced. "I... I've been troubled, Mother Prioress. Donna Sofia's gifts stirred up memories of what happened last year. Of Gian Paolo Osio's crime. Of the role I played in that whole terrible affair. I've been... struggling with guilt."

It was true, as far as it went.

Mother Imbersaga studied her face. "Guilt over refusing Donna Sofia's pleas for mercy?"

"Yes. And guilt over eventually granting it. Wondering if I made the right choice. If justice was served or abandoned. These questions have haunted me."

"I see." Mother Imbersaga sat back. "And these questions have manifested in distraction and illness?"

"Yes, Mother Prioress."

Sister Bianca spoke for the first time. "It seems convenient that your spiritual crisis happens to coincide with gifts from the Osio family. One might almost think you were expecting them. Waiting for them, perhaps?"

"I wasn't expecting anything," Virginia said, which was technically true. "Donna Sofia's generosity surprised me completely."

"Surprised you so much that you nearly collapsed?" Sister Bianca's eyes glittered. "I've watched nuns receive news of family deaths with more composure than you showed yesterday over a box of silk flowers."

Virginia had no response.

Mother Imbersaga raised a hand, silencing Sister Bianca. "Sister Virginia, I'm going to speak plainly. The Osio family brings nothing but scandal. First the murder, then the pardon, now these gifts. Every interaction with them puts this convent at risk."

She paused. "I want you to understand the position you're in. Your family's reputation, and by extension this convent's, rests in part on your conduct. I cannot allow any whiff of scandal to touch you. Especially not scandal involving the man who murdered your family's agent."

"There is no scandal, Mother Prioress. I have done nothing improper."

"Not yet." Sister Bianca's voice carried dark certainty. "But I've seen how this begins. Gifts. Letters. Innocent at first, then gradually less so. We'll ensure you're not tempted further."

Mother Imbersaga stood, signaling the end of the meeting. "You're dismissed, Sister Virginia. But know this. You are being watched now. By me. By Sister Bianca. By other sisters who care about this community's welfare. If I see any further sign that you're compromising yourself or this convent, the consequences will be severe. Do I make myself clear?"

"Yes, Mother Prioress."

Virginia left the study, her legs barely holding her weight. She found a stone bench in the cloister as afternoon shadows lengthened. Through the arches, the boundary wall stood solid and immovable. Somewhere beyond it, Gian Paolo waited.

And despite Mother Imbersaga's warnings, despite Sister Bianca's suspicions, despite the danger pressing in from all sides, Virginia knew with absolute certainty: this was only the beginning.

* * *

TWO DAYS LATER, a servant arrived at the Osio palazzo in Milan just after dawn, mud-splattered from hard riding. Gian Paolo met him in the stables before his mother could intercept.

"Well?"

The servant handed him a letter, sealed with plain wax. "The sister with the sharp face gave it to me. Told me to deliver it directly to you, not to Donna Sofia."

Gian Paolo broke the seal. His hands trembled.

Virginia's handwriting was elegant, the letters perfectly formed:

Your generous gifts surprised me with their arrival today, bringing beauty and grace to our humble convent...

And then, at the bottom, in letters so small he had to squint to read them:

The roses will never wilt.

Five words. That was all. But they told him everything.

She understood. She accepted. She was his, despite every barrier between them.

Gian Paolo burned the letter immediately in a stable lantern, watching Virginia's words blacken and curl. But the message remained, seared into memory.

The convent would accept Donna Sofia's gifts because refusal would insult a noblewoman known for her piety and generosity. And with each gift, Virginia would be bound more tightly to him.

Gian Paolo walked back toward the palazzo through the breaking dawn and began planning his next move: books this time, devotional works his mother would approve, with passages marked in ways only Virginia would understand.

* * *

Early July

THE PACKAGE SAT on Virginia's copying table like a trap. Fine wood. Brass hinges. Sister Costanza had brought it during None, interrupting the scriptorium's silence.

"For you, Sister Virginia. From *Signora* Osio. I inspected it. All proper."

Virginia's quill stopped mid-stroke. Ink pooled on the vellum, spreading into an ugly blot. Her fingers tightened around the quill shaft until the wood bit into her palm.

Signora Osio. Gian Paolo's mother. Again.

Around her, the other sisters had already abandoned their work. Even Sister Bianca craned her neck to see.

Virginia set down the quill and reached for the latch. The brass was cool beneath her fingertips, solid and real and dangerous.

She opened it. Inside, nestled in white parchment, lay an illuminated prayer book bound in crimson velvet. The cover was worked with gold thread in an intricate pattern of vines and lilies, and at its center, a small silver crucifix gleamed. The pages were thick vellum, each one painted with elaborate borders of miniature saints and angels rendered in brilliant colors and gold leaf that caught the light like fire.

Beneath the prayer book lay additional treasures: ivory rosary beads carved with tiny flowers, and a small reliquary pendant on a silver chain, its crystal window revealing what appeared to be a fragment of cloth, some saint's relic.

A card rested beneath, elegant feminine script:

For Sister Virginia Maria, with the affection and prayers of Signora Maria Osio.

Recognition coiled low in her belly and spread through her limbs.

These had not come from Gian Paolo's mother. The timing, the extravagance, the way each item seemed chosen specifically for her. This was his work, disguised under family protection.

Sister Benedetta materialized at her shoulder. She lifted the card, studied it with the same expression she used for convent accounts—neutral, assessing, revealing nothing.

"Another gift. The *signora* is certainly building a reputation for charitable works." Benedetta set down the card. "I wonder if she sends such gifts to other religious houses."

Sarcasm delivered with the smoothness of consecrated oil.

"You should write and thank her," Sister Candida suggested. "Such generosity deserves proper acknowledgment."

Virginia's hands shook as she folded the parchment back over the gifts. She pressed her palms flat against the box's wooden lid to still them. "Of course. I'll compose something this evening."

The other sisters returned to their work. Only Benedetta remained.

Benedetta's voice dropped to a thread. "Interesting that she would send more gifts. Or perhaps the son uses his mother's name to gain access where his own would be refused. Either way, accepting such gifts creates obligation. Debt. Connection."

Virginia's throat tightened. "It would be rude to refuse a gift from a respected noblewoman."

"It would be prudent to question why that noblewoman suddenly takes interest in a nun she's rarely spoken with." Benedetta straightened. "But courtesy demands a response. Write your thank you letter. I'll ensure it reaches the proper destination."

* * *

THAT EVENING, VIRGINIA sat at the writing table with a blank sheet before her. She dipped her quill and held it over the parchment. Ink gathered at the tip, threatening to drip.

What words could be safe for other eyes but still tell him what he needed to know?

The quill touched paper:

Most Honored Signora Osio,

Your generous gifts arrived today, bringing beauty and grace to our humble convent. The prayer book is exquisite, and the rosary will enrich my prayers during services. Please know that your kindness is remembered in our daily prayers. I remain your devoted servant in Christ, Sister Virginia Maria de Leyva

Perfect. Grateful but distant. The sort of letter any nun would write to a benefactress. She carried it to Benedetta, crossing the narrow cell where their three beds stood in shadow.

Benedetta read by candlelight, lips pursed. "Appropriate. Grateful but not effusive." She folded the letter. "I'll have it delivered."

"To the *signora* in Milan?"

"To wherever it needs to go." Benedetta met her eyes. "We both know the real recipient, Virginia. But maintaining the fiction protects everyone."

Virginia's fingers found the edge of Benedetta's writing table and gripped it. "Then he'll know I accepted them."

"He already knows. That's why he sent them in his mother's name, to force you to acknowledge the gift publicly, to create the appearance of legitimate connection between your families." Benedetta moved to her window. "It's brilliant, actually. No one can question a noblewoman's charitable gift to a convent. But every gift accepted is another thread in the web he's weaving around you."

Virginia's stomach turned. "What should I have done? Refused them in front of everyone?"

"No. Refusal would have created more questions than acceptance." Benedetta turned back, and the candlelight carved shadows beneath her eyes. "But understand what's happening. He's not just courting you anymore. He's building a framework of legitimate communication. Gifts from his mother. Letters of spiritual counsel. Public demonstrations of piety at Mass. Every interaction carefully crafted to appear innocent while serving his actual purpose."

Virginia's breath came shallow and quick. "Which is?"

"To make you his." Benedetta's voice held no judgment, no heat. Just flat assessment. "Not through force or scandal, but through patient strategy that binds you closer with each exchange until separation becomes impossible."

The words sat heavy in the air between them.

"He's being coached," Virginia said. Her voice came out rough, barely above a whisper.

"Father Arrigone." Benedetta confirmed what Virginia had already suspected. "He's advising every move. The letters, the gifts, probably even the timing of when Osio appears at Mass. Nothing is accidental."

Virginia sank onto the edge of Benedetta's bed. Her legs had started shaking. "Then what do I do?"

"You've already done it. Accepted the gifts. Written the thank you letters. Acknowledged the connection." Benedetta sat beside her. "The question now is whether you want to stop this before it goes further."

Silence stretched. Outside, the bell rang for Compline.

Virginia pressed her palms against her thighs to stop the shaking. "I don't know."

"Then we continue managing it." Benedetta's pragmatism cut through Virginia's paralysis. "Controlled risk is better than chaotic disaster. But know this: every gift accepted, every letter exchanged, every meeting arranged brings you closer to a point where management becomes impossible."

She stood, tucking Virginia's letter into her habit. "Go to Compline. Pray for guidance if you think it will help. I'll ensure this reaches him."

* * *

FIVE DAYS LATER, another package arrived. Virginia's hands went cold when Sister Costanza appeared in the scriptorium doorway.

This time, the wooden case contained six handkerchiefs. Linen so fine it felt like water between her fingers. Each one embroidered with Virginia's initials in silk thread. Hours of work by skilled hands, commissioned specifically for her.

She lifted one and pressed it to her cheek before she could stop herself. The fabric whispered against her skin, softer than anything she'd touched in years.

Her initials. ***V.M.*** worked in satin stitch, surrounded by tiny flowers. She traced the raised embroidery with one fingertip. The silk thread caught on her rough, work-worn skin. The intimacy stripped her breath away.

Again, *Signora* Osio's card expressed continued prayers and affection.

Virginia accepted them with proper gratitude. She wrote another careful thank you letter. The words came easier this time, the routine already establishing itself.

Benedetta's expression tightened when she collected the letter, but she said nothing.

By the third week of July, gifts arrived every few days. God forgive her, but Virginia began to watch for them. Her chest would tighten with anticipation when she heard footsteps approaching the scriptorium.

Scented soap infused with lavender and rosemary. A prayer book with gilt edges and Virginia's name stamped on the cover. A small silver crucifix on a delicate chain.

Each one more personal than the last.

The other sisters marveled at *Signora* Osio's remarkable generosity. Sister Candida suggested Virginia must have made a powerful impression during some prior meeting. Ottavia worried quietly but said nothing publicly.

Only Benedetta understood the truth.

"He's been visiting his mother in Milan." Benedetta stood in the doorway of their cell, arms crossed. "Making sure she writes the cards personally, using her servants for delivery. Everything appears legitimate because it is legitimate. She genuinely sends the gifts, but does she know her son selected each one specifically for you?"

Virginia held one of the handkerchiefs against her cheek. The embroidery pressed raised patterns into her skin. The fabric still carried the faint scent of lavender. She breathed deeper, and something dangerous unfurled in her chest.

"When does he plan to visit again?" The question escaped before wisdom could stop it.

Benedetta's jaw tightened. "You want to see him."

"I want to thank him properly. For his mother's kindness." The lie tasted bitter.

"His mother who's being used with or without her knowledge to facilitate an illicit relationship?" Benedetta stepped into the cell and closed the door. "I'm not judging. I'm clarifying reality. Each gift pushes you closer to a meeting. He knows it. I know it. The only question is whether you'll admit it to yourself."

Virginia's fingers clenched around the handkerchief. "One meeting. In the parlatory, properly chaperoned."

"Where he'll ask for another. And another. Until 'proper' becomes impossible and 'chaperoned' becomes a jest." Benedetta moved to the window. "But you're going to see him regardless of what I say. So, let's discuss terms."

She turned back, her face calculating.

"One meeting. Two weeks from now, after he's sent enough gifts that requesting an audience seems reasonable. You'll thank *Signora* Osio through her son. Ottavia and I will be present the entire time. You'll speak through the grating only. No opening the small door, no touching. Thirty minutes maximum."

Virginia's breath came quick and shallow. "You'll arrange it?"

"I'll manage it. There's a difference." Benedetta moved to the door, paused with her hand on the latch. "But Virginia, this is the path you're choosing. Every gift accepted, every meeting arranged, every rule bent brings you closer to complete ruin. Don't pretend otherwise."

The door closed. Virginia stood alone with the handkerchiefs spread across her narrow bed.

She lifted one to her face and breathed in the faint lavender scent. Then she pressed it to her lips, then to her throat where her pulse hammered.

She traced her embroidered initials again. Someone had spent hours creating these tiny perfect stitches. Had bent over this fabric in candlelight, working silk thread through linen, forming her identity in permanent beauty.

Two weeks until she could see him again. Fourteen days of waiting.

The gifts kept coming. And Virginia kept accepting them. And with each acceptance, the threads drew tighter around her wrists and throat—delicate as silk, strong as iron, and already too many to count.

* * *

Late July

VIRGINIA STOOD IN their cell, adjusting her veil with practiced fingers. She smoothed the black fabric, checked that no hair escaped beneath the wimple. Years of this routine had made the movements automatic.

Benedetta had arranged it exactly as promised. A formal meeting in the parlatory. Thirty minutes with Ottavia and Benedetta both present. Virginia would thank *Signora* Osio through her son for the generous gifts.

She pressed her palms flat against her habit. The coarse wool scratched beneath her fingers. Her breath came shallow, not quite steady, but she forced herself to walk to the parlatory with measured steps.

Through the corridor, she passed Sister Bianca near the refectory entrance. She paused in conversation, eyes tracking Virginia's progress.

Virginia took her place in front of the iron bars dividing the room. Benedetta and Ottavia positioned themselves near the inner door. Close enough to hear every word. Far enough to allow the appearance of privacy.

The exterior door opened. Footsteps crossed the outer parlatory.

Gian Paolo entered wearing a doublet of dark blue silk, gold embroidery tracing the collar and cuffs. His hair had been recently trimmed. The scent of bergamot oil reached Virginia even through the grating—warm, citrus-sharp, deliberate.

"Sister Virginia Maria." He bowed. "Thank you for receiving me."

"*Signor* Osio." Virginia kept her voice level. "I wished to thank your mother personally for her extraordinary kindness. The prayer book she sent was exquisite, and the rosary beads are treasures I will use in my daily devotions."

"My mother is pleased to support the holy work of this convent." His eyes held hers through the grating. Dark eyes, steady and intent. "She speaks often of the virtue she sees in you."

The lie sat between them, acknowledged by neither.

"Please convey my gratitude and assure her of my prayers for her continued health and happiness."

"I will." He moved closer to the grating. Not touching the bars, but near enough that the fine weave of his doublet came clear. The bergamot scent grew stronger. "Though I confess, I have brought something myself. Not from my mother, but from me. A token of my own devotion."

Benedetta shifted behind Virginia. The rustle of fabric carried clear warning.

"That would not be appropriate," Virginia said, though her voice lacked conviction.

"It is a holy object. A *reliquiario* containing fragments from a blessed saint." He reached into his doublet and withdrew something wrapped in silk. "Surely there can be no impropriety in sharing sacred relics between Christian souls."

Virginia leaned closer. Polished white stone, translucent and smooth, perhaps quartz. Gold bars encased the stone. The whole measured perhaps the length of her hand. Beautiful. Expensive. Deliberate.

"It comes from Rome," Gian Paolo said. "Blessed by holy fathers. Beneath the stone are bone fragments from a saint who knew the torments of devotion, who understood the struggle between earthly desire and divine calling."

"Which saint?" Virginia's throat tightened.

"Saint Mary of Egypt, who wandered forty years in the desert, who knew temptation of the flesh and overcame it through the grace of God." His voice carried absolute sincerity, smooth as altar wine. "Touch it, Sister. Feel the holiness within the stone."

Behind her, Benedetta spoke quietly. "Virginia, I don't think—"

"It is a relic," Virginia interrupted. The words came too quickly. "There is no harm in touching a blessed object."

She extended her hand through the bars. Her fingers passed through the iron barrier into the outer room, crossing the boundary that should have kept them separate. Gian Paolo placed the reliquary in her palm.

The stone was warm—fever-warm, as if it had been held close to his body for hours. Smooth under her fingertips. She turned it slowly, examining the craftsmanship. The stone caught the afternoon light and held it, glowing pale and luminous.

"Kiss it," Gian Paolo said softly. "As the faithful kiss relics to receive blessing."

Virginia glanced back at Benedetta. Her friend's face showed disapproval, jaw tight, eyes hard, but she said nothing. What objection could be raised to kissing a holy relic?

Virginia raised the reliquary to her lips. The stone pressed fever-warm against her mouth, smooth and faintly slick. She kissed it, tasted mineral and metal, and then, following instinct or compulsion, her tongue darted out and pressed onto it.

"Virginia, no." Benedetta's voice cut sharp through the air.

But it was already done.

The world narrowed. All sensation focused on that single point of contact. Stone and metal and salt, bitter as crushed herbs, sweet as honey wine. The taste coated her tongue and throat. The channel between the gold bars pressed sharp-edged where her tongue lay trapped, not quite cutting but close. Her flesh clung to the quartz with unnatural tenacity. She tried to pull back but couldn't.

Heat radiated from the contact point down through her chest, spreading through her veins. Foreign. Intrusive. Her saliva turned thick and metallic, tasting of copper and something else—medicinal, like the tinctures mixed for fevers. Her hands gripped the reliquary until the gold edges bit into her palms.

Through the grating, Gian Paolo leaned forward. His hand gripped the iron bars, knuckles white. His breath had gone shallow, quick, and his eyes fixed on her mouth with an intensity that made her stomach drop. For just a moment, his expression shifted. The polite concern fell away, replaced by something raw and hungry and calculating. A predator watching his prey take the bait.

“Step back from the grating.” Benedetta’s voice, low and furious. “Now.”

The command broke through the haze. Virginia’s hand jerked. Her tongue tore free from the stone with a sensation like ripping silk. The inside of her mouth burned.

The reliquary fell from her grip and clattered against the grating. It dropped to the floor on Gian Paolo’s side with a dull thud.

Virginia stumbled backward from the bars. Her legs wouldn’t hold steady. Her tongue felt swollen, raw, coated with residue that clung to every surface of her mouth. The heat remained, spreading through her chest, pooling low in her belly.

Benedetta’s hand clamped onto Virginia’s arm, fingers digging in hard enough to bruise. “What did you do?” Her voice shook.

“I don’t know.” Virginia’s voice came out rough, barely above a whisper. “I felt something. When my tongue touched it, something held it.”

“What was that?” Benedetta turned on Gian Paolo, her voice cutting. “What did you give her?”

“A blessed relic. Nothing more.” Gian Paolo bent to retrieve it, unhurried. When he straightened, his expression showed only polite concern, the mask firmly back in place.

But Virginia had seen what lay beneath it.

“Perhaps the holiness within it was too powerful,” Gian Paolo said.

“That was not holiness.” Virginia’s hands gripped the edges of her scapular. The heat in her chest continued to spread, pulsing in time with her heartbeat. “That was something else.”

“Sister Virginia,” Benedetta’s voice held barely leashed fury. “This meeting is concluded. Thank Signor Osio for his time and his mother’s generosity. Now.”

Virginia forced the words out through numb lips. “Thank you for coming. Please convey my gratitude to Signora Osio.”

“Of course.” Gian Paolo wrapped the reliquary in its silk covering with deliberate care. His eyes held Virginia’s through the grating. “I hope you are well. You look pale.”

“I am perfectly well. Good day, Signor Osio.”

He bowed and left. The sound of his footsteps faded, then silence.

Virginia stood frozen at the grating, staring at the empty space where he had been. The taste lingered in her mouth, coating her tongue and throat. The heat continued to pulse through her body in waves that made her skin flush and her breath come shallow.

Benedetta's grip on her arm tightened. "Come. Now."

They crossed into the corridor. Sister Bianca stood ten paces away, wrinkled face unreadable. She must have been waiting. Watching.

"Sister Virginia." Her voice carried through the corridor, thin but sharp. "A word, if you please."

Benedetta's hand tightened. "Sister Virginia is unwell. She needs to rest."

"I can see that." Sister Bianca's eyes narrowed. "Curious, how meetings with the Osio family always seem to leave you unwell, Sister Virginia. One might begin to wonder about the nature of such visits."

Virginia's mouth was too dry to form words. The metallic taste coated her tongue.

"There is nothing to wonder about," Benedetta said, her voice cold. "Signor Osio delivered a message from his mother. Sister Virginia thanked him for his family's charitable gifts. That is all."

"Is it?" Sister Bianca took a step closer. "Then why does she look as though she's seen a vision? Or perhaps experienced something rather less holy?"

The accusation hung in the air.

"We are late for Vespers," Benedetta said. She steered Virginia past Sister Bianca, who watched them go with eyes that missed nothing.

* * *

BENEDETTA CLOSED THE door to their cell and leaned against it, her face carved from stone. Ottavia stood near the window, arms crossed, face drawn and frightened.

"Tell me exactly what happened," Benedetta said. Each word came precise and controlled.

Virginia's mouth still tasted of stone and metal and that sickly medicinal sweetness. The heat in her chest had settled into a constant warmth that spread through her limbs, making her skin hypersensitive.

"He gave me a reliquary. I kissed it as one would kiss any sacred relic. But then my tongue—" She stopped. "It stuck to the stone. I couldn't pull away at first. And the taste wasn't just stone. It was medicinal. Like something had been applied to the surface."

Benedetta pushed off the door and crossed to her. "You put your tongue on an object handed to you by a man who has been pursuing you for months. A man who killed for you. A man who manipulates his own mother to reach you. Tell me you understand the madness in that."

"It felt wrong," Virginia said. Her hands wouldn't stop shaking. "Not holy. Something else entered me through that stone. I felt it spread through my body."

"A spell." Ottavia's whisper carried through the small space, trembling. "He put a spell on you. A love philtre or some dark working."

Benedetta turned to her. "Perhaps. The possibility exists." She turned back to Virginia. "Did he? I don't know. Does it matter? Spell or desire or your own willing participation, you're bound now either way. That's what matters."

"What do you mean?" Virginia pressed her hand to her throat where the heat still burned.

"I mean that whether he used some compound hidden in that reliquary or whether you simply tasted his skin where he held it and convinced yourself it was magic, the result is the same." Benedetta's voice held the sharp edge of fear beneath the anger. "You crossed a line. Put your mouth on something from his hand. Created a moment of shared intimacy disguised as devotion. And now you'll tell yourself it was outside your control."

"I felt it," Virginia insisted. The warmth continued to pulse through her body in waves. "Something that was not right."

"What you felt was desire." Benedetta moved closer. "Whether he helped it along with compounds or enchantments, I cannot say. Men have used such things before—ground beetle wings, herbs from the East, tinctures that heat the blood and cloud judgment. So yes, perhaps he did use dark arts. Perhaps that reliquary held more than blessed bone. Perhaps some potion was applied to the stone, something that entered your body through your tongue and now works its way through your blood."

She paused.

"But here is what I know with certainty: he gave you a way to absolve yourself. To say 'I was enchanted, I had no choice'. And that absolution is the most dangerous gift of all. Because once you believe forces beyond your control compel you, you will stop resisting. You will surrender to what you tell yourself is inevitable."

Virginia sank onto Benedetta's bed, gripping the rough wool blanket. Through the narrow window, a strip of sky turned gold with evening light.

"So, what do I do?"

"You decide." Benedetta sat beside her. "Do you want to stop this now, today, before it destroys you? Before it destroys all of us? Because I can help you stop it. We go to Mother Imbersaga tonight. Tell her everything. Accept whatever punishment comes. It will be severe—confinement, penance, surveillance. Sister Bianca already suspects. But it ends the danger."

She paused, watching Virginia's face.

"Or you acknowledge what you truly want and accept the consequences. But no more pretending. No more excuses about spells or divine tests or any other fiction. You choose this. You bear responsibility for what follows."

Silence filled the cell. Outside, the bells began to ring for Vespers. The familiar sound rolled across the courtyard, calling the sisters to prayer.

The taste of the reliquary lingered. The warmth pulsed through her chest. Gian Paolo's eyes holding hers through the grating. That moment when his mask had slipped, when the hunger and calculation beneath became visible. Predator and prey. And she had put her tongue on the stone anyway.

The alternative: confession to Mother Imbersaga. Confinement. Endless penance. Surveillance that would follow her for years. Sister Bianca's accusations. A life lived under suspicion.

And beneath all of it, the same routine. The same bells. The same prayers. The same walls. Year after year until death released her.

"I don't want to stop." The words tore from somewhere deep in her chest. "God help me, I don't want to stop."

Ottavia made a small sound of distress, quickly muffled. Benedetta's expression did not change. She sat silent for a long moment.

"Then we move forward with open eyes," she said finally. Her voice held neither judgment nor comfort, only flat assessment. "No more pretending. No more excuses about enchantments or forces beyond your control. You chose this. When everything falls apart, when Mother Imbersaga discovers the truth, when your family learns of the scandal, when Sister Bianca brings her accusations to the Chapter, when the consequences come as they inevitably will, remember that you chose this."

Virginia nodded. Her hands would not stop trembling, so she clasped them together in her lap and held them still through force of will.

"I understand."

"Do you?" Benedetta stood and moved to the window. "I wonder. But we'll find out soon enough."

* * *

THAT NIGHT, VIRGINIA lay in her narrow bed, staring at the darkness above her. Her tongue still felt tender where it had stuck to the stone. The warmth in her chest had faded to a dull glow that pulsed in time with her heartbeat. The metallic taste remained.

Real or imagined, she could not say. Did not care. Benedetta's words circled through her mind: *You chose this.*

Yes. She had reached through the grating, had put her tongue on the reliquary despite Benedetta's warning, despite the hunger in Gian Paolo's eyes, despite knowing this would change everything. Had said no to confession and yes to whatever came next.

Tomorrow she would go to the window that overlooked his garden and watch for him. When he sent word that he wanted to meet again, and he would, she would find a way to go to him. Not because a spell compelled her. Because she wanted to.

* * *

August

SISTER SILVIA HAD always been observant. Convent life rewarded those who noticed what others missed—the missing rosary that revealed a sister's distraction, the faint scent of wine on breath after Compline, the small betrayals that whispered through stone corridors.

Lately, she had noticed Virginia. The way Sister Virginia requested parlatory visits with increasing frequency, especially during feast days when the Prioress's attention divided itself among other obligations. The way Sister Benedetta and Sister Ottavia accompanied her to these meetings, positioning themselves like sentinels while voices murmured through the iron grating. The way Virginia emerged with color high in her cheeks, hands trembling, her eyes holding a brightness that had nothing to do with holy contemplation.

One afternoon in early August, curiosity won.

Silvia moved through the narrow corridor adjacent to the parlatory on silent feet. The stone was cool against her palms as she pressed herself inside the small alcove near the room. She held her breath at the voices she overheard.

A man's voice, low and urgent, roughened: "I cannot stop thinking of you. Every hour. Every moment. You consume me entirely."

Silvia's fingers dug into her habit.

Virginia's response came too quietly to distinguish words, but the tone, soft as silk, tender as confession, carried clearly through the oak.

This was not the prescribed exchange between a grateful nobleman and the nun who had saved him. This was something else entirely.

Footsteps approached from the opposite end of the corridor. Silvia pulled back, flattened herself further back into the shadowed alcove.

Sister Ottavia emerged first. She checked the corridor with nervous precision, eyes darting left and right. Virginia followed moments later, pressing one hand to her mouth as though holding something precious inside.

Silvia waited until their footsteps faded, then moved back toward the chapel, her pulse racing.

* * *

THE NEXT MORNING, Silvia found them in the music room.

Virginia's fingers stumbled over the organ keys. Benedetta sat perfectly still on the bench near the wall. Ottavia perched on the edge of a chair like a bird ready to take flight.

"I heard voices in the parlatory yesterday." Silvia kept her tone gentle. "A man's voice. Speaking to you with... familiarity."

Virginia's hands fell still on the ivory keys. For a moment, the only sound was the creak of wood settling.

"It was a permitted visit." Virginia's voice came out carefully controlled. "The Prioress approved it."

"Does the Prioress know what he says to you through that grating?" Silvia moved closer. "Does she know how your breath changes when he speaks?"

The silence that followed pressed heavy enough to crush bone.

Then Benedetta spoke. "Signor Osio requests formal visits to express his gratitude for Sister Virginia's mercy. Nothing improper occurs. The iron grating remains between them at all times. As the Holy Rule requires."

"The grating separates your bodies," Silvia said, meeting Virginia's eyes. "But not your hearts. That much is plain to anyone with eyes to see."

Virginia braced for condemnation, for the inevitable march to the Mother Superior's chambers.

Instead, Silvia asked, "Does he compromise you physically?"

"He cannot." Benedetta's interjection was swift. "The iron grating prevents any physical contact. Every visit is chaperoned. Me or Sister Ottavia remain present throughout. We observe every word, every glance. Nothing passes between them but conversation."

The lie was technically true. Silvia studied Virginia for a long moment.

"The barrier protects your body," Silvia said finally, her voice barely above a whisper. "But not your soul. You know this, don't you, Sister Virginia?"

Virginia's throat tightened. "Yes."

"Then I will not report this." Silvia smoothed her hands down the front of her habit. "But you must be more careful. If I can hear the intimacy in your voices through stone, others can too. And the grating that keeps you from touching will not save you from scandal if anyone suspects what passes between you."

Virginia's shoulders loosened. "Thank you."

Silvia's smile carried a sadness that aged her beyond her nineteen years. "Do not thank me yet. Nothing good can come of this, Virginia. Love that can only exist through a barrier is not love at all." She paused at the doorway. "It's longing dressed as devotion. And longing without hope is just another name for hell."

Her footsteps faded down the corridor.

Benedetta turned to Virginia. "She's right, you know. These parlatory visits grow more frequent. More dangerous. People are beginning to notice the pattern."

"What would you have me do?" Virginia's whisper scraped raw. "He comes. The Prioress permits it. I cannot refuse without raising more suspicion than acceptance ever could."

"You could show less eagerness." Benedetta's tone was dry as old parchment. "You could remember that every word spoken through that grating is a thread binding you tighter to your own destruction."

But the visits did not stop. Gian Paolo came weekly now, sometimes more. Each time, he brought gifts—books bound in tooled leather, flowers that wilted within hours, small tokens carved from wood or bone that Virginia hid beneath her mattress.

He spoke to her about his life beyond the walls. Of hunts through forests she would never see. Of political intrigues in Milan's great houses. Of the world that continued spinning beyond her cage, vast and varied and forever out of reach.

And she listened, starved not just for his voice but for the life it represented.

They discovered ways to create the illusion of touch. Pressing palms flat against opposite sides of the same vertical bar, cold iron between their skin but their hands aligned so perfectly the heat of him radiated through metal. Reaching fingers through the gaps as far as the spacing allowed, close enough to sense the warmth without quite making contact.

"This is madness," she whispered during a visit in early August. "We can never be together. Not truly. What is the purpose of this torture?"

"We are together now." His face was so close to the grating she could count the dark lashes framing his eyes. "We speak. We see each other. We share what no iron can prevent—our thoughts, our hearts, the truth of who we are beneath the roles the world has assigned us."

"We are separated by iron," Virginia interrupted, gripping the grating until the metal bit into her palms. "By vows I cannot break. By walls I cannot cross. What we have is shadow, Gian Paolo. Smoke and mirrors and pretty lies."

"Then we will learn to love through iron." His voice dropped lower, intimate as a caress. "And find freedom within walls. Is that not what you've done all these years? Survived by discovering spaces between the rules where you could still breathe?"

The truth of it struck clean through her defenses. Yes. That was precisely what she had done.

* * *

BY MID AUGUST, Virginia's physical deterioration had become impossible to hide.

In the refectory one afternoon, Sister Candida set down her spoon with a clatter that drew Sister Bianca's attention two places down the table.

"Sister Virginia." Candida's voice carried concern. "You haven't touched your soup. Are you unwell?"

Virginia stared at the thin broth in her wooden bowl. The smell turned her stomach. She lifted her spoon, watched the liquid drip back into the bowl, and set the spoon down again. Her hands shook.

"I'm fine. Only tired."

"You've been 'only tired' for weeks." Candida reached across the narrow table. Her fingers closed around Virginia's wrist, loose where the bones jutted sharp beneath skin. "You're wasting away."

Sister Bianca leaned forward, eyes narrowing. "When did you last sleep through the night, Sister Virginia?"

Virginia pulled her wrist free. "I sleep. I simply... the heat makes rest difficult."

But she didn't sleep. She lay awake replaying every word Gian Paolo had spoken, every near-touch, every moment when their eyes had met through the grating. Her habit hung loose on her frame now, the cincture requiring an extra knot to stay cinched at her waist.

Benedetta watched it all with precision. One evening, as Virginia lay on her narrow cot too exhausted to rise for Compline, Benedetta spoke.

"You're destroying yourself for a man you can never touch."

Virginia closed her eyes. "I know."

"Does it feel worth it?"

Virginia thought of Gian Paolo's voice through the grating, the way he looked at her as though she were the only woman in the world.

"Yes," she whispered into the gathering darkness. "God help me, yes."

* * *

THE LETTER ARRIVED on the Feast of the Assumption, delivered through the usual channels: Apollonia slipping it to Sister Silvia, who brought it to Virginia with worry etched in her face.

Virginia broke the seal in the privacy of the cell, Benedetta and Ottavia watching.

The parchment was expensive beneath her fingers, smooth as skin.

Most cherished Sister Virginia,

The iron grating that separates us has become both my salvation and my torment. I see you but cannot hold you. I hear your voice but am denied the simple grace of your hand in mine. This measured existence, these stolen moments under watchful eyes, no longer suffice. I write to request what I know borders on impropriety. Could you find the means to meet me in the parlatory at night? After Compline, when the convent sleeps? The grating would still divide us as it must. But the privacy of darkness would allow us to speak freely, without constraint of daylight or witnesses. I know the parlatory is secured at night. I know what I ask requires courage beyond measure. But this hunger for more than stolen moments under scrutiny consumes all reason.

Yours in devotion, G.

Virginia's hands shook so violently the parchment rustled.

"What does it say?" Ottavia's whisper barely disturbed the air.

Virginia looked up at Benedetta. "He wants to meet in the parlatory at night. After Compline. When it's locked and we'd be alone."

"Still separated by the grating," Benedetta observed. "So not breaking enclosure in the physical sense but breaking every other rule that governs this place."

"I know."

"The parlatory is locked after Vespers." Ottavia's voice quivered. "Sister Costanza secures it each evening. How would he even enter?"

She stopped. Her eyes went wide.

"You have a key," Virginia said quietly.

Ottavia's face drained of color. "I help Sister Costanza with the evening rounds sometimes. She trusts me to lock the side doors. But the parlatory key—"

"Could be thrown over the garden wall," Benedetta finished. Her tone remained calm, matter-of-fact. "Where Signor Osio could retrieve it. He'd enter the parlatory from the outside entrance. You and Virginia would go to the inner parlatory door. The grating would still separate them, as it must."

The words fell heavy in the room.

"You're describing treason against our vows," Ottavia whispered.

"I'm describing the method," Benedetta corrected. "What anyone does with that information is their own choice."

Virginia's pulse raced with possibility. The iron grating would still separate them. They would not be breaking the physical boundaries of enclosure. Gian Paolo would enter from outside; she'd remain on her side of the barrier. They would just be meeting at night instead of day.

"After the meeting, he'll leave the key somewhere you could retrieve it," Benedetta continued, her sharp eyes on Ottavia. "You'll return it before Sister Costanza begins her morning duties. No one would know it was ever missing."

"Unless we're caught." Ottavia's hands twisted in her habit. "If anyone sees us in the corridors after Compline..."

"Which is why I would accompany Virginia," Benedetta said. "Stand watch. Ensure no one approaches without warning."

"Why?" Virginia couldn't keep the shock from her voice. "Why would you risk yourself like this?"

Benedetta was quiet for several moments. "Because you're going to do this regardless of whether I help. And I'd rather manage the danger than watch you stumble into disaster through carelessness."

Ottavia made a small sound of distress. "How many times? Once?"

Virginia looked down at Gian Paolo's letter. The parchment trembled in her grip. "I don't know."

"Once will not be enough," Benedetta said flatly. "It never is. But perhaps we set a limit. Once weekly. During the darkest hours between Compline and Lauds. Any more frequent and the risk of discovery multiplies."

Virginia nodded slowly, her mind already leaping ahead. The parlatory in darkness. Gian Paolo's voice without the constraint of daylight propriety. The grating still between them, but the privacy to speak freely for the first time.

"I haven't agreed yet," Ottavia whispered, though her voice lacked conviction.

Benedetta looked at her, then at Virginia. "You both agreed the moment Virginia didn't tear that letter to pieces."

* * *

VIRGINIA WROTE HER response that night.

> *Your request troubles me deeply, yet I confess it also calls to something within me that I can no longer deny. I make no promises. But I will explore whether what you ask might be possible. If it is, you would need to approach the parlatory from the outside at a specific hour, late enough that the convent sleeps. Wait in the road behind the garden wall. The grating would still separate us, as it must. But we would have privacy that daylight denies us. Give me time to consider how this might be accomplished without discovery. If I can find a way, I will send word. V.*

She sealed it with wax, pressing her thumb into the warm red surface, and gave it to Apollonia the next morning in the herb garden. The woman's bruised face betrayed nothing as she tucked the letter into her apron alongside the silver coin Virginia pressed into her palm.

Virginia watched her disappear toward the Osio palazzo and stood alone in the garden, lavender releasing its scent in the morning heat.

Soon, perhaps as soon as tonight, Ottavia would take the parlatory key and throw it over the garden wall where Gian Paolo would be waiting. He would let himself into the outer parlatory. Virginia would go to the inner door. They would meet in darkness, separated by iron, but alone for the first time.

The grating would still divide them. The barrier would remain intact. As long as the grating stood between them, Virginia told herself, she hadn't truly broken her vows. It was a lie. But it was a lie she needed to survive what came next.

* * *

September

THE PARLATORY HELD the accumulated cold of centuries, stone walls that wept moisture in summer and froze breath in winter. Virginia stood on her side of the iron grating, the cold metal bars beneath her palms. The borrowed keys sat heavy in the pocket of her habit.

Everything had gone according to plan. Ottavia had thrown the keys over the garden wall after Compline. Gian Paolo had retrieved them and would let himself into the outer parlatory. Ottavia waited just outside in the corridor now, listening for footsteps, ready to knock three times if anyone approached. Behind Virginia, deeper in the convent, Benedetta stood watch in the shadows.

This was different from the daytime visits. This was active defiance. Deliberate sin, executed with premeditation and planning. She could still leave. Could slip back to her cell. Gian Paolo would wait on the other side and eventually understand she had changed her mind.

But even as the thought formed, she knew she wouldn't leave. Couldn't leave.

The faint scrape of the outer door. Footsteps crossed the outer parlatory, and then Gian Paolo appeared on the other side of the grating.

The faint candlelight caught the edge of his jaw, the curve of his shoulder. Leather and horses and something male that made her mouth go dry.

"Virginia." Her name on his lips sent heat through her chest.

"You came." His voice held wonder, but beneath it something else. Hunger barely restrained.

"I shouldn't have." Her voice came out breathless.

"But you did." He moved closer to the bars, his hands reaching through to find hers. His fingers closed around her wrists, warm and strong, and the touch, the first real touch they'd shared, jolted through her body. "You're here. You're real."

He pulled her closer until the iron pressed against her chest, the cold metal biting through her habit.

"We cannot stay long," she whispered. "If anyone discovers us..."

"Then let us not waste the time we have." His grip tightened on her wrists. Too tight. "Tell me I'm not alone in this madness. Tell me you feel it too."

She should deny it. Should maintain the pretense. But in the darkness, with his hands on her wrists and his eyes burning into hers through the bars, the lies wouldn't come.

"I feel it," she whispered. "God help me, I feel it."

His breath released in a rush. "Say my name. I've hungered to hear you speak it without formality."

"Gian Paolo." The word came out as barely more than a breath.

"Again."

"Gian Paolo." Louder this time, and saying it felt dangerous, intimate.

His hands released her wrists and reached higher through the grating, finding her face through the bars. His fingers worked at her veil, loosening it, pushing it back. She should have stopped him, but she didn't.

"This iron between us is torture." His voice roughened with frustration. "To be this close to you and still separated. I cannot bear it."

"The grating must remain," she whispered. "We agreed. I promised Benedetta."

"Damn the grating. Damn all of it." His hands withdrew from the bars. Movement on his side—the scrape of wood on stone as he tested the side door that connected the two halves of the parlatory, the door secured with only a simple bolt on her side.

"No." The word came out sharp with alarm. "You cannot cross to this side. That's breaking enclosure."

“Opening a door?” His voice held bitter amusement. “Virginia, we passed breaking rules the moment you arranged these meetings. This barrier is a lie we tell ourselves. Open it. Let me come to you properly. Let me hold you without this damned iron between us.”

Her hands trembled as she stared at the bolt. She should refuse. Should maintain this final barrier. The grating was the last pretense of propriety.

But his words echoed in her head. The grating *was* a lie. She had stolen keys. Had snuck through the convent like a thief. To hold him without iron between them, just to be held, to feel his arms around her, was that not what she’d wanted all along?

Her hand moved to the bolt before her mind fully registered the decision. One twist and the bolt released with a soft click.

Then everything shattered.

The door exploded inward with sudden violence, hinges shrieking. He didn’t step through. He lunged. His hands gripped her shoulders, fingers digging into flesh through layers of wool, and before Virginia understood what was happening, he drove her backward with enough force to empty her lungs.

Her shoulders struck the floor. Stone met bone. Cold seeped through her habit immediately. She tried to draw breath and couldn’t, her lungs paralyzed, vision sparking.

“No!” The word tore from her throat as soon as air returned. “My vows...you cannot.”

But he was already on her, his weight pinning her to the unforgiving stone. She tried to push him away, hands shoving against his chest with all her strength, but he caught her wrists in an iron grip and forced them to the floor above her head. His body pressed down, heavy and inescapable.

“I am the daughter of Count de Leyva,” she gasped. “I am a bride of Christ. You must not. My honor.”

A sound low in his throat. His mouth found her neck, her jaw, her lips. She turned her face away, cheek scraping against rough stone, skin tearing.

“Please,” she whispered, and hated herself for begging. “Please do not do this.”

He did not stop.

Pain. Sharp and wrong. Brutal and fast, happening on the cold parlatory floor that smelled of damp stone and fear, witnessed only by shadows and regret.

When it ended, he collapsed against her with his full weight, crushing her chest. Then, finally, he pulled away, rolling off her and onto the stone floor beside her.

Virginia lay motionless, staring up at the vaulted ceiling she could barely see. The cold seeped through her habit into her back, her hips, her thighs. Between her legs, wetness spread. Blood or seed or both. Her body felt wrong, changed, ruined.

Footsteps. The rustle of clothing being adjusted. His footsteps crossing back to the other side of the grating. The small dividing door of the parlatory clicked shut.

"I will write to you from Milan." His voice came through the darkness, through the iron bars again, steady and calm, as though nothing had changed. "Wait for my letters."

She couldn't speak. Couldn't move. Couldn't do anything but lie on the cold stone.

His footsteps retreated. The outer door opened. Ottavia's hissed whisper. His response too low to make out. The door closed. Silence settled.

For a long moment, Virginia simply lay there. Then, slowly, she dragged herself to sitting. Every motion sent fresh pain radiating through her pelvis. Her hands shook as she tried to straighten her habit, but her fingers fumbled with the fabric, clumsy and numb.

Ottavia's face appeared, pale, her mouth opening to ask questions Virginia couldn't answer.

Then Virginia ran. She pushed past Ottavia, stumbling through the doorway and down the corridor to their shared cell, her feet loud on the stone floor, past caring who heard. Behind her, Ottavia followed, as did Benedetta, her voice sharp with alarm.

But Virginia didn't stop, and didn't slow. She fled, with shame burning hotter than any fever.

Virginia reached their cell. The door slammed behind her. She pressed her back against the wood and slid down until she sat on the cold floor, knees drawn tight to her chest.

The shaking started then. Great shudders rattled through her frame, making her teeth chatter. She buried her face against her knees and tried to make herself small.

Between her thighs, the wetness had begun to cool. Sticky and wrong. The fabric of her habit clung to her skin. Proof of what had happened, written in her flesh and blood.

She had imagined her first time differently. During those fevered nights she had built fantasies of gentle hands and soft words. Not this. Not brutal violation on cold stone.

Hot shame rose in her throat. She had enabled this. Had arranged these meetings. Had stood in that parlatory willingly. Had opened the door with her own hands.

But beneath came the cold truth. She had wanted to be held. Had wanted closeness without iron between them. But wanting had never meant *this*. The fault was not in her desire but in his hands that had pushed her down, that had held her wrists against stone, that had taken what she never offered.

And then, deeper still, the practicalities. The blood on her habit, unmistakable. The bruises forming on her wrists. The way she would move tomorrow, stiff and careful. How would she hide this?

What if she quickened with child? What if her courses didn't come? What if her body swelled with evidence no amount of loose habits could hide?

Would he return? Would he expect more now that the threshold had been crossed?

A soft knock at the door made her flinch.

"Virginia?" Ottavia's voice, barely a whisper. "Let us in."

Virginia didn't move. Couldn't lift her head. Couldn't speak.

"Please." Benedetta's voice now, low and commanding. "You need help. Open the door."

When Virginia didn't respond, Benedetta spoke again. "Virginia. Open this door now, or I will wake Sister Bianca and tell her you've fallen ill. Your choice."

The threat cut through Virginia's paralysis. Moving like an old woman, she dragged herself upright. Her legs protested. She lifted the latch with shaking hands.

Benedetta pushed the door open and stepped inside. Her gaze swept the small cell—Virginia's torn habit, the blood visible even in darkness. Ottavia followed, carrying the basin of water and clean linen from across the room. Benedetta shut the door and shot the bolt home.

"Sit on the bed." She moved to light the candle. The flame illuminated her face, revealing no shock, no horror, only grim assessment.

Whatever Ottavia saw in Virginia's face made her own crumple. "Oh, Sister."

"Don't." Virginia's voice came out hoarse, broken. "Don't say anything."

"Sister Ottavia." Benedetta's interruption was swift. "Set the basin on the table. The keys need to be returned before dawn. You'll need to do that within the hour. Can you manage it?"

Ottavia nodded, her face pale. "I'll go now."

Benedetta removed the keys from the pouch beneath Virginia's habit and handed them to Ottavia.

"Good. Take the back route past the kitchen. If anyone sees you, you were fetching hot water for Sister Virginia's illness. Then return here immediately."

Ottavia slipped out, and Benedetta turned her full attention to Virginia.

"How badly are you hurt?" The question was clinical, matter-of-fact.

Virginia couldn't answer.

"Can you stand without assistance?"

A small nod.

"Good. That limits the visible damage." Benedetta's mind was already working through implications. "I need to examine what we're dealing with. What injuries will be visible tomorrow, what excuses we'll need. Can you remove the habit yourself or do you need help?"

"Help," Virginia whispered.

Benedetta moved closer and began helping Virginia out of her habit, her movements careful. They stripped away the stained layers, revealing the evidence written on her skin. Fingerprint bruises on her upper arms, clear as signatures. Scrapes on her back from the rough stone floor. Blood on her inner thighs, dried brown at the edges, still red where it had pooled.

Benedetta catalogued every mark with clinical precision. "The bruises on the upper arms, those we can attribute to a fall if questioned. The scrapes on your back... we say you slipped on the stairs and caught yourself against the wall. Rough stone. Plausible."

She moved to the basin and began washing Virginia's skin with efficient strokes. "Listen to me carefully. I need you to answer questions. Can you do that?"

Virginia managed a small nod.

"Did anyone see you in the parlatory besides Ottavia and myself?"

"No."

"Are you certain?"

"Yes."

"Did you cry out? Make any sound that might have carried beyond the parlatory walls?"

Shame burned through Virginia. "No."

"Good." Benedetta's hands paused briefly, and when she spoke again, her voice carried an edge Virginia had never heard before. "What he did was his choice. His crime. Not yours. Do you understand that?"

Virginia couldn't answer.

"I need you to understand that, Virginia. Because what happens next depends on your survival. Our survival." Benedetta resumed washing. "You opened the door. That was foolish. But what he did after you opened it, that was assault. His decision. His violence. Not something you caused by wanting him. Do you understand?"

"I... yes."

"Tomorrow, you will be stiff and move carefully. We will say you fell on the stairs this evening. Sister Ottavia and I heard the commotion and came to your aid. You scraped your back against the wall and bruised your arms catching yourself. Understood?"

"Yes."

"If your courses don't come next month, we have a more serious problem. But we'll address that if it happens. For now, we focus on immediate survival."

The door opened and Ottavia slipped back inside, carrying a larger basin of steaming water. "The keys are back in the porter's room. No one saw me."

Benedetta took the basin and began the washing again, more thoroughly. When Virginia was clean, Ottavia helped her into a fresh shift.

Benedetta gathered the stained habit and examined it. "Too much blood to explain away. The fabric is torn here, and here. This burns tonight. I'll do it myself in the kitchen fire."

"What do I say if someone asks about the missing habit?" Virginia's voice was barely audible.

"You spilled wine at supper. The stain wouldn't come out. You gave it to me to dispose of. I have permission to burn damaged linens as part of my sacristy duties." Benedetta's gaze fixed on Virginia. "Can you repeat that without hesitation if asked?"

"Yes."

"Say it back to me. Now."

Virginia forced the words out. "I spilled wine at supper. The habit was ruined. I gave it to Sister Benedetta to burn."

"Good. Again."

Virginia repeated it until Benedetta was satisfied.

"Sister Ottavia, help her into bed." Benedetta moved to the small table where she kept some medicinal herbs. She selected several items. "These will help with pain and swelling. And these..." She paused, measuring out a different mixture with careful precision. "These will help bring your courses if they're delayed. You'll drink this tea every morning, starting tomorrow. I'll bring it to you myself. I took them from the infirmary some time ago."

In case a child quickened. Herbs to bring blood. To prevent what might already be taking root. Virginia's stomach clenched, but she nodded.

"One spoonful in hot water. Every morning. No more, no less. Too much will make you violently ill and raise questions. Understood?"

"Yes."

"Get into bed."

Virginia climbed onto the narrow bed, moving stiffly. Ottavia tucked the blanket around her, but it was Benedetta who leaned close.

"He won't come back. I'll make certain of it." The words carried absolute conviction. "I'll monitor his whereabouts. I'll track his patterns. I'll make sure you're never alone in any location he could access. And if he tries..." Her jaw tightened. "If he tries, I'll ensure the Prioress learns of his presence in ways that bring the authorities down on him so fast he won't have time to flee."

The promise had teeth. Not empty comfort, but real planning.

"But you need to understand something, Virginia." Benedetta straightened. "What happened tonight changes everything. The conspiracy we've been managing just became exponentially more dangerous. Physical evidence. Possible pregnancy. Visible injuries that must be explained. This isn't letters and glances anymore. This is assault. And that means the stakes just went from social ruin to prison or worse if we're discovered."

Virginia's breath caught.

"So, here are the new rules." Benedetta's voice was flat, unyielding. "No more meetings. Ever. No more parlatory visits. No more windows. If he writes, the letters still come to me first. I read them. I decide if you see them. If he tries to approach you directly, you report to me immediately. And if you feel unsafe at any moment, you find me. Day or night. I don't care where I am. You find me. Understood?"

"Yes."

"I mean it, Virginia. Our survival depends on discipline from this point forward. One mistake, one moment of weakness, and we all face the Holy Office." She moved toward her cot. "And I have no intention of dying in a Spanish dungeon because of choices I didn't make."

Ottavia moved to her cot and extinguished the candle. Darkness swallowed their small cell.

But before settling, Benedetta spoke once more. "Sister Ottavia. I'll stay awake in case I hear anything unusual."

"You're staying awake all night?" Ottavia's voice trembled.

"One of us needs to remain alert. Besides we don't know if she'll feel worse, if she'll attempt something foolish. So, I stay awake."

Silence settled over the cell. Virginia lay in the darkness and stared at the ceiling she couldn't see. Outside, a nightingale sang.

She had wanted him. Had arranged these meetings with eyes open. Had stood in that parlatory willingly. Had opened the door with her own trembling hands. And now she would pay the price for that wanting. Not just once, but every day for the rest of her life.

The assault had bound them together in ways more permanent than vows. More damning than any sacrament.

And somewhere beyond these walls, Gian Paolo walked free beneath the same stars. He would write to her, he'd said. As though what had happened was merely another step in their romance. As though he hadn't just destroyed the last barrier through force and violence.

He would not let her go. Whatever had been awakened in that parlatory would not be satisfied by a single violation. This was not an ending. It was a beginning.

From her cot, Ottavia's breathing gradually evened into exhausted sleep. And by the window, Benedetta remained motionless. Not sleeping. Not resting. Simply there, a silent guardian organizing tomorrow's excuses, planning for every contingency, ready to act if needed.

The nightingale sang on. The moon traced its arc. The convent walls stood solid and silent, keeping their secrets as they had for centuries.

"Try to sleep, Virginia," Benedetta said into the darkness, her voice softer now. "Tomorrow requires clear thinking. And we have work to do."

Dawn would come eventually. It always did. But Virginia had crossed a threshold into darkness from which there was no return.

* * *

October

VIRGINIA PRESSED HER face into the pillow and wished for death. Three days had passed since she took to her bed. Three days of lying motionless while autumn light crept across the stone floor and retreated again, marking time she could not fill with prayer or duty. Her muscles ached from stillness, her joints stiff. Still, she could not rise.

The door creaked open. Footsteps crossed the threshold, light, hesitant.

"Sister Virginia, I've brought you some broth." Ottavia's voice trembled. "You must eat something."

Virginia kept her face turned away. The whitewashed plaster bore hairline cracks that spread like tributaries on a map. She had traced their patterns a thousand times, memorizing their branches as though they might lead somewhere beyond this cell, beyond remembering.

"Please." Desperation threaded through Ottavia's words. "You frighten me."

The mattress shifted as Ottavia sat on the edge. Steam curled from the wooden bowl, carrying chicken broth and herbs—rosemary, thyme. Virginia's stomach twisted.

"I'm not hungry."

"You haven't eaten since Sunday. It's Wednesday now. Three days, Virginia."

The gentleness made Virginia's throat tighten. If she looked at Ottavia, if she witnessed the concern in her friend's face, her careful control might shatter.

"Leave me be."

"I can't." Ottavia's fingers tightened on Virginia's shoulder. "Whatever troubles your heart, starving yourself won't cure it."

But that was precisely what Virginia hoped it might do. Reduce her body to something too weak to feel. Transform flesh and blood into stone, immune to hunger, to violence, to the awful humiliations of wanting.

The parlatory. The corridor. Cold stone beneath her shoulder blades. His weight crushing her as darkness swallowed everything but his breath and her panic. The shame that followed, relentless.

She had not gone to any window since. Had not answered his letters. Had pulled the blanket over her head and tried to disappear.

"I'll fetch Sister Benedetta." Ottavia stood. The floorboards creaked. "Perhaps she can talk sense into you."

Virginia lay very still. Her body had responded even as her mind screamed refusal. Some treacherous part of her had softened to him despite the violence, despite the shame.

That was the sickness eating her from within. Not fever or ague. But the terrible discovery that even after he had used her with such callousness, left her crumpled and bleeding, she lay here aching not with outrage but with the horrible compulsion to see him again.

Footsteps in the corridor announced Benedetta's arrival. She entered without knocking, carrying a wooden tray bearing bread, cheese, and wine. Her sharp features showed no sympathy, only calculating assessment.

"Sit up." Benedetta set the tray on the table with a decisive thud. "This performance has lasted long enough."

"I'm ill."

"You're melancholy." Benedetta's correction came swift. "There's a difference. One requires a physician. The other requires will."

Virginia turned her head enough to meet Benedetta's dark eyes. In them she found no moral judgment, only pragmatic concern.

"I can't face them." The admission escaped before she could stop it. "I can't walk through these corridors and pretend."

"Pretend what? That you're still untouched?" Benedetta sat in the single chair, spine rigid. "That is all gone now, Virginia. The question now is whether you'll drown in self-pity or learn to navigate the deep waters you've entered."

Virginia pushed herself upright. The cell tilted. She gripped the mattress edge, knuckles white, until the dizziness passed.

"He forced me." The words came out as a whisper.

"I know what he did." Benedetta's voice held no surprise.

Warmth crept up Virginia's neck. Ottavia knew. Benedetta knew. How long before everyone knew?

"Then you understand why I can't get up."

"What I understand," Benedetta interrupted, leaning forward, "is that you're confusing shame with grief. You're not lying here because he violated you. You're lying here because part of you welcomed him."

The accusation hung in the air. Virginia opened her mouth to deny it.

No words came.

Because it was true.

She had gone to that parlatory knowing what he intended. Had opened the door. And when he had taken her with rough urgency, she had experienced not violation alone but a sick confirmation of what she had always suspected about herself. That beneath the habit and vows, she was wanton.

"My soul is lost." Virginia's voice broke.

"Your soul was in peril the moment you answered his first letter." Benedetta's tone remained blunt. "What's done is done. The question is what comes next."

"I want nothing more to do with him."

"Liar." The word landed soft but final. "If that were true, you'd have thrown his letters in the fire months ago."

Virginia stared at her hands, clasped tight.

"And you promised me," Benedetta continued, "that if he wrote again, the letters would come to me first."

Virginia's breath caught.

Benedetta's gaze sharpened. "So, you've already broken the only rule that mattered."

"He won't leave me in peace."

"Of course he won't." Benedetta rose and crossed to the window, pushing open the shutters. Afternoon light flooded in, turning the dust motes into suspended gold. "Men like Gian Paolo Osio never leave anything in peace. They take what they demand and demand more."

Virginia shut her eyes against the brightness.

"That's why you must decide now," Benedetta said, "before he escalates further, whether you're strong enough to refuse him."

"I've tried. I've prayed until my knees bled. I've fasted. I've begged God to free me from this torment."

"And yet here you lie," Benedetta said, "waiting."

The observation pierced. Virginia tried to deny it.

But in the silence of her cell, with Benedetta watching with those knowing eyes, she could not sustain the lie even to herself.

She was waiting. Had been waiting since she took to this bed. Not for death or illness, but for some sign that he had not forgotten her. That despite her absence, he still craved her.

The realization turned her stomach.

"Eat something," Benedetta said, pressing the cup of wine into Virginia's hands. "You'll need your strength for what's coming."

"What's coming?"

Benedetta's expression held grim certainty. "He won't be satisfied with one stolen encounter. He'll demand more. Regular access. Complete control. And he'll use every tool at his disposal to wear you down until you surrender it."

Virginia raised the cup with trembling hands and drank. The wine burned her throat, sharp and sour.

"There are two paths before you," Benedetta continued. "Refuse him and face whatever vengeance he devises. Or surrender and manage the consequences as they come."

"Those are the only choices?"

"Those are the only choices that don't end in disaster for everyone who knows your secrets." Benedetta's voice softened imperceptibly. "Choose quickly, Virginia. He won't wait much longer for an answer."

A knock at the door made them both turn.

Ottavia entered, her face flushed and anxious. "Gioseffo Pesseno is at the gate. He says it's urgent." She held out a folded parchment sealed with red wax.

"And who else saw him?" Benedetta asked at once.

Ottavia swallowed. "Sister Costanza."

Benedetta closed her eyes briefly. "Of course she did."

Virginia's hand shook as she took the letter. The seal bore Gian Paolo's mark, the Osio crest pressed deep into wax. She broke it open.

The words leaped out at her, written in his bold hand.

> *Your absence grieves me. Your silence wounds me worse than any blade. I have had enough of corridors, of improvisation, of discomfort. When you are cured of your illness, you will allow me to come to your bed like any lover to his mistress. This is not a request.*

Virginia read it twice. Then a third time. The command in those final words made her body respond before her mind could form objections. Heat spread through her belly, shameful and undeniable.

"What does it say?" Ottavia asked.

Virginia folded the letter and tucked it into her sleeve. "He demands entry to the convent. To my bed. When I am well enough to receive him."

Benedetta nodded slowly, as though this confirmed something she had already suspected. "And your answer?"

Virginia picked up the bread from the tray and broke off a piece. The crust crackled under her fingers. The simple act of chewing, of swallowing, of choosing sustenance over starvation was choosing a path.

"I don't know yet." She met Benedetta's eyes. "But I'm no longer trying to starve myself free of him."

It was not an answer. But it was motion.

* * *

THE LETTERS CAME daily after that.

Sometimes Pesseno brought them, pressing folded parchments into Ottavia's hands at the gate. Other times Susanna de Regiubus carried them, the elderly woman who had served in the convent for so many years that her presence raised no questions. She would find Virginia in the scriptorium or garden, slip the letters into her hand, and disappear like smoke.

Virginia told herself she would not read them. That she would burn them unopened.

But each time, she broke the seal. Each time, she unfolded the parchment and let his voice enter her mind through ink and paper.

I think of you constantly. Your face haunts my dreams. Allow me to serve you as I once served you in the parlatory, with devotion and respect...

The gifts accompanied the letters. Cloth-covered baskets appeared at irregular hours. Virginia unwrapped candied fruits from Bologna—quinces glazed amber, apricots soft as velvet. Silk handkerchiefs embroidered with delicate patterns. Scented soaps from Venice that smelled of lavender and distant seas.

She should refuse them. Should return every offering with a stern rebuke.

Instead, she kept them.

The quinces sat in a bowl on her night table. The handkerchiefs lay folded in her trunk. The soap she used each morning, breathing in the forbidden luxury, marking herself with his scent.

"You're feeding the fire you claim to extinguish." Benedetta's observation came one afternoon as Virginia sat in their cell, turning over a new letter in her hands. The seal was still intact, but Virginia's fingers traced the edges, the ridges of wax.

"I'm doing no such thing." Virginia set the letter down without opening it.

"Then burn it." Benedetta gestured toward the sealed parchment. "Throw it in the brazier. Prove you're capable of refusing him."

Virginia's hand moved to protect the letter. An instinctive gesture she regretted the moment Benedetta's knowing eyes marked it.

"I will. When I'm ready."

"When you're ready." Benedetta's voice held bitter amusement. "And when will that be?"

"I'm trying to end this properly. With courtesy and clarity. So, that he understands."

"Understands what?" Benedetta moved closer. "That you're a participant who occasionally suffers attacks of conscience. Every letter you read tells him you're still engaged. Every gift you accept confirms you crave what he offers. You're not ending anything, Virginia. You're negotiating terms."

The accusation struck too close to truth. Virginia turned away, crossing to the narrow window that overlooked the inner courtyard. Below, young novices walked in pairs, their voices rising in afternoon prayers. Simple Latin phrases repeated, memorized, empty of meaning.

She had been one of them once. A young postulant who believed prayer and obedience would be enough. Who had entered this place terrified but determined.

When had that girl died?

"I don't know how to stop." The admission came out raw. "I've tried, Benedetta. God knows I've tried. But every time I resolve to refuse him, my hands won't obey. My will crumbles."

"You keep hoping he'll come back." Benedetta finished the thought Virginia couldn't speak aloud. "Keep imagining that next time will be different. That next time he'll be gentle."

Virginia blinked rapidly. Weeping had accomplished nothing these past days.

"He sends letters asking forgiveness for his roughness." She gestured to the unopened parchment. "He claims he was overcome by passion. That next time—"

"Next time will be exactly the same." Benedetta's certainty cut like a blade. "Because men like Gian Paolo Osio don't change. They simply find new ways to justify taking what they demand."

Ottavia entered, breathless. "Gioseffo Pesseno was here again." She held out another cloth-covered basket. The linen was fine-woven, expensive. "He says Signora Osio sent these for you. Fresh bread and honey."

Virginia took the basket. Beneath the cloth, she smelled yeast and butter, the sweetness of honey still warm from the hive.

"His mother didn't send this." Benedetta's flat statement made Ottavia flinch. "He did. Using her name as cover."

She handed the note to Virginia. The seal was already broken.

> *From Signora Osio, with her prayers for your swift recovery and her hope that you will accept her son's devoted service.*

"He's building a foundation," Benedetta said, taking the note and holding it to the candle flame. The parchment caught quickly, curling and blackening, edges glowing orange before crumbling to ash. "Pesseno for letters and small gifts. Susanna for movement within the convent. His mother's name for larger offerings. He's ensuring he can reach you constantly, through multiple channels, so you're never free of his presence."

Virginia watched the note burn, the last fragments floating upward before dissolving.

"What should I do?"

"Refuse it all." Benedetta dropped the last burning fragment into the brazier. "Send back every gift. Return every letter unopened."

It was the right answer. The only answer that might protect her. Virginia knew this with certainty.

But when she opened her mouth to agree, different words emerged.

"I can't."

Ottavia made a small sound of distress. Benedetta's expression hardened.

"Then you've made your choice." Benedetta moved toward the door. "Don't pretend otherwise. You've chosen him. Chosen this path. All that remains is seeing how much it will cost you."

She left. The door closed with a hollow thud.

Ottavia remained, wringing her hands, the gesture making her look younger than her years.

"She's angry because she's frightened." Ottavia's voice trembled. "We're all frightened, Virginia."

“I know.” Virginia set the basket on the table. “I know the danger. I know what we’re risking.”

“Then why won’t you stop?”

Because stopping meant returning to the numbness that had sustained her since she entered this place. Because stopping meant accepting that the rest of her life would pass in silent observation of rules that meant nothing to her heart. Because for the first time since her father locked her behind these walls, she felt something beyond resignation.

But she couldn’t say any of that to Ottavia.

“I don’t know.” The lie tasted bitter. “But I’ll try to be more careful.”

It was not the answer Ottavia craved. Disappointment clouded her friend’s features. But Ottavia nodded and moved toward the door.

“Be careful, then.” She paused on the threshold. “Because Benedetta’s right. He’s building something larger than secret letters. And whatever he’s building, it won’t stop until he has exactly what he demands from you.”

After Ottavia left, Virginia sat alone with the basket. She unwrapped the bread slowly, reverently. The smell of yeast filled her senses, mixing with honey and butter, the scent of something made with care.

She tore off a piece and ate it. The crust crackled between her teeth. Then another piece. The sweetness coated her tongue, rich and indulgent, forbidden.

With each bite, her resistance crumbled. Not because the bread was delicious, but because accepting it, savoring it, prepared her for the larger surrender she knew was coming.

She finished the bread and licked the honey from her fingers, one by one.

She longed to look at him. To stand at a window and watch him. To hear his voice. To believe, for a moment, that she was something other than a disappointment buried alive.

* * *

VIRGINIA FOLLOWED BENEDETTA and Ottavia to the bakehouse three days later, the first time she had left their cell for anything beyond required

Offices. The Feast of Saint Teresa had passed. October's chill crept through the corridors now, turning stone floors cold underfoot.

The bakehouse smelled of yeast and wood smoke, of dough risen and bread baked. Flour dust hung in the air, turning afternoon sunlight into a hazy blur that coated the tongue.

"Here." Ottavia pressed her palm against the wooden shutter. "This window looks directly onto the side of his garden."

Benedetta shoved the shutter open. Cool air rushed in, carrying the scent of dying leaves and distant smoke from kitchen fires. She leaned out, surveying the sight lines with care. "The Lichini house is there. They can see this window clearly. Anyone standing here would be visible."

"But they can't see down into the garden from that angle." Ottavia had already worked out the geometry. "They'd see us but not him."

Virginia joined them at the window, her hands gripping the rough sill. Gian Paolo's garden spread in autumn colors, grass fading to gold, bare branches reaching like skeletal fingers, the last roses clinging to thorny stems. Closer than the scriptorium window had been. Close enough that she could see individual stones in the path, moss growing in the cracks.

"The table." Benedetta gestured to the large wooden frame in the corner, its mesh screen dusty with flour. "If we position it beneath the window, we gain another foot. Enough to lean out."

They dragged the table across the floor together, their movements synchronized. The legs scraped against stone, leaving marks that would need explaining later. For now, Virginia needed to see.

She climbed onto the table. The wood creaked under her weight. From this vantage, the garden lay clear: the bench where he often sat reading, the tree he'd once climbed, the gate toward the street where servants came and went.

"This is madness," Benedetta said. "Domenico Ferrari checks all the windows every evening. He'll find this open and close it."

"Then we'll open it again." Virginia surprised herself with the firmness in her voice. "We'll come here during the day when he's occupied elsewhere. And at night..."

"At night you're visible to anyone passing in the street." Benedetta climbed up beside her, steadying herself against the sill. "The Lichinis' son reads by candlelight until well past Compline."

"Then we'll be careful." Virginia stared out at the garden, her mind filling with images of him there in the dusk, his voice reaching to her. "We'll watch for lights in their window. We'll move quickly."

"We'll get caught." Benedetta's hand closed on her arm. "Listen to me. Candida's window was risky but manageable. This is something else entirely. Every element of this plan invites discovery."

"I have to see him." The admission came out raw, desperate. "I've tried to stay away. I've tried to satisfy myself with letters and gifts. But it's not enough. I need to look at him. To hear his voice. To know that he still—"

She couldn't finish.

Benedetta studied her. Something flickered in her eyes, pity, perhaps, or weary recognition of a battle already lost.

"Then limit yourself to daylight hours when we can claim legitimate reasons for being here," she said finally. "Ottavia is assigned to the bakehouse twice a week. I have access for gathering supplies. We can create a rotation that gives you time at this window without raising immediate suspicion."

"That's not enough." Virginia's hands tightened on the sill. "I need to speak with him. To make arrangements."

"To arrange for him to enter the convent." Benedetta finished the thought. "That's what this is about. You're not satisfied with seeing him from a distance. You want him here. In your cell. In your bed."

The bluntness brought relief more than shock.

"Yes." Virginia met Benedetta's eyes. "Yes, that's what I need."

Ottavia gasped. "Virginia, you can't mean that. If he comes into the convent regularly, there will be consequences beyond scandal."

"I know." Virginia climbed down, her legs unsteady. "I know all the consequences. Pregnancy. Discovery. Ruin. I've considered them all."

"And you've decided they're worth the risk?" Benedetta's question held no judgment, only grim curiosity.

Virginia looked out one last time before they closed the window. In the gathering dusk, the garden lay empty, but she saw him there anyway, standing below, looking up at her with that intensity that made her breath catch.

"I've decided I can't live without it," she said. "Without him. Whatever that makes me, I've stopped caring. I need what he offers even if it destroys me."

Benedetta slid the shutter closed. The bolt clicked home with a finality that echoed through the bakehouse.

"Then we'll need to be smarter than you've been so far," she said, pushing the table back into position. "Domenico checks this room every evening after Vespers. We leave no evidence of our visits. No flour disturbed. No marks on the floor."

They worked together, erasing signs of their presence. Virginia swept the flour dust with her sleeve, careful to leave the surface as they'd found it. As they finished, a shadow moved across the Lichini window opposite. Candlelight flared briefly like an opening eye, then vanished.

The three women froze, breath held.

Only when the light disappeared did Benedetta exhale.

"How often?" Ottavia asked as they prepared to leave, gathering empty baskets to justify their presence. "How often will you come here?"

Virginia picked up a basket of bread, the loaves still faintly warm from the afternoon's baking. The heat seeped through the woven reeds into her palms.

"As often as necessary." She met Ottavia's worried gaze. "Until he agrees to come to me properly. Until we find a way to manage what's between us that doesn't require standing on tables and hiding in bakehouse shadows."

"That's not a plan." Ottavia's voice rose. "That's hoping something impossible will somehow become possible."

"Then it's a good thing I've become skilled at impossible things." Virginia stepped into the corridor, the scent of bread following her. "I've survived eight years in this place. I've learned to live with vows I never chose and a future I never accepted. Surely, I can learn to manage one determined lover."

"There's a difference," Benedetta said as they climbed the stairs, their footsteps echoing off stone, "between surviving and living. What you're doing now isn't survival. This is running toward disaster with your eyes open."

"Perhaps." Virginia shifted the basket to her hip. "But at least I'll know I chose it. That's more than my father ever gave me."

That night, she lay awake listening to Domenico's rounds—the soft click of iron on iron as he tested latches, secured windows. A sound so ordinary the convent barely noticed it anymore, woven into the fabric of evening prayers and sleep.

Virginia noticed.

She understood something with cold clarity.

The summons was coming.

* * *

REVEREND MOTHER IMBERSAGA'S summons arrived three days after Virginia began visiting the bakehouse window.

A note came during afternoon prayers, delivered by a younger sister whose eyes would not meet Virginia's: *My study. Now.*

Virginia found the Prioress standing at her window, hands clasped behind her back, posture rigid. Autumn light cast angular shadows across the room, turning the space into a place built for judgment.

"Close the door, Sister Virginia."

The latch clicked too loudly. Virginia remained near the entrance, her back against the wood.

"The Lichini family came to see me this morning," Mother Imbersaga said, still facing the window. "They expressed concerns about activities they've observed from their house across the road."

Virginia's throat tightened.

"What concerns, Reverend Mother?"

"Don't insult my intelligence with feigned ignorance." The Prioress turned. Disappointment, sharpened into grief, hardened her features. "They report that you and several other sisters have been frequenting the bakehouse window. The one that overlooks Signor Osio's garden."

"We've been gathering supplies."

"They say you stand on the table." The interruption was final. "That you lean out the window for extended periods. That you appear to be watching something, or someone, in the garden nearby."

"The window offers a pleasant view, Reverend Mother. When the work grows tedious, we simply go there to catch some fresh air."

"Do you think me a fool?" The words cracked like a whip. "Do you imagine I don't know exactly what you're doing at that window? What you've been doing at every place that offers sight of that man's property?"

Virginia flinched. The accusation was not a guess. It was a verdict already rendered.

"After everything, after the scandal with Molteno," Mother Imbersaga said, moving closer, pale eyes boring into her with an intensity that made Virginia want to look away. "After your father's intervention. After the magistrate's mercy and the Pope's dispensation that allowed you to remain here rather than face harsher judgment. After all the risks we took to protect you from consequences you seemed determined to invite, still you persist with this obsession."

"It's not an obsession."

"Then what would you call it? This compulsion to seek him out? This inability to leave well enough alone despite every warning, every consequence, every plea for your own protection?"

Virginia had no answer that did not confess too much.

"Domenico reports the bakehouse window is often found open nearly every morning." The Prioress's tone turned measured, each word precise. "He secures it each evening after Vespers. By dawn, it's open again. The table has been moved repeatedly, the marks are visible in the flour dust. And several neighbors, not just the Lichinis, have noticed nuns appearing at that window at irregular hours."

Each detail landed like a stone.

"Reverend Mother, I can explain."

"No." One syllable restored full authority. "You will not explain. You will listen."

Virginia lowered her gaze to the floor, the worn tiles familiar now from previous summons. She nodded once.

"Gian Paolo Osio is not a lover from some troubadour's song," Mother Imbersaga said. "He is a man who killed for wounded pride. Who evaded justice through family connections and papal influence. Who sees in you not a person but a conquest to be claimed and displayed."

"You don't know him."

"I know his kind." The correction was swift. "Wealthy young men who believe their birth entitles them to whatever they desire. Who ruin women without consequence and move on to the next entertainment."

Virginia tried to argue. She also remembered the parlatory floor, the cold stone, and the speed with which tenderness turned into appetite, into violence barely restrained.

"He won't leave me alone," she whispered. "I've tried to refuse him, but he persists. He sends letters daily. Gifts arrive constantly. He recruits others—Pesseno, Susanna, Apollonia—to keep contact despite my silence."

"Because you are not silent." Mother Imbersaga's gaze did not blink. "You read his letters. You accept his gifts. You seek out any place that might offer a glimpse of him. Those are not the actions of a woman refusing advances. Those are the actions of a woman negotiating terms."

The truth of it made Virginia's eyes sting. She swallowed hard against the tightness in her throat.

"I don't know how to stop craving him."

The admission arrived like a surrender, the words barely audible.

Mother Imbersaga's shoulders sagged for a heartbeat, then straightened. "Then I will stop him for you."

Virginia's head snapped up.

"From this moment forward," the Prioress said, "you are forbidden the scriptorium window, the bakehouse, the parlatory except under direct command from myself, and any location from which his house or garden can be seen. Any letters addressed to you will be delivered directly to me. Any gifts from the Osio household will be refused on behalf of the convent. You will not speak to him. You will not look for him. You will not so much as glance toward his wall. Do you understand?"

"Yes, Reverend Mother."

"This is not punishment." Her voice softened slightly, though her eyes remained hard. "This is protection—from him, and from yourself. Because whatever wound in you drives this compulsion, he has learned to exploit it with considerable skill."

Virginia's hands tightened inside her sleeves, nails biting into her palms.

"If you disobey," Mother Imbersaga continued, "the matter goes beyond my authority. The Holy Office would take an interest. And their concern for your soul would express itself through methods you would not survive intact. The Inquisition does not treat lightly with nuns who break their vows repeatedly. Do not force my hand in this."

"I won't," Virginia whispered.

"We shall see." The Prioress moved behind her writing table, signaling the end of the audience. "You are dismissed. Return to your cell. Sister Benedetta will be assigned formal responsibility for your conduct from this day forward. She will report to me weekly."

As Virginia turned to the door, Mother Imbersaga added, without looking up from the document she had picked up, "And Sister Virginia, whatever you tell yourself about this man, whatever pretty words he writes in his letters, remember who he is. A man who killed for wounded pride. A man who sees you not as a person but as a conquest to be claimed. Do not mistake his persistence for devotion."

Virginia left the study on unsteady legs, the echo of those words following her into the corridor like a shadow she could not shake.

* * *

BACK IN THEIR cell, Benedetta listened without interrupting as Virginia repeated the Prioress's orders, her voice flat, mechanical.

"So," Benedetta said at last. "The game has changed again. Letters go to Mother Imbersaga. Windows are closed and watched. Officially, it ends here."

"It won't end," Virginia said, sitting on the edge of her bed. The rope frame creaked. "He'll find another way. Another messenger. Another window."

"Yes," Benedetta agreed. "He will."

Virginia looked up sharply. "You're not telling me to stop? Not lecturing me about the dangers?"

"I told you to stop months ago," Benedetta said quietly. "You didn't. The Prioress has now done what I could not, she has cut off the most obvious channels. What he builds next will be more dangerous, less visible, harder to control. The risks will escalate."

"Then what do we do?"

"We survive," Benedetta said. "We watch. We lie when necessary. We prepare for the day when all of this comes to light and hope we've arranged things so that when the ruin falls, it doesn't crush us entirely."

Ottavia's rosary beads clicked faster in the shadows, the rhythm anxious.

"And you," Benedetta added, turning back to Virginia, "must finally decide whether you will spend what remains of your life trying to kill this craving, or whether you will follow it to its end and accept whatever waits there."

Virginia thought of the parlatory, of the bakehouse window, of bread and letters and blood on stone. Of his promise to come to her bed "like any lover to his mistress." Of Mother Imbersaga's warning about the Inquisition, about methods she would not survive intact.

"I don't know how to kill it," she said.

"Then learn," Benedetta answered, her voice hard. "Or be prepared to burn with it. Those are the only futures left to you now."

Outside, the bells began to ring for Vespers. The sound rolled across the cloister, deep and resonant, unchanged, indifferent to the dramas unfolding within these walls.

Virginia rose. Her legs still trembled, but she stood.

"I'll go to prayers," she said.

"Good." Benedetta's voice softened, just for a moment. "One step at a time, Virginia. Even toward damnation, one still walks by steps."

Virginia stepped into the corridor, the sound of bells filling the air, and walked toward the chapel. She carried within her a desire that law, threat, and violence had all failed to extinguish. A flame that burned brighter for every attempt to smother it.

* * *

November

VIRGINIA'S BLOOD HAD dried black on the knotted cords by the time All Saints Day arrived.

She knelt in the pre-dawn darkness of her shared cell, turning the scourge over in her hands, studying the evidence of last night's penance with the detachment of someone examining another woman's failure. The stains looked almost decorative in the candlelight, like some macabre embroidery, sin and salvation woven into hemp.

She had beaten herself until her arm gave out. Until blood soaked through her chemise and pooled in the small of her back. Until pain eclipsed every thought of him.

It had worked for perhaps an hour.

Then, as consciousness returned from that pure hurt, her first thought had been his name. Not God's. Not Mary's. His.

Virginia set the scourge aside and pulled her habit over the fresh wounds, welcoming the sting as wool adhered to torn flesh. At least physical pain was honest. It demanded nothing but endurance.

Outside her window, fog pressed against the convent walls like something trying to seep through stone itself, as if even the weather sought to breach what should remain separate.

* * *

SISTER BIANCA HAD become Virginia's shadow. Never quite visible, but always felt.

The older nun possessed the particular vigilance of women who believed rule-keeping was not merely virtue but weapon. Who understood that power in a convent came not from birth or beauty but from seeing what others wished to hide. When she passed Virginia in corridors, her gaze lingered with precision, a needle testing fabric for the exact location where pressure would tear it.

That scrutiny had changed how Virginia inhabited space. She learned to move with deliberate ordinariness, to make every gesture unremarkable, every expression carefully neutral. Her hands stayed busy with legitimate tasks. Her eyes never strayed toward windows. Her face revealed nothing when his name arose in conversation.

But surveillance, she discovered, could not eliminate longing. It merely taught her how to steal.

A heartbeat's glimpse through an interior casement while carrying linens. A reflection caught in diamond-paned glass. The high window in the infirmary where she'd volunteered to tend Sister Lucia's fever—a window that overlooked rooftops and bare branches and, if one stood in precisely the right position, the corner of his garden wall.

She had become a thief of moments. It was, she thought with bitter humor, probably the most honest thing she'd done in months.

Once, positioning herself in the short corridor near the sewing rooms, Virginia found the exact angle that offered a sliver of view toward his property. Only rooftops and skeletal trees were visible, but her body responded as if she'd seen his face—pulse jumping, breath shortening, heat pooling low in her belly.

The physical betrayal disgusted and thrilled her in equal measure.

She busied her hands smoothing her habit, adjusting her wimple, while her eyes drank in those bare branches like a woman dying of thirst.

Footsteps echoed behind her.

She did not turn. Did not flinch. Simply continued her manufactured task with steady hands while her pulse hammered in her throat so violently, she was certain it must be visible beneath her wimple.

A shadow fell across her shoulder. The scent of medicinal ointment and starched linen, Sister Bianca's distinctive smell, sharp and clean and unforgiving.

"Is something needed here, Sister Virginia?"

The voice was soft as silk drawn over steel.

"No, Sister." Virginia's voice emerged steady, blessedly, miraculously steady. "I was asked to fetch thread for the sewing room."

Silence stretched. Virginia counted her own heartbeats. One. Two. Three. Four. Five.

Sister Bianca's footsteps continued down the corridor, measured and unhurried.

Virginia remained frozen until the sound vanished entirely. Only then did she allow herself to breathe, her exhalation shaking with the knowledge of how narrowly she had escaped.

Or perhaps she hadn't escaped at all. Perhaps Sister Bianca knew exactly what Virginia had been doing at that window, and was simply waiting, gathering evidence the way one gathers kindling, patient and methodical, knowing that eventually there would be enough to start a fire that would consume everything.

The crackdown had not ended Virginia's obsession. It had simply taught her the architecture of survival. How to feed her hunger in ways so subtle they left no evidence, how to exist in the space between desire and discovery.

It had taught her, she realized, how to be a better wrongdoer.

* * *

THAT NIGHT, ALONE in her cell with Benedetta and Ottavia assigned elsewhere, Virginia made her confession.

Not to a priest. To the Madonna.

She knelt before the small statue in the corner and said the words she could never speak in the confessional: "I don't want to stop."

The admission emerged as a whisper, but in the silence, it sounded like a shout.

"Everyone thinks I'm fighting this. Benedetta thinks I'm trying to resist. The confessor thinks Satan is attacking me. But the truth," her voice cracked, "the truth is I stopped fighting weeks ago. Maybe months. I don't even know when it happened."

She stared up at the Madonna's face, searching for condemnation in those painted features.

"I keep waiting to feel guilty enough to stop. To be frightened enough to confess. But I don't feel guilty. I feel *alive*. For the first time since they locked me in here, I feel like a person instead of a ghost."

The statue's expression remained serene, neither judging nor absolving, simply witnessing.

"Does that make me evil?" Virginia asked. "That I would rather be damned and alive than saved and dead?"

The Madonna offered no answer. Perhaps there wasn't one.

Virginia pressed her forehead against the statue's base, her next words barely audible even to herself: "I'm going to let him in. And I'm going to pretend it wasn't my choice. I'm going to tell myself he forced my hand, that I had no choice, that his threats left me powerless. But we both know the truth."

She lifted her head and looked directly into those painted eyes.

"I *want* this. God forgive me, I want this more than I've ever wanted salvation."

She remained kneeling for a long time after that, but she did not pray. What was the point of praying when you'd already decided to embrace your own damnation?

When she finally rose, she had spoken truth to carved wood that living ears could never safely hear.

She wondered how many women before her had knelt here and confessed the same thing: *I don't want to stop.*

* * *

THE FIRST FROST arrived three days later and killed the last stubborn herbs in the garden beds. It also brought the next letter.

Susanna delivered it during evening prayers, her elderly hands shaking as she pressed the parchment into Virginia's palm. The old woman's fear was palpable. She knew she was facilitating something dangerous, but Virginia's family name and Gian Paolo's money had made her complicit long ago.

Virginia waited until she was alone before breaking the seal.

> *I have had enough of stolen glimpses and careful letters. I have had enough of improvisation and discomfort. When you are ready, and you will be ready, you will allow me to come to you properly. This is not a request. I am done waiting. Your Gian Paolo*

Virginia read it three times, her fingers tracing the violent slash of his signature.

Something about that possessive tone made her stomach drop and heat simultaneously. As if he'd branded her with ink.

She should be outraged. Should be frightened. Should recognize this as the ultimatum it was—comply or face uncontrolled scandal.

Instead, she felt something that horrified her: relief.

He had made the decision for her. Had taken the choice out of her hands. She could surrender now and tell herself she'd had no option.

It was a lie, but it was a comfortable one.

* * *

THAT EVENING, VIRGINIA sat at her writing table copying accounts by candlelight. Beside her, Benedetta reviewed inventories with the careful attention of someone looking for discrepancies. Ottavia sat near the window mending.

The domesticity of the scene felt like mockery. Three women performing ordinary tasks while conspiracy crackled in the air between them.

"He sends letters daily now," Benedetta said without looking up from her ledger. "Pesseno delivers them directly to Susanna, who passes them to you. The system has become... efficient."

Virginia's quill paused over the parchment. "Yes."

"And your replies?"

"I leave them in my pillowcase when I make my bed. Silvia collects them during cell inspections."

Benedetta finally looked up, her dark eyes sharp. "You're organizing an ongoing deception. An illicit intrigue."

"Perhaps this is the only kind of intrigue I'm allowed to build."

"It's the kind that ends with you pregnant or dead."

"Yes," Virginia said, and the calm acceptance in her own voice startled her. "I know."

Benedetta stared at her for a long moment. "You've given up, haven't you? You're not trying to stop this anymore."

"I was never trying to stop it," Virginia said quietly. "I was only trying to control *how* it happened."

The truth hung between them like smoke.

Ottavia's mending dropped into her lap. "Virginia, no."

"God help us all," Benedetta whispered.

* * *

THE LETTERS DID not stop after that. The gifts did not stop. But the methods evolved with frightening sophistication.

Susanna carried messages within the walls, her decades of service granting her invisible access. Pesseno handled deliveries through the gate, his brutal efficiency ensuring silence. Apollonia, with her laundry baskets and downcast eyes, connected both worlds, too valuable to be easily dismissed.

A basket of preserves would arrive from a grateful widow. Inside, beneath the jars, a note wrapped in waxed cloth. A devotional book would appear among donated volumes, a ribbon marker placed too precisely, hiding folded parchment between specific pages. Linens contributed for altar use arrived with embroidered patterns Virginia recognized. Roses and thorns worked in thread that matched the color of his doublet, each flower marking a date, each thorn an hour.

Virginia kept everything that could be kept. The notes went into the false bottom of the writing table. A space she'd discovered one sleepless night and deepened with a small knife, working at the wood with the patience of someone building her own coffin. The compartment now held a sheaf of letters thick enough to hang her.

The respectable objects she arranged in plain sight because plain sight was the safest hiding place. A prayer book was just a prayer book unless someone knew to look for the marks on page forty-seven.

She sent replies back through the same channels. Folded notes hidden in her pillowcase for Silvia to collect. Small gifts for his mother that carried private messages only he would understand—a handkerchief embroidered with specific flowers, each bloom a word in a language only the two of them spoke. Everything appearing innocent while serving forbidden purpose.

Gossip followed, spreading through the convent like fever.

One evening at supper, Sister Francesca made a veiled remark about "certain sisters who seem to attract unseemly attention from the world beyond our walls."

The refectory fell silent. Fifty faces turned, waiting.

Virginia set down her spoon with deliberate care and met Sister Francesca's gaze with the expression she'd learned from her father. A look that reminded lesser nobility exactly where they stood in relation to a de Leyva.

"The world beyond these walls takes interest in many things," Virginia said, her voice carrying in the sudden quiet. "Including the generous dowries that keep roofs intact and mouths fed. I trust we all remember who provides such generosity."

Sister Francesca's face went white. "Of course, Sister Virginia. Forgive me."

"I'm certain you meant nothing."

The whispers did not stop after that. They simply became quieter, more careful, discussed in corners where Virginia would not overhear.

And quiet, Virginia learned, was far more dangerous than open accusation. Quiet meant watching. Quiet meant waiting for proof that would overwhelm even her family's protection. Quiet meant gathering evidence for the day when her name would no longer be enough to shield her.

* * *

THAT SAME NIGHT, Virginia found a scrap of linen tucked beneath her mattress, blank, folded twice, placed with obvious care where she would discover it when she retired.

No one left cloth like that by accident.

She held it to the candlelight, searching for hidden ink, for codes, for some message that would appear under flame. There was nothing.

She understood immediately. A test.

If she hid it, someone could claim to find it as proof of secret communications. If she left it visible, they would observe whether she'd moved other hidden items. If she destroyed it, the act itself suggested guilt.

A test designed so that any response would provide information to whoever had planted it.

Virginia held the linen over her candle flame and watched it catch. The fabric curled and blackened, releasing a brief scent of burning that she wafted toward the window. When only ash remained, she ground it beneath her heel and swept it into the cracks between floorboards.

Then she lay awake in darkness, listening to the convent settle into night silence, wondering which sister had planted the test. Wondering how many others were watching her even now, documenting her every movement, building their case against her one observation at a time.

Sleep, when it finally came, brought dreams of being hunted. Endless corridors where she ran while shadows followed, never quite catching her but never falling behind, patient as stone, inevitable as dawn.

* * *

ON THE NEXT confession day, Virginia knelt behind the carved screen in the small chapel and spoke to the convent confessor, an elderly Franciscan who visited weekly and knew her only as one voice among many anonymous penitents.

She confessed in careful fog: impure thoughts, temptations of the flesh, rebellion against her vows. Abstractions that revealed nothing specific, nothing he could hold or report or use against her.

She did not speak Gian Paolo's name. Did not mention the parlatory or the letters or the way her own body betrayed her at the mere thought of him.

The confessor's questions stretched through long pauses weighted with uncertainty. His counsel arrived worn and tired by repetition: more prayer, more fasting, more discipline. The flesh must be subdued through denial and penance.

"I have already tried, Father." The words came out too raw, stripped of the careful neutrality she'd maintained. "It does not change what I feel."

Silence fell. When the confessor finally spoke, his voice carried the gravity of a man naming an ancient enemy.

"Daughter, what you describe is spiritual warfare. The Enemy takes particular interest in consecrated souls, seeking to corrupt what has been devoted to God. These feelings are not your own. They are temptations sent to test your resolve."

Virginia bowed her head and let the explanation settle over her like a cloak.

Satan was convenient. He transformed her from architect of her own destruction into victim of demonic assault. He allowed her to be blameless while feeling everything she should not feel.

She left the confessional lighter. Not because she believed the explanation, but because she had successfully performed the role expected of her. The mask had held. No one suspected how completely she had already surrendered.

* * *

THE FIRST SNOW arrived in late November, transforming the convent's gray severity into something deceptively clean and pure. White blanketed the courtyard, softening harsh angles, making the world look innocent when nothing beneath that surface had changed.

The ultimatum arrived the next morning, delivered by Susanna with trembling hands that betrayed how thoroughly she understood what she carried.

> *I am done with patience. Your Prioress travels to Milan on December third. I have sources, and I know her schedule. You will ensure the garden door can be opened from within. You will meet me at midnight. You will give me what I have waited for. This is your last opportunity to control how this happens. Refuse, and I will find my own way in. The scandal will be far worse without your cooperation. December third. Midnight. Be ready. Your Gian Paolo*

Virginia read it three times, each repetition making her hands colder.

He had weaponized everything. Her fear of uncontrolled scandal, her need to manage risk, her terror of discovery. He knew the threat of chaos would drive her to arrange controlled access. He understood that she would choose complicity over catastrophe.

He was forcing her hand by offering the illusion of choice.

She sat at her writing table and pulled fresh parchment. Dipped her quill in ink. Her hand did not shake as she wrote:

> *I am ready. Mother Imbersaga travels to Milan on December third. I will see that the garden door can be unlatched from within. Come at midnight. The convent will be silent after Compline. Come quietly. Do not make me do this twice. V.*

She sealed it with plain wax—no signet, nothing that could identify her if it were intercepted. Tomorrow, she would give it to Susanna. Susanna would pass it to Apollonia. Apollonia would give it to Pesseno. Pesseno would deliver it to Gian Paolo.

The chain would hold. It always did.

* * *

THAT EVENING, VIRGINIA returned to the Madonna statue in the corner of her shared cell. The painted face gazed at her with an expression that could have been compassion or condemnation or simple indifference.

"I lied to you before," Virginia whispered. "I said I wanted to feel alive. But that's not quite true."

She moved closer to the statue, her voice dropping even lower.

"The truth is... I want to know what it feels like to choose. Just once. Even if I choose wrong. Even if it destroys me. After so many years of having every choice made for me, I want to know what it feels like to say *yes* to something, instead of endlessly saying *no*."

She reached out and touched the Madonna's wooden hand—cold, unyielding, offering no comfort.

"Is that evil? To want the freedom to choose my own damnation?"

The statue remained silent, as it always would.

Virginia returned to her bed and lay down fully clothed, staring at the ceiling beams barely visible in the darkness.

December third was five days away. Five days until she would unlock the door and step across a threshold she could never cross back over.

She closed her eyes and realized, with a clarity that felt like ice water, that she wasn't afraid anymore.

She had spent months terrified of discovery, of consequences, of sin, of desire itself.

But fear had finally exhausted itself. What remained was simpler, cleaner, more honest than anything she'd felt in years.

Want.

Pure and uncomplicated and utterly damning.

She wanted him. She wanted to feel his hands on her skin. She wanted to know what it was like to be touched with desire instead of duty. She wanted one night when she wasn't Sister Virginia Maria de Leyva, bride of Christ, daughter of obligation and disappointed fathers.

She wanted to be, for just a few hours, simply Virginia.

A woman who could say yes.

And if that wanting destroyed her?

She had been dead for nine years already. At least this death would be one she chose.

Outside her window, snow continued to fall, silent, inevitable, covering everything in white that would melt away by morning, leaving no trace it had ever existed at all.

Somewhere in the convent, beyond her locked door, Sister Bianca moved through corridors with keys at her waist and rules in her bones. The kind of woman who did not miss wrongness forever, who waited with the patience of stone for evidence to accumulate beyond deniability.

But Virginia no longer cared.

She had written the letter. Set the date. Chosen her path.

December third was coming.

And she would be ready.

* * *

December

VIRGINIA'S HANDS HAD been steady all day. Through Vespers and supper, through the final prayers before Compline. Steady as she moved through familiar rituals, her body performing piety while her mind counted the hours until transgression.

Now, standing at her chamber window watching moonlight silver the snow-covered courtyard, her hands began to shake. The night of December third had arrived.

Mother Imbersaga had departed for Milan that afternoon, her traveling cloak dusted with early snow, her voice sharp with last instructions to Sister Bianca about maintaining order in her absence. Virginia had watched from a window, ensuring the Prioress's departure.

Three days. Mother Imbersaga would be gone for three days. Tonight was the first.

The convent had settled into its nightly silence an hour past Compline, but the quiet felt wrong, stretched too thin, as though the building itself sensed something unnatural pressing against its order. Virginia's ears caught sounds she normally wouldn't notice: the creak of old wood settling in cold, the distant scrape of a shutter, someone coughing two floors below.

Behind her, Ottavia sat on the edge of her cot, fully dressed, hands twisting in her lap with the mindless repetition of prayer beads without the beads. Her face had gone pale, lips moving in silent prayer or perhaps simply counting breaths until this ended.

Benedetta stood near the door, a shadow among shadows, her silhouette rigid with the stillness of a woman who had already decided this was happening and moved past protest into calculating survival. She held a small candle, unlit. When the time came, she would light it and lead the way.

"It's a quarter before midnight," Benedetta said. Her voice carried no inflection. A statement of fact, nothing more.

Virginia turned from the window. Her legs felt disconnected from her body as she crossed the cold stone floor. Each step required a conscious decision—lift, move, place. Again. Again.

"You don't have to do this," Benedetta said as Virginia reached the door that led into the rear corridor. No judgment in her voice, only weary clarity. "Even now, you could send word you've changed your mind. Silvia could intercept him in the garden."

Virginia's hand found the iron latch. The metal bit into her palm, real and solid and cold as condemnation.

"I haven't changed my mind."

Benedetta's mouth tightened. For a moment she looked as though she might say more, some final warning, some last attempt at wisdom. Instead, she simply nodded.

"Then God help us all." She lit the candle. Shadows leapt across the walls, making the narrow space seem vast and strange. They slipped into the corridor.

The stone was ice beneath Virginia's feet even through her leather shoes. She felt every irregularity of the floor. The walls pressed close on either side, and the flame from Benedetta's candle threw its shadows huge and distorted against ancient plaster.

Neither spoke. Even their breathing seemed loud in the silence.

They moved carefully in the uncertain light. Down the corridor toward the rear of the convent, past the kitchens, past the workrooms to where the practical spaces existed. The rooms where deliveries arrived, where work was done, where the convent touched the world beyond in necessary, mundane ways.

At the rear of the building stood a heavy service door that opened onto the convent garden. A single barrier between cloister and world. In moments, she would open it.

Benedetta stopped a few paces from the door and turned. In the candlelight, her face looked carved from stone, ancient and weathered.

"Four hours," she whispered. "He must be gone before Lauds. No more."

Virginia closed her fingers into fists. Her nails bit into her palms, and she welcomed the small hurt. Physical pain was honest, demanded nothing but endurance.

"Sister Virginia." Benedetta's hand closed on her wrist, surprisingly strong. "Listen to me. Once you open this door, everything changes. Not just for you. For all of us. Do you understand?"

Virginia met her eyes. "I understand."

"I don't think you do," Benedetta said quietly. "But you will."

She released Virginia's wrist and stepped back. "I'll watch from the stairwell. If anyone comes, I'll knock three times on the wall. You'll have perhaps thirty seconds to hide him."

"And I will watch the far end of the corridor," Ottavia whispered from behind them, her voice trembling. "If Sister Bianca wakes, if anyone—"

She couldn't finish. The enormity of what they were risking choked off speech.

Behind her, she heard Benedetta and Ottavia retreat back to their watching posts, back to the dangerous vigil that would keep them all safe or see them all destroyed.

She was alone now.

Virginia approached the service door, heavy wood reinforced with iron straps, built to keep the world out and the consecrated in. She stopped before it.

This was the final threshold. The last moment she could turn back.

Her hands found the bolt that secured the door and turned it. The bolt scraped against its iron brackets as she drew it free. Then she found the latch and pulled.

The door swung inward. Cold air rushed in, carrying the scent of snow and winter darkness and the dangerous world beyond convent walls.

Beyond that, she saw the garden, snow-covered and silent, touched with moonlight. And at the edge of the shadows, a figure waited.

Gian Paolo Osio crossed the snow quickly, his dark clothing making him nearly invisible against the night. His breath came in pale clouds. When he reached the doorway, he stopped and looked at her.

"You came," he said, voice low.

"I said I would."

For one heartbeat, they simply looked at each other across the threshold—she inside, he outside, the doorway between them like a border between two countries, two lives, two versions of who she might become.

Then she stepped back.

He entered.

She pushed the door closed behind him and dropped the latch into place. The sound of it, solid, final, irrevocable, seemed to echo through her bones.

She had done it. Had opened the convent not by force or accident but by will, by hand, by deliberate choice.

Gian Paolo caught her before she could speak. His mouth found hers; his hands gripped her through layers of fabric that suddenly felt too thin. The kiss was not tender. It was claiming. Possession disguised as passion, ownership masquerading as desire.

Virginia's body answered even as her mind recoiled at the violence of it, the way he took without asking, assumed rather than requested.

"Where?" he asked against her mouth, breath hot on her skin. "Where can we go?"

"Not here." Her voice came out unsteady. "Too dangerous. If someone wakes..." His hands moved with purpose, finding the ties of her habit.

"No." She pulled back. "If anyone comes down from the sleeping quarters, they'll see us. There is a storage room nearby."

Impatience flashed across his face, there and gone so quickly she might have imagined it. Then he smiled, and the expression carried such warmth it made her previous fear seem foolish.

"Show me," he said.

She led him down the passage. In darkness, her feet found the way by memory and feel. Seven steps to the third door on the right.

Virginia opened it.

Inside, a single candle burned on an overturned crate. Ottavia had prepared the space. The candle. A blanket spread on the floor over old rushes. Nothing else. Just privacy carved from a room meant for storing altar linens and ceremonial vessels.

The air smelled of soap and old wool, of lavender and something musty that might have been mice or simply age. The stone walls wept with condensation despite the cold, and Virginia could see her breath misting in the candlelight.

It was not a bedchamber. It was not even comfortable.

It was simply private. And privacy, in a convent, was the most forbidden luxury of all.

Gian Paolo shut the door behind them and turned.

For a moment they simply looked at each other across the small space. Virginia saw him truly for the first time in months, not glimpsed through windows or across iron gratings, but close enough to touch. Close enough to see the hollow beneath his cheekbone where candlelight carved shadow, the pulse beating in his throat, the way his chest rose and fell with breath that matched the rhythm of her own.

"Now," he said, and the single word contained everything—command and plea and promise. "Finally."

He crossed over to her in two strides.

This time would be different, Virginia told herself. This time she had chosen it. Had arranged it. Had unlocked the doors with her own hands and invited him in with full knowledge of what would follow.

This time it would be what she'd imagined during long nights of yearning, tenderness and passion, desire tempered by care, the transcendence poets wrote about. This time she would feel what she was supposed to feel.

He pushed her habit from her shoulders with hands that shook, whether from cold or need, she could not tell. The fabric fell away and Virginia felt suddenly exposed, but not with the shock of that first time in the corridor outside the parlatory. She knew what came next. Had known since July.

"Virginia." Her name in his mouth carried the same possession it had before. He kissed her throat, her shoulder, the hollow at the base of her neck where her pulse beat.

She waited for desire to kindle. For her body to answer the way it was supposed to, the way she'd convinced herself it would if only she controlled the circumstances, if only she chose the time and place.

Instead, she felt her muscles tense with memory. Her body remembered what her mind had tried to forget—the corridor floor, the pain, the way he'd covered her mouth to silence her.

It will be different this time, she told herself desperately. I chose this. That changes everything.

His hands found the ties of her chemise. She did not stop him. Had come too far to stop now, had risked too much to turn back at the threshold.

The linen fell away.

Cold air struck her skin. She was naked before him for the second time, and somehow it felt more vulnerable than the first, as if that initial violation had left her with no protection, no barrier between her flesh and his gaze.

"Beautiful," Gian Paolo whispered, and the word sounded the same as it had in July. "My God, Virginia."

He pulled her down to the blanket. The floor was hard beneath the thin wool as they settled. Virginia felt every stone, every irregularity.

And then his weight was on her, and her body tensed involuntarily, bracing for pain it remembered even if her mind had tried to reframe it as something chosen, something wanted.

"Do not tense," he murmured against her throat. "You're so stiff. It's all right. You want this, don't you?"

She did want it. Or thought she did. Had convinced herself she did through months of yearning and careful planning.

So why did her body refuse to cooperate?

He entered her. Not with the violence of that first time, but not gently either. Her body resisted, still remembering trauma, and there was a moment of sharp discomfort before flesh yielded to pressure.

Not the tearing pain of virginity lost. That threshold had already been crossed, but hurt, nonetheless. The ache of a body used before it was ready being used again.

Virginia bit her lip to stay silent and waited for the pleasure to begin. For the transcendence. For the feeling that would justify all of this.

It didn't come.

Gian Paolo moved above her with increasing urgency, his breath hot against her neck, his hands gripping her hips hard enough to bruise. She stared past his shoulder at the ceiling and counted cracks in the plaster visible by candlelight.

Seven major fissures. Dozens of smaller ones radiating out like blood vessels.

Why don't I feel it? she thought with growing desperation. I chose this. I arranged it. Why is it exactly the same as before?

She had believed, needed to believe, that choosing would transform the act. That it would convert violation into union, force into passion.

But her body understood what her mind refused to accept: choosing the circumstances didn't change the fundamental transaction. She was still a vessel for someone else's need. Still enduring rather than experiencing.

The realization was more devastating than any physical pain.

She had traded everything, her vows, her safety, her soul, for this. For something that felt no different than it had when it was taken from her by force.

The only difference was that now she had no one to blame but herself.

"Virginia." His voice had gone ragged. "Tell me you want this."

"I want it," she whispered, because he needed to hear it and because maybe if she said it enough times it would become true.

The lie tasted familiar. She had been lying for so long, to others, to herself, that one more untruth cost nothing.

Gian Paolo shuddered against her with a sound caught between prayer and curse. His full weight settled on her, pressing her onto the hard floor, making it difficult to breathe.

For a moment they lay tangled together, his heart thumping against her ribs, his breath coming in ragged gasps against her throat. Then he lifted his head to look at her. In the candlelight his face held an expression of such satisfaction, such tender possession, that Virginia had to look away.

"That was better, wasn't it?" he said softly. "Better than before. You felt it too, didn't you? The difference when you choose it, when you want it?"

She could have told him the truth. Could have said that it felt exactly the same, that her body couldn't distinguish between violation invited and violation forced.

But he was looking at her with such hope, such certainty that this time had been transcendent.

"Yes," she whispered. "It was better."

Another lie. Easier than the truth. Kinder, perhaps, though to whom she couldn't say.

He kissed her forehead with unexpected tenderness, as though that could make up for everything else. As though gentleness after the fact could retroactively transform the act into something it wasn't.

"I knew it would be," he said, satisfaction rich in his voice. "I knew once you stopped fighting what you wanted, once you let yourself feel."

He kept talking, but Virginia stopped listening. She stared at the ceiling and felt something inside her go numb and cold.

She had believed choosing would save her. Had told herself that choice was the difference between victim and lover, between violation and union.

But lying here on the cold floor with aches in places that would hurt for days, she understood. She had not chosen transcendence. She had only chosen to participate in her own diminishment. And somehow that was worse than having it forced upon her.

Time fractured after that.

She had no idea how long they lay there—minutes or hours, seconds or eternities. The candle burned lower. Wax pooled on the crate in pale stalactites. Virginia's body began to register individual discomforts: the hard floor beneath her hip, the cold raising gooseflesh on exposed skin, the sticky warmth between her thighs that might have been blood or seed or both.

She needed to move. Needed to stand and dress and restore some measure of the self she'd lost. But her limbs felt disconnected, as though the strings that should animate them had been cut.

Two sharp knocks sounded through the wall. Ottavia's signal. Time to end this before dawn found them.

The sound penetrated Gian Paolo's contentment. He stirred, kissed her once more, gently this time, almost sweet, then rose to dress.

Virginia watched him from the floor. He moved with the easy confidence of someone who had just taken what he wanted and found it satisfying. Pulling on his hose, tying his doublet, running fingers through disordered hair. Making himself presentable again, erasing evidence of sin as simply as buttoning a collar.

She envied that ease. That ability to separate body from consequence, pleasure from price.

She forced herself upright. Her thighs ached. Between her legs, rawness announced itself with every movement. She reached for her chemise with hands that had started shaking again and pulled it over her head.

The linen felt wrong against her skin now. Contaminated. Or perhaps she was the contamination, and the fabric simply absorbed it.

Her habit followed. Layer after layer, each one restoring the fiction that she was still Sister Virginia Maria de Leyva, bride of Christ, bound by sacred vows.

The fiction had never been thinner.

At the door, Gian Paolo paused and looked back. His face held satisfaction and something else. A warmth that made Virginia's stomach turn.

"I'll return," he whispered. "Tomorrow night, if you'll permit it."

Every rational impulse screamed refusal. Every scrap of self-preservation she still possessed demanded she tell him no, send him away, bar the door and never unlock it again.

"Yes," she heard herself say. "Tomorrow."

The word emerged from some part of her she didn't recognize. Some self that had survived the last hour and decided that since the worst had already happened, there was no point in stopping now.

His smile was radiant. He kissed her once more, briefly, chastely, as though they were proper lovers parting after a proper courtship. Then he slipped out the door and was gone.

Virginia stood alone in the storage room. The candle had burned down to a stub, wax pooled in congealed puddles on the crate. The blanket lay rumpled on the floor, stained now with proof of what had happened here.

She should feel something. Regret or satisfaction, shame or triumph. Poets insisted coupling was transcendent, that it elevated or destroyed, sanctified or damned.

She felt only hollow.

Outside, she Ottavia and Benedetta waiting. In the pre-dawn darkness, Benedetta's face was a pale blur, all sharp angles and exhausted resignation.

"It's done?" Benedetta asked quietly.

Virginia nodded.

"Then God help us all."

They made their way back to their cell and slipped inside. Ottavia sat on her cot, knees drawn up to her chest, arms wrapped around herself as though holding her own body together through sheer force of will. She'd been crying. Her face was blotched and swollen, eyes red-rimmed and glazed.

She looked at Virginia. Just looked, without speaking.

Virginia couldn't hold that gaze. She turned away and went to the basin, poured cold water that shocked her hands, began to wash. The rawness between her thighs announced itself with every movement, a physical reminder that would last for days.

Finally, she climbed into her narrow bed, still dressed, and lay staring at the ceiling. Lauds would ring soon. She would rise, join her sisters in the chapel, kneel among them as though nothing had changed.

But everything had changed.

The woman who had walked to that storage room no longer existed. In her place was someone new, someone who had chosen damnation with open eyes and found it disappointingly ordinary.

"Virginia." Benedetta's voice came soft from the darkness. "Are you well?"

No, Virginia thought. I will never be well again.

"Yes," she said. "I'm fine."

The lie tasted familiar on her tongue. She had been lying for so long now, to Mother Imbersaga, to the confessor, to herself, that one more untruth cost nothing.

She closed her eyes and waited for sleep that would not come.

Outside, the first birds began their pre-dawn chorus, greeting a day Virginia had no idea how to face.

He returned the following night. And the night after that.

Three weeks later, Gian Paolo arrived with a leather satchel slung across his shoulder. He set it on Virginia's writing table in the storage room with the careful handling of something precious.

"A gift," he said, unbuckling the straps. "Or perhaps a solution. I've been consulting Father Arrigone about our situation."

Virginia's stomach clenched. "You told him? About this?"

"Arrigone has been my confessor for years. He understands that Church law isn't always as absolute as it seems." He drew out a thick, leather-bound volume. Latin words tooled into the cover in gold leaf: *Summa Theologica*.

"Aquinas," Gian Paolo said, opening to a page marked with ribbon. "His work on cases of conscience. Father Arrigone thought it might ease yours."

Virginia stared at the dense Latin text. Even by candlelight she could see it was complex—the kind of theological argument that required extensive training to parse correctly.

"Here." Gian Paolo's finger traced a passage. "The excommunication you fear. It's meant for nuns who leave the convent, not for men who enter it. You might face discipline if discovered, yes. Penance, certainly. But not excommunication. Your soul remains intact."

He looked up at her with such earnest concern that Virginia almost believed he cared about her soul more than her body.

"I can't read this," she said quietly. "Not well enough to be certain. The Latin is too archaic."

"Then take it on faith." He closed the book and pressed it into her hands. "Trust that I, that Father Arrigone, would not mislead you about something so grave."

Virginia held the volume, felt its weight. She wanted desperately to believe him. Wanted the comfort of thinking that what they were doing, while sinful, wasn't the mortal kind. That some part of her remained salvageable.

"Leave it with me," she said finally. "I'll try to read what I can."

After he left that night, Virginia sat at her writing table with the *Summa Theologica* open before her and a candle burning low. She struggled through the Latin, her convent education proving inadequate for Aquinas's complexity. Words swam before her eyes, meanings slipping away just as she thought she'd grasped them.

She wanted it to be true. Wanted to believe that some loophole existed, some technicality that would let her keep doing what she was doing without losing her immortal soul in the process.

But in the cold hour before dawn, when she finally gave up and closed the book, Virginia understood with terrible clarity:

It didn't matter what Aquinas said or didn't say. It didn't matter whether the technicality existed or if Gian Paolo and Father Arrigone had simply invented it to salve her conscience.

She was going to continue regardless.

The book, the arguments, the careful parsing of Canon law—these were just prettier lies to tell herself. Ways to pretend she still cared about salvation when the truth was simpler and more damning:

She had chosen this. Was choosing it. Would continue choosing it. Not because she believed it was permissible. But because she no longer cared whether it was or not.

That realization should have terrified her. Instead, it brought a strange, cold peace.

She set the *Summa Theologica* aside and went to bed, and for the first time in weeks, she slept without dreaming.

* * *

ONE NIGHT IN mid-December, two weeks after Mother Imbersaga's return from Milan, Gian Paolo caught Virginia's wrist as she prepared to leave the storage room.

"I'm tired of this," he said. The warmth had left his voice. "Sneaking about in storage rooms like common servants. Meeting in places that smell of mice and mildew."

Virginia's pulse quickened. "We're fortunate to manage even this. The Prioress returned from Milan watching everything more closely. Sister Bianca reports to her daily."

"Which is precisely why we need to be bolder." His grip tightened. "I want to come to your chamber. On Christmas Eve, when the convent is distracted by Mass and noble visitors. When even your Prioress will be occupied with hospitality."

"No." The refusal came automatically. "That's the one place...my cellmates sleep there. Benedetta and Ottavia would have to find somewhere else to sleep."

"They'll endure it." His tone brooked no argument. "Just as you've asked them to endure everything else. Christmas Eve is perfect. The Prioress will be managing visitors until late. She won't be prowling corridors. Or are you saying you want this to end?"

* * *

THE NIGHT BEFORE Christmas Eve, Virginia sat on her cot and faced Benedetta and Ottavia across the small chamber.

"Tomorrow night," she said quietly. "He's coming here. To our cell."

Ottavia's face drained of color. "No." The word came out strangled. "No. Virginia, you cannot ask this of us."

"I tried to refuse him, but he insisted."

"You didn't try hard enough!" Ottavia was on her feet, shaking. "The storage room was already an abomination. But this? This is our home. The place where we sleep. Where we pray. You would bring him *here*?"

"He wouldn't accept my refusal."

"Then let him not accept!" Ottavia's voice rose dangerously. "Tell him it's over. Tell him he can't have this. Has the Devil so addled your reason that you cannot see the madness in this?"

Benedetta remained seated, but her hands were clenched white-knuckled in her lap. When she spoke, her voice was ice. "You're not asking our permission. You're informing us. There's a difference."

Virginia couldn't meet her eyes. "I'm sorry."

"Sorry." Benedetta's laugh was bitter. "Do you understand what you're making us? Not just accomplices now. Witnesses. You're forcing us to watch while you desecrate the one space we have left that is ours."

"I'll report you." Ottavia's voice broke. "I'll go to Mother Imbersaga right now. I'll tell her everything. I don't care what happens to me. I won't do this."

"Then we all burn," Benedetta said flatly. "Virginia. Me. You. Silvia. Candida. Everyone who's kept her secrets. Is that what you want, Ottavia? To destroy us all to save your conscience?"

Ottavia sank back onto her cot, sobbing. "This is wrong. This is so wrong."

"Of course it's wrong." Benedetta turned to Virginia, and there was something like hatred in her eyes. "But you stopped caring about wrong months ago, didn't you? You only care about what you want. And you want him more than you want our safety, our souls, or our sanity."

"That's not true."

"Isn't it?" Benedetta stood. "Then tell him no. Send word through Apollonia that it's over. Refuse him this one thing and prove me wrong."

Virginia opened her mouth. Closed it. The silence stretched.

Benedetta's expression hardened into something cold and resigned. "We'll do it. Not because we want to. Not because we agree. But because if we refuse, you'll simply arrange it anyway and we'll lose what little control we have left over our own fate."

"And because you're a de Leyva," Ottavia said bitterly, wiping her eyes. "Your father's money pays for this roof. Your family name protects you in ways we'll never have. If we report you and you're caught, you might face penance. We'd face the streets, or the loss of our families. Or worse."

The truth of it hung in the air like poison.

Virginia had never spoken the words aloud, had tried not to think them. But they both knew. The daughter of a count, even a disgraced one living as a nun, still carried weight that common-born sisters could never match.

"So, we'll endure it," Benedetta said, her voice flat. "We'll turn our backs and pray and pretend we don't hear. We'll keep your secrets as we've kept them all along. Because we have no choice."

"You always had a choice," Ottavia whispered. "We never did."

Benedetta moved to her cot and turned her back. "Tomorrow night, then. May God forgive us all."

Virginia stood to leave, but Ottavia's voice stopped her at the door.

"I used to think you were a victim, Virginia. Forced into this life, trapped by your father's cruelty. But you're not a victim anymore. You're just like him now, using your power to force others to bear the cost of your choices."

The words hit harder than any blow.

Virginia fled to the corridor and stood shaking in the darkness. Behind the door, she heard Ottavia's broken weeping.

She had lost them. Whatever friendship they'd shared, whatever loyalty had bound them together, she had destroyed it.

But she was going to let him come anyway.

Because even knowing what it cost, even understanding that she had become exactly what her father was, someone who used rank and power to make others suffer for her desires, she couldn't stop.

* * *

ON CHRISTMAS EVE, the chapel blazed with candles and noble families crowded into the visitors' section, their fine clothes and jewels making the small space feel even more cramped. Virginia did not search for familiar faces in the congregation. She kept her eyes on the altar, her hands folded, her expression serene.

But her mind counted the hours. Counted the moments until the noble families departed, until the convent settled into its Christmas night quiet, until he would come.

Waiting.

Always waiting.

After Mass ended, when the congregation rose to depart, Virginia remained kneeling. Several nuns stayed as well. It wasn't unusual for sisters to continue private prayers after Mass. Ottavia knelt beside her, lips moving in silent supplication. Benedetta stood near the door, eyes tracking movement with the vigilance of someone expecting catastrophe at any moment.

The noble families filed out. One by one, the sisters left until only a handful remained in the dimly lit chapel.

Virginia waited until the last possible moment, then rose. After going to the garden door and unbolting it, she made her way toward the dormitory stairs. Behind her, she heard Ottavia and Benedetta following, their footsteps measured and careful. They reached their cell and slipped inside. Benedetta closed the door with a soft click and leaned against it, eyes closed.

Ottavia sank onto her cot. Her rosary beads emerged from her pocket and the counting began, click-click-pause-click, marking time until the violation they were all complicit in arrived.

"How long?" Ottavia asked after a moment.

"Soon," Virginia answered. "He'll wait until the convent sleeps. Perhaps an hour."

They sat in silence and darkness, three women waiting for the catastrophe they'd all agreed to facilitate.

Across the corridor, Silvia's door stood slightly ajar, a sliver of darkness beyond where their friend kept watch. One more woman drawn into the conspiracy, one more soul endangered by Virginia's choices.

The hour stretched interminably. Virginia tried to pray but couldn't remember the words. Tried to justify what was coming but couldn't construct the lie. She simply sat on her narrow bed and waited for the inevitable.

Footsteps sounded in the corridor. Soft and measured, but wrong. The stride too long, the weight too heavy. A man trying to pass for something he could never be.

Ottavia made a sound like a wounded animal, quickly stifled. Her rosary beads clattered to the floor.

Three soft knocks.

Virginia's hand reached for the latch without conscious decision. The metal was cold beneath her palm. For one terrible moment she thought her body would refuse.

Then the latch lifted with a whisper.

Gian Paolo stood in the corridor draped in black fabric that might pass for a nun's habit in darkness, though everything about him screamed wrongness—

shoulders too broad, height too tall, the cloth hanging on a body built for violence instead of prayer. A black veil covered his hair.

He slipped inside. Benedetta followed him, pulling the door closed and locking it. She moved immediately to her cot and sat with her back to the room, spine rigid, presence declared even as she granted what privacy she could.

For a moment, no one moved. Four people in a space meant for three, the air suddenly too thick to breathe.

The scent of him, leather and wine and woodsmoke and something unmistakably male, filled the chamber, transforming it from a place of prayer into something else entirely.

From her cot, Ottavia began to weep.

Not quietly. Not the suppressed sobs she'd managed before. This was broken, desperate grief that she couldn't control no matter how hard she pressed both hands over her mouth. Her body shook with the force of it, tears streaming down her face in the moonlight.

Benedetta's hands clenched white-knuckled against her thighs. Her breathing had gone rapid and shallow, the onset of panic barely controlled. Her lips began to move in silent prayer, but no sound emerged. Just that desperate repetition of words she could no longer voice.

"Sister Ottavia. Sister Benedetta." Gian Paolo's voice cut through the darkness, low and almost respectful. As though acknowledging witnesses at a wedding rather than accomplices to sacrilege.

Ottavia's weeping intensified. She turned her face into her pillow, trying to muffle the sounds, her whole body convulsing with sobs.

Benedetta's prayer became audible, ragged and broken: "*Ave Maria, gratia plena, Dominus tecum...*" Over and over. Not for absolution. Not for Virginia. For herself. For the strength to endure what she was about to witness.

Gian Paolo moved toward Virginia slowly, each step measured, giving her time to refuse even as they both knew she wouldn't. Moonlight caught the planes of his face, and Virginia saw hunger there, barely restrained, predatory, patient only because patience had proven successful.

She did not move. Frozen between terror and want, between what she knew she should not do and what she was about to choose anyway.

A sound from the corridor froze them all.

Footsteps. Soft but distinct. Someone moving past their door.

Virginia's heart stopped. Ottavia's weeping cut off mid-sob. Benedetta's prayer died on her lips.

They waited. Four people barely breathing, while the footsteps grew louder.

Closer.

A shadow appeared in the crack beneath the door. Virginia could see it moving, hear the soft rustle of fabric. Someone was right outside. Right there.

Ottavia made a strangled sound, pressing both hands over her mouth so hard her knuckles went white. Benedetta had gone completely still, terror radiating from her in waves.

The shadow paused.

Virginia thought she might die. Gian Paolo was three steps from the door, too far to hide, too close to explain. If that door opened, if Sister Bianca or Mother Imbersaga or anyone pushed it open and saw...

The footsteps continued. Faded. Gone.

The silence that followed felt heavy enough to crush them.

"Sister Silvia," Benedetta whispered, her voice hoarse. "Going to the privy. Or checking windows. She knows and is keeping watch."

Ottavia grabbed the basin and began to retch. Nothing came up. She hadn't eaten since morning, but her body convulsed with dry heaves she tried desperately to silence, tears streaming down her face.

Benedetta's prayer resumed, more desperate now: "*Sancta Maria, Mater Dei, ora pro nobis peccatoribus, nunc et in hora mortis nostrae...*" At the hour of our death. As if they were already dying, already standing before judgment.

The danger should have stopped Virginia. Should have sent her to her knees in gratitude for the narrow escape, in recognition that God Himself was warning them away from this precipice.

Instead, it sharpened everything.

Her heart thumped in her chest, every nerve alive with terrible awareness. The nearness of catastrophe made every sensation more vivid. The cold floor beneath her feet, the rasp of wool against her skin, the sound of Gian Paolo's breathing in the darkness.

His hand found hers. His fingers wrapped around hers with pressure that made every nerve light, and Virginia understood with sudden, awful clarity that danger was not deterrent but stimulating. That the possibility of discovery had become part of what made this irresistible.

"Virginia." Her name in his mouth sounded like prayer and curse at once.

Behind them, Ottavia's retching had subsided into broken sobs. She whispered something that might have been "God forgive us, God forgive us, God forgive us" in endless, mindless repetition.

Benedetta's breathing was wrong, too fast, ragged at the edges. Her shoulders had started to shake, and Virginia realized with shock that she was crying. Silent tears that would go unwiped because wiping them would mean acknowledging they existed.

Gian Paolo's free hand rose to Virginia's face, traced the line of her cheek with terrible gentleness. A mockery of tenderness.

"Tell me to leave," he whispered against her temple. "If you want me to go, tell me now, and I swear I will never come back."

Virginia's hand lifted to his chest. She felt his heart beating beneath wool and linen, fast, hard, alive.

This was the moment. The precipice. One word would end this. One refusal would send him away and return her to the life she'd known, gray and safe and dead.

Her lips parted.

"No."

The word escaped before wisdom could stop it. Not yes. She couldn't bring herself to say yes with Ottavia weeping and Benedetta praying and the whole edifice of their shared life crumbling around them.

But no to his leaving. No to safety. No to the life she'd been forced into and had never chosen until this moment.

She reached up and pulled him down to her. Found his mouth in the darkness. Tasted wine and want and her own damnation.

"Please," he whispered against her lips. "I need you."

And Virginia, God help her, said the only word that remained to her: "Yes."

Behind them, Ottavia sobbed harder. Benedetta's prayer broke into something that might have been despair or surrender or simply the sound of a soul breaking beneath a weight it was never meant to bear.

And Virginia knew, with cold and perfect clarity, that she had chosen damnation with open eyes. That nearly a decade of careful survival, of protecting herself behind walls and vows and careful lies, had led inevitably to this moment.

To saying yes in a room full of witnesses. To becoming, finally and irrevocably, exactly what her father had feared she would be.

Not a nun.

Not a bride of Christ.

Just a woman who chose desire over duty and would pay whatever price that choice demanded.

The candle guttered and went out, plunging them into darkness.

And in that darkness, Virginia stopped fighting and simply let herself fall.

Chapter Five
1599

March

MORNING LIGHT SLANTED through the high windows as Sister Virginia moved to her place in the choir. Prioress Imbersaga, stationed near the altar, watched Virginia's eyes track toward the eastern windows where Gian Paolo's garden lay beyond the walls. The younger nun's shoulders stiffened. She had caught herself and resumed her forward motion with deliberate composure.

Something had shifted with Sister Virginia.

Virginia knelt with proper devotion, her voice steady during the psalms, her posture impeccable. But awareness radiated from her now, a quality of being conscious, always, of being seen. Her body occupied space differently.

The bell for Prime rang out, its iron voice echoing off stone. The sisters rose in unison, and Imbersaga moved through the service with the ease of long tradition. But part of her attention remained fixed on Virginia.

After the service, Imbersaga walked through the corridors near the dormitories, her fingers trailing along the cool wall. The whispers had begun. Nothing concrete, nothing she could act upon, but whispers nonetheless. A servant had mentioned seeing Sister Virginia at the scriptorium window at odd hours. A kitchen nun had noticed Virginia's cheeks flush when Gian Paolo Osio's name was mentioned. Benedetta and Ottavia had grown secretive, their conversations ending abruptly when others approached.

Nothing provable. But patterns. Patterns were how sin revealed itself before it became scandal.

That afternoon, Imbersaga climbed the narrow stairs to the scriptorium, each step creaking beneath her weight. She found Sister Candida there, bent over an illuminated text, adding gold leaf to a manuscript border.

The Prioress settled in the chair near the window that overlooked the Osio gardens and pretended to examine a book of hours. The leather binding was smooth under her palm, still cool despite the afternoon heat. Her eyes drifted frequently to the glass, to the sightlines the window afforded. Below, newly bloomed roses released their perfume into the thick air.

Gian Paolo Osio stood in his garden wearing a peacock blue doublet that caught the light. He tended to the roses with focused attention, entirely unaware of being watched. Or entirely aware and unconcerned.

Sister Virginia appeared at the garden wall.

The Prioress did not see her arrive. One moment the window showed only roses and stone, and the next, Virginia was there, moving as if drawn by invisible thread. As if called.

Virginia's face, visible in profile, held an expression the Prioress had never seen before. Not the face of a nun in prayer or contemplation. The face of a woman who was starving.

Gian Paolo looked up.

Their eyes met across the wall. Virginia's breath caught, visible in the subtle rise and fall of her shoulders. Gian Paolo's hand stilled on the rosebud. Something invisible moved between them, binding them across the space that should have kept them apart.

Imbersaga's hands tightened on the book. The leather creaked under her grip. Her pulse thudded dully in her ears.

Then Virginia turned from the wall. She did not look flustered or guilty. She simply left with the measured calm of a nun going about her day.

Imbersaga remained in her chair, the book forgotten in her lap, watching as Gian Paolo returned to his roses. But his movements had changed. Slower. More deliberate. As if performing the act of gardening for someone who could no longer see him.

The Prioress closed her book with careful precision and rose. The sudden movement drew Sister Candida's glance, but Imbersaga was already at the door. She had suspected. Now she knew.

And knowing meant she could no longer remain silent.

* * *

IMBERSAGA SUMMONED VIRGINIA to her study as the afternoon light was beginning to fade. She sent Sister Costanza with a message that carried the weight of command, and Virginia appeared within the hour, her composure intact, her expression carefully neutral.

The Prioress did not invite her to sit.

Virginia's gaze flicked to the empty chair, then back to the Prioress. Her hands disappeared into her sleeves. The study smelled of parchment and old candle wax. Somewhere in the corridor beyond, footsteps passed and faded.

"Where were you during the third hour this afternoon?"

Virginia's face remained smooth. "At my devotions, Reverend Mother."

"In the chapel?"

A pause, barely perceptible. "In quiet contemplation. As is permitted."

Imbersaga moved from behind her writing table, positioning herself between Virginia and the door. Her fingers found the iron key that hung at her belt and worried it absently. "And did your contemplation take you to the garden wall?"

Virginia's jaw tightened. "Reverend Mother, I—"

"Do not compound one sin with another." The Prioress kept her voice level. "I was in the scriptorium this afternoon. I saw you at the wall. I saw how you looked at him. I saw how he looked at you."

The color rose in Virginia's cheeks, then drained away. Her hands clenched within her sleeves, the only movement that betrayed her.

"I have been in this convent longer than you have been alive," Imbersaga continued. "I have seen other young women arrive with ideals and fire, only to be tested by isolation and longing. I have sympathy for that struggle. Sister Serafina was sent to San Bernardino for less than what I witnessed today. Do you know what became of her?"

Virginia said nothing, but something flickered behind her eyes.

"She has not spoken a word in seven years. Not even her own name. But I will not tolerate scandal here, Sister Virginia."

"There is no scandal, Reverend Mother."

"Not yet." Imbersaga took a step closer. The stone floor was cold even through her shoes, a chill that seemed to rise from the very foundation. "But there will be if this continues. Gian Paolo Osio killed a man in cold rage and could have been executed for his crime. He is not a suitable object for a nun's attention, spiritual or otherwise."

Virginia's breath came shorter now. "As you know, the warrant for his arrest was withdrawn at my request. He was pardoned."

"Because I urged you to ask for his pardon." Imbersaga's voice cut like a blade. "You did not grant mercy out of Christian charity. You did so because you had already begun to care for him."

"That is not true."

"Explain what I saw in the garden, then. Explain why your entire body moves differently now when you are near the eastern corridors. Explain why Sister Benedetta has become your shadow, why Sister Ottavia weeps secretly in the chapel, why the entire mood within this convent has shifted because Sister Virginia has discovered desire."

The word hung in the air between them. The silence stretched, broken only by the distant tolling of bells marking the hour.

Virginia's face flushed crimson. "I am a nun, Reverend Mother. I have taken vows."

"Vows that are meaningless if the woman taking them does not honor them in her heart." Imbersaga held her ground, her fingers still worrying the iron key. "That is the sin, Sister Virginia. Not the act itself, but the intention. The choice you are making every moment you position yourself at those windows. Every time you look toward that garden."

She waited, but Virginia's lips pressed into a thin line.

"Every time you accept a message or token from a man who has no business contacting you."

"I have not accepted anything from him." But Virginia's voice had gone flat, carefully controlled.

"Then what is the carved stone concealed beneath your pillow?" The Prioress watched Virginia's face closely. "What is the meaning of the initial carved into its surface?"

Virginia went very pale. Her eyes cut away for the briefest moment, then returned, harder, more focused. Calculating.

"Yes." Imbersaga's voice dropped to barely above a whisper, and in the sudden quiet, Virginia's breathing seemed loud. "I know about that as well. This convent is my responsibility, and I am not blind to what occurs within its walls. I see everything, Sister Virginia. And what I see is a young woman of noble birth, accustomed to having her will respected, deciding that her vows are less important than her desires."

"You do not understand."

"I understand perfectly. And what I understand is that this ends now." Imbersaga returned to her writing table and placed both hands flat on its surface. The smooth wood marked with decades of use. "You will not return to the windows or stray close to the garden wall. You will not accept any further contact from Signor Osio. You and the entire congregation will submit to greater discipline—additional prayers, expanded periods of silence. And for you, reduced contact with Sisters Benedetta and Ottavia, who have become your accomplices in this transgression."

Virginia's throat worked as she swallowed. When she spoke, her voice had dropped to barely a whisper. "And if I refuse?"

Imbersaga studied the younger nun. The light from the window caught the fine bones of Virginia's face, the proud set of her jaw, so like her father's. "Then I will have no choice but to write to your family in Madrid, informing them that their daughter has violated her sacred vows and endangered the reputation of Santa Margherita."

She paused, letting the weight of it settle. The air between them grew heavier.

"Your father will arrange for you to be moved to San Bernardino alle Monache. You know of it."

Virginia's breathing quickened, almost imperceptibly.

"The nuns there do not speak except during confession. They sleep on stone floors in winter and summer alike. They do not receive visitors or correspondence. You will spend the remainder of your life in complete isolation, separated from everyone you know." Imbersaga kept her voice steady, almost gentle. "Your name will be stripped from you. Your family will be instructed to consider you dead. Sister Serafina tried to resist the silence in her first year. They say she screams sometimes, but only in her sleep, where it cannot be heard."

Virginia's hands had begun to tremble within her sleeves.

"I do not wish to do this. But I will if you force my hand. Your father placed you in my care, expecting that I would protect both you and this community. I will not fail because a young woman has mistaken forbidden attraction for something meaningful."

"It is meaningful to me," Virginia whispered, and there was something raw in her voice now, something stripped bare.

"It is sin." The Prioress's voice was not unkind, but it was final. "And sin, no matter how it feels in the moment, leads only to destruction. You will accept the discipline I am imposing. You will break off all contact with Gian Paolo Osio. And you will trust that in time, this longing will fade, and you will be at peace again within these walls."

Virginia did not respond. She stood very still, her hands clenched within her sleeves. But her eyes had gone distant, unfocused, her mind working behind the mask of her face.

"Do you understand me, Sister Virginia?"

A long pause stretched between them. Imbersaga could see it happening. The subtle shift in Virginia's expression. A slight narrowing of the eyes. The barely perceptible set of her mouth. Her gaze cut away to the window, then back, and when it returned, something had hardened there.

"Yes, Reverend Mother," Virginia said finally, her voice stripped of all inflection.

"You are dismissed. You will begin your additional prayers this evening. And Sister Bianca will be assigned to accompany you whenever you leave your dormitory, until I am satisfied that you have accepted this correction."

Virginia turned and left the study without another word. But as she walked down the corridor, the rigidity in her shoulders was unmistakable, the controlled grace of each step, like a thread pulled taut, ready to snap.

The Prioress returned to her writing table and sat heavily. The chair creaked beneath her weight. She looked out the window toward the garden where she had seen Gian Paolo Osio tending his roses. A falsehood, for no nobleman would abase himself in such a way. The light was fading now, turning everything amber and gold, casting long shadows across the stone.

She had confronted Virginia directly. She had challenged the younger nun's will. And in doing so, she had declared herself an obstacle.

Imbersaga had learned, through long years in power, that there were two types of dangerous people: those who acted from passion without thought, and those who acted from deliberate calculation. Sister Virginia, she understood with a sinking sensation in her chest, had just crossed over from the first category to the second.

It was time to escalate. Time to take more decisive action.

It was time to remove the temptation that was corrupting her most dangerous charge.

She reached for parchment and ink, her fingers finding the smooth surface of the brass inkwell, the one her predecessor had used in decades of correspondence. Cardinal Borromeo would need to be informed. The Osio family would need to be pressured. Perhaps a benefactor could be convinced to purchase the property, to force Gian Paolo away from the convent walls entirely.

Imbersaga dipped her pen. The nib scratched against parchment, a sound that seemed unnaturally loud in the quiet study. Outside, the evening bells began to toll, marking Vespers. The sound rolled across the garden, across the walls, into the gathering darkness.

She wrote quickly, with the practiced hand of authority. But as the words took shape on the page, a small doubt needled at her thoughts. What if removing the temptation only drove Virginia to more desperate measures? What if the wall between desire and action was thinner than she believed?

The Prioress pressed the seal into warm wax, leaving her mark.

Outside, shadows pooled in the garden where the evening light could not reach. The roses bent heavy on their stems, their perfume fading into the cooling air. And somewhere beyond the walls, someone was watching.

* * *

Spring

VIRGINIA WOKE TO darkness and the faint, intimate sounds of someone dressing. Gian Paolo sat at the edge of her bed, pulling on his boots. Beyond the shuttered window, no softening of dawn yet relieved the black.

She pushed herself up on one elbow. "What are you doing?"

"I must go early." His voice was low, shaped for the night. "My brother, Teodoro, needs me in Milan. Business with our uncle's estates."

"When?"

"Today." He found her hand beneath the wool blanket. "I'll be gone a week. Perhaps two."

Two weeks. The words sank into her like stones. She laced her fingers through his, feeling the roughness of his palm, the living heat that would be taken from her in a moment.

"Write to me," she whispered.

"Every day. Pesseno will bring the letters as always."

From the bed across the narrow cell, Ottavia's breathing ran steady. Too steady. She was awake, listening, as she always did. In this room even sleep had manners; they lay as though nothing were happening and called it obedience.

Gian Paolo rose and reached for the black habit draped over the wooden chest, a spare taken from the convent's stores, still not large enough for him, but darkness forgave much.

Virginia slipped from her bed, her bare feet finding the cold stone without a sound. She drew her own habit over her chemise and went with him down the stairs and along the corridor to the rear convent door, the one they always used.

They moved through this final passage together, his hand finding hers though the darkness hid it.

Virginia lifted the heavy bolt as softly as she could. Iron scraped against iron, small, but sharp in the hush. The door opened onto the garden. Damp air flowed in, smelling of earth and spent ash.

He turned and kissed her one last time, his beard rough against her cheek, his mouth tasting of wine and something she could not name.

Then he was gone.

Virginia stood a moment in the doorway, watching his shape dissolve into the murk, and then slid the bolt home again. She returned alone through the sleeping convent, listening for any answering stir, any cough, any shifting footfall, any door that sighed too long.

Virginia re-entered the cell, careful not to make a sound.

Silence.

"He's gone?" Ottavia's voice came low from across the room.

"Yes."

A rustle of linen. Benedetta sat up, her outline darker than the dark. "How long before he returns?"

"Two weeks. Maybe more."

"Good." Ottavia shifted, the mattress whispering under her. "Perhaps we may sleep without starting at every sound."

"No one hears anything, and even if they did, no one will speak," Virginia said, and heard the edge in her own voice as she said it.

Benedetta's tone held no comfort. "This cannot be hidden forever. One day you will be discovered."

Virginia lay back upon her cot and stared at what she could not see. Benedetta was right. Every night he passed through doors and corridors was another throw of the dice. Every letter Pesseno carried. Every gift Susanna brought under cloth. Every collar Virginia mended and returned, her stitches plain to any eyes that cared to look.

They were raising something too tall to stand long.

But not tonight. Not yet.

She shut her eyes and waited for the bell.

In the chapel, morning prayers left her mouth and went nowhere. Virginia knelt amid the smell of warm wax and frankincense and old psalters handled by a hundred hands. Around her, voices rose in plainchant, Latin flowing beneath the vaults like water under stone.

Deus, in adjutorium meum intende. O God, come to my assistance.

Her lips formed the words; her voice joined the others. Yet her thoughts had already gone after him, measuring days like coins, counting the hours until he would return, until she could cease this hollow piety and feel his weight and heat again in the narrow bed.

The Host touched her tongue—dry, thin, without taste.

She swallowed, and felt nothing.

Later, Pesseno arrived at the third hour past noon, his weathered face kept carefully blank as he passed the covered basket through the parlatory grating. Ottavia and Benedetta stood close by, their backs to the door, eyes on the corridor.

"From my lord," Pesseno said.

Virginia's fingers trembled as she lifted the cloth. Sweetmeats from Milan wrapped in silk. A small hand mirror, no larger than her palm, its polished silver back worked with delicate scrollwork curling around the edges, and at the center, a tiny, engraved rose. The silvered glass gave back her reflection with a soft, dream-like quality, as if she were seeing herself through water. It came in a small leather case lined with silk, to protect the precious glass. And beneath it, a letter sealed with red wax.

She broke the seal.

> *My soul, I am barely departed and already the hours drag like years. My bed is empty. My days are ash. I count each moment until I can return to you, until I can taste your mouth again, feel your body beneath mine, hear you cry my name in darkness...*

Heat rushed up her throat and into her face. The letter ran on for another page, too bold, too naked. She folded it quickly and tucked it into her sleeve where it pressed against her wrist like a secret weight.

"Tell your lord," she said, keeping her voice even, "that I have received his words. And I wait."

She handed Pesseno a wrapped packet containing mended collars and her own letter, less plain than it should have been, though she wrote with care.

When Pesseno had gone, Benedetta and Ottavia slipped into the parlatory.

"More gifts?" Benedetta asked.

"Of course." Virginia could not help the small smile. "And a letter. He writes as if we have been parted a season, not a day."

"You should burn them," Ottavia murmured. "Such a letter must not be found."

"I know."

But she would not. She could not. Each letter proved that this was not only sin and peril, but something that had a name and a voice, something meant for her. Not for her title, not for her family's shadow, but for her own flesh and breath. Even if the man who wrote them was a killer and a libertine, half in love and half in cruelty.

She took what was given.

The days dragged, one prayer into the next. Virginia moved through the hours by rote—Lauds at dawn, Prime, Terce, Sext, None, Vespers, Compline. Eight times each day the bells ruled their bodies. Eight times she knelt, rose, and knelt again, her limbs obedient where her soul was not.

At night she lay in her narrow bed with his letters hidden beneath the mattress and remembered: the weight of him, the heat, the way he spoke her name like a blessing and a threat. Memory made sleep a stranger.

One evening, as the convent settled and the last footfalls faded, she heard a pause outside their door—long enough to turn her blood to ice. A faint rustle, as if cloth brushed stone. She held her breath, waiting for the latch to lift.

Nothing.

The steps moved on, slow and measured.

In the dark Ottavia shifted once and Benedetta let out a breath, and Virginia knew they had heard it too.

"You wear yourself thin," Benedetta said one morning, her gaze resting on the shadows beneath Virginia's eyes.

"I am well."

"You are not." No reproach in Benedetta's voice, only the cold truth. "You are bound to it."

Virginia looked at her sharply. Benedetta did not often speak of desire, as though naming it might summon it.

"How do you bear the hunger for a man's touch?" Virginia asked, scarcely above a breath.

"It is not easy," Benedetta said, eyes lowered. "I pray. I work. I turn my mind to other things." She paused. "But it does not leave."

"No."

"So, we endure," Benedetta said. "And we are careful. And we wait."

"For what?"

Benedetta's hands stilled in her sewing. "For what comes to all things that grow too bold."

* * *

ON THE EIGHTH day, Gian Paolo returned. Again, Virginia let him in through the rear garden door, and together they moved through the darkness to the cell. He followed like a shadow. Once inside he shed the borrowed habit and reached for her.

No words. His mouth found hers with the fierce need of a week's absence, his hands already at the ties of her chemise. They stumbled to the bed, graceless and urgent, as if haste could outrun consequence.

Afterward, tangled in wool blankets while Ottavia and Benedetta breathed steadily across the room, he pressed something into her palm.

"I brought you something."

She felt the weight before she saw it: a fine gold chain, a small ruby catching what little starlight slipped through the shutters.

"I cannot take it," she breathed.

"Hide it," he whispered. "Under your habit, where only I know it lies." His fingers found the clasp and fastened it at her throat. The metal settled cool between her breasts. "I want you marked as mine, if only in secret."

She should have refused. Should have made him take it back. Another danger. Another proof.

Instead, she pulled him down and kissed him.

They lay quiet for a time, their breathing slowing, the ruby a secret weight against her skin. Virginia traced the line of his jaw in the darkness, feeling the scratch of stubble, the warmth of him. But something in his body felt different tonight, a tension that had nothing to do with passion.

"I should go before dawn comes," he said finally.

She nodded and rose with him. They dressed in silence, Virginia pulling her habit over her chemise, feeling the ruby settle into its hiding place. Gian Paolo donned the borrowed black habit over his clothes, becoming shadow once more.

Together they slipped from the cell and moved through the darkened corridors. Virginia knew these passages by heart, could walk them blind. Down the narrow stairs, past the Chapter house, through the passage that led to the rear of the convent.

At the garden door, she lifted the bolt as softly as she could. Iron scraped against iron, small but sharp in the hush. The door opened onto damp air that smelled of earth and the coming dawn.

He turned to her, but instead of the usual swift kiss and departure, he hesitated. His hand found hers in the darkness.

"You are bothered about something tonight. I can feel it. Tell me," Virginia asked.

"There is something I must tell you," he said quietly. "About Milan."

Something in his voice made her stomach clench. "What is it?"

"My uncle is dead."

The words fell flat, without ceremony. Virginia's hand tightened on his.

"Dead?"

"They found him three days ago. At his country estate." His voice carried no grief, only a strange, tight control. "Someone stabbed him in his study. The servants found him in his chair with a knife in his chest. Blood everywhere, they said. The carpet was ruined."

The casual detail of the carpet made something cold settle in Virginia's stomach. "Who would do such a thing?"

Gian Paolo was silent for a long moment. When he finally spoke, his voice was carefully neutral. "The authorities suspect Teodoro. Several witnesses saw him riding toward the estate that afternoon. Others remembered hearing them argue about money a few weeks earlier."

"Your brother." Virginia's throat had gone dry. "Teodoro murdered your uncle?"

"Does it matter?" His grip on her hand tightened. "The old man is dead. The inheritance is secure. My brother has taken refuge in Venice, where Milan's magistrates cannot touch him. Everything has worked out as it needed to."

Virginia pulled her hand free. "You're saying your brother killed him for money? For the inheritance?"

"I'm saying that family must protect family." His voice remained low, aware of the sleeping convent around them. "That sometimes difficult actions become necessary. That the world is more complicated than the Church would have us believe." He reached for her again. "You of all people should understand that. How many people in this convent protect you? Keep your secrets? Enable your sins?"

Your sins, not our sins. The comparison struck her like a slap. She took a step back, pressing against the doorframe.

"That is different."

"Is it?" She could hear the edge in his voice now. "We do what we must to go on living. We all compromise our principles when necessity demands it. The only difference between your sins and my brother's is that yours hurt no one but yourself."

But that wasn't true. Virginia's sins hurt Benedetta and Ottavia, Candida and Silvia. Hurt the convent's reputation. Her sins rippled outward like stones thrown into still water, the circles expanding far beyond what she could see or measure.

"Do not judge what you do not understand," he said quietly. "The old man was bleeding us dry with his charity. Every monastery in Lombardy, every artist with his hand out, every peasant who came begging. He promised us that inheritance years ago. We planned our lives around it. And then he decided to play saint with what should have been ours."

"It was his money to dispose of as he wished."

"Was it?" His eyes glittered in the faint light of the coming dawn. "When he gave his word? When we made decisions based on his promises?"

Virginia pressed both hands against the doorframe, needing something solid. She stared at the man before her and saw him clearly for the first time. A man who could speak casually of his uncle's murder. Who saw the world as a series of transactions where everything had a price, and nothing was sacred. Who would do whatever served his interests and justify it afterward with clever words.

"Your brother killed an old man for money," Virginia said, her voice tight. "And you helped him escape justice. And you tell me about it as though it means nothing."

"It means exactly what it means. No more. No less." He stepped closer. "I thought you would understand. Thought we were past the point of pretending to be better than we are."

"There is a difference between carnal sin and murder."

"Is there?" His laugh was bitter and soft. "Both break God's law. Both merit damnation. The magnitude seems irrelevant once you have crossed the line."

Virginia had no answer. He was wrong. He had to be wrong. But she could not explain why and could not turn the wordless knowledge in her bones into an argument that would stand against his cold logic.

Gian Paolo cupped her face in his hands. His touch was surprisingly gentle.

"I am not asking you to approve," he said softly. "Only to accept what cannot be changed. My brother is free. The inheritance is secure. We can continue as we have been. That is all that matters."

He kissed her forehead, then leaned close to her ear. "You will keep this to yourself."

It was not a question.

She nodded, unable to speak.

"Good." His thumb traced her cheekbone. "What's done is done. No one else needs to carry this burden."

He kissed her once more, quickly, and then he was gone, dissolving into the pre-dawn murk.

Virginia stood a moment in the doorway, then slid the bolt home. She returned alone through the sleeping convent, the ruby pendant cold against her skin and the knowledge of murder a heavier weight still.

When she slipped back into the cell, Benedetta's voice came from the darkness. "He is gone."

"Yes."

Silence. Then Ottavia, soft and tentative: "Are you well?"

Virginia climbed into her narrow cot and pulled the blanket to her chin. The ruby lay hidden beneath her chemise, a weight against her breastbone. "I am tired. Nothing more."

She could feel them awake in the darkness, sensing something had changed but not knowing what. This secret she would carry alone.

She was part of it now. Not just her own damnation, but complicit in murder and corruption. The knowledge of what Teodoro had done, of what Gian Paolo had arranged, made her a witness. If she said nothing, if she kept this secret as she kept so many others, she became part of the crime.

But who could she tell? And what good would it do? The deed was done. The old man was dead. Teodoro would return to Monza eventually, a free man. Justice had already been purchased and paid for.

She pressed her forehead into the thin pillow and tried to pray. But the words would not come. They stuck in her throat like stones, heavy, sharp, impossible to swallow.

Libera me, Domine. Deliver me, O Lord.

This time she no longer begged to be freed from him, but from the woman she had become.

But God was not listening. Or perhaps He was listening and had simply chosen to let her reap what she had sown.

And she knew that whatever protection her family's name provided, whatever power her position gave her, she was building something that would eventually collapse under its own weight.

The only question was when. And who would be crushed beneath it when it fell.

* * *

BY LATE MAY, the affair had taken on a household rhythm, as if sin could be made ordinary by habit. Gian Paolo came three or four times each week, staying an hour or a whole night depending on his temper and her fear. He sent gifts—poultry, fish, fruit from the markets—and she sent him things in return: embroidered handkerchiefs, mended shirts, little notes folded into cloth.

The whole convent knew.

That was the marvel of it. Even the youngest novices whispered during recreation, and the schoolgirls, daughters of good houses, passed the tale among themselves until Virginia's fury forced them into silence.

Yet no one spoke to authority. Not to Imbersaga. Not to the confessor. Not to Cardinal Borromeo in Milan.

Because Virginia was the Lady of Monza, and the de Leyva shadow reached farther than these walls. Into Lombardy, into Madrid. Because to accuse without hard proof was to invite ruin: from her brothers, from Osio's bravos, and from the Church itself, which could not risk scandal when heresy already gnawed at Christendom.

So, silence held, thin, trembling, and useful. It was fed by fear, by self-interest, and by that strange complicity forbidden love breeds in those who must live it.

Virginia felt it everywhere: eyes that slid away, mouths that closed too quickly, the weight of what was known and never named.

It should have frightened her.

Instead, it made her bolder.

She was crossing the cloister one evening when Mother Imbersaga appeared from the shadowed arcade. The Prioress's face was carefully composed, but her hands trembled.

"Sister Virginia. A word."

They moved to the rose garden where no ear would catch them. The air lay heavy with the promise of rain and the thick sweetness of late bloom.

"This cannot continue." Imbersaga's voice came hard, brooking no opposition. "You will cease these meetings with Osio. I know he comes here. I know the doors are opened for him. And I am commanding you, under holy obedience, to end this sacrilege."

Virginia met her eyes without flinching. "I do not know what you speak of, Reverend Mother."

"Do not lie to me!" The Prioress's voice cracked like a whip. "The whole house knows. The servants know. The neighbors know. Do you think me blind? Do you think God is blind?"

"If the whole house knows," Virginia said softly, "then surely you have witnesses. Proof. Something more than rumors and suspicion."

Imbersaga's mouth opened, then closed. They both understood: proof meant accusation, accusation meant investigation, investigation meant scandal, and scandal meant the de Leyva family's wrath.

"I do not need proof to command obedience," Imbersaga said, but her voice had lost its edge. "I am still Prioress of this house."

"Are you?" Virginia took a step closer. "Then command me. Write to Cardinal Borromeo. Summon the ecclesiastical visitors. Bring this matter to light." She paused. "Unless you are afraid of what that light will reveal. Not just about me, but about your failure to maintain discipline. About your weakness. About how little authority you truly hold."

The color drained from Imbersaga's face. "You would not."

"I would do nothing," Virginia said. "I am innocent of these baseless accusations. But my family..." She let the words hang. "My family does not take kindly to insults against their blood. And if you force an investigation that finds nothing, or worse, that brings scandal to a house under their protection, well. That would be most unfortunate for you."

Imbersaga's hands were shaking openly now. "This is a threat."

"This is reality." Virginia's voice softened, became almost gentle. "You know what I am doing. I know what I am doing. The whole convent knows. But no one will speak it, because speaking it destroys us all, you most of all. So, I suggest, Reverend Mother, that you continue to see nothing. To hear nothing. To know nothing."

"I am afraid," Imbersaga whispered, and suddenly she looked old, broken. "Of you. Of him. Of what this will bring down on all our heads. When this falls, and it will fall, Virginia, because towers like this always fall, it will crush everyone in its path. Not just you. All of us."

Virginia touched the hidden ruby pendant beneath her scapular, feeling its small, cold weight. A reminder of what she had chosen. Of who she belonged to now.

"Then pray it does not fall during your tenure," she said softly. "And leave me to my own conscience."

"Please." The word came out raw, all authority stripped away. "End this before it's too late. Before it destroys you."

For one heartbeat, something stirred in Virginia's chest: the ghost of the girl who had once believed in virtue, who had scourged herself bloody and begged the Madonna to tear this hunger from her.

"I cannot," Virginia whispered. "I will not."

Imbersaga closed her eyes. When she opened them again, they shone with tears. "Then may God have mercy on us all."

She turned and walked away; her footsteps unsteady on stone.

Virginia stood alone as the first drops of rain began to fall.

She had won.

But the taste of victory was ash.

That night, Gian Paolo came to her as usual. She told him nothing of the Prioress's words, nothing of her own growing unease about his brother's crime. Instead, she drew him into her bed with a fierceness that surprised them both, her hands in his hair, her mouth hungry against his.

"What is it?" he asked afterward.

"Nothing." She pressed her face to his chest, breathing sweat and wine and the sharp, clean scent of the soap he used. "Everything. I do not know myself."

"Do you want me to stay away?"

"No." The word came out like a command. "Never. I do not care for the risks. I do not care what comes. Only, we keep coming."

His arms tightened around her. "Then I will. Whatever comes."

They lay tangled together until the bells of Monza would soon toll across the sleeping town, calling the hours in distant houses and convents. Time for him to go. Time for her to become, again, what she pretended to be.

He dressed in the darkness, kissed her once more, and together they slipped out of the cell and down to the garden door. There they kissed again, quick, desperate, and then he turned away, his presence fading into the night.

Virginia returned to the cell and lay in her narrow bed listening to rain drum on roof tiles and wondered how long this could last.

Not forever.

But for now, for this stolen season, for this dangerous present, she had what she wanted. Even if it damned her. Especially if it damned her.

Outside, thunder rolled across Monza like a warning. Virginia closed her eyes and slept.

* * *

June

THE CHAPTER HOUSE smelled of old wood and bodies pressed too close in June heat. It was the triennial election, the day Imbersaga's term expired, and the convent's future would be decided. Virginia sat on the hard bench between Benedetta and Ottavia; hands folded to keep them from trembling and watched the Bishop's representative count ballots with maddening slowness. Each slip of parchment unfolded with a papery whisper. Each name read aloud hung in the humid air.

"Sister Beatrice."

Virginia's nails bit into her palms.

"Sister Beatrice."

Around her, sisters shifted on benches. Someone coughed. Three rows ahead, Sister Candida's rosary beads clicked softly, nervous and quick.

"Sister Beatrice."

The pattern held. Sixteen ballots. Twenty. Twenty-five. Each one another step closer to freedom.

When the final vote was counted, Beatrice had won by a margin that left no room for contest. Thirty-eight votes to Imbersaga's eight.

Virginia's lungs unlocked. Air rushed in too fast, making her dizzy. They had done it. The impossible thing. They had removed the woman who held absolute power over their lives, and they had done it through channels so legitimate that no one could call it rebellion.

Three rows ahead, Imbersaga sat with her spine rigid, hands perfectly still in her lap. Only the tendons standing out on her neck betrayed anything at all.

Sister Beatrice rose when her name was called. She was fifty-two, soft-spoken, with crow's feet that deepened when she smiled. She had been Vicaress before, a woman who listened before she spoke, who understood that rules existed to serve the community, not to crush it.

Imagination took hold. No more restrictions. No more Sister Bianca shadowing her through corridors.

Freedom.

At the investiture ceremony two days later, Imbersaga knelt before Beatrice and kissed her ring with a face carved from stone. From her place among the choir sisters, something dark and satisfying curled in her chest. The woman who had restricted her movements, censored her letters, threatened her with punishment cells, now knelt in submission to someone else's authority.

Over the following weeks, Beatrice dismantled Imbersaga's regime with quiet efficiency. The mandatory extra prayers—ended. The enforced silences—lifted. Sisters could move through the convent without requiring permission for every step.

The convent exhaled like a body that had been holding its breath.

No one followed Virginia anymore.

She watched it happen with satisfaction so profound it frightened her. This was her doing. Not directly, perhaps not entirely, but the whispers she had sent through her brother Luigi, the strategic conversations with influential families, the careful cultivation of Beatrice's trust—all of it had led to this moment. She had learned to wield power without appearing to touch it. To destroy obstacles without leaving fingerprints.

Then, two weeks after her investiture, Beatrice summoned Virginia to her study.

The walk down the corridor felt both endless and too short. Virginia's pulse thrummed in her throat. She didn't know what this meeting meant. Didn't know if her careful campaign had been too obvious, if Beatrice suspected the manipulation behind her election, if this was recognition or reckoning.

The door stood slightly ajar. Virginia knocked twice.

"Come."

Virginia pushed the door open. Mother Beatrice sat behind the table, once Imbersaga's, Virginia corrected herself with savage satisfaction, reviewing what looked like convent accounts.

She looked up. Her expression was unreadable.

"Sit, Sister Virginia."

Virginia obeyed and settled onto the wooden chair. Her hands wanted to fidget. She pressed them flat against her thighs.

Beatrice set down her quill. "I'm appointing you Vicaress."

The words landed like a stone dropped into still water. Ripples spread outward through Virginia's chest, her lungs, her limbs.

"The appointment will be announced at tomorrow's Chapter meeting," Beatrice continued. "You have the education, the administrative capability, and the temperament for the position. The convent will benefit from your service."

Vicaress. Second-in-command of the entire convent. Authority over daily operations, over the other sisters.

Over Imbersaga.

Virginia forced her voice to remain steady. "Thank you, Reverend Mother. I'm honored by your confidence."

"The position comes with responsibilities," Beatrice said, her gaze sharp and assessing. "You'll manage the sisters' daily duties, oversee discipline, handle disputes. You'll also control access to the keys."

The keys. Virginia felt the weight of that word settle onto her shoulders like a mantle.

"I understand, Reverend Mother."

"Do you?" Beatrice leaned forward slightly. "Because I'm not Imbersaga. I believe in allowing the women under my guidance some measure of dignity and autonomy. I was given the task of watching you over many weeks, and during that time I saw nothing improper. But I expect those in positions of authority to use their power wisely. Do we have an understanding?"

The question held layers Virginia didn't quite trust herself to parse. Was this a warning? An invitation? A test?

"Yes, Reverend Mother."

Beatrice smiled, but something in her eyes suggested she saw more than Virginia wanted her to see. "Good. You're dismissed."

Virginia rose on legs that felt disconnected from her body. She crossed to the door, her hand on the latch, when Beatrice spoke again.

"Sister Virginia?"

She turned.

"Your friendship with Sisters Benedetta and Ottavia is noted. I trust you'll use your new position to guide them wisely as well."

The words could have been innocent. Probably were innocent. But Virginia's skin prickled with awareness.

She knows something. Not everything, but something.

"Of course, Reverend Mother."

Virginia left the study and walked down the corridor toward her cell. Her footsteps echoed off stone walls that had witnessed centuries of women's secrets, women's compromises, women's small and terrible victories.

She had won. Not merely survived but won. From powerless postulant to Vicaress of Santa Margherita. From suspect and restricted sister to a position of genuine authority.

The satisfaction should have been pure. Instead, it tasted like ashes and triumph mixed together, inseparable.

That night, lying in her narrow bed while Benedetta and Ottavia slept, Virginia stared at the ceiling and let herself feel it. The pride. The vindication. The cold, sharp pleasure of having seized power from the woman who had tried to break her.

Imbersaga had taught her the most valuable lesson of all: that power was not granted by God or tradition but taken by those ruthless enough to reach for it.

Virginia had proven herself quite ruthless indeed.

Outside, somewhere beyond the walls, Gian Paolo would be waiting. Watching. Now, with the keys to every door hanging from her cincture, she could finally give him what he wanted. What they both wanted.

The thought should have terrified her. Instead, it felt like the beginning of something inevitable. Something she had been moving toward since the moment her father's carriage had carried her through these gates fifteen years ago.

She closed her eyes and waited for guilt to come.

It didn't.

* * *

July

THE CHAMBER ASSIGNED to the Vicaress was twice the size of the cell Virginia had shared with Benedetta and Ottavia, and now it belonged to her alone. The floorboards didn't creak under a single person's weight the way they had in her old cell. The writing table stood solid as an altar, its walnut surface bearing the scars of decades—ink stains, knife marks, the circular ghosts of cups set down by Vicaresses long dead. A window overlooked both the chapel and the inner garden, offering a view that felt less like privilege and more like surveillance. Most importantly, the door locked from the inside.

Virginia stood at that window now, her fingertips resting on the stone sill still holding afternoon warmth, and watched shadows creep across the garden paths below. One day in this room, and already her body moved differently—shoulders back, spine straight, footsteps deliberate instead of apologetic. The keys hung from her cincture, iron weight bumping her hip with each movement. Physical keys that opened every locked door within these walls. But also symbolic ones. The authority to permit and forbid. To grant access and deny it. To determine what could happen here and what could not. She had spent nine years powerless. Now she controlled everything.

On her third night as Vicaress, she tested that power.

Sisters Costanza and Bianca would be monitored constantly. Benedetta would note every visitor Costanza spoke with, every letter she handled, every moment she left her post. Sister Bianca would be followed everywhere. The spying was easy to justify. Prudent oversight during the transition, ensuring they maintained proper protocols under new leadership. Nothing personal. Simply administrative necessity.

But Costanza and Bianca would understand. The women who had been Imbersaga's watchdogs, who had tracked Virginia's movements and reported her every deviation, would now live under eyes that never blinked. They would feel scrutiny like a hand on the back of their necks and would learn what it meant to be measured and found wanting at someone else's discretion.

Something flickered in Virginia's chest as she'd given Benedetta the order. Not quite guilt. Not quite satisfaction. She didn't examine it too closely. The hunters had become the hunted. That was justice enough.

On her fifth night, Virginia met privately with Benedetta and Ottavia in her new chamber. She turned the key in the lock herself, the bolt sliding home with a soft click that meant safety. No one could enter without permission. No one could overhear what passed between them.

"Now that I am Vicaress, I plan to continue my relations with Gian Paolo but here in this room. You will no longer be bothered."

"You are? For how long?" Benedetta asked quietly, settling into the chair across from Virginia's writing table with the ease of someone who had waited for this moment.

"As long as necessary." The words came out lower than Virginia intended, steadier. The voice of someone who could ruin you. When had that happened? "Beatrice is not Imbersaga. She will not restrict us."

"She might if scandal becomes unavoidable." Benedetta leaned forward, elbows on knees. "The concern is not Beatrice. It is the outside world: The Cardinal's representatives. The families who have daughters here. Word of your relationship with Osio will eventually reach someone with the authority to act upon it."

"Then we will be careful." Virginia moved to the window, her reflection ghostly in the darkening glass. Somewhere beyond these walls, Gian Paolo would be waiting. Watching. "More careful than before. But we will also be smart about it. There are ways to arrange meetings that will not raise suspicion. Ways to manage communication that will not leave obvious traces. Ways to ensure that if questions are asked, the answers point elsewhere."

Ottavia's hands twisted together in her lap, knuckles white. "This is a great risk, Virginia. If you are discovered now, when you hold the position of Vicaress, the scandal will be exponentially greater. You will not simply be dismissed. You will be exposed to the world as a hypocrite and a traitor to your vows."

"Then I will ensure that I am not discovered." Virginia pressed her palm flat against the window glass, cold seeping into her skin. Her breath fogged the surface. Below, the garden paths stretched empty in twilight. She searched for Gian Paolo but he was not there. "My position gives me authority. Power over the other sisters. Access to the keys and the spaces of this convent. And it gives me a layer of protection, because people do not suspect those in positions of authority of transgression."

She turned to face them, her back to the window. "They expect the Vicaress to be righteous. Devoted to the rule. Incapable of the very violations that others might commit. My appointment makes me untouchable."

The words tasted like power on her tongue. Like corruption. Like freedom.

"It also makes me useful," she continued. "There are things that need to be managed within this convent. The discipline of sisters who step out of line, management of scandal if it threatens the community, control of information that must not reach the outside world. Beatrice is a good woman, but she is not equipped to handle the complexities of power. She will come to rely on me."

"And you will become indispensable." Benedetta's voice was soft, but her eyes were sharp as always, cataloging everything. It was not a question.

"Exactly."

Ottavia's rosary beads clicked softly in the silence that followed. She didn't object. Didn't protest. Virginia knew she understood what she had become. What the events of the past months had forced her to become. Not merely a nun violating her vows. But a woman willing to manipulate, to deceive, to use every tool at her disposal to ensure that her will was served.

The Vicaress had become the true Prioress of Santa Margherita.

And the convent, without fully understanding what had occurred, had granted her the authority to be.

* * *

September

REVEREND MOTHER BEATRICE poured two small cups of wine from the crystal carafe she kept on the sideboard of her study. The liquid was dark as garnets, catching the flicker of the candles that burned against the gathering gloom. The room smelled of dried lavender and the sharp, metallic tang of ink—the scent of administration.

She handed one cup to Virginia across the heavy walnut writing table, where documents from their evening meeting lay scattered like fallen leaves, accounts from the farm holdings, plans for the school expansion, the endless tally of grain and oil.

"You know, there are rumors about you," Beatrice said conversationally, settling back into her chair. The velvet cushion sighed beneath her. "In the town. About your connection to Signor Osio."

Virginia's hand stilled, her cup halfway to her lips. The wine aroma, suddenly cloying, filled her nose. She forced her fingers not to tremble, gripping the stem until her knuckles whitened.

"I do not credit such rumors," Beatrice continued, her voice gentle but deliberate, smooth as the wine she swirled in her glass. "Servants gossip about everything and nothing. It is the nature of empty minds to fill silence with noise. But I wish you to know that if there is anything you need to discuss with me, I am someone who believes rigid rules sometimes fail to account for the complexity of human nature."

Virginia set down her cup carefully. It clicked against the wood, a sound too loud in the quiet room. "I am not certain what you mean, Reverend Mother."

"I mean that I became Prioress because I was dissatisfied with how my predecessor managed this community." Beatrice met her eyes. Her gaze was soft, lacking Imbersaga's piercing judgment, yet it held a different kind of weight. The weight of complicity. "I believe a truly wise community finds ways to accommodate both spirit and feeling, rather than denying one entirely."

She paused, taking a sip of wine. Outside, the evening bell for Compline began to toll, its mournful bronze voice vibrating through the glass of the window.

"What I am saying, Virginia, is that you have my trust. I value your counsel and your work here. You have brought order where there was chaos. And I am not inclined to pry into how a sister under my charge maintains her spiritual balance, so long as the work of the convent continues and the reputation of Santa Margherita remains sound."

Virginia understood exactly what was being offered. Not permission, but willful blindness. An agreement sealed in wine and silence: as long as appearances were maintained, the actual details would remain undiscussed.

"Thank you, Reverend Mother," Virginia said softly. The words tasted like ash on her tongue. "Your trust means a great deal to me."

"I am certain it does." Beatrice reached across the table and patted Virginia's hand. Her palm was warm, dry, motherly. "We are fortunate in each other, I think. You need someone who understands you. And I need a Vicaress who makes my burden lighter."

The conversation moved to other matters, the price of wax, the repair of the bell tower, but something fundamental had shifted. The air in the room felt heavier, charged with the static of an unholy pact.

As Virginia left the study that evening, walking through the candlelit corridors where shadows stretched long and thin like accusing fingers, she understood the full implications. Her position gave her not merely authority, but protection. The Prioress would trade ignorance for invaluable service.

It was the perfect arrangement. Virginia could pursue what she wanted without the constant fear that had characterized life under Imbersaga. She had authority that would discourage questioning. She had a superior who had made clear that certain things were better left unexamined.

She should have felt relief. Instead, a cold certainty settled in her bones, sharp as a winter frost. Beatrice's willful blindness was not merely protection. It was a noose that would tighten slowly, giving Virginia just enough rope to hang herself when the inevitable reckoning came.

Back in her own chamber, Virginia bolted the door. The sound of the iron sliding home was usually a comfort, but tonight it felt insufficient.

She moved to her writing desk, her fingers brushing against the iron keys that hung from her cincture. As Vicaress, she held the keys to every gate and door in Santa Margherita. They were heavy, cold, and pitted with age. They were the symbol of her authority, but also a tether. Every time Gian Paolo wished to enter, she had to be there to unlock the way. She had to stand shivering in the damp passageway, waiting for his signal, risking discovery with every minute she spent loitering by the door.

It was a risk she no longer needed to take.

She lit a second candle, the flame sputtering before catching hold. From the bottom of her small wooden chest, she retrieved a block of soft jeweler's wax she had procured from the sacristy supplies under the pretense of sealing official correspondence.

Her hands moved with steady precision. She detached the heavy iron key for the garden service door from the ring at her waist. She pressed it into the wax, bearing down until the metal bit deep, capturing every ridge and ward. She turned the key and repeated the process, creating a perfect impression of the other side.

The mold was crude, but sufficient. Gian Paolo would give it to Pesseno would take it to a smith, someone discreet, someone who asked no questions when paid in silver, and return with a copy.

A spare key. For him.

Virginia stared at the wax impression, the negative space where the metal had been. Giving Gian Paolo his own key was a crossing of a different threshold. It was not just allowing him entry; it was surrendering control. It was declaring that the walls of Santa Margherita no longer applied to him, that he could come and go as he pleased, a shadow king in a kingdom of women.

A tremor of fear fluttered in her chest. Not of discovery, but of the finality of it. She was dismantling the convent's defenses from the inside, one lock at a time.

But then she remembered his hands. The heat of his breath against her neck. The way he looked at her, as if she were the only living thing in a world of stone.

She wrapped the wax mold in a piece of linen and tied it with a ribbon. When Pesseno came to the parlatory tomorrow, she would pass it to him beneath a basket of mended shifts. She would place the tool for her own destruction directly into his hands, and she would call it love.

Chapter Six
1600

Early 1600

SISTER COSTANZA STOOD in the narrow passage and stared at the garden service door. The heavy bolt lay drawn back in the predawn gloom, a tongue of iron exposed where it should have been secured.

This was the third time in a month she had found it unbolted.

She pushed the heavy oak panel. It swung inward with a well-oiled silence that betrayed recent careful use. Beyond the threshold, the garden lay silent beneath gray dawn.

"Sister?" The servant girl stood behind her, gripping her broom. "Is something wrong?"

"Did you bolt this door before Compline last evening?"

"I did, Sister. I swear it upon the Virgin." The girl's voice rose with anxiety. "I checked it twice, as you taught me. The bolt was fast when I left it."

"I believe you, child." Costanza shoved the door closed and rammed the bolt home with a clang that echoed off stone. "Someone has been playing tricks on us, it seems."

But she knew it was no trick. It was a route, carefully maintained, repeatedly used by someone who moved through the convent's enclosure as if the Holy Rule meant nothing.

Costanza thought of reporting it to Reverend Mother Beatrice. But what would she say? That she suspected someone was violating enclosure based on shadows and unbolted doors? Without proof, her concerns would sound like nervous imaginings.

And there was something else. She had noticed how Beatrice managed certain situations with deliberate blindness. How certain sisters, Virginia de

Leyva in particular, seemed to move with unusual freedom that went unremarked.

She would need to catch them. To see with her own eyes who was violating the sacred enclosure. Only then could she bring irrefutable proof.

* * *

THAT EVENING, AFTER Compline, Sister Costanza slipped into one of the small storage rooms adjacent to the garden service door. She left the door barely ajar and positioned herself in the darkness where she could watch.

The hours bled by. Cold from the stones seeped through her thin sandals until her feet went numb. The darkness pressed close. Her back cramped into knots. Her bladder grew heavy. Still, she waited.

Then, sometime in the deepest part of the night, she heard footsteps. Quick and quiet, approaching from deeper within the convent.

A shadow moved along the corridor toward the garden door. Tall. Broad-shouldered. Moving with the confidence of someone who had walked this route many times before.

The figure reached the garden door. Costanza heard the bolt being drawn back, then the whisper of hinges. Cold night air rushed into the corridor. The shadow slipped through and disappeared.

A man. Inside the sacred enclosure.

"Who is there?" The words left her mouth before fear could stop them. She stepped into the corridor. "Is someone here?"

"I cannot see you properly in this darkness."

Costanza spun. Sister Benedetta stood in the corridor perhaps ten paces away, a pale shape in the gloom. She carried no candle. Offered no explanation for her presence during the hours meant for sleep.

How long had Benedetta been standing there?

"Sister Benedetta?" Costanza pressed her palm against her breastbone. "You startled me."

"What are you doing down here at this hour?"

"I couldn't sleep. I thought I heard something." Costanza gestured toward the open door. "The garden door. It's open."

"Is it?" Benedetta moved past her and pulled the door closed with a solid thud but didn't slide the bolt home. "The latch must have failed. These old mechanisms loosen with time. I'll mention it to the carpenter tomorrow."

The explanation came too quickly. Too perfectly formed.

"Sister Benedetta, I saw someone."

"You should return to your cell, Sister." Benedetta's voice cut through her protest like a blade. "The night air is unwholesome for those of advancing years. I will fetch a lamp so we might inspect the door properly."

Costanza followed her to fetch the lamp, her mind racing. She had seen someone leave. A man. And Benedetta had appeared mere seconds later, positioned perfectly to intercept.

When they returned, Costanza's blood ran cold.

The door stood closed and bolted. Someone had secured it while they were gone.

Sister Benedetta examined the mechanism, her face smooth and blank as polished marble. "You see? The door is properly secured. The bolt holds fast." She straightened. "You're exhausted, Sister. Imagining things in the darkness. It happens to all of us, especially at your age. The shadows play tricks."

The scheme was perfect. Costanza could prove nothing.

Benedetta's eyes held a message that required no words: *See nothing. Speak of nothing. Because what you saw has already been erased.*

"Of course, Sister Benedetta. You're quite right. I must have been mistaken."

"I'm certain you were." Benedetta took the lamp. "Come. I'll walk with you to the dormitory."

As they climbed the stairs, Costanza felt the weight of what she'd witnessed. Someone had re-secured that door while they were fetching the lamp. Someone was watching, managing, controlling every piece of evidence. The conspiracy was larger and more careful than she had imagined.

* * *

THE NEXT MORNING, Costanza found the village blacksmith, Giovan Pietro Mollo, waiting by the service entrance as she had arranged. She closed the heavy oak door behind him, the click of the latch sounding like a pistol shot in the quiet morning.

"Messere Mollo. I need your help."

He looked up, cap in hand, his weathered face curious. "Sister Costanza. Is the hinge broken again?"

"No. The garden door. Someone is using it during the Great Silence. I need it secured properly. With a new lock that cannot be opened without a specific key."

His face went still. "That door already has a bolt."

"It is not adequate now." Her hands clenched inside her sleeves. "I need a new lock installed. One that requires a key only I possess."

"Such work costs money. The Reverend Mother would need to approve."

"I will pay for it myself. From my own allowance. And I do not want the Reverend Mother told."

The silence was terrible. She watched understanding move across his face.

"What did you see, Sister?"

"Nothing I can prove. But I know someone is coming through that door. And I need it stopped."

He studied her for a long moment, then nodded. "I will install it tomorrow evening during Vespers. But Sister Costanza if there is real danger here, hiding it from the Reverend Mother may not be wise."

"The Reverend Mother sees what she wishes to see." The bitterness surprised even her. "And what she doesn't wish to see, she ignores."

His jaw tightened. "Be careful. If someone is bold enough to violate enclosure repeatedly, they will not take kindly to being thwarted."

* * *

MOLLO ARRIVED THE following evening during Vespers. Costanza stood guard while he worked. He tested the new iron mechanism again and again until the heavy bolt moved with smooth certainty, driven by the turn of a complex key. When he finished, he held out two heavy iron keys.

"One for you, one for the Reverend Mother."

"Thank you." Costanza closed her hand around both keys.

"This lock will hold," he said quietly. "But Sister... if someone wants in badly enough, there are other doors."

"I know." She closed her fingers around the keys, feeling their teeth bite into her flesh. "But at least these are mine."

After he left, she stood alone in the corridor. She had done something irrevocable. Had taken action without permission, commissioned work in secret.

She threaded one key onto a leather cord and hung it around her neck, tucking it beneath her habit. The second key she hid at the bottom of her trunk.

A small act of defiance against whatever darkness was moving through Santa Margherita's corridors.

That night, she pressed her hand against her chest, feeling the outline of the key against her skin. It gave her no comfort. Only the cold certainty that she had declared herself an obstacle.

And obstacles had a way of being removed.

Three days later, the removal began.

Costanza was scrubbing the refectory floor when a shadow fell across her work. She looked up to see Sister Virginia standing over her. Sister Ottavia stood just behind her, her face pale and tight.

"Sister Costanza." Virginia's voice was low, trembling with strange energy. "I understand we have you to thank for the new lock on the garden door."

Costanza scrambled to her feet, wiping her hands on her apron. "I…I thought it necessary for the convent's safety, Sister."

"Safety?" Virginia stepped closer. The air around her seemed to vibrate. "Or arrogance? You take it upon yourself to modify the enclosure? To restrict the movements of your sisters?"

"I restrict only those who violate the Rule," Costanza said, her voice shaking but her chin high.

The blow came out of nowhere.

Virginia's hand struck Costanza's face with a force that sent her staggering back against the heavy table. The sound of the slap echoed through the empty hall.

Costanza gasped, clutching her cheek. She tasted blood.

"You insolent cow," Virginia hissed. She grabbed the front of Costanza's habit, bunching the rough wool in her fists. "You think a piece of iron gives you power over me? You think you can lock me in like a child?"

"Sister Virginia!" Ottavia grabbed Virginia's arm, pulling her back. "Stop! Someone will hear!"

Virginia shoved Costanza away. Costanza hit the stone wall hard, the breath leaving her lungs.

"Let them hear," Virginia spat, though she allowed Ottavia to pull her back. Her eyes were black with fury. "Let everyone know what happens to those who spy on their betters."

She pointed a shaking finger at Costanza. "This isn't over. You may have your key, Sister. But you have no idea what you've started."

They swept out of the room, leaving Costanza sliding down the wall to the floor. She touched her throbbing cheek, her fingers coming away red.

She had been right. The darkness wasn't just moving through the corridors. It was already in control.

* * *

THREE NIGHTS LATER, Virginia stood at her chamber window watching darkness settle. Behind her, Benedetta sat mending.

"Costanza has sealed the garden door," Virginia said. "A new lock. Two keys, both in her possession."

The needle paused. "She is the portress. You knew she would eventually."

"Yes. But I thought we'd have more time."

For over a year, Gian Paolo had been entering through that door. Three times a week, sometimes four. They had perfected the timing, the choreography of violation.

And now it was gone.

Virginia moved to her writing table and pulled open the bottom drawer. Inside, wrapped in cloth, was the heavy iron ring that held keys to every exterior door in the convent.

She lifted it. The weight felt obscene in her hands.

"If I give these to him, he can have copies made."

"Then you've enabled his access to every entrance in this building," Benedetta said. "Not just one door. All of them."

Virginia stared at the keys. "I could stop this. Right now. Tell him the risk is too great."

The silence stretched.

"But you won't," Benedetta said.

"No. I won't." Virginia looked up. "Because if I stop now, what was it all for? A year of risk and sin, and then I just walk away?" She picked up the keys again. "It's too late for repair. I'm already damned. Might as well be damned for something worth the price."

"That's not true."

"It's true." Virginia wrapped the keys in their cloth, her hands shaking. "At least when he touches me, I feel something. At least when he looks at me, I exist as something other than the Count's discarded daughter."

She tucked the wrapped keys inside her habit.

"I'll pass them through tonight. In the herb garden. He'll take them to Cesare Ferrari."

"Domenico's son?" Benedetta looked up sharply. "The blacksmith?"

"Yes. Cesare is discreet. Not like that fool Mollo who Costanza hired. Cesare understands the value of silence. Gian Paolo says he can have copies made and return the originals before dawn."

"And if you're seen?"

"Then I'm seen. I'm tired of being careful, Benedetta. Tired of living like I'm already dead."

"Virginia, wait."

But she was already gone.

* * *

VIRGINIA WAITED UNTIL deep night, then made her way through darkened corridors toward the herb garden. The key ring hung heavy inside her habit. Her hands trembled. Every shadow looked like Costanza.

The herb garden window was set low in the eastern wall, partially hidden by overgrown rosemary. She had chosen this spot carefully, isolated, shadowed, difficult to observe.

Her hands shook so badly it took three tries to push the window open. The hinges creaked. She froze, listening. Heard only her own ragged breathing.

She pulled the wrapped keys from her habit and set them on the stone windowsill. The metal scraped against stone. Then she withdrew into the shadows and waited.

Minutes crawled by. Then, soft as breath, a shadow appeared at the window. A hand reached through, male, large, familiar. Fingers found the wrapped keys, lifted them with practiced ease.

The hand withdrew. The keys were gone.

Virginia pressed against the cold wall. Hours stretched ahead while those keys were copied by Cesare Ferrari's forge, while evidence of her betrayal was multiplied and made permanent.

She couldn't stay here. She had to return to her chamber.

As she turned to leave, she heard footsteps. Soft. Approaching from the dormitory stairs. Virginia's blood turned to ice. She pressed herself against the wall.

A shape appeared at the corridor's end. Tall. Slender. Sister Costanza.

She carried no candle. She moved directly toward the herb garden window. Directly toward Virginia.

Virginia couldn't breathe. Her mind raced through a thousand excuses and discarded them all. *She's seen me. It's over.*

Ten paces away. Virginia's hand twisted her habit into knots. Five paces.

Then Costanza stopped. Turned her head. Looked directly at the shadows where Virginia stood frozen. Costanza took a step toward her.

"Sister Virginia." The voice came from behind Costanza. Sister Ottavia appeared at the corridor's end, her face pale. "Sister Virginia, are you there? I heard sounds."

Ottavia stopped and stared at Costanza. At the open window. At Virginia pressed against the wall.

"I couldn't sleep," Ottavia said quickly. Too quickly. "I went to look for Sister Virginia. To ask for help with my prayers."

The lie was clumsy. Transparent. But it broke the moment.

Costanza turned from Virginia to Ottavia. The bruise on Costanza's cheek from days ago was still yellow and purple in the moonlight. She touched it instinctively as she looked at them.

"Sister Ottavia. You should be in your cell."

"I know. I'm sorry." Ottavia moved forward, positioning herself between them. "I was worried. About my spiritual state. Sister Virginia has been helping me."

It gave Virginia room to move. To step away from the wall. To cross to Ottavia's side.

"Yes," Virginia heard herself say. "We've been meeting to discuss Sister Ottavia's spiritual concerns. I must have left the window open by accident. The air grows stale in these corridors."

Costanza looked at the open window. At the two women standing together. "The window should not be open during the Great Silence. It poses a security risk."

"Of course." Virginia moved to the window. Closed it with shaking hands. "You're quite right."

She met Costanza's eyes. Saw the knowledge there. The certainty. The understanding that something had just happened, something that couldn't be proven but couldn't be denied.

"Thank you for your vigilance, Sister Costanza. Your attention to the convent's security is... admirable."

Costanza's jaw tightened. "Someone must protect this place. Even when those charged with that duty fail to do so."

"Indeed," Virginia said softly. "We must all do our duty. No matter the cost."

They stood in silence. Then Costanza turned and walked away. Her footsteps faded.

Only when she was gone did Virginia's legs give out. She sagged against the wall. Ottavia caught her.

"Did she see him take the keys?" Virginia whispered.

"I don't know. I don't think so. But she knows something happened. She knows you were here."

"She can't prove it."

"She doesn't need to prove it. She just needs to watch. To wait. To catch you the next time."

Virginia had thought she could control the risk, manage the exposure. But she'd been seen. Almost caught.

"We need to go," Ottavia said urgently. "Before she comes back."

Virginia nodded. Let Ottavia guide her back toward her chamber, back toward the narrow bed where she would lie awake until dawn, listening for the sound of returning footsteps.

Listening for the moment when those copied keys would appear at the window. When she would have to leave her chamber again, exposed and watched, to retrieve them before sunrise.

The affair had just become infinitely more dangerous.

And there was no way to stop it now.

* * *

Late 1600

THE LATIN DECLENSION faltered. The novice, a miller's daughter with hands too rough for the quill, stared at the parchment as if it were a cipher.

Virginia's hand moved before thought could check it.

Crack.

The sound ricocheted off the stone walls. The child stumbled back, palm pressed to a cheek already blooming crimson, eyes wide and wet.

"Again." Virginia's voice carried the brittle snap of dry wood. "And this time, demonstrate rudimentary intelligence."

The girl stammered through the conjugation. Around the long table, other novices kept their heads bowed, faces carefully empty. They had learned the lesson well: sympathy only drew the hawk's eye.

Sister Costanza waited in the corridor shadows after the lesson.

"That was excessive." Costanza kept her voice low, barely stirring the dust motes. "She is thirteen. She attempts her best."

"Her best is inadequate." Virginia swept past, her habit brushing the limestone. "If she cannot master simple grammar, she has no place in this order."

"She has a place because her family purchased it." Costanza's footsteps followed, soft but persistent. "As your father did. As ours did. Some of us, however, remember the terror of those first nights."

Heat flushed Virginia's neck. She spun. "You lecture me on compassion? You, who added a lock to the garden door to bar a man you had no right to judge?"

Costanza's face drained of color. Her fingers drifted to her cheek, hovering over the faint yellow bruise that remained from weeks ago.

"I performed my duty." The older nun's voice trembled. "I protected the sanctity of this house. A concept you seem to have discarded."

"Leave me." The command emerged as a whisper, sharper than a scream. "Before I forget myself again."

Costanza fled.

Virginia stood alone in the empty passage, hands trembling. The silence stretched, heavy and accusing. She had become the thing she once loathed—a tyrant using power to mask the rot inside, inflicting pain because her own burden had grown too heavy to carry.

* * *

REVEREND MOTHER BEATRICE folded her hands over the open ledger. The parchment smelled of gall ink and old paper.

"The household expenditure reduction is noted, Reverend Mother," Virginia said from the table's far end. She did not sit. "Page forty indicates the properties yield more revenue now than in a decade."

Beatrice studied the columns. Impeccable figures. Too impeccable. Under Virginia's hand, the convent's income had surged, and in the margins lay those anonymous donations, sums appearing without explanation, like manna or bribes.

The source required no guessing.

"Your management is efficient," Beatrice said, refusing to look up. "But efficiency is not the sole virtue of religious life. Humility. Obedience. Charity."

"I demonstrate charity by ensuring this community eats." Virginia's voice hardened. "I demonstrate obedience by enforcing the Rule. And as for humility..."

She let the word hang, severed.

The assembled sisters stared at their hands. The air in the Chapter house grew thin. They feared the young Vicaress more than their Prioress.

"Sister Virginia." Beatrice met her gaze. "We are mothers to these women, not jailers."

"Discipline is a form of love, Reverend Mother." Virginia closed her ledger. The heavy thud made two sisters flinch. "If standards slip, we fail our duty to God. I ensure this house remains orderly."

She turned and swept from the room, habit billowing like a judge's robe. The remaining sisters did not exhale until her footsteps faded.

Beatrice touched the silver cross at her breast. She had prayed for Virginia to find strength. God had answered, but the strength now served only to crush them.

* * *

NIGHT TRANSFORMED THE convent. Ottavia and Benedetta moved through the corridors after Compline, extinguishing lamps. Doors crashed against frames, sudden, violent slams that sent vibrations through the floorboards.

Something dangerous walks tonight.

Virginia made her own rounds. She drifted through the dark like smoke, checking latches, pausing at cracks in the wood. The boldness of it should have sickened her. Instead, a savage satisfaction curled in her gut.

Let them listen. Let them know. Who will they tell?

The dormitories lay silent. Fear had taught them to sleep.

* * *

BUT WALLS COULD not contain the rot. In the schoolrooms, girls exchanged glances and smothered giggles. The scandal had become as familiar as the Angelus.

Dusk settled over the courtyard. Virginia crossed the stones after Vespers, the scent of damp earth rising with the chill. Near the well, a cluster of students huddled.

"...Sister Virginia and Signor Osio..."

"...mother says he enters through the church..."

"...in her very cell..."

Virginia halted. The blood roared in her ears, drowning the distant chant of prayer.

"Repeat that. "Her voice sliced across the courtyard. The students froze. Sisters emerged from doorways, drawn by the tone.

The speaker, a merchant's daughter, paled.

"Nothing, Sister Virginia," another whispered.

"Nothing?" Virginia advanced. "You spread filth like base creatures and call it nothing?"

The group scattered. Virginia moved faster.

She seized the nearest girl. Fingers dug into soft flesh, finding the bone.

The child screamed. A high, thin sound that shattered the evening peace.

"I should take your eyes." Virginia leaned close, hissing into the girl's face. "I should tear the lying tongue from your mouth and nail it to the chapel door."

"Sister Virginia!"

Reverend Mother Beatrice's voice cracked the air. "Release that child."

Virginia's hand sprang open. The girl stumbled back, sobbing, clutching her arm where red crescents already darkened the skin.

Silence descended. Virginia stood in the center of the ring, chest heaving, hands curled into claws. The faces around her reflected her own image. Madwoman. Monster.

"Go to your cell," Beatrice said. Her voice shook. "Go, before I forget my vows."

Virginia walked through the parting crowd, chin high, refusing to shrink. Only when the heavy oak of her cell door clicked shut did she slide to the floor.

She had threatened a child. She had peeled back the mask.

Yet the consequences defied expectation. No punishment came. Beatrice pretended the incident had never occurred. But the silence in the corridors deepened. The students no longer whispered; they simply ceased to breathe when she passed.

* * *

WEEKS BLED INTO months. One night, Virginia approached Ottavia's and Benedetta's cell. The door, usually ajar, sat firm in its frame.

She knocked.

No immediate answer. Then, the scuff of furniture. The rustle of linen.

A low laugh, masculine and quickly stifled, roughened the silence.

Virginia's breath hitched.

The door creaked slowly open. Ottavia filled the gap, wimple askew, cheeks flushed with high color. Behind her, shadows stretched long and thin.

"Virginia." Ottavia's eyes held panic and a strange, glittery defiance. "I did not expect you."

Virginia looked past her. Rumpled sheets. A wine cup on the table. And a figure rising from the edge of the bed, adjusting a doublet with unhurried grace.

"Gian Paolo?" The name tasted like ash. "Here?"

Ottavia said nothing. Her chin lifted.

Gian Paolo stepped into the light. "Virginia." His tone held the warmth of a greeting in the piazza, not a discovery in a nun's cell. "I believed you were occupied."

Virginia turned and ran.

She fled through the cloister, the stone biting through her slippers. In the chapel, she collapsed on a bench, pressing a fist to her mouth to stifle the scream tearing at her throat.

He was hers. She had damned herself for him.

Yet as the tears came, hot and bitter, cold logic settled beneath them. She had invited Ottavia into the conspiracy. She had opened the door.

And Gian Paolo, had she truly believed a man who seduced a bride of Christ would keep faith with her?

The grief hollowed her out. What remained was harder than rage. Resignation. She had woven this trap; now she must inhabit it.

* * *

THE ROT SPREAD. Within a week, Virginia found Benedetta in the sacristy, emerging from the priest's entrance.

Musk and male sweat hung heavy in the incense-laden air.

"You as well?" Virginia whispered.

Benedetta smoothed her habit. Her eyes remained dry, flinty. "Do not judge me, Virginia. You opened the gate. You made us watch. Did you believe we were carved of stone? That we could witness your ecstasy and feel nothing?"

She moved to the basin, plunging hands into the water. "This serves a purpose. When the investigation comes, and it will, three compromised women are harder to believe than one. Confusion protects us."

"Does he come to you often?"

"Often enough." Benedetta dried her hands. "Not as often as to you. You remain the favorite. We are merely... diversions."

Virginia left without a word. The demotion from beloved to preferred burned worse than the betrayal.

* * *

SISTER SILVIA JOINED the circle before the month turned. The knowledge moved through Santa Margherita like a fever. Gian Paolo walked the halls as a lord inspecting his holdings because she had given him permission to duplicate all the keys.

Virginia's jealousy became a physical weight, pressing on her chest. She searched his face for signs of waning affection, but his dark eyes revealed nothing. He smiled the same smile. He whispered the same lies.

She endured it. The alternative, absence, was a void she could not face. She would share him rather than lose him.

The affair settled into a grotesque domesticity. Gifts arrived openly: poultry, fish, exotic fruit. Virginia served the wine he sent to the senior sisters. In return, she sent preserves and embroidered handkerchiefs.

And she mended.

Susanna, the servant, arrived one morning with a bundle wrapped in fine linen. "For you, Sister Virginia. From the Osio household."

Virginia unfolded the cloth. Linen collars, frayed at the edges, stained with sweat.

She sat at her small table. The needle pierced the fabric, in and out, a rhythm of wives and mothers.

Sister Bianca paused in the doorway that afternoon. Her plain face crumpled in confusion. "Sister Virginia? What are you doing?"

Virginia looked up. For a heartbeat, the defiance flared. Then the mask descended.

"I mend Signor Osio's collars." Her tone brooked no argument. "Is he not my vassal? Our lands adjoin. We maintain mutual interests." She snapped the thread. "Besides, I do it for his mother. A poor woman losing her mind. Would you deny Christian charity when she has been so generous to the convent?"

Bianca nodded, mute, and withdrew. The pretense had worn so thin it revealed the bone beneath.

* * *

"SENATOR TAVERNA VISITED yesterday." Reverend Mother Beatrice stood at her study window, back to the room. The morning light haloed her veil.

"He investigates irregularities in Milanese convents," Beatrice continued. "He asked of you. Of gifts. Of visitors."

A chill settled between Virginia's shoulder blades.

"I told him you correspond with the Osio family regarding property boundaries." Beatrice turned. Her face looked carved from gray stone. "I told him Signora Osio, his mother, is a benefactor. That all is documented."

She leaned forward, hands gripping the chair back. "I cannot lie again, Sister Virginia. The next man who asks receives the truth. Do you understand?"

"Yes, Reverend Mother."

"See that he has no cause to return."

Virginia bowed her head. The line had been drawn, but she stood miles past it, looking back at a shore she could no longer reach.

* * *

VIRGINIA BECAME HOLLOW. Passion, once a fire, now smoked and sputtered, choked by routine and jealousy.

Nights without him meant sleepless hours staring into the dark. Who was he sleeping with tonight? Mornings meant kneeling before the Madonna, praying with a desperation that bordered on madness.

One evening during Compline, she knelt beside Ottavia. The Latin chant washed over them. In the flicker of the altar candles, the truth took shape.

She was damned. Not by a single act, but by the chain of choices. By the slow death of conscience.

The bronze bell tolled. Winter approached. Another year dying.

She returned to her cell. Gian Paolo waited inside by the window, silhouette cut against the moonlight. He reached for her. She went to him.

Later, alone, she pressed fists into her eyes until sparks danced.

God remained silent.

Outside, the Monza bells marked the hour. She was a coward. They all were. Their fear had built a hell and christened it a holy place.

As sleep dragged at her, a sound drifted through the thin wall. Soft laughter. A woman's voice, then a lower murmur. Virginia pulled the blanket to her chin. She bit down on her knuckle until the copper taste of blood filled her mouth.

Chapter Seven
1601

Early 1601

THE LOCK ON outer door of the parlatory was absurdly simple. A child with a bent wire could have picked it, yet the nuns of Santa Margherita believed it secured their virtue against the world. Father Paolo Arrigone didn't need a wire, of course; the door yielded to a firm push, the latch barely catching. He stepped into the room, the scent of cold stone and old incense greeting him like a familiar friend.

He didn't need to look around to know the state of the convent. He could smell the laxity in the air, the Prioress's weak authority, the servants running commissions for coin, the nocturnal darkness that concealed more sins than it absolved.

He moved to the grille and ran a finger along the iron lattice. Rust stained his skin. Even the barriers here were decaying.

Through Gian Paolo, he had studied Sister Virginia de Leyva for months now. He had seen the transformation, the way ecstasy had curdled into addiction, the way jealousy ate at her features when Gian Paolo's attention wandered. She was beautiful, intelligent, and desperately unhappy. She was a woman who had given everything for a man who treated her devotion as casually as he treated a tavern wager.

Arrigone smiled in the dim light. He would succeed where other men failed. The debt Osio owed him was substantial, but he did not want coin. He wanted the satisfaction of taking for himself what he had helped another man win. He wanted to prove that intellect and eloquent speech were more powerful than the crude physical fumbling of a soldier.

Steps echoed in the corridor. Three sets.

Virginia arrived with Benedetta and Ottavia flanking her like guards. She positioned herself behind the iron grille, hands folded in her sleeves. The winter light from the high window washed her face in gray, highlighting the dark circles beneath her eyes.

"Father Arrigone." Her voice was a flat line, stripping the title of reverence. "Sister Benedetta said you had something of importance to tell me."

Arrigone leaned forward, resting his hands on the wooden ledge. He let the silence stretch, watching her breath plume in the biting air.

"Indeed, Sister Virginia. I thought you should know that your friend Gian Paolo Osio has been... active. Outside these walls." He kept his tone solicitous, heavy with paternal concern. "The Lady Clara Rabbia has arrived in Monza. They have been seen together. At the theater. Walking in the public gardens."

He watched for the flinch. It was small. A tightening at the corner of her mouth. A sudden stillness in her posture.

"What does it matter to me?" She lifted her chin, staring somewhere past his shoulder. "Signor Osio's affairs are no concern of mine."

The denial was too quick. Too practiced.

"Sister Virginia." Arrigone dropped his voice, an intimate murmur meant to slip through the iron bars. "There is no need for pretense. Not with me." He paused, allowing the words to land. "Tell me... does he still write to you? Does he still call your soul a 'white garden waiting for the sun'?"

Virginia froze. Her eyes snapped to his face, wide and dark. That phrase. It was from the third letter. The one she kept folded beneath her mattress.

"Or perhaps," Arrigone continued, his smile slight, "he has run out of the phrases I lent him."

Her hands emerged from her sleeves, gripping the iron bars. Her knuckles bleached white. "What are you saying?"

"I am saying that Gian Paolo Osio cannot distinguish a sonnet from a grocery list." Arrigone stepped closer, close enough that the scent of wine and parchment clinging to his cassock would reach her. "Every refined phrase. Every reference to Petrarch and Dante. Every profession of spiritual yearning that made you weep... I wrote them."

The silence in the parlatory was absolute.

"You..." Her voice cracked. "You are telling me he didn't write them?"

"Not a word." The admission tasted sweet. This was the moment he had rehearsed in the dark. "Osio wanted you, but he lacked the wit to court a woman of your intelligence. I remedied that deficiency. I translated his crude desires into the language of courtly love."

He watched the horror dawn on her face. It wasn't just shock; it was a fundamental unmooring of her reality.

"It was my eloquence that seduced you, Virginia. My mind that understood yours. Every time your heart quickened at the poetry, you were responding to me. To what I created for you."

He waited for the inevitable shift. The moment she realized that the connection she cherished belonged to him, not the brute who delivered the paper.

But Virginia didn't soften. She backed away as if he were a leper. "You wrote them," she whispered, the words mechanical. "All of them. The prayers. The vows."

"Precisely." Arrigone spread his hands. "Which is why I am here. To offer you the reality, not the proxy. I am in love with you, Virginia. I have been consumed by it for months. I want to do what Gian Paolo has done. I want what he has taken from you."

"You're mad."

"I am devoted." He pressed against the ledge, his voice urgent. "Don't you see? You gave yourself to him based on my words. You let him into your bed because of my thoughts. Logic dictates that I am the true object of your affection."

"I don't believe you." She shook her head, a violent, jerky motion. "You're lying. You're trying to manipulate me."

"Then I will prove it." He straightened, smoothing his cassock. "I will write a letter to Sister Ottavia. I will use the same script. The same phrasing. The same ink. You will see with your own eyes that the hand that wrote your love letters belongs to me."

Virginia stared at him, her chest heaving with shallow breaths. Then, with a sudden, violent motion, she struck her palm hard against the grille. The sound cracked like a pistol shot in the small room.

"I love you as a priest through Jesus Christ our Lord," she shouted through the wood, her voice trembling with hysteria. "I will pray for your soul. But that is all I will ever offer you. Now or in eternity."

Footsteps retreated, rapid, panicked, fading into the stone labyrinth of the convent.

Arrigone stood alone in the silence. The cold of the room pressed against his skin. His hands, resting on the ledge, trembled slightly. This had not gone according to plan.

But as the initial sting of rejection faded, calculation took its place. She hadn't threatened to expose him. She couldn't. She was too compromised, too deep in the mud herself to point a finger at his stains.

He adjusted his collar and turned to the door. She would need time. And proof. He would give her both.

* * *

THE LETTER ARRIVED the next day. It came through the usual channels—a servant to the portress, the portress to Ottavia. A simple piece of folded parchment, innocuous as a lender's receipt.

Ottavia opened it in the safety of Virginia's cell. Benedetta stood guard at the door. As Ottavia scanned the lines, the color drained from her round face.

"It's the same," she whispered. She held the parchment out as if it were contaminated. "The script. The slant of the letters. It's identical to the ones from Gian Paolo."

Virginia took the paper. Her fingers felt numb, distant.

> *Dearest Sister Ottavia, I write to you as proof of what I revealed yesterday... Observe the script, the phrasing, the learned allusions that follow...*

She recognized the hand. It was the hand that had courted her. The loop of the 'L', the sharp cross of the 't'. It was the handwriting of the man she loved.

Except it wasn't.

"It's true," Virginia said. The room seemed to tilt. "Everything he said. Gian Paolo couldn't have written those letters. He doesn't have the Latin. He doesn't know Petrarch." She pressed a hand to her mouth, stifling a sick laugh. "I corrected his grammar once, in the garden. He laughed and said he was a soldier, not a scholar. I thought he was being modest."

Benedetta took the letter, her sharp eyes dissecting the text. "This doesn't mean Osio felt nothing," she said, her voice pragmatic. "Many men hire scribes. It is a common deception."

"It means I fell in love with a ghost," Virginia said. She walked to the window. The garden below was dead, skeletal branches scratching at a gray sky. "I gave myself, my body, my soul, my vows, for words. And the man who wrote them is a priest who thinks I am payment for services rendered."

"What will you do?" Ottavia asked.

Virginia stared at her reflection in the dark glass. A stranger looked back, hollow-eyed, gaunt, a nun in a costume that no longer fit.

"I will do nothing," she said. "I cannot confront Gian Paolo. I cannot demand honesty when my entire life is a lie." She turned back to them, her face hardening. "But Arrigone has made a mistake. He thinks revealing this gives him power. He thinks I will be impressed."

She took the letter from Benedetta and tore it. Once. Twice. The sound of ripping parchment was loud in the quiet cell.

"He is worse than Gian Paolo. At least Osio's sins are honest. He is a brute, but he is a sincere brute. Arrigone..." She dropped the pieces into a cloth bag. "He prostituted his mind to help one man seduce me and now tries to claim me as a prize. He is a parasite."

* * *

THREE DAYS LATER, another letter arrived. Virginia recognized the script before the seal was broken.

My dearest Virginia, I cannot sleep for thinking of you...

It was a masterpiece of rhetoric. It spoke of celestial perfection, of martyrs, of a love that transcended the physical even as it begged for it. It was exactly the kind of letter that had once made her heart race.

Now, it made her stomach turn.

"He thinks this will work," Benedetta said, reading over her shoulder. "He is arrogant enough to believe the strategy will succeed twice."

"He forgets one thing," Virginia said. She didn't read past the first paragraph. She tore the paper into confetti with deliberate, vicious movements. "Those letters worked because I thought they came from a lover. Knowing they come from him... it is like finding a maggot in a peach."

She handed the bag of scraps to Benedetta. "Give this to him. Tell him this is my answer. The only answer he will ever get."

"He won't stop," Benedetta warned. "Men like him interpret silence as a pause, not a refusal."

"Let him try," Virginia said.

But the bravado felt thin. Arrigone was a priest. He walked in circles she could not touch. If he chose to talk, if he chose to whisper the right words to the right Bishop...

* * *

A WEEK PASSED. The tension in the convent tightened like a winch.

In the classroom, young Isabella Marchetti stood before Virginia's desk, tears trembling on her lashes. The girl had butchered the Latin conjugation for the third time.

"Again," Virginia said. The cold from the window was seeping into her bones.

Isabella stammered. "*A-amo... amas... amat...*" She faltered on the plural.

Virginia's hand moved before her mind engaged. The slap was sharp, a crack of flesh on flesh that silenced the room. Isabella stumbled back, a red mark blooming on her pale cheek.

"Again!" Virginia commanded. Her voice wasn't her own. It was a vessel for the rage boiling in her gut, the humiliation, the fear. "Do not waste my time with your incompetence!"

Isabella sobbed, shaking too hard to speak.

Virginia raised her hand again.

"Sister Virginia." Benedetta's voice cut through the red haze. She stood in the doorway, her face pale.

Virginia froze. She looked at her hand, suspended in the air. She looked at the terrified child.

"A moment," Benedetta said, her voice steel.

In the corridor, Benedetta gripped her arm hard enough to bruise. "What are you doing? These are children. Daughters of our patrons. You cannot strike them like a stable master."

"Don't tell me what I can do," Virginia snapped. She pulled away, breathless. Then she caught her reflection in the polished brass plate on the wall.

The face looking back was twisted, ugly. It was the face of a woman who hurt children because she could not hurt the men who used her.

"I..." The anger drained away, leaving her hollow. "I will dismiss them early."

She stood alone in the empty classroom for a long time, pressing her palms against the wooden lectern until the shaking stopped. Arrigone had taken even this from her. He had poisoned her sanctuary.

* * *

THAT EVENING, THE strategy shifted. This letter from Arrigone was different. Formal. Businesslike.

Sister Virginia, I write regarding my two nieces. I wish to place them in your care as students at Santa Margherita...

It was a trap. A brilliant, administrative trap.

Virginia stared at the parchment. Refusing the nieces without cause would raise questions she couldn't answer. The convent needed the tuition. The Prioress would demand an explanation for turning away the kin of a priest.

But accepting them meant he had a legitimate reason to visit. To write. To check on their progress. To stand in the parlatory and discuss their education while his eyes undressed her.

He had found the crack in the wall.

She picked up her quill, her hand heavy. She wrote a note to the Prioress, confirming the enrollment for the spring term, but adding a specific instruction: *All communication regarding the Arrigone girls must be directed to the Office of the Prioress.*

She tore the rest of his letter, the paragraphs where he slipped back into professions of love and burned them in the brazier.

That night, the wind howled around the convent towers. Virginia lay in the dark, listening to the old wood groan. She had won the skirmish, perhaps. She had blocked his direct path.

But she realized now that Arrigone was not a man who accepted defeat. He was a man who studied the board, who looked for the loose pawn, the unprotected flank. He would keep pushing. Keep testing.

And eventually, he would find one.

Chapter Eight
1602

Early 1602

TERROR ARRIVED EACH morning, sharp as the nausea that drove Virginia from her bed to kneel over the chamber pot. She pressed her palms to the cold tile and waited for her body to finish its daily betrayal.

Several months had passed since Gian Paolo began using the duplicate keys. Several months since the last fragile boundaries had dissolved, since she surrendered what remained of her vows in the darkness of her chamber while Benedetta kept watch.

And now this. Three months, perhaps four, since her courses had failed to arrive. Tenderness in her breasts made even the coarse wool of her habit scour like sand. Sickness arrived with cruel predictability at dawn, leaving her hollow.

Virginia rose on shaking legs and went to the basin. She splashed icy water over her face until the room stopped spinning.

Two taps, then three. Benedetta's signal.

Virginia opened the door. Dawn light caught the hard angles of Benedetta's face. Behind her stood Ottavia, twisting her hands in her scapular.

"Again?" Benedetta asked. No sympathy softened her tone. She scanned Virginia's pale skin with a merchant's calculating eye.

Virginia nodded. Her throat remained too raw for speech.

Benedetta slipped inside, Ottavia following, and eased the door shut. The Vicaress's chamber afforded them this small mercy, a space where they could speak without the convent's ears pressing against the wood.

"How many weeks since the bleeding should have come?"

"Twelve. Maybe fourteen. I cannot be sure."

Silence filled the room. Benedetta did not flinch. She warned of this months ago, but a pragmatic coldness settled into her features.

Ottavia sank onto the chair by the desk, hands clamped over her mouth. "Oh, Virginia."

"You must consult Rainerio Roncino," Benedetta said. "The apothecary near the market square. Today. Before the swell of your belly betrays us all."

"I cannot."

"You can, and you will." Exhaustion carved lines into Benedetta's face, but her stance remained iron-rigid. "If you will not go, then I will order the herbs. He is discreet. He asks no questions when the silver is clean."

She paused. "I never imagined I would cross this line. I have written letters. I have arranged meetings. I have stood watch while you violated every vow we took. But this..." Her hand swept toward the chamber pot, the sour air. "This is different."

Virginia managed a nod.

"I make myself guilty in ways that damn me beyond what we have already done," Benedetta continued, her voice threaded with a fine tremor. "Not just of aiding your affair, but of something darker. I do this because friendship has bound us since childhood. Because I cannot watch you face this alone."

"Benedetta..."

"But do not mistake weakness for willingness." The words cut clean. "Do not assume that because I help you now, I will do so again without cost. Every time you allow Gian Paolo past these gates, you roll dice with our futures. Eventually, your body will refuse to expel what it was designed to carry. No herbs from Roncino will save you then."

She stepped closer. "I will not abandon you. But you test the limits of what I can bear. There will come a day when I have nothing left to give. On that day, Virginia, you will be alone."

The truth hung between them, spoken without cruelty, yet without gentleness.

Ottavia rose and laid a hand on Virginia's shoulder. "We will help you," she whispered, tears streaking her round cheeks. "Whatever you need. But please, Virginia, be careful. I cannot bear much more of this fear."

Virginia covered Ottavia's hand with her own. Sweet, faithful Ottavia, drawn into this conspiracy by loyalty alone.

The three women stood as first light filtered through the window, bound by secrets that grew heavier with the rising sun.

* * *

RAINERIO RONCINO'S MAIN shop occupied a narrow building near the square, wedged between a chandler and a cloth merchant. His windows displayed jars of dried herbs, glass bottles of tinctures glinting amber and green, wooden trays of roots. The public face of his trade, legitimate offerings that let wives and mothers enter without shame.

Inside, the shop smelled of wholesome things: chamomile and rosemary at the front, dried lavender hanging from the rafters, peppermint and fennel in neat rows. Housewives came here for tisanes to soothe colicky babies; merchants came for salves to heal winter-chapped hands. Everything clean, proper, fit for open talk in Monza's streets.

But Roncino also maintained a second establishment down a narrow alley branching off the square. This shop boasted no bright displays. Only a weathered door marked with a small carved mortar and pestle signaled its purpose. The single window, small and dusty, revealed nothing.

Behind those thick walls, darker transactions occurred. Preparations wives could not request in daylight. Herbs whose purposes remained unspoken. To this second shop women came after nightfall, faces hidden beneath heavy veils, silver coins clutched in trembling hands. It was too early in the day, so Benedetta went to the main shop instead.

Virginia sent Benedetta with silver hidden in her sleeve. Benedetta went alone in the quiet hour after None, when most sisters were occupied. She knew which door to seek.

She pushed the weathered wood open and stepped into a dim interior reeking of bitter roots. Roncino stood alone behind the counter, grinding something in a stone mortar. He glanced up. His expression remained as neutral as carved stone. He was a small, neat man in his middle years, sleeves rolled to reveal forearms roped with muscle. His hands moved with quick precision. His eyes, the color of winter mud, revealed nothing. In the main shop, he played the affable neighbor. Here, he asked no questions and met no gaze longer than necessary.

"Sister," he said. Voice empty.

Benedetta approached the counter and withdrew the coins, setting them down with a soft clink. No need to explain. Nuns did not come here for chamomile.

"Herbs to dispel a babe from the womb," she said. "Enough for a full course."

Roncino did not blink. "Pennyroyal, tansy, rue, savin."

His hands moved to the shelves, selecting jars she could not see clearly in the murk. He measured and weighed with clinical attention, wrapping each portion in clean linen, tying the packages with twine, arranging them in a larger cloth bag.

His hands stayed steady. He never once looked at her face. When he finished, he slid the bag across the counter and swept the silver into his palm. "Steep in boiling water. Morning and evening. Proportions are marked. Do not deviate. Too much creates poison; too little creates tragedy."

Benedetta tucked the bag beneath her scapular, its weight pressing against her ribs.

"Will you speak of this?"

Roncino met her eyes for the first time—winter-mud brown and utterly unreadable. "I sell herbs, Sister. What people do with them is not my concern. My business depends on discretion, not judgments."

Beneath the neutral words, the threat lingered. Men like Roncino did not need questions to recognize desperation. He knew. And that knowledge was leverage.

She left without another word, pulling her veil forward. The bag burned against her skin with every step back to the convent.

At Vespers, Benedetta knelt beside Virginia. The altar candles flickered, casting long shadows. Incense thickened the air until Virginia's stomach clenched.

"He did not ask who the herbs were for," Benedetta murmured, lips barely moving. "He worked as if it were chamomile. But he knows, Virginia. Men like Roncino always know. For these type of herbs should never be requested by nuns in a convent. And that knowledge can become a noose."

Another man now held her ruin in his hands. Another thread in the web that tightened with each passing day.

* * *

THAT EVENING, AFTER the Great Silence settled, Virginia went to the kitchen. She measured the dried leaves with trembling fingers, spilling precious fragments onto the table—pennyroyal and tansy, rue and savin. She poured boiling water over them. The bitter scent filled the space, acrid and wrong.

She forced herself to drink. The scalding heat seared her throat; the taste turned her stomach. She clamped a hand over her mouth to keep from retching.

Nothing happened that night. Nor the next.

The herbs did nothing but deepen the sickness. She continued the infusions morning and evening, each cup harder to finish. By the third day, desperation drove her to increase the portions.

Her hands developed a tremor. Dark spots swam at the edges of her vision. Twice during the Divine Office she nearly fainted, clinging to the choir stall until the stone floor stopped tilting.

Sister Bianca noticed. Her plain face creased first with concern, then with something sharper. Not quite suspicion, but awareness. Virginia felt those eyes during meals, cataloging symptoms, drawing conclusions.

On the fourth day, the cramps began.

Pain started low in her belly and radiated outward, as if invisible hands wrung her organs like wet cloth. By midafternoon, the agony broke her composure. She stumbled back to her cell and collapsed onto the bed, knees drawn up beneath her habit.

When Bianca appeared in the doorway an hour later, Virginia's shift clung to her skin, damp with sweat. The room smelled of herbs, fear, and the copper tang of blood.

"Shall I send for the infirmarian?" Bianca's voice held concern, but her gaze took in the pallor, the clenched hands, the rigid jaw. Knowledge sharpened in her eyes.

"No." The word tore through gritted teeth. "Only my monthly courses. They are difficult. It will pass."

"I have never seen them affect you so." Bianca stepped closer. "If the infirmarian examined you—"

"No!" The word rang too loud, edged with panic. Virginia forced her voice down. "Thank you, Sister, but truly, I need only rest."

A lie.

Bianca lingered, mouth pressed into a thin line. Her eyes held Virginia's for a long moment. In that silence, Virginia understood that Bianca suspected. Perhaps not the full truth, but enough to be dangerous.

"I will pray for you, Sister Virginia," Bianca said.

The door closed. Virginia turned her face to the wall and let the silent, scalding tears come.

* * *

THE PAIN INTENSIFIED with the dark. Waves of cramping blinded her. At fourteen weeks, what her body tried to expel was no longer mere tissue.

By Compline, the bleeding began, heavy and dark. Benedetta moved with efficiency, stripping soaked linens. But she did not work alone.

Candida and Silvia slipped into the room, their faces shadowed by the single flickering lamp. The circle was complete now: Benedetta, Ottavia, Candida, Silvia. Four women bound by sin.

"The water is hot," Candida whispered, setting a basin near the bed. She dipped a cloth and wiped Virginia's forehead. Her hands were gentle, but her eyes were terrified.

Silvia stood by the door, listening for footsteps in the corridor. "The others are asleep," she murmured. "But we must be quiet."

Virginia bit into her pillow to smother a scream as a fresh contraction seized her. Benedetta gripped her hand, squeezing until the bones ground together.

"Breathe," Benedetta commanded. "It must come."

Time dissolved into red haze. The smell of iron and sweat filled the small cell. And then, a final, tearing pressure.

Virginia collapsed back against the pillows, gasping.

Benedetta moved between her legs. There was a moment of terrible stillness. The rustle of linen. A pause that stretched too long.

Virginia lifted her head, neck muscles straining. "The child?"

Benedetta held a small bundle wrapped in white cloth. She did not look at Virginia. She looked at Candida, then Silvia. A silent communication passed between them, a shared weight that bowed their shoulders.

"A tiny son," Benedetta said. Her voice was hollow.

Virginia turned her face to the wall. Her hand moved to her empty belly. A son. An heir to the de Leyva name. A son she might have borne with pride in another life. Now, he was refuse. Evidence.

"Is he...?"

"Perfectly formed," Candida whispered, peering over Benedetta's shoulder. Tears tracked through the dust on her cheeks.

"Wrap him," Virginia said. The words tasted like ash. "Do not let me see."

Benedetta wrapped the body with deliberate care, swaddling the small form as if he might still feel the cold. She placed the bundle in the corner, in the shadows.

"What now?" Silvia asked, her voice trembling. "We cannot keep him here. If Bianca returns..."

"Gian Paolo," Virginia said. The name left her lips with the weight of a curse.

"He must take him," Virginia whispered. "He must see what he has done."

Benedetta hesitated. "He does not know?"

"No." Virginia struggled to sit up, though the room swayed violently. "Bring him here. Tell him nothing but that I ask for him. Let him think it is love that calls him."

The women exchanged glances. It was madness to bring him inside now, with the convent waking soon. But Benedetta saw the resolve in Virginia's eyes, the frantic, grief-stricken need to force the man to witness this ruin.

"I will fetch him," Benedetta said.

* * *

TWO HOURS BEFORE dawn, the door creaked open. Gian Paolo entered first, a smile touching his lips, his dark cloak sweeping the floor. He stepped into the room with the easy confidence of a man expecting a lover's embrace. Benedetta followed him in, then turned and locked the door, her back pressing against it.

Gian Paolo's smile faltered.

The room did not smell of perfume or lavender. It smelled of iron, sweat, and sickness. He saw the blood-stained basin on the floor. He saw Candida and Silvia standing like sentinels in the shadows, their faces gray.

And then he saw Virginia.

She sat propped against the pillows, her skin the color of parchment, her hair matted to her skull. She did not look like the woman he wooed in the garden. She looked like a specter.

"Virginia?" He took a hesitant step forward. "Benedetta said—"

"Come here," Virginia rasped.

She pointed a shaking finger at the small table beside the bed. A bundle lay there, wrapped in white linen, motionless in the flickering lamplight.

Gian Paolo stopped. He looked from Virginia to the bundle, confusion knitting his brow. He did not understand. He *could not* understand.

"Look at it," she commanded.

He moved to the table, his movements slow, wary. He reached out and peeled back the linen.

The breath hissed out of him.

He stared down at the tiny, perfect form. A boy. His son. Small enough to cup in one hand, yet undeniably human, undeniably dead.

The silence in the room stretched, heavy and suffocating. The arrogance that usually carried him like armor dissolved. He gripped the edge of the table, his knuckles white.

"You..." He looked up at her, his voice cracking. "I did not know."

"No," Virginia said. Her eyes were dry, burning with a feverish light. "You did not know the pain. You did not know the blood. You only knew the pleasure, Gian Paolo. This is the cost."

He looked back at the child. His jaw tightened, a muscle jumping beneath the skin. For the first time, Virginia saw fear in his eyes, not of discovery, but of the reality of death lying cold under his hand.

"Take him," Virginia said.

"Virginia—"

"Take him!" Her voice rose to a thin shriek. "Take your son and bury him where the dogs cannot reach. He is yours now."

He hesitated, then reached out with hesitant hands. He tucked the small bundle beneath his cloak, against his chest, shielding it from the world. When he looked at her again, the desire was gone, replaced by a haunted, hollow shock.

"I will bury him," he whispered.

He turned and fled the room, vanishing into the corridor like a ghost, the evidence of their sin pressed against his heart.

Candida and Silvia began to strip the ruined bed sheets, their movements silent and frantic.

"It is done," Benedetta said. She did not move from the door. Her face was drawn, her eyes red-rimmed.

"Understand this, Virginia," she said. "What we did tonight, standing here while you labored, disposing of a life, crosses a line I never imagined. I have helped you with letters. I have stood watch. But this..." Her gaze lingered on the empty table. "This is a different sin."

"I know."

"I am complicit now in the destruction of a life," Benedetta said. "However unformed. However unwanted. I carry that ghost alongside you."

She walked to the bed, her voice dropping to a whisper that cut like glass. "Do not mistake my weakness for willingness. Do not assume that because I helped you once in this darkness, I will do so again without cost. You test the limits of what I can bear, and those limits are not infinite."

She straightened. "There will come a day when I have nothing left to give you. On that day, Virginia, you will be alone."

Virginia lay in the dark, listening to the silence where a baby's cry should have been. She knew Benedetta was right. She was playing a game whose rules guaranteed loss.

But as she remembered the look on Gian Paolo's face, the terror, the recognition, she felt a twisted, bitter satisfaction. He knew now. He carried the weight too.

She was damned. But at least she was not damned alone.

* * *

Late 1602

THE LETTER ARRIVED three days after Gian Paolo returned from Rome. Pesseno delivered it with his usual discretion. Virginia held the sealed parchment and felt the weight of expensive paper against her fingertips. The wax still bore the impression of his signet ring. She stood in the narrow corridor outside the refectory. Autumn light slanted through the high windows, dust motes swirling in the drafts.

He wanted to come inside the convent again. Wanted to resume their nocturnal meetings in the shadows. The familiar hunger stirred in her belly at the thought, an ache that had survived years of prayer and fasting. But something else rose alongside it now. A visceral terror that made her stomach clench and her hands shake. She remembered the herbs. The bleeding that had soaked through every cloth Ottavia could find. The fever that had brought her so close to death that even Benedetta had knelt and prayed. The son she had killed.

She broke the seal and read by the failing light. Each line was practiced seduction wrapped in devotion she had heard too many times to believe. He missed her beyond endurance. He had obtained absolution from the Pope himself for his sins, knelt in Saint Peter's basilica, confessed everything to a cardinal. He returned to her purified, transformed, worthy at last of her love. The past could be forgotten if she would only allow him entry one more time.

She could not stop him from entering the convent for he possessed the full set of duplicate keys. But she would lock her own door against him.

Virginia carried the letter through the cloister to the brazier in the common room. Its coals were banked low for heating irons and warming hands. She fed Gian Paolo's elegant script to the flames. The parchment curled and blackened. His careful lies dissolved into ash and smoke that rose toward the vaulted ceiling.

She watched until nothing remained but gray dust settling among the coals. The acrid smell reminded her of the herbs, how they had stunk when she brewed them, like rotting vegetation mixed with iron. How she had forced herself to drink cup after cup, knowing what they would do to her body, knowing she had no other choice.

"I refuse him," she said aloud to the empty room, as though speaking the words might make them true.

* * *

IN HER PRIVATE chamber, Virginia lowered herself onto the cot and pulled the thin blanket around her shoulders. The decision sat uneasily in her chest, making breathing difficult and turning food to sawdust in her mouth.

A soft knock announced Benedetta's arrival. She entered without waiting for permission, carrying a torn altar cloth and her mending basket. Her sharp eyes took in Virginia's condition with a single sweeping glance.

"You refused him," Benedetta said. Not a question. She settled in the chair by the window and began her needlework with steady, precise movements. "God has been merciful in letting all this business remain secret. It could have been discovered so easily."

"I will not tempt His patience further." Virginia closed her eyes against the afternoon light. But what she saw in the darkness behind her eyelids was worse: memories of her hands pressed against her belly, feeling for movement that would signal disaster. The relief when her courses came. The terror when they didn't.

The door opened again. Ottavia entered carrying a tray with bread and watered wine. Her round face was creased with concern that had become permanent in recent months. "You look unwell, Virginia. You must eat something."

The suggestion held more truth than Ottavia intended. A bone-deep exhaustion had settled into Virginia's body in recent weeks. It came not from physical exertion but from the work of holding herself together while everything inside her fractured. And beneath that, a physical memory her body would not release: the cramping that had bent her double, the blood that had flowed until she thought there could be none left, the tiny form that had been her child before the herbs did their work.

"Leave it there. I'll try to eat later."

"You said that yesterday. And the day before." Ottavia set the tray down with more force than necessary. "At least drink the wine."

But Virginia had already turned her face to the wall. After a long moment, she heard Benedetta's quiet voice: "Let her rest. We'll come back after Vespers."

Their footsteps receded. The door closed with a soft click, leaving Virginia alone in the silence that had become both refuge and prison. The private chamber that should have been a mark of her status as Vicaress now felt like a tomb.

But rest brought no relief. The narrow cot became her fortress against the world and against herself. She rose only for the canonical hours, dragging her body through the prayers with lips that moved while her mind wandered through darker territories. The fever that had plagued her since Gian Paolo's departure to Rome continued its work, burning through her on some days until the sheets soaked with sweat. On other days, a coldness settled into her bones, the same coldness that had gripped her when the pennyroyal had nearly killed her, when Ottavia had stayed with her through three terrible nights, wrapping her in every blanket she could find while Virginia's teeth chattered until she bit her tongue and tasted blood.

* * *

BENEDETTA DISCOVERED THE first object when she came to wake Virginia for Lauds. Frost had begun to silver the convent's garden walls. Virginia heard the door open but could not rouse herself from the half-sleep that had become her only escape. Then Benedetta's sharp intake of breath cut through the gray silence.

"What manner of devilry is this?"

Virginia struggled upright. Her head swam with the sudden movement. "What have you found?"

Benedetta stood beside the cot, her face twisted with an expression Virginia had never seen before, not merely disgust but something closer to fear. A small bone rested between her thumb and forefinger at arm's length. Yellowed with age and no larger than the first joint of a finger.

"This was next to your bed. I just noticed it on the floor. It must have worked its way through the straw. Tucked where you lay your head each night."

Virginia stared at the object. "I did not put it there. I swear before God and the Virgin, I know nothing of how it came to be in my bed."

"Then someone placed it there." Benedetta set the bone on Virginia's writing table with careful precision. "Someone who had access to this chamber. Who could move freely while you slept. Who wished to work some dark purpose against you."

More followed in the days after. A dead rat appeared between her sheets one night, positioned where her hand would encounter its cold fur when she sought warmth. Virginia woke with her palm pressed against stiff fur and reeking corruption. Her scream brought both Benedetta and Ottavia running.

After that, they took turns checking her chamber throughout the day. Iron crosses materialized in the straw of her mattress despite their vigilance, their edges filed sharp as razors. Small wounds appeared on her back and thighs, weeping but refusing to heal cleanly.

"He has done this," Virginia whispered to Ottavia one morning. They were alone in Virginia's chamber, Ottavia helping her change the bloodstained linens while Benedetta kept watch outside. "Gian Paolo. He means to bind me with spells. To make my refusal so unbearable that I will have no choice but to relent."

They burned what they could discover. Ottavia carried the bewitched objects to the brazier in the common room when the other sisters were at prayer. The stench of burning marrow filled Virginia's chamber for hours afterward despite open windows, clinging to the tapestries and bed curtains.

But burning changed nothing. The fever continued. The coldness remained. And the longing, that shameful hunger for Gian Paolo, only grew stronger, fed by absence and memory and the treacherous workings of her own damaged heart.

* * *

SISTER CANDIDA BROUGHT the suggestion on an afternoon when early winter rain drummed against the high windows. Entering without knocking, her narrow face was pinched with the expression of someone about to share information that both scandalized and thrilled her.

"I have heard something," Candida began, her voice dropping to barely more than a whisper. "From my cousin in Milan, who has connections to wise women learned in the old ways. There is a remedy for your condition."

Virginia's stomach clenched. "My condition. You mean my inability to stop loving a man who has destroyed me and endangered my immortal soul."

"If one consumes the excrement of the man she loves, for three nights in succession, the passion will turn to hatred." Candida delivered this information with the calm authority of someone reciting a recipe for bread. "The body recognizes the defilement and rejects not merely the substance but the source. Love transforms into its opposite. You will be freed."

The words hung in the damp air between them. Virginia's gorge rose at the mere thought. "You cannot be serious."

"I am entirely serious." Candida's gaze did not waver. "The remedy is unpleasant, yes. But measured against eternal damnation and the continuing destruction of your soul, what is three nights of temporary discomfort?"

Virginia turned toward the wall. Everything in her recoiled from what Candida proposed. To consume filth, to defile herself in pursuit of purification, violated every principle that had governed her existence since childhood.

"This is madness. I would rather die."

"Would you?" Candida's interruption carried surprising sharpness. "Because death is precisely where this path leads if nothing changes. You waste away in this bed while Gian Paolo works his spells from beyond these walls."

The brutal assessment struck with the force of truth. Virginia closed her eyes and saw herself as Candida must see her: gaunt and fevered, hollow-eyed and broken, clinging to the wreckage of her faith while the tide pulled her toward destruction. Prayer had failed. Fasting accomplished nothing. The bewitched objects multiplied no matter how many they discovered and burned. What other remedy remained?

"Even if I agreed to this obscenity," Virginia said slowly, "how would we obtain such a thing? I refuse to see Gian Paolo. Refuse him entry to the convent."

Candida's smile held triumph. "Leave that difficulty to me. The man has servants, and servants can be persuaded to part with many things for the right price."

The plan took shape over whispered consultations in empty corridors. Three days later Candida returned with a small cloth bundle wrapped in waxed linen and tied with coarse string. She placed it on the table without a word.

They dried it first. Spread the material thin on an iron pan held over low coals until moisture evaporated, leaving only a brown residue that could be ground to powder. The smell made Virginia gag—an animal wrongness her body recognized and rejected at the most primitive level. Like meat gone bad mixed with something sharper, more acrid. The stench coated her throat and made her eyes water.

Candida mixed the powder with finely chopped liver and onions, cooking the mixture until the ingredients blended into an unidentifiable mass. But the smell persisted, seeping through the other flavors like corruption through thin gauze.

The small refectory felt cold and dark when Virginia made her way there after Compline. Candida waited with a wooden bowl and a cup of watered wine. Virginia raised the spoon to her lips. The smell alone nearly defeated her. Forcing herself to open her mouth, she took the first bite. Her throat closed. Her body's wisdom recognized defilement and refused passage. The texture was worse than anything she could have imagined—gritty and slick at once, coating her tongue with a film that no amount of wine could wash away. The taste was unspeakable. Bile and rot and something metallic that made her think of blood.

She swallowed through sheer force of will and immediately reached for the wine. But the wine came back up almost before it reached her stomach, along with everything it contained. Virginia leaned over the wooden bucket and vomited until nothing remained but bitter bile that burned her throat raw and brought tears streaming down her face.

The second attempt came the following evening. This time Virginia drank the mixture rather than eating it, powder dissolved in wine and honey. But even diluted, even masked by sweetness, her body recognized what it was. The wrongness of it made her skin crawl. She managed to retain it for nearly an hour, sitting perfectly still and breathing through her mouth before the nausea became unbearable and her body's revolt could no longer be contained.

By the third night, Virginia's hands shook so violently she could barely hold the cup. She drank in frantic gulps, ignoring taste and texture and knowledge. But her body proved wiser than her will. Within moments she was on her knees again, retching into the bucket while Candida held her back and murmured useless comfort.

When the ordeal finally ended, Virginia lay on the cold stone floor and wept. She had debased herself beyond imagining. Swallowed filth and shame. Subjected herself to degradation that made her previous sins seem almost innocent by comparison. And still she burned for him with a hunger that made her previous desire seem modest and manageable. The cure had failed. The love remained, stubborn as a weed with roots driven so deep into poisoned soil that no remedy could reach them.

* * *

VIRGINIA DRAGGED HERSELF to chapel the next morning. She knelt before the crucifix with her arms outstretched, a posture of supplication that bordered on blasphemy. Cold stone bit into her knees through the thin fabric of her habit. She welcomed the pain as proof that her body still worked, still felt, even if her soul had fled beyond reach.

Words tumbled from her lips in broken Latin and Italian. *Libera me, Domine, de morte aeterna.* Deliver me, O Lord, from everlasting death. Free me from this bondage. Release me from captivity. Break the chains that bind me to sin and damnation.

The crucifix gazed down with carved wooden eyes that offered no comfort, no sign that her pleas reached beyond the chapel's vaulted ceiling. She prayed until her voice gave out, until the Latin dissolved into wordless cries. Sisters came and went for the canonical hours, kneeling and rising and moving in ordered ranks while Virginia remained fixed in place, held there by anguish and the desperate hope that enough suffering might buy what prayer alone could not.

On the third day of this vigil, she sought out the convent's confessor. He listened from behind the carved wooden screen that preserved confessional anonymity. Virginia poured out her sins in whispered fragments. The adultery. The dead child, not born dead but killed with herbs before it could draw breath, poisoned in the womb by her own hand through cups of bitter tea. The magic spells. The degrading remedy that failed to cure her unnatural attachment. She spoke until her throat was raw, confessing everything except the one thing that might actually help her: Gian Paolo's name.

The confessor remained silent for a long moment after she finished. When he finally spoke, his voice carried the weariness of a man who had heard too many confessions and granted too many absolutions that changed nothing. "You have committed grievous sins, my daughter. Sins that endanger your immortal soul and violate the sacred vows you made before God."

"I know, Father. Tell me how to make amends."

"Prayer. Hours of prayer each day, beginning before dawn and continuing until Compline. Fasting—bread and water only for forty days. The discipline, twenty lashes each evening until the flesh is properly mortified."

Virginia accepted the penance without protest, welcoming it even.

That evening after Vespers, she embraced the scourge. Kneeling in her chamber, she counted each stroke. Leather bit into flesh already raw from previous penitential exercises, drawing crimson that ran warm down her spine and soaked into the wool of her habit.

Where once the physical pain of the scourging accomplished nothing beyond temporary distraction, it now offered no relief whatsoever because the guilt was too deep. Fasting weakened her frame without touching the hunger that gnawed at her heart. Prayers rose from her lips while her mind wandered through forbidden territory, replaying memories of Gian Paolo's hands on her skin, his mouth against hers, the weight of him pressing her into shadow and surrender.

* * *

THE WELL STOOD in the convent's garden, a stone structure as old as the walls that enclosed them. On an afternoon when the other sisters were occupied with their various duties, Virginia walked there through a garden that lay empty beneath a sky heavy with unshed rain. She moved like a sleepwalker through rows of winter vegetables and dormant herb beds. Her feet carried her toward the well with the inevitability of water seeking its level.

Stone felt cool beneath her palms when she leaned forward and looked down into the yawning chasm below. No reflection gazed back. Only blackness met her gaze, absolute and complete, promising oblivion and the end of all her torments. An escape from the hunger that devoured her from within. From the shame that poisoned every prayer. From the knowledge that taking Gian Paolo back meant opening herself to the same danger that had nearly killed her before.

The solution was so simple it made her want to laugh. One movement. One moment of surrender to gravity's pull. And all of this would be finished. No more fever. No more bewitched objects. No more degrading remedies. No more lying awake through endless nights while her flesh betrayed her with its persistent longing. No more terror of another pregnancy, another desperate trip to Rainerio's apothecary, another dance with death in the form of bitter herbs that might cure the problem or might simply kill her.

Leaning farther forward, she let her weight tilt over the lip of the well. The void below reached up toward her, welcoming and patient. Just a little farther. Just one more movement and—

"Virginia, no!"

The shout came from behind. Hands seized her habit and dragged her backward with such force that they both fell onto the damp earth. Virginia landed hard. The impact drove air from her lungs. Ottavia's considerable weight pinned her to the ground. Her friend's round face loomed above her, streaked with tears and contorted by fury.

"How dare you." Ottavia's voice shook. Each word was forced through clenched teeth. Her fingers dug into Virginia's upper arms hard enough to bruise. "How dare you even consider leaving me alone in this place with only your death and your sins for company."

"Please." Virginia could barely force the word past the knot in her throat. "I cannot bear this any longer. Every breath is agony. Every moment, a torment. Better to end it now than continue this slow descent into madness."

"Look." Ottavia's grip tightened painfully. "Look at Her and tell me you still wish to throw away the life Her son died to save."

Virginia turned her head, staring directly at the image of the Madonna that occupied a small niche near the base of the garden wall. Painted plaster had weathered over years of exposure. The Virgin's blue robe was faded to gray in places. Her body was worn smooth by decades of reverent fingers. Someone had placed fresh flowers at Her feet—roses, their petals brown at the edges but still clinging to life.

She had prayed before that image countless times. Lit candles in the niche below it. The Madonna had witnessed her transformation from reluctant postulant to professed nun. She had looked on during her first tentative explorations of authority as mistress of the schoolgirls. Had maintained Her silent vigil through all the years of Virginia's affair with Gian Paolo and the consequences that followed.

Now those painted eyes held her, anchoring her to this world through the sheer force of divine attention.

"She watches over you," Ottavia whispered, her rage giving way to something gentler. "She knows your suffering because She suffered too. She will not abandon you in this trial if you do not abandon Her."

Virginia pressed her face into Ottavia's neck and wept, the exhausted grief of someone who has lost a battle but must somehow find the strength to continue the war. Weeping for the child she had poisoned before it could fully form. For the innocence she could never reclaim. For the woman she might have been if her father had made different choices. Weeping for Ottavia, who deserved better than a friend who contemplated suicide in the garden's well. And for herself, who would wake tomorrow to face the same impossible situation that had driven her to the well's edge.

* * *

THE STRANGE ATTACKS grew worse after her moment at the well's edge. What had been occasional discomfort in her mouth and stomach became constant agony, spreading from throat to belly, sharp as knives and relentless as waves battering a shore. Virginia could barely eat without throwing up. She could not drink without feeling fire course down her throat.

One night she woke from fevered sleep unable to move. Her body was lead, impossibly heavy, pinned to the mattress by invisible hands. She tried to scream but her throat was stone. Her eyes were open. She could see the familiar ceiling beams, the window's pale rectangle, but she could not turn her head. Could not lift a finger. Terror flooded through her, electric and absolute, worse than physical pain because it came with the awful understanding that her body had become a prison.

Then the sounds began. Footsteps thundered through the corridors beyond her door, dozens of them, running in panic. Doors slammed with violence that shook the walls. Women's voices rose in alarm, calling for help, screaming warnings she could not quite make out. The noise swelled until it filled her skull, pressing against the inside of her forehead like a physical weight.

She felt them then, the other nuns, gathering around her bed. Pressing close. Reaching for her with hands she could sense but not see. Their presence was suffocating, crushing down on her chest until she could not draw breath. She was drowning in air while invisible fingers pawed at her face, her arms, her throat. The terror was absolute—a certainty that she would die here, paralyzed and helpless, smothered by ghosts or demons or the weight of her own guilt made manifest.

Then, like a rope snapping, the paralysis broke. Her eyes opened. Truly opened this time, as though she had been seeing through a veil before. The chamber was silent. Still.

Virginia lay gasping. Her nightgown was soaked with sweat. Her hands trembled as she pressed them against her face, checking that she could move, that her body was her own again.

Whatever she had experienced existed only in her mind, or in some realm no one else could perceive.

Another night, the pillow moved. She woke to find it sliding from beneath her head, rising slowly into the air as though lifted by invisible hands. She was frozen again, unable to cry out or struggle, able only to watch as the pillow hovered above her for a long moment before settling back into place with deliberate, careful precision. The message was clear. Something had power over her even here. Even in this holy space. Even surrounded by her sleeping companions.

"Demons," she whispered after one particularly vivid episode. "Demons sent to punish me for my sins."

But even as she spoke the word, doubt gnawed at her certainty. Were they truly demons? Or visions from her own damaged mind, given form by guilt and fever and the poison she had forced into her body months before? The distinction mattered less than the effect. Real or imagined, supernatural or born in her own fractured psyche, the nightly visits wore away at her resistance with patient, methodical erosion.

* * *

THROUGHOUT THE ORDEAL, Gian Paolo's strategy shifted. He still came to the convent. She heard his footsteps in the corridors after Compline, heard the soft click of his keys in the garden door lock, heard the muffled sounds from Benedetta's chamber or Silvia's cell. But he no longer came to her.

Not because he couldn't. The keys gave him access to any chamber he wished. But because Virginia had made it clear, through Ottavia's whispered messages and Benedetta's cold interventions, that if he tried to force his way into her private chamber, she would scream. Would wake the entire convent. Would bring down consequences he couldn't control, even with all his power.

So instead, he wrote letters. Dozens of them, carried by Pesseno or left tucked beneath her door in the dark hours when he visited the others. Some she burned immediately, recognizing manipulation. But others she kept, reading them until the parchment grew soft with handling. Not because the words moved her, she had learned to see through his craft years ago, but because they proved she still mattered to him in ways the others did not.

He came to the parlatory twice during permitted visiting hours, requesting audiences through proper channels. A public performance of courtship, as though they hadn't already destroyed each other in private a dozen times over.

At their second meeting, he looked thinner than she remembered. His handsome face was hollowed by what might have been genuine suffering. Dark circles shadowed his eyes, giving him a haunted quality that appealed to something maternal in her nature despite everything.

"You are killing me," he said. His voice was rough with emotion that sounded too raw to be entirely fake. "Every day you turn from me is torment. I walk these corridors at night and know you lie awake in your chamber, so close I could reach you in twenty steps. But you've made yourself unreachable."

Virginia gripped the wooden arms of her chair, forcing herself to meet his eyes through the grating's iron bars. "You have Ottavia. You have Benedetta. You even have young Silvia now. And likely others, too. Surely that's enough to satisfy you."

"They are nothing." The words came out harsh, dismissive. "You know that. You've always known that. I don't want convenient bodies in the dark. I want you. My Virginia. The woman who opened that door for me years ago."

"That woman is dead." The words tasted of ash and truth. "You buried her the night you took that bundle from my table. The night I bled for three days and nearly died expelling the child you planted in me."

The silence that followed was absolute.

Gian Paolo went utterly still. The haunted look in his eyes deepened, not with confusion, but with recognition. His gaze dropped to his hands, the same hands that had cradled the linen-wrapped weight of his son, before returning to her face.

"I have not forgotten," he whispered. "Do not think I have forgotten."

"Haven't you?" Virginia's voice was steady, cold as winter stone. "You stand here speaking of desire as if that night never happened. As if you didn't see the blood on the sheets. As if you didn't feel the coldness of your own son against your chest."

His hands gripped the grating's iron bars so tightly his knuckles went bone white. "It haunts me," he said, his voice cracking. "Every time I close my eyes, I see him. Small. Perfect. Dead. I buried him where the earth is deep, Virginia. I said the prayers myself because no priest could say them."

"And yet you returned," she said, leaning forward. "You buried him, you washed your hands, and now you come back to the very place where we destroyed him, asking to begin again."

"Because I need you." The words were a plea, stripped of his usual arrogance. "Because without you, the guilt is the only thing I have left. When I am with you... the darkness recedes."

"Does it?" She watched him carefully. "Or do you simply want to use my body to forget what we did? To prove that we are still alive, that the sin didn't kill us?"

He pressed his forehead against the cold iron. "Is that so wrong? To want comfort? To want to feel something other than this... hollowness?"

"It is not wrong to want it," Virginia said softly. "But it is impossible to have it. Not from me."

He looked up, desperate now. "Why? We have survived the worst. The secret is buried. The danger is past. We can be careful. I will use herbs myself, precautions."

"Precautions?" The word came out sharp as breaking glass. "You think this is about fear of another child? It is about the fact that I look at you and I don't see my lover anymore, Gian Paolo. I see the man who carried my dead son out into the night."

She rose from her chair, her knees trembling but her spine rigid. "You ask for access to my bed. But you forget what lies between us now. It isn't just a door or a lock. It is a grave."

"Virginia, please." He reached through the bars, his fingers brushing the empty air inches from her habit. "Do not do this. Do not condemn us both to this solitude."

"I am not condemning us," she said. "I am saving us. Or at least, I am saving what little is left of me."

She moved toward the door. "If you force your way into my chamber, if you violate the one boundary I have left, I will scream. I will wake this entire convent. I will bring down consequences neither of us can control. Do you understand me?"

He stared at her through the grating, his hand still extended in that futile, reaching gesture. For a long moment neither of them moved. Then he pulled his hand back. The defeat in his posture was total.

"I never wanted to hurt you," he said quietly.

"I know." Her hand rested on the door latch. "That's what makes it worse."

She left him standing there. The door closed with a soft click that sounded like the end of everything.

In the corridor beyond, Virginia pressed her back against the cold stone wall and closed her eyes. She hadn't told him the whole truth. She hadn't told him that she wanted him still, that the hunger for him was a physical ache that rivaled the pain of the abortion.

But she had told him the truth that mattered.

She drew a breath. Another. Then she straightened her habit and walked back toward her chamber with her head high and her steps steady.

Behind her, she heard him leave the parlatory. His footsteps receded down the corridor. Tonight, he might go to Ottavia. Tomorrow to Benedetta. But he would not come to her.

She had drawn a line. For the first time since that night in the parlatory years ago when she'd opened the door in the grating, she had claimed something back. It wasn't freedom. She would never be free of him, not while he walked these halls, not while her friends lay in his arms. But it was something. A small, cold satisfaction that lived in her belly where their child had died.

She reached her chamber. Locked the door. And only then, alone in the darkness, did she let herself weep.

* * *

VIRGINIA SAT ALONE in the chapel as the afternoon light faded to gray. Her hands pressed against her belly in the old gesture, checking for the swelling that would signal disaster. But there was nothing there now. Only the hollow absence where a child had been before the herbs did their work.

And then, unexpected, unbidden, laughter bubbled up from somewhere deep in her chest. It started as a small sound, almost a cough, but grew until it filled the empty parlatory with its bitter music. She laughed until tears ran down her face, until her sides ached, until the absurdity of her situation struck her with the force of revelation.

She had consumed excrement to cure her love. Had debased herself with folk magic while demons visited her at night. Had nearly thrown herself down a well to escape a man who thought her suffering unfortunate. She had murdered her own child with herbs and prayer and lies, and still she wanted him. Still, she lay awake at night imagining his hands on her skin. Still, she kept his letters hidden like treasures rather than burning them as she should.

The laughter died as quickly as it had come, leaving her hollow and cold. But something had shifted. A small crack in the dam that had been holding back the inevitable. She understood now what she had been resisting. Not Gian Paolo himself. She had never truly resisted him, not in any way that mattered. What she had been fighting was the knowledge of her own nature. The truth that he had spoken before he left.

She was not a victim. She was a willing participant in her own destruction. And that made everything so much worse, because it meant she could not blame him for what she chose freely, again and again, knowing the cost.

* * *

THE SIEGE CONTINUED through early winter. More bewitched objects appeared in her bed. More letters arrived from Gian Paolo. More nights passed in fever and cold and the strange paralysis that might have been demonic or might have been her own mind turning against itself.

Virginia moved through the days like a woman already dead, going through the motions of prayer and duty while waiting for the moment of final surrender. And when it came, when she finally kept her door unlocked late one December night and found him waiting in the shadows exactly as she knew he would be, she felt nothing but a weary relief that the waiting was over.

He reached for her. She went to him. And as his arms closed around her and his mouth found hers in the darkness, she thought of the deadly herbs waiting in Rainerio's shop. The herbs she would need again, sooner or later, when the inevitable consequence of this moment made itself known.

But that was a problem for another night. Tonight, there was only this: his hands on her body, his breath against her neck, the familiar weight of him pressing her back against the cold stone wall. Tonight, there was only the choosing of damnation with open eyes and steady hands.

The Lady of Monza had fallen. Not to siege or storm or overwhelming force, but to the simple truth that some hungers cannot be starved, some wants cannot be prayed away, some choices make themselves inevitable through the slow accumulation of smaller surrenders.

She had known this ending from the beginning. All that remained was living through whatever came next.

Chapter Nine
1603

Early 1603

THE MONTHS BLURRED together. Gian Paolo came to her three or four times each week. Always at night. He moved through the convent like smoke—silent, familiar, impossible to grasp.

Virginia stopped pretending to resist. Stopped pretending she wanted him to stop coming. The magic spells ceased. The bewitched objects stopped appearing in her bed. The demonic visits ended as suddenly as they had begun. Her body had needed only permission to want what it wanted. Once she stopped denying him entry, the torments vanished, and somewhere in the back of her mind a small voice whispered that this felt less like deliverance than a bargain accepted.

By late March, the garden had begun to green. One morning Virginia stood at her chamber window and watched new leaves unfurl on the trees. She listened to birds singing their territorial claims and felt the sun warm on her face through the old glass. Everything should have felt different. But nothing had changed. She still woke each morning and dressed in her habit, proceeded to chapel for canonical hours, taught the younger sisters their letters, supervised the convent's accounts. The only difference was the guilt that sat in her chest like a stone—heavy, impossible to dislodge.

"You look troubled," Benedetta observed one afternoon. They sat together in the scriptorium copying manuscripts. The scratch of quills on parchment provided a soothing rhythm. Ink stained Virginia's fingers black. The familiar smell of it filled the small room.

Virginia set down her quill. The letter she was copying blurred before her eyes. "I am damned. There is no other word for what I have become."

"We are all damned." Benedetta's voice held neither comfort nor condemnation. A simple statement of fact delivered with precision. "All four of us, or more."

The words hung in the air. Virginia's hands stilled. She did not ask what Benedetta meant. They both knew. "The question is whether we can live with it."

"Can you?"

Benedetta considered this for a long moment. Her sharp features were softened by the afternoon light slanting through the scriptorium's high windows. "I stopped asking myself that question years ago. I survive. That is enough."

"It is not enough for me."

"Then you will carry a heavier burden than necessary." Benedetta returned to her copying. Her quill moved with practiced efficiency across the vellum. "Suffering without grace brings no redemption. It only marks the hours".

Virginia wanted to argue. To insist that guilt served some purpose. That remorse mattered even when it could not undo what had been done. But Benedetta's face held no invitation to debate. She had drawn her conclusions about how to live with sin, built her survival on practical acceptance rather than impossible redemption. Perhaps she was right. Perhaps suffering was merely self-indulgence dressed as piety.

The thought should have brought comfort. Instead, it left Virginia hollowed out. Empty of everything except the basic animal needs that drove her to Gian Paolo's arms again and again despite knowing better.

* * *

GIAN PAOLO CAME to her one night in late April carrying news that sat strangely on his handsome features. Not quite grief, and certainly not the tension that had ridden him for months. It was the loose-limbed satisfaction of a gambler who has finally raked in the pot.

They lay together in her cell. The air had grown warm with spring's advance. Honeysuckle bloomed somewhere nearby, its sweet scent drifting through the open window along with night sounds—crickets, a distant dog barking. The ordinary noises of a world that continued its business while they sinned in darkness.

"It is finished," Gian Paolo said. His fingers traced idle patterns on Virginia's bare shoulder. The touch was gentle, absent-minded. "The negotiations are concluded. Teodoro is coming home."

Virginia turned her head to look at him. His face was unreadable in the dim moonlight, but the tightness that had defined his jawline since winter had smoothed away. "The Governor has agreed to lift the ban?"

"The Governor agrees to what serves the state. And I have made sure this serves him." He shifted, propping himself on one elbow so he could see her face more clearly. "My brother is leaving the Veneto. He will be back in Monza before the summer heat sets in."

"I am glad for your mother," Virginia said, though the words felt heavy on her tongue. She remembered the terror of the previous autumn, the news of the stabbing, the uncle dead in his chair, Teodoro's desperate flight across the Adda to escape the Milanese magistrates. "But I do not understand. You said the evidence against him was overwhelming. Witnesses saw him on the road; the servants heard the arguments about the inheritance."

"Evidence is fluid, Virginia. Like water. It takes the shape of the vessel that holds it." Gian Paolo's mouth curved into something that was not quite a smile. "I simply provided a more attractive vessel."

"You bribed the magistrate?"

"Better. I gave them a trade." He spoke with the casual pride of a merchant discussing a favorable shipment. "The authorities in Milan have been plagued by contraband running across the border. They needed heads to display. I gave them three."

Virginia sat up slowly. The thin blanket fell away from her shoulders, the night air raising gooseflesh on her arms. "What do you mean?"

"I arranged for three smugglers, men who have been a thorn in the Duchy's side, to be captured and delivered to the authorities," he said, his voice steady, conversational. "In exchange, the Senate has agreed to issue a pardon for

Teodoro. The state gets three criminals for the galleys. My family gets my brother back. Justice is served".

"You bought his freedom with human lives?"

"I bought it with leverage. The smugglers were criminals anyway; they merely met their fate a little sooner than expected." He reached for her, his hand warm against her waist. "Do not look at me like that. This is how the world works. My uncle is dead, and his miserly grasp on our inheritance is broken. Why should my brother rot in Venetian exile when the problem is already solved?"

"Because he killed a man," Virginia whispered. "Because he murdered his own flesh and blood for money."

"He did what was necessary to secure our future. Just as I have done what is necessary to bring him home." His fingers tightened on her hip, possessive and grounding. "Family protects family. You, of all people, should understand that. How many people in this convent protect you? Keep your secrets? Enable your sins?"

The words landed like blows. "That is different."

"Is it? We do what we must to go on living. We all compromise our principles when necessity demands it." His mouth found the sensitive spot behind her ear. "The only difference between your sins and my brother's is that yours hurt no one but yourself."

But that was not true. Virginia knew her sins rippled outward like stones thrown into still water. They hurt Benedetta and Ottavia, Candida and Silvia, who risked their souls to guard her door. And now, she lay in the arms of a man who traded human beings to wash away the stain of fratricide.

"In any case," Gian Paolo continued, his voice light now, "I have sold the estate at Barzanò, the one with the mill and the orchards along the Lambro, to cover the costs of the arrangement. The funds greased the necessary palms".

"You treat justice as if it were a market stall."

Gian Paolo laughed. The sound was bitter as unripe fruit. "It is a market stall. Power determines the price. The sooner you understand that the less disappointed you will be."

Virginia pulled away from him. The floor was icy beneath her bare feet as she stood and retrieved her discarded habit. Her hands shook as she dressed. Not from the chill in the room, but from the dawning understanding of what kind of man she had bound herself to. A man who could speak casually of corruption, who saw the world as a series of transactions where nothing was sacred.

"You are upset," Gian Paolo observed. He remained in her bed, watching her with those dark eyes that saw too much.

"Your brother killed an old man. You bartered three men into chains to save him. And you tell me about it as though you were reading it from a business ledger."

"It means the inheritance is secure. It means the Osio name is safe." He rose finally, collecting his scattered clothing. "I thought we were past the point of pretending to be saints, Virginia. We are both knee-deep in this life."

He finished dressing and crossed to where she stood, cupping her face in his hands. "I am not asking you to approve. Only to accept that it is done. Teodoro returns in a few weeks. We can continue as we have been. That is all that matters."

He kissed her forehead. Then he was gone, slipping out the door and down the darkened corridor with the ease of long practice.

Virginia stood alone in the room that smelled of sex and sin and the fading sweetness of honeysuckle. She pressed both hands against her stomach and tried to slow her racing breath. She was part of it now. By knowing, by staying, by loving him, she had made herself a silent witness to his brother's return. Justice had been purchased and paid for with the bodies of three strangers she would never know, whose names she would never learn, who would spend the rest of their lives chained to oars or hung by the neck because a nobleman needed his brother pardoned.

She sank to her knees on the stone floor. *Libera me, Domine.* Deliver me, O Lord.

But the prayer stuck in her throat like a stone. She was no longer begging to be freed from him, but from the woman staring back at her from the dark surface of her own soul. A woman who knew of murder and corruption, and yet, when the sun rose tomorrow, would do nothing but wait for him to return.

* * *

Summer

TEODORO RETURNED TO Monza in early June. Virginia watched from a window as he rode through the street below. A free man. Pardoned. The sentence vacated as though it had never been.

He looked much like his brother. The same dark hair and handsome features. The same easy confidence of men born to privilege. He waved to someone Virginia could not see. Smiled. Laughed. As though he had been away on holiday rather than fleeing murder charges.

"Justice purchased," Benedetta observed from her place by the door. She had been mending a torn altar cloth but now stood watching the street below. "The natural order of things among the wealthy."

"It is obscene."

"It is reality." Benedetta returned to her mending. Her needle flashed in the afternoon light. "The sooner you stop being surprised by wickedness, the easier your life will become."

But Virginia did not want to stop being surprised, did not want to accept corruption as inevitable. The moment she surrendered that last shred of moral outrage would be the moment she lost whatever remained of her soul.

The summer heat pressed down on Monza like a heavy hand. Stone walls held the day's warmth and released it slowly through the night. Virginia lay in her cot. Sweat trickled between her breasts. The air was thick. Too hot for blankets. Too warm for sleep.

Gian Paolo's visits continued without interruption. Three or four times each week he came to her. They made love in her cell or sometimes in the garden itself when the night was warm enough. Hidden by shadows and late-blooming roses that climbed the convent walls.

Virginia had stopped pretending this was anything other than what it was. Addiction. Need. The terrible hunger that could be satisfied only temporarily and always demanded more.

* * *

November

VIRGINIA'S MONTHLY COURSES stopped. At first, she told herself it meant nothing. Strain could stop a woman's cycles. Lack of sleep, constant anxiety. But by mid-November, denial became impossible. She was pregnant again.

The knowledge settled over her like a burial shroud. Heavy. Suffocating. Inescapable. Another child. Another life growing inside her that she could neither keep nor acknowledge.

"You are certain?" Benedetta asked when Virginia told her. They sat in their chamber with the door barred. Ottavia had gone to the kitchens. They had perhaps an hour of privacy.

"Certain enough. I recognize the signs."

Benedetta's sharp gaze mapped Virginia's face, looking for weakness, for denial, for anything that might complicate what needed to be done. "Then you must act quickly. Before your body shows what you wish to hide."

"I know."

"Rainerio?"

The name hung in the air between them. Rainerio Roncino the apothecary. The man who asked no questions and supplied what should not be supplied.

"I have no choice," Virginia said.

"There are always choices." Benedetta's voice was matter of fact. "The question is whether we can live with the consequences."

But what choice was there really? Bear the child and watch it taken away? Better to end it now. Before it became real.

Virginia sent word to Rainerio through Benedetta, as they had done before. Silver coins. The same illness as before. The same remedy required.

Benedetta returned two hours later, her face tight with something between anger and fear. She closed the chamber door and set the coins on the writing table, untouched.

"He refused?" Virginia asked, her stomach dropping.

"Not refused. Demanded." Benedetta's voice was clipped. "He said the remedy requires specific information about the patient's condition. That he must speak with you directly in the parlatory to ensure proper dosage and timing." She paused. "We both know that's a lie. He wants to know the nun who needs such remedies, wants you visible, wants you implicated in a way you weren't before."

Virginia stared at the returned coins. "What did you tell him?"

"That I would convey his request." Benedetta sat down heavily. "Virginia, this is a trap. He's asserting control. Once you meet him face-to-face, he has leverage he didn't have when I was the intermediary. He'll know you and your desperation firsthand. He'll be able to name his price."

"What choice do I have?"

"You could refuse. Find another apothecary."

"There is no time." Virginia pressed both hands against her stomach. "And any other apothecary would be the same risk. At least Rainerio already knows. At least the damage is already done."

"The damage is not already done," Benedetta said sharply. "Right now, he knows I purchased herbs once before. If questioned, I could claim they were for my own purposes. But if you meet him in the parlatory, if any sister sees you conducting business with an apothecary, there will be questions."

Virginia knew Benedetta was right. But the alternative, bearing this child, watching her body swell and betray her, was impossible to contemplate.

"Send word that I will meet him," Virginia said quietly. "Tomorrow. During the permitted visiting hour."

Benedetta's jaw tightened, but she nodded. "I'll arrange it. But understand what you're doing. You're giving him power over you that he doesn't have yet. Power he will use."

"I know."

* * *

RAINERIO CAME TO the parlatory the next afternoon. He was smaller than Virginia remembered from Benedetta's description. His clothes were fine but not ostentatious—dark wool and white linen, the costume of a respectable tradesman. But his eyes were sharp, calculating, the color of tarnished silver. They moved constantly as though totaling sums visible only to him. A dark stain marked his left cuff, rust-brown and irregular.

"Sister Virginia?" He inclined his head as he acknowledged her identity. Respectful but not servile. "How kind of you to see me personally. I do apologize for the inconvenience, but in matters of such delicacy, I find direct consultation essential."

The lie was transparent. Virginia forced herself to meet his gaze. "Sister Benedetta said you required information to explain the dosage."

"Indeed." His smile showed too many teeth. When he breathed, she caught the scent of something medicinal and faintly sweet, like rotting fruit masked with cloves. "Though I confess, I remember your constitution quite well from our previous arrangement, even though I did not know your name at the time. The remedy you require is similar to what I provided before, but stronger. More certain in its effects."

So, he was admitting it. The demand to meet her had nothing to do with medical necessity.

"How much?" Virginia asked, keeping her voice steady.

"Thirty *scudi.*" He watched her face carefully, gauging her reaction, measuring her desperation. His tongue darted out to wet his lips. "For the herbs and my discretion."

Virginia's jaw tightened. "That is three times what you charged before."

"Prices rise. Risks increase." He shrugged as though discussing the weather. "You understand how these things work, Sister. Supply and demand. A woman in your position has limited options for obtaining such remedies. Particularly now that I know it is you specifically who requires my services, not merely some anonymous sister sending intermediaries."

There it was. The real reason for this meeting. He wanted her to understand that her anonymity was gone. That he held her secret in his hands.

"Very well. Thirty *scudi*."

"I will have the preparation delivered tomorrow evening. Through your usual intermediary." He turned to go, having gotten what he wanted—her fear, her acknowledgment of his power. Then he paused as though a thought had just occurred to him. "You know, Sister, a woman in your position might benefit from having a reliable friend. Someone who could assist with various difficulties that might arise in the future."

"What do you mean?"

Rainerio's smile widened. His eyes glittered in the dim light. "I mean that I am a man of many talents. Discretion chief among them. For the right compensation, I can solve many problems. Provide many services. It would be wise to cultivate such a friendship."

Understanding dawned cold and clear. This meeting had never been about dosage or medical consultation. It had been about establishing dominance. About forcing her into visibility so he could look her in the eye and make certain she understood the leverage he now held.

This was blackmail dressed in the language of mutual benefit.

"I understand," Virginia said. Her voice was steady and gave away nothing of the fear churning in her stomach. "Thank you for your assistance."

"Always a pleasure, Sister." His bow was mocking. Theatrical. "I look forward to our continued friendship."

He departed. His footsteps echoed away down the corridor, fading slowly like a threat whispered in darkness.

Virginia sat alone in the parlatory. Gian Paolo had been the trap, but now the larger snare closed around her. Rainerio held her secrets in his quick hands. He could destroy her with a word and would bleed her dry for as long as she had anything left to give.

* * *

WINTER LIGHT SLANTED thin and gray through the high window. Virginia stood between her cot and the wall, adjusting her wool habit. The fabric would not lie flat over the new curve of her belly, no matter how she shifted or how tightly she cinched the cord.

"Again," Benedetta said quietly. "Let it fall."

Virginia released the wool. It whispered against her linen shift and draped itself around the unmistakable swell.

Ottavia made a small, wounded sound. "Perhaps it is only swelling. From all the lying in bed. From the draughts."

"Swelling does not quicken." Candida's knuckles were white around her rosary. "You felt it. You told us."

The memory rose unbidden: that small flutter beneath her hand as she lay in the dark two nights ago, counting days since she had choked down Rainerio's bitter powders and waited for the blood that never came.

"Once," Virginia whispered. "It might have been my imagination."

"It was not your imagination." Benedetta stepped closer, her fingers cold when she pressed them flat against Virginia's abdomen through the layers of wool and linen. "Be still."

The room held its breath. Beyond the stone walls, a bell tolled Terce. Inside the cell there was only the rasp of four women breathing and the faint creak of floorboards as Ottavia shifted her weight.

Then, beneath Benedetta's palm, a small push. Distinct. Stubborn. As if the life inside had heard itself discussed and answered back.

Benedetta's eyes closed. Just for a heartbeat. When she opened them again, whatever softness had been there was gone. "It is alive," she said.

Candida crossed herself quickly, her lips shaping words that sounded more like accusation than prayer. "God have mercy."

"On you," Silvia said from her post at the door. She had stationed herself there without being asked, back pressed to the wood, one ear turned toward the corridor. "If this is discovered, it is your name they will speak first. Not ours."

"Our names will follow soon enough." Benedetta let her hand fall and stepped back. "Do not pretend otherwise. Rainerio's herbs have failed."

The words landed like a fist to the stomach. The knowledge had lived in her for days, but hearing it named aloud stripped away the last threadbare pretense of denial. Her knees threatened to give. She pressed one palm flat against the cold stone wall to steady herself.

"There must be something else," Ottavia said, desperation fraying the edges of her voice. "If we ask him for a stronger dose, perhaps—"

"Stronger?" Candida rounded on her. "You would have her drink poison until she kills herself along with it? Then we may as well prepare two shrouds and be done."

"Enough." Benedetta's tone sliced cleanly through the rising panic. "We will not go back to him. He has her name now. Her face. He has counted the silver she gave him and measured exactly how much fear lives behind her eyes." Her dark gaze found Virginia's. "He will use all of it when it suits him."

The memory flashed vivid and unwelcome: the iron grating between them in the parlatory, Rainerio's smile too patient and too knowing, the rust-brown stain on his cuff. Thirty *scudi* for the herbs. More, unspoken, for his silence.

"Then what would you have me do?" Virginia's voice came out flat, distant. "I cannot wish this away. I have tried."

Benedetta did not look away. "You carry it. We hide what we can, for as long as we can. Keep you from Chapter meetings, from the refectory when your body begins to show. We give Bianca reasons to shield you instead of asking questions. And when your time comes, we bring it into the world and get it out of this convent before anyone can count back the months and do the arithmetic."

"As if it were simple," Candida murmured. Her fingers had gone still on the rosary. "Another child born in mortal sin. Another soul marked by what we have chosen to hide."

"Would you prefer the alternative?" Silvia's question was quiet but edged. "The Prioress at your door before dawn? Monsignor Barca summoned from Milan because the Vicaress has grown round in the belly while claiming to suffer from nervous ailments?" She shook her head. "We chose this path when

Benedetta went to Rainerio. When we let Osio climb the garden wall for the first time and did not raise the alarm. What comes now is only the consequence of those choices."

"It is a child." Ottavia's voice broke on the word. Tears shone in her eyes. "Not a consequence. Not a path. A child."

The word lodged itself beneath Virginia's ribs like a splinter of bone. Child. Not sin, not evidence to be hidden in a sack and smuggled through a gate. A small life assembling itself cell by cell from the wreckage of her vows.

"I cannot do this again." The confession came raw, stripped of pious language. "Not the lying. Not the pretending."

Something shifted in Benedetta's expression, not softness, but a loosening around the edges. "You have no choice," she said, and her voice had lost its sharpness. "Not anymore. The remedies failed. The child did not. Whatever we decide in this room will not change those facts."

Silence settled over them. From somewhere below came the muffled clatter of wooden bowls in the refectory, the bright high voice of a novice reciting her catechism. Ordinary sounds. The convent carrying on as though nothing had shifted.

But everything had.

Virginia straightened slowly, her palm still pressed to the cold wall for balance. A wave of nausea rolled through her, and she swallowed hard against it. At last, she nodded. The motion felt like sentencing herself. "Very well. We hide it. We carry it to birth. And when the time comes, you will help me." Her gaze moved from Benedetta to Ottavia to Candida, finally to Silvia standing watch at the door. "All of you."

One by one, they inclined their heads. No oaths spoken aloud, no hands clasped over a Bible. Only the grim, wordless understanding that their fates were bound now to the life inside her as tightly as to one another, that none of them could betray the rest without condemning herself.

Virginia smoothed her habit over the curve of her belly. The wool caught slightly on the new shape, resisting her hand. Rainerio's medicines had not saved her. The birth would come, arriving with the same inevitability as Compline bells or the turn of seasons. Something she could not stop, only endure.

She could only pray that when it was done, when the child had been carried out through some gate in the dark and given to Osio to raise or abandon as he saw fit, the walls of Santa Margherita would still be standing around her. That she would still be standing within them.

The winter light shifted. A cloud passed over the sun. The cell darkened by a shade, and Virginia felt the cold seep up through the stones beneath her feet, ancient and patient and impossible to escape.

Chapter Ten
1604

Early 1604

VIRGINIA'S FINGERS HAD gone numb long before Reverend Mother Beatrice stopped breathing. Frost crept along the window beside the bed, a pale lattice that caught what little light the January morning allowed into the infirmary. Around her, the sisters whispered prayers, their breath clouding the air. Beatrice's chest lifted once. Twice. Then no more.

The silence dropped like a curtain. No one moved. Somewhere in the convent a bell began its slow, measured toll. In the narrow room Virginia heard only the echo of another night, five years earlier, when Beatrice had drawn her aside and said, "You are not alone here." The words rose now like a promise revoked.

They buried her three days later, when the ground finally yielded. The gravediggers' picks struck frozen earth with a hard, metallic ring, each blow jolting through Virginia's teeth as she stood at the edge of the open pit. Soil flecked her hem as clods of dark earth thudded onto the coffin lid until the wood disappeared beneath it.

By the end of the week, the convent had a new Prioress. In the Chapter house, the sisters' votes settled on Sister Bianca—practical, steady, her ink-stained fingers folded neatly as she accepted. Virginia kept her gaze on the floor. Bianca's eyes passed over her, assessing, measuring. They had never been friends. Bianca's piety was the exacting kind, the sort that noticed absences from choir and lingered too long in doorways. With Beatrice gone, no one remained to deflect those watchful glances.

Bianca rose and addressed the house in her calm, deliberate voice. "Sister Virginia will continue to serve as Vicaress."

Virginia's head snapped up. Around the room, faces turned toward her—some surprised, some carefully neutral. Bianca met her gaze with a thin smile that did not reach her eyes. "Your experience will be invaluable to me as I learn my duties."

The words sounded like courtesy. They felt like a leash. Virginia lowered her eyes and murmured her thanks, her hands clenching in her lap. To refuse would raise questions she could not afford to answer. To accept meant serving under a woman who already suspected her of something.

Virginia returned to her chamber and closed the door. The latch clicked. Alone in the narrow quiet, she released the breath she had held since Beatrice died. Bianca would be watching now, waiting for a misstep. Whatever came next would begin here, behind this door, in this sliver of privacy that felt less like a gift than a cage with a lock she could reach from the inside.

* * *

THE NEXT DAY, Bianca came to Virginia's chamber. She knocked softly before stepping inside, her round face calm and unreadable. "You were not at the morning meeting."

Virginia sat on the edge of her cot, bracing herself. "I was unwell. I apologize."

Bianca stepped farther into the room, her eyes sweeping over the unmade bed and the washbasin. But her gaze didn't linger. It passed over everything with practiced indifference, as though she had decided not to see. "You are often unwell these days."

"I—"

"Which is why," Bianca continued smoothly, moving to the window and looking out onto the street rather than at Virginia directly, "I've decided to relieve you of some of your duties. Sister Francesca can handle the morning meetings and the inspections. You need to rest and recover your strength."

Virginia stared at her. This was not the rebuke she'd expected. "I don't understand. I am still Vicaress. These are my responsibilities."

"And you will remain Vicaress," Bianca said, her tone pleasant but firm. "Your title, your rank, your position—all unchanged. But the daily work can be delegated when one of our senior sisters is indisposed." She turned from the window, offering Virginia a brief, professional smile. "It's a practical arrangement, nothing more."

Virginia's hands twisted the fabric of her habit. The kindness seemed almost worse than accusation. "The other sisters will notice."

"They already have. Which is why it's important that we manage this sensibly. For the good of the community."

Something in the way she said 'manage this' made Virginia's pulse leap beneath her jaw.

"I want you to know," Bianca continued, sitting down on the chair at the writing table, "that if you require anything, privacy, rest, certain accommodations, you need only ask. Discreetly, of course. I'm not interested in creating difficulties where they can be avoided."

Virginia's mouth went dry. "What are you saying?"

"I'm saying that I understand you've been under considerable strain." Bianca's voice remained carefully neutral. "Reverend Mother Beatrice managed this convent with great wisdom. She knew when to enforce rules and when to exercise pastoral discretion. I intend to follow her example."

The words were maddeningly oblique, yet their meaning pressed against Virginia like a hand on her chest. Bianca knew something. But she wasn't going to name it.

"I appreciated Reverend Mother Beatrice's guidance," Virginia said slowly.

"As did we all." Bianca stood, smoothing her habit. "She had a gift for protecting this community from scandal. For handling delicate situations before they became public problems." She paused at the door, her hand on the latch. "If you find yourself facing any difficulty in the months ahead, I ask that you come to me early. The sooner I know what practical arrangements need to be made, the more easily they can be managed. Quietly."

Virginia's surprise must have shown, because Bianca's expression softened slightly, though whether with pity or something else, Virginia couldn't tell.

"You seem surprised."

"I am." Virginia's voice came out barely above a whisper. "I thought you would be less understanding."

"Understanding?" Bianca repeated the word as if considering its weight. "I'm not sure that's what I'm offering, Virginia. What I'm offering is discretion. There's a difference." She opened the door, then paused. "I'm not Beatrice. I won't give you the warmth she gave, or the latitude to move freely. But neither am I interested in exposing what can be kept private, if it's handled properly. For the sake of Santa Margherita's reputation, not for yours."

The distinction hung in the air between them, sharp and clear.

"Do we understand each other?"

Virginia nodded.

"Good. Then rest today. Tomorrow, you'll join us for prayers, so the community sees you haven't vanished entirely. But the morning meetings, the parlatory inspections, Sister Francesca will handle those for now." She stepped into the corridor, then looked back. "And Virginia? If your condition worsens, if you need a physician or other assistance, send word through Sister Francesca. I'll arrange it. No questions asked, no explanations required. But only if you ask before it becomes a crisis I cannot contain."

She left. The door clicked shut.

Virginia sat in stunned silence. She had prepared herself for confrontation, for condemnation, for careful probing questions. Instead, Bianca had offered her something far more unsettling: complicity wrapped in cool pragmatism.

Not protection born of affection, like Beatrice had given her. Not even forgiveness. Just a businesslike willingness to manage an inconvenient situation, provided Virginia didn't force Bianca's hand by letting it spiral into public scandal. Beatrice had protected her out of love. Bianca was protecting the convent's reputation, and Virginia just happened to be part of the calculation.

The moment Virginia became more liability than asset, that protection would evaporate like morning mist. And the most disturbing part was Bianca's absolute refusal to name what she clearly suspected. As long as nothing was spoken aloud, as long as Virginia managed her situation discreetly, Bianca would look the other way. But that unspoken arrangement came with a price: Virginia would owe her. Bianca would collect that debt whenever it suited her purposes.

Virginia pressed her hands against her abdomen. The subtle changes there would soon become impossible to hide. She had privacy now, and Bianca's tacit permission to handle things quietly. Yet every protection came with invisible chains. The child inside her shifted, a flutter against her palm. Bianca's unspoken bargain coiled around Virginia's ribs like an iron band.

* * *

BY LATE FEBRUARY, managing perception became harder as Virginia's body changed. Her habit strained across her middle. She took to wearing her scapular loose, arranged to disguise the swell, and walked with her arms folded across her stomach, a posture that could pass for contemplation or cold. She avoided the refectory during communal meals, claiming persistent ailments.

The sisters whispered. Virginia caught the knowledge in their eyes or the way they looked away when Virginia passed in the corridors. But fear of Virginia's rank, or fear of what knowing might require them to do, kept them silent. And whenever the whispers grew too loud, Bianca reassigned the curious ones to distant parts of the convent, scattering them before they could form a coherent story.

* * *

SPRING ARRIVED IN March with purple and yellow crocuses pushing through the last patches of melting snow. They looked fragile from Virginia's window, yet they bloomed anyway, stubborn in their refusal to wait for safety.

The child inside her had grown strong. It moved constantly now, pressing against her ribs during Vespers, kicking when she tried to sleep, reminding her of its existence with every breath. The first child had come and gone in darkness, barely real, a grief she could name but never fully feel. This one was undeniably alive, asserting its claim to existence despite everything she had done to prevent it.

Sometimes, in the quiet hours before dawn, Virginia found herself speaking to it. Not words exactly. Just sounds, meaningless murmurs that might have been prayer or apology.

One afternoon in mid-March, Benedetta stormed into Virginia's chamber and slammed the door with enough force to rattle the latch.

"That man is unbearable."

"Which man?" Virginia asked, looking up from her mending.

"Arrigone. The priest who cannot keep his thoughts or his hands to himself." Benedetta paced the small room. "He cornered me after confession. Said he had been admiring me for months. That he saw in me a woman of intelligence and strength who deserved better than the half-life we live here." Her voice dripped contempt. "Then he put his hand on my arm and squeezed, as though I was a piece of fruit he was testing for ripeness."

Virginia's stomach clenched. She remembered that touch, that presumption of ownership.

"What did you say?"

"I told him to remove his hand before I removed it for him." Benedetta dropped onto Virginia's bed. "He looked genuinely surprised, as though he could not fathom why any woman would refuse him."

A chill spread through Virginia's chest. "He will not take the rejection well."

"Men like him do not accept refusal," Benedetta said. "They simply look for an easier target."

Within a week, Arrigone had fixed his sights on Sister Candida. Letters began arriving, carried by Domenico. From her window, Virginia watched Candida retrieve the first one, that quick, nervous glance over her shoulder before tucking the paper into her sleeve. Virginia knew that gesture. Had made it herself, years ago, when Gian Paolo's letters had first begun arriving.

Candida's face changed over the following weeks. The pinched anxiety gave way to something that looked like excitement. She smiled more. Hummed while she worked. Started wearing better-quality wimples, a rosary with polished beads.

Virginia watched and saw herself five years earlier, eager, terrified, convinced she could control what she was beginning.

One evening, Benedetta brought news. She had overheard Candida whispering to Domenico. "Arrigone wants to come inside," Benedetta said, her voice flat. "He told her she must leave the garden door unlatched."

"What did Candida say?"

"She told him no. But her voice was weak, Virginia. She did not tell him to stop writing."

"Then she will let him in," Virginia said. The certainty tasted like ash. "She will tell herself she had no choice, that he overwhelmed her resistance. But in the end, she will open the door."

"As you did," Benedetta murmured.

"Yes." Virginia did not deny it. "I have no grounds to warn her."

They sat in silence, three women trapped by stone walls and the choices they had made, watching another sister step onto the same dark path.

* * *

BY EARLY MAY, as spring turned to summer and heat began to settle over Monza, the truth could no longer be hidden. The child inside her was enormous, restless, ready. Her habit no longer closed properly. Her face had acquired the fullness of late pregnancy. She looked exactly like what she was: a pregnant woman trying desperately to hide.

Benedetta confronted her one morning after Ottavia had gone to fetch water. "Not long to go now."

"Only six months. Perhaps seven." Virginia had stopped counting.

Benedetta's expression remained practical. "You must prepare."

"How?" The word came out too sharp, too desperate. "I cannot give birth here. Someone will hear. Everyone will know."

"Everyone will know soon enough if we do nothing," Benedetta said. "The only question is whether you give birth in secret with our help, or whether you wait until the pain takes you in the middle of the day and you scream your sin for all the convent to hear."

Virginia pressed both hands against her stomach. The baby moved immediately, a strong flutter against her palms. It was no longer an abstract problem. It was a life, stubborn, insistent, undeniably real.

"What do I need?"

"Swaddling cloths. A cradle. Clean linens. Wine for the pain." Benedetta listed the items as calmly as if planning a meal. "And we must send word to Gian Paolo. He must be ready to take the child the moment it is born."

The practicality of it helped steady Virginia's nerves. It turned a nightmare into a list of tasks.

She began her preparations that afternoon. Fine linens meant for headdresses became strips for swaddling. The repetitive motion of the scissors soothed her. She folded each piece and hid them in the wooden chest at the foot of her bed, beneath the winter blankets.

Ordering a cradle was more dangerous. She sent Ottavia to the market with careful instructions. "Tell them it is for the orphanage."

Ottavia returned with a small wooden basket lined with soft cloth. Simple, the kind a peasant woman might use. The smell of fresh pine still clung to it, raw and clean and wrong. It smelled exactly like the coffins being built in the carpenter's workshop next door.

Virginia set the cradle in the corner farthest from the door, where shadows gathered even at midday. She had paid silver for something she would use for hours at most before handing her child to Gian Paolo and never seeing it again.

The child kicked hard. A tiny foot, or perhaps an elbow, pressed against her from within. She touched her side where it pushed.

"It is strong," Benedetta observed from the window. "That is good. Weak babies do not always survive."

Virginia stared at the empty cradle. How could she wish for this child to live when its existence threatened to destroy her? Yet the movement inside her felt undeniable, precious. She had tried to kill it with Rainerio's poison, and it had refused to die. She pressed her palm to the spot where the baby had kicked. Another flutter came, gentler this time. As if in response.

The child would come whether she wanted it or not. All she could do was prepare and pray that their secrets would hold.

In the corner, the pine cradle waited. Small and empty and smelling of death. Virginia turned away and returned to cutting linen into strips, each snip of the scissors marking another step toward an ending she could not yet imagine.

* * *

VIRGINIA STOOD AT her window watching a pattern repeat itself. As usual, Domenico carried his market basket through the garden. He would cross to the fountain, always the same spot, and set the basket down among the herbs before going back inside.

Moments later, Candida appeared, kneeling as if to pray with her hands clasped and her head bowed in an attitude of devotion that fooled no one who understood what to look for. Her fingers darted into the basket, searching beneath the arranged produce until they found the folded paper. The letter disappeared into her sleeve with that practiced gesture Virginia had perfected five years ago, when she'd convinced herself no one was watching her do something similar. But everyone had been watching.

"Four letters yesterday," Benedetta said as she entered with a tray of food Virginia's stomach wouldn't accept. She set the dishes on the writing table with a soft clatter. "Domenico's hands shake when he sets down the basket. He knows people are watching, knows the pattern has become too obvious to ignore, but Candida keeps demanding he continue."

Virginia pressed her palm to her belly where the child rolled beneath her skin. "And Candida?"

"Smiles during prayers. Hums while she works." Benedetta sat on the edge of the bed, the ropes supporting the mattress creaking. "Her face glows the way yours did five years ago, when you first started meeting Gian Paolo in the parlatory."

"I remember." Virginia's voice came out flat, drained.

"Yes." Benedetta's words landed between them, and Virginia didn't argue because there was nothing to argue against.

* * *

THE LETTER THAT shifted everything arrived on a Tuesday morning in late May, delivered through the usual channels but different in a way Virginia noticed even from her window. Domenico crossed the garden with jerky, uneven movements, the careful pretense of normalcy abandoned in favor of speed. He set the basket down and hurried away without his usual glance around, and Virginia's chest tightened.

Candida emerged moments later, moving with her usual cautious grace until she retrieved the letter and unfolded it. All color drained from her face in an instant. Her hand flew to her mouth, pressing against her lips as if to hold back sound, and she read the letter once, twice, three times before tucking it away with trembling fingers. She stood frozen for a long moment, staring at nothing, before turning and fleeing back inside with quick, unsteady steps.

That evening, Ottavia brought confirmation. "Domenico showed me the letter before delivering it," she whispered, closing the door to Virginia's chamber and turning the lock. The click of the latch echoed. "Arrigone wants to climb the wall. He wants to enter the convent proper, not just meet in the parlatory. The language, what he intends to do with her once inside, no priest should write such things to anyone, let alone to a nun."

Virginia closed her eyes, pressing both hands against her belly where the baby kicked hard. "And Candida?"

"She wrote back to him this afternoon. I didn't see the full text, but Domenico said she told Arrigone he mustn't say such things, that she doesn't want it." Ottavia sat on the stool by the writing table, the wood creaking. Her round face showed the strain of carrying these secrets. "But she's still writing to him, Virginia. She could have refused to respond. Could have brought the letter to Prioress Bianca and exposed him. Instead, she engaged with his proposal."

"She's already decided and is performing reluctance to absolve herself when it happens," Benedetta said from the doorway before entering and closing the door behind her. "Women do that. Say no while arranging circumstances that make yes inevitable. Creating the fiction that they were overwhelmed rather than admitting they chose it."

Virginia opened her mouth, but her throat constricted. How many times had she done exactly that with Gian Paolo? Protested his visits while leaving the garden door unlocked. Performed reluctance while arranging every circumstance that made surrender possible.

The thread in her hands had snapped.

* * *

THREE DAYS LATER, Virginia woke past midnight to footsteps in the corridor outside her chamber—soft, furtive, moving with the careful quiet of someone who understood the consequences of discovery. She lay still, one hand pressed to her belly where the child shifted restlessly, and listened. The footsteps moved past her door, heading toward the stairs that led down to the ground floor.

Virginia rose, one hand braced against the bedframe and the other supporting her belly. She shuffled to her door and opened it just wide enough to see down the dim corridor. A single figure descended the stairs at the far end. Candida, visible for just a moment in the faint moonlight from a high window before she disappeared from view.

Virginia closed her door and returned to her window, looking down into the empty garden below. Moonlight illuminated the fountain, the herb beds, the gravel paths—all still and silent. The garden revealed nothing. She couldn't see the parlatory from here, couldn't see the street, couldn't see where Candida had gone or why.

But she knew. The midnight hour. The furtive movements. Ottavia had told her about the letter—Arrigone's demand to enter the convent proper, to meet Candida without the constraint of the grating. Virginia pressed one hand against the cold glass. Somewhere below, in corridors and rooms she couldn't see, the pattern was repeating itself. Another woman opening a door that should stay locked. Another man crossing a threshold he should never approach.

She returned to bed with slow, careful movements, lowering herself onto the mattress. The baby kicked against her ribs, hard, insistent jabs that stole her breath, and she pressed her hand to the spot where the small foot pushed back against her palm. She lay awake in the darkness, staring at the ceiling beams barely visible, imagining what she couldn't witness but understood too well.

Three hours later, she heard the footsteps return. Quick and light this time, moving up the stairs with less caution than before. Then a door closing somewhere down the corridor, and silence stretching through the darkness until dawn began to gray the eastern sky and the bells called the sisters to Lauds.

* * *

AT MASS THE next morning, Candida's face was flushed with color that had nothing to do with the warmth in the chapel, and her eyes held a bright, glittering quality. Her wimple sat askew, the fabric bunched on one side where she'd pinned it hastily without taking the time to arrange it properly, and when she caught Virginia watching from across the chapel, her gaze skittered away. After prayers, Virginia summoned her with a gesture that left no room for refusal, and Candida followed in silence with her hands twisting together and her breathing quick and shallow as they walked through the corridors to Virginia's chamber.

Virginia closed the door, the latch clicking, and turned to face the younger woman who stood just inside the threshold looking as though she might bolt at any moment. "Tell me what's happening between you and Father Arrigone."

"Nothing. I don't know what you mean." Candida's voice came out high and thin, the lie transparent even as she spoke it.

"Don't lie to me." Virginia moved away from the door, though walking required careful negotiation now with her shifted center of gravity and the constant pain in her hips. "I heard you last night. I know you let Arrigone into the convent. I know you stayed with him for three hours."

Candida's face crumpled. Tears spilled down her cheeks in sudden streams, but she made no sound beyond the sharp, hitching breaths that shook her shoulders. She just stood there with her hands clenched in her habit, and the sight sent Virginia's mind back five years to her own face in the mirror, the same tears, the same posture.

"How long has this been going on?" Virginia kept her voice level.

"Two months. Maybe three. I've lost track of when it started, when the letters became something more than simple spiritual guidance." Candida's voice emerged as barely a whisper. "It started with letters about faith and devotion. He said he'd been watching me during Mass, that he saw something special in me that no one else had noticed. That I deserved better than this half-life we live here, trapped behind walls, our gifts wasted on endless repetition of prayers no one really hears."

The same words Gian Paolo had used. The same seduction disguised as concern. The same promise that she was special and different. "And last night?"

"He wanted to meet in person. Said we needed to talk without the constraint of letters, that what he had to say required seeing my face, hearing my voice respond." Candida's hands clenched tighter in her habit until the knuckles whitened. "I told Domenico it was urgent spiritual business, that you'd given permission for the meeting because I needed counsel that couldn't wait for daylight. I'm sorry. I shouldn't have used your name, but Domenico wouldn't help me otherwise."

"What happened when Arrigone arrived?" Virginia pressed both hands to her belly where the child shifted, rolling from one side to the other in movements that were becoming more constrained as it ran out of room.

Candida's flush deepened, spreading from her throat to her hairline. "We talked. That's all, I swear. He told me I was beautiful, that he'd been thinking about me constantly since our first conversation. That he wanted—" She stopped, the words catching in her throat.

"Wanted what?" Virginia's voice came out harder than she'd intended.

"To touch me. To hold me. To know what it felt like to—" The confession broke off in a sob that Candida tried to muffle with her hand.

Virginia turned back to the window, gripping the sill until her knuckles ached and the wood bit into her palms. "Did he touch you?"

"Through the grating. Just my hand." Candida's voice dropped so low Virginia had to strain to hear it. "He held it and said it was the softest thing he'd ever felt, like touching grace itself. That every moment we spent apart was torture, that the iron between us was a cruelty neither of us deserved. It felt wrong, Sister Virginia, but also... as though God had brought us together for a purpose we didn't yet understand."

Virginia had spoken those exact words to herself five years ago when she'd been trying to reconcile her vows with her desire. She had wrapped sin in the language of divine providence to make it bearable. "He's using you, Candida. Every word he's saying, every promise he's making, every gesture of concern—they're tools he's perfected through practice. Techniques he's refined on other women before you and will use on others after you're no longer useful to him."

"You don't understand. What we have is different." Candida protested.

"It's not different." Virginia's voice carried absolute certainty born from bitter experience. "You think you're special. That your situation is unique. That the rules applying to everyone else don't apply to you because what you feel is so powerful it must be sanctioned by God." She turned from the window to face Candida directly, letting the younger woman see the consequences written in her distended belly and the exhaustion carved into her face. "I told myself exactly those words. I wrapped every boundary I crossed in the language of destiny. I convinced myself my connection with Gian Paolo transcended ordinary sin because surely such intense emotion couldn't exist if it wasn't meant to be."

Candida's eyes dropped to Virginia's belly, and something shifted in her expression. "Arrigone told me about you and Gian Paolo. He said you fell because you didn't have proper spiritual guidance. That with him, it would be different because he knows how to protect me from—" She gestured helplessly at Virginia's pregnant form.

"From this?" Virginia's laugh came out bitter as wormwood. "He told you the same lies he helped craft for Gian Paolo to use on me. Did he mention that?

That he wrote those beautiful letters you've heard about? The ones that convinced me I was special and chosen and beloved?"

Candida's face went white. "He said he helped advise Gian Paolo on spiritual matters. That he guided him toward—"

"He guided him toward my bed." Virginia's voice cut through the excuse like a blade. "And now he's using the success of that seduction as proof of his skill. You're not the first woman he's practiced on, Candida. You're just the latest. He chose you because I succeeded, because my fall proved his methods work. He's using what happened with me to seduce you."

Silence stretched between them, broken only by the distant sound of bells calling the sisters to prayer and the softer sound of Candida's ragged breathing. Outside the window, a bird sang with cheerful obliviousness.

"You need to stop seeing him," Virginia said, forcing the words out through a throat that wanted to close. "Stop writing to him. Stop meeting him. Stop this before it goes further than hand-holding through a grating, because it will go further if you let it continue. First comes the accidental touch. Then the deliberate touch. Then the kiss. Then more, always more, until you've crossed so many boundaries you can't remember where the lines were supposed to be."

"He says he loves me." Candida's voice carried desperate need.

"He doesn't." Virginia's voice held no doubt, no hesitation. "He loves what you represent. The challenge of seducing a nun, the proof of his skill, the trophy he can display to other men when he brags about his conquests. Whatever he claims to feel is performance designed to lower your defenses. And whatever you think you feel for him is built on lies and manipulation, constructed from the words he's carefully chosen to make you surrender."

Candida shook her head, fresh tears streaming down her flushed cheeks even as her jaw set. "You're wrong. What Arrigone and I have is real. He's promised to take me away from here, to Venice where no one knows us. Where we can be together properly without these walls between us. He has it all planned, the route we'll take, the house where we'll live, the new names we'll use. And he's told me how to avoid what happened to you. He loves me enough to risk everything and wise enough to protect me from the consequences you suffer."

Virginia could have recited every detail because she'd heard these exact lies before, had wrapped them around herself like armor when Gian Paolo whispered them in the darkness. The promise of protection from pregnancy had been one of them. "Go," she said, exhaustion crashing over her with sudden force that made her legs shake. "Just go, Candida. I can't help you if you won't help yourself."

After Candida left, Virginia sank onto her bed with slow, careful movements, the ropes supporting the mattress creaking. The baby rolled beneath her hands, pressing against her bladder and her ribs and her lungs until she couldn't draw a full breath. Movement brought pain. Standing brought pain. Lying down brought pain. Everything hurt now, and she couldn't stop what was happening to Candida any more than she could stop what was coming for herself.

* * *

THE LETTERS INTENSIFIED over the following week, arriving multiple times each day according to reports from Benedetta and Ottavia who tracked the pattern. Five letters in three days, then six, then two more parlatory meetings late at night when the convent slept. Domenico's fear was palpable. His hands shook so badly he could barely manage the basket, his eyes darted constantly toward the convent windows, his wife reported that he wasn't sleeping, that he paced their quarters at night muttering about consequences and discovery.

"She's planning something," Benedetta said one evening, standing at the window and watching the garden below where Candida walked among the herbs with a distracted expression. "That particular look people get before doing something they know is wrong but can't stop themselves from attempting. The look of someone who's decided to jump and is just waiting for the right moment to let go."

Virginia pressed her hand to the wall. "She's going to let him in. Not just to the parlatory for supervised meetings. Into the convent proper, where there are no barriers, no witnesses, no pretense of maintaining boundaries."

"How can you be certain?" Benedetta turned from the window.

"Because that's the natural progression. The pattern is predictable once it starts." Virginia shifted her weight, trying to ease the constant ache in her hips. "Letters lead to meetings. Meetings lead to touch. Touch leads to more intimate contact. Each boundary crossed makes the next one easier to justify until there are no boundaries left."

Benedetta's expression remained carefully neutral, but her jaw tightened almost imperceptibly. "You could still stop it. Go to Prioress Bianca and report what you know. Give her the evidence she needs to intervene before Candida destroys herself completely."

"And say what?" The words tasted bitter on Virginia's tongue. "That I notice the signs of seduction because I'm carrying the evidence of my own fall? That I'm qualified to judge Candida's sins because I've committed worse ones? Bianca would ask how I know so much about Arrigone's methods, how I can predict his moves with such certainty. Any explanation I offer will expose me as thoroughly as it exposes Candida. I have no ground to stand on, Benedetta. No credibility left."

"So, you'll just watch it happen."

"I don't have a choice." But even as Virginia spoke the words, she understood they weren't quite accurate. She had choices. Simply none that wouldn't destroy her in the process of saving Candida.

* * *

JUNE BROUGHT A heat that turned the stone corridors into ovens and the air in Virginia's chamber into something thick enough to choke on. She woke before dawn on the first day of the month with her chemise soaked through with sweat and her heart pounding from a dream that had already dissolved into fragments. The baby kicked hard against her ribs, once, twice, three times in rapid succession, and she pressed her palm to the spot where the small foot drummed its restless rhythm.

She pushed herself upright, the effort leaving her breathless. Her ankles had swollen so thick that when she swung her legs over the side of the bed, the skin pulled tight and shiny across the bone. She pressed her thumb into the flesh below her ankle. The indentation remained long after she removed her hand, a pale crater in the swollen tissue that took minutes to fill back in.

A knock on her door brought Benedetta into her cell. "You should stay in bed today. You're not strong enough for the stairs."

"I have to attend Mass." Virginia stood with effort, one hand braced against the bedframe. The room tilted, and she waited for her vision to clear before taking another step. "If I stop going entirely, they'll know for certain."

"They already know." Benedetta rose and moved to help her, one arm around Virginia's waist to support her weight. "Sister Agnes asked me yesterday if you were with child. I told her you suffered from dropsy, but she didn't believe me."

The words settled into Virginia's chest with the weight of stones, but she forced herself to take another step toward the washbasin. If she acknowledged the danger, if she let herself think about what would happen when the whispers became accusations, she would lose what little courage remained.

* * *

THE CHAPEL WAS stifling despite the early hour. Virginia knelt in her usual place near the back. Her mind drifted through the Latin prayers she had recited so many thousands of times that the syllables moved on their own. Around her, the other sisters knelt with heads bowed and hands clasped, their voices rising and falling in the familiar rhythm of morning prayer.

Attention pressed against her like hands. Sisters watched the way she climbed the chapel steps more slowly each day, the way her breathing shortened when she rose, the way her habit strained across her middle despite Benedetta's careful work with folds and pins.

The priest at the altar lifted the Host; a bell rang; the choir responded. Virginia kept her gaze fixed on the crucifix and counted. Breaths. Heartbeats. The subtle shifts of the child inside her. The minutes until she could leave this suffocating air and lie down.

When Mass ended, the sisters filed out in pairs and small clusters toward the refectory. Virginia remained kneeling until the press of bodies thinned, then pushed herself upright, one hand on the pew to steady her. The room tilted. By the time she reached the cloister, sweat ran down her spine beneath the wool.

Benedetta appeared at her elbow. "You're swaying."

"I'm walking," Virginia said, though her knees had begun to shake.

"Barely." Benedetta slid an arm around her waist, taking some of the weight as they crossed the cloister toward the stairs. "You should rest."

Before they reached the first step, Sister Costanza hurried toward them, breathing harder than the distance required.

"Sister Virginia," she said, dipping her head. "Prioress Bianca asks you to go to the parlatory. Father Arrigone from San Maurizio has requested to speak to you about 'parish business.' She said it would cause more talk to refuse him without reason."

Of course. Arrigone would not risk being seen inside the convent chapel unless duty required it; he preferred safer ground, where iron bars still gave the appearance of propriety.

"I'll go," Virginia said.

As Sister Costanza walked away, Benedetta's arm tightened in warning. "Be careful."

"It will be brief." Virginia drew a breath that scraped her ribs. "If I refuse, he'll only try again."

* * *

SHE TOOK HER place on the convent side of the grate, lowering herself onto the narrow bench with care. A moment later, footsteps sounded, then Arrigone stepped into view. The iron pattern chopped his face into narrow vertical strips, but the smile needed no clarity.

"Sister Virginia," he said. "Thank you for seeing me. I know rising for morning prayers has become... taxing."

Incense still clung to his cassock; somewhere, he had already said his Mass at San Maurizio. His gaze drifted over her face, then down to the swell of her belly, lingering there with frank curiosity.

"What business brings you, Father?" Virginia kept her hands folded in her lap so he could not see them tremble.

"Only concern," he replied, moving closer until his fingers curled around the bars. "For the spiritual and physical welfare of the sisters of Santa Margherita. You look unwell. Is there anything I can do?"

"No, Father. Thank you."

"I am here to help the sisters with any burden." The words came mild; the look did not. His eyes moved once more from her face to the arc of her habit, then back. "Some secrets grow heavy when carried alone. Confession can lighten the load."

The iron between them suddenly felt too thin. He had not said the word, but his gaze made it unnecessary. Pregnancy was not an illness one caught. It had a cause, and he knew enough of her history with Gian Paolo to guess the rest.

"I have no secrets beyond the usual sins," Virginia said. Her voice held steady; her pulse did not.

"Is that so?" One corner of his mouth lifted. "How fortunate. Though I wonder if Prioress Bianca would share your confidence. Or the Cardinal's agents who were in Monza last week, asking such very pointed questions about this convent."

Her chest clenched. "I don't understand you, Father."

"Don't you?" He slipped one hand between two of the bars as far as the angle allowed and closed his fingers around the iron directly in front of her. "You understand that discretion is... valuable. That some truths are safer in the dark. And that when a man has been unjustly thrown into prison once already, he develops a very keen appreciation for what other people's secrets are worth."

His voice never rose, but every syllable landed like a weight.

"I'm sure your parishioners at San Maurizio benefit from your concern," Virginia said. "As for this convent, those matters belong to Prioress Bianca. If you have questions, you should address them to her."

"I prefer to gather information from the source." He eased his hand back from the grate. "But very well. I won't keep you from your rest. I'll pray for your swift recovery from your… condition. And if you find yourself in need of guidance, you know where to find me."

She stood before he could say more and offered the barest inclination of her head, enough courtesy to satisfy form, not enough to smell like gratitude. The corridor beyond the parlatory blurred as she walked; by the time she reached the stairwell, her heart pulsed so hard that each beat pushed against her throat.

Benedetta waited at the base of the stairs. One look at Virginia's face and she moved to support her again without a word.

"What did he say?" she asked as they began the climb, one step at a time.

"He knows," Virginia said. Breath came short between words. "Or close enough. He wondered aloud what the Cardinal's agents might pay for certain truths. He offered 'help.'"

"Men like him don't help," Benedetta muttered. "They hoard."

Each step demanded thought. One foot, then the other. Both hands on the railing now, Benedetta's arm still firm at her waist. Heat rose from the stone, the stairs themselves radiating the June sun trapped in the walls.

"He's building leverage," Virginia said when they reached the first landing. "Watching. Waiting. If everything collapses, he wants to be the one holding the rope."

"We need to move faster," Benedetta said quietly. "The birth is still some time away, but not so much that we can waste time. Once the child is out of this house, Arrigone's hold weakens. Until then, that babe inside you gives every fool in Monza a weapon."

* * *

August

THE HEAT OF August turned the convent into a kiln. In the small chamber where Virginia labored, the air hung thick and stifling, heavy with the smell of sweat, vinegar-soaked rags, and the copper tang of blood.

Virginia gripped the edges of her mattress until her knuckles turned white. Pain rolled through her in waves, each one higher than the last, threatening to pull her under. A scream rose in her throat, but she caught it behind her teeth and bit down hard on the rolled cloth Benedetta had given her.

There could be no noise. No screams that might echo through the corridors. The silence was as vital as the breath in her lungs, and far more difficult to maintain.

Benedetta knelt between Virginia's legs, her black habit pulled up to her elbows. Her face was set in grim concentration. Sweat beaded on her forehead despite the cloth tied around her head.

Ottavia hovered near the door like a nervous bird, her round face pale as tallow. Her hands twisted in her habit, ready to bar the way if anyone approached. From the corner, Sister Candida's low murmur of prayer drifted out like smoke.

"Push," Benedetta whispered. Her voice cut through the haze of pain. "Now, Virginia. Push."

Virginia bore down with everything she had left. The agony tore through her center, a blinding white flash that seemed to split her body. She arched her back, pressing her head into the pillows. Tears leaked from the corners of her eyes. Sweat ran in rivulets down her face and neck.

"Again," Benedetta urged. "I see the head. One more. Give me one more."

One final, wrenching effort drained the last reserves of Virginia's strength. She collapsed back onto the pillows, gasping for air. Blood raced in her veins. The room tilted and swam.

But there was no cry.

The silence that followed was not the silence of safety or relief. It was the silence of the grave.

"Why does it not cry?" Virginia whispered, pushing herself up on trembling elbows. "Benedetta, why?"

Benedetta moved with terrible speed. The baby was a girl, small and slick with blood. But her face was wrong, dark, bruised purple. Her tiny mouth hung open in a silent scream. The umbilical cord was wound tight around the infant's neck like a noose.

"The cord," Benedetta hissed. "It is wrapped."

There was no time to be gentle. Benedetta hooked two fingers under the slippery loop where it dug into the baby's throat. With a sharp, decisive movement, she snipped the cord.

For a terrible second, nothing happened. The baby lay limp and motionless. Virginia's heart stopped. The room went utterly still. Even Candida's prayers had ceased.

Then, with a small, hitching gasp, the infant's chest expanded. Her mouth opened wide. A thin, reedy wail pierced the heavy air.

"Quiet!" Ottavia hissed from the door, though tears were already streaming down her round cheeks. "Please, God, quiet!"

Benedetta quickly placed one hand over the baby's mouth, muffling the sound to a soft whimper. With the other hand, she worked efficiently, dipping a cloth in warm water and cleaning the child. She wrapped the infant in the linen strips Virginia had hidden months ago, swaddling her tight.

"She lives," Benedetta said. Her voice was flat with exhaustion and something that might have been wonder. She held the bundle out to Virginia. "Your daughter lives."

Virginia reached out with a shaking hand and touched the baby's cheek. The skin was soft beyond anything she had ever felt. Warm. Real.

"Alma," she whispered. The name came from nowhere, or perhaps from everywhere at once. *Soul.*

There was no time to rest. Reality crashed back into the room with the sound of the convent's gate bell ringing.

"The doctor," Ottavia whispered. The blood drained from her face. "He is scheduled to see you today for your illness. I had forgotten. Virginia, what do we do?"

Panic spiked through Virginia's chest. If the doctor entered this room now, he would smell the blood. He would see the exhaustion carved into her face, the way her belly had deflated.

"Take her," Virginia said, thrusting the bundle toward Ottavia. "Hide her in your room. Quickly. Go now."

Ottavia took the baby and slipped out of the chamber like a shadow.

Benedetta moved with the speed of a soldier under siege. She stripped the bloody sheets, kicking them under the cot. She threw a fresh blanket over Virginia. She crossed to the window and threw open the shutters, letting the summer breeze chase away the coppery smell.

"You are ill," Benedetta commanded, wiping Virginia's forehead with a damp cloth. "You have a fever. You are too weak to be examined closely. Do you understand?"

Virginia nodded.

A knock at the door. Benedetta opened the door to reveal the doctor, a gray-haired man with tired eyes. He entered and approached the bed, Sister Costanza behind him. Virginia lay against the pillows, forcing her breathing to remain shallow and quick. She let her eyelids droop as though keeping them open was too great an effort.

"How long have you felt poorly?" he asked.

"Weeks," Virginia whispered. "My stomach. No appetite. Weakness."

The doctor made a noncommittal sound. He felt her forehead with the back of his hand. After a few minutes of cursory examination, he stepped back and shook his head.

"A lingering stomach ailment. Rest and light meals. Broth and bread. I will send a tonic."

He stayed only a few minutes longer before taking his leave. He never heard the soft whimper from the room next door. He never saw the blood-soaked linens hidden beneath the bed.

Once his footsteps had faded, Ottavia returned. She carried the baby back into the room, her shoulders sagging with relief. She placed the child in the wooden cradle in the corner.

"She slept," Ottavia said, her voice trembling. "Through the whole thing. She slept."

Virginia closed her eyes. They had survived the birth. They had survived the doctor. Now, only the final surrender remained.

* * *

NIGHT FELL OVER Monza, but it brought no relief from the heat. The baby fussed occasionally in her cradle, making small mewling sounds that tore at something deep in Virginia's chest. Ottavia had sent the signal hours earlier. Now, they waited.

Virginia tried to sit up, wincing as her body protested. Everything hurt. But the worst pain was not physical. It was the knowledge that in a few moments, she would hand over her daughter and never see her again.

A soft sound at the garden door signaled his arrival. Ottavia went to let him in while Benedetta stood watch. Gian Paolo entered the chamber, bringing with him the scent of the outside world—cool night air, leather, earth.

He did not look at Virginia first. His eyes went straight to the cradle.

He stood over it for a long moment. His expression was difficult to read in the dim candlelight. The line of his jaw was tight. His hands opened and closed at his sides.

"A girl," Benedetta said from the shadows.

Gian Paolo nodded slowly. He reached down and picked up the bundle with hands that were surprisingly gentle. He studied her face, tracing the small nose and rosebud mouth with his eyes.

"She looks like me," he said quietly. There was wonder in his voice. "She has my nose. My chin."

He turned to Virginia then. "You did well," he said.

The words should have meant something. But all Virginia felt was a terrible emptiness.

"Take her," she whispered. Her voice broke. "Take her now, before I change my mind."

It was a lie. She could not change her mind. There was no place for a child within these walls. But the lie gave her a moment of agency.

Ottavia stepped forward, arms outstretched. "I will carry her to the gate. It is safer if you walk empty-handed through the garden."

Gian Paolo hesitated, then handed the baby to Ottavia. He bent down and pressed his lips to Virginia's forehead. His breath was warm against her clammy skin. "Rest now. I will take care of her. I swear it."

Virginia watched them leave. Ottavia carrying the child in her swaddling. Gian Paolo following close behind. The door clicked shut behind them with a sound of terrible finality.

The room was suddenly, utterly empty. Virginia stared at the empty cradle in the corner and felt something inside her break that she knew would never heal.

* * *

GIAN PAOLO CARRIED his daughter out of the convent grounds and into the dark streets of Monza. The night was warm and moonless. He kept the bundle close to his chest, shielding her from the world. The baby was mercifully quiet, lulled by the movement and warmth.

He could not simply walk through the front gates of his estate with an infant. Instead, he circled to the rear of his property, where a small garden gate opened onto an overgrown path. Once inside, he climbed the back stairs to his private chambers, moving quickly through corridors he knew would be empty.

The baby began to whimper.

Gian Paolo had fought in battles. He had killed men. But this small, fragile creature terrified him in a way no enemy ever had.

He laid her carefully on his bed and lit a candle. In the flickering light, he unwrapped the swaddling to check if she was injured or wet. She seemed whole and unharmed, but her face was screwing up in preparation for a wail. He quickly rewrapped her, his large hands clumsy.

The baby cried. Not loudly, but persistently. A thin, mewling sound that set his nerves on edge. He picked her up and tried bouncing her the way he had seen peasant women do. It did nothing. She only cried harder.

By dawn, both were exhausted. The baby had finally fallen into fitful sleep against his chest. Gian Paolo sat in his chair, afraid to move and wake her.

He spent the following day hidden in his private rooms, keeping the child away from prying eyes. The baby fussed and cried, her tiny face screwing up in protest. She was hungry, confused, searching with her small mouth for milk.

Gian Paolo had not arranged for a wet nurse in Monza. Secrecy had been paramount. He would have to make do until he could transport the child to Milan.

In his study, with the curtains drawn, he tried to think. The baby's cries filled the room. Finally, an idea came. He went down to the kitchen himself and warmed milk in a small pan, testing it against his wrist. Then he returned to his study and locked the door.

He took one of his fine leather riding gloves from the drawer. The leather was supple and well-oiled, soft from years of use. He poured the warm milk carefully into the largest finger of the glove. Then, using the tip of his dagger, he pricked a tiny hole in the fingertip.

He sat in the high-backed chair and settled the baby in the crook of his left arm. She was so small, so light. He had held hunting falcons that weighed more. He offered the leather finger to her searching mouth.

For a moment, she resisted. But hunger won out. Her small lips latched onto the leather, and she began to suck. The milk flowed slowly through the tiny hole, and she drank with desperate intensity. Her tiny hand emerged from the swaddling and grasped his thumb, her fingers curling tight with surprising strength.

Gian Paolo watched her drink. His chest tightened. His throat constricted. This was his daughter. She carried the de Leyva name in her veins and the Osio pride in her bones. She would not be hidden away. She would have a name. She would have a place in the world.

* * *

TWO DAYS LATER, when the child seemed strong enough to travel, he wrapped her securely in fine linen and placed her in a wicker basket lined with silk. He summoned his closed carriage and set out for Milan.

He went to the Church of Sant'Andrea, one of the finest in Milan. Senator Count Francesco d'Adda was already waiting. D'Adda was a man of immense wealth and influence, his family one of the oldest in Lombardy, and long time friends of the Osio family. He had agreed to be Alma's godfather. His presence here was a statement. It elevated this child, born in secret and sin, into something approaching legitimacy.

The priest who performed the baptism asked no awkward questions. He simply poured the holy water over the infant's head.

"I baptize thee Alma Francesca Margherita," the priest intoned, his voice echoing in the cool, incense-scented air.

Gian Paolo watched the water run down his daughter's forehead. *Alma* for the soul, the name Virginia had whispered. *Francesca* for her godfather, binding her to the d'Adda family and their protection. *Margherita* for the convent where she had been born and that could not hide her.

She was a secret no longer. She was his daughter, baptized and claimed.

After the baptism, he took her to the wet nurse he had hired. The woman lived in a respectable house near the Duomo. She was clean and healthy, with milk enough for two babies. She took Alma into her arms with practiced ease.

"I will care for her as though she were my own," the woman promised.

Gian Paolo paid her well. Enough to ensure her silence and devotion. Then he left his daughter in her care and returned to Monza.

* * *

A WEEK AFTER the birth, Gian Paolo returned to the convent. The August heat had finally begun to break. Virginia was recovering in her cell, her body slowly knitting itself back together.

The danger had passed. The child was gone, safe with her wet nurse in Milan. The doctor had suspected nothing. Reverend Mother Bianca had expressed concern about Virginia's continued weakness but had not pressed for details.

But the bond between Virginia and Gian Paolo had not been severed. If anything, it had been strengthened. They had created a life together, hidden it, saved it, and sent it out into the world. That kind of shared secret forged chains stronger than any marriage vow.

He came to her room deep in the night. When he entered, Virginia was sitting up in bed, unable to sleep. Her body ached with a loss that had nothing to do with physical pain.

Gian Paolo sat on the edge of her narrow bed. "How do you feel?"

"Empty," Virginia said. The word was inadequate, but it was the only one that fit.

Her breasts were swollen and painful with milk that had no baby to drink it. They ached constantly, a dull throb that reminded her with every breath of what she had lost. Ottavia had brought her cloths to bind them, to stop the milk from coming, but that process took days.

Gian Paolo's eyes moved to her chest, where the fullness was visible even through her nightdress. He knew what she needed. He knew what he wanted.

Without a word, he reached out and began to undo the ties of her nightdress. His fingers were deft and sure. Virginia did not stop him.

"Let me help you," he whispered.

He lowered his head to her breast. His mouth found her nipple, and he began to draw the milk that flowed there. The relief was immediate and intense. The pressure that had been building for days eased as he drank from her body. Virginia gasped at the sensation—part pain, part relief, part something darker she could not name.

But it was more than physical relief. His tongue was warm against her skin. His breath was hot. His hand cupped her other breast, thumb rubbing slowly across the fabric. This was not a baby's innocent feeding. This was possession. Claiming. A ritual that bound them together in a way that went far beyond the joining of lovers in the night.

He was consuming what she had made for their child. The wet sound of his swallowing filled the quiet room. His other hand moved to her thigh, fingers pressing through the thin fabric.

Virginia closed her eyes and let him drink. She ran her fingers through his dark hair, feeling the strands slip between her fingers. The sensation pulled at something deep in her belly, something that had nothing to do with maternal feeling and everything to do with the hunger that had always existed between them.

The baby was gone. The child who should have been drinking this milk was miles away in Milan, being fed by a stranger. But Gian Paolo was here, and he would always be here, because they were bound together by blood and sin and secrets that could never be spoken aloud.

This, too, was sin. But it was the only gift she had left to give.

The sin remained. It had never left. And in the dark, silent room, with the cool breeze drifting through the window and the moonlight painting silver stripes across the floor, the cycle began again.

* * *

September

THREE WEEKS HAD passed since Virginia gave birth to her daughter. The baby was gone, carried away by Gian Paolo, baptized and raised in his house in Milan, and Virginia's body was slowly healing. But the exhaustion that had settled into her bones ran deeper than physical weakness.

It was in this vulnerable state when she first noticed the change in Sister Candida.

The younger nun drifted through her duties like a sleepwalker, her attention elsewhere. During Vespers, her gaze would slide toward the windows that overlooked the parlatory. During meals, her hands would tremble when she lifted her cup. She jumped at sudden sounds and flushed crimson when anyone addressed her directly.

Virginia recognized the signs because she had worn them herself. The distraction. The nervous energy. The way ordinary moments became unbearable when your mind was consumed by thoughts of forbidden meetings.

It was Benedetta who brought confirmation on a cool evening when the first hints of autumn had begun to creep into the stone corridors. She entered Virginia's chamber without knocking, closed the door behind her with deliberate care, and moved to the window to check that no one lingered in the courtyard below.

"Candida is meeting someone," Benedetta said. Her voice was clipped, efficient. "At night. In the parlatory."

Virginia's hands stilled on the account book she had been pretending to review. "Who?"

"Arrigone." The name fell between them like a stone dropped into dark water. "Domenico has been letting him in."

The news should not have surprised her. Arrigone had been circling the convent for months like a carrion bird, first pursuing Benedetta, then turning his attention to Candida when she refused him. But hearing it stated so baldly, knowing that Candida had succumbed to the same seduction that had nearly consumed Benedetta, made her stomach clench with something that felt uncomfortably like guilt.

"How long?"

"At least a week. Perhaps longer." Benedetta moved away from the window and perched on the edge of the wooden chair. "I saw Candida returning from the parlatory three nights ago. She thought everyone was asleep, but I was awake. The next night, I followed. I watched from the shadows while they spoke through the grating."

The account book closed with more force than necessary. "And Domenico?"

"Candida tells him she has permission from you to use the parlatory for spiritual counsel at unusual hours." Benedetta's mouth twisted into something that was not quite a smile. "He believes her because she is the convent chancellor. Because she speaks with authority, and men like Domenico do not question women who sound confident in their lies."

The betrayal stung more than expected. Not Candida's deception. That was almost understandable. But the way the nun had used Virginia's name, had hidden behind her authority while committing the same sins that had nearly destroyed them all.

"Domenico unlocks the main door in the evening and leaves the keys in the inner door," Benedetta continued. "Candida retrieves them when she arrives, locks herself in the parlatory with Arrigone, and returns them to a hiding place beneath a stone near the entrance when they finish. Domenico collects them in the morning and replaces them on their hook. A perfect system. Clean. Untraceable."

Virginia stood and moved to the window. Below, the garden lay peaceful in the fading light. The last roses of summer still clung to their vines, their petals beginning to brown at the edges. In a few weeks, the first frost would kill them. Everything beautiful died eventually.

"I will watch first," Virginia said finally. "I need to understand what we are dealing with before I act."

Benedetta nodded slowly. "Then watch tonight. They meet after Compline, when the convent has settled. Position yourself in the corridor that leads to the parlatory. You will hear everything through the door."

* * *

THAT NIGHT, VIRGINIA waited in the shadows. The stone corridor was cool despite the lingering warmth of the day. She pressed her back against the wall of a storage room where she could see the corridor through the slightly open door. Chill seeped through her habit. The darkness was absolute, broken only by a sliver of moonlight that fell through a high window and painted a silver line across the floor. The air smelled of damp stone and old incense.

The soft sound of footsteps announced Candida's arrival. Virginia's breath caught. She held perfectly still as the younger nun passed within arm's reach, so close Virginia could hear the rustle of her habit and the quick, nervous rhythm of her breathing.

The quiet scrape of metal against stone. Candida retrieving the key.

The lock turned with a well-oiled click. The door swung open and closed again, sealing Candida inside the parlatory.

Virginia stepped out into the corridor.

Then Arrigone's voice drifted through the heavy wood, warm and pleased and utterly false.

"You came. I was afraid you might lose your courage."

"You said it was important." Candida's voice trembled. "You said there was urgent business to discuss."

"There is. The most important business in the world. The business of my heart."

Candida made a small sound that might have been protest. "Father, you should not speak this way. It is not proper for a priest."

"Why not?" Arrigone's interruption was smooth as silk. "Because I am a priest? Because you are a nun? These are merely roles we play. Costumes we wear. Beneath them, we are still man and woman. God made us with hearts that yearn for connection, for love, for the touch of another soul. It is not sin to acknowledge what He created within us."

Virginia's hands clenched in the folds of her habit. She had heard these arguments before. The theology twisted but seductive, transforming lust into divine calling, reframing sin as sacred truth. It was the kind of reasoning that made you doubt your own certainty.

Candida would be powerless against such arguments. The girl was lonely and inexperienced, starved for affection in a place where warmth was rationed like bread in winter.

They spoke for perhaps an hour. Arrigone painted pictures with his language, describing a love that transcended earthly vows, a connection blessed by God despite what narrow-minded churchmen might claim. Candida resisted at first, her responses hesitant and uncertain. But gradually, inexorably, the younger nun's defenses crumbled. Her voice grew softer, more yielding.

"Tomorrow night," Arrigone said when they finally parted. "Come back tomorrow night. There is so much more I need to tell you."

"I should not," Candida whispered. But there was no conviction in the words. "If anyone discovers us..."

"No one will discover us. I promise you." A pause, weighted with meaning. "Tomorrow, Candida. Please. I cannot bear another day without seeing you."

Virginia slipped back inside the storage room.

The rustle of fabric. The key turning. Footsteps retreating down the corridor, quick and furtive.

Virginia remained hidden in the shadows, her legs cramping from standing so still, until long after the sounds had faded. Only then did she allow herself to move, flexing stiff muscles and breathing deeply of the cool night air.

* * *

THE FOLLOWING EVENING, Candida came to Virginia's chamber. Her face was flushed, her eyes bright with something that might have been fever.

"Father Arrigone brought me something," Candida said without preamble. She held out her hand. In her palm lay a small black object wrapped in crimson silk. "He said there was a note inside it. That I should open it when I was alone and read his message."

Virginia stared at the package. "Have you opened it?"

"No." Candida's hand trembled. "I've heard stories. About magic practices. About priests who use charms and enchantments to bind women's hearts. The way it's wrapped, the color of the silk... I was afraid to touch it."

"Show me," Virginia commanded.

Candida placed the package on the desk. Virginia used the corner of her habit to lift it, turning it carefully without making direct contact with the silk or the object beneath.

"Put it on your window sill," Virginia said finally. "Don't touch it with your bare hands. Don't unwrap it. In the morning, we'll see if it's still there."

Candida's eyes widened. "You think it's witchcraft?"

"I think Father Arrigone is desperate. And desperate men turn to dark practices when honeyed words fail them."

* * *

THE NEXT MORNING, Candida burst into Virginia's chamber, her face pale.

"It's gone," she gasped. "I looked everywhere. It's not on the sill. It's not on the floor. It's simply... vanished."

Virginia felt cold certainty settle over her. "Tell Benedetta. She should know that Arrigone has moved beyond seduction into darker arts."

Candida nodded, but Virginia could see the fear in her eyes. Magic practices were whispered about in the convent but rarely encountered directly. This was something else. This was proof that Arrigone would use any means necessary to bend women to his will.

* * *

THE FINAL MEETING happened several nights later. The air carried a bite that spoke of winter coming, and the first leaves had begun to fall from the trees in the garden.

Virginia positioned herself in the now-familiar spot, her body fitting into the hollow she'd worn against the stone. The cold seeped through her habit, but she barely noticed. All her attention was focused on the voices beyond the door.

Arrigone was coaxing, pleading, his voice rough with need that was entirely physical. Candida's responses came slowly, her protests growing weaker with each exchange.

"Touch me," Arrigone whispered. The words were raw, stripped of poetry. "Please, Candida. I need to feel your hand. Just that. Nothing more."

There was a long pause. Then Candida's voice, so quiet Virginia almost missed it. "How?"

"Through the grating. Reach through. I will guide you."

What followed made Virginia's hands clench into fists. Arrigone's instructions, each one more explicit than the last. Candida's small gasp of shock. The moment when resistance crumbled. The soft, wet sounds that needed no interpretation.

When it was over, Candida fled. Her footsteps echoed down the corridor, running now, no longer caring who might hear. The nun's ragged breathing, the small sounds that might have been sobs, faded into the darkness.

Arrigone remained on the other side of the grating for a moment longer. Virginia heard him adjusting his clothing, heard him humming softly to himself with the satisfaction of a man who had gotten exactly what he wanted.

Virginia waited until he left. Then she returned to her chamber, fury and disgust warring in her chest.

She knew what Candida was feeling now. The shame. The revulsion. The sick awareness that she had crossed a line that could never be uncrossed. That was why the girl had run. Not from discovery, but from the truth of what she had just done.

Candida would not go back. Virginia was certain of it. The physical violation had accomplished what all of Virginia's watching and planning could not. It had shattered the illusion that this was about love or spiritual connection.

It was about power. About a man taking what he wanted and leaving a woman to live with the shame.

* * *

THE NEXT MORNING, Virginia summoned Candida to her chamber. The younger nun arrived with fear etched into every line of her body, but beneath the fear was something else: disgust. Self-loathing.

"Sit," Virginia commanded. Her voice came out softer than intended.

Candida perched on the edge of the wooden chair like a bird ready to take flight.

"Tell me everything," Virginia said. She moved to stand at the window, unable to look at Candida while hearing this. "Leave nothing out. Every meeting. Every letter. Every gift. I want to know it all."

The confession poured out in a torrent of words. Candida described the first letter, delivered by Domenico with claims of urgent spiritual business. Described the first meeting in the parlatory, how Arrigone had transformed discussion of faith into discussion of love. Described the subsequent meetings, each one pushing boundaries a little further.

She spoke of the letters she had sent in return. The gifts she had commissioned. The quills she'd given Domenico to sharpen, with messages written inside the hollow shafts. The way she had lied to everyone and had used Virginia's name without permission.

And finally, haltingly, with shame choking every word, she described the final meeting. What Arrigone had asked her to do. How she had agreed despite knowing it was wrong. How his pleasure had left her feeling dirty and used.

"I cannot see him again," Candida whispered. "I know I should never have begun this. I know I have sinned. But after last night... I felt his touch and I wanted to vomit. I wanted to scrub my hand until the skin came off. Whatever spell he had over me, it broke the moment I realized what I was truly doing."

Virginia nodded slowly. This was the crucial difference. Candida had chosen to end it herself. Had recognized the ugliness beneath Arrigone's pretty words and recoiled from it.

"You will not see him again," Virginia said. "You will not write to him. You will not accept any communication from him. Do you understand?"

"Yes," Candida said, and this time her voice carried certainty.

"And you will tell me exactly how your system works. Where the keys are hidden. When you meet. How Domenico is involved. Everything."

Candida described it all. Virginia listened, cataloging every detail, planning her next move with the cold precision of a general mapping a battlefield.

When Candida left, Virginia stood at the window for a long time, looking at the garden below. Arrigone had not only seduced a nun under her authority. He had used Virginia's own seduction as his calling card. Had boasted about his authorship of the letters that had helped destroy her. Had laughed about it. Had turned her suffering into a demonstration of his power.

And now he would pay for it.

* * *

SEVERAL DAYS PASSED. Candida did not return to the parlatory. The physical encounter had broken whatever spell Arrigone's words had woven. She could not erase the memory of his touch, the ugliness beneath the poetry, the sick awareness of what she had allowed herself to become.

But shame has strange effects on the mind. Unable to accept that she had been so thoroughly manipulated, Candida wrote one final letter. Not a love letter. Something else. An attempt to preserve some dignity. To frame what had happened as something she had chosen, not something done to her.

She gave the letter and the *Agnus Dei* to Domenico. "For Father Arrigone," she said, her voice carefully neutral. "He asked for spiritual guidance on a matter of conscience."

Domenico took them without question.

* * *

BUT VIRGINIA WAS watching now. She intercepted Domenico in the wine cellar before he could leave the convent grounds.

The air in the cellar was cool and damp, thick with the smell of old stone and fermenting grapes. The space was narrow, the ceiling low enough that she had to duck beneath a wooden beam. Barrels lined the walls, their surfaces slick with condensation.

Domenico looked up when she entered, his expression shifting from mild curiosity to wary alarm when he saw her face.

"Vicaress," he said tentatively.

"You have been carrying letters," Virginia said. She did not raise her voice. Did not need to. The fury in her tone was unmistakable. "Between Sister Candida and Father Arrigone."

The color drained from Domenico's face. "She said she had permission. She said you had approved."

"She lied." Virginia stepped closer. "And you are a fool for believing her."

"I didn't know, Vicaress. I swear to you, I had no idea."

"Where is the *Agnus Dei*?" Virginia interrupted. "And the letter she asked you to deliver today?"

Domenico's hand moved unconsciously to the pocket of his jerkin.

"Give them to me," she said. "Now."

Domenico hesitated for only a moment before reaching into his pocket. His fingers emerged clutching a small package wrapped in cloth and a sealed letter. He held them out with a hand that trembled visibly.

Virginia unwrapped the cloth. Inside was the wax medallion, stamped with the Lamb of God. She broke the seal on the letter and unfolded the paper.

The words inside were not what she expected. Not declarations of love or pleas for another meeting. Instead, they were confused, halting, an attempt to make sense of what had happened:

> *Father Arrigone, I do not know how to write what I must say. What passed between us troubles my conscience greatly. You spoke of love and devotion, but what occurred was not what I understood those words to mean. I believed your intentions were pure, as you claimed. I do not know what to think now. I pray you will help me understand what this was, so I may confess it properly and receive absolution. I cannot meet you again, but I beg you to tell me if I have sinned as grievously as I fear.*

Virginia read it twice. The letter revealed everything—Candida's confusion, her shame, her desperate attempt to frame the encounter as something other than what it was. She was not pursuing the affair. She was trying to escape it while preserving some shred of dignity.

But the letter was still evidence. Evidence of the correspondence. Evidence of the meetings. Evidence that Arrigone had been inside the convent at night.

"Tear it up," Virginia commanded.

"But Vicaress—"

"Tear it up, or I will have you brought before the Cardinal." Virginia's voice cut through his protest. "I will tell him you have been facilitating sin within these walls. You will lose your position. Your wife will lose hers too. You may well lose your freedom. Is that what you want?"

Domenico's hands shook as he took the letter back and tore it into pieces. The sound of ripping paper echoed in the stone cellar, strangely loud in the confined space.

"The *Agnus Dei* stays here," Virginia said. "You will not deliver it. You will not carry any more letters for Sister Candida. You will not carry letters for anyone without my explicit permission. Do you understand?"

"Yes, Vicaress."

"And if Father Arrigone comes to this convent seeking entry, you will turn him away. If he asks about Candida, you will tell him nothing. If he offers you money, you will refuse it." Virginia leaned closer. "And if I discover you have disobeyed me in any way, I will see you chastised publicly in the town square. The Cardinal will hear of your role in this sordid affair, and I will personally ensure that the consequences are severe."

Domenico nodded, shoulders slumped in defeat. "I understand, Vicaress. It will not happen again."

Virginia took the torn pieces of the letter and the *Agnus Dei* and left him standing there among the wine barrels, a broken man contemplating the wreckage of his foolishness.

* * *

WHEN CANDIDA RECEIVED no reply to her letter, she feared it was because of Virginia. She found Domenico working in the same cellar the next day, rolling barrels into position for the winter storage.

She stopped in the doorway, her hands clenched in her habit. "The letter and the Agnus Dei I gave you yesterday. Did you deliver them?"

Domenico didn't look up from the barrel he was positioning. "No, Sister."

"Why not?"

"Because the Vicaress took them." He straightened slowly, his weathered face carefully neutral. "She knew about them."

Candida's breath caught. "And?"

"She took them from me. Both the letter and the Agnus Dei you wanted returned." His eyes met hers now, steady and unapologetic.

"She had no right."

"She's the Vicaress." Domenico's voice was flat. "She has every right."

Candida's face flushed red. "How dare you? I am the convent chancellor. I can write and send out all the letters I want."

Domenico straightened, meeting her gaze. His jaw was set, his expression no longer fearful but resolute. "I'll take letters only if the Vicaress passes them to me directly and not before."

Candida's body shook with rage and something else, desperation. "Then I'll go to the parlatory myself. Tonight. I'll demand answers from him directly."

"The Vicaress has forbidden Father Arrigone from visiting the parlatory." Domenico's voice held no sympathy. "She gave the order to the portress this morning. He's not to be admitted under any circumstances."

Candida stared at him, the words not quite penetrating. "She can't. I'm the chancellor. I can override her orders."

"She's the Vicaress and daughter of the Count of Monza." Domenico turned back to his work. "Who do you think the portress will obey?"

The reality of her powerlessness settled over Candida like a shroud. Virginia had cut off every avenue. The letters intercepted. The gifts taken. The parlatory barred. There was no way to reach Arrigone, no way to demand the explanations she desperately needed.

“He promised me,” she whispered, more to herself than to Domenico.

The old servant’s expression softened slightly. “Men like Father Arrigone make many promises, Sister. I’ve carried his letters for years. You’re not the first, and you won’t be the last.”

The words landed like stones in still water, ripples spreading outward. *Not the first.* Candida felt something inside her chest crack and collapse.

But Candida never went to the parlatory again. Never wrote any more letters. The affair was over, ended not by Virginia’s intervention alone, but by Candida’s own recognition of what Arrigone truly was. The physical encounter had shattered the illusion. Virginia’s complete severing of all contact, and Domenico’s revelation that she was never special, had broken what remained of her hope.

The shame would remain. But at least it would not grow worse.

* * *

WORD REACHED VIRGINIA a week later through channels she preferred not to examine too closely. Father Arrigone was furious. When Domenico told him what had happened, he blamed Virginia for the end of his liaison with Candida. He cursed her name in taverns. He spoke of her with contempt to anyone who would listen, describing her as a hypocrite who judged others for sins she herself committed regularly.

“He says you have no right to interfere,” the servant reported, clearly uncomfortable delivering such news. “He says you are no different than Candida, except that you have been at it longer and borne children by your lover. He says—” The woman stopped, flushing.

“He says what?” Virginia’s voice was dangerously quiet.

“He says you’re jealous. That you cannot bear knowing his letters were wasted on you. That you treasured his words like they were scripture, never understanding that you fell in love with his art, not Count Osio’s soul.”

The accusation struck home with devastating accuracy. Not because Virginia had been fooled. She had known the truth for years. But because Arrigone was still using her as a trophy, still displaying her seduction as proof of his power, still refusing to acknowledge that she had seen through him long ago.

Virginia dismissed the servant and sat alone in her chamber while the afternoon light faded. The shadows lengthened across the floor, creeping up the walls like dark water rising.

Arrigone had not only seduced a nun under her authority. He had used Virginia's own seduction as his calling card. Had boasted about his authorship of the letters that had helped destroy her. Had laughed about it. Had turned her suffering into an advertisement for his skill.

And now he was spreading poison about her through Monza, painting himself as the victim of her interference.

Virginia could not forgive that Arrigone had been the author of Gian Paolo's love letters. But more than that, she could not forgive that he had turned her private fall into public proof of his cleverness. That he had made her pain into his achievement. That he refused to let her suffering remain her own.

This is what rankled her so deeply that it finally drove her to an explosion of rage.

She sat at her desk and pulled out paper and ink. Her hand did not shake as she began to write.

> *From Sister Virginia Maria de Leyva to Priest Paolo Arrigone:*
>
> *You infamous, shameful creature. I am informed that your arrogance has reached such heights that you now spread the vilest lies against me, lies only a perverse and sacrilegious man like you could invent. God's mercy is astounding that He does not strike you down at the altar and have you dragged to Hell by a hundred devils. But I swear by the holy baptism I bear, and by who I am, that I will expose you. I will show the world why you invented these fantasies against me. I will reveal the true cause of your revenge.*

I will make you known for the infamous scoundrel you are. Your true profession has always been wickedness, your public dealings with whores, your keeping of three sisters as concubines, your attempts to seduce women in the confessional. You know this is true.

And having committed all these abuses, as all the world knows, you then had the audacity to pursue even the brides of Christ within these walls. You tried in every way to corrupt this convent's reputation. You wrote many amorous and shameful letters to Sister Candida, trying everything to make her break her vows. I have your letters as proof. They clearly came from your hand, even though you did not sign your name.

You, who wanted to climb the walls of this convent for your indecent purposes. You, who had the gall to come to the parlatory many times between midnight and Matins, always dealing with her licentiously and immorally in word and deed. It makes me ashamed even to write of it. But we know everything, down to the loosening of your trousers and your shameless acts with her.

You were seen and heard from the parlatory grating. That person will testify under oath. Your victim will be forced to confess everything. At the proper time and place, she will be compelled to speak the truth that has been hushed up until now out of respect for her position.

I will see to it she will testify with oaths and other proofs about that night, throwing her kisses and other indecencies. You were plainly recognized by other nuns who pretended to be your friend in order to catch you in your schemes. Domenico and his wife will have to confess about the letters they carried and confirm that you came to the parlatory at night. Believe me, I will expose you before all, with witnesses.

And so, I will have you. I will make it known why you acted so wickedly against me in revenge. It was only because I, by my conscience and my position as Vicaress, took steps to stop your shameful schemes. I will make Domenico and the nun herself testify that after I intervened, there were no more letters and no more opportunities in the parlatory.

Know that you will be brought to account by my brother, Luigi de Leyva, who God willing will come soon. You deserve punishment for trying to destroy the honor of a family as noble as mine. Your punishment will be delivered by my family's hand. If they have waited until now, it is only because I must inform them of the reason for your schemes and revenges. You will be exposed to the world as the wicked creature you are, while I will remain the noble and honored woman I profess to be.

I expect a reward from God for my zeal in preventing this poor convent from being dishonored by you. We will punish you for your crimes against my honor by naming you the deceiver and exposing you as the liar you are. Otherwise, God will not receive me in Paradise, not if I fail to see you suffer this punishment, not if I fail to see justice done.

I will also charge you with the designs you had on my own person. You sent your servant with love letters, for which I drove her away, as you know. I made the Prioress denounce her wickedness to her face and had your shameful presents returned to you.

Sister Virginia Maria de Leyva

She sealed the letter and had it delivered that same day.

The relief was immediate and intoxicating. Throughout her affair with Gian Paolo, she had been tormented by a rooted sense of guilt. Every sin weighed on her conscience. Every transgression reminded her of her own weakness.

But now, turning her fury on Arrigone, she gained relief through the illusion that others were far more guilty and censurable than she. If Arrigone was the true villain, the seducer, the manipulator, the author of her fall, then she was merely his victim. Her sins became his responsibility. Her shame became his creation.

It was a lie, but it was a comforting one.

* * *

October

THE MORNING AFTER sending the letter, Virginia woke before Lauds with her chest feeling strangely light, as though someone had removed stones she had been carrying for so long, she had forgotten their weight. She lay in the darkness of her cell and waited for the familiar crushing guilt to descend. The litany of sins that usually greeted her upon waking remained oddly distant, muted somehow.

She pressed her palm against her sternum, feeling for the constriction that had lived there for years. Nothing. Just her heartbeat, steady and calm beneath her nightshift.

During morning prayers, Virginia found herself able to focus on the Latin words rather than the endless internal accounting of her transgressions. Her voice joined those of the other sisters in the familiar cadences of Lauds, and for the first time in years, perhaps, the prayers did not taste like ashes in her mouth. She glanced sideways at Sister Candida kneeling three places down, and instead of seeing a mirror of her own failings, she saw a victim. A young woman who had been manipulated by a predator.

Not like me at all, Virginia thought, and the distinction felt important, felt true, felt like a rope thrown to a drowning woman.

At the midday meal, she met Prioress Bianca's eyes across the refectory without the usual shame that made her want to look away. Let Bianca look. Let her see a Vicaress who had acted righteously to protect the convent from corruption.

"You seem at peace today," Benedetta observed when they were alone in the scriptorium that afternoon. Her tone was carefully neutral, but Virginia caught the question beneath the words.

Virginia's hand remained steady on the manuscript she was examining. "I have clarity about the situation. About where the true fault lies."

Benedetta set down the quill she had been mending, her sharp eyes studying Virginia's face with uncomfortable intensity. "Do you."

It was not quite a question, not quite a challenge. Something in between that made Virginia's shoulders tighten defensively. "Arrigone crafted those letters specifically to seduce me. Without his manipulation, without his calculated poetry designed to break down my defenses, none of this would have happened."

"When you first saw Gian Paolo in the chapel and felt that first pull of attraction? And the night you first let Gian Paolo through the garden door?" Benedetta's voice remained quiet, pitched low so the younger nuns would not overhear. "Was Arrigone responsible for that as well?"

Virginia's fingers tightened on the parchment. "I made mistakes. I have never claimed otherwise. But I was manipulated by a man who has made seduction his art and his weapon. That changes the nature of my culpability."

Benedetta said nothing for a long moment. The silence stretched between them, filled with the soft scratch of quills on parchment from the younger nuns at the far end of the room. When she finally spoke again, her voice carried something that might have been resignation. "If that belief brings you peace, I will not take it from you."

The words should have felt like absolution. Instead, they lodged somewhere in Virginia's chest like a splinter—small, sharp, impossible to ignore. She pushed the discomfort aside and returned her attention to the manuscript, determined not to let Benedetta's skepticism poison the relief that had finally granted her respite.

Over the following days, Virginia moved through the convent's rhythms with an ease she had not felt since before Gian Paolo first appeared in the garden.

She supervised the younger nuns without distraction. She reviewed convent accounts without her mind wandering. She knelt in prayer without the constant internal recitation of transgressions that had made devotion feel like mockery.

At night, she still dreamed of Gian Paolo, his hands on her skin, his voice in her ear, the way he had looked at her with hunger that made her feel desired rather than judged. But upon waking, instead of the familiar shame that used to flood through her, she felt only a distant sadness. As though those memories belonged to a different woman, someone who had been victimized by forces beyond her control.

Sister Ottavia watched this transformation with visible relief. "You seem yourself again," she said one evening as they prepared for Compline. "The darkness that was eating at you has lifted."

Virginia smiled, and the expression felt genuine. "I understand now what happened. Where the true blame lies. It has brought me peace."

Only Benedetta remained skeptical, her sharp eyes tracking Virginia's movements with the intensity of someone watching a wound for signs of infection. But she said nothing more, and Virginia told herself that Benedetta's silence meant acceptance rather than judgment deferred.

* * *

IT WAS RAINING by the time Virginia sat down to write her second letter. Three days had passed since she had sent her accusations to Arrigone, three days during which her newfound lightness had settled into something more solid and permanent.

She positioned fresh parchment on her writing table, this one finer than the paper she had used for Arrigone. This letter required more care, more precision. Where the first had been filled with rage, this needed to be strategy dressed in righteousness.

The afternoon light was cold and clear through her window. Virginia dipped her quill and began to write, each word chosen with the precision of someone laying stones in a foundation that must bear enormous weight.

Most Esteemed Signor Marcellino,

The salutation emerged in her most formal script. Appio Marcellino was a functionary of the Archdiocese, one of Cardinal Borromeo's most trusted advisors. If anyone could bring her accusations to the Cardinal's attention, it was Marcellino.

Virginia wrote of spiritual concerns and institutional duty, positioning herself as a reluctant witness compelled by conscience to bring troubling matters to the attention of those with authority to address them. Each phrase was calibrated to present her in the most favorable light. Not as a vengeful woman striking back, but as a guardian of convent virtue forced to act despite personal cost.

The quill scratched across the parchment with satisfying regularity. She described Arrigone's pursuit of Sister Candida with clinical precision, laying out dates and witnesses, physical evidence and documented patterns. The midnight meetings in the parlatory. The explicit letters she had confiscated. The physical acts witnessed through the grating.

She wrote of his broader corruption, the attempts to seduce other nuns, the abuse of the confessional to proposition women, the systematic pattern of predation.

> *Father Arrigone's response to my intervention has been to spread malicious lies about my character and that of this holy institution. He has attempted to deflect attention from his own sins by accusing others of the very crimes he himself has committed.*

Virginia paused, reading the sentence back. It was theoretically true. Arrigone had been spreading rumors about her affair with Gian Paolo. But the sentence made it sound as though his accusations were fabrications rather than uncomfortable truths. She told herself the distinction did not matter. The important thing was protecting Santa Margherita from scandal.

She continued writing, building her case with methodical precision. Every accusation was framed as established fact. Every witness was positioned as reliable and credible. The picture that emerged was of systematic corruption demanding official response.

> *I bring these matters to your attention not out of personal animosity, but out of concern for the souls under my care and the reputation of Santa Margherita. As Vicaress, I have a sacred duty to protect the women entrusted to my spiritual guidance. I cannot in good conscience remain silent when I have witnessed such abuses.*

The words looked noble on the page, righteous and proper. Virginia read them three times, checking for any hint of the personal vendetta that actually motivated this letter. Finding none, she continued.

The afternoon light had shifted by the time she reached the conclusion. Her hand cramped from gripping the quill, but she forced herself to maintain perfect penmanship through the final paragraphs. Appearance mattered in correspondence with Church officials.

She sealed the letter with red wax and pressed her signet ring into it, the de Leyva crest proclaiming her noble lineage. Let Marcellino see exactly who was bringing these accusations. Let him understand that this was not some hysterical complaint from a woman of no consequence, but a serious allegation from someone whose family name carried weight.

Virginia held the letter in both hands, feeling its weight. Somewhere in the back of her mind, a voice whispered warnings about consequences and exposure, about the danger of inviting powerful men to examine the convent's operations too closely. But she pushed the warnings aside. The satisfaction of striking back at Arrigone was too sweet to abandon now.

She sent the letter the next morning.

And so, through her own folly, Virginia's affairs came forcibly to the notice of Cardinal Federigo Borromeo.

She told herself it was necessary. That Arrigone had to be stopped. That other nuns needed protection from his advances.

But in her heart, she knew the truth. This was revenge. Pure and simple. Arrigone had used her as a trophy, and she would destroy him for it.

Let him feel what it was like to be displayed. To be reduced to an object lesson. To have his private sins dragged into public view.

Let him suffer as she had suffered.

* * *

FATHER ARRIGONE SAT in his study at San Maurizio Church, reading the letter that had arrived from the Archbishop's office that morning. The language was formal, carefully neutral, but the message was clear enough: accusations had been made against him regarding improper conduct with nuns at Santa Margherita. His presence would be required in Milan to answer questions, should His Eminence deem an investigation necessary.

He read it three times, his anger building with each pass.

Virginia.

It had to be her. Who else would dare? Who else had reason to strike at him now, after he'd moved his attention from Benedetta to the more pliable Candida? The timing alone made it obvious.

Arrigone set the Archbishop's letter aside and pulled a fresh sheet of parchment toward him. His hand trembled slightly—not with fear, but with rage barely contained. She thought she could destroy him with accusations? She, who had violated every vow she'd ever taken?

He would show her what a real accusation looked like.

The afternoon light slanted through the window, illuminating the parchment as his hand moved across the page with practiced elegance, each word chosen for maximum effect.

To His Eminence Cardinal Federigo Borromeo, Archbishop of Milan:
I write to defend myself against the false and malicious accusations leveled by Sister Virginia Maria de Leyva, Vicaress of Santa Margherita, who has sought to destroy my reputation through lies born of personal vendetta.

He paused, dipping his quill again, savoring the moment.

The said Sister Virginia accuses me of improper conduct with Sister Candida Colomba, but I submit that these accusations arise not from any concern for the convent's purity, but from her desire to silence one who knows too much of her own transgressions.

Arrigone leaned back in his chair, reading what he'd written. Not enough. He needed to be more direct without being so explicit that the Cardinal would be forced to investigate immediately. A delicate balance.

I have served faithfully as parish priest to Santa Margherita for many years. During this time, I have observed irregularities that I chose to overlook out of Christian charity and respect for the de Leyva family's position. However, when falsely accused, I cannot remain silent about what I have witnessed.

His lips curved into a smile.

Gian Paolo Osio has been granted access to the convent at unusual hours under circumstances that violate the sacred enclosure. This has occurred not once, but repeatedly over a period of years. The connection between Osio and Sister Virginia is well known

throughout Monza, yet no action has been taken despite the scandal it brings to the Church.
Furthermore, there are children—

He stopped. Too far. The Cardinal would have to act on such a direct accusation, and Arrigone wanted this petition to serve as a shield, not a sword. Not yet.

He scratched through the last line and began again.

I mention these matters not to accuse, but to explain why Sister Virginia has sought to destroy me. A guilty conscience often attacks most viciously those who might reveal its secrets.

Better. Much better.

I ask only that Your Eminence consider the source of these accusations. A woman who has violated her own vows repeatedly cannot be trusted to judge the conduct of others. If there has been any impropriety at Santa Margherita, I submit that the investigation should examine the Vicaress herself, not those she seeks to destroy. I remain Your Eminence's humble and obedient servant, Father Paolo Arrigone

He set down the quill and read the entire petition through twice. Perfect. It denied Virginia's accusations while insinuating his own without making claims specific enough to force an investigation. It positioned him as the victim of a powerful woman's vendetta. And it planted seeds that could grow later, if needed.

Most importantly, it gave the Cardinal an easy resolution: dismiss both accusations and let the matter rest. Virginia couldn't pursue him without exposing herself to counterattack. And if she tried, he had this petition on record as his defense.

Arrigone folded the parchment carefully and sealed it with wax. He would send it to Milan tomorrow through a reliable courier. Then he would wait to see if the Cardinal took the bait he'd offered—the chance to avoid scandal entirely by taking no action at all.

And if Virginia ever moved against him again, he would have far more than a petition ready.

* * *

WEEKS CRAWLED PAST. Virginia moved through the convent's rhythms in a state of suspended dread, waiting for consequences that never came.

No summons arrived from the Archbishop's palace. No investigators appeared at Santa Margherita's gates. The autumn turned colder, frost replacing rain on the garden paths, and still Virginia heard nothing.

Finally, a young priest arrived bearing a brief letter from Marcellino's office. Virginia broke the seal with trembling hands, scanning the formal script.

> *The Cardinal thanks you for bringing these matters to his attention. He assures you that appropriate steps will be taken should circumstances warrant further investigation.*

That was all. No mention of Arrigone. No promise of inquiry. Just polite acknowledgment and vague assurance.

Virginia read it three times, searching for meaning between the carefully chosen words. Finding none, she crumpled the letter in her fist.

It was Benedetta who explained what the letter actually meant, appearing in Virginia's chamber later that afternoon when the initial shock had worn off.

"They've filed it away," Benedetta said without preamble, standing in the doorway. "No inquiry will be conducted."

Virginia's throat constricted. "How do you know?"

"Because I know how these things work." Benedetta moved into the room, her voice quiet but certain. "The Cardinal has no interest in creating a scandal that would bring the Church into conflict with the de Leyva family. Marcellino likely advised him that the matter was nothing more than a private dispute between a high-strung feudal lady and an intractable priest."

* * *

WORD REACHED HER three days later through channels she preferred not to examine too closely. A servant who knew someone who worked in the taverns near San Maurizio Church. The information arrived in whispers, second-hand and unreliable, but Virginia knew in her bones it was true.

Father Arrigone had somehow learned about her complaint to the Cardinal and that he had taken no action against him.

His celebrations were loud and public. He bought drinks for anyone who would listen to his account of how he had defeated the false accusations of a vengeful nun. He described Virginia as a hypocrite who judged others for sins she herself committed regularly. He painted himself as an innocent priest persecuted by a powerful woman who could not bear to have her schemes disrupted.

And worse, much worse, he had begun gathering evidence.

"Not for immediate use," Benedetta explained when she came to Virginia's chamber with more detailed information. "He is building a case to hold in reserve. A weapon to deploy if you ever move against him again."

Virginia's hands trembled in her lap. "What kind of evidence?"

"Witnesses who can testify to Gian Paolo's late-night visits to the convent. Servants who saw the children, both of them. Physical evidence of violations of enclosure that occurred repeatedly over years." Benedetta's voice remained clinical, detached, as though she were describing someone else's life. "He is documenting everything, Virginia. Every detail that would prove your own corruption as thoroughly as you tried to prove his."

The irony was not lost on Virginia. She had started this war, had fired the first shot with her letter full of accusations and threats. Now Arrigone was preparing his counterstrike, methodically compiling the same kind of evidence she had gathered against him.

"What should I do?" The question emerged as barely a whisper.

"Nothing." Benedetta's answer was immediate and final. "You have already done too much. Every action you take now will only make things worse. The Cardinal has chosen not to investigate. Accept that mercy, because it is a mercy, Virginia, whether you recognize it or not, and do not give him reason to reconsider."

But gratitude was impossible. Virginia lay awake that night, staring at the darkness above her narrow bed, imagining Arrigone's testimony before Church investigators. Imagining her own examination under oath, forced to choose between perjury and confession. Imagining the destruction of her family's name, the exposure of every secret she had fought so hard to keep hidden.

The relief she had felt after writing her accusations now seemed like the cruelest joke. For a few brief weeks, she had believed that blaming Arrigone could absolve her own guilt. That positioning herself as a protector of convent virtue could transform her from hypocrite to hero. That striking first would ensure victory.

Instead, she had merely revealed her own position to an enemy who was now fortifying his defenses and preparing to strike back harder.

* * *

ARRIGONE'S HATRED INCREASED even more after he learned the Cardinal had dismissed both their accusations. He began plotting his revenge, spreading rumors, seeking allies. He wrote letters to anyone who would listen. He denied her accusations publicly. He painted himself as a victim of a vindictive woman who could not bear to see others find happiness.

The battle between them was far from over. It had only just begun.

And neither of them could see where it would lead. How their mutual hatred would fuel the events to come. How their war would eventually consume not just themselves but everyone around them.

The first shots had been fired. Blood would follow.

* * *

November

THE AUTUMN DEEPEND to winter. Snow replaced frost, covering the garden in white that looked pure from a distance but showed dirt and decay up close. Virginia moved through the convent's rhythms with the knowledge that somewhere in Monza, Arrigone was compiling evidence that could end her. And in Milan, her own letters waited in the Cardinal's archives, ready to provide context if scandal ever erupted.

She tried to pray, but the words stuck in her throat like stones. The temporary relief she had felt, that beautiful, seductive illusion that someone else bore responsibility for her fall, had evaporated completely. What remained was worse than the original guilt. Because now she carried not only the weight of her sins, but the additional burden of knowing she had made everything infinitely worse through her own vengeful stupidity.

Benedetta watched her with knowing eyes but said nothing. Ottavia fretted and brought her extra food, as though Virginia's problem were simple hunger that could be solved with bread and cheese. Candida avoided her entirely, perhaps sensing that Virginia's protection had become a liability rather than a shelter.

Only Prioress Bianca confronted her directly, calling Virginia to her private chamber one afternoon when sleet rattled against the windows.

"You wrote to the Archbishop," Bianca said. It was not a question.

Virginia's spine straightened. "I did. To report corruption that threatened this convent's reputation."

"And succeeded only in drawing attention to that very corruption." Bianca's voice remained calm, but Virginia heard the steel beneath. "The Cardinal's mercy in choosing not to investigate is a gift you should treasure, Sister Virginia. Do not mistake it for approval or vindication."

"I acted to protect—"

"You acted to strike back at a man who humiliated you." Bianca's interruption was sharp. "Do not compound your errors with self-deception. I know what you did, and why. The question now is whether you have learned from your mistake or whether you will continue down this path until you destroy not only yourself but everyone in this convent."

Virginia's throat tightened. "I have learned, Reverend Mother."

"Have you?" Bianca studied her with the penetrating gaze that had always made Virginia feel transparent. "Then learn this as well: the letters you sent are not forgotten. They wait in archives, patient and permanent. Should scandal touch this convent in the future, those documents will be retrieved and examined. Your name is now connected to accusations of clerical corruption and moral decay within Santa Margherita. That connection cannot be severed."

The weight of it pressed down on Virginia's shoulders. She had thought herself so clever, so righteous. Instead, she had been a fool who handed her enemies the weapons to destroy her.

"You are dismissed," Bianca said. "But remember what I have told you. Silence and discretion are your only protections now. Guard them well."

Virginia left the Prioress's chamber with legs that barely supported her weight. The corridor stretched endlessly before her, cold stone and colder shadows. Somewhere ahead lay her chamber, her narrow bed, the long night of sleepless dread that awaited her.

* * *

DECEMBER ARRIVED WITH bitter cold that made the convent's stone walls weep with condensation. Virginia stood at her window one morning, watching ice form delicate patterns on the glass. Beautiful from this angle. But fragile. The slightest warmth would melt it away, leaving only water and the harsh truth beneath.

Her anger had subsided, replaced by something closer to despair. The righteous fury that had sustained her through writing the letters now seemed like a fever dream, intense while it lasted, but ultimately hollow. She had accomplished nothing except to make herself vulnerable.

"You should occupy yourself with something useful," Benedetta said one afternoon when she found Virginia staring at nothing in the scriptorium. "Idleness feeds melancholy."

"What would you have me do?"

"What you have always done. Manage the convent's affairs. Supervise the younger nuns. Maintain the routines that keep Santa Margherita functioning." Benedetta set down a stack of account books. "The world does not stop because you have made a mistake."

Virginia looked at the books with something like revulsion. The minutiae of convent administration, grain inventories, servant wages, repairs to the roof, all of it seemed trivial against the weight of what she had risked. But Benedetta was right. Life continued whether she participated or not.

She opened the first ledger and forced herself to focus on the columns of figures. The familiar work brought a kind of numbness that was not quite comfort but was better than the constant circling of anxious thoughts.

* * *

THE DAYS GREW shorter. Virginia threw herself into preparations for a pilgrimage. Not her own, she could not leave the convent, but one she would finance and orchestrate from within these walls.

"Bernardo Grosso will travel to the Madonna of Loreto," she told Benedetta one afternoon in early December. "I am sending offerings. Prayers for the convent's welfare."

Benedetta's sharp eyes studied her. "What are you really praying for?"

Virginia turned to the window. "Freedom."

"From what?"

"From this." Virginia gestured vaguely, encompassing everything, the affair, the guilt, the endless cycle of sin and repentance that had consumed her for years. "I cannot seem to break free on my own. Perhaps the Madonna will grant what my own will cannot achieve."

She had assembled the offerings with methodical care. A silver god of love that Gian Paolo had given her years ago, that pagan trinket she had kept hidden in her chamber despite knowing what it represented. She had it melted down and remade into sacred images. The transformation felt symbolic, as though she could transmute her own corruption into something holy through sheer force of will.

She added coins from her personal funds. A letter to be left at the shrine, detailing her desperate need for divine intervention. Everything carefully arranged to petition the Madonna for what Virginia could not achieve through her own strength.

Benedetta said nothing for a long moment, her expression unreadable. "This is not the first pilgrimage you have commissioned to Loreto."

"No." Virginia's voice was quiet. "The third, I think. Perhaps the fourth."

"And yet you remain bound to Gian Paolo."

The words landed like stones. Virginia wanted to argue, to insist that this time would be different, that this time the prayers would take hold. But they both knew it was a lie. Each previous pilgrimage had been accompanied by the same desperate hope. Each time, Virginia had failed to sustain her resolution more than a few weeks before she found herself back at the garden door, lifting the bar to let Gian Paolo through.

"The Madonna of Loreto works miracles," Virginia said, hearing the defensiveness in her own voice.

"The Madonna cannot free you from choices you continue making." Benedetta's tone was matter of fact rather than judgmental. "Only you can do that. And you have shown no inclination to make that choice, no matter how many silver trinkets you send to shrines."

Virginia closed her eyes. "I am trying."

"Are you?" Benedetta moved closer. "Or are you simply performing the ritual of trying while knowing full well that you will return to him the moment he calls for you?"

The accuracy of the observation cut deep. Virginia wanted to protest, but exhaustion made the effort impossible. Benedetta was right. She had been performing repentance for years, the prayers, the pilgrimages, the moments of anguished guilt, all of it theater designed to convince herself she was something other than what she knew herself to be.

A woman who could not let go. A woman who would rather damn herself than live without the one thing that made her feel alive.

"Bernardo leaves for Loreto in three days," Virginia said finally. "I have given him six ducats for the journey and one for an offering at the shrine. Whether the prayers work or not, at least I will have tried."

Benedetta's expression softened slightly. "Trying is not nothing. But do not fool yourself into thinking that effort alone absolves you of the need to change."

After Benedetta left, Virginia remained at her writing table, staring at the carefully prepared offerings. The melted-down god of love, transformed into images of saints. The coins that represented months of careful hoarding from her allowance. The letter that laid bare her soul to the Madonna in words she could never speak aloud.

All of it desperate. All of it probably futile.

But she would send them anyway, because the alternative was surrendering completely to despair.

* * *

BERNARDO GROSSO DEPARTED for Loreto three days later. Virginia watched him ride away through the convent gates, his saddlebags heavy with her offerings and petitions. The December morning was bitterly cold, frost coating everything in crystalline white.

She stood at the window long after he disappeared from view, one hand pressed against the cold glass. Somewhere ahead of him lay the road to Loreto, the shrine where miracles were said to happen, the Madonna who listened to the desperate prayers of women who had no one else to turn to.

Let this work, Virginia prayed silently. *Let this be the time I am finally freed.*

But even as she formed the prayer, she felt its hollowness. She had prayed the same words before. The Madonna had not answered then. Why would she answer now?

"He is gone?" Ottavia appeared in the doorway, her round face worried.

"Yes." Virginia turned from the window. "The pilgrimage has begun."

"Do you truly believe it will help?"

Virginia studied Ottavia's earnest expression. Sweet, faithful Ottavia, who still believed that prayers could transform hearts and miracles could break the chains of sin. Once, Virginia had believed that too. Now she was no longer certain what she believed, except that she was trapped in a pattern she could not seem to break no matter how desperately she tried.

"I believe," Virginia said carefully, "that we must try everything within our power. And when our own power fails, we must petition those who possess power we lack."

It was not quite an answer, but it seemed to satisfy Ottavia. She smiled and squeezed Virginia's hand. "The Madonna will hear you. She always hears us when we cry out in true need."

Virginia wished she shared that certainty. But she had cried out so many times, and the Madonna's silence had been absolute. Perhaps some sins were too deep for even divine intervention. Perhaps some women were too thoroughly corrupted to be saved.

The thought settled over her like frost, cold and pervasive. But she pushed it aside and returned to her duties, because standing at windows contemplating her own damnation accomplished nothing.

* * *

WORD REACHED SANTA Margherita three days later that Cardinal Borromeo would be visiting Monza. The news sent a ripple of anxiety through the convent. Any visit from the Cardinal required preparation, scrutiny of every corner to ensure nothing would offend his reforming eye.

But as more details emerged, it became clear this would not be the inquisitorial visit Virginia had feared. The Cardinal was conducting a pastoral tour of convents in the diocese, a ceremonious progress intended to demonstrate his care for religious communities under his authority.

Prioress Bianca summoned Virginia to her chamber the morning after the announcement.

"His Eminence will wish to speak with you," Bianca said without preamble. "As feudal lady of Monza, you represent this convent to the world. He will expect a gracious conversation befitting your rank."

Virginia's pulse quickened. "Does he intend to question me about—"

"He intends to make a ceremonial visit." Bianca's interruption was sharp. "If he had meant to investigate, he would have sent his vicar, not come himself. This is theater, Virginia. Political theater designed to demonstrate the Cardinal's benevolent oversight of his convents. Your role is to play the noble lady, grateful for his pastoral care, devoted to the spiritual welfare of your sisters."

"And if he asks about my letters?"

Bianca was quiet for a long moment, her expression grave. "Then you will say you were concerned about irregularities you had observed, that you brought them to his attention as your conscience demanded, and that you are grateful for his wise handling of delicate matters. You will not elaborate. You will not press for action. You will accept whatever he says with humble gratitude."

Virginia heard the warning beneath the instructions. The Cardinal had chosen not to investigate. Pressing him further would be worse than foolish. It would be suicidal.

"I understand, Reverend Mother."

"Do you?" Bianca's gaze was penetrating. "Because if you make any misstep during his visit, if you give him any reason to reconsider his decision to file your accusations away, you will not be the only one who suffers. Every woman in this convent who has kept your secrets will face consequences. The de Leyva name may protect you from the worst, but it will not protect us."

The weight of responsibility pressed down on Virginia's shoulders. She had been thinking only of her own survival, her own fear of exposure. But Bianca was right. Her actions had endangered everyone. Benedetta, who had conspired from the beginning. Ottavia, who had opened doors and kept watch. Candida and Silvia, who had witnessed everything. Even the servants who had carried messages and looked the other way.

All of them vulnerable because of choices Virginia had made.

"I will play my role perfectly," Virginia said, her voice steadier than she felt. "The Cardinal will see exactly what he expects to see. A grateful, pious noblewoman devoted to her convent's welfare."

Bianca studied her for another long moment before nodding. "See that you do."

* * *

THE CARDINAL ARRIVED on a cold December morning with a retinue of priests and functionaries. The convent chapel had been decorated with fresh greenery despite the season, candles lit at every altar, the best vestments brought out for the occasion. The nuns had spent days cleaning and preparing, ensuring that Santa Margherita would present itself as the model of religious devotion and proper order.

Virginia stood with Prioress Bianca in the parlatory, waiting to pay homage through the iron grating. She had dressed with meticulous care, her habit freshly cleaned and pressed, her veil arranged to perfection. Every detail of her appearance proclaimed what she was, not a desperate woman who had gambled everything on a vengeful accusation, but a de Leyva, noble and proud, worthy of respect.

The Cardinal entered with the bearing of a man accustomed to authority. His face was stern but not unkind, his penetrating gaze seeming to see through walls and pretense. At forty-seven, Cardinal Federigo Borromeo was at the height of his power, his reputation for zealous reform well-established throughout the Church.

He moved through the required rituals with practiced efficiency—the blessing, the prayers, the formal exchange of courtesies with Prioress Bianca. Then his attention turned to Virginia.

"Sister Virginia Maria." His voice was measured, neither warm nor cold. "I am pleased to see you well."

Virginia sank into a deep curtsy, her movements precise and elegant. "Your Eminence honors us with his presence."

"The Lady of Monza." Something flickered in his eyes, recognition, perhaps, or calculation. "Your family has long served the Church with distinction. Your father's service to the Crown is well-known."

"My family takes great pride in serving both Crown and Church, Your Eminence."

The Cardinal moved closer to the grating. His next words were pitched low enough that only Virginia and the Prioress could hear. "I understand you have taken your duties as Vicaress seriously. That you concern yourself with the spiritual welfare of the women under your care."

Virginia's heart hammered. "I do what my position requires, Your Eminence."

"Admirable." The Cardinal's gaze held hers through the iron lattice. "Though one must be careful that zeal does not outpace wisdom. The Church has many enemies who would seize upon any scandal to discredit her work. Discretion is as much a virtue as vigilance."

The message could not have been clearer. *I know what you did. Do not do it again.*

"I understand, Your Eminence." Virginia kept her voice steady. "I am grateful for your guidance in all matters."

"Good." The Cardinal stepped back, his public voice returning with the smoothness of a man who had spent decades navigating the politics of the Church. "I am pleased to find Santa Margherita in such excellent order. Prioress Bianca, you and your sisters do honor to the Benedictine rule."

The conversation moved to safer topics—the convent's accounts, recent repairs, plans for the coming year. Virginia stood silently, playing her role with the skill of someone who had spent years perfecting the art of performance. She answered when spoken to, her responses carefully calibrated to demonstrate piety without drawing attention.

The Cardinal asked about the convent's relationship with the town, about Virginia's role as feudal lady, about the spiritual formation of the younger nuns.

Each question felt like a test, and Virginia navigated them with the caution of someone walking across ice that might crack at any moment.

"Your devotion to the Madonna is well-known," the Cardinal observed at one point. "I understand you have commissioned another pilgrimage to Loreto."

Virginia's pulse spiked. How did he know about that? Had someone reported it? Or was this simply the thoroughness of a man who made it his business to know everything that happened in his diocese?

"Yes, Your Eminence. I sent my administrator Bernardo Grosso just days ago, with offerings and prayers for the continued welfare of this convent."

"Admirable." The Cardinal's expression was unreadable. "The Madonna of Loreto is a powerful intercessor for those who seek her aid. I trust your petitions will be heard."

The words could have been simple pastoral encouragement. But Virginia heard the undercurrent—the suggestion that she needed intercession, that her prayers were not merely pious gestures but desperate pleas for help. He knew. Perhaps not every detail, but enough to understand that Virginia was a woman struggling against forces she could not control.

"I trust in the Madonna's mercy, Your Eminence."

"As we all must." The Cardinal inclined his head slightly. "But we must also remember that divine mercy works through human cooperation. The Madonna can grant us strength, but we must choose to use it wisely."

Another warning, this one even less veiled. Virginia bowed her head in what she hoped looked like humble acceptance. "I will remember, Your Eminence."

When the Cardinal finally departed, Virginia remained in the parlatory long after the others had left. Her legs felt boneless, her hands trembling with relief she could barely contain. She pressed them against the rough stone of the window ledge, grounding herself in something solid.

He had known. Had reviewed her letters, considered her accusations, and chosen to do nothing. But rather than exposing her, rather than pressing for investigation, he had come to deliver a message wrapped in pastoral courtesy: *Be silent. Be discreet. Be grateful I am allowing you to escape the consequences of your own stupidity.*

Virginia pressed her forehead against the cool iron of the grating and allowed herself one moment of pure, overwhelming relief. She had been spared. For now.

But the Cardinal's warning had been clear. This was her final chance. Any further scandal, any hint that she was continuing to cause trouble or invite scrutiny to Santa Margherita, and his mercy would evaporate. Next time, there would be investigation. Next time, there would be consequences.

Virginia straightened, forcing her breathing to steady. She had survived this encounter. She would survive whatever came next, provided she was careful. Provided she gave no one, not Arrigone, not the Cardinal, not anyone, reason to look too closely at what happened behind Santa Margherita's walls.

* * *

NOT LONG AFTER the Cardinal departed, word reached the convent that a new vendetta had erupted between Gian Paolo and Arrigone.

"They say Arrigone spoke to the Cardinal during his visit," Ottavia reported breathlessly one afternoon, appearing in Virginia's chamber with her cheeks flushed from excitement. "That he whispered things about you and Gian Paolo. That's why the Cardinal warned you about discretion."

Virginia's chest tightened. "How do you know this?"

"The servants are talking. Everyone in Monza believes Arrigone betrayed you to save himself." Ottavia's round face was troubled. "Gian Paolo is furious. They say he confronted Arrigone in the street yesterday."

The details emerged over the following days through the gossip network that connected convent to town. Gian Paolo had indeed confronted Arrigone, demanding to know what he had told the Cardinal. Arrigone had denied saying anything, but his denials had the hollow ring of obvious lies. Everyone knew Arrigone had submitted his own counter-petition to the Archdiocese. Everyone knew he had been eager to defend himself and, by implication, to attack Virginia and Gian Paolo.

The confrontation had not satisfied Gian Paolo. Within a week, authorities had raided the sacristy of San Maurizio and discovered illegal firearms, harquebuses hidden in a closet behind the altar vestments.

Arrigone was arrested and imprisoned pending investigation.

"It was Gian Paolo," Benedetta said flatly when she heard the news. "He planted those weapons and then reported them. Revenge for what he believes Arrigone told the Cardinal."

Virginia pressed her hands against her temples where pressure was building. "This will only make things worse. If Arrigone is imprisoned because of Gian Paolo, he will retaliate when he is released."

"If he is released." Benedetta's tone suggested she thought this unlikely. "Possession of forbidden weapons is a serious offense. Especially for a priest."

But Virginia knew better. Arrigone had powerful connections of his own. He served wealthy families, heard confessions, said masses for those who paid well. Someone would intervene on his behalf. Someone would ensure his release. And when he emerged from prison, his hatred would burn hotter than ever.

She had started this war with her letter of accusations. Now Gian Paolo had escalated it, and Arrigone would have no choice but to respond in kind. The vendetta would spiral outward, drawing more people in, creating more opportunities for exposure.

Virginia stood at her window, watching winter clouds gather over Monza. Somewhere in the town, Arrigone sat in a prison cell, nursing his rage and plotting revenge. In Milan, her letters waited in the Cardinal's archives. And in Loreto, her offerings lay before the Madonna's shrine, petitioning for freedom she knew she would never find.

She had thought writing those letters would destroy Arrigone. Instead, she had merely ensured that when destruction came, it would consume them all.

* * *

CHRISTMAS CAME WITH its familiar rituals—midnight Mass, the singing of ancient hymns, the brief relaxation of convent discipline that allowed for small celebrations. Virginia moved through the festivities with a performance of devotion that felt hollow even to herself. She sang the familiar carols, her voice joining the others in harmonies that had once moved her and now simply filled time. She knelt for prayers, her body going through motions while her heart remained elsewhere.

On Christmas night, after Compline, Virginia made her way through the silent convent to the garden door. She unlocked the door and lifted the bar with practiced ease, the movement so familiar her hands found their way in darkness.

Gian Paolo slipped through like a shadow given form. He pulled her close without a word, his lips finding hers with the hunger of weeks of separation. Virginia melted into him, all her resolutions evaporating in the heat of his touch.

"I thought they had taken you from me," he murmured against her throat. "When I heard the Cardinal had come—"

"Hush." Virginia pressed her fingers to his lips. "It is over. We are safe."

It was a lie, but in that moment, wrapped in Gian Paolo's arms, she needed desperately to believe it. They were not safe. They would never be truly safe. But for tonight, she could pretend that nothing had changed, that her gamble with Arrigone had not made everything infinitely more dangerous.

Gian Paolo lifted her in his arms and carried her through the darkened corridors to her chamber. Benedetta and Ottavia had taken up their positions as lookouts with the practiced efficiency of years of conspiracy. Virginia's bed awaited, and for a few hours she could lose herself in the only thing that had ever made her feel truly alive.

Afterward, they lay tangled together in the darkness, Gian Paolo's breathing gradually slowing to the rhythm of sleep. Virginia remained awake, staring at shadows on the ceiling cast by moonlight filtering through her window.

* * *

THE PILGRIMAGE TO Loreto had accomplished nothing. The Madonna had not answered her prayers, had not granted the freedom she had begged for.

Bernardo Grosso had made the journey, had left her offerings at the shrine, had carried her desperate petitions to the Mother of God.

And Virginia had learned that Gian Paolo was coming into the convent again this night, and she had been waiting at the garden door before the bells for Compline had finished ringing.

Some chains could not be broken by prayer. Some addictions ran too deep for even divine intervention to cure. Virginia had known this, on some level, even as she commissioned the pilgrimage. But she had needed to try, needed to perform the ritual of seeking freedom even knowing it was futile.

Because the alternative was admitting that she was exactly what she feared. A woman who had chosen her own damnation, who continued choosing it every time she lifted that bar and let Gian Paolo through.

"You are thinking too much," Gian Paolo murmured, his eyes still closed. "I can feel it."

"I always think too much."

He pulled her closer, his hand settling warm against her hip. "About what?"

Virginia was quiet for a long moment. "About whether we can continue like this. About how long before everything collapses."

"We have been asking that question for seven years." Gian Paolo's voice was drowsy. "And yet we are still here."

"Are we?" Virginia turned to face him. "Arrigone is in prison because of you. The Cardinal knows about us. My letters are in his archives. How much longer do you think we can pretend we are safe?"

Gian Paolo opened his eyes, suddenly more alert. "Arrigone deserved what he got. He tried to destroy you."

"And you have given him more reason to destroy us both when he is released." Virginia's voice was sharper than she intended. "This vendetta between you serves no purpose except to draw more attention to all of us."

"Would you rather I did nothing? Let him spread his poison without consequence?"

"I would rather," Virginia said carefully, "that we had never started any of this. That I had never written those letters. That you had never planted weapons in his church. That we could simply exist without creating new enemies every time we act."

Gian Paolo was quiet for a long moment. When he spoke again, his voice carried an edge Virginia had not heard before. "Do you regret us? Is that what this is about?"

"No." The answer came immediately, instinctively. "But I regret the consequences. I regret that my love for you has created so much danger for so many people."

"Love always creates danger," Gian Paolo said. "Especially love like ours. We knew that from the beginning."

Virginia wanted to argue, but exhaustion pulled at her bones. He was right, of course. They had always known their affair would end badly. Had known from that first night in the corridor, from the first time he climbed through her window, from the moment she chose passion over prudence.

The question was not whether there would be consequences. The question was when those consequences would finally arrive, and whether anyone would survive them.

Chapter Eleven
1605

THE YEAR UNFOLDED with deceptive calm, like the stillness before thunder. Virginia moved through the rhythms of convent life with the knowledge that she was living on borrowed time. The Cardinal's warning still rang in her ears. Arrigone remained imprisoned, but his release was inevitable. And somewhere in Milan, her daughter grew under the care of strangers.

Virginia tried to occupy herself with convent duties, but her mind drifted constantly to that baby she had held for only moments before handing her to Gian Paolo. Alma Francesca Margherita. The name carried weight, noble, carefully chosen, as though proper baptism could sanctify what had been conceived in sin.

"You are distracted," Prioress Bianca observed one afternoon in early spring, finding Virginia staring at account books without seeing the numbers. "The convent requires your attention."

"Forgive me, Reverend Mother." Virginia forced her gaze back to the ledger. "I was considering repairs to the south wall."

Bianca's expression suggested she knew this was a lie, but she said nothing more. The unspoken understanding that had always existed between them, that Bianca would not look too closely at what Virginia did, provided Virginia maintained the appearance of proper conduct, remained in force. But the foundation had become fragile. One more scandal, one more misstep, and even Bianca's protection would evaporate.

* * *

SPRING BROUGHT WARMER weather and the resumption of normal rhythms. Gian Paolo continued visiting the convent at night, slipping through the garden door with the ease of long practice. Virginia had tried, briefly, to refuse him after the Cardinal's visit. Had stood at her window one night and watched him in the garden below, waiting for a signal that did not come.

He had returned the next night. And the next. Until finally Virginia's resolve had crumbled and she had unlocked and lifted the bar herself, unable to bear another night of separation.

"You cannot stay away from me," Gian Paolo had said, pulling her close in the darkened corridor. "Any more than I can stay away from you."

It was true. Whatever the Cardinal had said, whatever warnings Virginia had received, the bond between them remained unbreakable. She belonged to Gian Paolo in ways that transcended reason or prudence. The affair continued as it had for years. Secret meetings in her chamber, Benedetta and Ottavia standing watch, the practiced choreography of sin that had become as familiar as prayer.

But something had shifted. Virginia found herself increasingly unable to maintain the illusion that this could continue indefinitely. Every time Gian Paolo left through the garden door, she wondered if it would be the last time. Every morning, she woke expecting news that Arrigone had been released, that denunciations had been filed, that the Cardinal's patience had finally run out.

The waiting was its own kind of torture.

* * *

SUMMER ARRIVED WITH oppressive heat that turned the convent's stone walls into ovens. Virginia spent long afternoons in her chamber, too drained to perform even basic duties. Prioress Bianca's earlier complaint, that the Vicaress should help with the things needed in the convent more and that she should be present at conversations in the parlatory, had become more pointed.

"You are always ill in bed," Bianca said one afternoon, her tone edged with frustration. "The other nuns notice. They whisper."

“Let them whisper.” Virginia’s response was sharper than she intended. “They have always whispered.”

“But before, you gave them no cause beyond speculation.” Bianca moved closer, lowering her voice. “Now your absences are so frequent that even those who wish to defend you find it difficult. What am I to tell them when they ask why the Vicaress never appears at Chapter meetings?”

Virginia had no answer. The truth, that she spent her nights with Gian Paolo and her days recovering from exhaustion and guilt, could not be spoken aloud. So, she remained silent, and Bianca left with an expression that mingled pity and exasperation.

* * *

AUGUST BROUGHT NEWS that changed everything.

“The baby is coming back to Monza,” Ottavia reported breathlessly one afternoon, bursting into Virginia’s chamber with her round face flushed. “Gian Paolo is bringing her from Milan. He says the wet nurse there was not clean enough, not careful enough. He’s bringing Alma Francesca to his house here, where he can watch over her himself.”

Virginia’s heart lurched. “When?”

“Within days. He’s already sent a carriage to Milan to fetch her.”

Virginia rose from her bed, suddenly energized despite the heat. Her daughter. After a year of separation, after months of imagining that small face, wondering if she’d recognize her own child, Alma Francesca would be in Monza. Close enough to see, to touch, to hold properly for the first time.

“I must see her,” Virginia said, her voice urgent. “When she arrives, you must find a way.”

Ottavia’s expression turned worried. “How? Gian Paolo will keep her in his house.”

“Apollonia.” Virginia gripped Ottavia’s arm. “Apollonia can bring her to the parlatory. She comes and goes freely between the house and the convent. No one would question it if she brought the baby to show the nuns.”

"Virginia, if people realize she is yours..."

"I do not care what people realize." Virginia's voice rose, then she caught herself and lowered it again. "I need to see my daughter. Arrange it. Please."

* * *

WHEN ALMA FRANCESCA arrived in Monza, Gian Paolo installed her in his house with a new wet nurse, a young woman from a good family, healthy and clean, whose milk he'd had a physician evaluate before hiring her. Virginia learned these details from Ottavia, who heard them from servants who heard them from Apollonia, who lived in Gian Paolo's household with her husband Pesseno.

The first time Virginia saw Alma Francesca was through the parlatory grating. Apollonia brought her during the day, when visitors were permitted, the baby bundled in fine linens that Virginia recognized as far too expensive for a servant's bastard. Virginia pressed her face close to the iron lattice, straining to see through the dimness.

The baby had grown. No longer the tiny newborn Virginia had birthed in blood and terror, but a sturdy child of one year, with dark hair and features that reminded Virginia painfully of Gian Paolo. She was learning to pull herself up, Apollonia reported, would soon be walking. But Virginia could only glimpse her through the shadows and the narrow spaces between the iron bars. It was not enough. She needed to hold her, to feel that small weight in her arms, to know this child was truly hers.

"Bring her to the convent door tomorrow," Virginia whispered urgently. "Where I can see her properly. Where I can touch her."

Apollonia hesitated, glancing around the parlatory with nervous eyes. She knew the risk. Everyone in Monza whispered about the Lady of Monza and Gian Paolo Osio. Everyone suspected the baby was more than just his bastard. But Apollonia had a kind heart beneath her peasant practicality.

"Tomorrow," she agreed quietly. "At None, when the sisters are at prayer."

The second time Virginia saw Alma Francesca was at the convent entrance door itself. A breach of every rule, an indiscretion so blatant it made even

Benedetta nervous. But Virginia did not care. Apollonia placed the baby in her arms, and for a few precious moments Virginia held her daughter.

She cried. The baby seemed strange to her at first, bigger than Virginia had imagined, no longer the tiny newborn she'd birthed a year ago but a child with her own expressions, her own personality already forming. But then Alma Francesca reached up with a chubby hand and touched Virginia's veil, and something broke open in Virginia's chest.

She caressed the baby, delighting in her warmth, her weight, the way she babbled nonsense sounds and grabbed at Virginia's fingers with surprising strength. Whispered endearments that meant nothing and everything. Pressed her lips to that small forehead, breathing in the scent of milk and soap and innocence.

For those few moments, she was not Sister Virginia Maria, Vicaress of Santa Margherita. She was simply a mother holding her child.

Apollonia watched with knowing eyes. Later, Virginia would realize that Apollonia had guessed the truth at that moment, that this baby was not merely Gian Paolo's bastard, but Virginia's own child. The evidence was written in Virginia's face, in the way she held Alma Francesca, in the tears that streamed down her cheeks.

"She is beautiful," Virginia whispered.

"Yes, my lady." Apollonia's voice was gentle. "She is."

"Tell me everything. How she sleeps, what she eats, if she cries. I want to know everything."

Apollonia glanced toward the garden, where Benedetta kept watch. "She's healthy. Growing strong. The new wet nurse is good, better than the one in Milan. Signor Osio watches over her like a hawk. He barely sleeps, checking on her through the night."

Virginia closed her eyes and held her daughter tighter. Gian Paolo loved Alma Francesca. Truly loved her, in ways that should have brought Virginia comfort. Instead, it highlighted her own exile from their child's life.

"I've sewn things for her," Virginia said suddenly. "Shifts and caps. I'll give them to you next time."

"My lady, you must be careful."

"I know." Virginia kissed Alma Francesca's forehead one more time, then reluctantly handed her back to Apollonia. "I know. But I cannot help myself."

* * *

FROM THAT DAY forward, Virginia behaved with blind, almost unbelievable indiscretion. She had Apollonia bring the baby to the convent repeatedly. Sometimes through the parlatory grating, sometimes to the convent door itself where Virginia could hold her properly. She made clothing for Alma Francesca, tiny garments sewn in secret, cutting up her own linens and embroidering them with careful stitches during hours when she should have been sleeping.

The nuns noticed. How could they not? Virginia's absorption with Gian Paolo's baby was obvious to everyone. Sister Paola whispered to Sister Imbersaga. Sister Costanza reported to the Prioress that Apollonia came to the convent far too often with the Osio baby. Some guessed the truth immediately. Others whispered speculations that came close enough to the mark.

But no one spoke openly, because to do so would be to invite catastrophe for the entire convent.

"You are being reckless," Benedetta warned one night after Gian Paolo had left. "Every time Apollonia brings that baby here, you risk discovery. The entire convent talks of nothing else. Even the schoolgirls whisper about it."

"I know."

"Then why continue? Why not content yourself with knowing she is alive and well-cared-for?"

Virginia turned to face her friend, and Benedetta saw something desperate in her eyes. "Could you? If you had a child living in a house you could see from these windows, could you simply pretend she did not exist? Could you hear her cry at night and not go mad with wanting to go to her?"

Benedetta was quiet for a long moment. "No," she admitted finally. "I could not."

The affair continued as before. Gian Paolo came to Virginia's chamber several nights each week. But now there was a new dimension to their meetings, hushed conversations about Alma Francesca, reports on her progress, arguments about her care.

"You've changed wet nurses again," Virginia said one night, lying in the darkness beside Gian Paolo. "Apollonia told me. That's the second time in as many months."

"The first one ate too much garlic. It soured the milk and made Alma fussy." Gian Paolo's voice carried the edge of obsession. "The new one is better. Cleaner. More careful."

"You cannot keep dismissing them for minor issues."

"Minor?" Gian Paolo sat up, his silhouette dark against the window. "Our daughter nearly became ill because I wasn't there to supervise her care. I will not make that mistake again. I will hire and dismiss as many nurses as necessary until I find one who meets my standards."

Our daughter. The words should have brought comfort. Instead, they highlighted Virginia's powerlessness. She had borne this child, had nearly died in the process, had sacrificed everything. And yet she had no say in how Alma Francesca was raised, no right even to acknowledge her publicly. She could only sew tiny clothes and steal moments at the convent door while Gian Paolo made all the decisions.

"I want to see her more often," Virginia said quietly.

"It's too dangerous. People are already talking."

"I don't care."

"You should care." Gian Paolo lay back down beside her. "The Cardinal's mercy has limits. Arrigone sits in prison, but he will be released eventually. When that happens, we'll need every advantage we have. Drawing attention to Alma will only make things worse."

Virginia said nothing, because he was right. But rightness did nothing to ease the ache in her chest.

* * *

ONE NIGHT IN late summer, perhaps out of curiosity, perhaps out of recklessness, Virginia did something she had never done before. She went out.

It was midnight when she slipped through the garden door, not to let Gian Paolo in but to follow him out. Benedetta and Ottavia had arranged it, setting up their usual watch system but this time to facilitate Virginia's escape rather than Gian Paolo's entrance. They waited on the loggia near the attic with a bell beside them, a string hanging down into the garden.

The night air was cold and sharp, utterly unlike the stale atmosphere of the convent. Virginia pulled her cloak tight around her habit and followed Gian Paolo through the darkness, her heart pounding with equal parts fear and exhilaration.

They walked to the edge of Monza, to places Virginia had not seen since she was a child. The streets were mostly empty at this hour, just drunks stumbling home and prostitutes calling from doorways. Gian Paolo kept Virginia close, shielding her from view, guiding her through shadows like he knew every alley in the town.

For a few hours she was not a nun but simply a woman with her lover, free to move through the world without walls or rules or consequences. They stood on a bridge over the Lambro and watched moonlight shimmer on dark water. Gian Paolo held her hand, his thumb tracing circles on her palm, and Virginia felt something she had not felt in years, possibility. The sense that life could be different, that she could be different, that the walls enclosing her were not permanent structures but temporary barriers that might someday fall.

But freedom was an illusion. When the night grew late and Virginia's fear began to outweigh her exhilaration, she pulled the cord that rang the bell, signaling Benedetta and Ottavia. Gian Paolo walked her back to the convent door and waited while she slipped inside, back into her cage.

The excursion should have satisfied something in Virginia. Instead, it made everything worse. Because now she knew what she was missing. Knew exactly what it felt like to walk beside Gian Paolo under open sky, to move without walls pressing close, to breathe air that did not smell of incense and stone and the accumulated prayers of centuries.

And knowing this, returning to convent life became almost unendurable.

* * *

OCTOBER BROUGHT CRISIS. The fever came in the night.

Virginia woke in darkness with dread sitting cold in her stomach. She sat up in bed and pressed her hand to her chest where something had pulled tight, some thread stretched taut between her body and the daughter she could not claim.

She did not know yet what had happened. But she knew. The way a mother knows.

The news came at Prime, but not through official channels. Ottavia appeared in the corridor outside the chapel, her face pale, her hands twisting in her habit. She caught Virginia's arm as the sisters filed past.

"Come," she whispered. "Quickly."

Virginia followed her to an empty parlatory, her heart hammering. "What is it?"

"Apollonia sent word through the kitchen servants. The baby is ill." Ottavia's voice broke. "Very ill. The fever came last night, and they cannot break it."

The words struck Virginia's chest, stealing her breath. She gripped the edge of the table between them, her knuckles going white. "How ill?"

"The physician has been sent for. Gian Paolo's mother—" Ottavia hesitated. "She fears the child may not live."

Not live. Her daughter burned with fever in Gian Paolo's house while Virginia stood trapped behind these walls, useless, powerless, unable even to go to her.

"I must do something." Virginia stopped. What could she do? She could not go to Alma Francesca. Could not hold her, could not comfort her. Could not do anything except stand here and feel her heart being ripped from her chest.

"There is more," Ottavia said quietly. "Apollonia asks if we might pray. She knows you cannot request it openly, but she thought, perhaps privately."

Virginia's mind raced. Prayers. The convent could pray for a sick child. It happened often enough. Families requesting intercession for ailing relatives. But to ask for prayers for Gian Paolo's baby would be to admit publicly what everyone already whispered. Would be to connect herself openly to that child, to make her interest explicit rather than merely suspected.

And yet. Her daughter was dying.

"I will speak to the Prioress," Virginia heard herself say.

"Virginia, no. If you ask directly—"

"My daughter is dying." Virginia's voice was flat. "I will not let her die without the prayers of this community simply because I am afraid of gossip."

* * *

THE NEXT MORNING brought a formal request.

Prioress Bianca announced at Chapter that she had received a petition from the household of Gian Paolo Osio. His mother humbly requested that the sisters of Santa Margherita pray for a child in their care who had fallen gravely ill with fever.

Virginia's hands clenched in her lap beneath her scapular. She kept her face carefully blank, her eyes fixed on the floor, while her heart hammered against her ribs.

"The request comes through proper channels," Bianca continued, her voice neutral. "We will, of course, honor it. A child's life hangs in the balance, and it is our duty to intercede with prayer."

Murmurs of agreement rippled through the assembled nuns. Virginia felt eyes sliding toward her—Sister Paola, Sister Imbersaga, others whose gazes she could feel like brands on her skin. They knew. Or suspected. Or were making calculations that would lead them to the truth soon enough.

"We will pray at Sext and None," Bianca said. "And continue throughout the day as our offices permit. Sister Virginia, as Vicaress, perhaps you will lead us?"

The words landed like a blow. Virginia's gaze snapped up to meet Bianca's. The Prioress's expression was impassive, but her eyes held something else, a test, perhaps. Or a warning.

"Of course, Reverend Mother." Virginia's voice came out steadier than she felt. "It would be my honor."

After Chapter dismissed, Virginia remained in her seat while the other nuns filed out. Her legs would not support her. The baby, Alma Francesca, was dying, and she had to stand before this community and lead prayers as though it were any other sick child in Monza. As though her heart were not being torn from her chest.

Bianca paused at the door. "Sister Virginia. A word."

Virginia rose on trembling legs and followed the Prioress to her private chamber. Once inside, Bianca closed the door and turned to face her.

"The request came from the Osio household," Bianca said carefully. "Proper and formal, as it should be. We pray for many children. This should be no different."

Virginia said nothing. Could not speak.

"And yet." Bianca moved closer, her voice dropping. "I have observed, Sister Virginia, that you take unusual interest in this particular child. The servants report that the woman Apollonia brings the baby here frequently. That you see her in the parlatory. That you have... become fond of her."

The words hung carefully between them. Not an accusation. Not quite.

"She is an innocent child," Virginia managed. "She deserves prayers."

"All children deserve prayers." Bianca's gaze was penetrating. "But I wonder if you understand what it will cost you to lead these prayers. Every nun in this convent will watch your face. They will hear your voice. They will measure your grief and draw their own conclusions about why the Vicaress cares so deeply for Gian Paolo Osio's bastard."

Virginia flinched at the word.

"You see?" Bianca's voice softened slightly. "You cannot hide what you feel. I would not ask you to. But you must understand that this moment will be remembered. When trouble comes, and it will come, this will be part of the evidence against you."

"What would you have me do?" Virginia's voice was barely a whisper. "Refuse to pray for a dying child?"

"No." Bianca turned to look out her window. "I would have you pray with everything you possess. I would have you beg God for mercy. And I would have you accept that in doing so, you reveal yourself."

Virginia pressed her hand against her chest where her heart felt like it might burst through her ribs. "She is innocent. Whatever sins have been committed, she is innocent of them all."

"Yes," Bianca said quietly. "The child is innocent. But you are not, Sister Virginia. And neither am I, for I have watched this affair unfold and said nothing. We are all complicit in our silence. The question is how much longer that silence can hold."

She turned back to face Virginia, and her expression was grave. "Lead the prayers. Do not stint in your petitions. If God chooses to spare this child, then we will all give thanks. But know that every word you speak today will be weighed against you when the reckoning comes."

Virginia met her eyes. "I accept that."

Bianca nodded slowly. "Then go. And pray for the child as you see fit. I will not ask you to explain why she matters to you. Some truths are better left unspoken until they can no longer be denied."

* * *

THE CONVENT PRAYED. Not publicly, not with the full ceremony that might have drawn attention, but in quiet intercession during the canonical hours. Bianca announced that a child in the town was gravely ill and requested prayers for her recovery. She did not name the child or the family.

But everyone knew. The whispers started immediately. Virginia felt the eyes on her during Sext, during None, during Vespers. Saw the glances exchanged between nuns who thought themselves subtle. Sister Paola whispered to Sister Imbersaga. Sister Costanza looked at Virginia with something like pity.

Virginia knelt in the chapel and prayed with an intensity that left her shaking. She made bargains with God; promises she could not keep. *Take anything,* she prayed. *My life, my soul, anything you want. Only let her live.*

But God did not answer. Or perhaps He did, and the answer was silence.

News came in fragments throughout the day, carried by Ottavia who heard it from Apollonia through the network of servants who moved between convent and town. The fever had not broken. The baby would not take milk, would not take water, only cried in thin wails that tore at everyone who heard them. The physician had bled her, had applied poultices, had done everything his art allowed, but the fever raged on.

Virginia moved through the hours in a fog of dread. She stood in choir, and her mouth formed the words of psalms while her mind was elsewhere, in Gian Paolo's house where her daughter burned. She sat in the refectory and could not eat. She tried to sew, and her hands shook so badly she had to put the needle down.

Benedetta and Ottavia watched her with worried eyes but said nothing. What could they say? The child was dying, and Virginia could do nothing but wait and pray and feel something vital being ripped from her chest one beat at a time.

* * *

ON THE SECOND day, Virginia could bear it no longer. She sent word through Ottavia to Apollonia that the nuns would pray specifically to Saint Monica, protector of children. Perhaps it would help. Perhaps it would do nothing. But she had to try.

Prioress Bianca agreed without comment and gathered the community in the chapel. They knelt together and raised their voices in petition.

Virginia's voice cracked on the Latin. She pressed her forehead to her clasped hands and felt tears slide hot down her cheeks, dropping onto stone that had absorbed the prayers and tears of women for generations. How many women had knelt here begging God to spare their loved ones? How many had lost them anyway?

Please, she prayed. *Please, please, please.*

After the prayers ended and the other sisters filed out, Virginia remained kneeling. The chapel was quiet except for the sound of her breathing and the occasional creak of old wood settling. Afternoon light filtered through the windows, painting the floor in patterns of gold and shadow.

She stayed until Vespers' bells rang and her knees had gone numb.

* * *

THE NEXT MORNING, word came that Gian Paolo had returned from Milan.

He had been away on business when the fever struck. His mother had not sent word, perhaps thinking the illness would pass quickly. But Apollonia had taken it upon herself to send a servant riding hard to Milan with news that the baby was dying, and Gian Paolo had come home in a fury.

Virginia pieced the story together from whispers between servants, from Ottavia who had it from Apollonia herself.

He had arrived at dawn, his horse lathered from being ridden through the night. He went straight to the room where Alma Francesca lay burning with fever, took one look at his daughter's flushed face and glazed eyes, and turned on his mother with rage.

"Why didn't you tell me?" His voice had carried through the house, loud enough that servants in the kitchen had stopped their work to listen. "My daughter is dying, and you didn't think to send word?"

His mother had tried to explain. The fever had come so suddenly, the physician had said such illnesses were common in small children, she had not wanted to worry him unnecessarily. But Gian Paolo had cut her off with words so sharp that Apollonia had flinched in the retelling.

He blamed her. Told her she had failed in her duty, that if Alma Francesca died it would be because his mother had been too proud or too stupid to send for him when it mattered.

Then he had dismissed everyone from the room except the physician and the wet nurse, and no one had seen him since.

Virginia stood in the garden when she heard this, her hands gripping the wall that separated convent ground from the Osio property. He was there. Just beyond this wall. Sitting with their daughter while she fought for her life, and Virginia could not go to either of them.

The unfairness of it choked her. He could hold Alma Francesca, could stroke her fevered forehead and whisper comfort in her ear. He could call physicians and dismiss servants and rage at his mother. He could do everything a father should do.

And Virginia could only kneel in the chapel and pray to saints who might not listen.

* * *

ON THE FOURTH day, the fever broke.

The news came at midday through Ottavia, who had it from Apollonia. Alma Francesca had woken that morning clear-eyed and asked for milk, her skin cool to the touch, the crisis passed. The physician declared her out of danger. The household exhaled. Gian Paolo's mother wept with relief.

Virginia's legs became weak. She sat down hard on the bench in her chamber, her hands pressed flat against her thighs and breathed. Just breathed. In and out while her vision blurred and her chest loosened and something that had been clenched tight inside her for four days finally let go.

"Thank God," Ottavia whispered.

"Yes." Virginia's voice was hoarse. "Thank God."

She went to the chapel and knelt before the altar, her body shaking with exhaustion and relief. She had asked for prayers. Had risked exposure, had revealed her connection to that child for all the convent to see. And her daughter had lived.

Whether the prayers had worked or the fever had simply run its course, Virginia would never know. But she whispered thanks to the Madonna and Saint Monica and every saint who might have carried her desperate petitions to heaven.

Later, when the community gathered for Vespers, Prioress Bianca announced that the child had recovered and they should give thanks. Virginia felt the eyes on her as she sang the psalm of thanksgiving, saw the knowing looks exchanged between nuns.

She had revealed herself. Everyone knew now, or guessed close enough to the truth that it made no difference. The Lady of Monza cared about Gian Paolo Osio's baby. Cared enough to risk scandal, to ask for public prayers, to kneel in the chapel and weep for a child she could not claim.

The secret was no longer a secret. And Virginia found she did not care.

Her daughter had lived. That was all that mattered.

* * *

GIAN PAOLO THREW threw himself into Alma Francesca's care with an intensity that bordered on obsession. Virginia gathered the details from Ottavia, who heard them from Apollonia.

He supervised everything. The wet nurse's diet, to ensure the milk was rich and healthy. The temperature of the room where the baby slept. The frequency of feedings and the quality of linens. Whether the child was gaining weight properly, reaching the milestones she should reach.

In the months following the crisis, Gian Paolo changed wet nurses three times, each time seeking someone healthier, cleaner, more careful. One wet nurse ate too any onions, and he said it soured the milk. Another let the baby cry for more than a minute before picking her up. A third had a cough that might spread to Alma Francesca.

He housed each nurse in his own home at his own expense, not trusting them to care for his daughter properly if they lived elsewhere. His house was filled with nurses and servants whose sole purpose was to ensure Alma Francesca's comfort and safety.

"He cannot bear the thought of losing her," Ottavia whispered one evening as they sat in their chamber. "Apollonia says he barely sleeps. He goes to the nursery at night just to watch her breathing. Sometimes he sits beside her cradle for hours, making sure she's still alive."

Virginia's throat tightened. She bent over the tiny shift she was embroidering and did not answer.

Each detail that reached Virginia opened something raw inside her chest. He loved their daughter. Truly, deeply, with the fierce protectiveness of a man who had almost lost something precious. He was a good father in ways that shamed her, because all she could do was sew tiny clothes and weep in the chapel and steal moments to hold the baby when Apollonia brought her to the gate.

She should have been grateful. Should have thanked God that their child had a father who cared for her so completely. And she was grateful. She was.

But gratitude did nothing to ease the ache of being shut out from her own daughter's life, of hearing about fevers and wet nurses and daily routines secondhand, of loving someone she could never claim and watching other women, Gian Paolo's mother, his hired nurses, Apollonia, raise the child she had borne in blood and terror.

* * *

LATE AUTUMN BROUGHT word that the authorities were investigating the harquebus affair found in possession of Father Arrigone. They had discovered that Gian Paolo, or an agent of his, had obtained the sacristy keys from the church custodian of San Maurizio. The guns found hidden there were Gian Paolo's own weapons. He had planted them deliberately to incriminate Arrigone.

The evidence was mounting. Witnesses had come forward. The magistrates were preparing their report.

"Arrigone will be released," Benedetta said flatly when the news reached the convent. "It's only a matter of time now. The investigation proves he was framed. By spring, he'll walk free."

Virginia stood at her window, watching gray clouds gather over Monza. Winter was returning. And with it, all the consequences she had been running from for years.

Arrigone had remained imprisoned for over a year now, but everyone knew it was ending. When spring came and the investigation concluded, he would be released. And Virginia's letters to the Cardinal, those foolish, vengeful letters, would be waiting for him to use as weapons. He would have proof that she had tried to destroy him. Proof that she had accused him of corruption while conducting her own sinful affair.

The vendetta between Gian Paolo and Arrigone had spiraled into something dangerous. And Virginia had started it all with her jealous rage, her need to strike back at a man who had humiliated her.

"Let him come," Virginia said, her voice hollow. "I am tired of running."

But she was not tired enough to stop. That night, when Gian Paolo came through the garden door, Virginia went to him with the same desperate hunger that had ruled her for seven years. She could not change. Could not break free. Could not do anything except continue down the path she had chosen until it led to its inevitable end.

* * *

THE LEAVES TURNED gold and fell. The air grew cold. Alma Francesca recovered fully, grew rosy and fat and healthy in ways that made Virginia ache with relief and longing every time she saw her. The baby was walking now, Apollonia reported. Taking her first wobbling steps, laughing when she fell, pulling herself up again with determination.

Virginia had missed it. Had missed her daughter's first steps, her first words, all the moments a mother should witness. She heard about them secondhand, through whispered reports from Apollonia, and each detail was a knife in her chest.

Winter settled over Monza like a shroud. Virginia stood at her window on the last day of the year, watching snow fall on the garden below. Somewhere in the town, Arrigone waited in prison, counting the days until his release. Somewhere in Gian Paolo's house, Alma Francesca slept in her nursery, watched over by nurses and servants who knew nothing of the nun who sewed clothes for her in secret. And somewhere in Milan, the Cardinal reviewed reports and made decisions that would determine Virginia's fate.

The year had passed without catastrophe, but also without resolution. Virginia remained trapped in the same patterns, making the same choices, unable to break free from the life she had built through years of accumulated sin.

"What are you thinking?" Ottavia asked, appearing in the doorway with her perpetually worried expression.

"I am thinking," Virginia said slowly, "that this cannot continue much longer. That something will break. And when it does, all of us will be swept away in the flood."

"Then why do you continue? Why not end the affair with Gian Paolo, send him away, protect yourself while you still can?"

Virginia turned from the window. "Because I would rather be swept away with him than survive without him. Because this life, the convent, the prayers, the performance of devotion, means nothing to me compared to the few hours I have with Gian Paolo each week. Because I am already damned, Ottavia. And if I am damned, I might as well have the one thing that makes me feel alive."

Ottavia said nothing. What could she say? They both knew Virginia was right. The choices had been made years ago. All that remained was to see them through to their conclusion, whatever that might be.

The bells rang for Compline. Virginia straightened her habit and followed Ottavia to the chapel, her feet carrying her along paths worn smooth by repetition. The year 1605 was ending. Tomorrow would bring 1606, and with it whatever reckoning awaited.

But tonight, Virginia would kneel and mouth prayers she did not believe. Would sing hymns with words she no longer felt. Would perform the role of Sister Virginia Maria one more time, because that was all she knew how to do.

And later, when the convent slept, she would go to the garden door. Would lift the bar. Would let Gian Paolo through. Because in the end, she always did.

Chapter Twelve
1606

THE AUTHORITIES TOOK their time with the harquebus affair. Weeks stretched into months while investigators questioned servants and examined locks and traced the path of forbidden weapons to the narrow closet where they had been found. Justice moved with the slow deliberation of men who understood that accusing a nobleman required certainty.

Eventually the truth emerged in ways that pleased no one.

The sacristy keys had been borrowed from the church custodian by someone acting on Gian Paolo's orders. The guns themselves belonged to Gian Paolo, as everyone had half-suspected. He had admitted as much to the chancellor, explaining with elaborate courtesy that he kept harquebuses for hunting and had stored them at the church temporarily while his own armory was being repaired. A thin excuse that convinced no one, but what could the authorities do? Gian Paolo Osio was not a man they could afford to prosecute without ironclad evidence of intent.

In the end, they released Arrigone. Not with fanfare or apology, but with a curt notation in the court records that he had been found innocent and was free to resume his duties as priest of San Maurizio.

The news reached the convent during a cold afternoon in February. Ottavia brought it from the portress who had seen Arrigone walking through town in his dusty cassock, thinner than before and blinking in sunlight his eyes had not seen for months.

"They let him out," Ottavia said, keeping her voice low. "Yesterday morning. He went straight to the church."

Virginia set down the infant's cap she had been hemming. "Did he say anything? About who put him there?"

"What could he say?" Ottavia's mouth twisted. "Everyone knows it was Gian Paolo. But knowing and saying are different things, especially for a man who has just been released from prison and would like to keep his freedom."

Virginia nodded. The knot in her stomach tightened. Arrigone was free, and he would know exactly who had arranged his imprisonment. The question was what he would do with that knowledge.

* * *

ARRIGONE WENT TO Gian Paolo's house three times in the weeks that followed. The visits came to Virginia through the usual channels—servants who liked to talk, sisters who gathered information at the gate.

The first visit was brief and formal. Arrigone arrived in the late afternoon, stayed less than an hour. When he left, his face was pale and set, his hands clenched at his sides. No one overheard what was said behind the closed door, but the household staff whispered that Gian Paolo's voice had been pleasant throughout, the kind of pleasant that made smart people nervous.

The second visit was shorter. Arrigone came in the evening and left before the church bells rang Compline, his expression angry when he emerged, his jaw tight and his eyes burning with something that might have been rage or humiliation or both.

The third visit was the last. Arrigone stayed only long enough to exchange a few words in the doorway, then turned and walked away without looking back, his shoulders rigid beneath the worn cassock.

After that, he stopped coming.

The friendship, such as it had been, was finished. Whatever words had passed between them, threats, perhaps, or warnings dressed in courtesy, had made it clear that the easy alliance of nobleman and priest was over. They were enemies now, the kind who smiled when they met in public and plotted in private.

Virginia received each fragment of this news with a sick dread she could not shake. Two men who knew her secrets, who could destroy her with a few well-placed words, now hated each other with the intensity of former allies turned bitter.

* * *

ARRIGONE RESUMED HIS duties at San Maurizio. He said Mass in the mornings, heard confessions in the afternoons, performed baptisms and marriages and funerals with the proper solemnity. To the casual observer, he was the same priest he had always been, a little dissolute, perhaps, but diligent enough in his sacred obligations.

But the careful observer would have noticed changes. He was thinner after his time in prison; his cassock hung loose on a frame that had lost flesh to bad food and worry. His eyes held a wariness that had not been there before, the look of a man who understood that the world was more dangerous than he had thought.

He was also, despite everything, still pursuing the nuns.

This news arrived with a mixture of disbelief and weary recognition. The man had been imprisoned, humiliated, made to understand exactly how much danger his actions carried, and still, he could not help himself. Still, he sent notes and wrote letters and found ways to make contact with women who were supposed to be brides of Christ and nothing more.

* * *

THE GOSSIP, WHICH had always simmered beneath the surface of Monza life, now began to boil over. The affair between the Lady of Monza and Gian Paolo Osio had become common knowledge. Not whispered speculation but accepted fact. Servants talked openly in the markets. Merchants exchanged knowing looks when the Osio name was mentioned. Even the schoolgirls in the convent whispered about it, giggling behind their hands about things they only half understood.

And everyone knew about the baby.

Gian Paolo kept little Alma Francesca in his house with a procession of wet nurses, changing them with obsessive frequency, supervising every detail of her care with an intensity that made his own household staff uncomfortable. He claimed the child as his own bastard, naming the mother as an unknown Isabella Montini. But nobody believed it.

The baby had been brought to Monza too publicly. She looked too much like Gian Paolo, yes, but also, those who had glimpsed her said, like the Lady of Monza herself. And Virginia's interest in the child was far too obvious, too desperate, too maternal to be anything but what it appeared.

"The whole town knows," Benedetta said one evening, her voice tight with worry. "They speak of it openly now. No more pretense, no more careful words. They say the baby is yours and Gian Paolo's, and they wonder what the Cardinal will do when he hears."

"He has heard," Virginia said flatly. "He has known for months. And he has done nothing."

"Perhaps he is waiting."

"For what?"

Benedetta had no answer to that.

* * *

THE DAY CAME in late spring when three young women took the veil at Santa Margherita. The church filled with families and well-wishers, the choir rang with voices raised in praise, and the three novices knelt before the altar to speak their final vows.

One of them was called Arresina.

Virginia watched from her place in the choir as the girl, barely seventeen, with a round face and frightened eyes, promised stability and obedience and conversion of life. She remembered her own profession, remembered kneeling on this same cold stone and speaking these same words while her father watched with satisfaction in his eyes. How young she had been. How little she had understood about what those words would cost.

The ceremony concluded with prayers and blessings. The new novices rose from their knees and filed back into the convent, their white veils bright in the afternoon sun. Virginia followed, her mind already on the evening meal.

She was crossing the cloister when the commotion started.

Arrigone's housekeeper stood at the convent gate, a woman Virginia vaguely recognized from town. She was speaking to the portress, her voice rising with insistence.

"I must speak with Sister Arresina. Father Arrigone has sent me with an urgent matter for her."

The portress, an older woman with no patience for nonsense, shook her head firmly. "Sister Arresina has just taken her vows. She is in seclusion and cannot receive visitors."

"But Father Arrigone insists."

"Father Arrigone should know better." Prioress Bianca had arrived, drawn by the raised voices. She stood with her spine straight and her hands folded, every inch of her radiating disapproval. "You will tell your master that newly professed sisters are not to be disturbed by anyone, priest or otherwise."

The woman's face flushed. "He said it was important."

"I do not care what he said." Bianca's voice cut through the protest with precision. "You will leave this gate immediately, and you will tell Father Arrigone that he is to attend to his church and say his Masses and stop meddling with the nuns of this convent. If he has business to conduct, he can conduct it through proper channels during visiting hours with a chaperone present. Is that understood?"

The woman opened her mouth as if to argue, then seemed to think better of it. She nodded stiffly and turned to go, her footsteps quick on the cobblestones as she hurried away.

Prioress Bianca watched her until she disappeared around the corner, then turned to find Virginia standing in the cloister archway.

"You heard?" the Prioress asked.

"I heard."

Bianca's mouth tightened. "This is not the first time he has tried to contact our sisters, is it?"

The question hung in the air between them. Virginia could lie, could pretend ignorance, could protect Arrigone from consequences he had earned ten times over. But something in her had reached its limit. She was tired of protecting men who did nothing but cause harm, tired of keeping confidences that served no purpose except to let fools continue being foolish.

"No," Virginia said. "It is not the first time."

Prioress Bianca waited, her sharp eyes steady on Virginia's face.

Virginia took a breath. "He sent love letters to me and to Sister Candida. His housekeeper brought them back and forth." The words came easier than she expected, truth emerging clean and sharp. "He tried everything to arrange meetings in the parlatory at night. He wrote shameful things, promised shameful things. Sister Candida refused him, but he persisted until I ordered Domenico to stop delivering anything from him."

Bianca's expression did not change, but something cold moved behind her eyes. "When was this?"

"More than a year ago. Before his trouble with Gian Paolo Osio."

Bianca nodded slowly as understanding settled into place. "And you did not report this because?"

Virginia met her gaze. "Because I was afraid it would bring scandal to the convent. Because I thought I could handle it quietly. Because I was a fool."

"You were protecting your own affairs, I think. Not the convent's honor."

The accusation was fair. Virginia did not flinch from it. "Yes."

"And now?"

"Now I am telling you. Do with the information what you will."

Prioress Bianca looked toward the gate where Arrigone's housekeeper had stood moments before. "He learns nothing, this priest. Prison did not teach him wisdom." She turned back to Virginia, her face unreadable. "I wonder what will."

Virginia had no answer to that. She stood in the cloister while Prioress Bianca walked away, her footsteps echoing on stone, and felt something shift in her chest, relief, perhaps, or simply the exhaustion that came from holding too many things inside for too long.

* * *

THE LETTER ARRIVED at the Archbishop's palace in early summer.

It was anonymous, written in a careful hand that disguised its author's identity. The messenger who delivered it could not, or would not, say who had paid him to carry it. It was addressed to Cardinal Federigo Borromeo himself, and when his secretary opened it and read the contents, he went pale and immediately took it to the Cardinal's private study.

The letter denounced both Father Paolo Arrigone and Sister Virginia Maria de Leyva.

It accused Arrigone of corrupting nuns, of sending love letters into the Convent of Santa Margherita, of attempting to seduce brides of Christ with shameful proposals. It detailed his pursuit of Sister Candida, his meetings in the parlatory at night, his use of servants to carry messages back and forth.

But that was not the worst of it.

The letter also revealed the affair between Virginia and Gian Paolo Osio. Not in vague terms or careful suggestions, but with specifics that left no room for doubt. It described Gian Paolo's nocturnal visits to the convent. It mentioned the baby he kept in his house, naming her as Virginia's child. It accused Virginia of conducting a years-long liaison, of birthing children in secret, of violating every vow she had taken with full knowledge and deliberate intent.

The letter ended with a plea for the Cardinal to investigate, to cleanse the convent of corruption before the scandal destroyed not only Santa Margherita but the entire Church's reputation in Monza.

Cardinal Borromeo read the letter three times, his expression growing darker with each reading.

He had known there were rumors. Had heard whispers, had even received Virginia's own petition against Arrigone the year before. But he had dismissed it as a private quarrel, a matter best left alone to avoid conflict with the de Leyva family. He had visited the convent, had spoken to Virginia, had come away uncertain but unwilling to push further without clear evidence.

Now he had evidence. Or at least an accusation detailed enough that he could not ignore it.

He sat for a long time with the letter in his hands, staring at the words without seeing them. Then he called for his secretary and began drafting orders for an investigation.

But not yet. Not immediately. He needed to be careful. The de Leyvas were powerful, and Virginia was the daughter of Don Martino, feudal lord of Monza. To move against her without absolute certainty would be to invite a war between Church and aristocracy that could tear Milan apart.

He would wait. Would gather information quietly. Would build a case so strong that when he finally acted, no one, not Virginia, not her family, not even the Spanish Governor himself, could claim he had been rash or unfair.

The letter was filed away carefully, marked with a notation of the date it had been received. And the Cardinal began to plan.

* * *

IN MONZA, LIFE continued with an illusion of normalcy. Virginia did not know about the letter. Gian Paolo did not know. They went on as they had for years, meeting in secret, maintaining the pretense that nothing was wrong, believing that their power and position would protect them forever.

But the rumors continued to spread. Servants talked. Merchants gossiped. The schoolgirls whispered. And slowly, inexorably, the weight of public knowledge grew too heavy to ignore.

Virginia sensed it in the way people looked at her when she appeared at the parlatory grating. In the careful way Prioress Bianca spoke to her now, with a wariness that had not been there before. In the silences that fell when she entered a room, the conversations that stopped mid-word and did not resume.

"Something has changed," she said to Gian Paolo one night in the darkness of her chamber. "I can feel it."

"Nothing has changed." His voice was confident and dismissive. "People have always talked. Let them talk."

"This is different."

"How?"

Virginia could not explain it, this sense of walls closing in, of time running out. "I think the Cardinal knows."

"The Cardinal has always known. Or suspected. It makes no difference." Gian Paolo pulled her closer. "My status protects me. Your family protects you. What can he do?"

Virginia wanted to believe him. Wanted to accept his certainty, his arrogance, his absolute conviction that they were untouchable. But she could not shake the feeling that something fundamental had shifted, that the ground beneath them was no longer solid.

"I am afraid," she whispered.

"Don't be." He kissed her forehead, her cheeks, her mouth. "I will never let anything happen to you. I swear it."

The promise should have comforted her. Instead, it made her more afraid. Because she knew, had always known, deep in the part of herself that saw clearly even when she wished she could not, that Gian Paolo could not protect her from what was coming. No one could.

* * *

SUMMER DEEPENED. THE heat grew oppressive. In his house across the wall, Gian Paolo doted on Alma Francesca, changing wet nurses again when he decided the current one was not careful enough. The baby thrived despite, or perhaps because of, his obsessive attention, growing sturdy and bright-eyed, learning to say simple words that made him weep with pride.

Virginia watched from her window sometimes, catching glimpses of him in his garden with the child in his arms. Each time she saw them together, something twisted in her chest. Love and grief and longing so intense it was almost unbearable.

That was her daughter. Her child. And she could only watch from a distance while others raised her, while Gian Paolo made all the decisions, while the world went on pretending she had no claim to the life she had brought into being.

* * *

THE CHANGE CAME gradually at first, then all at once.

Virginia noticed it in small things. The way Sister Paola stopped talking when Virginia entered the refectory. The careful neutrality in Prioress Bianca's voice during Chapter meetings. The portress who wouldn't quite meet her eyes when Virginia passed through the cloister.

But it was more than the usual whispers. Those had always been there, a low hum of speculation and judgment that Virginia had learned to ignore. This was different. Sharper. More certain.

One afternoon in late summer, Virginia stood at the parlatory grating to receive a visitor—a distant cousin come to discuss some matter of family business. The woman's manner was stiff, formal in ways it had never been before. When they finished and the woman rose to leave, Virginia saw something in her face. Pity, perhaps. Or disgust carefully masked as courtesy.

"You should be more careful, cousin," the woman said quietly, glancing toward the portress to ensure she was out of earshot. "People are talking. Not whispers anymore. Open talk. In the markets, in the churches, everywhere."

Virginia's throat tightened. "Let them talk."

"It's not just gossip now." The woman leaned closer to the grating. "There are those who say someone has written to the Archbishop. That formal complaints have been made."

The words struck like a blow. Virginia kept her face carefully blank. "What complaints?"

"About you. About the Osio man. About..." The woman's eyes dropped. "About the child everyone knows is yours."

After the woman left, Virginia remained at the grating, her hands gripping the iron bars. Someone had written to the Cardinal. Formal complaints. The phrase echoed in her mind, each repetition bringing fresh dread.

She had always known this moment would come. Had felt it approaching like a storm on the horizon, inevitable and terrible. But knowing and experiencing were different things. The abstract threat had become concrete. Someone she did not know who, had put her sins in writing and sent them to Milan.

* * *

THAT NIGHT, WHEN Gian Paolo came through the garden door, Virginia met him in the corridor rather than her chamber.

"We need to stop," she said without preamble. "At least for a while. Until things calm down."

Gian Paolo's expression hardened. "We've had this conversation before."

"This is different. Someone has written to the Cardinal. Formal denunciations. My cousin told me today."

"Your cousin is repeating gossip." He reached for her hand, but Virginia pulled away. "They've been talking for years. Nothing has changed."

"Everything has changed." Virginia's voice rose, then she caught herself and lowered it to a harsh whisper. "Don't you understand? Before it was rumors. Now someone has made official accusations. The Cardinal will have to investigate."

"Let him investigate." Gian Paolo's confidence was absolute, infuriating. "What will he find? Gossip from servants? Speculation from jealous nuns? He needs proof, Virginia. Real proof. Witnesses willing to testify under oath. And who would dare?"

"Anyone," Virginia said quietly. "Everyone. They're not afraid anymore. That's what I'm trying to tell you. Something has shifted. The protection we've had, the silence people maintained because they feared us, it's dissolving."

Gian Paolo studied her face in the dim light of the corridor. Then he pulled her close despite her resistance, his arms wrapping around her with familiar strength. "I will not lose you. Not to the Cardinal, not to your family, not to anyone. Do you understand me?"

Virginia wanted to believe him. Wanted to let his certainty wash away her fear, to pretend that love and status could protect them from consequences that had been building for seven years. But she could not shake the memory of her cousin's face, the pity in those eyes, the careful warning that had really been a condemnation.

"I'm afraid," she whispered against his chest.

"I know." His hand moved to the back of her head, fingers tangling in her veil. "But fear changes nothing. We've come too far to turn back now."

He was right, of course. They had passed the point of redemption years ago. The only path left was forward, into whatever reckoning awaited them.

That night they made love with a desperation that had not been there before, as though each touch might be the last, each whispered word a farewell they were not yet ready to speak aloud.

* * *

AUTUMN CAME WITH cold winds that stripped the trees bare. Virginia moved through the daily offices like a ghost, her body present while her mind circled endlessly around the same questions. Would Arrigone make good on his threats of revenge? Would the gossip that had intensified after Imbersaga's removal as prioress finally reach ears that mattered? When would someone, anyone with power, decide that the rumors demanded investigation? Or was it all still just talk, whispers building on whispers until they became their own kind of truth?

The not-knowing was torture. At least with certainty she could prepare. But this suspended state, where danger felt imminent but remained shapeless, left her constantly on edge, jumping at shadows, reading threat into every glance.

The gossip intensified. Servants who had once been careful now spoke openly in the markets, their voices carrying through the square when Virginia's name was mentioned. The schoolgirls whispered in corners, giggling over scandals they only half understood. Even priests from other churches, included pointed remarks about the corruption of religious houses in his Sunday homilies.

Monza knew. All of Monza knew. The secret that had been maintained through years of careful silence had finally broken into the open, and there was no way to contain it now.

One evening, Prioress Bianca summoned Virginia to her private chamber.

"Sit," the Prioress said, gesturing to a chair.

Virginia sat, her hands folded in her lap, her spine straight. Whatever was coming, she would face it with dignity.

Bianca was quiet for a long moment, studying Virginia's face with those sharp eyes that saw too much. Finally, she spoke.

"I received a letter today. From the Archbishop's office." She paused. "It was not addressed to you. It was a general inquiry, sent to all the convents in the diocese. Questions about discipline, about adherence to cloister, about any irregularities that should be brought to the Cardinal's attention."

Virginia's heart beats increased. A general inquiry. That meant the Cardinal was looking, searching, building a case perhaps. Or perhaps it meant nothing, perhaps he sent such letters routinely. She could not tell, and Bianca's careful neutrality gave no clues.

"And what will you answer?" Virginia's voice was steady despite the terror clawing at her throat.

"Nothing. Yet." Bianca's expression was unreadable. "But I cannot protect you anymore, Sister Virginia. You understand that, don't you? If the Cardinal sends investigators, if he demands testimony under oath, I cannot lie to protect you. I will not lie."

"I understand."

"Do you?" Bianca leaned forward. "Because I wonder if you truly grasp what is coming. This inquiry, it may be routine, or it may be the first step toward something far worse. Either way, the Cardinal is paying attention now. And once his attention is fixed on Santa Margherita, your family name will not save you. Your status will not save you. Nothing will save you."

Virginia met her eyes. "I know."

"Then why do you continue? Why not end the affair now, before the final blow falls? Send Osio away. Confess your sins. Throw yourself on the Cardinal's mercy while you still can."

"Because I love him." The words came without thought, truth emerging stark and clear. "Because I would rather be destroyed with him than saved without him. Because this love, however sinful, however doomed, is the only real thing in my life."

Bianca's expression softened slightly, something like sadness moving behind her eyes. "Then God have mercy on you, Sister Virginia. Because no one else will."

* * *

AFTER VIRGINIA LEFT, she walked through the cloister in the gathering darkness. Above her, stars emerged in a sky gone deep blue with evening. The chapel bells rang for Compline, calling the sisters to prayer.

Virginia went to the chapel and knelt in her usual place. Around her, the other nuns filed in, their habits rustling in the silence. They sang the psalms together, voices rising in practiced harmony, the ancient words washing over Virginia without touching her.

She had prayed for years. For strength, for deliverance, for God to remove this love from her heart or at least to make it bearable. But God had remained silent, or perhaps His answer had been the silence itself, permission to choose, to fall, to find whatever grace or damnation awaited at the bottom of her descent.

When the office ended and the others filed out, Virginia remained. She stayed until the chapel was empty and dark except for the single lamp burning before the altar. Stayed until her knees ached and her back cramped. Stayed until she could no longer distinguish prayer from simple exhaustion.

Finally, she rose and made her to her cell. Gian Paolo had sent word through Apollonia that he would be away in Milan for several days. Business with the Spanish governor, some matter requiring his presence at court.

So, Virginia lay alone in the darkness and listened to the wind rattle the shutters. Somewhere beyond these walls, perhaps letters were being written.

Perhaps denunciations were being drafted. Perhaps the Cardinal was already building his case, gathering testimonies, preparing the machinery that would eventually crush her.

Or perhaps not. Perhaps it was all still just talk, rumors that would fade as they always had, leaving her to continue this dangerous dance indefinitely.

The not-knowing was its own kind of torture.

She closed her eyes and thought of Gian Paolo, miles away in Milan, confident in his power and status. Thought of Alma Francesca sleeping in her nursery, innocent of all the sins that had brought her into being. Thought of the Cardinal in his palace, reading reports or perhaps thinking nothing of Santa Margherita at all.

And she waited. Because waiting was all she had left. Waiting to see if the axe would fall or if the rope would hold just a little longer.

* * *

The 19th of April

THE DOCUMENT ARRIVED on a morning when spring rain drummed against the convent windows and turned the courtyard into a maze of puddles. Ottavia brought it to Virginia's chamber wrapped in oilcloth, the wax seal still intact, Gian Paolo's mark pressed deep into red wax.

Virginia broke the seal with trembling fingers. Inside were two sheets of parchment, the ink dark and official, the language precise in the way of legal documents that changed lives.

> *Be it known that I, Gian Paolo Osio, do hereby acknowledge and legally recognize Alma Francesca Margherita Osio as my legitimate daughter, born of an unknown woman by the name of Isabella Montini.*

Virginia read the line again. Unknown woman. As if the mother who had carried the child and birthed her in secret could be reduced to those two words. Unknown. A fiction written in ink and sealed with wax.

The second document was the baptism certificate from the Church of Sant'Andrea in Milan.

> *Alma Francesca Margherita. Baptized August 1604. Godfather: Senator Count Francesco d'Adda. Mother: Isabella Montini, whereabouts unknown.*

Virginia set the documents on her table and stared at them until the ink blurred and reformed, until the words lost meaning. Her daughter had a name now. A legal name. A father who claimed her. And a mother who was nobody, unknown, a ghost invented to satisfy the law.

She should have felt relieved. The documents protected Alma Francesca, gave her legitimacy, ensured she would inherit property and bear the Osio name without the stain of bastardy.

But all Virginia felt was hollow.

* * *

ONE AFTERNOON IN early May, Virginia stood at the parlatory grate waiting for Apollonia to bring the child. She arrived with the wet nurse in tow, and Alma Francesca bundled against the spring chill. Virginia's throat tightened at the sight of that small face, those dark eyes beginning to show intelligence beyond her two years.

"Come closer," Virginia whispered through the iron bars. "Let me see her."

Apollonia shifted the child nearer to the grate. Alma Francesca reached out with chubby fingers, trying to grasp the metal, and Virginia pressed her palm against the bars, so their skin almost touched through the narrow spaces.

"Oh, my lady Alma Francesca." The endearment escaped before Virginia could stop it, her voice breaking. "My little girl. My sweet baby."

Behind her, footsteps stopped.

Virginia froze, her palm still pressed to the grate, her face turned toward the child. She did not need to look to know someone stood in the shadows, listening. The quality of the silence had changed, grown thick with attention.

Apollonia's eyes widened. She took a small step back, clutching Alma Francesca tighter.

Virginia turned slowly. Sister Candida stood in the doorway, her face stricken, gripping her rosary so tightly her knuckles had gone white. Their eyes met. Something passed between them. Not discovery, for Candida had been there that August night when the child was born, but horror at the recklessness, the sick awareness that Virginia had just spoken words that could destroy them all.

"Sister Virginia," Candida whispered, her voice shaking. "Anyone could have been standing here. Anyone."

The rebuke landed like a slap. Virginia opened her mouth to respond, but no words came.

Candida glanced toward the gate where Apollonia still stood frozen, then back to Virginia. "You have to be more careful. You have to—" Her voice broke. She shook her head and fled, her footsteps quick on the stone floor.

Virginia turned back to the grate, but Apollonia was already backing away, murmuring something about needing to return home. The wet nurse's face had gone carefully blank, the expression of someone who understood that survival meant seeing nothing, hearing nothing, remembering nothing. They disappeared through the gate with Alma Francesca in Apollonia's arms, and Virginia was left alone with the iron bars and the sound of rain beginning again outside.

She stood there until the cold seeped through her habit, until her fingers went numb from gripping the metal. Candida was right. Virginia had been reckless, stupid, careless in ways that endangered not just herself but everyone who had helped her.

* * *

"PEOPLE ARE TALKING," Benedetta said that evening as they sat in their chamber. Rain lashed the windows, and candles flickered in the draft. She kept her voice neutral, but her hawkish features were tight with worry. "About you and the child."

Virginia's needle stilled on the little shift she was hemming. "People always talk."

"Not like this." Benedetta set down her own sewing with deliberate care. "After what Candida heard today... Virginia, the whole convent knows. And if the convent knows, then—"

"Then they know." Virginia pulled her thread through the fabric with more force than necessary. "What would you have me do about it?"

"I would have you stop." Benedetta leaned forward, her voice dropping to barely above a whisper. "Stop seeing the child. Stop sewing for her. Stop giving people more ammunition to use against you."

Virginia looked up at Benedetta. "I can't."

"You have to."

"I. Can't." Each word came out separately, hard as stones. "She's my daughter."

"She's Gian Paolo's acknowledged child. Legally. On paper. You're nobody to her except a nun who takes too much interest in a neighbor's baby." Benedetta's voice turned urgent. "That's what you need to be. That's the only way this ends without destroying you."

Virginia looked down at the shift in her lap, at the careful stitches she had worked in candlelight. "And if I can't be nobody to her?"

Benedetta had no answer to that. She picked up her sewing again, and they sat in silence while rain drummed against stone and the candles burned lower.

* * *

GIAN PAOLO'S OPENESS with Alma Francesca grew worse. He walked through Monza's market square with the child in his arms, her dark hair catching sunlight, her laugh carrying across the stalls. He showed her off to visitors who came to his house, spoke of her constantly with pride that bordered on recklessness.

Each report arrived from servants and sisters, another nail in the coffin of discretion. The more openly he displayed the child, the more certainly people drew their conclusions. Gian Paolo Osio had a daughter. The mother was supposedly some Isabella Montini, whereabouts unknown. But everyone had eyes. Everyone had seen the nun at Santa Margherita sewing infant clothes and weeping over a baby that belonged to her neighbor.

The facts were simple enough for a child to work out.

Anger rose in Virginia some days, sudden and hot. She would be in the garden pulling weeds or in the chapel kneeling on cold stone, and fury would sweep through her. Rage at Gian Paolo for his carelessness, at herself for her stupidity, at God for making a world where women paid for sins that men walked away from.

But the anger never lasted. It would burn bright for a moment, then collapse back into the weariness that had become her constant companion.

* * *

ARRIGONE'S CONTINUED SCANDALS had made everything infinitely worse. The seminarians at San Bernardino had refused to keep him as their confessor, and the rejection rippled through Monza's churches and market squares. Every story about the disgraced priest seemed to circle back to Virginia, connecting his name to hers with increasing frequency.

Virginia was crossing the market square one morning in June, accompanied by Sister Ottavia as they returned from delivering alms, when she heard two women talking near the baker's stall. Their voices carried in the warm air.

"—bleeding him dry, they say. Goes to Osio's house three times a week now."

"Not for friendship anymore, that's certain."

"What else? He knows about the nun and he's making Osio pay to keep him quiet."

Virginia's steps faltered. Ottavia's hand found her elbow, steadying her, but blood drained from Virginia's face.

The women noticed them and fell silent, their eyes widening as they recognized the nun standing close enough to have heard every word. One of them had the grace to flush. The other simply stared, bold and curious.

Virginia forced her legs to move, to carry her past the stall and the staring women and the whispers that followed in her wake. Ottavia stayed close, her grip firm on Virginia's arm, but she said nothing until they were safely back inside the convent walls.

"You shouldn't go into town anymore," Ottavia said quietly as they stood in the cloister. "It's not safe."

"Not safe from what? Words?"

"Words can kill just as surely as knives. You know that."

Virginia did know. She leaned against the cool stone wall and closed her eyes. Around her, the convent hummed with its usual rhythms—sisters walking to prayer, the distant clang of the kitchen, birds singing in the garden. Normal sounds. Safe sounds. But the walls felt thinner now, as if the gossip seeping through might dissolve them entirely.

Whether the blackmail rumors were true or invented hardly mattered. The damage was in the telling, in the way each repetition connected Arrigone's scandals more firmly to Virginia's name, until the two were inseparable in the town's collective imagination.

* * *

THE ENTIRE TOWN was aroused and buzzing with talk. Not whispers anymore but open discussions in the market square, in the churches, in the houses of noble families who suddenly wanted to know what really went on behind Santa Margherita's walls.

The convent itself had become a hive of tension. Sisters who had once pretended not to notice Virginia's strange behavior now watched her openly, their eyes following her movements. The younger nuns looked frightened, their faces pale when Virginia entered a room. The older ones looked grim, mouths pressed into hard lines. And Prioress Bianca looked like a woman trying to hold back a flood with her bare hands while the water rose higher every day.

It pressed in from every side. The gossip. The rumors. The knowing looks and the careful silences. The way Gian Paolo continued to walk through town with Alma Francesca as if scandal meant nothing. The way Arrigone lurked at the edges of everything, a constant reminder that some secrets could not stay buried.

The trap was tightening. The walls closing in. And Virginia carried the approaching disaster in her bones the way animals sense storms before the first clouds appear, a pressure building, a charge in the air, the certainty that something was about to break and when it did there would be no going back.

The only question was who would break first, and how much damage they would do on the way down.

* * *

THE IDEA CAME to Virginia on a morning when sunlight slanted through the chapel windows during Chapter meeting. Prioress Bianca sat conducting the week's business, her voice steady as she reviewed accounts and assigned duties. But her term would end in July. The elections were only weeks away.

Virginia watched from her place among the senior nuns and let the thought take shape. Why not her? Why shouldn't she be Prioress?

The position would solve everything. As Prioress, she would have real authority, not the nominal power of Vicaress, which depended entirely on the Prioress's goodwill, but actual control over who came to the parlatory and when, over which sisters spoke to whom, over what information reached the Cardinal's office in Milan. She could silence the gossip or at least contain it. She could refuse Arrigone access to the convent entirely. She could present herself to Cardinal Borromeo as a reformed and pious leader.

The more she considered it, the more inevitable it seemed. She was Sister Virginia Maria de Leyva, daughter of the Count of Monza, feudal lady of this town. Her rank alone made her the natural choice. Add to that her years of service as Vicaress, her administrative experience, her connections to Milan's most powerful families—who else could possibly compete?

After the meeting ended and the sisters filed out, Virginia remained in her seat. Benedetta and Ottavia lingered near the doorway, waiting.

"Well?" Benedetta said quietly once they were alone. "You're thinking about it."

It was not a question. Benedetta's sharp eyes missed nothing.

"Yes," Virginia said. "I'm thinking about it."

Ottavia's face brightened. "You should do it. You'd make a wonderful Prioress."

"Prioress Bianca has been perfectly competent," Virginia said, though the words tasted diplomatic rather than true. "But she lacks vision. And she's too cautious with the Cardinal's office. Always trying to appease, never pushing back."

"Exactly." Benedetta moved closer, her voice dropping. "You wouldn't let people walk over this convent the way she does. You'd protect us."

"I'll need support," Virginia said. "Not just from you two. From the other sisters."

"You'll have it," Ottavia said with confidence. "Everyone respects you. You're the feudal lady. Who would dare oppose you?"

Virginia allowed herself a small smile. "Then we begin."

* * *

THE CAMPAIGN BEGAN quietly. Virginia spoke to sisters individually after Mass, in the garden, during recreation hours. She never asked directly for their votes. That would have been too crude, but she let it be known that she was considering standing for election.

The younger nuns seemed enthusiastic. Sister Silvia promised her support immediately, as did several others from the middle ranks. They saw Virginia as a patron, someone whose noble connections could benefit them and whose authority might shield them from harsher aspects of convent discipline.

"You would bring honor to Santa Margherita," Sister Candida said one afternoon as they walked together in the cloister. The young nun's voice carried genuine admiration. "The great families would respect a Prioress of your lineage."

"I hope only to serve," Virginia replied with calculated modesty. But inside, satisfaction bloomed warm and steady.

The lay sisters were harder to read. They nodded and murmured respectfully when Virginia spoke to them, but their faces remained carefully neutral. Virginia attributed this to their lower station and did not press them further. Peasant girls like Caterina da Meda could hardly be expected to understand the politics of convent leadership.

Over the following days, Virginia refined her approach. She made strategic visits to the infirmary to sit with elderly sisters, listening to their concerns with apparent sympathy. She reviewed the convent accounts and spoke knowledgeably about fiscal management during recreation periods when other sisters could overhear. She positioned herself as both spiritually grounded and administratively capable—the complete package for leadership.

Prioress Bianca herself seemed genuinely pleased when Virginia mentioned her intention.

"I think you'd do very well," she said one afternoon as they walked together in the cloister. The June air was warm and heavy with the scent of roses. "You have the intelligence and the experience. And your connections to the great families would certainly benefit Santa Margherita."

Virginia studied her face for signs of insincerity but found none. "I'm glad you think so. I was concerned you might feel I was presuming."

"Not at all." Bianca paused beside the fountain, trailing her fingers through the cool water. "The convent needs strong leadership. These past years have been difficult. The tensions with the Cardinal's office, the questions about discipline.

A new Prioress with your authority might be exactly what's needed to restore order."

The words should have reassured Virginia. Instead, something in Bianca's tone, a careful neutrality, perhaps, or a hint of something left unsaid, made her uneasy. But the feeling passed quickly, and Virginia chose to take the words at face value.

"I hope to serve the community well, if the sisters choose to honor me with their confidence."

Bianca smiled, but the expression didn't quite reach her eyes. "I'm certain they will consider your candidacy with all the seriousness it deserves."

* * *

WHILE VIRGINIA COUNTED her supporters, another campaign moved through the convent's shadows.

Sister Crocifissa, one of the oldest and most respected nuns, had been watching Virginia for years with growing disapproval. She had said nothing publicly, one did not cross a de Leyva lightly, but privately she had spoken to other senior sisters about the scandal, about Gian Paolo's visits, about the child everyone knew belonged to Virginia despite the fiction of Isabella da Meda.

"She thinks we're fools," Sister Crocifissa said one evening to a small group gathered in Sister Agnese's chamber. They kept their voices low, aware that even walls had ears in a convent where Virginia held the keys. "She parades her sin before us and expects we'll make her Prioress anyway because of her name."

Sister Agnese, whose family had been prominent in Monza for three generations, nodded grimly. "My brother says the whole town is talking. They're saying Santa Margherita has become a brothel."

"And whose fault is that?" Sister Crocifissa's hands clenched in her lap, the only visible sign of her agitation. "She's Vicaress. She's supposed to uphold the rule, not break it nightly in her own chamber."

"But what can we do?" Sister Paola asked. She was younger than the others, less certain. "Her family—"

"Her family is in Spain," Sister Crocifissa interrupted. "Her father hasn't set foot in Italy in years. Her brothers don't care what happens here. The de Leyva name carries weight, yes, but it's not invincible."

"We could oppose her openly," Sister Agnese suggested, though her voice lacked conviction.

"And have her retaliate? Look what happened to Father Arrigone when he crossed her." Sister Crocifissa shook her head. "No. We work quietly. We speak to the sisters we trust. We make sure enough of them vote against her that she loses."

"Will there be enough?" Sister Paola's doubt hung in the air.

"There will be if we're careful," Sister Crocifissa said. "Many of the older sisters feel as we do. They're simply afraid to say so. We need to show them they're not alone."

Sister Agnese leaned forward. "And we need to remind them what's at stake. If Virginia becomes Prioress, the scandal will only grow. The Cardinal will have no choice but to intervene. Santa Margherita could be placed under censure. We could all suffer for her sins."

The threat was real enough to make even Sister Paola straighten her shoulders with resolve.

The conspiracy spread through the convent in whispers, traveling from chamber to chamber in the hours after Compline when the younger nuns slept and the older ones lay awake with their grievances. Sister Crocifissa proved a skilled organizer, identifying sympathetic sisters and speaking to each with arguments tailored to their particular concerns.

To the devout, she emphasized Virginia's violations of sacred vows. To the pragmatic, she stressed the danger of scandal bringing Church censure. To those who had suffered under Virginia's authority as Vicaress, she offered the possibility of a different leadership style. Someone who valued consensus over command.

Within two weeks, Crocifissa had assembled a coalition of perhaps fifteen sisters committed to voting against Virginia. It wasn't enough to guarantee defeat, not yet, but it was a foundation to build upon.

* * *

VIRGINIA, MEANWHILE, GREW more confident with each passing day. She counted votes in her head as she moved through the convent—Sister Silvia, Sister Candida, most of the younger nuns who looked to her for patronage. The middle-ranking sisters who benefited from her administrative efficiency. Even allowing for some opposition from the older, more conservative nuns, she would have more than enough support to win.

She kept careful mental tallies, categorizing sisters by their level of commitment. Certain supporters. Probable supporters. Neutral. Unlikely. She needed twenty-four votes out of forty-six to secure the majority. By her count, she had at least thirty.

Gian Paolo encouraged her ambitions during his nightly visits. He slipped through the garden door as he always did and found Virginia waiting in her chamber.

"Prioress," he said, testing the word as he settled beside her on the narrow bed. "It suits you."

"It's not certain yet." But Virginia smiled despite herself.

"It will be. You're a de Leyva. These provincial nuns won't dare vote against you once they understand you're serious." He traced a finger along her jaw. "And once you're Prioress, you'll have real power. You can shut Arrigone out completely. Tell the Cardinal whatever story you want."

"That's what I'm thinking." Virginia leaned into his touch. "As Vicaress, I'm always subject to Prioress Bianca's authority. But as Prioress..."

"As Prioress, you answer to no one but the Cardinal, and he's in Milan, too busy with his reforms to pay much attention to one prosperous convent in Monza." Gian Paolo's smile turned wicked. "We could have years more of this. Decades, even."

The thought sent heat through Virginia's chest. Power and safety and control, all wrapped together. The ability to protect herself and Alma Francesca and the fragile web of secrets that held their lives together.

"July twenty-ninth," she said. "That's when Monsignor Barca comes from Milan for the election."

"Less than two months." Gian Paolo kissed her temple. "You'll win. I'm certain of it."

Certainty settled into Virginia's bones, solid and sure. She would win. She had to. Because if she lost, if the sisters rejected her despite her name and her rank and everything she had done for this convent, then she would be left with nothing. No authority, no protection, only the weight of her sins and the gossip that grew louder every day.

But she would not lose. She was Sister Virginia Maria de Leyva, and she had never lost anything she truly fought for.

* * *

JUNE PASSED INTO July. The summer heat pressed down on Monza, turning the convent into a maze of stifling corridors and airless chambers. Tempers grew short. Small disputes flared between sisters who normally kept their disagreements private.

Virginia attributed the tension to the approaching election and the heat. She did not notice how the convent had divided itself into factions, how certain sisters no longer spoke to each other at recreation, how groups formed and reformed in the refectory based on allegiances she did not recognize.

She was too focused on her own campaign, on securing the final votes she needed, on planning what she would do once she held the Prioress's authority. She imagined herself in the Prioress's chambers, the spacious rooms with their view of the garden, the writing desk where she would compose letters to Milan with her own seal.

In her mind, she was already drafting the letter she would send to Cardinal Borromeo. A humble expression of gratitude for the sisters' confidence. A commitment to maintaining the convent's reputation and spiritual discipline. Careful words that would position her as a safe, conventional choice, nothing to alarm the Archbishop's office.

She practiced walking with the measured dignity befitting a Prioress. She modulated her voice during Chapter meetings, speaking with authority but without aggression. She was building the persona she would inhabit for the next three years, or six, or however long the sisters continued to elect her.

Sister Ottavia noticed the transformation. "You carry yourself differently now," she observed one evening. "Like you've already won."

"I'm simply preparing," Virginia replied. But she knew Ottavia was right. In her own mind, the election was a formality. The outcome was inevitable.

Only Benedetta seemed troubled. "You're very confident," she said one afternoon, her tone carefully neutral. "Perhaps too confident."

"I've counted the votes," Virginia said. "I have the support I need."

"Have you?" Benedetta's sharp eyes studied her face. "Or have you counted only the sisters who will tell you to your face that they support you?"

The question lodged like a splinter beneath Virginia's confidence. "What do you mean?"

"I mean that not everyone who smiles at you in the corridors will vote for you in secret ballot. I mean that resentment runs deeper than politeness reveals. I mean that you should prepare yourself for the possibility that you've miscalculated."

Virginia's jaw tightened. "You think I'm going to lose."

"I think you've made assumptions about how others see you. About whether your authority as Vicaress has earned you loyalty or merely compliance." Benedetta paused. "There's a difference."

But Virginia pushed the warning aside. Benedetta was always cautious, always pessimistic. She saw danger everywhere. Virginia trusted her own assessment—the enthusiastic promises from younger sisters, the respectful deference from those who benefited from her patronage, the general acknowledgment that she was the most qualified candidate.

She would win. She had to win.

Prioress Bianca watched it all with troubled eyes but said nothing. She was Prioress for only a few weeks more. Whatever came next would be someone else's problem to solve.

* * *

THE ELECTION WAS set for July twenty-ninth, the feast of Santa Marta. Monsignor Barca would arrive from Milan to oversee the voting, as Church law required. Forty-six nuns would cast their ballots, and whoever received the majority would become the new Prioress of Santa Margherita.

Virginia went to bed each night counting those votes in her head. Twenty-four would be enough. She was certain she had at least thirty. She rehearsed her acceptance speech—humble, gracious, emphasizing service and community. She planned her first acts as Prioress: reviewing the accounts, meeting with the convent's legal advisors, sending that carefully crafted letter to Cardinal Borromeo.

In her imagination, everything was perfect. Orderly. Under control.

She was so focused on the election that she barely noticed the lay sister called Caterina da Meda, who had been causing minor disturbances throughout the convent for weeks. The girl was insolent and lazy, prone to gossip and complaints. But she was only a peasant's daughter, a conversa who cleaned the floors and hauled water, beneath Virginia's notice.

Caterina had come to Santa Margherita as a servant, one of those girls from poor families who were taken in by convents to perform menial labor in exchange for food and shelter. She had grown into a difficult young woman, sullen, resentful of authority, constantly testing boundaries. Several sisters had suggested dismissing her, but Virginia had kept her on out of a vague sense of charitable obligation.

It never occurred to Virginia that this insignificant lay sister, this girl she had kept at the convent out of pity when everyone else wanted her dismissed, would be the one to destroy everything.

Virginia counted her votes and planned her victory while the ground shifted beneath her feet. She felt secure in her position, confident in her calculations, certain that her name and her authority would carry her to triumph.

She did not see the resentment festering among the older sisters. Did not recognize that her confidence looked like arrogance to those who had been watching her sins for years. Did not understand that every display of certainty made the opposition more determined to deny her what she seemed to consider her birthright.

In less than a month, the world she had so carefully constructed would collapse, and the fall would be so complete that nothing, not her name, not her rank, not even the desperate measures she would take to save herself, could stop it.

The machinery of her destruction was already in motion. She simply didn't know it yet.

On the evening of July twenty-eighth, Virginia knelt in the chapel during Compline and offered a prayer for guidance. The words came easily, automatically, shaped by years of practice. But underneath the rote recitation, a whisper of unease finally penetrated her certainty.

What if Benedetta was right? What if she had miscalculated?

Virginia pushed the thought away and rose when the office ended. Tomorrow would prove her fears groundless. Tomorrow she would become Prioress, and all her careful planning would bear fruit.

She walked back to her chamber through darkened corridors, her footsteps echoing off stone walls. Somewhere in the distance, a door closed with a soft thud. The night settled over Santa Margherita like a held breath, waiting for morning to release it.

Virginia lay in her narrow bed and stared at the ceiling, too keyed up to sleep. In less than twelve hours, Monsignor Barca would arrive. The sisters would cast their votes. Her future, and the future of everyone whose secrets she protected, would be decided.

She closed her eyes and waited for dawn, still certain of victory, still blind to the trap closing around her.

* * *

July

CATERINA DA MEDA had been at Santa Margherita for three years, and in all that time she had mastered every aspect of her work except discretion. She was a lay sister, the daughter of a peasant from Meda who had sent her to the convent when she was fifteen. She had no vocation, no piety, and no particular interest in learning the quiet discipline that convent life required.

She did the heavy work, scrubbing floors, hauling water, washing linens, and she waited on Virginia personally, bringing her meals and tending her chamber. In exchange, she received food, shelter, and the dubious privilege of living among women who considered her beneath them.

What she also did, constantly and with a peasant's blunt disregard for consequence, was talk.

"I saw him again last night," the girl said one morning in early July as she emptied Virginia's chamber pot. She did not bother to lower her voice, even though the door stood half-open. "Coming through the garden gate after Compline. He thinks he's so clever, skulking about in the dark."

Virginia, who was braiding her hair before the small mirror, went very still. "You'll keep your observations to yourself."

"Why? Everyone already knows." The lay sister straightened, wiping her hands on her stained apron. She was plain-faced and broad-shouldered, with the sturdy build that came from generations of fieldwork. "The whole convent knows. The whole town knows. You and your nobleman, carrying on like that."

"Enough." Virginia's voice sliced the words clean. She turned from the mirror and fixed the girl with a look that had made smarter women fall silent. "You will not speak of such things. Do you understand?"

Caterina met her gaze with the particular insolence of someone who had nothing left to lose. "Or what? You'll dismiss me? Send me back to Meda where everyone will know I couldn't even manage to stay at a convent?" She laughed, a harsh sound. "At least at home I won't have to watch nuns sneaking about at night pretending to be holy."

The urge to strike her rose so fast and fierce that Virginia's hand actually moved before she stopped it. She forced her fingers to uncurl. "Get out."

"Gladly." The girl hefted the slop bucket and crossed to the door. She paused on the threshold and looked back. "You should know the other sisters have been asking questions. About who stays up all night. About why your chamber door is always bolted after Compline." Her smile twisted. "I tell them I don't know anything. But I don't think they believe me."

Then she was gone, leaving Virginia alone with her fury and the sick certainty that the lay sister had become a problem that would not solve itself.

* * *

THE COMPLAINTS MULTIPLIED as July wore on. Sister Silvia came to Virginia three days later with a pinched expression and careful words.

"The lay sister assigned to your service has been indiscreet."

They were standing in the cloister after Mass, the morning sun already hot. Virginia kept her face neutral. "In what way?"

"She speaks disrespectfully of you. And of Signor Osio." Sister Silvia's discomfort was visible in the way she would not quite meet Virginia's eyes. "She told Sister Paola that you and he meet at night. That other sisters help you. That the whole affair is common knowledge among the servants."

Virginia's stomach tightened, but she kept her voice steady. "The girl is foolish and given to wild stories. You know how servants gossip."

"Yes." Sister Silvia's tone suggested she did not believe this was mere gossip. "But her stories are specific. She claims to have seen things. To have hidden in your chamber and watched." She stopped, her face flushing. "I won't repeat what she said. It's too shameful."

"Because it's a lie." Virginia forced certainty into the words even as her mind raced. Had the servant truly hidden in the chamber? Had she seen Gian Paolo come through the door?

"She's bitter and spiteful. She resents her position here and invents scandals to make herself interesting."

Sister Silvia nodded, though the doubt remained in her eyes. "Perhaps. But others have heard her too. Sister Agnese. Sister Crocifissa. They're concerned."

"I'll speak to her," Virginia said. "She'll stop this gossip or she'll be dismissed."

But even as she said it, she understood the impossible position she was in. Dismiss the girl now, and she would leave the convent with a head full of secrets and no reason to keep them. Keep her, and she would continue spreading poison through Santa Margherita.

There was no good choice. Only ways to limit the bleeding.

* * *

VIRGINIA HAD KEPT the lay sister at Santa Margherita against everyone's advice. Prioress Bianca had wanted to dismiss her a year ago, after she had been caught stealing food from the kitchen and lying about it. The other sisters had united in their disapproval. The peasant girl was lazy, impertinent, disrespectful. She had no place in a respectable convent.

But Virginia had intervened. She had pleaded the case with careful compassion, saying the girl was young and foolish but could be reformed with patience. That sending her back to Meda in disgrace would ruin whatever small chance she had at a decent life. That Christian charity demanded they give her another opportunity.

The Prioress had agreed reluctantly, and the servant had stayed.

Now, watching her move through the convent with her sullen face and her dangerous mouth, Virginia wondered what madness had possessed her to show such mercy.

Compassion, she had called it. But perhaps it had been something else, some unconscious need to prove she was still capable of goodness, still able to perform acts of kindness despite the sins that stained her soul.

Whatever the reason, it had been a mistake.

* * *

THE INCIDENT WITH Sister Degnamerita happened on July twenty-fourth, five days before the election.

Virginia discovered it when she went to visit her friend in the afternoon. Sister Degnamerita Rivolta was one of her closest allies, a sharp-minded woman from a good family who had supported Virginia's candidacy from the beginning.

When Virginia entered the chamber, she found her friend standing beside the bed, face gone white with fury.

"Look," Sister Degnamerita said, pointing to the bedding. "Look what that little demon has done."

Virginia looked. The smell hit her first, sharp and foul, unmistakable. Someone had defecated on Sister Degnamerita's bed, smearing it across the blanket and into the straw mattress beneath.

"The lay sister," Virginia said. Not a question.

"Who else?" Sister Degnamerita's hands shook. "I reprimanded her yesterday for being lazy with the washing. She stood there with that insolent look on her face and said nothing, but I saw it in her eyes. She was planning this even then."

Virginia stared at the ruined bedding and felt rage rise up her throat, hot and bitter. This was not just spite. This was deliberate provocation, calculated to humiliate Sister Degnamerita in the most degrading way possible.

And the timing, five days before the election, could not be coincidence.

"She's trying to damage you," Sister Degnamerita said. "The election. Your campaign. She knows what this will do."

"Yes." Virginia's voice came out flat and cold. "She knows."

"Then you'll dismiss her now? Before she does worse?"

Virginia shook her head slowly. "If I dismiss her now, she'll go straight to the taverns and tell every drunk in Monza her complaints against everyone in this convent. By tomorrow the whole town will know details of her embellishments or lies." She turned to face her friend. "No. We can't let her leave. Not yet. Not until after the election."

"Then what?"

"We punish her. We lock her away where she can't spread more poison. And we make sure she understands that if she speaks one more word against us, the consequences will be far worse than confinement."

Sister Degnamerita's eyes widened slightly. "You're going to frighten her into silence."

"I'm going to do whatever is necessary to protect this convent." Virginia touched her friend's arm. "Go to Prioress Bianca. Tell her what the girl has done. Tell her about the disrespectful words, the gossip, everything. I'll speak to the confessor. Together we'll make sure she's dealt with properly."

* * *

THE PROCESS MOVED quickly once Virginia set it in motion.

She went to the convent's confessor and laid out the offenses with careful detail. The foul act against Sister Degnamerita. The constant gossip and disrespect. The loose words she had spoken about Virginia and other sisters.

The priest listened with a grave face. He was an old man, cautious and conservative, but he understood the politics of convent life.

"This girl has become a source of scandal," he said when Virginia finished. "She must be disciplined."

"I agree." Virginia kept her hands folded, her expression composed. "Prioress Bianca should impose a severe penance. Confinement, perhaps. Away from the other sisters where she can cause no more harm."

"Where would you hold her?" the priest asked slowly.

"There is the room off the poultry yard," Virginia said. "Where the linens are washed. It's small and isolated. Near the outside road, but with a strong door that can be bolted."

"Perfect," he responded.

Virginia allowed herself a small nod. "Let her spend some time there in prayer and reflection. Perhaps it will teach her the value of silence."

The priest agreed. He went to Prioress Bianca and ordered her, in his authority as confessor, to impose the penance.

The Prioress complied without argument. She had wanted the servant gone for months.

* * *

THAT EVENING, AS the sun began its descent and shadows lengthened across the courtyard, Prioress Bianca and several other nuns went to fetch the girl from the kitchen where she had been scrubbing pots.

"Come with us," Bianca said. "You are to be confined as punishment for your behavior."

The lay sister's face went from sullen to frightened in an instant. "Confined? Where?"

"The washing room by the poultry yard. You'll stay there until you learn proper respect and humility."

"No." She backed away, her hands still dripping with greasy water. "You can't lock me up. I haven't done anything wrong."

"You defiled a sister's bed," Sister Agnese said sharply. She was one of the nuns who had come to help, and her disapproval was written plainly on her severe features. "You've gossiped and spread lies. You've shown nothing but disrespect since you arrived here."

"I told the truth!" The servant's voice rose, shrill and panicked. "That's my crime, isn't it? I told the truth about what goes on in this place, about Sister Virginia and her lover, about—"

Prioress Bianca moved forward and gripped her arm with surprising strength. "You will be silent. Now come."

The girl struggled, but she was outnumbered. Sister Agnese took her other arm, and together they half-dragged, half-marched her through the cloister toward the back of the convent.

Other sisters joined them along the way, Sister Paola, Sister Silvia, even young Sister Candida, drawn by the commotion.

Virginia watched from the shadows of the arcade, her face hidden in the gathering dusk. She did not join the procession. Better to stay removed, to let Prioress Bianca handle the discipline.

But she followed at a distance, keeping to the edges, making sure everything went as planned.

They reached the washing room, a small stone chamber with one narrow window set high in the wall. The floor was damp from the trough where linens were scrubbed, and the air smelled of lye and mildew.

"Inside," Prioress Bianca said, pulling the servant toward the threshold.

"Please." The struggle had turned to pleading now, her voice breaking. "Don't lock me in there. I'm sorry. I'll be good. I'll stop talking. Please."

"You should have thought of that before." Bianca pushed her through the doorway and stepped back. "Monsignor Barca arrives in five days for the election. When he comes, he will hear of your behavior, and he will decide your punishment. Until then, you'll remain here and reflect on your sins."

"Monsignor Barca?" The servant's eyes went wide with fresh terror. "You're going to tell him? He'll...he'll have me beaten."

"He'll do what is just." Prioress Bianca pulled the door closed. The bolt slid home with a heavy thunk that echoed in the courtyard.

Inside the washing room, the girl began to scream. She pounded on the door, her fists making dull thuds against the thick wood, her voice rising in incoherent pleas and curses.

The nuns who had helped confine her stood in a half-circle, their faces uncertain. This was harsher than most of them had expected.

But Prioress Bianca's expression remained firm. "She'll quiet down soon enough," the Prioress said. "Leave her. She needs time to consider her actions."

The group dispersed slowly, heading back toward the main convent building as the last light faded from the sky.

Virginia waited until they were gone, then approached the washing room door. Inside, the screams had subsided to ragged sobs.

She stood outside that door and listened to the weeping, and felt nothing. No pity, no remorse, no guilt. Only grim satisfaction that one threat had been neutralized, at least for now.

In five days, Monsignor Barca would arrive. In five days, the election would take place, and Virginia would become Prioress.

Behind the locked door, the peasant girl wept and cursed and beat her fists bloody against wood that would not yield.

And in the gathering darkness, Virginia turned away and walked back to the convent, already planning her victory.

* * *

THE FIRST SISTER to bring food was Sister Paola, who arrived at the washing room door the morning after the confinement with bread and watered wine balanced on a wooden tray.

She knocked softly. "Caterina? I've brought your breakfast."

The silence that answered stretched long enough that Sister Paola wondered if the girl had somehow escaped. Then footsteps shuffled across the stone floor inside, and the voice came through the thick wood, hoarse from screaming.

"I don't want it."

Sister Paola crouched and set the tray on the ground, sliding it carefully under the narrow gap at the bottom of the door. "You have to eat something."

"The Prioress can rot in hell." The voice had changed overnight, Sister Paola realized with growing unease. Gone was the pleading desperation of yesterday, replaced by something harder and more dangerous. "Along with Sister Virginia and all her whores."

Sister Paola's hand flew to her mouth. "You mustn't say such things. If you show proper humility and repent your disrespect, perhaps they'll release you before Monsignor Barca arrives."

"Release me?" The laugh bordered on madness, bitter and uncontrolled. "They'll never release me. Not while I know what I know."

A pause, and Sister Paola heard movement, the servant coming closer to the door, pressing herself against it.

When she spoke again, her voice had turned sly and calculating. "But Monsignor Barca will let me out. When I tell him what goes on in this holy convent of ours."

Sister Paola straightened, her legs suddenly unsteady. "What do you mean?"

"You know exactly what I mean." Confidence had crept into the tone now. "Sister Virginia and her nobleman, sneaking about after Compline. The baby that's supposed to belong to some imaginary woman in Milan. I've seen things the rest of you only whisper about."

"You're lying."

But Sister Paola's voice wavered, because some part of her knew the accusations were true.

"Am I?" The laugh came again, sharper this time. "Then why am I locked in here like a criminal? Why are they so desperate to keep me quiet until after the election?"

Movement inside the chamber, footsteps approaching the door. "I've hidden in the chest in Sister Virginia's chamber. I've watched them together, her and Gian Paolo Osio. I know everything."

Sister Paola backed away from the door as if the words themselves might contaminate her. The breakfast tray sat untouched where she had pushed it through the gap.

She turned and hurried back toward the main convent building, her heart pounding, her mind racing with the implications of what she had just heard.

Behind the locked door, the servant smiled and returned to her pacing. She had all day to refine her accusations, to practice the words she would use when Monsignor Barca finally arrived.

* * *

WORD OF THE threats spread through the convent with the speed of plague. Virginia was in the garden when she heard about it, kneeling among the herb beds with dirt under her fingernails and sweat dampening the back of her habit.

Sister Silvia found her there, stepping carefully between the planted rows with her face tight with worry. She glanced around to make sure they were alone before speaking.

"Sister Virginia. You need to know what the lay sister is saying."

Virginia's hands stilled on the rosemary stem she had been cutting. She did not look up. "What is she saying?"

"Terrible things." Sister Silvia crouched beside her. "Sister Paola brought her breakfast this morning, and the girl told her she's going to report everything to Monsignor Barca when he arrives. About you and Signor Osio. About the child. She claims she hid in a chest in your chamber and saw..." Sister Silvia trailed off, her face flushing.

"What exactly did she tell Sister Paola?"

Virginia kept her voice steady through sheer force of will, though her fingers had tightened on the rosemary until the woody stem bit into her palm.

"That she'll tell Monsignor everything when he arrives in five days for the election. That she'll have you put in prison instead of her." Sister Silvia's hands twisted together. "She's not just gossiping anymore, Sister Virginia. She's making specific accusations. She's threatening to destroy you."

Virginia set down the herbs with careful deliberation. Her mind raced through calculations and contingencies, weighing options that grew darker and more desperate with each passing moment.

Monsignor Barca would arrive on the twenty-ninth for the election. If Caterina managed to speak to him, if she told him even half of what she claimed to know, there would be no election, no Prioress position, no carefully constructed future.

"We need to calm her," Virginia said, though the words felt hollow. "Someone she trusts. Someone who can make her understand that threats will only make her situation worse."

Sister Silvia's expression suggested she understood how futile that hope was. "Who does she trust? The only person she's ever relied on is you, and you're the one she hates most."

"Someone will have to try," Virginia said, rising from the herb bed and brushing dirt from her knees. "We have five days until Monsignor arrives. Surely, we can find some way to reach her before then."

But even as she said it, Virginia knew they would not.

* * *

THAT AFTERNOON, SISTER Benedetta took food to the washing room without being asked, driven by the same fear that had been tightening in Virginia's chest.

Benedetta understood better than most what the accusations would mean, not just for Virginia but for all of them who had helped conceal the affair over the years. She had kept watch while Gian Paolo visited. She had hidden him when the manhunt grew too close. She had lied to Church officials and fellow sisters alike.

She knocked on the door with more force than Sister Paola had used. "Caterina. It's Sister Benedetta. I've brought you dinner."

"I don't want your food." The response came immediately.

"Then you'll starve, which would be foolish when you need your strength." Benedetta kept her voice hard and authoritative. "But hear me first before you refuse. These threats you're making are worse than foolish. They're dangerous. You think Monsignor Barca will reward you for taletelling? He'll see you as exactly what you are, a spiteful servant trying to bring down her betters out of malice."

A crash from inside the room made Benedetta step back, the breakfast tray being kicked against the door with enough force to send it clattering across the stone floor.

"My betters?" The voice had gone shrill with fury. "You mean the whores who break their vows every night while I scrub their floors and empty their piss pots? Those betters?"

"Mind your tongue before you say something that can't be unsaid."

"Why should I mind anything?" The shrillness intensified. "You've all treated me like dirt since the day I arrived. Made me do the filthiest work, looked down on me because my father was a peasant, never let me forget I was beneath you. Well, now I have something you want. My silence. And I'm not giving it to you. Not for any price."

Benedetta pressed her palm flat against the door. She could feel the rage vibrating through it like a living thing.

"If you accuse Sister Virginia of what you're threatening to accuse her of, you'll destroy yourself along with her. Do you understand that? The Church doesn't reward informers. They punish everyone involved in scandal, guilty and innocent alike."

"Then we'll all burn together." The laugh bordered on madness now, wild and uncontrolled. "At least I'll have the satisfaction of watching Sister Virginia fall first. At least I'll see her dragged away in chains the way I've been locked in this hole."

Benedetta stood outside that door for a long moment after the girl stopped speaking, listening to the pacing footsteps that suggested she had lost whatever thin grasp on prudence she might once have possessed.

When she found Virginia in her chamber, she did not need to speak. Virginia saw the answer written plainly in Benedetta's grim expression.

"She won't listen," Benedetta said, closing the door behind her and leaning against it. "She's beyond listening now. All she wants is revenge, and she doesn't care what it costs her as long as you pay the price too."

Virginia sat at her table with her hands folded in front of her, the posture of prayer though no prayers moved through her mind. "Then we have a problem that ordinary solutions won't fix."

"Yes." Benedetta met her eyes across the small chamber. "We do."

The words hung between them, heavy with implications neither woman was ready to voice aloud.

Not yet.

But soon.

* * *

The 27th day of July

THE NIGHT AIR hung thick and heavy over the convent courtyard. Virginia stood in the kitchen doorway waiting for the soft knock that would signal Gian Paolo's arrival. Her hands twisted together so tightly that her fingers had gone numb. Behind her, Ottavia paced between the long wooden tables, each footstep creating a rhythm that matched Virginia's own racing pulse.

Benedetta remained perfectly still near the window, her sharp profile outlined against the darkness beyond. She had not spoken for the past hour.

The knock finally came, three soft taps. Virginia's hands shook as she lifted the iron latch and pulled the door open just wide enough for Gian Paolo to slip through. He entered with rain still glistening on his dark hair and cloak. His eyes found hers immediately.

"Where are the others?" His voice was low, barely above a whisper.

"Sister Candida is keeping watch near the main gate." Benedetta stepped forward. "Sister Silvia is in the chapel, ready to ring the bell if anyone approaches."

Gian Paolo nodded. His hand rested casually on the knife he always wore at his belt.

"Tell me everything Caterina said."

Benedetta stepped into the circle of candlelight. "Two days ago, she told Sister Paola that when Monsignor Barca arrives for the election, she will demand an audience with him. She intends to tell him everything, about you and Virginia, about the nights you spend in the convent, about the child, about how she hid in a chest in Virginia's chamber and watched you together."

Virginia's throat closed as the specific accusations were spoken aloud.

"There's more." Ottavia's voice came from the shadows, trembling. "She told Sister Paola that she would see Virginia imprisoned, that she would make sure all of us who helped conceal the affair were punished. She said she didn't care what happened to herself as long as Virginia suffered."

For a long moment, no one spoke. When Gian Paolo finally spoke, his voice carried a certainty that made Virginia's blood run thick with dread. "Then she has to die."

Ottavia gasped, her hand flying to her mouth. Benedetta went very still.

Virginia found she could not breathe.

"There's no other solution." Gian Paolo moved closer to the table, leaning forward so the candlelight illuminated his face fully. Virginia saw no madness there, no wild rage, only calm pragmatism. "If Monsignor Barca hears what Caterina knows, we're all ruined. Virginia will be locked away. The rest of you will face the Inquisition. And I'll be excommunicated at minimum, probably imprisoned."

"We could send her away," Ottavia said desperately. "Tonight. Give her money, help her reach Milan or Venice."

"And have her spend the rest of her life telling everyone she meets about the scandalous nun of Monza?" Gian Paolo shook his head. "Within a month, the story would reach the Cardinal's ears. Within two months, investigators would arrive with orders to examine every sister under oath."

Benedetta spoke finally. "He's right. Caterina has moved beyond the point where normal solutions will work. All she wants now is revenge against Virginia, and she's willing to destroy herself to achieve it."

"Then we frighten her into silence." Virginia forced the words past the constriction in her throat. "We threaten her family, everything she cares about."

"She doesn't care about anything except hurting you." Gian Paolo's tone allowed no room for argument. "I've dealt with people like Caterina before, peasants who develop a grievance and nurture it until it consumes all reason. You can't negotiate with that kind of rage. You can only eliminate it."

The word hung in the air between them.

"I can't." Ottavia's voice broke. "I can't be part of killing someone. It's a mortal sin."

"We're already damned." Benedetta's laugh was bitter. "Or have you forgotten the vows we've all broken? The lies we've told? The sacraments we've profaned?"

"That's different from murder."

"Is it?" Benedetta turned to face Ottavia fully. "We've been accomplices to adultery, to sacrilege, to the corruption of holy vows for years. What makes you think God will forgive those sins but draw the line at this one?"

Ottavia had no answer.

"If we do this..." Virginia's voice sounded strange to her own ears, distant and hollow. "How would we accomplish it without being discovered?"

Gian Paolo straightened, satisfaction flickering across his features. "The room where she's confined is isolated, accessible from the garden. The door can be broken from the outside to suggest forced entry. We move the body somewhere it won't be found immediately."

"Where would we put the body?" Benedetta's question was clinical.

"The chicken house. No one searches it regularly. We can hide her there temporarily, then move her later when attention has shifted."

"What about witnesses?" Virginia forced herself to think practically. "Caterina will scream. She'll fight."

"There's a storm coming." Gian Paolo gestured toward the window where lightning had begun to flicker. "Thunder will cover any sounds. And we'll include everyone who has reason to fear Caterina's testimony—Sister Candida, Sister Silvia, anyone who helped conceal your affair. That way, no one can betray us without condemning themselves."

The calculated cruelty of it took Virginia's breath away.

"I need an answer." Gian Paolo's gaze moved from Virginia to Benedetta to Ottavia. "We do this tonight, all of us together, or we wait for Monsignor Barca and prepare ourselves for the consequences. There's no middle path. Choose."

Virginia looked at Ottavia, who sat with her face in her hands. She looked at Benedetta, whose expression revealed nothing except grim acceptance. She thought about the election in two days, about the position of Prioress that would give her real power.

And she thought about Caterina, locked in that small room, believing dangerous knowledge made her powerful, not understanding it had made her a target.

"We do it." The words emerged from Virginia's mouth quiet and final. "We do it tonight. All of us together."

Ottavia's sob cut through the kitchen, but Benedetta merely nodded once, and Gian Paolo smiled.

* * *

THE STORM ARRIVED as darkness settled fully over Monza, thunder rolling across the valley and shaking the old convent walls. Virginia stood in the corridor listening to rain hammer against stone while she tried to quiet the wild beating of her heart.

Benedetta emerged from the shadows. "Caterina's been calling for company. She told Sister Paola she's frightened of storms, that she doesn't want to be alone."

"Will you go to her?"

"I already offered. She accepted." Benedetta's expression remained carefully neutral. "I'll stay with her for two or three hours, keep her calm. When it's time, I'll signal you."

Virginia nodded. The plan was simple. Benedetta would keep Caterina occupied and unalarmed while Gian Paolo entered through the garden. They would gather the others, and then they would go to that small room where Caterina waited.

"Virginia." Benedetta's hand found her arm, fingers pressing hard. "Once we start this, there's no going back. If you have doubts, voice them now. Not later."

Virginia met her friend's dark eyes. "I have no doubts," Virginia lied, and Benedetta released her arm and turned away, disappearing down the corridor.

Virginia watched her go and tried to remember a prayer, any prayer, that might give her courage for what was coming. But her mind remained blank, empty of everything except terrible certainty.

* * *

BENEDETTA FOUND CATERINA sitting on the straw pallet in the small washing room, arms wrapped around her knees and face pale with fear. The girl looked younger than her eighteen years in the dim light—vulnerable, almost innocent.

"You came." Caterina's voice trembled with relief. "I thought everyone had forgotten me."

"The storm is bad." Benedetta settled herself on the floor near the door. "Sister Virginia was concerned you might be frightened. She asked me to sit with you until it passes."

Something flickered in Caterina's eyes, suspicion, perhaps, but fear of the storm won out. The girl nodded and pulled her knees tighter as thunder shook the walls.

"It sounds like the world is ending," Caterina whispered.

"Just summer weather. It will pass." Benedetta kept her voice calm and soothing. "Are you hungry? Thirsty?"

"No. I just don't want to be alone."

They sat together while the storm raged, not speaking. Gradually Caterina's fear eased. Around the second hour, she began to talk. Complaints about the other sisters, but then inevitably her grievances turned to Virginia.

"She thinks she's better than everyone," Caterina said, her voice hardening. "Noble blood and fine education, as though that makes her less of a whore for what she's done."

Benedetta made no response, simply let the girl talk.

"In two days when Monsignor arrives for the election, I'm going to tell him everything." Caterina's voice grew stronger. "About how she sneaks that man into the convent, about the baby, about how all of you help her and lie for her."

"You should rest," Benedetta said quietly. "Save your voice for when he arrives."

"I'll rest when she's locked away where she belongs." Caterina lay back on the straw. "I'll rest when I've seen her face when they drag her out in chains."

Benedetta watched the girl's eyes close and listened to her breathing slow. When she was certain Caterina had drifted into sleep, she rose silently and moved to the window to signal Virginia that everything was ready.

* * *

VIRGINIA MOVED THROUGH the darkened convent with Ottavia, Silvia, and Candida flanking her. They collected Gian Paolo who had climbed over the garden wall, then crossed to the workroom. The night was humid and oppressive despite the rain.

The workroom door creaked as Virginia pushed it open. She held the lamp high while Gian Paolo moved among the spinning wheels and looms, testing implements until finally he settled on the base of the wool-winder, a heavy wooden piece.

"This will do," he said, lifting it to test its heft.

They made their way to Caterina's laundry room, moving in single file. The window stood waist-high in the wall. Virginia opened the door silently, then entered first. Ottavia, then Candida, Sister Silvia, and finally Gian Paolo followed her in with his terrible burden.

The room was dark and stifling. Against the far wall, a figure stirred in sleep before bolting upright.

"Who's there?" Caterina's voice was thick with sleep but sharpening with alarm. "Virginia? What are you doing here?"

Light flared as Virginia raised the lamp. The sudden brightness illuminated Caterina's face; confusion giving way to recognition, then to terror.

"Please," Virginia heard herself say. "Caterina, please. If you swear before God that you'll keep silent about what you've seen, if you promise never to speak of it to Monsignor Barca, we can end this now."

“Swear?” Caterina scrambled backward until the wall stopped her. “Why would I swear anything to you? You’re all going to burn in hell.”

“So arrogant,” Virginia said, and something cold and final clicked into place inside her chest. “Even now, even at the end, you can’t stop running your mouth.”

Caterina’s face twisted with fury. “The end? You think you can silence me? When Monsignor Barca finds me missing, he’ll tear this convent apart. You’ll all hang.”

“He’ll find you dead of natural causes,” Virginia said flatly. “A tragedy. A young woman’s weak heart giving out. These things happen.”

The words drained the color from Caterina’s face, and for the first time real understanding dawned in her eyes.

“Virginia,” she whispered, using the Christian name in a last desperate attempt. “Please. I’m sorry. I won’t say anything. I swear before the Madonna herself, please.”

“Your Madonna can’t help you now.” Gian Paolo moved with brutal efficiency, and Caterina tried to dodge but the space was too small. She opened her mouth to scream.

Benedetta’s hand clamped over it, muffling the sound.

The base of the wool-winder came down.

The crack of wood against bone was sickeningly loud. Blood sprayed across the whitewashed wall in an arc that caught the lamp’s light and glistened. More blood ran down Caterina’s neck, soaking into her servant’s dress and pooling on the floor.

Gian Paolo struck again. And again. Each blow accompanied by sounds Virginia’s mind tried desperately to block—the wet crack of breaking bone, Caterina’s muffled screams fading to whimpers and then to nothing. Blood spattered onto Virginia’s habit, hot and sticky.

After the third blow, Caterina’s struggles weakened to mere twitches. After the fourth, she stopped moving entirely except for one final shudder before absolute stillness claimed her.

The silence that followed was profound and terrible. Virginia could hear her own heartbeat thundering, could hear Candida's ragged breathing, could hear the soft drip of blood falling from the wool-winder to the floor.

"Is she dead?" Candida's voice broke.

"Dead," Benedetta said, having moved to check. Her fingers pressed to Caterina's throat where no pulse beat. "She's dead."

Ottavia wept and Silvia stood stunned while Virginia stared at the body slumped against the wall. She waited to feel something, horror, remorse, the crushing weight of mortal sin, but instead she felt only a vast emptiness.

The girl's eyes were still half-open, glazed and unseeing. Blood matted her hair and ran in dark rivulets down her temples.

She was someone's daughter, Virginia thought with strange detachment. Someone held her as an infant and hoped for her future.

"Good," Virginia heard herself say. "Now we make it look like thieves broke in from outside."

Gian Paolo moved to the connecting door and raised the bloody wool-winder, bringing it down against the wood near the latch. The door splintered. He pushed through into the adjoining drying room and crossed to the fireplace, using his sword to chip at the chimney stones until he had created a hole large enough for a man to crawl through.

"The garden wall next," he said. "I'll breach it from outside to make it look like they came that way."

While he worked creating the false trail, the women stood guard around Caterina's body. Virginia held the lamp, and in its flickering light she studied the dead girl's face, noting how the blood had already begun to darken and thicken, how the skin was losing its warmth.

"It's done," Gian Paolo announced, returning from the garden with scratches on his hands. "The wall's breached convincingly. Any investigator will assume thieves forced their way in from the street."

"The body," Benedetta said, ever practical.

"The chicken house for now," Ottavia whispered. "I have the key. We could hide her there until morning."

"Yes," Virginia agreed. "Help me."

They pulled Caterina's body through the door, the dead weight heavier than expected. Blood left a smeared trail on the threshold that would need to be cleaned before dawn.

Outside, the rain fell harder. They carried Caterina between them through the darkness, Virginia and Ottavia supporting the shoulders, Silvia her head, while Benedetta and Candida took the feet. Gian Paolo kept watch.

The chicken house stood at the far edge of the convent grounds. Ottavia fumbled with the key in trembling hands. Inside, they propped Caterina's body upright in the corner among the nesting boxes. When she slumped sideways, Benedetta braced her against the wall with boards and old planks. They surrounded the body with firewood and other detritus.

"Good enough," Gian Paolo said, surveying their work. "When they find her, they'll see exactly what we want them to see."

Virginia stared at the body propped in its corner. The girl looked smaller in death, diminished somehow. Blood had soaked through her shift and dripped onto the straw beneath her.

"I'm going to Milan immediately," Gian Paolo said. "I'll return tomorrow night. If anyone asks, I've been there for days on business that can be verified."

He kissed Virginia's forehead with unexpected gentleness despite the blood still staining his hands, and then he slipped through the hole in the garden wall and disappeared into the rainy darkness.

* * *

BACK IN THE laundry room, Ottavia scrubbed blood from the wool-winder while Virginia held the lamp and watched water in the bucket turn pink, then red, then a dark muddy brown.

"It won't come clean," Ottavia whispered through tears. "The wood's soaked it up too deep. Everyone will see, we'll be discovered."

"Put it back with the others," Virginia said, her voice hollow. "Put it back in the workroom. No one will look closely at equipment that's used every day."

Silvia took the wool-winder and returned it to its place among the other tools while the rest washed away the blood from the floor and the door's threshold. They then dispersed through the convent by different routes, each woman returning to her chamber alone.

Virginia climbed the stairs to her cell with legs that felt disconnected from her body. Once inside she stripped off her bloodstained habit and burned it in the small brazier, watching fabric blacken and curl and release smoke that smelled of wool and copper and something else.

She washed herself with cold water from the basin, scrubbing at her skin until it hurt, but no amount of water could wash away the stain she carried now. The water turned pink with diluted blood.

When she finally climbed into bed, the sky beyond her window was beginning to lighten with the first gray promise of dawn. In a few hours the bells would ring for Lauds. Someone would discover Caterina missing.

Virginia lay in the darkness and waited for guilt to come crashing down, for God's judgment to fall, for some sign that what she had done mattered.

Nothing came except silence and the sound of rain and the slow steady beat of her own heart proving she was still alive while Caterina lay dead in the chicken house.

I killed her, Virginia thought, testing the words. *I helped arrange it. I watched her die. I am a murderer.*

But the words felt abstract, disconnected. It was easier to think of Caterina as a problem that had been solved rather than a person who had been ended.

Sleep came eventually, and with it dreams. Not of Caterina's death but of the election, of accepting the Prioress's ring while blood dripped from her fingers onto the Chapter house floor, of kneeling before Monsignor Barca while Caterina's ghost stood behind him and smiled.

* * *

The 29th of July

BY FIRST LIGHT on the morning of the election, every nun in Santa Margherita knew that Caterina had vanished.

Virginia woke to the sound of voices drifting through her window, sharp with alarm. She lay motionless in her narrow bed, hands still aching from the work of the previous night.

A quick knock came at the door. Before Virginia could respond, it swung open and Ottavia and Benedetta appeared, their faces bearing the same sleepless pallor as Virginia's own. "Someone has discovered the room. The entire convent knows," Benedetta said quietly.

A moment later, Silvia slipped inside, her jaw tight. Candida followed, closing the door with deliberate care. "I watched from the corridor," Silvia announced, voice hushed. "They know Caterina's gone. Some are blaming men. Some are saying she forced open the door by herself."

"I overheard Reverend Mother Bianca telling Imbersaga about the bolt and the rope. They're organizing a search," Candida added.

Virginia crossed to the window. In the courtyard below, clusters of nuns gathered like dark birds, their habits rustling as they turned toward the washing room where Caterina had been confined. Monsignor Barca would arrive in six hours to oversee the election. Six hours to maintain the story that would either save them or condemn them all.

"We should be there before Imbersaga calls for us," Benedetta said. "If we're absent when the search begins, we appear more suspect."

"If anyone looks pale, let them think it's because they believe Caterina really escaped and will denounce us outside," Candida said. "We must look desperate, not guilty."

Ottavia's hands twisted nervously. "What if someone saw us last night? On the stairs?"

"No one saw," Silvia interjected with unexpected steadiness. "I watched the main hall. The others were in their cells."

Virginia nodded, drawing from grim reserves of composure. "The story is what we agreed. She broke the door and used something to break through the chimney's mortar. We need only maintain calm and answer truthfully about everything except what happened after dark."

Together, they descended through corridors that smelled of tallow smoke and yesterday's incense.

* * *

THE MORNING SUN hit the courtyard with brutal clarity. Imbersaga stood before the damaged washing room with Reverend Mother Bianca, examining the broken door and scattered stones. Virginia and her allies joined the outer ring, each silent, their glances quick but loaded, a mutual understanding binding them.

"Sister Virginia, approach," Bianca's voice carried across the courtyard.

Virginia crossed the space with measured steps, acutely aware of every watching eye. Benedetta, Ottavia, Silvia, and Candida followed close behind.

"Reverend Mother." Virginia inclined her head.

"Caterina has disappeared." Bianca gestured toward the broken door that led to the drying room and crumbled chimney, where morning light slanted through. "She broke through the confinement with considerable force. The damage is extensive."

"How could she have managed this?" Virginia kept her tone even as her pulse hammered. "The wall is stone."

"Old mortar, weakened by decades of damp." Sister Imbersaga crouched, brushing at crumbled stone. "Desperation gives people strength they don't normally possess."

"Or perhaps she had assistance." Sister Crocifissa's voice came sharp from behind. "Men possess greater strength than desperate girls, after all."

The implication hung between them, ugly and undeniable. Several nuns murmured agreement.

Bianca straightened. "Sister Crocifissa, do you have accusations to make?"

"I make no accusations, Reverend Mother. I merely observe that Caterina made specific threats before confinement, threats about certain nuns and gentlemen. If she managed to contact those gentlemen—"

"She was locked in a room," Virginia interrupted, cold and precise. "How do you imagine she contacted anyone?"

Sister Crocifissa's smile was thin. "Perhaps you might enlighten us, given your apparent familiarity with what transpires after the convent retires for the night."

A hush fell.

"Innuendo serves no purpose," Benedetta cut in. "Caterina was confined for her disrespect, her gossip, her threats. If she's gone, it's because she feared the punishment coming when Monsignor Barca questioned her."

"Speaking of whom," Imbersaga added, "Monsignor Barca arrives this afternoon. Let's prepare for him, not give in to rumors."

Bianca raised a hand. Silence ruled. She turned to Ottavia: "You hold the key to the chicken house."

"Yes, Reverend Mother," Ottavia managed.

"I want it searched. Immediately."

The assembled nuns processed toward the chicken house. Ottavia's hand shook so hard the key threatened to drop. Silvia brushed a hand against her back, steadying her.

Imbersaga stepped through the open door, disappearing into the chicken house's shadow. For a heartbeat, no one breathed.

"There's nothing here," Imbersaga called, finally emerging. "The girl has fled, just as it appears."

"*Deo gratias*," Ottavia whispered, voice nearly soundless.

But Sister Crocifissa edged forward again. "Reverend Mother, please, we should move the wood."

"There is no time now." Bianca's voice cracked like a whip. "Monsignor Barca will be here soon. We cannot spend the morning searching in vain. The girl is gone."

She turned to address them all: "Caterina was troubled, disrespectful. We'll notify the authorities after the election. But know this. Her disappearance comes at a dangerous time. When Monsignor Barca arrives, I will inform him not only of this, but of irregularities that demand investigation."

Virginia's heart stilled.

"The Monsignor will be encouraged to question those sisters Caterina named," Imbersaga continued, her gaze resting heavily on Virginia and her allies. "And I'll recommend postponing the election until proper inquiry."

Whispers spread. Promised votes felt like water slipping from Virginia's grasp.

* * *

IN VIRGINIA'S CHAMBER, Benedetta locked the door. The room had filled quickly—Ottavia, Silvia, Candida. They arranged themselves with practiced precision.

"We need to hold firm," Silvia said, voice stripped of all innocence. "If anyone shows nerves, the others will turn on us first."

Candida nodded. "Sister Imbersaga means to split the house. Some sisters might break. We keep our story. If they question us separately, we repeat it until we believe it."

"We have six hours," Benedetta said. "Six hours to convince enough nuns to stand with us, to undermine Bianca and Imbersaga."

"If we don't?" Ottavia began.

Virginia stopped her with a look. "We all know what happens if we don't. We must campaign harder, appear more devoted, more certain of Caterina's guilt and our innocence than anyone."

"Sister Candida, Silvia, you both have influence among those who are wavering," Benedetta instructed. "Quiet the nervous ones. Promise them reassurance, stability, protection."

Silvia squared her shoulders. "We keep the others close and get through this day."

Candida's nod was somber. "We hold together."

Virginia moved to the window. Below, nuns still huddled in anxious clusters. "We do not lose our nerve. We do not contradict each other. We have six hours. We do this together, or not at all."

* * *

VIRGINIA MOVED THROUGH the convent with practiced grace, visiting cell after cell, speaking in low voices with sisters who had promised support, but whose eyes now flickered with uncertainty. She found Sister Degnamerita in the scriptorium and reminded her of past favors, of confidences kept. Sister Degnamerita nodded, but her agreement rang hollow.

In the refectory during the midday meal, Benedetta worked her own territory, cataloging every hesitation, every averted gaze. The knowledge she gathered was grim. Support was collapsing faster than they could firm it up.

Ottavia found Virginia in the corridor near the Chapter house. "Sister Agnes approached me after prayers," she whispered. "She asked if I had seen anything strange the night Caterina disappeared. She said she heard footsteps in the main hall past midnight."

Virginia's stomach clenched. "What did you tell her?"

"That I was in my cell, asleep. That she must have been dreaming." Ottavia's hands twisted. "But she looked at me as though she didn't believe it."

"Then we pray she says nothing to Monsignor Barca." Virginia placed a hand on Ottavia's arm. "Go find Silvia and Candida. Make sure they're prepared for questions. If anyone asks about that night, we were all in our cells. No one saw anything."

By the time the bells rang for None, Virginia had spoken with twenty-three nuns directly. She reminded them that postponing the election would invite months of investigation. She promised stability, discretion, and the continuation of comfortable arrangements.

But even as she spoke, the ground was shifting. Sisters who had been enthusiastic supporters now offered only cautious nods. Promises evaporated under the weight of scandal. The political architecture she had constructed over months was crumbling.

In the garden, she found Silvia and Candida together near the herb beds. They looked up as Virginia approached, exhaustion and fear written in lines too deep for their young faces.

"How many?" Virginia asked quietly.

"Perhaps fifteen who will hold," Silvia said. "But even they're frightened."

Candida's gentle features were drawn tight. "Sister Crocifissa has been speaking to the older nuns. She's telling them that supporting you means complicity in whatever scandal Caterina threatened to reveal. She's making it clear that anyone who votes for you will be remembered when the investigations begin."

Virginia absorbed this with dull recognition. "Then we've lost."

"Not if the election happens," Benedetta said, appearing from the arcade. "As long as the vote proceeds, there's still a chance. But if Bianca convinces Monsignor Barca to postpone—"

"Then it's over," Virginia finished. "And we have nowhere left to hide."

When the gate bell rang announcing the arrival of Monsignor Barca's carriage, something inside Virginia went very still and very cold.

* * *

THE FEAST OF Santa Marta proceeded with all the ceremony such an occasion demanded. The church was massed with flowers in honor of Monsignor Carlo Barca, canon of Sant'Ambrogio in Milan, vicar of all the diocese's nuns, and a doctor of theology. His reputation preceded him, an experienced and profound observer who had penetrated the innermost recesses of cloistered life and could read his subjects' thoughts from their faces. Therefore, he was greatly feared.

His carriage drew up before the convent entrance, and all the nuns assembled in the courtyard. Virginia stood among them, her spine straight and her hands folded. Reverend Mother Imbersaga and Sister Bianca positioned themselves at the front.

Monsignor Barca descended with the dignity of his station, his bearing that of a man accustomed to authority. His face was lean and intelligent, his eyes sharp as they swept across the assembled nuns. Virginia held his gaze when it passed over her, knowing that to flinch would invite suspicion.

The ceremonies went off with the usual ritual. First in the church, with the adoration of the Most Holy and the benediction. Then they processed to the Chapter house, where Reverend Mother Imbersaga intoned the ancient hymns.

Yet neither the prayers nor the chanting could clear the atmosphere. Caterina's flight had left a general sense of anxiety that oppressed all hearts. Virginia could see it in how the other nuns held themselves, in the tension that radiated through the Chapter house.

There were forty-six voting nuns, and none were absent.

The ballot box sat on the table before Monsignor Barca's seat. One by one the sisters approached to cast their votes, each movement scrutinized by the monsignor's penetrating gaze. Sister Degnamerita approached with obvious reluctance, her hands trembling. Sister Crocifissa walked with triumph barely concealed. The younger nuns looked frightened, uncertain.

Virginia cast her own vote with steady hands, though her heart pounded. She had campaigned for months for this moment. She had murdered for it. And now she was watching her support evaporate before her eyes.

Benedetta voted with her characteristic composure. Ottavia's hands shook so badly she nearly dropped her ballot. Silvia and Candida approached together, slipping their votes through the slot in silent solidarity.

Then the counting began.

Monsignor Barca opened each ballot with deliberate precision, announcing the name written there. Sister Angela. Sister Angela. Sister Angela. The repetition built with devastating momentum. Virginia's name appeared occasionally—once, twice, three times scattered among dozens of votes for her opponent.

When the final ballot had been read, the numbers were brutal.

Sister Angela had been elected Prioress by a clear majority of thirty-four votes.

Virginia had received eleven.

The shock hit like a fist to the stomach. Months of work, undone in a single morning. Years of building influence, destroyed by one servant's threats and one night's desperate violence.

She had not even been retained as Vicaress. In her place, the nuns had chosen Sister Imbersaga, her enemy.

Virginia kept her expression composed, revealing nothing of the devastation that roared through her mind. But inside, something was breaking apart.

Beside her, Benedetta sat rigid as stone. Ottavia's face had gone white, and Silvia's hands gripped her rosary so tightly the wooden beads creaked. Only Candida maintained perfect composure, though the rigidity of her spine suggested shock.

The sudden news of Caterina's flight, with the comments it had aroused, had dealt the deathblow to Virginia's hopes. Taken by surprise and with no time to repair the damage, Virginia's supporters had found themselves isolated. Those who had wavered made up their minds in favor of safety and distance from scandal.

And so, the puritans returned to power in the Convent of Santa Margherita.

Monsignor Barca proceeded directly to his sermon, a long succession of strict injunctions, each point of monastic discipline ending with the formula: "The nun who does this sins, and sins mortally."

Virginia heard the words as if from a great distance, her mind already racing ahead to the implications. Without the protection of becoming Prioress, she was vulnerable to investigation, to questioning, to scrutiny that would inevitably uncover what must never be revealed. Each hour the body remained in the chicken house increased the danger of discovery.

When the ceremony was over, the newly elected Reverend Mother Angela and Sister Imbersaga approached Monsignor Barca. They informed him of Caterina's flight, and Virginia watched with sinking dread as they made additional disclosures, their voices too low to hear but their gestures unmistakable. They were telling him about her. About the suspicions.

Monsignor Barca listened with the focused attention of a confessor. Then he asked a question, his voice carrying across the Chapter house.

"What does one look out on from Sister Virginia's window?"

Reverend Mother Angela answered with precision. "She was in the Vicaress' cell. It looks out onto the house of a neighbor, a good youth, but too gay for our dear sisters. The proximity has been a source of concern. But now that she is no longer Vicaress, she will be moved."

"Ensure her new cell is sealed off at once." Monsignor Barca's command was immediate and absolute. "The Devil can enter even through a crack. For charity's sake, let us not leave the doors open to him."

The pronouncement landed on Virginia's chest with crushing weight. Her one remaining connection to the world beyond these walls, her one source of contact with Gian Paolo, ordered closed.

"Sister Virginia." Monsignor Barca's voice cut through her paralysis. "A word, if you please."

She rose on legs that threatened to buckle and approached where he stood with Reverend Mother Angela and Sister Imbersaga.

"You are to be moved to another chamber," he said. "One that does not overlook the property of young men whose presence might prove distracting to a woman vowed to contemplation of divine rather than earthly matters."

"Yes, Monsignor."

"I am also ordering the dean of Monza Cathedral to undertake a discreet inquiry into certain rumors that have been circulating in the town." His gaze held hers with uncomfortable intensity. "I trust you will make yourself available to answer whatever questions he may have about the governance of this convent and the incidents that have occurred here recently."

It was not a request. It was a warning. He suspected. Perhaps he did not know the full truth, but he suspected enough to warrant investigation.

"I am always at the service of the Church, Monsignor," Virginia said, the words tasting of ash.

He dismissed her with a gesture, and she retreated from the Chapter house. In the corridor outside, Benedetta waited with Ottavia, Silvia, and Candida. Their faces told her they had heard everything.

"We're finished," Ottavia whispered, her voice breaking.

“Not yet.” Virginia forced steel into her spine. “An inquiry is not a trial. Suspicion is not proof. As long as the body stays hidden, as long as we maintain our story, there is still a chance.”

But even as she spoke the words, their hollowness echoed back at her. The day that had begun with desperate hope had ended in devastating defeat. The power she had pursued so relentlessly had been stripped away, and in its place, she had gained only enemies empowered to investigate, to question, to search until they uncovered the truth.

Virginia and her allies, reeling from their defeat, spent that long afternoon anticipating the ordeal that loomed ahead. For there was still one matter left unfinished. One task that could not wait any longer.

Caterina’s body had to be moved, and tonight was their last chance to do it before the investigation began in earnest.

The sun set slowly over Santa Margherita, painting the walls in shades of blood and shadow. And as darkness gathered, Virginia began to plan the second crime that would be necessary to conceal the first.

* * *

NIGHT FELL OVER Santa Margherita with agonizing slowness, the summer twilight stretching long past Compline until true obscurity finally settled over the convent walls. Virginia lay rigid in her narrow bed, listening to the sounds of the community settling into sleep.

They had lost the election. Angela now ruled as Prioress, and Sister Imbersaga, Virginia’s enemy, held power as Vicaress. The new regime would be watching, suspicious, eager for evidence. Moving through the convent tonight would be far more dangerous than it had been two nights ago when they had hidden Caterina’s body.

But the body could not wait. The July heat was already working its corruption beneath the stacked firewood. Another day, perhaps two, and the smell would become undeniable. The dean of Monza Cathedral had been ordered to investigate. Discovery was not a possibility but an inevitability unless they acted tonight.

Virginia rose from her bed when the convent bells tolled midnight. She dressed in the blackness with hands that trembled. They had all agreed on the plan that afternoon in whispered consultation. Gian Paolo would come, they would move the body, and somehow they would survive this night.

Virginia encountered Benedetta and Ottavia at the garden door. Every corner seemed to hold a watching face. Every creak sounded like footsteps approaching.

They reached the garden door and waited. Then came the soft scratch at the wood—three quick taps, a pause, then two more. The signal.

Virginia lifted the heavy bar and opened the door. Gian Paolo slipped inside, his clothing black against the deeper gloom. His face was grim, all traces of his usual arrogance stripped away.

"To the chicken house," he said, his voice barely above a whisper.

"But first we need Silvia and Candida." Virginia closed and barred the door behind him. "We'll need everyone to carry the body through the convent."

"Through the convent?" Gian Paolo's voice sharpened. "Why not over the garden wall? It would be faster, safer."

"Sister Angela has posted watchers." Virginia's throat was dry. "I saw them this evening from the upper windows. Two nuns stationed where they can observe the garden. They're watching for exactly what we planned to do."

Gian Paolo swore softly. "Then we carry it out the main door? Past the parlatory? That's madness."

"It's our only option." Virginia turned toward the stairs just as Silvia and Candida appeared, both pale but steady. Candida carried a large cloth sack, the one she used to store her viola and music books, now emptied for a more terrible purpose.

"This is big enough," Candida whispered, holding it out. "I've removed everything. There's nothing to identify it as mine if anyone finds it later."

Gian Paolo's eyes moved over the group. "Six of us to carry one body?"

"Four to carry, one to scout ahead, one to follow and watch behind," Benedetta said. "We can't afford to be surprised."

They moved as a unit toward the chicken house, Silvia leading the way. The chickens stirred as they entered. The stench hit Virginia first, not just present now but aggressive, sweet and putrid. Her stomach heaved. She pressed her sleeve to her nose and mouth, fighting the nausea that rose hot in her throat.

Gian Paolo and Benedetta began removing the firewood. The logs came away with soft scraping sounds. Virginia and Ottavia helped, working quickly, piling the wood to the side until the corner where they had stood Caterina's body was finally revealed.

The corpse had stiffened in the July heat, the rigor making it difficult to maneuver into Candida's sack. Gian Paolo lifted the shoulders while Benedetta took the feet, both grimacing at the dead weight. Virginia held the sack open, turning her face away as they worked the body inside. The smell intensified, thick and cloying. Behind her, Ottavia retched into her sleeve.

Finally, the body was contained, the sack tied shut. Gian Paolo lifted one end, testing the weight. "It's heavy. You'll need to work in shifts."

"No time for that," Benedetta said. "We carry it straight through without stopping. Four of us on the sack, one ahead, one behind."

They arranged themselves. Gian Paolo and Benedetta at the front taking most of the weight, Virginia and Ottavia at the back, Silvia scouting ahead, Candida following to watch behind. They lifted together, and Virginia's arms screamed immediate protest. The sack sagged between them, the weight shifting and unbalanced.

They moved through the convent with agonizing slowness. The burden was worse than Virginia had imagined, not just the physical weight but the constant awareness of what they carried. Her shoulders burned. Her fingers cramped around the fabric. Sweat soaked through her habit.

The first doorway loomed ahead. Silvia checked it, listened, then waved them forward. They had to turn the sack sideways to fit through the frame. Virginia's arms shook with the effort.

Down the corridor. Past the refectory. Virginia's breath came in gasps she tried to muffle. Ahead, Benedetta's arms trembled visibly. Gian Paolo bore his portion with grim determination, but even he was sweating.

A sound from above. Footsteps on the floor overhead.

They froze. Virginia's arms burned with holding the weight motionless, her whole body rigid with terror. The footsteps moved across the ceiling, slow and deliberate. Someone awake. Someone walking. The steps approached the stairwell.

Silvia pressed herself against the wall, gesturing frantically toward an alcove. They moved as one, shuffling sideways, trying to maneuver the unwieldy burden into the small space. Virginia's end knocked against a protruding stone. The sound seemed deafening.

The footsteps above paused.

Virginia stopped breathing. Beside her, Ottavia had gone pale as burial cloth. The weight in their hands threatened to slip. If they dropped it now, if the sound carried to whoever stood listening above.

The footsteps resumed. Moving away from the stairwell. Fading into distance.

They waited. Thirty heartbeats. Forty. Finally, Silvia gestured them forward again. They extracted themselves from the alcove and continued, every movement now laden with the awareness of how close they had come to discovery.

Through the Chapter house. Virginia's arms had gone from burning to numb, her hands locked into position around the canvas through sheer will. Her back screamed. Her shoulders felt as though they were pulling apart. But they could not stop.

The parlatory loomed ahead, and beyond it the heavy main door. Silvia waited there, her face white in the faint lamplight. "The way is clear," she whispered. "But hurry. I heard voices from the upper floor."

They reached the door and set the sack down while Gian Paolo worked the locks. Virginia's arms shook from the released weight. The locks turned with soft clicks. The door swung open on hinges that had been recently oiled.

Beyond the threshold lay the piazza, open and exposed under a sky full of stars. The church of San Maurizio stood silent across the square, and beyond it the narrow street that led to Gian Paolo's property.

"From here, just Benedetta and I," Gian Paolo said. "The rest of you stay inside. If we're caught, you can claim ignorance."

Benedetta was already removing her white wimple and black veil, replacing it with a dark shawl that Candida handed her. "Two people carrying a burden in the night look less suspicious than one struggling with something heavy."

She wrapped the shawl around her head and shoulders, transforming from nun to anonymous woman in an instant. The white parts of her habit were still visible, but the dark shawl concealed enough to provide some measure of disguise.

Gian Paolo lifted one end of the sack, Benedetta the other. They stepped through the doorway and into the open, their figures quickly swallowed by the blackness as they moved toward the piazza.

Virginia stood in the doorway with Ottavia, Silvia, and Candida, watching them disappear. The distance was perhaps one hundred paces to Gian Paolo's house, but every step took them further into danger. Any citizen returning home late might see them. The night watch made irregular rounds. A resident might look out a window.

But the piazza remained empty. Gian Paolo and Benedetta moved with steady purpose. They reached his home and disappeared as they went around to the back, out of Virginia's sight, the blackness absolute.

Minutes passed. Five. Ten. Virginia counted her own heartbeats. Beside her, Ottavia whispered prayers. Silvia kept watch on the upper windows. Candida stood rigid, her hands clasped so tightly her knuckles showed white.

More minutes. Fifteen. Twenty. Virginia's mind raced through possibilities, each more terrible than the last. What if someone had seen and raised an alarm?

Then, finally, a figure emerged from the gloom and entered the piazza. Alone. Moving quickly. Virginia's breath caught. Where was Gian Paolo? But then she recognized the determined stride, the dark shawl. Benedetta.

She walked alone, keeping close to the buildings. She reached the convent door and slipped inside, and Virginia closed it behind her with hands that shook with relief so intense her knees threatened to buckle.

"It's done," Benedetta said, unwrapping the shawl and revealing her white headdress beneath. "The body is buried in Gian Paolo's cellar. He had a place prepared, the earth already dug. We put the sack in the hole, and he covered it while I returned."

"Did anyone see you?" Silvia asked.

"No one. The streets were empty. God or the Devil was with us tonight." Benedetta's face was drawn with exhaustion, her habit marked with dirt and sweat. "But we can't do this again. The next body that needs burying will have to be our own, because we'll have run out of luck."

They made their way back through the convent to their cells, moving separately now, each nun returning by different routes to avoid suspicion. Virginia climbed the stairs with legs that felt boneless, her arms still aching from the weight they had carried. In her chamber, she found her bed exactly as she had left it. It seemed impossible that less than two hours had passed since she had risen.

She lay down without undressing and stared at the ceiling while her heart gradually slowed its frantic pounding. They had done it. Caterina's body was gone from the convent, buried where no search would find it unless someone thought to excavate Gian Paolo's entire property. The immediate danger had passed.

But the investigation would continue. Questions would be asked. The dean of Monza Cathedral would interview nuns, examine the evidence, probe for inconsistencies. And somewhere beyond her window, Gian Paolo was dealing with the reality of having a murdered woman buried in his cellar.

She had lost the election. Murdered a servant. Transported a corpse through a convent and out into the piazza. And somehow, despite all of this, she was still alive, still undiscovered, still clinging to the desperate hope that she might survive what she had become.

But as the first pale light of dawn began to touch her window, Virginia understood with cold certainty that survival was no longer the same as salvation. She had crossed too many lines, committed too many sins, destroyed too many lives in service of preserving her own.

And the worst part was that she would do it all again if that was what it took to avoid the consequences of what she had already done.

* * *

August

THE DAYS FOLLOWING the Feast of Santa Marta brought no relief from scrutiny, only a different quality of attention.

The nuns of Santa Margherita spoke of nothing but Caterina's disappearance. In the refectory, in the corridors, during work periods, every conversation circled back to the same questions. How had she managed to break through solid stone? Where had she gone? And most persistently, had Gian Paolo Osio helped her escape?

Virginia heard her lover's name spoken a hundred times in those first days, always with knowing looks, always with suggestions of impropriety.

The nuns remembered Caterina's rough manners, but they also remembered that she had been young and fresh-faced, with the kind of unrefined vitality that might appeal to a man of Gian Paolo's appetites.

Caterina had made no secret of wanting to leave the convent.

The conclusion was inevitable. Gian Paolo had seduced the servant, promised her freedom, and spirited her away to some distant city where they now lived as lovers beyond the reach of ecclesiastical authority.

Virginia listened to these speculations with her face composed into appropriate concern. Inside, her mind raced through implications. The theory was wrong, but it was also useful. As long as the nuns believed Caterina had fled willingly, they would not be searching the grounds for a corpse.

The church authorities pressed their investigation with bureaucratic thoroughness. Signor Capitaneo, the civil administrator, summoned Caterina's father from Meda. Ludovico della Cassina arrived three days after the feast, a man weathered by agricultural labor and confused by his summons.

Virginia stood with the other nuns in the courtyard while Reverend Mother Angela, the title still scraped against Virginia's pride every time she heard it, escorted Ludovico to the washing room to show him the evidence.

The man examined the hole in the wall with blunt practicality. He ran his fingers along the crumbling mortar, peered through to the alley beyond, and shook his head. "She always wanted more than her station allowed," he said, his voice carrying across the courtyard. "I told the sisters she would be trouble. But the convent needed servants, and I needed one less mouth to feed." He did not sound grief-stricken. He sounded as though he were discussing failed livestock.

Signor Capitaneo wrote to the vicar, requesting guidance on how to proceed with the search.

The vicar's response arrived within the week: they would find her soon enough. Runaway servants rarely stayed hidden for long. Caterina would surface eventually, either returned by necessity or discovered by authorities.

Virginia read the vicar's letter when Sister Imbersaga left it briefly unattended, her eyes scanning the formal Latin phrases that promised continued investigation while simultaneously suggesting that the matter was not urgent enough to warrant extraordinary measures.

For the first time since Caterina's death, Virginia allowed herself to breathe without the constant constriction of imminent discovery.

* * *

THE RELIEF DEEPENED when Gian Paolo slipped into the convent four days after they had buried the body. He came after midnight, using the garden door that Virginia had left unbarred. She met him in the same arcade where they had stood on the night of the murder, and this time Benedetta and Ottavia were already present.

"It's done," Gian Paolo said without preamble. His face was haggard, marked by sleepless nights. "After Benedetta left that night, I went back down to the cellar. I couldn't leave her whole. If anyone ever searched my property, if they ever found the grave..."

"Tell us what you did," Benedetta interrupted, her voice flat and practical. "Spare us your conscience and give us the facts."

Gian Paolo's jaw tightened. "I cut the body into pieces. It took hours. I wrapped each part separately and buried them in different locations around my property—some in the cellar, some in the garden, some beneath the floor of the stable. No single grave holds enough to identify as human remains."

Virginia's stomach turned, but she forced herself to remain still, to show nothing of the revulsion that rose in her throat.

"And the head?" Benedetta asked.

"I took it away from Monza entirely. There's a well about two miles outside the city walls, deep and long abandoned. I threw the head down there along with her headdress and the clothing we couldn't risk burning. No one will ever find it."

The precision of his account, the distribution of evidence across multiple locations, the disposal of the most identifiable remains far removed from the scene—Virginia recognized the experience and knowledge that had gone into these decisions.

"The search will continue," Ottavia whispered, her voice thin with barely suppressed panic. "They'll keep looking, they'll question people."

"They'll find nothing," Gian Paolo said. "I've been thorough. There's no blood left in the cellar, no tools that couldn't be explained by ordinary household work, no evidence that anyone died in my house. And even if they search the grounds, they'll find only scattered bones that could belong to animals slaughtered for food."

He looked directly at Virginia, his eyes holding hers with intensity. "We're safe. As long as we maintain the story, as long as no one breaks under questioning, we're safe."

They parted shortly after. But Virginia carried his words with her through the following days, repeating them whenever fear threatened to overwhelm her fragile calm. We're safe. We're safe. Yet even as she repeated those words, sleep became elusive. She lay awake at night staring at the ceiling of her new chamber, the one that faced away from Gian Paolo's house, the one that reminded her with every glance that her power had been stripped away.

The murder marked a turning point, a boundary crossed that could never be recrossed. In the convent, her prestige had been damaged by the scandal and by her crushing defeat in the election. Sister Angela ruled as Prioress with the support of the puritan faction, and Sister Imbersaga wielded power as Vicaress with barely concealed satisfaction at Virginia's reduced circumstances.

The younger nuns who had once sought Virginia's favor now looked elsewhere for patronage.

The older nuns who had whispered their support now kept their distance.

For the first time in eight years, Virginia was not the center of convent politics. She was not the woman whose approval was sought, whose displeasure was feared, whose influence could make or break a nun's position. She was simply another nun, middle-aged and disappointed, living out her vowed existence in an institution that no longer bent to accommodate her desires.

She had always bullied and threatened as though her liaison with Gian Paolo was her natural right, as though the rules that governed others did not apply to someone of her intelligence and breeding. She had moved through Santa Margherita with the confidence of someone whose power was unassailable.

Now, for the first time, vulnerability pressed down on her with crushing weight. She was no longer just an unhappy woman trapped in religious life. She was a criminal living in constant fear of discovery, dependent on the silence of accomplices who might crack under pressure, trapped in a web of lies that would unravel if any single thread was pulled too hard. And underneath that fear was an even deeper terror: that she might lose Gian Paolo, that the man who had loved her might decide the risk was too great.

The proud ruler she had been before Caterina's death seemed to belong to another woman entirely.

That Virginia had believed herself invincible.

This Virginia had learned otherwise through blood and terror and defeat.

* * *

THE SEARCH CONTINUED, but with decreasing intensity. Church officials made inquiries in surrounding towns, asking if anyone had seen a young woman matching Caterina's description. Civil authorities checked records of recent departures, investigated reports of unfamiliar faces in nearby cities, followed leads that inevitably dissolved into nothing. They found no trace of Caterina de Meda anywhere.

As weeks passed, the nuns began to accept what seemed the only reasonable explanation. Caterina had escaped through the hole in the wall, had met Gian Paolo Osio outside the convent grounds, and had fled with him to some distant location, perhaps Milan, perhaps Venice, perhaps even abroad.

The more imaginative nuns constructed elaborate narratives of Caterina's new life. Some pictured her installed as Gian Paolo's mistress in a house outside Monza. Others imagined her abandoned after a few weeks, inevitably falling into prostitution as women without protection always did.

Sister Crocifissa predicted darkly that the girl would come to a bad end, punished by God for her wickedness.

Virginia listened to these speculations with increasing detachment. The nuns were creating a story to fill the void left by Caterina's absence, weaving gossip and assumption into something that hardened through repetition. And the more they told this story, the more it became fixed in the collective memory of Santa Margherita.

Daily rhythms returned, the bells marking hours, the prayers recited by rote, the work assignments distributed according to the new Prioress's preferences. The convent resumed its ordinary patterns. But Virginia herself did not return to what she had been before.

* * *

BUT THE VULNERABILITY did not last. Slowly, as summer gave way to autumn and the investigation ground to its inconclusive end, Virginia's spirits revived. The fear receded to a manageable level, present always but no longer paralyzing. The humiliation of her political defeat stung less sharply as time created distance. And most importantly, Gian Paolo kept coming to her, kept risking everything for their stolen hours together, kept proving through his presence that her worst fear, abandonment, was unfounded.

She was not a woman capable of resignation. She was not someone who could accept defeat gracefully and retreat into pious obscurity. Whatever she had lost in the convent's political structure, whatever damage had been done to her reputation, whatever vulnerability she now carried, none of it was enough to make her renounce the passion that had defined her adult life. She would not give up Gian Paolo. She would not surrender to the puritans who had seized power. She would not transform herself into the kind of nun the church wanted her to be.

She had committed murder to protect her secrets. She had allowed Gian Paolo to dismember and bury a woman to conceal her crimes. She had lied to investigators, manipulated grieving family members, and used every tool of deception available to preserve her freedom to love as she chose. And she would do worse, if necessary, to keep what she had fought so hard to hold.

The autumn rains came to Monza, washing the summer dust from the convent walls and filling the garden with the rich smell of wet earth.

Virginia stood at her new window, the one that did not overlook Gian Paolo's property, the one that Monsignor Barca had ordered sealed to prevent further temptation and looked out at the transformed landscape. She had survived. Against all odds, against every reasonable expectation, she had survived. And survival was victory enough.

* * *

Autumn

THE BAKER'S WIFE told the butcher. The butcher told his apprentice. The apprentice told the washerwomen at the public fountain, and soon, the story had circulated through every shop and household within Monza's walls. Sister Caterina had vanished.

The official version, proclaimed from the convent's gates, maintained that the foolish young nun had fled through a hole in the garden wall. Probably seduced by some passing merchant. Probably halfway to Venice by now.

But Monza was a small town where people knew their neighbors' business better than their own prayers. Within days of Caterina's disappearance, a different truth took hold, one that made far more sense given what everyone already knew about the Convent of Santa Margherita and the man whose property shared its wall. Gian Paolo Osio had something to do with it. Of that, people were certain.

At taverns, men gathered over wine and spoke in voices low enough to avoid his bravos' ears. In the market square, women exchanged meaningful glances when his name was mentioned. In the cathedral after Mass, families clustered and whispered about the scandal.

The evidence was impossible to ignore. It lived in Gian Paolo's house, visible through windows when shutters stood open. A child. A little girl, more than two years old now, with dark hair and features that reminded some of the de Leyva nobility. Alma Francesca, they called her. Raised by Gian Paolo's mother as though she were legitimate family, though everyone knew no marriage had produced her. And if the child belonged to Gian Paolo Osio, then whose daughter was she?

Anyone who had watched the convent over the past years knew the answer. Virginia de Leyva had given birth in secret. The child now lived openly in Osio's household. And poor Sister Caterina, who must have discovered the truth or threatened to expose it, had conveniently disappeared. The logic was impeccable.

Within a fortnight, the entire town had woven the scattered threads into a complete tapestry.

* * *

RAINERIO the apothecary was grinding valerian root when the merchant arrived requesting tincture for sleeplessness.

While Rainerio measured and mixed, the man leaned across the counter. "They say the nun who disappeared knew about the baby," the merchant whispered. "They say she threatened to tell the Cardinal, and that's why she's gone."

Rainerio's pestle stilled in the mortar. "These are accusations that could get a man killed for repeating them."

"I'm only saying what everyone already knows. That child in Osio's house didn't appear from nowhere. And nuns don't vanish into thin air without help."

After the man left, Rainerio stood at his shop window and looked across the narrow street toward the convent's high walls. He had sold the convent, and specifically Virginia de Leyva, medicines, herbs for women's complaints, remedies for monthly discomforts. And in the months before the child appeared in Osio's house, he had filled requests that made him wonder what illness required such specific treatments.

He was not a fool. He understood what those herbs were meant to address. And now, with Caterina gone and speculation spreading through town, the pieces he had tried not to examine too closely formed a pattern he could no longer ignore.

His wife appeared in the doorway. "What troubles you?"

"Nothing that concerns us." The lie came easily after years of learning when to speak and when to guard his tongue.

But that night, as he lay beside his sleeping wife, Rainerio stared at the ceiling and calculated risk with the precision he usually reserved for measuring medicines.

His shop sat near Osio's villa and convent property, positioned perfectly to see and hear things others missed. He had provided herbs that now, in retrospect, told a story the authorities would pay handsomely to hear. He had children to consider. A daughter nearly old enough to marry, a son apprenticed to the silversmith, a business that fed his family. Speaking could destroy them all. Osio's bravos were thorough, and the graves outside Monza held men who had made the mistake of knowing too much.

But staying silent while knowing the truth was its own kind of corruption, wasn't it? Its own kind of sin. The decision would come soon. Already he could feel it approaching, inevitable as winter.

* * *

IN THE CHURCH of San Maurizio, Father Paolo Arrigone blessed the Eucharist and tried not to think about the confessions he'd heard that week. Seven penitents had knelt in his confessional, seven variations on the same theme.

The missing nun. Lady Virginia. Gian Paolo Osio's child. Whispers that had hardened into conviction.

He elevated the Host above the altar. *Hoc est enim corpus meum.* This is my body, broken for you. The words stuck in his throat with the bitter taste of hypocrisy. What right did he have to speak of Christ's sacrifice while concealing his own role in the sins everyone now discussed? He had written the letters that seduced Virginia, had crafted the words that unmade her defenses, had enabled the affair from its inception. And then, with breathtaking arrogance, he had used the same technique on Candida.

The Mass ended. Parishioners filed out into autumn sunlight.

Arrigone removed his vestments in the sacristy, each motion practiced and automatic.

A knock at the sacristy door made his heart hammer once, hard. "Enter."

One of Osio's servants stood in the doorway. Not Pesseno, but one of the lesser bravos, young and eager, with his hand resting on the knife at his belt.

"Signor Osio sends his regards, Father. He hopes you continue in good health."

The message beneath the courtesy was clear as church bells. Stay quiet. Remember who protects you. Remember what happens to those who forget.

"Give the Signore my thanks." Arrigone kept his voice steady. "Tell him I pray for him daily."

"He knows you do, Father. He values your prayers. And your discretion." The young bravo's smile didn't reach his eyes. "He wanted to be sure you knew how much he values your discretion."

After the man left, Arrigone sank onto the bench. His hands shook now that no witness remained to see them. The threat had been subtle in its delivery but absolute in its meaning. He could confess everything and tell the authorities what he knew about the affair, the murder, the conspiracy. He could purchase his own redemption through testimony that would destroy everyone else involved. And die within a week, throat cut in some alley, his body left as warning.

The choice wasn't really a choice at all. It was survival masquerading as morality, self-preservation disguised as wisdom.

And Arrigone had always been better at surviving than at virtue.

* * *

AT THE PUBLIC fountain where the town's women gathered each afternoon, three women worked the pump while a fourth kept watch for approaching bravos.

"My cousin works at the convent," the youngest said while water splashed into her jug. "She says Sister Caterina was locked in a room as punishment before she disappeared. Says the prioress and Lady Virginia ordered it herself."

An older woman with gray threading through her hair frowned. "Why would a noblewoman of Virginia de Leyva's standing care about some poor lay sister?"

"It makes perfect sense if the lay sister knew about the baby." The young woman glanced around. "If Caterina threatened to tell the authorities what she'd seen, Virginia would have every reason to want her silenced."

"You're saying the Lady of Monza murdered her?"

A third woman crossed herself. "A consecrated nun killing another nun?"

“Not with her own hands, surely.” The first woman tilted her head toward Gian Paolo’s villa. “Everyone knows Osio would do anything for her. She speaks the word; he makes it happen.”

The women fell silent, the weight of what they were discussing pressing down. To speak such things about the daughter of Don Martino de Leyva was to invite disaster. But the truth, or what passed for truth, demanded acknowledgment.

“The poor girl,” the older woman finally said. “If she was murdered, she deserves justice. Someone should speak for her.”

“Justice?” The young woman’s laugh was bitter. “Against a de Leyva? Against Osio and his hired killers? There is no justice for people like us.”

* * *

CAPTAIN NIGUARDA OF the Spanish Territorial Guard stood at his office window and watched the afternoon shadows lengthen across Monza’s main square. Behind him, his lieutenant waited for orders. The garrison commander had spread a map of Monza across his writing table that morning, marking Osio’s various properties with careful precision. The villa that shared a wall with the convent. The vineyard outside town. The warehouse near the Porta d’Agliate. And there, pressed against Santa Margherita’s eastern boundary, the house where a child now lived as proof of crimes no one could officially acknowledge.

“More reports, sir,” his lieutenant said. “Three more citizens came to the garrison this morning demanding we investigate Sister Caterina’s disappearance.”

“Demanding what evidence can’t support.” Niguarda didn’t turn from the window. “We have speculation. Theory. Public conviction strong enough to hang a man. Not one piece of proof that would survive scrutiny before a magistrate.”

“The child in Osio’s house.”

“Is a child. Legally, she could be his by any number of women. Proving the mother’s identity requires testimony we don’t have, from witnesses too frightened to come forward.”

"Sister Caterina's disappearance."

"Could be flight, seduction, any of a dozen explanations that don't require murder." Niguarda finally turned to face his lieutenant. "You know what we're facing here. The moment we move against Osio without irrefutable proof, the aristocracy and the de Leyva family closes ranks. The Cardinal defends his convent's reputation. And we find ourselves caught between forces that can crush us without breaking stride."

The lieutenant's jaw tightened with frustration. "So, we do nothing? We let them believe they're above the law?"

"We wait for a mistake." Niguarda moved back to his writing table. "Crimes this elaborate always unravel eventually. Someone gets frightened and talks. Someone decides their own safety matters more than loyalty. When that happens, when someone comes forward with real testimony, with evidence that will stand, we'll be ready to move."

"And if no one talks? If fear keeps them all silent?"

Niguarda was quiet for a long time. Through his window, he could see the ordinary life of Monza continuing—merchants calling their wares, housewives hurrying home, children playing. All of them living under a system where justice stopped at the walls of wealth and power.

"Then I'll write a report for Governor Fuentes," he said finally. "And I'll explain in careful language why pursuing this case further would create more problems than it solves. And we'll document everything, so when this inevitably explodes, the record shows we saw it coming."

"That's all we can do?"

"For now." Niguarda's voice carried the weight of experience. "But I'll keep watching. And waiting. Because people like Osio and Virginia de Leyva always make mistakes eventually. Pride makes them careless. And when they slip, we'll be there."

* * *

GIUSEPPE PESSENO stood before Gian Paolo's writing table and delivered his report with the economy of words that came from years of service.

"The whole town talks, Signore. They've connected the child to the Lady Virginia, the Lady to Sister Caterina's disappearance and murder. The story has hardened from rumor into conviction."

Gian Paolo's wine glass was half-empty. He'd been drinking since Vespers. "Let them talk. Suspicion without evidence is powerless. They can believe what they like as long as no one can prove it."

"Belief becomes action when it reaches the right ears." Pesseno's scarred face remained impassive, but his tone carried warning. "If Captain Niguarda hears enough complaints, political pressure will force him to investigate regardless of your family's connections."

"Then we make certain he finds nothing concrete enough to act on." Gian Paolo set down his wine glass with deliberate care. "Anyone who moves beyond vague speculation into specific accusations will discover why precision can be dangerous. Make that clear to whoever needs to hear it."

"The apothecary." Pesseno's voice sharpened slightly. "Rainerio. His shop sits between your villa and the convent. He sees everything, hears everything, and he's been supplying medicines to Sister Virginia for years. If anyone knows enough to be truly dangerous, it's him."

"Then watch him carefully. If he shows signs of talking to the authorities, we'll address the problem. But subtly, Pesseno. Carefully. Too much violence right now would only confirm what people already suspect."

"Domenico and his son Ferrari the blacksmith who has been making keys all these years. Them too?"

"Them too. Watch everyone who served us. Fear keeps people silent, but fear can also make them desperate. We need to know the moment anyone's loyalty wavers."

After Pesseno left, Gian Paolo remained at his writing table while dusk painted the convent walls gold, then orange, then red. Everything had seemed manageable once. The affair had been a calculated gamble. The child had been a private arrangement. Even Caterina's death had seemed like an unfortunate necessity, a problem solved rather than a disaster created. But decisions had accumulated, risk had compounded, and now the entire structure was unstable.

From upstairs came Alma Francesca's voice, his daughter chattering in the half-formed words of a two-year-old. His mother's patient responses drifted down as she taught the child simple prayers. The baby whose very existence might destroy them all had grown into a bright, curious toddler who had no idea she was the center of a scandal that threatened to consume everyone around her. He should move her, find a nurse in Milan or a remote villa where her presence wouldn't fuel speculation. But moving her now would be tantamount to confession.

Gian Paolo poured another glass of wine and stood at his window, looking toward the convent where Virginia knelt at evening prayers. Or perhaps she didn't pray at all anymore. Perhaps she simply went through the motions while her mind raced through the same calculations: who might break, who might talk, how long the silence could hold.

The wine tasted bitter despite its quality. He drank it anyway, staring at the walls that separated him from the woman who had become both his greatest passion and his certain doom.

* * *

VIRGINIA KNELT BESIDE her bed, rosary beads sliding through her fingers with automatic rhythm. *Ave Maria, gratia plena, Dominus tecum.* Hail Mary, full of grace, the Lord is with thee. The words were empty of meaning, her mouth forming syllables while her mind raced through calculations.

Domenico had delivered his report hours ago, his weathered face tight with fear. The town knows about the child. The authorities suspect murder. Everyone who aided you will face interrogation when the investigation comes. Not if—when.

Behind her, the door opened without preliminary knock. Benedetta entered and closed it again. "The Prioress is asking questions. Quiet ones, careful ones, but questions nonetheless. About Caterina's final days. About finances that don't quite match the records. About correspondence and visitors."

Virginia's hands stilled on the rosary beads. "What does she know?"

"Enough to be curious. Not yet enough to accuse directly." Benedetta moved to the narrow window. "She'll protect the convent's reputation as long as possible. Reverend Mother Angela understands that Santa Margherita's standing depends on discretion. But if investigation becomes inevitable, she'll sacrifice individuals to save the institution."

"Meaning she'll sacrifice me."

"Meaning she'll sacrifice all of us if that's what it takes." Benedetta turned from the window, strain showing around her eyes. "Ottavia is terrified, barely eating. Candida and Silvia spend hours in the chapel praying. Everyone who participated is waiting for the blow to fall, and that kind of fear makes people unpredictable."

Virginia stood, the rosary still hanging from her fingers. "Then we ensure the blow never lands."

"How? When the entire town believes—"

"The town believes a story without proof." Virginia moved to her writing table and drew out fresh parchment. "Belief is powerful, I grant you. It shapes perception. But belief without evidence cannot sustain itself indefinitely. We need only outlast it."

"And if evidence surfaces? If someone's fear overcomes their self-interest and they decide to talk?"

"No one will talk because everyone shares the guilt." Virginia dipped her quill in ink. "Ottavia was present at the murder. You helped dispose of the body. Candida and Silvia carried Caterina through the corridors. Domenico and his son provided access and keys. Susanna carried messages. Even Apollonia knew what was happening and chose to stay silent. Everyone is implicated. Everyone has compelling reasons to maintain that silence."

"Silence maintained by mutual fear isn't stable over time."

"It doesn't need to be stable forever." Virginia continued writing, each word chosen with care. "It only needs to last until attention shifts elsewhere. Until some new scandal captures the town's interest. Until the authorities conclude that without Caterina's body, without witnesses willing to testify under oath, without confession from any of us, they have no case worth pursuing against a de Leyva and an Osio."

The letter took shape beneath her hand, careful phrases, strategic omissions, words designed to reassure and deflect.

Benedetta watched from the window. "You're writing to him."

"I'm reminding Gian Paolo of what's at stake for both of us. Of why recklessness now would destroy everything we've worked to protect." Virginia paused, her quill hovering over the parchment. "And I'm telling him to come to me tonight. We cannot let fear drive us apart. That would be the only true defeat."

Virginia sealed the letter with wax and pressed her signet ring into the hot red pool. The de Leyva crest emerged, a symbol of power that had protected her family for generations. She handed the letter to Benedetta. "Have Susanna deliver this tonight when the streets are dark. And tell Ottavia to stop looking terrified every time someone speaks to her. Fear draws attention. We need to appear untouched by accusations too baseless to merit our concern."

After Benedetta left, Virginia returned to the altar and knelt again before the small crucifix. She took up the rosary and let the beads slide through her fingers.

But she didn't pray for forgiveness or divine intervention or any of the things a truly penitent soul would seek. Instead, she planned. Calculated who could be trusted absolutely, who might break under pressure, who needed reassurance or threats or careful management to maintain the silence on which everything depended. The town could whisper. The authorities could suspect. Public opinion could rage against her. None of it mattered without proof. And proof, Caterina's body, the murder weapon, testimony from witnesses willing to face Osio's bravos, was buried too deep to surface. Virginia had made certain of that.

She had survived her father's betrayal and abandonment. Had survived forced vows and years of bitter captivity within these walls. Had survived the loss of her child and the murder of a woman who had trusted her protection. She would survive this too. She had no choice. Survival was all that remained.

And tonight, when darkness fell and Gian Paolo slipped through the garden door, she would prove to both of them that their bond was stronger than fear, stronger than scandal, stronger than the judgment of an entire town.

Because if she surrendered him now, after everything they had done to stay together, then Caterina's death would have been for nothing. And Virginia refused to let that be true.

* * *

December

CESARE FERRARI WORKED the bellows with steady rhythm, watching the coals pulse from dull red to angry orange. Heat washed over his face, familiar as the weight of his own skin. The smithy smelled of char and hot iron, scents he'd breathed since his father, Domenico, first lifted him onto a stool thirty years ago.

He pulled the glowing bar from the coals and set it on the anvil. A hinge bracket for the miller's barn door. Simple work that required no thought, leaving his mind free to circle the worry it had circled for four days.

The tavern. His own voice rising above the others, wine-loosened and foolish. *She didn't flee. That girl died in the convent.*

Each hammer blow rang through the December air. Behind him, his apprentice Pietro swept metal shavings while humming off-key. The boy had no idea his master had marked them both for attention they couldn't afford.

"Cesare." Lucia appeared in the doorway with bread and watered wine. Her face was lined from bearing five children and burying one, from thirty years of smithy smoke and worry. "Your father was here earlier."

Ferrari plunged the bracket into the water bucket. Steam hissed and billowed. "What did he want?"

"Asked about keys." She set the meal on the workbench. "Whether you'd made any recently for the convent."

The bracket had already cooled but Ferrari left it in the water, watching bubbles rise and burst. "The convent orders through the Prioress. Always has."

"That's what I told him." Lucia's hand found the worn wooden cross at her throat. "He seemed curious about other arrangements. Private commissions."

Ferrari lifted the bracket and examined it. The metal had warped slightly in cooling. He'd have to heat it again, waste time correcting his own carelessness. "I make keys for half the town. Can't remember every order."

"No." Lucia's voice carried something harder than her usual care. "I don't suppose you can."

She studied his face the way she'd studied their children's faces during fever, looking for signs of how bad the sickness might become. Then she crossed herself and returned to the house, her footsteps fading across the packed earth courtyard.

Ferrari stared at the ruined bracket. The truth sat in his chest like an ingot of lead, gaining weight with each hour. Fifty keys, perhaps more. All duplicates. All commissioned Gian Paolo Osio over the course of years, quietly, at night, always with good silver coin and the kind of smile that suggested questions would be unwelcome.

He'd asked none. Had simply taken the impressions pressed into soft wax, had filed the teeth with patient precision until each forgery matched its original, had accepted payment and watched Osio disappear into the night with keys that opened doors he had no lawful right to enter.

Santa Margherita's doors. Every lock from the main entrance to the Chapter house to the bolt on the sacristy. The entire convent laid open, its protection stripped away one key at a time.

Four months had passed since Caterina de Meda vanished. Four months of whispers in the market square, of knowing glances, of rumors that grew teeth with each retelling.

But Cesare Ferrari had seen something those months ago that transformed rumor into certainty.

He'd been returning from a delivery to the Taverna estate, his cart empty and the November night cold enough to make his breath steam. The streets were empty. Only a fool or a criminal had business abroad past midnight.

Or a blacksmith whose wealthy client demanded work delivered before dawn.

He'd been passing the convent when movement caught his eye. Two figures emerging from the main entrance, struggling with a burden between them. They moved in fits and starts, pausing to adjust their grip, their heads turning constantly to check the empty street.

Even in darkness Ferrari recognized Gian Paolo Osio's height and bearing. The other figure was smaller, dressed in a nun's habit that gleamed pale in the starlight.

The burden was wrapped in cloth. But its shape was unmistakable—the length of it, the weight that made even two people strain, the awkward way a human body refuses to cooperate when carried by limbs rather than will.

Ferrari had stopped his cart. Not from courage but from shock, his hands frozen on the reins while his mind struggled to make sense of what his eyes reported. The two figures dragged their burden across the piazza toward the Osio palazzo, disappearing through a side entrance.

He should have driven on immediately. But he'd sat paralyzed for long moments before finally gathering his wits and continuing home.

For months he'd succeeded in not knowing. Had pushed the memory down whenever it surfaced and told himself it was none of his business what the nobility did at night.

But three nights ago, at the tavern, wine had unlocked what caution had kept sealed.

His friend, Matteo, had mentioned Caterina's name, poor girl, probably spreading her legs for Venetian merchants by now, and something in Ferrari had snapped.

"She didn't flee." The words had escaped before prudence could stop them. "That girl died in the convent. And not a natural death, either."

The table had gone silent. Five men staring at him with varying expressions of shock and hunger.

"How would you know that?" Matteo's eyes were bright with interest.

Ferrari had shrugged, trying to sound casual while his heart hammered. "I know what I know. Mark my words. She never left Santa Margherita alive."

Someone laughed nervously. The conversation had moved on. But Ferrari had seen the way information passed between them in glances and nods, the way knowledge flowed from one mind to another like water finding cracks in stone.

By morning, half of Monza would know what he'd said. By afternoon, the other half would hear it secondhand.

And eventually, perhaps already, it would reach Gian Paolo Osio's ears.

* * *

THE DECEMBER SUN sank toward the horizon. Cesare continued working though his hands shook and the bracket seemed determined to warp no matter how carefully he heated it.

A shadow fell across the doorway.

Ferrari glanced up, expecting Lucia. Instead, Pesseno stood motionless in the street, his face bearing the scars of old violence. His arms were crossed over his chest.

Osio's chief bravo. The man who'd held Molteno down while his master struck the killing blow, or so the rumors claimed.

Their eyes met. Pesseno didn't smile or nod. He simply stood watching, a butcher weighing livestock, calculating exactly where to make the first cut.

Then he turned and walked away, disappearing around the corner.

Ferrari's hammer slipped from nerveless fingers and clattered on the floor. He gripped the edge of the anvil with both hands, his breath coming in short gasps.

They knew. Osio knew.

The wolves weren't circling anymore. They were already at the door.

* * *

RAINERIO RONCINO MEASURED dried valerian root into a cloth pouch, his fingers moving with the automatic precision of three decades' practice. The apothecary shop smelled of sage and lavender, of remedies that healed and preparations that destroyed. The distinction between them was often a matter of dosage. A matter of intent.

Through the window, he watched December afternoon fade toward evening.

His wife, Elisabetta, entered from the back room carrying folded linens. "I heard the strangest thing at market."

Rainerio tied off the pouch, his hands steady though his pulse had begun to quicken. "What sort of strange thing?"

"Ferrari the blacksmith." Elisabetta set the linens on the counter. "Claiming that de Meda never fled the convent at all. Says she died there. Murdered."

Rainerio's hands went still. "Ferrari said this? Publicly?"

"At the tavern. Three nights ago." Elisabetta leaned closer, her voice dropping. "Half the town heard him. They're saying he knows something. That he saw something that night she disappeared."

Rainerio set down the pouch and reached for a jar of dried mint, not because he needed it but because his hands required occupation. "People say many things after drinking too much wine."

"This wasn't wine talking." Elisabetta moved around the counter to stand beside him. "His wife came to market this morning. Wouldn't meet anyone's eyes. She's frightened."

She should be frightened. They all should be frightened.

Rainerio had seen things too. Had witnessed more than a blacksmith glimpsing bodies carried through the night. He'd seen Gian Paolo Osio arriving at dawn all those months ago, his fine clothes disheveled, his hands bearing fresh scratches, his eyes wild with something that might have been fear or triumph or both.

"Strong spirits," Osio had said, his voice hoarse. "For medicinal purposes. The strongest you have."

Rainerio had sold him a bottle of *grappa* that could dissolve wood. Had watched Osio drain half of it standing there in the shop, hands shaking as he tilted the bottle.

"Bad night?" Rainerio had ventured.

Osio had wiped his mouth with the back of his hand, smearing dirt across his face. "The worst." Then he'd laughed, a sound with no humor in it. "Or the best, depending on how you measure these things."

He'd left the bottle half-empty on the counter and walked out without paying. Three days later, Pesseno had arrived with double the bottle's cost and a message: *The master values your discretion.*

Translation: *Keep your mouth shut or discover what happens to those who don't.*

Rainerio had kept his mouth shut. For months. Through all the rumors about Caterina's disappearance, through the whispers about Sister Virginia's increasingly obvious relationship with Osio, through the speculation about whose bastard that baby really was.

He'd sold abortifacient herbs to the convent for years—pennyroyal and tansy, savin and rue—always through intermediaries, always with the falsehood that they were for 'women's ailments' rather than for ending unwanted pregnancies. He'd asked no questions when the orders increased in frequency.

He'd even witnessed Osio slipping into the convent grounds at night, moving through shadows with the confidence of someone who possessed keys he shouldn't have.

All of this Rainerio had seen and kept silent about. Because silence was how an apothecary survived in a town where nobles made the rules.

But Ferrari had broken that silence. Had spoken aloud what everyone whispered in private.

"Someone should warn him," Elisabetta said. She'd moved to the window; her arms wrapped around herself. "Ferrari doesn't understand the danger."

"What danger?" The lie came automatically. "A girl fled the convent. Rumors spread. None of it concerns a blacksmith."

Elisabetta turned to face him. Her eyes were red-rimmed. "Don't lie to me. Not after thirty years. I know you know something. I've known for months, watching you flinch every time someone mentions the convent."

The accusation hung between them. The weight of what he knew had grown too heavy for one person to carry alone.

"If I know something," he said carefully, "speaking of it would accomplish nothing except making us the next targets. Ferrari will learn that lesson soon enough."

"So, we do nothing? Say nothing?" Elisabetta's voice rose. "Let him walk into whatever's coming without warning?"

"Warning him means admitting what I know. Admitting what I know means becoming implicated." Rainerio crossed to the window and pulled the shutters closed. "And implication leads to the ditch outside town. Or worse."

"There's worse than the ditch?"

Rainerio thought of Molteno's widow, who'd come begging for herbs to help her sleep, her hands shaking so badly she could barely hold the coins. Thought of Caterina, who'd vanished so completely, it was as though she'd never existed. Thought of Osio's scratched hands and wild eyes.

"Yes," he said. "There's worse."

The shop door opened. Its bell chimed, a cheerful sound utterly at odds with the leaden dread settling in Rainerio's gut.

Apollonia entered. Pesseno's wife, her face pale beneath her kerchief, her eyes downcast. A fresh bruise darkened her left cheekbone. Not her first. Wouldn't be her last.

"Signor Roncino." Her voice barely carried across the small shop. "My husband requires your services."

Rainerio's throat constricted. "What manner of remedy does he need?"

"Not a remedy." Apollonia's fingers twisted in her skirt. She still hadn't raised her eyes. "He wishes to speak with you. At the Osio house. Tonight, after Vespers."

The shop seemed to tilt. Rainerio gripped the counter's edge. "About what matter?"

"He didn't say." But her eyes, when she finally looked up, told a different story. She knew. "He said to come to the kitchen entrance. Quietly."

* * *

THAT EVENING, RAINERIO walked through Monza's streets carrying his herbal bag though he'd packed none. Only the knowledge that weighed more than any remedy.

Pesseno met him at the Osio palazzo's kitchen entrance, torchlight casting harsh shadows across his ravaged features. "This way."

He led Rainerio across the courtyard to a storage building where Gian Paolo waited, seated on a barrel.

"Signor Roncino." Osio's voice was pleasant. Almost friendly. "Thank you for coming."

Rainerio bowed, his heart hammering. "How may I serve you, Signore?"

"I understand there's been talk." Osio leaned back against the wall, casual as a man discussing the weather. "About the convent. About Sister Virginia. About matters that should remain private." He paused. "You serve the sisters. You hear things. I'm curious what you've heard."

The trap was elegant in its simplicity. Deny hearing anything, and Osio would know he lied. Admit hearing too much, and he'd reveal his own dangerous knowledge.

Rainerio chose his words with the care of a man crossing a frozen lake. "I've heard that Ferrari the blacksmith spoke unwisely at the tavern."

"Ah. Ferrari." Something shifted in Osio's eyes. Sharpened. "And what did our drunken blacksmith claim?"

"That Caterina didn't flee. That she died in the convent."

"Interesting." Osio examined his fingernails. "Ferrari saw something, perhaps. The night of July twenty-ninth. Something that disturbed him enough to speak of it months later, after sufficient wine."

The casual admission struck like a physical blow. Osio wasn't asking for information. He was confirming what he already knew. Testing whether Rainerio would add lies to his other sins.

"Ferrari should guard his tongue," Rainerio managed.

"Yes. He should." Osio stood in one fluid motion, moving with the easy grace of a predator. "But some men lack the wisdom to recognize danger until it's too late. They speak without thinking. Share knowledge that isn't theirs to share."

He moved closer. Three steps. Two. "You're not such a man, are you, Signor Roncino?"

"No, Signore." Rainerio's throat had gone desert dry.

"I thought not. You're careful. Discreet." Osio smiled. "A man who understands that discretion has kept his shop prosperous, his wife comfortable, his children fed and clothed. A man who would hate to see those things endangered."

The threat was clear. But Osio continued anyway.

"Your daughter is what, fourteen? Marriageable age." His eyes held Rainerio's. "Pretty girl. I've seen her in the market. It would be unfortunate if her prospects were damaged by scandal attached to her father's name." He paused. "Or worse things than scandal."

Rainerio's hands clenched into fists at his sides. Rage and terror warred in his chest, but terror won. "I understand perfectly, Signore."

"Good." Osio stepped back. "Then we understand each other. You'll continue serving the convent with your usual discretion. You'll hear things, people always talk to their apothecary, but you'll remember that some knowledge is better kept locked away."

He gestured to Pesseno. "Show Signor Roncino out."

* * *

WALKING HOME RAINERIO understood with perfect clarity what would happen next. Osio had confirmed Ferrari's dangerous knowledge. Had learned that the blacksmith's tavern talk had spread through Monza. Had recognized the threat Ferrari represented.

Ferrari was a dead man walking. He simply didn't know it yet.

Rainerio should warn him. Should find the blacksmith tonight and tell him to flee.

But warning Ferrari meant defying Osio. And Osio had been clear about the cost of defiance. Not just Rainerio's death, but his daughter's ruined reputation. His wife's widowhood. His son inheriting nothing but a destroyed name.

He climbed the stairs to the rooms above his shop. Elisabetta looked up from her mending when he entered, her face flooding with relief.

"Thank God. I thought—" She stopped. Read something in his expression. "What did they want?"

"To remind me of the value of silence." Rainerio crossed to the brazier and held his hands out to its heat, but the chill was inside him, bone deep. "To ensure I understand my place."

"And Ferrari?"

Rainerio said nothing.

Elisabetta's needle stilled in her lap. "You're going to let them kill him." Her voice was flat. Not accusation. Just acknowledgment. "You're going to say nothing and let them kill him."

"What would you have me do?" Rainerio turned to face her. "Warn him? Osio would know it came from me. We'd be next. Is that what you want? Should I sacrifice our children to save a man who was foolish enough to speak truths that should have stayed buried?"

"No." Elisabetta resumed her mending, but her hands shook. "I want you to be the man I married. The man who became an apothecary because he wanted to heal people. But I don't recognize that man anymore."

The accusation stung worse than any physical blow. Because she was right.

He went to bed without answering. Lay awake while Elisabetta's breathing eventually evened into sleep beside him. Through their window, he could see stars burning in the December sky.

Two streets away, Ferrari was probably sleeping too. Completely unaware that tomorrow would never come. That he'd already spoken his last words, eaten his last meal, kissed his wife for the final time.

Rainerio knew this with certainty. And did nothing. And that nothing became its own kind of action. Participation through silence, guilt through inaction.

* * *

CESARE FERRARI STAYED late in his smithy. The apprentice had gone home at sunset. Lucia had called twice from the house, reminding him that supper was getting cold.

But Ferrari continued hammering, shaping a lock plate that didn't need shaping. Keeping his hands busy. Keeping his mind occupied.

The forge's coals had been banked for the night, their glow fading from orange to dull red. The smithy held only one tallow candle on the workbench, its flame guttering in drafts.

Outside, the December night was still. No wind. The kind of silence that should have been peaceful but instead felt like held breath before a scream.

Ferrari set down the lock plate and flexed his hands. They ached from a full day's work, the good ache of honest labor. His father had worked this forge before him. His grandfather had built it. His father, elderly now, worked at the convent and had passed the forge to him so that one day his son could inherit it.

Now he wasn't sure he would get the chance.

Pesseno had been watching the shop again today. Standing across the street for an hour at midday. Not hiding. Not threatening. Just... present. A reminder.

"Working late, Ferrari?"

The voice came from the doorway. Casual. Almost friendly.

Ferrari spun, his hand reaching for the hammer he'd set down moments before. But his fingers closed on empty air. The hammer was three feet away.

Gian Paolo Osio stood silhouetted against the street beyond, blocking the doorway. Behind him, another figure appeared. Pesseno, filled the doorway completely, cutting off escape.

"Signore Osio." Ferrari's voice cracked. He swallowed, tried again. "I was just closing."

"I know." Osio stepped inside. Behind him, Pesseno followed. "I wanted to speak with you. About a conversation. At the tavern."

Ferrari's bladder loosened. Warm urine soaked his breeches, running down his leg. The shame barely registered beneath the terror. "That was wine talking. Nothing more. I was drunk. Said foolish things I didn't mean."

"Didn't mean?" Osio moved closer, circling the anvil. "Or didn't mean to say out loud? There's a difference, Ferrari."

"I saw nothing." The lie came desperately, uselessly. "I swear on my children's lives, I saw nothing."

"Don't." Osio's voice went cold. "Don't swear on your children when you're lying."

He'd reached the workbench now and was examining Ferrari's tools. "The night of July twenty-ninth. You were returning from the Taverna estate. Late delivery. The streets were empty except for you." He picked up a chisel, tested its edge. "And except for two people carrying something heavy."

He set down the chisel. Met Ferrari's eyes. "You know what it was."

Ferrari's legs shook. He gripped the workbench for support. "Please. I have a wife. Four children. Another on the way. Whatever you need, I'll pay it. I'll swear any oath you want."

"The problem with oaths," Osio said quietly, "is that you've already broken the one that mattered. Silence. You promised that when you took my silver to make those keys. Instead, you talked."

He nodded to Pesseno.

Ferrari tried to run. His body made the decision before his mind caught up, animal instinct toward the back door that led to the courtyard.

He made it two steps before Pesseno's arm locked around his throat from behind. The bravo moved with brutal efficiency, no wasted motion.

Ferrari clawed at the arm choking him, kicked backward, connected with something that earned a grunt but didn't loosen the grip cutting off his air. His vision was already narrowing. He couldn't breathe. Couldn't scream.

Then the knife entered below his ribs.

Not a stab. A punch, almost gentle, followed by profound cold spreading through Ferrari's gut like water soaking through cloth. Distant pain, almost ignorable. His mind hadn't yet processed what his body already knew—that he was dying, that this spreading cold was blood filling spaces blood was never meant to occupy.

Pesseno twisted the blade.

The cold became fire. Agony exploded through Ferrari's core so intense that his struggles ceased immediately. His hands dropped from Pesseno's arm, fell to his own stomach where they encountered the wooden handle protruding from his body.

His legs gave out. Pesseno lowered him almost gently to the floor, guiding his descent like a father settling a child into bed. The knife remained buried in his gut. Pesseno left it there.

Ferrari found himself lying on his side, his cheek pressed against packed earth littered with iron filings. Through the gaps in the floorboards, he could see the dirt beneath his shop, could smell it mixing with the metallic scent of his own blood.

Osio crouched beside him, just outside the growing puddle. His face was calm. Almost regretful. "I take no pleasure in this."

He paused as though waiting for Ferrari to respond, but Ferrari's throat had filled with something wet and hot. When he tried to speak, only bubbles emerged.

"You should have stayed quiet," Osio continued. His voice was almost kind. Teaching a lesson, not gloating. "Now you're simply a warning."

He stood. Brushed invisible dirt from his knees. Then he left, Pesseno following. They disappeared through the front door, leaving it open. Night air rushed in, making the candle flame dance before it guttered out.

Ferrari lay in sudden blackness. The pain in his gut had spread to his chest, making each breath a labor that accomplished less and less. He could feel blood pumping out with each heartbeat, could feel his body emptying itself onto the floor.

He tried to call for Lucia. Tried to scream. But his lungs weren't working anymore. Only wet gurgles emerged, pathetic sounds that wouldn't carry beyond these walls.

Through the back door, he could hear domestic sounds. Lucia talking to their oldest daughter. A pot clattering. The ordinary noise of evening routines continuing while Ferrari bled out twenty feet away.

He wanted to tell them he loved them. Wanted to warn Lucia about the danger. Wanted to tell his son that the shop was cursed now.

But he couldn't speak. Could barely think through the fog creeping over his mind.

The forge's coals provided the only light, just barely visible across the room, pulsing red like a slow heartbeat. Their glow was fading as they cooled. Soon they'd be nothing but ash.

Ferrari's vision narrowed. Through it he could see a single point of red, the last living coal, growing dimmer.

The convent bell rang Compline. It had marked his hours since childhood. Had rung when he was born, when he married Lucia, when each of his children entered the world.

The sound faded. Or perhaps his hearing was fading.

The last coal winked out. The smithy went black.

And Cesare Ferrari, blacksmith, father of four, keeper of dangerous secrets, died on the floor of his shop with his wife's name on his lips and blood soaking into the earth where three generations of his family had worked iron into useful things.

* * *

LUCIA FERRARI WOKE at first light. The space beside her in bed was empty, the sheets cold.

She'd fallen asleep waiting for Cesare to come in from the shop. He did that sometimes, worked late into the night when something troubled him. She'd learned over thirty years not to push.

But he'd never stayed out all night before.

She dressed quickly, pulled her shawl around her shoulders, and crossed the courtyard to the smithy. The door stood open. Strange. Cesare always closed it.

"Cesare?" Her voice echoed in the empty space.

No answer.

She stepped inside. The forge was dead, just cold ash. The candle on the workbench had burned down to nothing. And there, on the floor near the anvil—

Lucia's mind refused to make sense of what her eyes reported. A shape. A man-sized shape. Lying in something dark that had spread across the packed earth like spilled wine.

Not wine.

She moved closer. Her slippered feet made no sound. Everything felt distant, as though she were moving through a dream.

But she didn't wake.

The shape resolved into her husband. Lying on his side, his face peaceful as though he'd simply decided to rest there. But his eyes were open. Staring at nothing. And the dark stain beneath him was blood, so much blood, soaked into the earth, pooled in the spaces between his fingers where he'd pressed his hands to the wound that had killed him.

Lucia opened her mouth to scream. Nothing emerged. Her throat had closed.

She knelt beside him in the blood that was already sticky and congealing. Touched his face. His skin was waxy and cold, cold as the December morning, cold as stone.

"Cesare." The word came out as a whisper. "Cesare, please."

But he was gone, had been gone for hours while she slept peacefully twenty feet away, while their children dreamed in their beds.

The scream finally came. It tore from her throat like something with claws, raw and animal and endless.

* * *

VIRGINIA WAS DESCENDING the stairs when Sister Ottavia intercepted her. The other nun's face had gone the color of whey. Her rosary dangled from her hand, beads swinging wildly with each tremor.

"Cesare Ferrari is dead."

The words reached Virginia through a strange distance, as though Ottavia were speaking from the far end of a tunnel. The corridor tilted. Virginia's hand shot out, found stone wall, held on.

"What?"

"The blacksmith." Ottavia's voice was barely audible. She kept glancing toward the refectory where other sisters were gathering. "They found him this morning. In his shop."

Virginia's fingers scraped against mortar between the stones. The convent had stood for nearly one hundred years. These walls had witnessed countless tragedies. The stone's permanence was oddly comforting while everything else fell apart.

"How?" The question emerged hoarse.

"Stabbed." Ottavia glanced over her shoulder. "His wife found him at dawn. The servants are saying there was so much blood. So much so that it soaked into the ground. They'll never get it out."

Virginia pressed her palm flat against the wall. Stone. Solid. Real. While her mind catalogued another death to add to the list she carried like a ledger of debts unpaid.

Molteno. Caterina. Now Ferrari.

Three dead because of what connected them to her and Gian Paolo.

"Do they know who—" She stopped. The question was pointless.

"They're saying thieves." Ottavia's fingers twisted in her rosary until the wooden beads creaked. "That he surprised robbers in his shop."

"At night? When the forge was already banked?" Virginia's voice went flat. "When there was nothing left to steal except tools too heavy to carry?"

"I know." Ottavia's eyes held fear mixed with accusation. "No one believes it."

Virginia forced her legs to move, descending the stairs. Ferrari had made the keys. Gian Paolo had told her that himself. Fifty keys duplicated over years. Every door in Santa Margherita laid open by forged iron.

And now Ferrari was dead.

She reached the refectory and took her place at the long table. The hall smelled of porridge and bread. Ordinary scents that belonged to ordinary mornings. But nothing was ordinary anymore.

Prioress Angela led them in grace. Virginia bowed her head, moved her lips in the familiar Latin, but the words were hollow. Empty vessels containing nothing. God wasn't listening to her prayers. Perhaps He'd stopped listening years ago.

She picked up her spoon. The porridge tasted like paste. She forced herself to swallow. Around her, sisters were whispering behind their hands.

"His poor wife," Sister Candida murmured from across the table. "Four children and another coming. How will they survive?"

"Perhaps the Prioress will commission work from her," Sister Silvia suggested.

"The convent," Benedetta interrupted quietly, "will do nothing that draws attention to its connection with Ferrari." She met Virginia's eyes across the table. Her gaze was steady. "Some associations are best forgotten quickly."

The unspoken message was clear. Ferrari had worked for the convent. Had made keys for doors that should have remained locked. Had possessed knowledge that could damage not just Virginia but the entire community.

His death was terrible. Tragic. Worthy of brief mourning.

But it was also convenient.

Virginia set down her spoon. Her stomach had clenched into a fist that refused to accept food. She stared at the porridge congealing in her bowl and thought about patterns. About the way death followed certain people like a loyal dog, always circling back, always hungry.

Molteno first. Her family's advisor and tax collector who'd been murdered on a lonely road because Gian Paolo needed to avenge an insult to his honor.

Then Caterina. The lay sister who'd threatened to expose the affair, who'd been strangled and dismembered and buried in pieces.

Now Ferrari. The blacksmith who'd forged the keys, who'd witnessed something that night in July and been foolish enough to speak of it.

Three deaths. And the intervals between them were shrinking.

"Sister Virginia." The Prioress's voice cut through her spiraling thoughts. "You're not eating."

Virginia looked up to find the entire table watching her. Prioress Angela's face was stern, but her eyes held something else. Suspicion. Or perhaps just exhaustion.

"Forgive me, Reverend Mother." Virginia picked up her spoon again. "I was praying for Ferrari's soul."

"We all pray for the dead." Angela's voice was flat. "But the living must still eat. Finish your meal."

Virginia forced herself to swallow three more spoonfuls. The porridge sat in her stomach like stones. Around her, the meal continued, sisters eating, whispering, speculating about Ferrari's death.

By the time grace was said, Virginia's hands were shaking.

* * *

SHE CLIMBED THE stairs to her chamber. Morning sun slanted through the window, painting the floor in geometric patterns. Virginia stood in one of the bright squares and felt nothing. No warmth. Just the weight of three corpses pressing down on her shoulders.

"He's eliminating witnesses." Benedetta's voice came from behind her. She'd followed Virginia up, had closed the door firmly. Ottavia stood next to her. "First Caterina because she knew about the baby and threatened to expose everything. Now Ferrari because he knew about the keys and couldn't keep his mouth shut." She paused. "The question is who's next."

"Don't." Virginia pressed her palms against her temples. A sick throbbing had begun behind her eyes. "Don't say it."

"Someone has to say it." Benedetta moved into the room. "Because you're standing there pretending this isn't a pattern. Pretending each death is separate. Unconnected. But they're not, Virginia. They're all connected to you. To him. To what you've been doing together for years."

"I didn't ask him to kill anyone." The protest sounded hollow.

"You didn't have to ask." Benedetta sat on her cot by the window. "You created the situation. You brought him into this convent. You involved servants and blacksmiths and apothecaries in covering your sins. And now he's cleaning up the mess the only way he knows how. With blood."

Virginia turned from the window. "What would you have me do? I can't bring Ferrari back. Can't undo what's been done."

"No. But you can recognize the danger we're all in." Benedetta leaned forward. "Rainerio is next. You know that, don't you? The apothecary who's been selling you abortifacient herbs for years. Who's likely seen Gian Paolo coming and going at dawn. Who knows too many pieces of the story. He's already nervous. And once Gian Paolo realizes that Rainerio might talk..."

She trailed off, not needing to finish. They both knew how that sentence ended.

"And after Rainerio?" Ottavia's voice came from the doorway. She'd entered silently, was now standing with her back pressed against the door. "After the apothecary, who's next? Apollonia? Domenico? Us?"

The question hung in the air like smoke, poisonous and inescapable.

Virginia sank onto her own cot. She stared at her hands in her lap, hands that had carried Caterina's body through the convent, that had written love letters to a murderer, that had opened doors and broken vows and destroyed everything they'd touched.

"We're already dead," Ottavia whispered. She'd begun crying silently, tears running down her face unchecked. "We just don't know it yet. We know too much. We've done too much. And one day he'll decide we're more dangerous alive than dead, and we'll end up like Ferrari. Like Caterina."

"No." Benedetta's voice was hard. Certain. "We survive. Because unlike Ferrari, we're smart enough to keep our mouths shut. Unlike Caterina, we're valuable enough that killing us would create more problems than it would solve." She looked between them. "But that only works if we maintain absolute silence. No confessions to priests. No tearful admissions to family. No drunken revelations at market. We survive by becoming invisible. By knowing everything and saying nothing."

"For how long?" Virginia asked. "How long can we maintain that silence? Months? Years? The rest of our lives?"

"However long it takes." Benedetta's expression was grim. "Because the alternative is Ferrari's fate. Bleeding out on a dirt floor while your family sleeps twenty feet away."

Silence settled over the chamber. Through the window, Virginia could hear ordinary sounds—sisters moving through the corridors below, the gardener's spade striking earth, the convent bell marking Terce. The routines that had structured her days for eight years continuing unchanged while everything beneath the surface had transformed into nightmare.

She thought of Ferrari's wife discovering his body at dawn. Thought of his children waking to learn their father was dead. Thought of the baby not yet born who would never know the man whose blood had soaked into the smithy floor.

And she thought of Gian Paolo, somewhere in Monza, believing he'd solved a problem. Believing that violence could answer every question, could silence every witness, could protect their secret indefinitely.

He was wrong. She understood that now with terrible clarity. The violence wasn't protecting them. It was consuming them. Each death created ripples that spread outward, touching more people, raising more questions, making the secret harder rather than easier to keep.

Eventually, perhaps soon, the ripples would reach someone with enough power to demand answers. A magistrate who couldn't be bribed. A bishop who couldn't be intimidated.

And when that happened, when the truth finally emerged into daylight, everyone even peripherally connected to this affair would burn.

"We should never have started this," Virginia said quietly. "Any of it. I should have refused him that first night in the garden. Should have sent him away and never looked back."

"Yes," Benedetta agreed. "You should have. But you didn't. And now we live with the consequences."

She stood. Ottavia remained by the door, still crying silently. Virginia remained on her cot, staring at her hands. Benedetta moved to the window.

Three women in one small room. Bound together by blood they hadn't shed but were nonetheless complicit in. By choices they couldn't undo. By knowledge that was both their protection and their doom.

Outside the window, the December sun climbed higher. The garden trees stood bare and black against gray sky, their branches reaching upward like drowning men grasping for salvation that wouldn't come.

The convent bell rang. Virginia rose and followed her sisters toward the chapel, where they would kneel and pray for the soul of Cesare Ferrari, blacksmith, murdered in his own shop for the crime of speaking truth.

She wondered if God would accept those prayers. Or if He'd long ago stopped listening to anything that emerged from Santa Margherita's walls.

The wolves weren't circling anymore. They were feeding. And they wouldn't stop until everyone who'd touched this secret had been devoured.

Chapter Thirteen
1607

Early January

RAINERIO RONCINO LOCKED the shop door as twilight bled into night. January air bit through his cloak. He tucked his hands beneath his arms for warmth and started the walk home, barely fifty paces, a journey he'd made thousands of times without thought.

Tonight, every shadow held menace.

Three weeks had passed since Ferrari had been found dead in his smithy. Three weeks of watching Monza transform from a town where people whispered behind closed doors into one where silence itself had become a kind of speech. No one spoke Osio's name aloud anymore. Everyone understood which deaths were accidents and which were warnings written in blood.

Rainerio's boots crunched on frost-rimed cobblestones. His breath steamed white. Ahead, the narrow street curved past the Church of San Maurizio, its bell tower a black spike against the purple sky.

Familiarity brought no comfort. Not anymore. Not since Ferrari.

The shot came from the alley beside the church.

A concussive boom punched through the evening stillness. Something hissed past his ear with a sound like cloth tearing, so close that heat seared his skin. Stone exploded from the wall beside his head in a shower of fragments that stung his face and neck, opening hot lines.

For one frozen instant Rainerio's mind went blank. Then his body moved.

He threw himself sideways, feet tangling in his cloak. He crashed against the opposite wall hard enough to knock the breath from him. His herbal bag flew from his grasp, contents spilling across cobblestones.

Another boom shattered the evening. The ball struck cobblestones where he'd stood a heartbeat before, throwing orange sparks before ricocheting away with a high metallic whine.

Rainerio ran.

Not toward home. That meant death. Whoever waited in that alley would have time to reload. Not back to the shop. Only one place close enough to offer sanctuary: the church itself.

His legs pumped beneath him while terror screamed that he was too slow, too old, too soft from years measuring herbs. Behind him came footsteps, boots pounding cobblestones, chasing, closing the distance.

The church door. Twenty paces. His vision narrowed to that single point of salvation.

Fifteen paces. His cloak caught on something and nearly yanked him off his feet. He tore free, kept running.

Ten paces. Five paces.

His palms found the iron ring slick with evening frost. He pulled with desperate strength. The door was never locked. San Maurizio welcomed sinners at all hours.

The hinges shrieked as the door swung inward. Rainerio threw himself through into darkness that smelled of incense and old stone and beeswax candles. He slammed the door behind him, his entire body shaking.

Silence settled around him like a shroud.

He stood frozen, waiting for the door to burst open, for the final shot. Nothing happened.

Slowly, his hearing returned. Not footsteps. Not pounding on the door. Just his own ragged breathing and somewhere deeper in the church the small sounds of evening prayer.

Rainerio's legs gave out. He slid down the door until he sat on flagstones so cold they burned through his breeches. His fingers trembled so violently they wouldn't close. Shock—the signs were there. Trembling. Cold sweat. Thundering pulse.

Blood welled from where stone chips had opened his cheek. He touched the wounds with quaking fingers. Minor injuries. Nothing that wouldn't heal.

He was alive.

By pure luck. The shot fired a fraction too early, his stumble at exactly the right moment, the church door unlocked. He was alive when by all rights he should be lying in the street with his skull shattered.

The message had been delivered with perfect clarity: *Stop talking or the next time we won't miss.*

* * *

VIRGINIA KNELT IN her cell as dusk gathered outside, her rosary beads sliding through her fingers without conscious thought. The prayers were automatic, leaving her mind free to circle obsessively around the same question.

How many more would have to die before this ended?

The door opened without warning. She didn't look up. She knew his footsteps by heart.

"You're praying." Gian Paolo's amusement made her stomach clench. "How devout you've become."

Virginia's fingers stilled on the rosary. "Someone tried to kill Rainerio tonight."

"I know." He crossed to her narrow bed and sat. "I was there."

Her head snapped up. In the dim candlelight, his face was half in shadow. No guilt. No shame. Just casual satisfaction.

"What?"

"I fired the shots myself." He said it the way another man might mention attending Mass. "Borrowed Pesseno's harquebus. Waited in the alley by San Maurizio until he walked past. Two shots from fifteen paces."

Virginia's rosary clattered to the floor, wooden beads scattering across stone. "You, not Pesseno? You did it yourself?"

"Pesseno's too recognizable. Everyone knows his face, knows he's mine." Gian Paolo leaned back against the wall. "Better to handle certain matters personally. Less chance of witnesses connecting it back to me."

"You missed." Flat. Not quite relief. Not quite accusation.

"Yes." His jaw tightened. "The light was failing. He stumbled at the wrong moment. But next time—"

"There won't be a next time." Virginia surged to her feet, rosary forgotten. "No more. Do you hear me? No more murders. No more blood."

"He's been talking."

"I don't care!" The words tore from her throat. "Molteno, Caterina, Ferrari—how many bodies do you need piled at your feet before you're satisfied?"

Gian Paolo stood and stalked toward her with predatory ease. "This is necessary. You know it's necessary."

"Necessary?" Virginia backed away, putting the small table between them. "You tried to murder an apothecary in the street because he gossips. That's not necessary. That's madness."

"You think I'm mad?" His tone went quiet in a way that was more dangerous than shouting. "I'm protecting us. Protecting what we have together."

"Our secret." The words tasted like ashes. "When did loving you turn into shooting people in the street like animals?"

"Then what would you have me do?" He moved around the table, backing her toward the wall. "Let them talk? Let them speculate? Let the rumors spread?"

"I would have you stop." She couldn't keep the break from her words. "Just stop. No more violence. No more blood. We find another way, we leave Monza."

"There is no other way!" His palm slammed against the wall beside her head hard enough to send plaster dust drifting down. "This is the only way. Silence the witnesses before they can testify."

He leaned closer. "Arrigone. Months ago, when I wanted to silence him, you begged me. Pleaded with me to spare him because he was a priest." His fingers gripped her chin, forcing her to meet his eyes. "So, I spared him. And what happened?"

Virginia tried to pull away but his grip tightened. "Let go of me."

"He talked. To Rainerio, to Ferrari, probably to half of Lombardy. Made everyone brave because they saw I wouldn't act against a priest." He dropped to barely above a whisper. "If I'd killed Arrigone when I wanted to, the others would have learned. Would have been too frightened to whisper our secrets. But you stopped me."

"So, this is my fault now?" The accusation struck like a physical blow. "Every death, every murder, all of it my responsibility because I tried to show mercy to one man?"

"Yes." The word landed hard and certain as a hammer blow. "Your choices led here. Your mercy destroyed us both."

They stared at each other in the flickering candlelight.

"Get out," Virginia whispered.

"What?"

"Leave." Louder now, steady despite the tremors running through her. "Get out of my room. Out of the convent. I don't want you here tonight."

For a long moment she thought he would refuse. But something in her expression must have penetrated his rage because his grip loosened and he stepped back.

"You can't dismiss me." Wonder, soft and dangerous. "After everything we've done together, you think you can simply send me away?"

"Tonight, I can." Virginia pulled what remained of her dignity around herself. "Go home. Think about what you've become. What we've both become. And ask yourself if this is worth the price we're paying for it."

He stared at her for a heartbeat longer. Then he turned and left without another word.

Virginia sank onto her bed, strength draining from her legs. She'd sent him away. Chosen something other than his presence, even for one night.

But the victory felt hollow.

Because he would return. Because despite her brave words, she was as trapped in this as he was. Trapped by choices already made, by sins already committed, by blood already spilled.

And because somewhere in Monza, Rainerio Roncino was barricading his door and wondering if he would live to see morning.

* * *

THREE DAYS AFTER the assassination attempt, Rainerio stood outside the convent's parlatory, his palms slick with sweat despite the January cold. The servant who'd answered his knock had gone to fetch Sister Virginia, leaving him alone to contemplate exactly how much of his soul he was about to sell for the privilege of staying alive.

He'd spent three days weighing his options with the precision of a man measuring poison. Flee, abandoning everything he'd built over thirty years. Report everything to Captain Niguarda and pray the authorities could protect him. Do nothing and hope whoever had fired those shots would be satisfied with a warning.

Each path led to disaster in its own way.

So, he'd chosen the only option that offered any fragment of hope: bend the knee, show submission, become what they wanted him to be.

The door opened. Sister Virginia entered, her face composed but her eyes carrying wary exhaustion. She took her seat, folding her skirts with deceptive calm.

"Signor Roncino." Cool. Distant as Milan. "I was surprised to receive your request for an audience."

Rainerio bowed, deeper than necessary. "Sister Virginia. Thank you for seeing me."

"You came," Virginia interrupted, cutting through his prepared speech, "because someone tried to kill you three nights ago. And now you're frightened enough to make peace. Let's not pretend this is about conscience or remorse."

The accuracy stung. "You're right. I came because I'm terrified. Because I want to live."

"At least you're honest about your cowardice." She leaned back. "Tell me how it started. How much you told Ferrari before he died."

"He came to me months ago." Rainerio forced himself to meet her eyes. "He was troubled by something he'd seen. Wouldn't say what exactly. He asked if I'd heard anything unusual."

"And?"

"I didn't tell him anything specific. But I'd seen things too—Signore Osio at odd hours, the baby everyone whispers about, the herbs you've been ordering from me for years." He swallowed hard. "I didn't confirm his suspicions directly. But my silence confirmed enough."

"So, you told him he was right to be suspicious."

"I just didn't deny it. I thought maybe if people talked openly, if the scandal became public, someone with authority would intervene." He paused. "Instead, Ferrari ended up dead."

Virginia's laugh was bitter. "And you learned that talking doesn't stop anything. Just gets you killed."

"Yes." His fingertips brushed where scabs had formed on his cheek. "Three nights ago proved that conclusively."

"What exactly are you proposing?"

"Complete silence." Hoarse. Raw. "I'll stop answering questions about the convent. Stop nodding knowingly when people speculate. Stop doing anything that could confirm rumors or encourage gossip." He leaned forward. "I'll serve the convent as I always have, providing herbs when requested, asking no questions. And in return, I ask only that I be allowed to live. To continue my work. To raise my children without fear."

Virginia studied him through the iron lattice, her expression unreadable. "You've shown yourself unworthy of trust. Why should I believe your promises now?"

"Because I'm terrified." The admission, raw and unguarded, scraped his throat. "Because I have a wife who depends on me, children who need me. Because I've seen what happens to people who cross Signore Osio and I don't want to die bleeding in the street. I'm not a brave man, Sister Virginia. I'm not a hero. I'm just an apothecary who made terrible mistakes and wants desperately to survive them."

The honesty seemed to penetrate her reserve. Virginia's posture shifted, the rigid lines softening.

"If I agree to this, if I speak to Signore Osio on your behalf and try to convince him that you pose no further threat, you understand what you're accepting?"

"I think so."

"No." Steel returned to her bearing. "You need to understand it completely. You'll be complicit. Not just in keeping silent about what you've seen, but in actively participating in the deception. Providing herbs when requested without question. Looking the other way. Becoming part of the machinery that keeps this secret buried." She leaned closer to the lattice. "You'll be as guilty as any of us. Do you understand that?"

The weight settled over him like chains. "I understand. And I'm already complicit, aren't I? Have been for years. The only difference is now I'm acknowledging it openly instead of pretending I'm somehow separate from all of this."

Virginia nodded slowly. "Then we have an understanding. I'll speak to him. I'll try to convince him that killing you would only draw more attention. But Signor Roncino?" She dropped lower, nearly a whisper. "If you betray this agreement, if I hear even a breath of gossip that you've been talking, there won't be a warning next time. Do you understand?"

"Perfectly." Barely audible.

"Good." Virginia rose with fluid grace. "Continue serving the convent as you have been. Forget everything you've seen and heard. And pray that your discretion is sufficient to keep you alive."

She left without another word. Rainerio sat alone in the parlatory. Had he just saved his life or purchased a brief delay of his inevitable execution?

Either way, the cage door had closed around him. He was trapped now, kept alive only as long as he remained useful and silent and completely, utterly compliant.

He picked up his bag and left the parlatory. He stepped out into the January afternoon. The sun was setting early, painting the sky in shades of amber and rust and deep purple. Beautiful, he thought. The world could be so beautiful even while humans tore each other apart within it.

When he finally reached his door, Elisabetta looked up from her mending with eyes that asked questions her mouth didn't dare voice.

"I made peace," Rainerio said, setting his bag down with trembling fingers. "It's done."

She set down her needle. "At what cost?"

Rainerio crossed to the window. "Everything. I gave them everything they wanted. My silence. My complicity. My soul, probably, if such things can be bartered."

Elisabetta didn't ask for details. Instead, she crossed the room and took his hand in hers, her fingers warm against his cold skin.

They stood together in the fading light, two people who'd built a life through honest work, now trapped in circumstances neither had chosen.

"We'll survive this." Elisabetta's words held no conviction, just desperate hope wearing the mask of certainty.

Rainerio said nothing. Because he'd seen Ferrari's body, had heard about Molteno and Caterina, had felt harquebus balls hiss past his head. Survival wasn't guaranteed in a world where nobles killed with impunity and apothecaries bent their knees and begged for mercy.

It was the best they could hope for. The only card left to play.

* * *

Late January

THE WINTER SUN was setting behind Monza's rooftops when Captain Lorenzo Niguarda of the Spanish Territorial Guard stood in the town's small central square, listening to a delegation of citizens who'd gathered with the kind of nervous courage that came from collective outrage temporarily overcoming individual fear.

"Three times now in as many months," old Giovanni was saying, his weathered hands gesturing. "First Molteno murdered on the road outside town. Then Ferrari stabbed to death in his own shop. And now shots fired at Rainerio in the street."

"In the evening," someone corrected from the back. "Just after dark fell. My wife heard the shots from our kitchen."

"The point stands." Giovanni's tone rose with frustration. "We're not safe anymore. Not in our streets. Not in our homes. Not anywhere in this town as long as that man walks free."

Niguarda held up one hand, forestalling further commentary. He was a career soldier, forty years old, bearing scars from campaigns that had taught him more about human nature than he'd ever wanted to know.

"You're speaking of Gian Paolo Osio," Niguarda said, deliberately using the name everyone was dancing around. Forcing them to confront what they were implying.

The crowd shifted uncomfortably at the sound of the name spoken aloud. Several people looked away, suddenly fascinated by the cobblestones. The courage of collective complaint evaporated when forced to transform into specific accusation.

"We're not saying—" someone began.

"You are saying exactly that," Niguarda interrupted. "You're saying that a nobleman has been terrorizing this town through murder and attempted murder. You're saying he acts with complete impunity while honest citizens fear for their lives. And you're asking me what I intend to do about it." He paused. "Am I correct?"

Giovanni straightened his spine, meeting Niguarda's eyes directly. "Yes. That's exactly what we're saying. Someone needs to say it plainly instead of whispering it in corners."

Niguarda respected that. "I'll need evidence. Witnesses willing to testify before a magistrate. Something more substantial than rumor and suspicion, no matter how well-founded."

"Everyone knows," someone said.

"Everyone knowing isn't evidence," Niguarda cut across the protest with authority. "It's not enough for me to believe something is true. I need witnesses who will put their names on official documents and stand in a courtroom and point at Gian Paolo Osio and say 'I saw him do this thing'. I need physical proof that connects him directly to these crimes. Without that, my hands are tied."

The crowd exchanged glances, uncomfortable looks passing between neighbors. Because testimony meant risk. Meant putting their names on permanent records. Meant standing up in front of a man who'd already demonstrated his willingness to kill.

"That's what I thought," Niguarda said quietly. "You want justice. You deserve justice. But you want it without personal risk. Without individual sacrifice." He shook his head slowly. "I'm sorry, but justice doesn't work that way. Someone has to be willing to speak."

"Ferrari spoke," Matteo said bitterly. "He opened his mouth in a tavern and looked what it got him. A knife in the gut and his family left to starve."

"Yes." Niguarda's jaw tightened. "Which is precisely why I need to act before anyone else dies. But I can't act on gossip alone. Help me. Give me something I can use. Names of witnesses who saw something specific. Physical evidence. Without that, my hands are tied."

The crowd began to disperse. Some people left immediately. Others lingered longer before drifting away in twos and threes. Within minutes, Niguarda stood alone in the square with only old Giovanni still present.

"They're afraid," Giovanni said unnecessarily.

"They have reason to be afraid." Niguarda watched the last stragglers disappear. "Fear is often wiser than courage when it comes to staying alive."

"Then what happens now? We just wait for the next murder?"

"Now I write to Count Fuentes and report what's happening here. I request authorization to begin a formal investigation into Osio's activities." Niguarda turned to look at the older man. "But that takes time. Letters travel slowly. The Count will need to review the situation, consult with advisors, weigh the political implications. And during all of that, Osio remains free."

"So, we're helpless."

“Not helpless. Just constrained by law and procedure.” Niguarda clapped a hand on Giovanni’s shoulder. “Go home. Bar your door. Keep yourself and your family safe. And if you see or hear anything that could serve as evidence, send word to me immediately.”

* * *

NIGUARDA REACHED HIS office and lit the candles on his writing table. From a locked drawer he withdrew parchment and ink. Words on paper traveled farther than any blade could reach.

He began to write:

> *Your Excellency, Count Fuentes.*
>
> *I write to you concerning a matter of escalating urgency in the town of Monza that can no longer be ignored. Four serious incidents have occurred that bear the marks of coordination rather than random criminal activity:*
>
> *First, many years ago, Giacomo Molteno, a man of business for the de Leyva family of good reputation, was murdered on the road outside town. His death was initially attributed to bandits, but subsequent investigation revealed no robbery took place.*
>
> *Second, Sister Caterina de Meda, vanished from the convent of Santa Margherita in July 1606.*
>
> *Third, Cesare Ferrari, a blacksmith whose shop was located near the convent of Santa Margherita, was stabbed to death in his place of business in early December. Again, nothing was stolen.*
>
> *Fourth, and most alarming, three nights past shots were fired at Rainerio Roncino, an apothecary of this town, in what appears to be a clear assassination attempt. The weapon used was a harquebus fired in a public street during evening hours.*

The town's citizens are frightened, Excellency. They believe, though fear prevents them from testifying formally, that all three incidents stem from the same source: Gian Paolo Osio, nephew of the late Count Osio. The escalating brazenness of these acts suggests the perpetrator feels himself beyond the reach of justice.

I am a soldier, not a politician. I understand the delicacy required when moving against men of noble blood. But I must report honestly that without intervention from higher authorities, I believe additional violence is inevitable.

I request formal authorization to begin investigation into Gian Paolo Osio's activities and associations. I need the authority that comes from your office to compel testimony from witnesses who currently fear retribution too greatly to speak. Without such authorization, I am powerless to act.

Your servant in the service of His Majesty and Spanish justice,
Captain Lorenzo Niguarda

He sealed the letter with wax and his official stamp, then locked it in his writing table until he could have it messengered first thing in the morning. In three days, perhaps four, Count Fuentes would receive it in Milan. In a week, if fortune favored him, authorization might come.

By then, how many more would be dead?

Niguarda extinguished the candles and sat in his office surrounded by the trappings of Spanish authority—the king's standard, the official seals, the ledgers recording justice dispensed. All of it meaningless if he couldn't protect a frightened apothecary from a nobleman with blood on his hands.

Ferrari's widow with four children and another on the way. Rainerio barricading his door each night. An entire town living in fear because one man had decided he was above the law.

And Captain Lorenzo Niguarda, twenty-year veteran of the king's service, sat alone with the taste of ash in his mouth—impotence, powerlessness, the bitter residue of justice deferred.

He went home to his own quarters and barred his door and prayed that his letter would arrive in time to matter. But he'd been a soldier long enough to know that prayers and hopes were poor substitutes for action, and by the time authorization came from Milan, the situation in Monza might have deteriorated beyond any peaceful resolution.

In the darkness of his room, he checked his pistols and sword one more time before sleeping. Just in case the wolves came for him next.

* * *

THE BLACKSMITH'S WIDOW clutched her shawl tighter, her knuckles white against the dark wool. Her eyes darted to the door of Niguarda's office, once, twice, three times in sixty heartbeats.

"You understand, Signora Ferrari, that I require only the truth." Gentle—the tone he used with frightened witnesses. "Nothing more, nothing less."

"I've told you, Captain." Quick and breathless. "My husband worked for many men. The keys—he made keys for half of Monza."

"Including keys for the Convent of Santa Margherita."

Her throat worked. Her lips pressed white.

Niguarda leaned forward, resting his forearms on the scarred wood of his writing table. Morning sun slanted through the narrow window, catching dust motes that drifted between them like ash. "Your husband is dead, Signora. Murdered. You owe him justice."

"Justice." Bitter as wormwood. "What justice is there when the murderer walks free? When everyone knows his name, but no one dares speak it?"

"Then speak it now. Here, where only I can hear."

She looked at him fully for the first time. Fear lived in those reddened eyes, but something else flickered beneath it—rage, perhaps, or exhausted recognition that silence had bought her nothing. "Gian Paolo Osio killed my husband. Everyone in Monza knows it. And everyone in Monza is too terrified to say so."

Niguarda dipped his quill and began to write. The scratch of pen on parchment filled the small room. "Tell me everything."

* * *

THREE HOURS LATER, Niguarda sat alone in his office, his shoulders stiff from transcribing testimony. Winter light had shifted, stretching shadows across the documents spread before him like accusations. Outside, church bells marked Nones. Inside, only the occasional crack of settling timber broke the silence.

He read through his notes one final time:

Sister Caterina de Meda—vanished from convent, July 1606. Body never found.

Blacksmith Cesare Ferrari—murdered after speaking publicly about Caterina's fate, December 1606.

Apothecary Rainerio Roncino—shot in ambush, January 1607. Survived. Refuses to name his attacker.

Niguarda set down the last page and pressed his fingertips to his temples. The pattern was unmistakable. Two deaths and one attempted murder, all connected to one man, all serving to silence witnesses who knew too much about affairs at Santa Margherita.

But pattern was not proof. Not the kind that would hold before a magistrate when the accused bore a name like Osio.

He gathered the documents, tied them with cord, and reached for his cloak. Count Fuentes needed to see this. What the Governor chose to do with it was a different matter entirely.

* * *

THREE DAYS IN the saddle gave Niguarda too much time to rehearse arguments he knew would fail.

The Palazzo Reale in Milan rose against the February sky like a monument to Spanish power, all severe lines and martial elegance. Niguarda dismounted in the courtyard, his boots crunching on gravel still frozen from the previous night's cold.

A servant led him through corridors where tapestries muffled sound and made the air close. They climbed a marble staircase ascended by generations of petitioners seeking favor or justice or the careful line between the two.

Count Don Pedro Enríquez de Acevedo, Count of Fuentes, received him in a private study. Afternoon light filtered through tall windows, illuminating a room that spoke of power wielded with precision—maps on the walls, correspondence stacked in careful piles, a chess board positioned mid-game near the fire.

Fuentes did not rise. He sat behind an ornate writing table of carved walnut, his doublet midnight blue with silver fastenings that caught the light when he moved. Fifty years old, his beard trimmed close and going gray at the edges. His eyes, dark and shrewd beneath heavy lids, tracked Niguarda with the attention of a man who missed nothing.

"Captain." He gestured to a chair. "You've ridden from Monza with news that couldn't wait for regular dispatches. This concerns the Osio matter you recently wrote to me about?"

"It does, Your Excellency." Niguarda placed the bundle of documents on the writing table. The cord made a soft sound against polished wood. "I've compiled evidence regarding Gian Paolo Osio's recent activities."

Fuentes made no move to open the bundle. Instead, he leaned back in his chair, fingers steepled beneath his chin. "Recent activities. An artful phrase, Captain. What you mean is murders."

"Two deaths and one attempted murder in seven months, Excellency. And another many years ago. All connected to Osio. All serving to silence witnesses regarding his affair with Sister Virginia de Leyva."

"Ah." Amusement flickered in Fuentes' expression. "The nun. The de Leyva girl who was supposed to bring honor to her family by taking the veil and instead brings scandal by taking a lover."

Niguarda's jaw clenched, but he kept his words level. "The affair itself is a matter for Church authorities. The murders are not."

"And yet the two cannot be separated, can they?" Fuentes picked up the bundle, weighing it in his palm without opening it. "To prosecute Osio for silencing witnesses, we must acknowledge what those witnesses knew. Which means dragging the de Leyva name through public trial. Which means," he set the bundle down again, "complicating my relationship with Count Don Martino de Leyva, the Prince of Ascoli, who serves as secret counselor to His Majesty in Madrid."

"With respect, Excellency, two people are dead, and another barely escaped."

"Three people who had the misfortune to know dangerous secrets about dangerous people." Fuentes rose and moved to the window. He stood with his back to the room, looking out over the city. "Tell me, Captain. What do you imagine happens if I arrest Gian Paolo Osio?"

Niguarda hesitated. "Justice, Excellency."

"Justice." Fuentes turned. The light from the window cast his face half in shadow. "We would need a public trial. Testimony from the nuns of Santa Margherita. Evidence of the affair laid bare for every gossip in Milan to feast upon. The de Leyva family humiliated. Cardinal Borromeo forced to discipline his convent or explain why he didn't. And Osio's noble friends, of whom he has many, united in outrage that one of their own faces Spanish justice for the death of commoners."

"Innocent people."

"Were they innocent?" Sharp as a blade. "The blacksmith made duplicate keys knowing they'd be used to violate enclosure. The apothecary sold abortifacients to nuns and gossiped about her secrets. They profited from Osio's sins, Captain. That doesn't justify killing them, but it complicates the narrative of pure victims and evil nobleman, doesn't it?"

Niguarda's jaw tightened. "What would you have me do, Excellency? Pretend I found nothing?"

Fuentes returned to his writing table. He sat, opened the bundle, and began reading through the documents with methodical attention. Minutes passed. The fire crackled. Somewhere in the palazzo, a door closed with an echoing thud.

Finally, Fuentes looked up. "Your work is thorough, Captain. These witness statements are detailed. The timeline is damning." He tapped the papers with one finger. "But it's all circumstantial. Nothing that would compel conviction before a magistrate who knows Osio's connections."

"Then we gather more evidence."

"To what end?" Fuentes dropped to the register of someone explaining unpleasant truth to a child. "You cannot arrest Gian Paolo Osio. Not yet. Not without proof so overwhelming that even his allies cannot ignore it. And gathering such proof takes time."

"While he walks free. While he kills again if anyone else threatens to expose him."

"Yes." Fuentes met his gaze without flinching. "That is precisely what I'm saying. We move with subtlety, Captain. We watch. We wait. And when Osio makes a mistake, and he will, men like him always do, we strike with force sufficient to end this cleanly."

Niguarda stared at the Governor. Subtlety sat wrong in his mouth, tasting of compromise and expedience and the kind of calculation that sacrificed immediate justice for long-term strategy. "Your Excellency."

"Return to Monza." Command, clear and absolute. "Watch Osio closely but discreetly. Note where he goes, who he sees, what he does. Report to me weekly. Give me no cause to suspect you're moving openly against him."

"And if he kills someone else while I'm watching discreetly?"

The silence stretched. Fuentes' fingers stilled on the documents. Outside, a guard's boots echoed in the corridor, then faded.

"Then you will document that death as thoroughly as you've documented the others," Fuentes said finally. "And you will add it to the evidence we're building. Sometimes justice requires patience, Captain. Even when patience costs lives."

Niguarda stood. The chair scraped against marble. He gathered the documents Fuentes had finished reading, retying them with cord that felt heavier than before. "By your leave, Excellency."

"Captain." Fuentes stopped him at the door. "I understand your frustration. Truly. But understand this in return, I am not protecting Osio. I'm maneuvering around obstacles you cannot see. The de Leyva family's influence. The Cardinal's authority over his convents. The delicate balance between Spanish civil law and Church jurisdiction. Move too quickly, and we lose everything. Move with care, and we may yet achieve justice without igniting a scandal that destroys more lives than it saves."

Niguarda looked back. Fuentes sat outlined against the window, expression shadowed and unreadable. A man infatuated with his own power, some said. But something else was there, the exhausted pragmatism of someone who'd learned that governing required choosing between bad options and worse ones.

"Weekly reports," Niguarda said. "Discreet observation. Nothing that alerts Osio we're watching."

"Precisely."

* * *

GIAN PAOLO OSIO moved through Monza as though murder left no mark on him. He visited the convent under cover of darkness. Niguarda's men reported the garden gate opening at midnight, closing again before dawn. He rode to Milan twice, staying three days each time at his family's palazzo. He attended to his lands and business dealings with the casual confidence of a man who feared no consequences.

And Captain Niguarda watched. Documented. Reported to Count Fuentes with mounting frustration as the weeks accumulated and nothing changed.

The trap was being built, stone by patient stone. But in Monza's churchyard, the blacksmith and his secrets lay beneath frozen ground, and justice looked very much like abandonment.

* * *

The 27th of February

PAVIA WRAPPED ITS trade in celebration. Outside the city walls, along the broad field that served as both fairground and muster ground, stalls had been raised in uneven lines. Vendors shouted over one another, hawking blades and pistols, breastplates and helmets, powder and shot. The annual arms fair drew not only merchants and officers but half the surrounding countryside, and this year it coincided conveniently with carnival.

Masks mingled with morions. A jester's bells jangled beside the clink of steel. Wine flowed as freely as boasts, and the cold river wind carried the scents of oiled metal, roasting meat, and trampled earth.

Gian Paolo Osio walked through it as though born to its center.

He wore a black velvet domino that fell straight over his shoulders, his upper face covered by a half-mask worked in dark leather. Simple by carnival standards, but he moved with such easy self-possession that men stepped aside without knowing why. Women's glances followed him longer than politeness required.

Four months of scrutiny had not taught him to bow his head. Monza's gossips had sharpened their tongues. Captain Niguarda's men had shadowed his comings and goings. Governor Fuentes had glowered in Milan. Yet here he was, inspecting daggers and muskets like any other gentleman with coin to spend.

At one stall, he picked up a pistol, testing the weight in his palm. The gunsmith, face reddened by the brazier's heat, leaned forward with the greedy respect reserved for customers who clearly did not haggle.

"Spanish make," the man said. "Accurate at forty paces, if your hand is steady."

"My hand is always steady," Osio replied, sighting along the barrel. "The question is whether the steel deserves it."

The gunsmith laughed too loudly. "For you, Signore, it will."

Osio smiled beneath the mask. Men always promised perfection when they smelled profit.

He set the pistol down. Today, he had come less for commerce than for the pleasure of moving in a crowd where no one was supposed to see clearly. Carnival meant license. The arms fair meant distraction. Together, they offered a kind of freedom even a wary man found hard to resist.

If Fuentes truly intended to act, surely he would have done so already. Governors did not hesitate once they chose a course.

Osio had long experience with what men said and what they did.

* * *

ON A LOW rise at the edge of the field, Captain Niguarda stood beneath the brim of his plain felt hat, studying the fair below.

He was dressed without insignia, a dark cloak, sword ordinary enough not to draw attention. Two soldiers he trusted stood a little behind and to either side, likewise unmarked. From a distance, they might have been minor landowners come to haggle over muskets.

The sealed warrant lay in the inner pocket of Niguarda's doublet, its presence as tangible as cold metal.

Take Gian Paolo Osio into custody for reasons of State. Confine him in the Castle of Pavia until further notice. Signed with Count Fuentes' precise, uncompromising hand.

No mention of Ferrari bleeding out on a Monza street, or a lay sister who had vanished, or the apothecary who still limped and flinched at sudden noises. Only those three words—*reasons of State*—that wrapped scandal and necessity in a veil no court need pierce.

This moment had been inevitable. Still, Osio strolled between stalls as if the world existed for his amusement. Niguarda's jaw tightened.

"Third line of tents," one of his men murmured. "By the gunsmith with the blue awning."

"I see him."

Even masked, Osio was unmistakable. The confident pace, the straight back, the way people created space for him without being asked.

For months, that figure had moved through Monza while Niguarda took testimony from widows and shopkeepers, heard whispered names. Fear was there in the way people wrapped their shawls tighter when they spoke. Now the warrant in his pocket turned all that testimony into action.

He drew a slow breath. "We go down. No swords unless he draws. No spectacle."

"Among this many armed men?" the other soldier said. "If he chooses to fight..."

"He won't," Niguarda said. "He loves his own skin too well."

They descended from the rise, threading into the shifting lanes between stalls. A juggler in a harlequin mask nearly collided with them, muttered an apology, danced away. Somewhere, a piper struck up a tune wildly at odds with the sober business of buying weapons.

Niguarda's fingers brushed the warrant once more through the cloth, as if to remind himself this was not some private vendetta. The King's paper. The Governor's command. His duty.

* * *

OSIO WAS ADMIRING a Spanish rapier when the space around him changed.

It was subtle, the way conversation thinned, the way men who had been angling for the gunsmith's attention found urgent reason to step aside. But he'd spent a lifetime reading rooms where what was not said mattered more than what was.

He set the weapon down and turned.

"Signor Osio." Captain Niguarda stood three paces away, barefaced amid the masks, flanked by two men whose grips hovered near their hilts but had not yet closed.

Osio's mouth curved. "Captain. I thought Pavia's garrison had better ways to pass a carnival day than browsing among merchants."

"I'm not here to browse." Niguarda's gaze flicked briefly to the mask. "Remove your mask, if you please."

"Is it illegal now to hide an honest face in a dishonest world?" Osio's tone was light, but his mind had already leapt ahead. Pavia, not Monza. Niguarda here, not some local underling. Too many witnesses for a quiet quarrel, too much noise for words to carry far.

"By order of His Excellency," Niguarda said, low enough that it did not carry beyond their small circle, "I require you to uncover yourself."

There was a moment when Osio considered refusing, to see how far the captain would go. But defiance for its own sake had never appealed to him.

He removed the mask with a small bow, as though obeying a request from a hostess rather than a command backed by the Spanish crown.

"Better?" he asked.

Murmurs rippled outward as those nearest saw his face clearly. A merchant's wife's hand flew to her mouth. A young officer glanced quickly away, as though worried to be caught looking too long at a man about to fall.

Niguarda's expression did not change. "Gian Paolo Osio, by order of the Count of Fuentes, Governor of Milan, you are under arrest for reasons of State."

The words fell heavy despite their careful gentleness. A drummer somewhere skipped a beat. Then, with the heedless cruelty of crowds, the fair swallowed the moment, noise swelling to cover the slight hush.

Osio laughed once, softly. "Reasons of State. How those words do labor when men are ashamed to name what they fear."

"This is not a debate," Niguarda said. "Surrender your sword."

"And here I thought you might be inviting me to examine your purchases." Osio unbuckled his sword-belt with unhurried movements. "Very well, Captain.

Take good care of this one. It's served more honorable fields than this fairground."

He held it out hilt-first. Niguarda accepted it and passed it back without comment.

Fingers closed around Osio's arms, firm and impersonal, like the grip of the State itself. The circle around them widened a fraction.

Osio raised his voice just enough that those nearest could hear. "Remember, friends, if they can take a man like this, with no crime named aloud, imagine how easily they can come for you."

"Enough," Niguarda said, but he did not look around to see who had heard.

They led Osio away from the stalls toward the road that climbed gently to Pavia's walls. No one tried to intervene. A few men bowed slightly as he passed, whether in respect or relief that it was not their turn, he could not say.

* * *

THE CASTLE OF Pavia rose above the town like a lesson in permanence. Its broad brick bulk dominated the end of the avenue, battlements and towers etched against a washed-out morning sky. Once, princes had built it for hunting and feasting. Under Spanish rule, it had become something sterner: barracks, arsenal, prison.

They crossed the bridge over the moat, hooves ringing on planks still slick with frost. Within the outer gate, the noise of the fair dropped away as if someone had closed a door on the world.

A lieutenant in Spanish colors stepped forward, saluting Niguarda. "Captain. We were told by courier to expect a special prisoner."

"You've been told correctly." Niguarda swung down from his horse. "By the Governor's command, this man is to be held here under strict confinement. No visitors without written authorization bearing His Excellency's own hand. No letters in or out without being read and countersigned."

The lieutenant's gaze went to Osio and sharpened. Recognition flickered, followed by the quick, careful blankness of a man who understood both gossip and survival. "Name?"

"Gian Paolo Osio," Niguarda said.

The lieutenant's brows rose despite himself. "Ah. Then the rumors from Monza did not lie."

Osio inclined his head slightly. "Rumors seldom lie, Lieutenant. They merely choose their truths."

"Take him," the lieutenant said, ignoring the remark. "Use the inner cells."

Stone swallowed them: archways, narrow corridors, air that smelled of damp, old smoke, and the flattening weight of thick walls. Light came thinly through high slits, turning dust into slow, drifting ghosts.

At a heavy, iron-banded door, they stopped. A guard produced a key the length of a man's hand, turned it in a lock that grated protest.

Inside, the cell was smaller than Osio's dressing room in Monza. A pallet of straw, a bucket, a low stool, a slit of a window that admitted more cold than daylight.

The guard cut the rope binding his wrists. Osio flexed his fingers, feeling life sting back into them in sharp, needling bursts.

"Signor Osio," the lieutenant said, almost formally, "until His Excellency orders otherwise, this is where you'll remain."

"Reasons of State," Osio said, as if testing the phrase on his tongue. "Tell the Count I admire his delicacy. Not every man can bury an enemy and praise himself for prudence."

"If the Governor wishes you to have his thoughts, Captain Niguarda will bring them," the lieutenant replied. "We provide walls. What you think inside them is your affair."

The door closed. The key turned. The sound of the lock sliding home echoed once, then settled into the stone.

Osio sat on the pallet and looked around.

Four walls. One door. One window, high enough that even at full stretch he could not see more than a strip of pale sky and the corner of a roof. No hidden passages, no conveniently crumbling mortar, no obvious weakness.

But doors had hinges, hinges had pins, pins had men who oiled them. Walls had guards, guards had debts and vices. The world did not become less human because it had narrowed.

Outside, faint through layers of brick, a bell rang the hour. In the fields beyond the walls, the arms fair would be resuming its noisy commerce. Somewhere in Monza, Virginia would be hearing that he was finally caged.

Gian Paolo Osio leaned back against the chill stone and smiled into the dimness.

Let Fuentes have his triumph. Let the pious whisper that justice had at last caught up with him. A cell was only a move, not a mate.

The game, he knew as surely as he knew his own name, was not finished.

* * *

May

THE CELL AT Pavia Castle had grown smaller with spring. Warmth outside made the chill inside more offensive. Each day, sunlight traced a bright square high on the opposite wall for one hour, just long enough to remind Gian Paolo Osio what he was missing, before sliding away and leaving the stones to their damp gloom.

He lay on the pallet, hands folded behind his head, listening to the muffled sounds of the fortress waking—boots on distant stairs, a door banging somewhere in the barracks, the faint clatter of pots from the kitchen. Life went on, layer upon layer above his head, while he was expected to molder quietly out of sight.

Four months in Pavia had taught him two lessons. First, that the Spanish crown knew how to make a man disappear without the inconvenience of a trial. Second, that no wall was perfect if you could find the right crack in the mortar.

The crack, in this case, wore a professor's black robe.

When the key turned in his lock mid-morning and the guard announced a visitor, Osio swung his legs over the side of the pallet with practiced slowness, as if any movement cost him.

Doctor Pietro Paolo Orlando entered with the self-importance of a man used to lecturing youths who could not answer back. The professor's beard was neatly trimmed, his hair more gray than black. Ink stains marked the fingers that tightened on the medical bag he carried.

"Signor Osio." His gaze swept the cell, taking in straw, bucket, stool, barred window, then returned to its occupant. "I was told you required a physician."

"And one of Pavia's most esteemed comes himself." Osio inclined his head. "I am honored, Doctor."

The guard hovered in the doorway. Osio let his shoulders sag a fraction, drawing attention to the sharpness of his cheekbones, the shadows beneath his eyes.

"If we are to discuss my health," he said, "it might be more useful without an audience."

The guard hesitated, then shrugged. "Call if you need anything, Dottore." He pulled the door mostly closed, leaving it a hand's breadth ajar.

Orlando did not move closer at once. His gaze moved over Osio, cool, evaluating, taking in both body and opportunity. "You understand that I am here as a physician, not an advocate. My reputation rests on my judgment."

"So does my immediate future," Osio replied. "Which is why I chose you. Your opinion carries weight in Milan."

"Opinions must be grounded in observation."

"Of course." Osio smiled faintly. "And observation, as we both know, is never entirely free of interpretation."

Neither spoke. The unspoken matters of fee and risk hung in the air between them.

Osio broke it first. "I am prepared to show my appreciation for your time. Two hundred *scudi*. Half now, half upon delivery of a written statement describing the effects of confinement on my health."

"Two hundred." Orlando weighed the figure, and the man who offered it. "You are generous for someone who claims to be dying."

"I am generous because I have no intention of doing so here." Osio gestured at the walls. "This place is an insult, not a sentence. A word from you, properly phrased, might persuade His Excellency that further rigor is unnecessary."

"And if my word does not persuade him?"

"Then at least I will have tried every door." Osio spread his palms. "Better that than lie on this pallet waiting to see whether he remembers I exist."

Orlando's shoulders relaxed by a degree. He set down his bag, opened it with careful deliberation. "Very well. Let us begin with your pulse."

The examination was thorough enough to pass muster, cursory enough not to delay the business at hand. Orlando counted heartbeats, listened to Osio's chest, pressed fingers against ribs and abdomen. He asked about sleep, appetite, pains.

Osio answered with artless candor, painting a picture of declining strength: restless nights, poor food, air that never quite warmed. He did not need to feign the irritability or the ache in his spine from too many hours on too thin a mattress.

Orlando frowned at appropriate moments. He made notes in a small leather-bound book.

When he finished, he stepped back and clasped his fingers. "Your condition has indeed suffered from confinement. You are thinner than when I last saw you in society. Your pulse is irregular. The air here..." He glanced at the window slit, the sweating walls. "It does not favor recovery."

"Then you can say as much?"

"I can say," Orlando replied, voice taking on the measured cadence of a man composing his own testimony, "that Gian Paolo Osio is affected by a serious and dangerous weakening illness, and that in consequence he is in evident danger of his life if these conditions persist. That he urgently needs to be released from the rigors of this prison, for otherwise, without proper care, I fear his imminent death, given his present state of extreme debility."

The words hung in the air for a moment, tasting their own weight.

"Put that on parchment," Osio said, "add today's date and your seal, and we may yet convince the Governor he would rather have me someplace more comfortable."

Orlando closed his book. "I will draft the statement this afternoon. It will be ready for your signature tomorrow."

Osio reached beneath the pallet, where a loose stone in the floor hid the small purse he had managed to keep through transfer and searches.

He offered it to Orlando. The weight of coin made the leather sag.

"One hundred now," Osio said. "The rest when I see the document."

Orlando did not open the purse. He tucked it into his sleeve with practiced discretion. "Tomorrow, then."

When the door closed behind him, the cell was no larger. But the air seemed marginally less stale.

Walls could not be bullied. Men could. And men, not walls, decided how long he stayed here.

* * *

ORLANDO DELIVERED THE statement the next day, written in formal Latin and sealed with his academic insignia. Osio read it twice, lips moving slightly as he followed the phrases.

His body was there in the description, his strategy in the conclusion.

He signed where Orlando indicated. The castle's officer took the parchment with cautious respect, promising to forward it to Milan with the next courier.

It was not release. But it was leverage. And for a man like Gian Paolo Osio, leverage was the first step toward any door opening.

* * *

IN MONZA, THE May sun lay warm on the convent roof tiles, but the air inside Santa Margherita carried a new, uneasy chill.

Virginia sat in the small room she used for receiving those with business to discuss. Today, the visitor trembled on the threshold before he even crossed it.

"Domenico," she said. "Come in."

The convent's servant obeyed, cap clutched in both fists. Dirt streaked his sleeves. The lines around his eyes looked deeper than she remembered, carved by years of labor and, more recently, by fear.

"You sent for me, Sister Virginia."

"I did." Her tone was mild, almost conversational. Only the tightness in her clasped fingers betrayed the anger coiled beneath. "I hear you've been talking in the town."

"I... I don't know what you mean."

"I think you do." She leaned closer, voice sharpening. "At the baker's. At the tavern near San Maurizio. In the market, when you think no one of consequence is listening. You speak of little Alma Francesca. Of who you claim her real mother is."

Red crept up his neck. "I only said what everyone else is saying."

"Everyone else is not a servant of Santa Margherita whose place depends on his discretion." The words came out colder than stone. "You forget yourself, Domenico."

He swallowed. "I never meant any harm to Your Ladyship."

"You mean me harm every time you let my name drip from your tongue in such company." Virginia's fingers tightened on the arm of her chair. "Do you think this convent exists to provide you with stories to trade for ale?"

"No, Sister."

"Do you think the de Leyva family's honor is a bauble you can toss about a tavern for the amusement of drunkards?" The memory of whispers, of sidelong glances in Monza's streets, tightened her chest. "Or that there is no cost when you fan the embers of scandal?"

Sweat stood out on his forehead. "I was angry," he muttered. "Sometimes. For how I've been treated. For what I've seen. The work, the risk..."

"Ah." Her voice went dangerously soft. "So, this is about wounded pride. You risk my ruin to soothe your vanity."

He flinched. "No."

"It doesn't matter why." She straightened. "Here is what will happen now. You will go back to your work. You will keep your mouth shut. You will speak of me and my household to no one. Not in the square, not in the taverns, not even in your own home. If I hear my name linked to yours again in any whisper, I will have you beaten publicly and thrown in jail for slander. And there is not a magistrate in this province who will choose your word over mine."

He stared at the floor, chest rising and falling too quickly.

"Do you understand me, Domenico?"

"Yes, Sister."

"Say it."

"I understand." His voice came out hoarse. "I'll say nothing more."

"For your sake, I suggest you remember that vow more faithfully than any other you have ever made."

She rang for the portress. When the door opened behind him, she did not look back as he was led away.

Only when she was alone again did she let herself exhale. Her fingers trembled once, then stilled.

Fear, she told herself, would hold him for a time. But fear faded. Resentment ripened in its place.

She could not afford another man in Monza growing bold on the strength of what he thought he knew.

* * *

THREE DAYS LATER, Domenico was kneeling in the convent garden, turning the soil between rows of herbs, when the shadow of two men fell across his work.

He looked up.

The one on the left he recognized: a narrow face he'd seen at Gian Paolo Osio's house more than once, loitering in the courtyard with the casual watchfulness of a man used to waiting until his master needed something done quietly. The other was broader, his expression as blank as a butcher's block.

"Domenico Ferrari?" the narrow-faced man asked, though he already knew.

"Yes."

"We've a message for you."

He pushed himself up, wiping dirt on his trousers. "From who?"

The first blow drove the question back into his throat.

A fist slammed into his stomach, folding him. A second struck the side of his head, sending light flaring white behind his eyes. He reached for breath, for balance, found only air and the hard edge of the garden path as his knees hit it.

They did not speak after that. There was no need. Boots and fists delivered their own explanation.

Pain blossomed in his ribs, his back, his thigh. Each impact blurred into the next until time narrowed to the space between one blow and the one that followed. Somewhere, a bird shrieked and took off from a tree. The convent wall loomed to his right, solid and blind.

When they finally stepped back, Domenico lay curled on his side in the dirt, tasting blood and earth. Every breath was a knife.

The narrow-faced man crouched so that his words would reach him without needing to be shouted.

"That's for your tongue," he said. "Our master doesn't like it when servants forget who owns their secrets."

Domenico tried to speak. Only a wet sound came out.

"Next time," the man added, almost pleasantly, "he might send someone less careful."

They left him there. The other man laughed once, short and without amusement, as they slipped back through the side gate and into the lane beyond.

It was nearly an hour before one of the lay sisters found Domenico, drawn by the absence where his steady presence should have been.

By the time they managed to carry him inside, the story had already started its slow, inevitable spread beyond the convent walls.

That afternoon in Monza's market, a butcher's apprentice told a customer that Osio's men had nearly killed the convent's gardener and servant for running his mouth. By evening, a group of men at the tavern near San Maurizio were agreeing, with grave shakes of the head, that even locked away in Pavia, Gian Paolo Osio's reach was long.

Virginia heard of the beating before Compline. Sister Benedetta brought the news in a flat voice, her eyes searching Virginia's face for any sign of reaction.

Nothing came that she could easily name. Not triumph. Not pity. Only a grim, hollow steadiness.

She had warned Domenico. He had chosen not to believe her. Now the town had been reminded, brutally, that absence did not equal impotence.

* * *

FROM HIS CELL in Pavia, Gian Paolo could not see the gardener limping through the square days later, face mottled with yellowing bruises, conversations dying mid-sentence as he passed. He did not have to. The silence that followed Domenico was the true measure of his reach. Imprisoned or not, he, Gian Paolo Osio, remained dangerous as long as fear walked ahead of his name.

* * *

July

THE HEAT IN Pavia Castle did what the winter cold had not: it made the walls feel closer.

The air in Gian Paolo Osio's cell hung thick and unmoving, pressing against his skin like damp cloth. The square of light on the opposite wall had grown larger with the change of season, but it brought no relief, only the taunting reminder that summer ripened outside while he sat inside, caged and waiting.

Waiting had never suited him.

Four months of it had taught him patience, but not resignation. Fuentes's warrant had dropped on him like a trap, and the Governor's silence since had confirmed what Gian Paolo had always known: when power wanted a man gone, it preferred to do so without conversation.

If he wanted words, he would have to force them.

He had already played the physician's card. Orlando's declaration of grave illness, drafted and dispatched in May, had traveled up the chain of command toward Milan with all the proper seals. Nothing had come back down. No summons. No alteration of his conditions. No indication anyone in authority felt moved by the prospect of his imminent death.

So, he turned his thoughts higher. Not higher in rank, Fuentes held the temporal reins, but higher in reverence.

Cardinal Federico Borromeo.

Of all the men who might have a voice in his fate, the Cardinal knew least about his affairs. That ignorance was both danger and opportunity. The danger: rumors surely reaching the archbishop—whispers of murders, seduction, scandal within a convent that should have been a model of discipline. The opportunity: ignorance itself could be shaped.

Fuentes knew the worst of him and had chosen to bury him. The Cardinal might yet be persuaded to doubt.

Osio sat on the stool, elbows on the narrow writing shelf the castle had finally allowed him. The blank sheet lay before him. Ink and quill waited at his right. Beside them, Doctor Orlando's statement, folded but ready to be enclosed.

Piety alone would not move a prince of the Church. Men like Borromeo answered to God in public and to politics in private. If he wanted mercy, he needed to make mercy look like prudence.

He dipped the pen and began.

Most Illustrious and Reverend Lord and Most Honored Father...

The forms came easily. What mattered was not the courtesy but the story.

He reminded the Cardinal, first, his detention had been long and without clear cause.

Since my release is so long delayed without reason, and since I live with this desire to show my innocence and make myself known as Your Holiness' humble and devoted servant...

Innocence was a generous word for a man with blood on his conscience, but guilt in the world's eyes was not a simple ledger. He had enemies. Envy and malice had sharpened tongues against him. It cost nothing on paper to attribute his imprisonment to plots and slanders.

He laid that claim carefully at the feet of unnamed adversaries.

I wish to undeceive you and to ensure Your Holiness, will now know the truth about me, I having been deceived by those who plotted against me and slandered me to Your Holiness...

Not Fuentes. Not by name. He was not so foolish as to attack the Governor directly. But here and there, a suggestion others had moved rashly, information presented to Milan had been incomplete, a noble house had been sullied by calumny.

Where accusation could not serve him, gratitude might.

He sketched the debt his family owed to Saint Carlo Borromeo, the small ways he had continued that tradition. The wine he'd offered when Borromeo visited Monza two years past. Discreet assistance to young Count Giovanni Borromeo in certain delicate scrapes—that business when the youth had escorted Lady Margherita Taverna Visconta home from Loreto and found himself entangled in complications honor could not easily navigate.

Your Holiness will recall, perhaps, on more than one occasion I placed myself at the disposal of your noble nephew, Count Giovanni, when youthful ardor led him into difficulties. I did so happily, not for favor, but out of devotion to your name.

Family pride, wrapped in humility. Borromeo prided himself on continuing his cousin Saint Carlo's zeal; reminding him the Osios had once stood in that circle might soften his view.

He invoked his illness next, weaving Orlando's phrases into his own, then added a final touch to his portrait of piety: the Cappuccine Mothers of Santa Prasseda, who could testify to his devotion.

In closing, he returned to the posture of humble petitioner.

> *Trusting in God and in the blessed Carlo, I place myself wholly in Your Holiness' hands, confident you will work to have me released soon, that I may continue to serve you and all your house.*
> *From Pavia, the fourth of July, 1607.*
> *From Your Most Illustrious Holiness' most humble and devoted servant, Giovanni Paolo Osio.*

He sanded the signature, shook off the excess, and let the ink dry. Then he folded the sheets with care, placed Doctor Orlando's statement between them, and sealed the packet with what remained of his signet wax.

When the guard came to collect the afternoon correspondence, Osio handed the missive over with a look of grave hope.

"To His Most Illustrious Lordship Cardinal Federico Borromeo," he said. "See that it travels with the next pouch."

The guard nodded. "I'll give it to the lieutenant."

The door shut again. The heat pressed in as before. But now, somewhere on the road between Pavia and Milan, a new thread had entered the web.

He had moved a piece. Now he would see how the Cardinal answered.

* * *

IN THE ARCHBISHOP'S residence in Milan, the summer afternoon lay heavy on the city. Even the pigeons on the cathedral roof were subdued, their cooing a low mutter beneath the tolling bells.

Inside, in the cool half-light of his study, Cardinal Federico Borromeo sat at a large table strewn with petitions, reports, theological treatises, and correspondence from agents scattered across Europe.

A clerk entered quietly, carrying a new bundle tied with string.

"From Pavia, Your Illustrious Holiness," the man said, bowing as he laid the packet on the cleared corner of the writing table. "The castle's dispatches."

"Leave them."

When the door closed again, Borromeo finished the paragraph he had been annotating, then turned to the new arrivals.

Most of it was routine: notices about repairs, questions about chaplains, inventories. He set those aside for his secretary to answer.

One envelope, however, bore script neither bureaucrat's nor priest's. The seal, though smudged by handling, showed a device he knew only dimly.

He broke it and unfolded several closely written pages.

Most Illustrious and Reverend Lord and Most Honored Father...

The salutation alone told him what this was. Supplication had its own cadence.

He read on.

As he progressed through Gian Paolo Osio's appeal, his brows drew together. The man declared himself innocent. That was not unexpected; guilty men seldom wrote to confess. He blamed unnamed enemies for slanders, professed himself a humble servant of the Borromeo house, invoked Saint Carlo's name with reckless familiarity.

He spoke of a grave illness. Borromeo glanced at the attached sheet, recognized Pietro Paolo Orlando's careful Latin, the formal diagnosis: confinement endangered the patient's life.

He read references to past services, assistance to young Count Giovanni, a mention of Lady Margherita Taverna Visconta's journey from Loreto. That caught his attention more sharply. His nephew's more exuberant episodes had not always reached his ears, but enough had. Between the lines lay a hint of indiscretions quietly managed.

The further he went, the more unease stirred beneath his practiced pastoral calm.

For months now, vague reports had filtered to him of scandal in Monza. Conduct unbecoming a professed nun. Whispered names. The Governor's people had been close-fisted about their information, citing the need to avoid public disgrace. Borromeo had pressed, gently, for particulars and had been met with the kind of respectful stonewalling signaling Spanish reluctance to share control.

This petition, arriving from Pavia Castle rather than from any ecclesiastical channel, told him something he had not been fully apprised of.

Fuentes had moved from surveillance to action. A nobleman of his diocese was being held under reasons of State in a fortress, and the Archbishop had not been clearly informed.

That, more than Osio's pleas, pricked his pride.

He set the document down and steepled his fingers, eyes fixed on some middle distance beyond the page.

He was not inclined to take Osio's self-portrait at face value. Stories circulating in Milan painted a darker figure: seducer, murderer, corrupter of a convent. Yet he knew also Fuentes could be ruthless in the protection of Spanish interests, and not over-scrupulous about the niceties of ecclesiastical jurisdiction.

For one brief moment, the Cardinal's hand moved toward his pen—to write immediately, to assert his authority, to demand answers from the Governor.

Then prudence reasserted itself.

To intervene too quickly might put him at odds with secular authority without knowing exactly what he defended. To ignore the petition entirely risked appearing either callous or powerless if the matter later became public.

He needed time. Time to gather more precise information about the charges, about the state of the Monza convent, about the nature of Osio himself.

He reached for his pen, not to answer the appeal—that would require more thought—but to instruct.

At the top margin of the first page, in precise notation cutting across Gian Paolo's fervent script, he wrote for his secretary: *Petition from Giovanni Paolo*

Osio, held in Pavia, who begs to be helped and sends a doctor's certificate of his infirmity and speaks of his services to the Borromeo house. Reminder: give it to His Eminence in fifteen days' time.

Fifteen days to make inquiries. Fifteen days to speak, discreetly, with men who knew more of the Governor's actions. Fifteen days to decide whether mercy, in this case, would be justice or folly.

He sanded the brief note, shook the page gently, and handed the packet to his secretary when the man returned.

"Not now," Borromeo said. "In a fortnight. Remind me then."

"Yes, Your Illustrious Holiness."

The door closed. Outside, the bells began to ring the hour. In the streets below, people moved through the heat of another summer day, unaware a man in Pavia pinned his hopes on words that would, for the moment, be set deliberately aside.

* * *

WHEN WORD OF Virginia's scandal finally reached him in full, Cardinal Federico Borromeo felt the news like a blow that should have landed months earlier.

He sat in his Milan study while the Dean of Monza, hat in hand, recounted inquiries made, suspicions raised, testimonies half-won and then withdrawn. The shutters were half closed against the summer glare, casting the room in a tempered light that made the Dean's face look more lined, his gray hair thinner, than it had at their last meeting.

"You are telling me," Borromeo said at last, voice very quiet, "that for months a scandal has been brewing in a convent of my diocese. A noblewoman under solemn vows has given cause for grave suspicion. A man of notorious reputation has moved freely under those walls. Murders, or at least violent deaths, have followed, and I am only now being correctly informed, after the civil authority has already seized the man and locked him in Pavia?"

The Dean bowed his head. "Your Illustrious Holiness, I beg you to consider the circumstances."

"I am considering them," Borromeo replied. "They do not improve with examination."

Years of parish disputes, of wrestling with obstinate canons and negligent priests, had given the Dean a certain sturdy courage. He lifted his eyes now and met the Cardinal's gaze with something like defiance held carefully in check.

"This past spring," he said, "all my time and attention were demanded for the proceedings concerning the sanctification of my cousin, the blessed Carlo Borromeo. Your Holiness knows how exacting Rome has been. Every testimony examined, every miracle weighed. To neglect those duties would have been to fail not only your house, but the memory of the saint himself."

Borromeo's jaw tightened. The cause of Saint Carlo, his cousin, was indeed close to his heart. He had poured himself into it, seeing in his holy cousin's elevation a beacon for Milan's reform. That this very devotion had been used, however unintentionally, as reason to leave Monza insufficiently watched stung all the more.

"And yet," he said, "while we polished saints' halos on parchment, wolves slipped among my nuns."

"I did not ignore them," the Dean protested. "I questioned. I visited unexpectedly. I spoke with the Prioress, with confessors, with servants. But rumors do not make canon law. I could prove no specific count. The Lady Virginia Maria is of the house of de Leyva. To act precipitously, without firm evidence, would have meant provoking her family. They, in turn, might have brought their weight against this See. I feared to ignite a struggle between your authority and theirs before I had anything more than whispers."

He spread his hands, a weary gesture. "And there was the Governor."

"Fuentes," Borromeo said, the name tasting sour.

"His Excellency sent his own men to watch. Their presence unsettled the town. People grew cautious. Tongues that had loosed themselves earlier stiffened under the threat of the Spanish gallows. By the time I reached those who might once have spoken freely, they were suddenly afflicted with poor memory."

The Cardinal was silent for a while. Outside, the dull hum of the city rose and fell, punctuated by the occasional shout from the street. A fly traced aimless circles near the shutter slats.

"You did make inquiries," he said finally. "You did not simply close your eyes and hope the matter would vanish."

"No, Your Illustrious Holiness. I swear it. I chased every faint trail I could find. But without a confession, without a witness willing to stand by his words, I could not proceed to formal accusation. And then, before I could gather more, the Governor moved. He seized Osio for reasons of State and removed him to Pavia. We were forestalled."

"Adroitly so," Borromeo murmured.

If Fuentes had set out to ensure that the Church's hand came second in a matter touching both ecclesiastical discipline and public morality, he could not have chosen his moment better. The civil power had struck swiftly and without consultation, and now a man who should have faced canonical process for the corruption of a nun and sacrilege within a cloister sat instead under Spanish guard in a secular prison, subject only to civil decisions and beyond the reach of Church authority.

"I regret," the Dean said, "that I did not press you sooner. I thought, perhaps foolishly, that by delaying I might spare Your Holiness an open conflict with the de Leyva and with the Governor both. I misjudged the speed with which they would act."

Borromeo exhaled, a breath that stopped short of a sigh. Some of his initial anger eased. The Dean's reasons were not trivial. The cause of Saint Carlo. The danger of lashing out at noble patrons on imperfect proof. The Governor's encroachment.

But the sting remained.

"I am partly mollified," he said. "Not wholly. Matters of religious discipline within my diocese ought not to be left for the Spanish to handle first. That an Osio sits in Pavia without my having had the chance to examine a single witness in Monza offends both my authority and my conscience."

The Dean bowed again, more deeply. "Tell me how to remedy what can still be remedied, Your Illustrious Holiness, and I will obey."

Borromeo rose from his chair.

He had built his episcopate on visitations and reform, on not ruling from a distance. When Milan's clergy grew lax, he went to their parishes. When convents strayed from their rules, he passed their doors in person, cloaked in pastoral concern but carrying questions sharp as knives.

"Very well," he said. "We will not speak of this only in Milan. I will go to Monza myself. A pastoral visit will offend no one. A shepherd has the right to look into his own fold."

The phrase was mild; the resolve beneath it was not.

"I will speak with the Prioress. With the nuns. With those who serve them. I will see what can still be salvaged of discipline there, and what truth can be wrested from silence."

The Dean's shoulders straightened, relief and apprehension warring on his face. "Shall I precede you to prepare them?"

"No." Borromeo shook his head. "Forewarning breeds rehearsed answers. Let them be surprised. I will leave within days."

He turned toward the window and pushed the shutter wider. The light that spilled in was hard and clear, showing every dust mote in its path.

Fuentes had moved first, and cleverly. But the Church would not remain an afterthought in a scandal that touched its vows, its houses, its very claim to moral guidance.

If the Governor thought a fortress and a warrant for reasons of State could keep all accounts within secular hands, he would discover that bishops, too, had long memories and a duty to souls that did not always align with Madrid's convenience.

"Make the necessary arrangements," Borromeo said. "We travel to Monza."

"At once, Your Illustrious Holiness."

The Dean withdrew.

Left alone, Federico Borromeo turned back to his desk, one hand resting on the scattered papers before him. His eyes fixed on a map of the diocese where, beyond the city's edge, lay a small town, a troubled convent, and a tangle of sin and secrecy that now demanded his presence.

He had been late to it. That failure he could not undo.

But he would not be late again.

* * *

CARDINAL FEDERICO BORROMEO did not go straight to Santa Margherita. His carriage, bearing the archiepiscopal arms, rolled first to other houses in the area: a small community of Benedictines outside Monza's walls, a group of Ursuline sisters engaged in teaching girls, a confraternity chapel whose priests had been the subject of earlier complaints. At each place he descended with the same calm dignity, blessed the assembled religious, spoke of prayer and perseverance, asked after their needs.

It was not wasted effort. A shepherd ought to know all his flocks. But there was calculation, too. If he arrived at Santa Margherita alone, his purpose would be too obvious. Better that the town see his presence as part of a broader pastoral round.

Only after these visits did his carriage turn toward the convent that concerned him most.

Santa Margherita's walls rose pale and severe at the edge of town, their height sufficient to deny any easy view of the life within. The bell tower stood modestly above the roofline. From the street, the building looked like any other cloister: thick doors, small, barred windows, an air of withdrawal from the world it bordered.

Inside the parlatory, the Prioress and several senior sisters waited in careful order to receive him. Behind them, in the dimness, younger nuns watched with furtive curiosity through the grille.

Borromeo offered the customary greeting; hands raised in blessing. He spoke with the Prioress first, of ordinary matters: the observance of the Rule, the health of the community, the education of the schoolgirls.

Then he asked, as if casually, to see the sisters individually. "Since I am here, Reverend Mother, it would please me to speak with as many as time allows. To encourage them, to learn their concerns."

The Prioress could hardly refuse. She signaled to the portress. One by one, nuns were summoned to spend a few moments before their Archbishop.

He received them in a small room off the main corridor, a space usually used for private counsel. A table. Two chairs. A crucifix on the wall. The window shutter was open, letting in a rectangle of hot afternoon light.

Some sisters came trembling, others composed. He spoke with each in turn, inquiring after her vocation, her health, her struggles. To some he offered simple exhortation. To others he asked, lightly, how they found life in Santa Margherita, whether there was anything that weighed on their conscience.

He never once spoke the names that lay at the heart of his visit. Not Gian Paolo. Not Virginia. Not murder. Not scandal.

Even so, he watched closely for any flinch, any flicker of fear or resentment that might suggest deeper knowledge.

None came.

If anything, the nuns were too uniformly vague. They praised their Prioress's prudence. They spoke of the convent's good order. A few whose faces bore traces of old quarrels might have seized the opportunity to hint at faults in a rival if the matter had been a small one. Here, on this subject, they were united in silence.

Even those who had reasons to dislike Virginia kept their grievances carefully removed from anything that might touch the wider scandal.

They were protecting not her, Borromeo saw, but the house itself. To admit rot within would be to invite the world's hand to tear at their walls.

By the time he had spoken with a dozen, he knew he would not, in this manner, extract what he sought.

He asked, at last, that Sister Virginia Maria de Leyva be brought to him.

* * *

VIRGINIA ENTERED WITH measured steps, veil and wimple impeccably arranged, hands folded before her. Had one not known, one might have taken her for a model of composed religious virtue.

She knelt to kiss the cardinal's ring, then rose and stood with her eyes cast down, in the attitude convent training instilled when a nun faced authority.

"Come, daughter," Borromeo said, indicating the chair opposite his. "Sit. This is not a trial. It is a conversation."

"Yes, Your Illustrious Holiness." Her voice was soft, clear.

He studied her a moment before speaking. The traces of beauty that had so turned heads in Monza were still visible: the fine bones, the dark eyes, the carriage of someone born to nobility. But there was strain there now as well, a shadow in the gaze, a slight tightness about the mouth.

He began gently. "You were not born for this life. Few of our noble daughters are. Yet Providence placed you within these walls. You have received much: education, protection, a respected name in religion."

"Yes, Your Illustrious Holiness."

"With such gifts come obligations." His tone remained paternal, but there was steel beneath it. "You are of the house of de Leyva. You bear a name that carries weight in Lombardy and beyond. Here, within Santa Margherita, that nobility should not be an excuse for pride or privilege. It should be a spur to virtue."

She lifted her eyes slightly, just enough that he could see the dark flash within.

"In a convent," he continued, "every sister is bound to strive for piety. For modesty in words and deed. For charity toward her companions. But in your case, daughter, there is more. You must aspire to be the most conspicuous example of religious life here. Not because you are better by nature than your sisters, but because the world looks at you."

He let that sink in.

"People in Monza speak of this house. It is their custom. The common folk comment on every piece of news that escapes. They notice when a carriage stops at your door, when a letter is delivered, when a servant lingers too long at your gate. They whisper. They speculate. Their words travel farther than they know."

Virginia's fingers tightened in her lap.

"Up to now," Borromeo said, "you may protest that your conduct has been outwardly blameless. Perhaps in many respects it has been. Yet even so, one cannot deny that evil rumors have arisen. There has been talk of visits, of improprieties, of attachments. Whether those rumors are true or false, they cling."

He leaned forward slightly.

"It is now up to you, and no one else, to disprove them. To dissipate them. Not by argument, not by indignation, but by living henceforth in such a way that even the most ill-disposed tongue finds nothing to grasp. Your life must be irreproachable. Not merely correct, but exemplary."

For a moment he thought he saw something move in her expression—an instant of wounded pride, perhaps, or of weary resignation. Then it closed again.

"Do you understand what I am saying, daughter?" he asked.

"Yes, Your Illustrious Holiness," she replied. "You desire that I live more perfectly the vows I have taken, so that no one may have cause to speak ill of this house."

"I desire," he said, "that you remember who you are. A daughter of a noble family. A bride of Christ. A woman looked to by others for example whether you wish it or not. And I desire that you consider how your actions bind not only yourself, but this whole community."

He paused. There was another name he could no longer avoid.

"You know that Giovanni Paolo Osio is imprisoned," he said. "That the Governor has taken him to Pavia."

A faint flush rose in her cheeks. "I have heard, Your Illustrious Holiness."

"There are those," he continued carefully, "who say his dealings with this house, indeed, with you in particular, have not been what they should. I am not here to accuse you, Virginia. I am here to urge you, as your pastor, to free yourself from any tie that endangers your soul and the honor of this convent."

Her answer came calmly, but the words themselves were a gauntlet.

"As long as Signor Osio remains in prison," she said, "it will be a matter of my honor."

He felt, more than heard, the emphasis.

A matter of her honor that he not be further pressed? That his situation not be worsened by anything she might admit? That the Cardinal understand that to touch Osio was to touch something she considered bound up with her own name?

"As long as he is held," she repeated quietly, "I cannot speak."

The implication lay unvoiced: that any attempt to extract confession from her would be construed as cruelty to a woman already punished through the suffering of the man she loved.

For an instant, Borromeo saw not the composed nun before him, but the whole ruinous structure behind her: the pride, the passion, the tangled loyalties that had led her into sin and now held her there in chains of her own forging.

He had come hoping that an appeal to her better nature, to her sense of responsibility, might open some crack in her defenses. That if he approached not as a judge but as a father, she would yield something—remorse, a plea for help, a first admission of having gone astray.

Instead, she offered a condition. She set herself, even now, as guardian of a man whose crimes were already staining souls and streets alike.

He saw, with a clarity that saddened him more than anger could have, that she still believed herself in control. That she clung to the illusion that by choosing silence, by framing Osio's fate as bound to her honor, she held some power over how this story would end.

"I ask only," he said slowly, "that you examine your conscience before God. That you consider whether the loyalty you claim is owed to a man, or to the Lord who called you here. And that you remember no human honor is worth the loss of your soul."

She inclined her head. "I will reflect on your words, Your Illustrious Holiness."

He believed she would. Reflection, however, was not the same as repentance.

He blessed her, tracing the sign of the cross in the air.

"May God enlighten you," he said. "And may the blessed Carlo, whose blood you know has long been close to your house, intercede for you."

"Thank you," she murmured.

When she had gone, the little room felt emptier than it had when he began the day's interviews.

* * *

BORROMEO LEFT MONZA with his retinue as the sun slanted westward, casting long shadows from the town's walls across the surrounding fields.

The official account of his visit would record that the archbishop had made a pastoral tour, had found the convents generally in good order, had offered exhortations to greater fervor. There would be no mention in that neat summary of the unease that sat like a stone beneath his ribs.

He had not been deceived by Santa Margherita's outward composure. Too much effort had gone into presenting a flawless surface. Too many mouths had closed a little too quickly when certain topics brushed the edge of conversation.

His brief exchange with Virginia had confirmed what the silence of the others suggested: whatever had happened there, the truth would not come easily. It would require more than gentle admonitions. It would require formal inquiry, precise questions, the machinery of a canonical process he had hoped to avoid unleashing.

As the carriage wheels turned on the road back to Milan, Federico Borromeo sat with his hand resting on the rosary at his belt, fingers moving from bead to bead more out of habit than conscious prayer.

He had arrived in Monza troubled. He returned more so.

What he had seen there was not open rebellion or obvious disorder, but something subtler and, in its way, more dangerous: a community locked in a conspiracy of silence, and at its center a woman still convinced that by protecting her lover she could protect herself.

The time for pastoral visits was ending. The time for tribunals was drawing near.

* * *

August

HEAT TURNED THE air inside Virginia's cell thick as wool. Sweat gathered beneath her wimple and trickled down her spine despite the stone walls. She stood at the window in the late afternoon, watching cobblestones shimmer beyond the enclosure walls. Three months since the election stripped her of power as Vicaress. Three months waiting while nothing happened and everything remained suspended.

A soft knock. Sister Benedetta entered without waiting for permission, the usual rigid control stretched thin across her features.

"Mother Angela wishes to see you." Each word came precise and clipped. "Immediately."

Virginia's stomach contracted. The Cardinal has acted. The investigation begins.

The corridors seemed narrower as she followed Benedetta. Sister Candida appeared in the arcade ahead and looked away quickly, color draining from her round face. Near the chapel entrance, Sister Silvia made the sign of the cross. Even the younger nuns moved aside as Virginia approached, their whispers dying before she could catch the words.

Reverend Mother Angela stood at her writing table rather than seated behind it. Afternoon light illuminated papers spread across the wooden surface, correspondence bearing official seals, documents with dense script. The scent of sealing wax hung in the air, sharp and resinous.

"Sit down, Sister Virginia."

Virginia sat, folding her hands in her lap where their trembling wouldn't show. Admit nothing unless there's no alternative.

The Prioress remained standing, forcing Virginia to look up at her. "I have received disturbing news. Not from the authorities, though that may come soon enough. From other sources."

"What news, Reverend Mother?"

"The Cardinal has written to your family in Madrid." She set the letter down with deliberate care. "To your brother, Don Luigi. The correspondence suggests, delicately of course, that the wall between our property and Signor Osio's should be heightened. For security purposes, he claims. To better protect the sanctity of our enclosure."

The Cardinal knew. Or suspected enough to act. But why write to Madrid rather than confront her directly?

"I see." Virginia chose each word with caution. "His Eminence is concerned for our protection."

"His Eminence is creating a paper trail." The Prioress moved around the writing table, coming to stand directly before her. "He writes to your family months before taking any direct action here. Why would he do that, Sister Virginia?"

The question hung between them. Virginia met the older woman's gaze and saw knowledge there. Not proof, perhaps, but certainty born of years watching scandal and cover-up within convent walls.

"Perhaps he wishes to ensure cooperation from the de Leyva family before proceeding with whatever concerns him."

"Or perhaps he wishes to demonstrate that he gave proper notice to your relations before exposing them to scandal." Steel ran beneath Mother Angela's even tone. "So that when the storm breaks, and it will break, Sister Virginia, he can point to this letter and say he acted with appropriate caution and respect for a noble family's honor."

She knows. Not everything, but enough.

Virginia's fingers tightened against each other. "If His Eminence has concerns, surely he should address them directly rather than through correspondence to Spain."

"Should he?" The Prioress returned to her writing table and sat heavily, suddenly appearing every one of her sixty years. "Tell me, Sister Virginia. If the Cardinal were to question you about your conduct, about any improprieties that might have occurred within these walls, what would you tell him?"

"That I have served Santa Margherita faithfully according to my vows."

"Even under oath? Even under interrogation by the Holy Office?"

The threat was explicit now. Sweat gathered in the hollow of Virginia's throat. "I would tell the truth, Reverend Mother. As any faithful servant of God should."

"The truth." Mother Angela's mouth tightened into a thin line. "Yes. That is precisely what concerns me."

She pulled another document across the writing table, newer, the parchment still crisp. "I have also received notice from the Count of Fuentes' office. Nothing formal yet. No official summons. But his secretary writes that questions have arisen. Testimony has been collected. Witnesses have spoken of matters that reflect poorly on this convent and everyone within it."

Virginia's breath came shorter. How many have talked?

"What manner of questions?"

"You know what manner." The Prioress leaned forward. "Sister Imbersaga and I have done what we could to maintain order since the election. We have looked away when perhaps we should have intervened earlier. But if formal investigation begins, I cannot shield you. I will not perjure myself before God and the Church to protect crimes I neither committed nor condoned."

The words landed like stones dropped from a height. Virginia held herself upright, maintaining that steady gaze. "I understand, Reverend Mother."

"Do you? Because I fear you still believe your family name will save you. That the de Leyva influence extends far enough to make all this simply disappear." Mother Angela's voice softened slightly. "It will not, child. Not this time. The witnesses are too many. The scandal too great."

"What would you have me do?"

"Confess. Before formal charges are brought. Before the Holy Office becomes involved. Make full confession to Cardinal Borromeo, throw yourself on his mercy, beg forgiveness and accept whatever penance he deems appropriate." Urgency sharpened each word. "It is your only hope for anything resembling leniency."

Confess. Name Gian Paolo. Expose Benedetta, Ottavia, Silvia, Candida—everyone who helped or knew. *Destroy them all to save myself.*

Virginia's throat closed. "I need time to consider."

"Time is the one thing you do not have." Mother Angela stood again, her face hardening into something carved from marble. "But you will do as you think best. You always have."

The dismissal was clear. Virginia rose on legs that threatened to buckle and moved toward the door.

"Sister Virginia."

She turned back.

"Whatever you decide, do not compound your sins by dragging innocents into your fall. Too many have already paid the price for choices they did not make." Pity crossed the Prioress's features, brief and unmistakable. "I will pray for you. But I fear even prayer may not be enough at this stage."

* * *

THAT EVENING, SHE summoned Benedetta and Ottavia to her cell. Candida came too, slipping in after dark when the corridors stood empty. Silvia kept watch outside.

"The Cardinal has written to Madrid." Virginia dispensed with preamble. "To my brother. Suggesting the wall be raised between the convent and Gian Paolo's property."

Benedetta's sharp intake of breath was the only sound for several heartbeats.

"That is preparation." She spoke finally, each word measured. "He builds his case piece by piece. First the letter to your family, creating documentation that he expressed concerns months before acting. Then investigation. Then formal charges."

"He knows everything." Ottavia's voice came out as barely more than a whisper.

"He suspects everything." Benedetta's correction was knife-sharp. "Suspicion is not proof. But he clearly has enough to proceed cautiously toward accusation."

“Mother Angela says Count Fuentes’ office has also been collecting testimony.” Virginia sank onto her cot, the rope frame creaking beneath her. “Witnesses have spoken. They know about things that happened here.”

“What did the Prioress advise?” Benedetta asked.

“Confession. Full disclosure to the Cardinal before formal charges are brought.”

“Betraying everyone who helped you.” No judgment colored Benedetta’s tone, only flat assessment. “Naming names. Destroying us all to purchase whatever small mercy he might extend.”

“I did not say I would do it.” Virginia looked up. “I only said that is what she advised.”

“Then what will you do?” Ottavia leaned forward. “Because we are all bound to your choices now. Whatever you decide affects every one of us.”

Virginia stood and moved to the window. Darkness had settled over Monza. Somewhere in that darkness, Gian Paolo hid from the same forces closing around her.

“We fight.” She turned back to face them. “The Cardinal builds his case with letters and implications. We build ours with documentation that contradicts his narrative.”

“How?” Benedetta’s posture shifted, alert now. “What documentation could possibly counter testimony from witnesses?”

“A petition.” Virginia’s mind worked quickly, desperation sharpening into strategy. “Signed by every sister at Santa Margherita. Testifying that no evil has occurred within these walls. That all rumors are malicious lies spread by enemies of our order.”

Candida stared at her. “You think the nuns will sign such a document?”

“They will if they understand the alternative.” Virginia’s voice hardened. “If this convent falls under investigation, everyone suffers. Reputations destroyed. Families dishonored. The entire community disbanded and dispersed to other houses. Every sister here has something to lose if scandal erupts.”

“So, you will threaten them into complicity.” Benedetta’s observation held neither approval nor condemnation, just recognition.

"I will remind them of what they face if the Cardinal proceeds. And I will offer them a way to protect themselves and this community." Virginia pulled parchment from her writing table and reached for quill and ink. "A united front signed by all. Presented to Count Fuentes as evidence that the testimony against us comes from unreliable sources with axes to grind."

"It will not stop investigation." Benedetta spoke with flat certainty. "Not at this stage."

"No. But it may slow it. May give Gian Paolo time to do whatever he must to protect himself. May demonstrate enough institutional support that the authorities hesitate before moving against a convent with powerful connections." Virginia dipped her quill, watching ink gather at the nib. "It is a defense, even if not a complete one."

She wrote quickly:

> *We, the professed sisters and novices of the Convent of Santa Margherita in Monza, do hereby testify that no evil of any kind has occurred within our sacred walls. All rumors to the contrary are false witness borne of malice. We affirm the virtue and piety of our community and protest any investigation based on such unfounded accusations.*

"That is perjury." Ottavia's whisper barely carried across the cell. "For all of us."

"It is survival." Virginia set down the quill. "And every sister who signs it binds herself to silence. They cannot testify against us without admitting they lied in this petition."

The logic was ruthless. Benedetta nodded slowly. "Mutual destruction. We protect each other because exposing one exposes all."

"Exactly."

"And if they refuse to sign?" Candida asked.

Virginia met her gaze without flinching. "They will not refuse. I may no longer be Vicaress, but my name still carries weight."

"You sound like your father." The words escaped Ottavia before she could stop them.

Silence filled the cell.

"Perhaps I am like him." Virginia returned to the writing table and picked up the petition. "But unlike him, I fight to protect those I love rather than myself alone."

The lie tasted familiar in her mouth.

"I will begin tomorrow. After Prime. Every sister will be given opportunity to sign. The document will be complete within three days."

"And then?" Benedetta asked.

"Then I send it to Count Fuentes with a letter from Mother Angela attesting to its authenticity." Virginia folded the petition with careful precision. "Let the Cardinal write to Madrid. Let him build his careful case. We build ours as well."

* * *

THE NEXT MORNING after Prime, Virginia approached Sister Febronia in the arcade outside the chapel. The elderly nun had been at Santa Margherita longer than anyone else. Forty years of devotion and service that commanded respect from every sister.

"Sister Febronia, may I speak with you privately?"

They moved to a quiet corner where shadows still clung to the walls. Virginia kept her voice low.

"You have heard the rumors circulating about our convent."

The old nun's face tightened. "I hear many things. Not all of them should be repeated."

"These particular rumors threaten our entire community." Virginia withdrew the petition. "Count Fuentes' office has been collecting testimony. The Cardinal has expressed concerns to my family in Madrid. Without intervention, formal investigation may begin within weeks."

Sister Febronia's weathered hands trembled. "What manner of investigation?"

"The kind that examines every sister, questions every visitor, scrutinizes every aspect of our daily life." Virginia let that sink in. "The kind that finds irregularities even in the most carefully maintained houses. No convent survives such scrutiny with its reputation intact."

"What would you have me do?"

"Sign this petition. Testify that Santa Margherita is a house of virtue being maligned by those with malicious intent." Virginia unfolded the document. "Your name carries weight, Sister Febronia. If you sign, others will follow."

The old nun read slowly, her lips moving as she traced each word. When she finished, she looked up with eyes that had witnessed too much to be easily fooled.

"This asks me to swear that no evil has occurred here."

"It asks you to protect the community you have served for four decades." Virginia held her gaze without wavering. "Whatever private sins individual sisters may have committed, the institution itself remains holy. Would you see Santa Margherita destroyed because of rumors and unreliable witnesses?"

For a long moment, Sister Febronia stood silent. Then she reached for the quill Virginia offered, her fingers closing around it with visible effort. The nib scratched across parchment, leaving her shaky but legible signature.

"Heaven have mercy on us all," she whispered.

* * *

THE MORNING CONTINUED. Virginia moved through the convent with systematic efficiency, approaching each sister individually, calibrating her arguments to match what she knew of their fears and loyalties.

Sister Agatha stood at the ovens in the bakehouse, flour dusting her habit. Virginia waited until the loaves came out.

"I need your signature on a petition."

When Virginia mentioned investigation, Agatha's hands stilled.

"They would question everything," Virginia said quietly. "Every transaction. Every coin that changes hands. The wine you sometimes sell to townspeople despite regulations against such commerce—do you think that would escape notice?"

The color drained from Agatha's face. The extra income from wine sales kept her widowed sister and three nieces fed in Meda.

Her hand left a smudge of flour on the parchment as she wrote her name.

Sister Francesca, whose family had fallen on hard times, required different persuasion. Virginia found her in the scriptorium, copying a psalter.

"Your mother wrote last month requesting additional support," Virginia said. "The convent has been generous, but scandal might cause us to reduce such charitable assistance to impoverished relations."

Francesca's quill paused mid-stroke. Her mother and two younger sisters depended entirely on the convent's discretionary funds.

When she signed, her hand moved with the same careful control she brought to her manuscript work, but Virginia saw how white her knuckles went as she gripped the quill.

The younger nuns signed without much persuasion, trusting in Virginia's former authority and reassured by seeing their superiors' names already inscribed.

By midday, more than half the signatures had been collected.

* * *

SISTER DEGNAMERITA PROVED more difficult. She stood in the herb garden with the unsigned petition in her hands, reading it for the third time while bees hummed among the lavender.

"This feels wrong." She kept her eyes on the document. "Like we compound sin with lies."

"We protect our community from destruction based on unreliable testimony." Virginia kept her tone gentle. "Is that sin or duty?"

"I am uncertain."

"Then consider this." Virginia moved closer. "Your brother serves as notary in Milan. His position depends on maintaining a reputation above reproach. If Santa Margherita falls under investigation, every family connected to this convent faces scrutiny. Every relationship examined. Every business dealing questioned."

Sister Degnamerita's face went pale. Her brother's recent appointment had been hard-won after years of service.

"You would threaten my family?"

"I protect all our families." Virginia gentled her voice. "Including yours. Sign, and we present a united front that discourages investigation. Refuse, and you stand alone when the authorities come asking why you alone would not attest to our virtue."

The quill left ink stains on Degnamerita's fingers as she pressed it to parchment, the letters forming with jerky, uneven strokes. When she finished, she thrust the document at Virginia without speaking and fled through the garden gate.

* * *

BY EVENING, ONLY a handful of signatures remained uncollected. Virginia found Sister Costanza in the portress's room near the main entrance, sorting through keys.

"Sister Costanza, I need your signature on the petition."

The woman set down the keys with deliberate care. "I have been avoiding you all day."

"I noticed."

"This document asks me to lie before God and the authorities." Costanza turned to face her directly. "I cannot do that, Sister Virginia. My conscience will not allow it."

Virginia had prepared for this. She pulled a folded letter from her sleeve; one she had taken from the convent records weeks ago.

"Do you remember writing to your family last year? Asking them to send money beyond your usual allowance?"

Costanza's eyes widened. "That was private correspondence."

"It was correspondence that passed through my hands for approval before being sent." Virginia unfolded the letter. "You told your family the money was needed for charitable works. In truth, you used it to commission new vestments for the chapel without the Prioress's permission. A small deception, but one that violates our vow of obedience and poverty."

"You would blackmail me with that?"

"I would remind you that all of us have small secrets we would prefer remained private." Virginia refolded the letter. "Sign the petition, and this letter stays forgotten in the archives. Refuse, and I may need to bring it to Mother Angela's attention during the confusion of investigation."

Costanza's face flushed red, then drained white. Her hand trembled as she took the quill, and when she pressed it to parchment, the nib caught and left a blot that spread like blood. Her signature was barely legible.

* * *

BY THE END of the third day, only two signatures remained uncollected. Mother Angela's name needed to anchor the document, lending it the authority of the convent's highest office. And Sister Imbersaga, the new Vicaress, would need to sign as well.

Virginia found the Prioress in the Chapter house after Compline, when the rest of the community had dispersed to their cells. The older woman sat alone at the long table, a single candle illuminating her weathered features. She looked up when Virginia entered but did not speak.

"I have brought the petition for your signature, Reverend Mother."

Mother Angela did not reach for the document. "I wondered when you would come."

Virginia laid it on the table between them. Signatures covered the parchment. The document was beginning to show wear at the edges from being carried through corridors and gardens, unfolded and refolded.

The Prioress read slowly, her finger tracing down the long list of names. When she finished, she looked up at Virginia with disappointment carved into the lines around her mouth.

"You have forced them all to add their names to this perjury."

"I asked only that they affirm what protects us all." Virginia held out the quill. "That Santa Margherita is a house of virtue unfairly maligned by those who would see us destroyed."

"And if I refuse?"

"Then you stand alone against the united voice of your entire community." Virginia kept her tone level. "You call every one of these sisters liars. You invite investigation that will destroy not only me but everyone who has built their lives within these walls. Is that what you wish, Reverend Mother?"

The older woman's hand shook as she took the quill, the tremor so pronounced that ink splattered across the table. Her signature was firmer than Virginia expected, the letters formed with the authority of her position despite the visible reluctance.

"God have mercy on our souls," she whispered as she set down the quill.

"Sister Imbersaga will not sign so easily." Mother Angela's voice was flat. "She has been vocal in her opposition to protecting you."

"Then I will speak with her myself."

* * *

VIRGINIA FOUND IMBERSAGA in her new chamber, the same room Virginia had occupied for years when she was Vicaress. Sister Imbersaga looked up from her work with cold satisfaction etched into every line of her sharp face.

"Come to beg for my signature, Sister Virginia?"

"Come to remind you of what's at stake." Virginia set the petition on the writing table. "Every other sister has signed. Even Mother Angela. You alone remain."

"Because I alone have the courage to refuse." Imbersaga's voice dripped with contempt. She pushed back from the writing table, rising to her full height. "You destroyed this convent with your sins. Now you would bind us all to your lies."

"If this convent is destroyed, you will fall with it." Virginia leaned forward, placing her palms flat on the writing table. "You were Prioress when much of this occurred. You knew, or should have known, what was happening under your authority. When the Cardinal investigates, do you think he will distinguish between those who committed sins and those who failed to stop them?"

Imbersaga's face paled slightly, a flicker of uncertainty crossing her features.

"You will be held responsible for your failure of leadership." Virginia pressed her advantage. "Sign this petition and we present a united defense. Refuse, and I will ensure the Cardinal knows exactly how much you observed and ignored during your time as Prioress. How you maintained your position by looking away, by choosing institutional stability over moral courage."

The threat hung between them. Imbersaga's hand clenched into a fist, knuckles whitening.

"You are a monster."

"I am a survivor." Virginia placed the quill within reach. "As you will be, if you sign."

Sister Imbersaga stared at the petition for a long moment. Then, with visible fury radiating from every controlled movement, she seized the quill and scratched her name at the bottom. The strokes were violent, the letters harsh and angular, the final flourish leaving a tear in the parchment that Virginia would need to repair with wax.

Virginia collected the completed petition without another word. The document was heavy in her hands, weighted with more than parchment and ink. Every name represented a sister bound to silence, complicit now in whatever consequences followed.

* * *

THAT AFTERNOON, SHE drafted a letter to Count Fuentes' office:

Your Excellency, in response to disturbing rumors that have reached our attention, the entire community of Santa Margherita wishes to provide testimony regarding the virtue and conduct of our house. We are profoundly troubled by false accusations that threaten not only individual reputations but the sacred mission of our order. The enclosed petition, signed by every professed sister and novice within our walls, attests to the piety and devotion that characterizes life at Santa Margherita. We trust Your Excellency will give due weight to this united testimony when considering any further action.

She sealed it with the convent's mark, pressing the wax until the image came clear—a stylized marguerite flower, symbol of purity that now protected something far more complicated than innocence.

When everything was prepared, Virginia summoned the convent's lay steward to the parlatory. He appeared quickly, cap in hand, still accustomed to serving the woman who had been Vicaress until three months ago.

"Take this to Count Fuentes' office in Milan." Virginia pressed the sealed documents into his hands along with a purse. "Deliver it directly to his secretary. No one else. Do you understand?"

"Yes, Sister Virginia. Directly to the secretary, no one else."

"And speak to no one about the contents or purpose of your errand. Not in taverns, not to friends, not even to your wife."

"Of course, Sister. My lips are sealed."

She watched him depart through the front gates, the documents disappearing beyond the convent walls like messages sent into an uncertain void.

Benedetta found her at the window afterward, staring at the empty space where the steward had vanished.

"It is done."

"It is begun." Benedetta's correction came swift and certain. "The Cardinal moves. You move. He will counter. Then you must counter again. This is not an ending but the opening of a game where the stakes are everything we have."

"I know." Virginia pressed her palm against the cool glass. "But I will not go quietly into whatever fate the Cardinal has planned. If I fall, it will be fighting."

"You are your father's daughter, after all." Grim understanding colored Benedetta's tone. "And the de Leyvas have never surrendered without blood."

Virginia said nothing. Outside, evening bells began to toll across Monza—San Giovanni, San Maurizio, Santa Maria, their bronze voices overlapping in a conversation that had continued for centuries. The same bells that had marked canonical hours for all the years of her life within these walls.

But for now, she remained. And while she remained, she would fight with every weapon at her disposal—manipulation, intimidation, the weight of her name, and the desperate strength of someone with nothing left to lose.

The petition would not save her. She understood that with cold clarity.

But it might buy time. Might force authorities to move more cautiously when faced with united testimony from an entire convent. Might create enough doubt about witness reliability that formal charges became more difficult to sustain.

Time was the only currency she had left. And she had just purchased a few more weeks, possibly months, at the cost of binding every sister at Santa Margherita to her fate through the ruthless logic of mutual destruction.

Virginia turned from the window as the bells fell silent. Darkness gathered in the corners of the courtyard, advancing slowly as daylight retreated.

She moved toward the chapel for Vespers, her footsteps echoing in the corridor that would soon fill with sisters walking to prayer, all of them bound now by signatures on parchment and the shared weight of lies that might be the only truth that mattered.

* * *

September

SEPTEMBER ARRIVED WITH cooler mornings that promised autumn's approach, though midday heat still pressed down on Monza. Virginia sat in her cell with Ottavia and Benedetta. Four weeks since the petition had been dispatched to Count Fuentes' office. Four weeks without response, the quiet more ominous than any letter could have been.

"The Dean has been to town again." Sister Silvia slipped through the doorway without knocking, her round face flushed from hurrying. "Three times this week. The portress heard from the baker's wife who heard from her sister that he's been questioning people. Asking about Signor Osio. About visitors to the convent. About..." She hesitated, glancing toward the corridor before continuing in a whisper. "About the apothecary."

Virginia's hands stilled on the breviary she had been pretending to read. "Rainerio?"

"The Dean spent two hours at his shop yesterday. And this morning he returned with someone from the Cardinal's office in Milan. A notary, judging by the documents he carried."

The breviary slipped from Virginia's grip, pages fluttering as it struck the floor. Benedetta retrieved it without comment, setting it on the table while her sharp eyes fixed on Silvia.

"Did anyone hear what was discussed?"

"Only that when they left, Rainerio looked ill. White as altar linen, his wife said. And he closed the shop for the rest of the day, which he never does. Not even on feast days."

After Silvia departed, Virginia sank onto her cot. The rope frame creaked beneath her. Rainerio had supplied her with medicines for years, digestive tonics, sleeping draughts during the months after Caterina's murder when nightmares left her gasping awake. And other preparations, the ones she tried not to think about too directly. The abortifacient drugs after that second pregnancy, the compounds whose purpose she had never stated explicitly but which Rainerio had understood well enough.

"He knows too much." Ottavia's voice trembled. "About the herbs. About Gian Paolo visiting at night. About the child."

"He suspects much and knows some." Benedetta's correction was automatic, precise. "But suspicion and knowledge are different things when giving testimony under oath. The question is what he told the Dean, and what proof he can provide to support his claims."

Virginia pressed her palms against her thighs, steadying herself. "He's been frightened since spring. Since that business with the harquebuses and Father Arrigone's imprisonment. He knows Gian Paolo is dangerous, knows what happens to people who talk too freely."

"Yet he talked anyway." Benedetta moved to the window. "Which means either the Dean offered him something he wanted or threatened him with something he feared more than Gian Paolo's revenge."

"The Cardinal's authority outweighs even Gian Paolo's violence." Ottavia's observation was quiet but certain. "What good is avoiding murder if you face excommunication instead? Or prosecution for providing medicines that ended a pregnancy?"

The words settled into the room like ash. Virginia had never explicitly told Rainerio what the second set of drugs was for, had never admitted aloud that she sought to expel the child growing inside her. But he was an apothecary, trained in the properties of plants and compounds. Pennyroyal and rue, tansy and savin—the traditional arsenal of women desperate to undo what nature had begun.

"If he testifies about the herbs—" Virginia started.

"Then the Cardinal has physical confirmation of your attempts to end a pregnancy." Benedetta finished the thought with brutal efficiency. "Which implies there was a pregnancy to end. Which implies violation of your vows. Which opens investigation into every other aspect of your conduct."

Virginia crossed to the window. Below, Sister Agatha moved through the courtyard with a basket of bread, unhurried, her conscience apparently untroubled. What would it feel like to walk through the world that simply? To have no secrets eating away at your foundation?

"We need to know exactly what he told them." She turned back to face the others. "Every detail. Every name mentioned. Every date or circumstance he revealed."

"How?" Ottavia asked. "We cannot exactly march into his shop and demand an accounting."

"No." Virginia's mind raced, desperation sharpening into strategy. "But his wife talks to the other merchants' wives. And Sister Agatha buys our bread from the baker whose sister is married to the cooper who supplies Rainerio with barrels. Information flows through this town like water through channels. We simply need to position ourselves to catch it."

Benedetta nodded slowly. "Sister Agatha has been nervous since signing the petition. Eager to prove her loyalty by being useful."

"Then give her opportunity to do so." Virginia settled back onto her cot, forcing her breathing to slow. "Tell her we've heard disturbing rumors about the Dean's investigation. Ask if she might discreetly inquire through her contacts in town. Frame it as concern for the convent's reputation."

"She'll see through that excuse." Ottavia's doubt was evident.

"Of course she will. But she's already complicit through her signature on the petition." Virginia kept her voice level. "She cannot expose my sins without exposing her own perjury. That makes her safer than someone whose hands are clean."

The logic was ruthless but sound. Benedetta departed to find Sister Agatha, leaving Virginia and Ottavia alone in the gathering afternoon shadows.

"This will not end well." Ottavia spoke with the flat certainty of someone stating observable fact. "Even if Rainerio said nothing damning, even if the petition creates enough doubt to slow investigation, eventually the truth will emerge. There are too many witnesses, too much to hide, too many years of accumulated scandal."

Virginia said nothing because there was nothing to say that would not be either a lie or an admission of defeat.

* * *

SISTER AGATHA RETURNED before Compline with information gathered through the intricate network of merchant wives and household servants who formed Monza's real communication system. She stood in the corridor outside Virginia's cell, twisting her apron between flour-dusted hands while she delivered her report in whispered fragments.

"Rainerio's wife told the cooper's wife who told the baker's sister that the Dean questioned him for nearly three hours. Asked about remedies he supplied to the convent. About visitors he observed coming and going at unusual hours. About conversations he overheard between Signor Osio and various servants."

Virginia's chest tightened but she kept her face composed. "Did she mention specific medicines?"

"Sleeping draughts. Digestive tonics. And..." Sister Agatha's voice dropped even lower. "Preparations for women's complaints. That's what she called them. But the way she said it, like there was more meaning beneath the words..."

"There are many women's complaints that require treatment." Virginia kept her tone steady, dismissive. "Painful courses. Excessive bleeding. Conditions that afflict even cloistered women despite our removed lives."

Sister Agatha nodded eagerly, wanting to believe the innocent explanation. "That's what I thought as well, Sister Virginia."

"Did Rainerio mention anything else? Any specific incidents or dates?"

"The cooper's wife said something about a baby. About Signor Osio keeping a child in his house and Rainerio seeing a servant bring it to the convent gate." Agatha's discomfort was palpable. "But surely that's just malicious gossip."

"Perhaps seeking charitable assistance, as poor women sometimes do." Virginia's lie came smooth and practiced. "Or perhaps the story is entirely fabricated, invented by those who wish to cause scandal where none exists. You know how rumors multiply in small towns."

"Yes. Yes, of course." Relief flooded Sister Agatha's features. "I'm sure it's nothing but gossip and exaggeration."

After Agatha departed, Virginia remained standing in the corridor while evening bells began their call to Compline. The information was worse than she had feared but not as catastrophic as it might have been. Rainerio had confirmed medicines, problematic but potentially explained away. He had mentioned the baby and the wet nurse, damaging but not direct proof of Virginia's maternity. He had observed nocturnal visitors, suspicious but not conclusive.

What Rainerio apparently had not done was provide the Dean with explicit testimony about abortifacient drugs or detailed accounting of when and why Virginia had requested certain dangerous preparations. Either he had held back that information out of lingering self-preservation, or the Dean had not asked the right questions.

A temporary reprieve. But only temporary.

* * *

THAT NIGHT AFTER Compline, when the convent settled into the hushed rhythms that preceded sleep, Virginia knelt at her bedside. Moonlight filtered through the window, illuminating the simple crucifix on the wall, Christ suffering in bronze, his agony frozen in metal as permanent as the sins she could not undo.

She had stopped believing her prayers reached heaven sometime during the year before Caterina's murder. The words still formed on her lips out of habit and necessity, the performance of devotion required of a nun, but the faith that once animated those words had leaked away drop by drop until only the empty vessel remained.

Still, she knelt. Still, she whispered the familiar phrases.

"*Miserere mei, Deus.*" Have mercy on me, O God. The psalm her nurse had taught her as a child. "*Secundum magnam misericordiam tuam.*" According to your great mercy. Words offered up by sinners and saints alike, as if there might be no difference between the two when stripped of pretense and brought low by circumstance.

Footsteps in the corridor made her pause. Light and deliberate, someone moving with purpose despite the late hour. The steps stopped outside her door.

"Sister Virginia?" The Prioress's voice carried unmistakable authority despite its quietness. "I need to speak with you. Now."

Virginia rose from her knees, her joints protesting after too long on cold stone. She opened the door to find Mother Angela standing with a letter in her hand, sealing wax broken, the parchment creased as though it had been read multiple times.

"The Dean has submitted his preliminary report to the Cardinal." She held out the letter, her weathered face grave in the candlelight. "His Eminence has written to inform me that he will be visiting Santa Margherita personally within the month. Not a pastoral visit, Sister Virginia. An investigation."

The corridor tilted. Virginia gripped the doorframe, rough wood biting into her palm.

"What did the Dean's report say?"

"I was not shown its full contents. Only informed that serious allegations have been raised requiring His Eminence's personal attention." The Prioress's careful neutrality began to crack, anger bleeding through. "He will speak with each sister individually. He will examine our records and financial accounts. He will question servants and townspeople. And he will determine whether formal charges should be brought before the ecclesiastical court."

"The petition?"

"Your petition, signed under duress by every sister in this convent, will not save you from a Cardinal determined to uncover truth." Mother Angela's words came sharp now. "I warned you this would come. I told you to confess before it reached this point. But you chose manipulation over repentance, coercion over contrition, and now we will all face the consequences of your pride."

Virginia forced herself upright, releasing the doorframe. "When does he arrive?"

"The letter does not specify an exact date. Only that it will be within four weeks." The Prioress folded the letter with precise movements. "Which means you have perhaps three weeks, perhaps less, before His Eminence walks through our gates and begins asking questions you will not be able to deflect with noble bearing and carefully constructed lies."

She turned to leave, then paused. "I suggest you use that time to prepare yourself, Sister Virginia. Not to craft new deceptions, but to make peace with whatever God you still believe in. Because when the Cardinal finishes his investigation, there will be no peace to be found anywhere in this world."

The Prioress's footsteps faded down the corridor, leaving Virginia alone with moonlight and the crucifix and the certainty that the endgame had finally begun.

She returned to her knees, but no prayers would come. Only the sound of her own breathing in the darkness, and the image of Cardinal Borromeo arriving at Santa Margherita's gates with the full weight of ecclesiastical law behind him.

The bells of San Maurizio began to toll midnight across the sleeping town. Twelve strokes marking the passage from one day to the next. Virginia counted each one, and when the final note faded, she stood and moved to the window.

Somewhere beyond these walls, Gian Paolo hid from the same investigation that would soon consume her. Somewhere, Rainerio lay awake wondering if his testimony would be enough to save him or only enough to damn them all. Somewhere, the Cardinal prepared his questions and marshaled his authority.

Three weeks. Perhaps less.

Virginia pressed her forehead against the cool glass and closed her eyes. She had bought herself time with the petition, bought it at the cost of binding every sister in the convent to her lies. But time was a currency that could only be spent, never saved, and she had just learned that her account was nearly empty.

Tomorrow she would need to tell Benedetta and Ottavia about the Cardinal's letter. She would need to convene their diminished circle and plan whatever futile response might delay the inevitable.

But tonight, in these final moments before the knowledge spread and the panic began, Virginia stood alone at the window and watched moonlight silver the garden where she had once believed herself untouchable, protected by birth and rank and the conviction that some people were simply too important to be held accountable for their sins.

She had been wrong.

For the first time since that July night when she had helped carry Caterina's body through the convent to Gian Paolo's waiting hands, Virginia understood the difference between manageable anxiety and inevitable defeat. The Cardinal was not afraid of the de Leyvas. He was not susceptible to manipulation.

The game was ending. And she was going to lose.

Virginia turned from the window as the last echo of midnight bells faded. Every signature on the petition was a thread in the web she had woven, every name a promise that might hold or might shatter when the Cardinal's investigation finally broke through the walls she had built from desperation and threats and the solidarity of women who had nowhere left to turn.

Three weeks to prepare for the Cardinal's arrival. Three weeks to shore up defenses that would not hold. Three weeks to maintain the illusion of innocence while everyone involved knew the truth beneath it.

She moved back to her cot and lay down, staring at the ceiling where shadows danced in the moonlight. Sleep would not come tonight. Perhaps it would never come easily again. But she would endure these dark hours as she had endured everything else, with the determination that had sustained her through every crisis.

The Cardinal was coming. And when he arrived, there would be nowhere left to hide, no story left untold, no witness remaining silent.

But until then, she would fight. She always had.

* * *

VIRGINIA PRESSED HER thumb against the calendar scratch she had carved into the doorframe of her cell—seventeen marks since Mother Angela had delivered the Cardinal's letter. Seventeen days measured in chapel bells and the scrape of her thumbnail against wood. Each morning, she added another line, watching the tally creep toward the moment when His Eminence would arrive to examine her life like a ledger book full of damning entries.

The convent had settled into a strange, suspended atmosphere. Gian Paolo had been imprisoned since late January, nearly eight months now, and without his nocturnal presence the corridors no longer echoed with sounds that had once made sisters cross themselves and pretend not to hear. The quiet should have brought relief. Instead, it felt like held breath before a scream.

On the fifteenth day of September, Sister Silvia brought news that seemed almost irrelevant given Virginia's circumstances, but which illustrated how thoroughly corruption had saturated Monza's moral landscape. The Dean had written again to the Cardinal, this time about the priest of San Maurizio who kept his maidservant living openly in his house despite repeated warnings.

"The whole town is outraged," Silvia reported, twisting her hands in her apron. "The neighbors have complained to the sheriff. But Father Arrigone refuses to send her away, and apparently, it's easier to dissolve a marriage than to separate a bad woman from a priest determined to keep her."

Virginia listened, her attention drifting to the window where September light slanted across the garden. What did other people's sins matter when her own was about to be laid bare?

On the feast of San Michele, Mother Angela received another letter, this one from Madrid, bearing the de Leyva seal. Don Luigi had finally responded to the Cardinal's diplomatic inquiry about raising the convent walls. The Prioress read portions of it aloud to Virginia in the Chapter house, her voice flat with irony.

> *I can assure Your Eminence that we are arranging with Milan to heighten the walls of the Convent of Santa Margherita. I have spoken with my family, and we all agree that they shall be raised.*

Virginia listened to her brother's ornate deflections and felt only distant, bitter amusement. Don Luigi wrote as though the problem were architectural rather than moral, as though higher walls could retroactively undo years of violations that had occurred within them.

"He concludes by saying he is always happy to serve His Eminence in any way possible." Mother Angela set down the letter. "Your family plays the game well, Sister Virginia. They acknowledge the Cardinal's authority while giving him nothing that could be used against them."

"They have had generations of practice protecting the de Leyva name." Virginia's voice was flat. "Higher walls will not save me. We both know that."

The Prioress said nothing, which was answer enough.

* * *

THE CARDINAL ARRIVED three days later, at the end of September, when autumn had finally claimed victory over summer's lingering heat. He came without the formal procession that usually accompanied a Cardinal's visitation—no banners, no elaborate entourage, no advance notice. Instead, he slipped through Monza in a simple carriage with only two attendants, moving with the discretion of someone who wished to catch Santa Margherita unaware.

Virginia was in the garden when word reached her of his arrival. She had been kneeling before the small shrine to the Madonna beneath the apple tree, rosary beads slipping through her fingers while her lips formed words her mind could not hold. Sister Benedetta found her there.

"He is here. Mother Angela is with him in the parlatory." Benedetta kept her voice low. "He has asked to speak with you. Alone."

Virginia's hands clenched around the rosary, wooden beads biting into her palms. "When?"

"Now. Immediately." Benedetta moved closer and lowered her voice. "Virginia, whatever you say to him—"

"I know." Virginia stood, brushing dirt from her habit with hands that wanted to tremble but which she forced to steadiness. "I know."

She walked through the garden and into the convent proper, each step measured and deliberate. Sisters appeared in doorways and corridors as she passed, their faces anxious, curious, afraid. Virginia kept her eyes forward and her chin level.

Mother Angela stood outside the parlatory. "His Eminence wishes to speak with you privately. I am instructed to wait here and ensure you are not disturbed."

The Prioress opened the door. Virginia stepped through into the dim space beyond, and the door closed behind her with a finality that sounded like a tomb sealing.

Cardinal Federigo Borromeo stood at the window, his back to her, hands clasped behind him. He was not a tall man, but his presence filled the room with an authority that had nothing to do with physical stature. Late afternoon light filtered through the grating, illuminating dust motes suspended in still air that smelled faintly of beeswax and old wood.

When he turned to face her, his eyes were neither cruel nor kind, only penetrating, intelligent, and utterly focused on uncovering truth. His face was lean, ascetic, marked by years of scholarship and prayer and the weight of administering an archdiocese.

"Sister Virginia Maria de Leyva." His voice was measured, cultured, carrying the precision of someone accustomed to being obeyed. "Please, sit."

Virginia sat on the hard chair, the rough wood pressing through the fabric of her habit. She folded her hands in her lap where their trembling would not be visible. The room felt cooler than the corridor, as though judgment itself lowered the temperature.

He studied her, his gaze moving over her face with the careful assessment of someone reading a document written in a foreign language. Virginia met his eyes, summoning every ounce of de Leyva pride and breeding.

"I have received troubling reports about this convent." He spoke without preamble. "From the Dean of Monza. From townspeople. From servants. From the apothecary Rainerio. All describe irregularities that, if true, represent grave violations of your vows and the sanctity of this holy place."

Virginia said nothing. Better to wait, to see what proof he would present.

"Testimony suggests that Signor Gian Paolo Osio has been a frequent visitor to this convent, often at night, often for extended periods." The Cardinal's tone remained even, factual. "That he has been observed entering and leaving through passages that should have been secured. That you, Sister Virginia, have maintained an intimate relationship with this man for several years, despite your vows of chastity and enclosure."

Still Virginia remained silent. The distant sound of chapel bells tolling the hour drifted through the grating.

"There are also reports of a child." Now the Cardinal's voice sharpened slightly. "A daughter, kept in Signor Osio's household, visited by you with unusual frequency. The apothecary mentions remedies he provided—some for digestive complaints, some for sleeping difficulties, and some..." He paused, letting the silence stretch. "Some whose purpose is less innocent."

The room felt suddenly airless. Virginia forced herself to breathe normally, to keep her face composed.

"And there are whispers of violence." The Cardinal's eyes never left her face. "Of a lay sister named Caterina de Meda who disappeared, whose body has never been recovered. Of servants who know too much, silenced through fear or force. Of a convent that has become something very far from what God intended."

He leaned back slightly, creating distance between them. "I ask you now, Sister Virginia, to tell me the truth. Not the version you think will protect you, not the careful lies you have constructed. The truth, before God and the Church."

This was the moment. The precipice. Virginia could feel the weight of every decision she had made for the past years pressing down on her shoulders.

She lifted her chin, met the Cardinal's penetrating gaze, and spoke with all the authority her name and breeding could summon.

"Your Eminence, I cannot deny that I have known Signor Osio. That I have spoken with him, that I have taken interest in the welfare of his daughter, that perhaps my conduct has been less circumspect than a professed religious should maintain." She paused, letting those admissions settle into the space between them. "But I contest absolutely the charge that I have committed carnal sacrilege or violated my vows in the manner these reports suggest."

The Cardinal's expression did not change, but she saw the slight narrowing of his eyes, the minute tightening of his jaw.

"The vows I took were not freely given, Your Eminence." Virginia let each word fall precisely, like a chess piece placed with deliberate strategy. "I was brought to this convent as a child, not yet of the required age for profession. My novitiate was shortened, the prescribed years not fully elapsed before I was compelled to take vows I never desired. My father arranged my enclosure not out of concern for my soul but out of political convenience and financial calculation."

She watched his face carefully. His expression remained neutral, but he had not interrupted.

"I have lived here for eighteen years, Your Eminence, but I have never truly been a nun in my heart or by the proper forms of the Church. I was forced into holy orders against my will, enclosed before I reached marriageable age, compelled to profess before the law allows. If my vows were not freely and properly taken, then how can I be accused of violating them?"

It was her final card, the one defense she had been saving for exactly this moment. The Cardinal had spent years fighting against forced vocations, denouncing parents who treated convents as repositories for unwanted daughters. If any ecclesiastical authority might be sympathetic to this argument, it would be Federigo Borromeo.

"If I was never truly a nun, if my profession was invalid from the beginning, then whatever relationship I may have had with Signor Osio cannot be called sacrilege. I am of marriageable age. I have the right, as any woman does, to form attachments according to my own will rather than my father's dictates." Virginia's voice gained strength. "The sin, if any, lies with those who forced me into a life I never chose, not with me for seeking whatever small measure of human connection I could find within my imprisonment."

The silence that followed stretched until Virginia wondered if she had miscalculated catastrophically. The Cardinal sat motionless, his eyes distant, his hands still folded with perfect composure. From somewhere in the convent, the sound of sisters chanting Vespers drifted faintly through the walls.

Then he sighed—not the exasperated sound of someone confronting stubbornness, but something deeper and more troubled.

"Your argument touches upon concerns that have long occupied my attention." He measured each word carefully, as though weighing them on scales. "I have indeed spoken out against the practice of forced vocations. I have denounced parents who treat convents as convenient repositories for unwanted daughters. The suffering caused by such coercion offends both divine law and natural justice."

Something fragile kindled in Virginia's chest, not quite hope, but the possibility of it.

"However." The Cardinal's tone hardened like cooling iron. "However willing or unwilling your original profession, you have lived as a nun for years. You have held the position of Vicaress, exercising authority over other sisters. You have enjoyed the protections and privileges of religious life. Whatever the circumstances of your entry into Santa Margherita, you have had ample time to petition for release if your vocation was truly forced."

The fragile thing guttered and died.

"Moreover, the reports I have received suggest that your conduct has endangered not only your own soul but the souls of others under your influence. If the allegations about Caterina are true—" He left the sentence unfinished, the implication hanging heavy in the still air.

Virginia's throat closed. She swallowed once, twice, forcing words past the constriction.

"I did not harm Caterina." The words came out stronger than she felt. "Whatever happened to her, I bear no responsibility for her fate."

The Cardinal studied her for a long moment, his intelligent eyes searching her face for cracks in the façade.

"I am not convinced of your innocence in all these matters, Sister Virginia. But neither am I prepared, based on what has been presented to me, to bring formal charges that would destroy you and create enormous difficulty for your family before all of Milan." He stood, moving to the window where the light silhouetted him. "Your argument about forced vocation has merit, though not as much as you might hope. And the fact remains that you are a de Leyva, with all the political complications that name entails."

He turned back to face her, the light behind him making it difficult to read his expression clearly. "I will be lenient, Sister Virginia. Not because you deserve it, but because the alternative would cause more harm than good to the Church and to those innocent sisters who have been caught up in the consequences of your choices."

Virginia hardly dared to breathe.

"You will swear to me now, on your immortal soul, that you will never see or communicate with Signor Gian Paolo Osio again. Not in this life. Not by letter, not by messenger, not by any means whatsoever." The Cardinal's voice carried absolute authority. "You will dedicate yourself to genuine penitence. Not the performance of devotion you have been maintaining, but true spiritual reformation through fasting, prayer, and meditation on the gravity of your sins."

"I swear it, Your Eminence." The words tumbled out before he could change his mind. "I swear on my soul that I will never see or speak to Signor Osio again, that I will devote myself to penance and prayer."

"And you will submit yourself absolutely to the authority of your Prioress. No more special privileges. No more exercise of influence over other sisters. You will live as the newest novice lives—in obedience, humility, and constant examination of conscience." He moved toward the door, then paused with his hand on the latch. "I do this not because I believe you are innocent, Sister Virginia, but because I believe in the possibility of redemption even for the most fallen souls. Do not make me regret this decision."

The door opened. The Cardinal departed without further word, leaving Virginia alone in the parlatory with her oath hanging in the air and the scent of beeswax sharp in her nostrils.

She remained seated for a long time after he left, her hands gripping the arms of the chair until her knuckles whitened. Leniency. Mercy. An oath never to see Gian Paolo again, but no formal charges, no public trial, no exposure that would have destroyed what remained of the de Leyva name.

It was more than she had dared hope for. And somehow, sitting alone in that dim parlatory with afternoon fading into evening outside, it felt like the worst punishment imaginable.

* * *

WHEN SHE FINALLY emerged, she found Mother Angela waiting in the corridor. The Prioress searched her face with sharp, assessing eyes.

"The Cardinal has shown me mercy." Virginia's voice sounded strange in her own ears, hollow. "I am to remain here. To devote myself to penance. To never see or communicate with Gian Paolo again."

"And you agreed to these terms?"

"What choice did I have?"

Mother Angela nodded slowly. "Then perhaps, Sister Virginia, you have been given an opportunity very few receive, a chance to begin again, to become what you might have been if circumstances had been different. I suggest you do not waste it."

She turned and walked away, leaving Virginia standing in the corridor while the rest of the convent waited to hear what judgment had been rendered.

Virginia made her way back to her cell where Benedetta and Ottavia were waiting, sitting in tense silence, their faces anxious in the fading light.

"What happened?" Benedetta stood as soon as Virginia entered. "What did he say?"

Virginia sank onto her cot, the rope frame creaking beneath her. "He knows. Not everything, perhaps, but enough. Rainerio testified about the medicines. The Dean compiled reports. There were witnesses, testimony, evidence."

"And?" Ottavia's voice trembled.

"And he has shown mercy." Virginia spoke the words as though they belonged to someone else's story. "I swore an oath never to see or communicate with Gian Paolo again. To submit myself to the Prioress's authority. To dedicate myself to genuine penance."

"But no formal charges?" Benedetta's analytical mind grasped the essential point immediately.

"No formal charges. No trial. No public exposure." Virginia met her eyes. "The de Leyva name is protected. The Church's reputation is preserved. Everyone benefits from this arrangement except, perhaps, truth itself."

"And us?" Ottavia asked quietly. "Did he mention us?"

"He mentioned Caterina. He mentioned violence and witnesses silenced through fear." Virginia's hands clenched in her lap. "But he brought no specific accusations against either of you. I think... I think he chose to see what he could prove and ignore what he could only suspect."

The three women sat in silence as the last daylight faded from the window. The bells for Compline began to toll, calling them to evening prayer.

"What will you do?" Benedetta asked finally.

Virginia looked at her hands, pale against the black fabric of her habit. "What I swore to do. Submit. Obey. Pray. Become what they always wanted me to be—a proper nun, properly penitent, properly enclosed." She raised her eyes to meet theirs. "The performance continues. But this time, there is no audience but God, and no rebellion left to make the years bearable."

* * *

THAT NIGHT, LONG after Compline, Virginia knelt at the small altar in her cell. Moonlight filtered through the window, casting shadows that shifted and pooled across the floor. She whispered the words of her oath again, binding herself more completely than any convent walls ever had.

The Cardinal had given her mercy she had not earned, and in accepting it she had surrendered the last piece of herself that remained ungoverned by the institution that had claimed her at fourteen. She would live here now as she was meant to have lived from the beginning—in obedience, humility, and the endless repetition of prayers that might never reach heaven.

Somewhere beyond these walls, Gian Paolo sat in prison, nearly eight months now since his arrest, unaware that she had just sworn never to see him again. Somewhere, the Cardinal traveled back to Milan satisfied that he had resolved a difficult situation with minimal damage to the Church's reputation. Somewhere, her family in Madrid breathed easier knowing that the de Leyva name had been protected once again.

Virginia remained on her knees as moonlight tracked slowly across the floor, her joints aching from too long on cold stone. She would fast and pray and examine her conscience as the Cardinal commanded. She would become what everyone had always expected her to be.

This was mercy. This was redemption. This was the price of survival.

And Virginia, kneeling alone in the darkness, understood that she had traded one prison for another. But this new cell had no door at all, only walls that would close in slowly, year after year, until there was nothing left of the woman who had once believed herself too important to be held accountable for her sins.

The bells of San Maurizio began to toll midnight across the sleeping town. Virginia counted each stroke and wondered if it might have been kinder to have faced the Cardinal's judgment without flinching and been done with it.

But she had never been brave enough for that. She had only ever been cunning enough to survive.

* * *

THE WALLS OF Pavia Castle had never truly been as secure as they appeared. Gian Paolo Osio learned this on a night when the autumn wind carried the scent of rain and the guards' watches changed with the predictability of prayer bells. A captain with debts. A sergeant whose sister worked in the castle kitchens and had mentioned, carelessly, which locks stuck and which doors were poorly watched. Bribes calculated not in gold alone but in the careful elevation of men who had labored too long without advancement.

By the time Count Fuentes received word that the prisoner had vanished, Gian Paolo was already three leagues south on the road to Monza, riding through darkness with two trusted men and the knowledge that flight was the only remaining choice.

Clemency had never been Fuentes' way.

In his prison cell, the same narrow room that had held him since February, Osio had understood with absolute clarity what his continued captivity meant: years stretching toward decades, documents accumulating, the investigation broadening until the Church and the Crown had wrung everything useful from his imprisonment. Better to become a fugitive than a monument to Spanish justice.

His palazzo in Monza stood dark when he arrived near dawn, servants long since dismissed or scattered. He did not light the lamps. He moved through familiar rooms that now felt like a stranger's house, gathering what he would need: money hidden in places only he knew, clean clothes, correspondence that had to be destroyed before anyone could seize it as evidence.

He could not leave Monza permanently. To do so was to abandon everything—property, influence, the delicate web of loyalty and fear he had spent years constructing. But neither could he move openly. The town would know within hours that he had escaped. Captain Niguarda would have men watching the roads, the markets, anyone known to have served Osio in the past.

He would have to hide. And from hiding, he would have to act.

* * *

THE MESSAGES BEGAN within days, carried by intermediaries through channels he had spent years developing. A servant whose cousin worked at the convent. A priest with complicated loyalties. A merchant's widow in Milan whose son owed Osio favors worth any risk.

Within a week, intelligence reached him about the state of things in Monza. The Cardinal had visited Santa Margherita. Virginia had been questioned privately. The investigation was proceeding, carefully, methodically, building layer upon layer of testimony. And Rainerio, the apothecary, the man whose shop he had already tried once to reach with violence and failed, had opened his mouth to Count Fuentes' men and told them nearly everything.

Osio sat in the darkness of an upstairs room in his palazzo, the only room where he dared show a candle after nightfall and weighed his options. Rainerio alive meant testimony that would seal him in Pavia for decades, or worse, send him to the gallows. Rainerio had seen too much, supplied too many suspicious medicines, observed too many nocturnal comings and goings. The apothecary was the kind of witness whose detailed, specific testimony could overcome even the protection of the de Leyva name.

Rainerio dead meant silence. Meant a chance, however slim, that without his corroboration the case might weaken.

The decision, once he framed it that way, was simple.

He assembled his men, three of them, capable and reliable, men who understood that loyalty came with rewards but also with blood. He gave them clear instructions about timing and method. The apothecary kept irregular hours at his second shop, the smaller establishment he used for less legitimate commerce. Narrow street, few witnesses, easy escape routes.

But they would need a reason to draw Rainerio out at a specific time. They would need him vulnerable, distracted, believing himself safe.

Osio composed a brief message to Virginia and sent it with Pesseno, whose nervousness was barely concealed as he approached the convent gate with the folded parchment.

The note was deliberately vague:

> *I am returned to Monza but cannot move openly. Circumstances require immediate action regarding our mutual difficulties. The apothecary has informed against us both. I will address this matter. Do not reply directly. If questioned, know nothing.*

He did not tell her his plans. Did not seek her permission or cooperation. He simply informed her that he would act, and that she should maintain ignorance if authorities came asking questions afterward.

* * *

VIRGINIA HELD THE note in trembling fingers, reading it twice in the dim light of her cell before holding it to the candle flame and watching the parchment blacken and curl.

Gian Paolo had escaped. Was in Monza. Knew about Rainerio's testimony.

I will address this matter.

She understood what that meant. Had understood the moment she read those words. Osio, cornered and desperate, was about to do something that would make everything worse. Another act of violence. Another body. Another crime that would bind them together in mutual culpability.

She should refuse. Should find a way to send word that she wanted no part in whatever he planned. That she had sworn to the Cardinal never to communicate with him again, that she was trying to save what remained of her reputation and her life.

But she did nothing. Said nothing. Sent no reply, as he had instructed.

Her silence was its own form of consent.

Benedetta found her standing at the window, the note's ashes scattered in the ceramic dish beneath the loose stone.

"He has escaped," Virginia said quietly. "He is in Monza."

"And?"

"And he knows about Rainerio. About the testimony." Virginia's voice was flat, empty of inflection. "He says he will address the matter."

Benedetta's sharp eyes searched her face. "You know what that means."

"Yes."

"And you sent no word to stop him?"

Virginia turned from the window. "What word could I send? What power do I have to stop Gian Paolo when he has decided on a course of action? He informed me as a courtesy, not to seek my permission."

It was true, but it was also an evasion, and they both knew it. Virginia could have found a way to warn Rainerio, could have sent word to the authorities, could have done something other than simply accept what was about to happen.

Instead, she waited.

* * *

The 6th day of October

VIRGINIA HAD AWOKEN that morning with a familiar discomfort—throat rawness that made swallowing painful, the early warning of the sore throats that plagued her in autumn when the weather turned. By Vespers, her voice had grown hoarse, each word scraping against inflamed tissue.

After the service, she mentioned it to Ottavia. "My throat is worse. I'll need something from Rainerio—diamaron for a gargle, perhaps."

Ottavia's face showed nothing unusual. "I'll have Isabetta fetch it this evening. You should rest."

Virginia thought nothing of the request. Such errands were routine. The convent's relationship with the apothecary, though complicated by recent events, still involved the regular supply of medicines. She had ordered remedies from Rainerio dozens of times over the years.

The evening arrived with unseasonable warmth despite the advancing season. Virginia attended Vespers with the other sisters, her voice joining theirs in the familiar psalms though it hurt to sing, her hands folded in an attitude of devotion while her mind catalogued her discomfort.

When the service ended, she returned to her cell. The throat pain had intensified. She would not sleep without relief.

Ottavia appeared at her door as the last light faded from the sky. "Isabetta is going now for your medicine. She'll return shortly."

"Thank you." Virginia settled at her small table with her breviary, trying to read by candlelight, but the pain made it difficult to focus. She waited.

Time passed slowly. The convent settled into its evening rhythms. Sisters moving to their cells. The last offices sung. Lamps extinguished one by one until only the sanctuary light remained burning in the chapel.

Still Isabetta had not returned.

Virginia moved to her window, looking out at the darkening garden. From here she could see nothing of the town, only the walls and the shadows gathering beneath the trees. But somewhere out there, beyond the convent walls, an errand was being run on her behalf. A simple request for throat medicine.

She tried not to think about what else might be happening in those same streets. About Gian Paolo, escaped and hiding somewhere in Monza. About

Rainerio, who had opened his mouth to Count Fuentes' investigators and described things better left unspoken.

The sound, when it came, was distant but unmistakable. Two sharp cracks, like wood splitting. Then silence. Then running feet on cobblestones, faint and confused.

Virginia's hands tightened on the windowsill. Harquebus shots. She had heard them before, the night Ferrari died, and earlier, the night someone had fired at Rainerio and missed.

This time the shots came from the direction of San Maurizio. From the direction of Rainerio's smaller shop.

Her throat tightened, though no longer from illness.

Footsteps approached her cell. Sister Dionisia, the doorkeeper, her face troubled in the lamplight she carried.

"Sister Virginia, Isabetta has returned with your medicine, but there's been violence in the town." Dionisia held out a small phial. "The apothecary Rainerio has been shot."

Virginia took the medicine with hands that did not tremble, though her heart hammered against her ribs. "Shot? Is he...?"

"Gravely wounded, they say. Isabetta heard the shots as she was leaving the shop and saw a man running toward Porta Lecco. She was frightened and came directly back."

"How terrible." Virginia heard her own voice, steady and appropriate, expressing exactly the right degree of shocked concern. "We must pray for his recovery." She paused, as though a thought had just occurred to her. "Did Isabetta see who fired the shots?"

"A man in a cloak," Dionisia said. "He moved too quickly in the darkness to recognize. But she thought he carried something long under his cloak."

A harquebus. Of course.

"Thank God Isabetta was not harmed," Virginia said. "Please tell her I'm grateful she was brave enough to complete the errand despite such danger."

After the doorkeeper departed, Virginia stood alone in her cell with the phial of medicine in her hand. She had sent for it. Had created the errand that brought

Isabetta to Rainerio's shop at precisely the hour when someone, she would not let herself think who, had been waiting with a weapon.

She set the medicine on her table and stared at it in the candlelight. The liquid inside was perfectly ordinary. Diamaron for a gargle. A remedy she had requested dozens of times before.

But something about it felt wrong. Tainted.

What if Arrigone had been to the shop? What if he had cursed it somehow, put a spell on any herbs intended for her? The thought was irrational, born of years of magical thinking, of magnet stones and love potions and the constant fear that unseen forces were manipulating her fate.

But it was also useful. A reason to refuse the medicine. A way to create distance.

She opened her door and found Ottavia in the corridor. "I cannot take this curative. I don't trust it. What if Arrigone has been to the shop? What if it's cursed?"

Ottavia's eyes met hers with perfect understanding. "Then I'll send for fresh herbs. A different batch."

"At this hour? After what just happened?"

"Giuseppe de Regibus, Susanna's son and Appolonia's brother, returned to Monza today. He's young and brave. He won't refuse."

Within the hour, Ottavia returned with confirmation that Giuseppe had been sent. Virginia waited in her cell, the untouched first phial still sitting on her table like an accusation.

When Giuseppe returned, Ottavia brought not fresh herbs but news. "The apothecary's shop is in chaos. Giuseppe heard wailing inside. Rainerio may not survive the night."

Virginia received this information sitting at her small altar, rosary beads threaded through her fingers. "How dreadful. His poor family."

"Giuseppe managed to obtain a fresh remedy before the household descended into mourning. Shall I bring it to you?"

Virginia looked at the first phial, then at Ottavia's carefully neutral face. "No. I think... I think I will manage without it. My throat feels somewhat better. Prayer has helped, perhaps."

It was a transparent lie, and they both knew it. Her throat still ached. But the treatment felt impossible to swallow now. Not because of curses or spells, but because accepting it meant accepting everything it represented.

She had sent for a treatment she genuinely needed. She had not arranged for Rainerio to be at his shop at any particular hour. She had simply been ill and requested a remedy, as she had done countless times before.

But the timing. The coincidence. The fact that on this particular night, when Gian Paolo was desperate and Rainerio had become a dangerous witness, her ordinary request had drawn the apothecary to his shop after dark.

The bells of San Maurizio began to toll. Not the regular call to prayer but the urgent, irregular clanging that meant someone was calling for the Sacrament. Someone was dying. A priest was needed to administer last rites.

Virginia closed her eyes and tried to pray, but the words would not come.

She had not held the weapon. Had not given the order. Had not even known, when she sent Isabetta for herbs that morning, that tonight would be the night Gian Paolo chose to act.

But she had known he was free. Had known Rainerio had testified. Had known that sooner or later, violence would follow.

And when her throat had hurt and she needed treatment, she had sent for it anyway.

The distinction between innocence and guilt felt impossibly thin.

Hours later, when Benedetta found her still kneeling at the window, the bells had stopped ringing.

"It is done," Benedetta said quietly. Not a question.

"Yes."

"The whole town will know by morning that it was Osio's men."

"Let them know." Virginia's voice was hollow. "I sent for throat curatives because I was ill. What happened to Rainerio afterward is not my concern."

"Do you believe that?"

Virginia finally turned from the window. "I believe that I requested herbs I needed. That Isabetta went to fetch it on my orders. That violence occurred in the street while she was there, and that she was fortunate not to be harmed. These are facts. What authorities choose to make of them is beyond my control."

"They will ask questions. About the timing. About why you sent for herbs at night."

"My throat was painful. I needed relief to sleep. These are ordinary things." Virginia's hands were steady now, her voice taking on the cold precision she used when constructing useful fictions. "Sister Dionisia can attest that I remained in the convent all evening. You can confirm that I was ill. The doorkeeper will testify that Isabetta completed an errand on my behalf and returned safely, thank God, despite the violence she witnessed."

Benedetta studied her friend's face in the dim light. "You have become very skilled at this."

"At what?"

"At maintaining the appearance of innocence while knowing full well what transpires in the shadows."

Virginia was silent for a long moment. When she finally spoke, her voice was barely above a whisper. "I sent for medicine, Sister Benedetta. Nothing more. If Gian Paolo Osio chose this night to settle his grievances with the apothecary, that is his sin, not mine. I cannot be held responsible for coincidences."

"Can't you?"

The question hung in the air between them. Outside, the night was beginning to lighten infinitesimally toward dawn. Somewhere in Monza, Rainerio was dying or already dead. Somewhere, Gian Paolo was hiding, blood on his hands or on the hands of his men.

And here in the convent, Virginia knelt with her untouched medicine and her carefully constructed alibis and the knowledge that she had crossed another line she could never recross.

Not the line between planning murder and witnessing it. But the line between someone who sinned through ignorance, and someone who had learned to orchestrate her needs so perfectly that violence followed in their wake like a shadow.

Whether she had known the specific time or method no longer mattered. She had sent for a curative on a night when Rainerio's death served her interests. Had created the circumstance, however innocently, that drew him to his shop after dark.

Complicity did not require conspiracy. Sometimes it required nothing more than ordinary needs, expressed at convenient moments, and the willingness to look away from what followed.

"We should pray for him," Virginia said finally. "For Rainerio's soul."

"And for your own?"

Virginia did not answer. She simply knelt at her small altar and bowed her head, not in prayer but in acknowledgment of what she had become.

Outside, the bells began to toll for Matins. The convent stirred with the sounds of sisters rising for prayer. Soon they would gather in the chapel to sing the ancient psalms while somewhere in Monza a family grieved.

And Virginia would join them, her voice rising with theirs, her face composed in devotion, her hands folded in an attitude of piety that had become so practiced she could no longer remember what genuine faith had felt like.

The performance would continue. The lies would persist. The machinery of investigation would grind forward.

But in the darkest hours of night, alone with her conscience, Virginia understood exactly what she was.

And she chose to live with it anyway.

* * *

RAINERIO DIED BEFORE dawn. The news spread through Monza with the rising sun, carried by servants and merchants, growing more elaborate with each retelling. The apothecary had been shot twice. Had lingered through the night in agony. Had been unable to name his attacker before succumbing.

Virginia heard the details in fragments throughout the morning. Sister Silvia brought word from the portress who had heard from the baker's wife. Sister Candida whispered that Domenico, who had gone into town early, had returned saying the whole marketplace was in an uproar.

"They are saying it was Signor Osio's men," Candida said, her voice low and frightened. "That everyone knows he has returned to Monza. That this is revenge for Rainerio's testimony to Count Fuentes."

"What evidence do they have?" Virginia kept her tone calm, detached, as though inquiring about events that had nothing to do with her.

"Domenico says he saw one of Osio's servants, the one they call Redhead, walking near San Maurizio last night with something under his cloak. He recognized him by his walk and his red hair catching the lamplight. And Isabetta says the man she saw running had the same build."

Virginia felt the noose tightening with each new piece of information. Witnesses. Testimony. Connections being drawn between Osio and the murder, between the murder and the convent, between the convent and her.

She needed to create distance. Needed to muddy the waters before the pattern became too clear.

That afternoon, she had Rainerio's eldest daughter called to the convent. When the girl arrived, Virginia spoke to her through the parlatory grating, her voice gentle with concern.

"My dear child, I am so grieved to hear of your father's death. He was a good man who served this convent faithfully for many years." Virginia paused, letting her sorrow register. "I understand there is much confusion about who might have committed this terrible crime. Have the authorities said anything? Have they found the man responsible?"

The girl's face was blotched with tears. "They question everyone, Sister. They say it was one of Signor Osio's men, but Signor Osio has disappeared again. They cannot find him."

"How strange." Virginia allowed puzzlement to color her voice. "I wonder... Has anyone mentioned Father Arrigone? The priest of San Maurizio?"

The girl looked confused. "Father Arrigone? No, Sister. Why would they?"

"Only that I know there was some difficulty between your father and Father Arrigone. Some dispute about payments or services, I believe. And Father Arrigone's church is so close to where your father was attacked. It seems odd that no one has questioned whether he might have seen something. Or known something." Virginia let the suggestion hang delicately in the air.

It was a transparent attempt at misdirection, and in the days that followed it would gain no traction. But it was something. A seed of doubt planted. A suggestion that perhaps other enemies existed beyond the obvious one.

* * *

THAT NIGHT, BENEDETTA found Virginia at the window again, staring out at darkness.

"It is done," Benedetta said. Not a question.

"Yes."

"The whole town knows it was Osio's men. They are looking for him everywhere. And they are asking questions about his connections, his associates, those who might have helped him or known of his plans."

Virginia did not turn from the window. "Let them ask. I know nothing. I sent for throat medicine because I needed it. That Isabetta's errand coincided with Rainerio's death is unfortunate timing, nothing more."

"Do you believe that?"

"It does not matter what I believe." Virginia's reflection ghosted in the dark glass. "It matters only what can be proven."

"Domenico is saying that the murder was done on your orders. That you arranged for Rainerio to be at his shop at that specific hour. That you and Osio planned this together."

Now Virginia turned, her face pale but composed in the candlelight. "Who will believe him over a de Leyva?"

"The authorities might. If they find enough corroboration."

"Then we ensure they find none." Virginia moved away from the window, her voice taking on the cold precision of someone making practical calculations.

"I sent for medicine I genuinely needed. Sister Ottavia witnessed my illness. The doorkeeper can attest that I remained in the convent all evening. What happened in the streets of Monza is not my concern or my responsibility."

Benedetta studied her friend's face in the dim light. "You have become very skilled at maintaining useful fictions, Sister Virginia."

"I have become skilled at survival." Virginia met her eyes without flinching. "As have you. As have we all. We are bound together now, not by choice but by necessity. What happened to Rainerio is tragic, but it changes nothing about our situation except perhaps to buy us a small measure of protection by removing a dangerous witness."

"You feel no guilt?"

Virginia was silent for a long moment. When she finally spoke, her voice was barely above a whisper. "I feel many things, Sister Benedetta. Guilt. Fear. Exhaustion. But I also feel the cold certainty that we are too far down this path to turn back. Rainerio's death was not my doing—I gave no orders, made no plans, participated in no conspiracy. But did I know something was coming? Yes. Could I have warned him? Perhaps. Did I choose instead to do nothing?" She paused. "That is the question I will answer to God someday. But not today. Today I must simply survive."

Outside, the bells tolled for Matins. The convent stirred with the sounds of sisters rising for prayer. Soon they would gather in the chapel to sing the ancient psalms, their voices rising in the darkness while somewhere in Monza a family grieved and authorities searched for a fugitive who had disappeared like smoke.

Virginia knelt at her small altar, not to pray but simply to assume the posture of devotion that had become her constant disguise. Benedetta watched her for a moment, then turned and left without another word.

In the silence that followed, Virginia closed her eyes and tried to feel remorse for Rainerio's death. Tried to summon the horror and guilt that surely a decent person would feel at having enabled, even passively, the murder of a man who had only told the truth.

But she felt nothing beyond hollow weariness and the knowledge that she had crossed another line she could never recross. Not the line between innocence and guilt. That had been crossed long ago. But the line between someone who sinned through weakness and passion, and someone who maintained her position through calculated silence while others committed murder.

The performance would continue. The lies would persist. The machinery of investigation would grind forward, and she would meet it with the same cold composure she had shown the Cardinal; the same aristocratic disdain she had always wielded as both shield and weapon.

But in the darkest hours of night, alone with her conscience, Virginia understood exactly what she had become.

And she chose to live with it anyway.

* * *

The 10th of October

VIRGINIA STOOD AT her window, watching the cobbled square below where townspeople clustered in anxious knots. Four days since Rainerio's death, and the investigation showed no signs of abating. Senator Truffi had arrived from Milan with an authority that superseded local jurisdiction, and his methodical questioning had spread unease throughout Monza.

She turned from the window as footsteps approached. Ottavia, her face pale.

"They're questioning Domenico," Ottavia said quietly. "Senator Truffi sent for him this morning."

Virginia's hands tightened on the windowsill. Domenico, who had witnessed everything that night. Domenico, who had seen Redhead with the harquebus. Domenico, whom she'd had beaten last May for gossiping about Alma Francesca.

"He won't dare speak against us," Virginia said, though her voice lacked conviction. "He knows what happens to those who betray this house."

But even as she spoke, she remembered the look in Domenico's eyes after the beating. Not fear, but something colder. Calculation.

* * *

THE HOURS CRAWLED past. Virginia tried to occupy herself with her devotions, but the words of the psalter swam before her eyes. Around midday, Sister Dionisia appeared at her door.

"My lady, Domenico has returned to the convent."

Virginia rose. "Send him to me."

But Dionisia hesitated. "He's... in the garden, speaking with some of the other sisters. I thought you should know. His manner is strange. Almost... triumphant."

Triumphant. The word struck Virginia like a blow.

She descended to the garden where Domenico was bent over a row of herbs, his movements unhurried. Too unhurried. When he heard her approach, he straightened but didn't bow.

"You were summoned by Senator Truffi," Virginia said without preamble.

"I was." Domenico met her eyes, something he'd never dared before. "The good senator wished to know what I observed the night of Rainerio's death."

"And what did you tell him?"

"The truth, my lady." The title carried an edge of mockery now. "That I saw one of Signor Osio's servants, Redhead, passing behind me in the dark with a harquebus on his shoulder. That I recognized him perfectly by his walk, and by the lamp he carried."

Virginia's breath caught. "Nothing more?"

A smile played at the corners of Domenico's mouth. "I also told him that the shots were fired by your order."

The world tilted. For a moment, Virginia couldn't speak, couldn't breathe. When words finally came, they emerged as a hiss.

"You lying dog!"

"Lying?" Domenico's voice rose. "Lying? You had me beaten like an animal. You threatened to have me thrown in prison, chastised by the Cardinal himself. And for what? For knowing the truth everyone in Monza whispers behind your back?"

Other nuns had appeared now, drawn by the raised voices. Virginia saw Sister Angela, the new Prioress, watching from the cloister walkway. Sister Febronia near the chicken yard. Even Candida, keeping a careful distance.

"You will retract every word," Virginia said, her voice shaking with fury. "You will go back to Senator Truffi and tell him you were mistaken, that you lied."

"Out of what? Fear?" Domenico laughed bitterly. "I've spent years in fear, my lady. Fear of you, fear of Signor Osio and his bravos. But I've given my testimony under oath now. It's done."

Virginia stepped forward, her hand raised to strike him. Domenico didn't flinch.

"Go ahead," he said quietly. "Add assault to your crimes. Senator Truffi will be most interested to hear of it."

For the first time in her life, Virginia felt her power crumble beneath her. She lowered her hand, trembling with impotent rage.

"You will leave this convent," Virginia said, her voice low and dangerous. "You and your wife both. By nightfall."

Domenico's smile was bitter. "You have no authority to dismiss us, my lady. I serve the convent, not you. Sister Angela is Prioress now, or have you forgotten?"

The words landed like a slap. Virginia had forgotten, or rather, had been so accustomed to commanding servants that she'd failed to recognize how much her position had eroded.

"Then I will speak to Sister Angela," Virginia said, struggling to maintain her composure. "I will make it clear that your presence here is intolerable. That you have slandered me to Spanish authorities. That you cannot be trusted."

"Will you?" Domenico began removing his work gloves with deliberate slowness. "And will Sister Angela listen? She who has no love for you? She who knows what everyone knows?"

He turned and walked toward the servants' quarters without bowing, without permission to leave her presence.

Virginia watched him go, then turned sharply toward the convent offices where Sister Angela would be found.

* * *

SISTER ANGELA SAT at the Prioress's desk, the same desk where Sister Bianca had once sat, where Virginia herself had dreamed of sitting. Now it belonged to her enemy.

"Sister Angela, I must speak with you about Domenico and his wife."

The Prioress looked up, her expression carefully neutral. "I understand there was a scene in the garden. Half the convent heard your raised voices."

"He has made false accusations against me to Senator Truffi. Lies born of malice and resentment. He cannot remain here."

"False accusations?" Sister Angela set down her pen. "Are you certain they are false, Sister Virginia?"

The question hung in the air between them.

"He testified that I ordered Rainerio's murder. It is a vicious lie. He seeks revenge because I had him disciplined for gossiping."

"The beating in May, you mean. Where the injuries could have killed him." It was not a question. "When he spoke publicly about the child in Signor Osio's house."

Virginia's hands clenched. "His employment here is a matter for the convent to decide. I am simply informing you that his continued presence is... problematic."

"Problematic for whom, Sister Virginia? For the convent? Or for you?"

"They are the same thing," Virginia said coldly. "My family built this convent. The de Leyva name is inseparable from Santa Margherita. An attack on me is an attack on this institution."

It was her final card, and they both knew it. The feudal authority she could no longer wield as Vicaress, she could still invoke as a de Leyva.

Sister Angela was silent for a long moment. When she finally spoke, her voice was carefully measured. "I will speak with Domenico and Isabetta. If they wish to leave, I will not prevent it. But I will not dismiss faithful servants simply because they have given testimony to lawful authorities."

"Then suggest to them that their continued employment here may become... uncomfortable. That the convent is a small place. That it would be better for all concerned if they sought positions elsewhere."

"You want me to intimidate them into leaving."

"I want you to recognize that their presence here is disruptive and will only become more so as Senator Truffi's investigation proceeds." Virginia rose. "They have testified against me. Do you truly believe they can continue to work in a convent where I reside? That I can share these walls with people who have accused me of murder?"

Sister Angela's expression gave nothing away. "I will speak with them."

It was not the immediate acquiescence Virginia had once commanded, but it would have to suffice.

* * *

WITHIN THE HOUR, Domenico and Isabetta stood at the convent gate, their few possessions bundled in worn cloth. Sister Dionisia had opened the door with visible reluctance, and now the couple passed through without looking back.

Virginia watched from an upper window as they disappeared into the narrow streets of Monza. She'd meant the expulsion as punishment, as a demonstration of her authority. But even from this distance, she could see that Domenico walked with his head high, not as a dismissed servant, but as a man newly freed.

"You should have kept them close," Ottavia murmured beside her. "Now they have nothing to lose by testifying against us."

Virginia closed her eyes. She knew Ottavia was right. In her rage, she'd made a tactical error. But the damage was done.

"What will you do?" Ottavia asked.

Virginia drew herself up, smoothing her habit with hands that almost didn't shake. "We show grief, as is proper. We express shock and horror that Rainerio was killed. We pray for his soul and for justice against his murderer."

"But Domenico..."

"Is a lying servant with a grudge," Virginia said firmly. "His testimony means nothing. He's angry about being dismissed, so he's invented fantasies to take revenge."

Even as she spoke the words, she heard how hollow they sounded. But what else could she do? Admit the truth? Confess?

No. She would maintain her innocence. She would perform grief and outrage and wounded dignity. She would make them prove every accusation.

Below in the chapel, she could hear the nuns gathering for None. The bells rang out their measured call to prayer, the same as they had every day for decades. But everything had changed.

Virginia descended the stairs, composing her face into an expression of pious sorrow. Sister Dionisia glanced at her as she entered the chapel, then quickly looked away.

They know, Virginia thought. Or they suspect. But suspicion isn't proof.

She knelt before the altar, her lips moving in the familiar prayers. But her mind raced ahead to Senator Truffi's investigation, to the questions that would surely come, to the lies she would need to tell with utter conviction.

Behind her, she sensed the other nuns watching. Not with sympathy, but with something closer to fascination—the way one watches a building burn, unable to look away.

Virginia bowed her head and prayed. Not for forgiveness, but for the strength to maintain her denials. Not for mercy, but for the skill to survive what was coming.

The prayers echoed in the stone chapel, ancient and unchanging. But the woman who spoke them had crossed another line she could never recross.

* * *

The 11th of October

THE BELLS OF San Maurizio had scarcely finished tolling for Compline when Gian Paolo understood, finally and without evasion, that Monza would no longer endure him.

The church was dark, save for the single lamp that burned before the Sacrament. Its feeble light barely reached the side chapel where he had made his refuge these last nights—a pallet dragged in from his house at dusk, his cloak for cover, his saddlebag for pillow. The stone beneath him held the day's chill, seeping through the thin mattress, but he had grown accustomed to discomfort. It was the other sounds that unnerved him now: the distant murmur of voices in the streets, the hurried steps at odd hours, the way the great wooden doors shuddered whenever someone leaned against them as if to test the strength of their bolts.

He lay on his side, watching the faint, wavering aura of the sanctuary lamp, as Captain Niguarda's words repeated themselves in his mind.

Give him to the executioner. Give him to Bodot.

Monza had taken up the cry willingly. He could hear it in the market, in the courtyards, in the way shutters banged closed when he passed. Rainerio's blood had soaked into the apothecary's shop floor and from there into the very soil of the town, and now the earth itself seemed to reject the man who had spilled it.

A door creaked softly. Steps crossed the nave, not hesitant, but furtive, the gait of a man accustomed to moving unseen. Gian Paolo tensed, one hand sliding toward the knife he kept beneath his cloak.

"Gian Paolo."

The low voice belonged to Arrigone, whose thin shadow now detached itself from the darker mass of the choir screen. He had shed his vestments and wore only a plain cassock, belted in haste. The man looked older in this uncertain light, his face a landscape of resentment carved deep by years of envy and humiliation.

"You still skulk in shadows, priest," Gian Paolo said, rising to sit on the edge of the pallet. "Old habits die hard. Especially when one has spent so much time peeping through grates and whispering filth to nuns."

Arrigone's mouth tightened. "And you still imagine yourself the lord of Monza, sleeping on a beggar's pallet in a church whose priest despises you. We are both creatures of habit, it seems."

"Careful, Father," Gian Paolo said softly. "Remember who put you in prison the last time your tongue grew too loose. Those harquebuses found in your sacristy? Do you recall how surprised you were? How quickly the bishop acted on my information?"

"I recall everything," Arrigone said, moving closer until the lamplight caught the glitter of hatred in his eyes. "I recall the damp of the cell. The shame of the interrogation. And I recall who wrote the letters that won you your prize in the first place. Who taught you the words to seduce a woman you were too clumsy to win on your own. Who crafted the soul of the lover while you merely provided the body."

Gian Paolo laughed, a short, sharp sound in the quiet church. "And how it must gall you still. To know you wrote the poetry while I took the pleasure. To know she read your words but moaned my name. You tried to steal her from me, didn't you? Told her the truth, begged her to love the author instead of the man. And what did she do? She laughed. She threatened you. She called you 'infamous and shameful' in her letter and swore to see you punished if you ever dared speak of your desires again."

Arrigone's face went white, the skin stretched tight over cheekbones sharp with malice. For a moment, Gian Paolo thought the priest might strike him, and his hand tightened on the knife hilt beneath his cloak.

But Arrigone mastered himself, though his hands trembled at his sides. "Mock me if it comforts you, Osio. It changes nothing. You are a rat in a trap, and the water is rising. Captain Niguarda's men circle the piazza. The people howl for your blood. And I tell you frankly: I will not drown with you."

"You will do as you are told," Gian Paolo said. "As you always have. Because you are a coward. And because you know that if I fall, I can drag you down with me. One word to Truffi about your role in this affair, about the messages you carried, and you will burn long before I hang."

"Perhaps," Arrigone said, his voice dropping to a whisper that carried more venom than any shout. "Or perhaps I will simply open the doors tonight and let the mob find you. They say sanctuary is sacred, but accidents happen in the dark. A man who has murdered so many—who would question if justice found him hiding here?"

Gian Paolo stood, moving with sudden, fluid grace. He saw Arrigone flinch, saw the fear that lived just beneath the hatred.

"You won't," Gian Paolo said, looming over the smaller man. "Because you need me gone, not dead. Dead men leave confessions. Dead men's papers are examined. You want me to vanish. To disappear into the mists and take our secrets with me."

Arrigone held his ground, though his eyes darted toward the sacristy door. "Then go. Leave Monza. Cross the Adda tonight. Go into the Veneto and rot there. Just get out of my church before you bring the roof down on us both."

"I will go," Gian Paolo said. "But not because you wish it. And not to the Veneto."

"I care nothing for where you go," Arrigone spat. "Hell would be my preference, but Rome will suffice if it gets you out of Lombardy."

"Rome." Gian Paolo smiled, a cold expression that didn't reach his eyes. "Yes. Let them believe that. Spread the word tomorrow. Tell Niguarda I have gone to throw myself at the Pope's feet. Tell the nuns I seek absolution. It suits me to have eyes turned south while I move elsewhere."

"You intend to stay nearby?" Arrigone realized, horror dawning on his face. "You fool. You arrogant, blind fool. Do you think you can hide in the hedgerows forever? Truffi will find you. Niguarda will find you. And when they do..."

"When they do, I will be ready for them. Unlike you, who freezes when the wolf barks." Gian Paolo turned away, dismissing the priest. He moved to his saddlebag and began to gather his few belongings: a change of linen, a small purse of coins, a shirt that still smelled of Virginia's lavender.

"You will carry a message," Gian Paolo said without looking back. "To Niguarda. And to the governor's palace. That I am gone. That I have fled the duchy."

"And why should I carry your lies?"

"Because it is the only way you survive," Gian Paolo said, buckling on his sword. "If they think I am here, they will tear this church apart stone by stone. And they might find things you would prefer hidden. Your collection of obscene books, perhaps? Or letters from certain nuns? Evidence of the mistresses you kept here?"

Arrigone made a sound in his throat, a choked noise of impotent rage. "One day," he whispered. "One day, Osio, you will push too far. And there will be no one left to threaten."

"But not tonight." Gian Paolo turned, settling his cloak over his shoulders. "Tonight, we are allies. As Cain and Judas were allies, bound by the rope that waits for us both."

He walked past the priest, close enough to smell the sour scent of unwashed linen and fear. Arrigone did not move, but his eyes followed Gian Paolo with the flat, dead stare of a reptile watching prey.

At the sacristy door, Gian Paolo paused. "If you betray me, Arrigone, if you whisper a word of where I have truly gone, I will come back. And I will not need a harquebus to finish what we started."

"Go," Arrigone said, his voice suddenly quiet with a certainty that was more chilling than rage. "But you'll be back. You always come back. And when you do, these walls won't save you. The rope is already woven, Osio. You just refuse to see it hanging above your head."

Gian Paolo felt a cold finger trace his spine, but he forced himself to smile. "We shall see who hangs first, priest."

He stepped out into the nave, leaving Arrigone standing in the shadows, vibrating with hate. The great doors of San Maurizio loomed ahead, but Gian Paolo turned toward the side exit. The bolt slid back with a soft groan. Cold night air washed in, cleansing the staleness of the church.

Monza lay under a thin veil of mist. He slipped into the shadow of the wall, moving with the silent confidence of a predator in familiar territory. He passed the corner of the apothecary's shop without looking at it, though he felt its presence like a cold breath on his neck.

He did not take the main gate. Instead, he threaded his way through back lanes to the low section of the wall he had known since boyhood. The stones were slick with moss, but he climbed them easily, driven by the knowledge that behind him, in the church he had just left, a man was praying fervently for his death.

Crouched atop the wall, he looked back at the dark bulk of Santa Margherita. Somewhere within those stones, Virginia waited. He imagined her face, not the soft, pliant look of their early days, but the hard, desperate mask she wore now. She would hear the rumor of Rome tomorrow. She would know it for the lie it was.

"I will not leave you to them," he murmured.

He dropped down on the outer side, landing in the weeds with a jarring impact that shook his bones. His sword scraped against stone with a metallic shriek that seemed impossibly loud in the stillness. He froze, pressed against the wall, listening for shouts, for running feet, for the clatter of weapons.

But the night remained still. Even the watch, it seemed, no longer cared whether Gian Paolo Osio stayed or fled. The town had already pronounced its verdict. What remained was merely execution.

He set his feet on the path that led south and west, into the darkness that would hide him, but not far enough to save him.

* * *

BY THE MORNING, the rumor had already begun its work.

The portress of Santa Margherita heard it first from a woman delivering eggs. The woman crossed herself, eyes bright with the thrill of news.

"They say he is gone, Sister. Osio. Gone to Rome to beg the Pope's mercy. Captain Niguarda is beside himself."

The portress repeated this in the kitchen, where lay sisters whispered it to laundresses. By Terce, half the convent knew: Gian Paolo Osio had fled to Rome.

Mother Angela received the news with a tightening of the mouth that might have been relief. But when Sister Febronia brought the same news to Virginia, she found her target kneeling before the altar in the chapel, rosary beads threaded through fingers that did not move.

"Sister Virginia," Febronia said softly, approaching the communion rail. "There is news. About Signor Osio."

Virginia did not turn from the altar. The candles before the Sacrament flickered, casting dancing shadows across her profile.

"They say he has gone to Rome," Febronia continued, her voice carrying equal parts relief and uncertainty. "Captain Niguarda's men entered and searched his house at dawn and found it empty. The servants claim he had not been there. The sheriffs are beside themselves. They had the house watched, and yet..."

"Rome." Virginia spoke the word as though tasting something bitter on her tongue.

"Yes. To throw himself at the Pope's feet, they say. To beg absolution for his crimes." Febronia moved closer, lowering her voice. "You must be relieved, Sister. With him gone, perhaps the investigation will lose its urgency. Perhaps Senator Truffi will—"

"He has not gone to Rome."

Virginia's voice cut through the chapel's pious atmosphere like a blade through silk. She rose from the kneeler with slow, deliberate movements, smoothing her habit with hands that betrayed no tremor.

Febronia hesitated. "But everyone says it is true."

"Everyone says what he wishes them to say." Virginia turned, and Febronia saw something in her eyes that made her take an involuntary step backward. Not fear, but a cold, calculating certainty. "If Gian Paolo Osio announces he has fled to Rome, it is because he does not wish to be sought elsewhere."

"But where else would he go?"

"Closer." Virginia moved past her toward the chapel door, her footsteps echoing in the stone chamber. "Always closer than they know."

"I don't understand."

Virginia paused at the threshold, one hand resting on the ancient wood. When she spoke again, her voice was so quiet that Febronia had to strain to hear it.

“Rome is where he went once before, when the Cardinal first learned of our affair. He stayed there long enough to be absolved, then returned to me within the month. He has never possessed the discipline for genuine penance, only the cleverness to perform it.” She looked back over her shoulder. “If he says he has gone south, it means he is hiding north. If he claims to seek the Pope’s mercy, it means he trusts only his own cunning.”

“Then where is he?”

“Close enough to send messages. Close enough to interfere. Close enough to make one more mistake that will destroy us both.” Virginia’s hand tightened on the doorframe. “He cannot leave me, you see. It is his fatal weakness. And mine.”

She walked through the door without waiting for a response, leaving Febronia standing alone in the chapel with the candles and the silence.

* * *

VIRGINIA MOVED THROUGH the stone passages of Santa Margherita, her mind working with the cold precision that had become her only reliable ally. The other nuns she passed fell silent as she approached, their eyes following her with expressions she could no longer interpret—sympathy? Judgment? Fear?

It no longer mattered.

In her cell, she sat at her small writing desk and stared at the blank page before her. She should send word to her brother. Should alert her family’s advocates. Should begin constructing the legal defenses that might preserve what remained of the de Leyva name.

But her hand did not reach for the quill.

Instead, she found herself thinking of Gian Paolo crouched somewhere in the darkness beyond these walls. Watching. Waiting. Unable to fully flee because he could not bear to surrender the game.

We are bound together, she thought. *Not by love. That died years ago, if it ever truly lived. But by complicity. By shared guilt. By the knowledge of what we have done and what we have become.*

The investigation would continue. Senator Truffi would not be satisfied with Domenico's testimony alone. He would dig deeper, question more witnesses, follow the threads of connection that led from Rainerio's murder back through Ferrari's death, through Caterina's disappearance, through all the accumulated violence of their affair.

And when he had gathered enough evidence, the Church and the Spanish Crown would act.

Virginia understood this with perfect clarity. Understood that her title, her family name, the feudal power she had wielded so carelessly, none of it would save her in the end.

But not today. Today she would continue the performance. Would attend prayers with appropriate devotion. Would speak to the other nuns with careful courtesy. Would maintain the fiction that Sister Virginia Maria de Leyva was merely an unfortunate victim of malicious gossip.

The lie had become her life. And she would sustain it until the moment it became impossible.

Outside her window, the bells of Monza rang the hour, their sound carrying over walls and fields, reaching toward a man who walked through darkness under cover of mist.

He had not left her. He never would.

The trap was closing around them both, and neither possessed the wisdom to escape it.

* * *

IN THE TOWN, Captain Niguarda stood in the emptied rooms of Osio's palazzo and listened to the sheriffs report what they had found: nothing. No hidden cache of weapons. No incriminating correspondence. No evidence of where he had gone or who had helped him flee.

"Rome," one of the sheriffs said, but without conviction.

"Perhaps," Niguarda replied. "Or perhaps he simply wishes us to believe so."

He walked to the window and looked toward the convent's walls. Somewhere in that maze of stone and shadow, a woman prayed and lied and waited.

"Double the watch on Santa Margherita," he said quietly. "If Osio has fled, we will know soon enough. And if he has not..."

He did not finish the sentence. In the streets below, Monza continued its daily life, the scandal already fading into the background murmur of gossip that sustained every small town.

But Niguarda knew better. The storm had not passed. It had merely drawn breath before the final, devastating blow.

He turned from the window and descended the stairs, his footsteps echoing in the abandoned house where a man had once lived who believed himself beyond the reach of consequence.

The rope was already woven. It hung invisible above them all, waiting only for the moment when pride and passion would finally place their necks within its noose.

* * *

The 14th of October

THE DISPATCH FROM Captain Niguarda lay open on the governor's writing table, its edges curling in the damp air that seeped through the palace windows. Outside, Milan lay under a sullen sky, but inside the study of Count Fuentes, the atmosphere was sharper, charged with the dry, crackling heat of political opportunity.

Don Pedro Enríquez de Acevedo, Count of Fuentes and Governor of Milan, did not sit. He stood before the great map of Lombardy that dominated one wall, his hands clasped behind his back, his silhouette as rigid as the Spanish steel that kept this duchy tethered to Madrid.

"Rome," he said, testing the word as one might test a coin for counterfeit. "He claims to have gone to Rome."

"So, the rumor runs, Excellency," his secretary said from the shadows near the door. "Captain Niguarda reports that the man vanished from Monza two nights ago. His mother claims ignorance. The priest of San Maurizio wrings his hands and says Osio spoke of seeking the Holy Father's mercy."

Fuentes turned slowly. He was a man of precise movements, each gesture calculated to convey authority. At seventy, his face was a mask of parchment and bone, the eyes beneath the heavy lids dark and unreadable. He had ruled Milan for seven years with an iron hand, famously declaring that while the King commanded in Madrid, Fuentes commanded here.

But there was one power in Milan that even he could not easily bend: the Church. And specifically, its prince, Cardinal Federico Borromeo.

"Rome," Fuentes repeated, a thin smile touching his lips. "It is a desperate lie, of course. Men like Osio do not run to the Vatican unless they wish to trade a hangman's noose for a dungeon. He is likely hiding in some ditch in the Veneto or shivering in a barn on the Adda."

He walked to the writing table and looked down at the report. Molteno, dead. Rainerio the apothecary was dead, murdered in his own shop. The blacksmith Ferrari, dead. The nun Caterina de Meda, vanished and almost certainly dead. And through it all, the stench of scandal rising from the Convent of Santa Margherita like smoke from a hidden fire.

For months, Fuentes had watched Borromeo dither. The Cardinal was a saintly man, they said, obsessed with the purity of his clergy, tireless in his visitations. But in this matter of the de Leyva nun, his saintliness had looked suspiciously like paralysis. He had visited Monza, asked gentle questions, and allowed himself to be maneuvered by a woman's lies because he could not bear to tear open a wound that would shame a noble house and the Church itself.

There was more than politics at stake. Fuentes had held Milan for seven years, and in that time, he had made it clear that Spanish authority would not bend to Italian sensibilities—not to the nobility, not to the merchants, and certainly not to the Church. Every compromise was a crack in that authority. Every scandal left unpunished was an invitation to chaos.

The de Leyva family was powerful, yes. But they were in Madrid, not Milan. And here, in this city, at this moment, Fuentes commanded.

Laisser-aller, they called it in the diplomatic corridors. Let it go. Let sleeping dogs lie. Rome and Madrid both preferred a useless conflict of gestures to any real action that might upset the delicate balance of power in Italy.

But Fuentes was tired of balance. He was tired of the Cardinal's pious inertia.

"Borromeo waits for God to solve his problems," Fuentes said, his voice dry as dust. "He hopes that if he prays enough, the girl will repent, the lover will disappear, and the stain on the Church will fade in the sun. But God has given the sword to the magistrate, not the priest."

He picked up the quill, testing its point against his thumb.

"If Osio says he has gone to Rome," Fuentes murmured, "then let us take him at his word. Let us pretend we believe him."

"Excellency?"

"If he is in Rome, he is the Pope's problem. And if he is the Pope's problem, then the Cardinal has failed to keep order in his own diocese."

Fuentes sat, pulling a fresh sheet of parchment toward him. The strategy unfolded in his mind with the cold clarity of a military campaign. To bypass the Cardinal was a breach of protocol so severe it bordered on insult. To appeal directly to the Pope was to declare, before all of Europe, that the Church's administration in Milan was incompetent.

It would infuriate Borromeo. It would embarrass the de Leyva family in Madrid. It might even annoy the King, who disliked having his governors meddle in ecclesiastical affairs.

But it would trap Osio. And it would force the Cardinal's hand.

"Dictate," Fuentes said, dipping the quill.

The secretary scrambled for his own writing table, parchment rustling.

"To His Holiness, Pope Paul V," Fuentes began, his voice steady. "From his humble servant, the Count of Fuentes, Governor of Milan."

He paused, composing the phrases in his head—polite, deferential, and lethal.

"Preamble," he said, waving a hand. "The usual obeisances. Then this: '*Disorders of the gravest nature have arisen in the Convent of Santa Margherita in Monza, causing the greatest discontent in the countryside. This scandal has reached even the ears of the civil government, which sought to dispose of it with the least noise possible by imprisoning the principal agent of these crimes, one Gian Paolo Osio, in the Castle of Pavia.*'"

He looked up, his eyes hard. "Make sure His Holiness understands that we acted while his Cardinal did nothing."

"Yes, Excellency."

"Continue: '*But this Osio escaped, returning secretly to Monza and giving himself to a nauseous life of crime, culminating in the murder of a witness. Now, rumor reaches us that this assassin, this violator of nuns, has fled to Your Holiness's own city to appeal for absolution.*'"

The quill scratched loudly in the silence of the room.

"*Therefore,*" Fuentes said, leaning forward, "*the Count of Fuentes begs His Holiness to intervene where local authority has faltered. We ask that You authorize the Cardinal of Milan to raise Sister Virginia Maria de Leyva from the abyss into which she has fallen, and to deliver Gian Paolo Osio over to the authority of the King of Spain, should he arrive in Rome.*"

He sat back, dropping the quill. The ink glistened wetly in the dim light.

It was a masterstroke. If the Pope acted, Borromeo would be humiliated, forced to clean his own house under direct orders from the Vatican. If the Pope refused, he made himself complicit in the protection of a murderer. And Osio, if he truly was fool enough to go to Rome, would find the Holy City a trap waiting to snap shut.

"Send it by special courier," Fuentes ordered. "Tonight. I want this in the Vatican before the rumor dies."

"And the Cardinal?" the secretary asked, sanding the wet ink. "Should a copy be sent to the Archbishop's palace?"

Fuentes smiled, a thin, wintry expression that held no warmth.

"No," he said. "Let the Cardinal learn of it from Rome. Let him hear the thunder from the Vatican before he sees the lightning in Milan. Perhaps then he will understand that while he shepherds souls, I govern men."

The secretary paused, pen hovering over parchment. "And the nun, Excellency? Sister Virginia?"

Fuentes' expression did not change, but something cold flickered in his eyes. "The Cardinal will deal with her as he sees fit. My concern is civil order, not spiritual corruption." He paused, examining his hands as though studying the lines of strategy written there. "Though it would not displease me to see the de Leyva name somewhat tarnished in the process. Pride is Spain's sin, and that family has indulged it too long."

The secretary bowed, gathering the documents.

"One more thing," Fuentes said. "Have my secretary prepare letters to Captain Niguarda. I want daily reports on any movement in Monza. If Osio is fool enough to return, I want him taken alive. The King will want to make an example."

"And if he truly is in Rome, Excellency?"

"Then the Holy Father will have an interesting choice to make," Fuentes said, rising from his chair with the deliberate grace of a man who knew his power. "Protect a murderer or preserve the dignity of the Church. Either way, we win."

The secretary bowed and departed, leaving Fuentes alone with his maps and his calculations.

He stood and walked to the window, looking out at the gray stones of the courtyard below. Servants crossed the space with the hurried efficiency of those who knew they were watched. Beyond the walls, Milan continued its commerce and intrigue, indifferent to the machinations of the powerful.

The game had changed. He had thrown a stone into the pond, and the ripples would spread far beyond Monza. They would wash against the walls of the Vatican itself, and when they receded, there would be no place left for Osio to hide. No refuge in churches. No sanctuary in shadows. No forgiveness from Rome.

And Cardinal Borromeo? Fuentes allowed himself a thin smile. The Cardinal would learn that while he shepherded souls, Fuentes governed men. And in the contest between heaven and earth, earth always moved faster. The Church might claim dominion over the spirit, but the sword, the secular authority that could imprison, execute, and destroy, belonged to the Crown.

And the Crown had placed that sword in his hand.

Somewhere, in a convent in Monza, a woman waited. In Rome, perhaps, or more likely in some ditch in the Veneto, a man hid. Between them lay a trail of bodies: Molteno the de Leyva's agent, Ferrari the blacksmith, Rainerio the apothecary, the lay sister Caterina whose disappearance no one truly believed was flight. And threading through it all, the whispers of scandal that had reached even the Spanish court in Madrid.

The de Leyvas would rage, of course. They would write furious letters to their relatives in the King's circle, would protest that their daughter was being persecuted, that the Governor of Milan overstepped his authority by meddling in Church affairs.

Let them rage. Fuentes had learned long ago that power consisted not in avoiding conflict but in choosing which battles to fight, and ensuring you fought them on ground of your own selection.

He had chosen his ground. The Vatican. The Pope himself.

And now the machinery of Church and State ground forward with inexorable precision, each turning of the gears bringing Osio and his nun closer to the moment when all their lies would collapse beneath the weight of accumulated evidence.

Fuentes turned from the window. On his desk, the map of Lombardy lay spread beneath the lamplight, its territories marked in careful ink: Spanish holdings in red, Venetian in blue, Papal in gold. Monza sat at the convergence of three powers, and for years it had played them against each other, using proximity to the borders as both shield and weapon.

No more. This letter to the Pope would eliminate the nun's greatest protection—the Cardinal's reluctance to act against a noble family. Once Rome itself demanded action, Borromeo would have no choice but to investigate thoroughly, to interrogate rigorously, to root out every detail of the scandal that had festered in Santa Margherita for nearly a decade.

And when the investigation was complete, when all the testimony had been gathered and all the witnesses had spoken, there would be judgment. Not the gentle, pastoral correction the Cardinal preferred, but something harsher. Something that would serve as a warning to other noble families who believed their rank placed them above the law.

Fuentes allowed himself a moment of satisfaction. He had been patient. He had waited while Borromeo dithered, while the Cardinal made his polite inquiries and accepted implausible denials. He had even imprisoned Osio without revealing the full scope of the man's crimes, giving the Church time to handle its own affairs.

But patience had limits. And those limits had been reached the moment Rainerio's blood soaked into the cobblestones of Monza.

The end game had begun.

Outside, the bells of Sant'Ambrogio tolled the hour, their deep resonance carrying across the city. In palaces and hovels alike, people paused to cross themselves, to mark the passage of time with the rhythm that had governed Milan for centuries.

But time, Fuentes knew, was not neutral. It could be an ally or an enemy, depending on how one used it. He had used it well. Had waited for Osio to make one mistake too many. Had gathered evidence while appearing to do nothing. Had let the Cardinal believe he still controlled the situation while slowly, methodically, building the case that would force Rome's hand.

And now the trap was sprung.

Not with violence. Not with dramatic arrests or public executions. But with a letter. A carefully worded appeal to the one authority Cardinal Borromeo could not ignore or deflect.

The Holy Father himself.

Fuentes collected the documents on his desk, organizing them with the same precision he brought to all his affairs. Tomorrow, this letter would be in the hands of a courier riding south toward Rome. Within a week, it would lie on the

Pope's desk. Within a month, the response would come, and with it, the authorization for Borromeo to act with all the power the Church could muster.

The de Leyva nun would fall. Osio would hang, if they ever found him. And Milan would learn once again that while the Church might claim men's souls, the Governor claimed their lives.

And that, in the end, was all that mattered.

He extinguished the lamp and left the study, his footsteps echoing in the marble corridors of the palace. Behind him, the letter lay on the desk, its ink drying, its words already beginning to reshape the fates of everyone they touched.

In Monza, Virginia slept, or lay awake in her cell, wondering how much longer she could maintain the performance.

In some hidden refuge, Osio counted his dwindling options and planned his next desperate move.

In Rome, the Pope would soon receive news that would force him to choose between mercy and justice.

And in Milan, Count Fuentes retired to his chambers with the quiet satisfaction of a man who had just moved the most important piece on the board.

Checkmate was not yet declared. But the King was in check, and every remaining move led inexorably toward the same ending.

* * *

Mid-October

THE PETITION REACHED Rome folded into the thick packet of dispatches from Milan, its seal impressed with the arms of the King of Spain and the smaller device of his governor in Lombardy. Among letters on tariffs, troops, and quarrelsome Venetian envoys, the sheet bearing Don Pedro Enríquez de Acevedo's hand might have seemed of little consequence.

It was not.

Clerks unfastened ribbons, sorted papers, and stacked them according to urgency. Somewhere between the most urgent matters, the request from the

Count of Fuentes found its place, carried at last into one of the smaller antechambers where decisions were quietly made and just as quietly forgotten.

There, beneath the painted eyes of long-dead pontiffs, an official of the Secretariat of State broke the seal and read.

To His Holiness, Pope Paul V,

From Don Pedro Enríquez de Acevedo, Count de Fuentes,

Governor of Milan.

Most Holy Father,

It is with the deepest reluctance that your humble servant presumes to lay before Your Holiness a matter of such grave and scandalous nature, yet conscience and duty alike compel this appeal.

Disorders of the most serious character have arisen in the Convent of Santa Margherita in Monza, within the Duchy of Milan. A certain Gian Paolo Osio, a layman, a minor nobleman of that town, has for many years maintained criminal relations with the nuns of that house, most particularly with Sister Virginia Maria de Leyva, daughter of the noble house of that name. Murder, sacrilege, and the most abominable offenses against chastity have followed in the wake of this unholy connection.

This has caused the greatest discontent in the countryside, which even reached the ear of the Count de Fuentes, who, thinking to dispose of it with the least noise and scandal possible, had the said Osio imprisoned in the Castle of Pavia without revealing the cause. But this Osio escaped, returning secretly to Monza and giving himself to a nauseous life of crime, culminating in the murder of a witness who had dared to speak of what he knew.

Therefore, the Count de Fuentes humbly begs His Holiness to authorize the Cardinal Archbishop of Milan to raise Sister

Virginia Maria de Leyva from the abyss into which she has fallen, and to deliver the said Gian Paolo Osio over to the authority of His Catholic Majesty the King of Spain, in the event that he arrives in Rome to appeal for absolution.

Your Holiness's most humble and obedient servant,

The words were respectful enough. The substance was not.

To ask the Pope to 'authorize' a cardinal to correct his own convent was already an implied rebuke. To request that a lay murderer, if he set foot in the Holy City, be handed over to the King of Spain for civil punishment was something more, an intrusion of the secular arm into the most jealously guarded sphere of ecclesiastical authority.

Had Cardinal Borromeo known of it, he would have been outraged. For a governor, however powerful, to bypass the Archbishop of Milan and address the Pope directly about the discipline of a Lombard convent was an affront to the intangible sovereignty of a prince of the Church. It said, without saying: *Your Eminence has failed. Permit me to correct your negligence.*

But Borromeo did not know.

In Rome, the petition was examined, weighed, and quietly put aside. The Holy See had no desire to encourage a precedent by which governors might run to the Vatican whenever they found their local bishops inconvenient. Nor did it relish being drawn into a quarrel between a zealous cardinal and a proud old soldier who liked to declare that, though the King commanded in Madrid, he commanded in Milan.

"A regrettable business," someone said, folding the parchment. "Let it rest. The cardinal can answer for his own nuns. As for this Osio, if he comes to Rome, we shall see. Until then, there is no need to give the Governor more importance than he already grants himself."

So, the petition was filed, as so many petitions were, neither granted nor refused, but buried. No rescript was sent to Milan. No instruction went forth to Borromeo.

But in the archives of the Vatican, the document remained. A loaded weapon that could be drawn forth at any moment, should circumstances change. A record that the civil authority had appealed to Rome about disorders the Cardinal had failed to address.

In time, such records had a way of becoming inconvenient.

* * *

IN LOMBARDY, NOTHING had dissolved.

While Roman clerks smoothed papers and dipped their quills, the *birri* of Milan scoured the countryside for a man who seemed to have melted into the autumn mists.

All during the last half of October, the search for Gian Paolo Osio went on without respite. Parties of mounted sheriffs clattered through the gates of Monza at dawn, their breath steaming in the chill air as they spread out along the roads toward Lecco, toward Bergamo, toward the Adda. They questioned innkeepers and carters, ferrymen and charcoal burners. They peered into haylofts and wine cellars, barns and roadside shrines.

They found nothing.

In Monza itself, Captain Niguarda had Osio's house watched day and night. At first, that vigilance had yielded small fruits. While Gian Paolo slept beneath the dubious shelter of San Maurizio's altar, he had spent his days in his own rooms, slipping back and forth under cover of the crowd. Now even that trace had vanished. The shutters of the Osio palazzo remained closed. No light showed at night. No familiar figure crossed its threshold by day.

His mother, gray and pinched with fear, wrung her hands and protested ignorance.

"He is my son, *signori*," she sobbed when the sheriffs pressed her. "Do you think I would hide him from you if I knew where he had gone? He will be the ruin of us all. May God forgive him. May God have mercy on him. I do not know where he is."

She was eighty-four years old, her house already marked for destruction, her other son Teodoro still suspected of their uncle's murder. The ruin of the Osio name was nearly complete. One son a fugitive murderer, the other an accused murderer, and she herself reduced to begging the authorities for mercy while her neighbors whispered and pointed.

Yet even now, she would not betray Gian Paolo. Whatever else he was, seducer of nuns, killer of witnesses, he was still her son.

Perhaps she spoke truth. Perhaps not. In either case, it did not help them. The man they sought had disappeared as though the earth had opened and swallowed him.

In a sense, it had.

* * *

LA CANONICA LAY far from the main roads, among low hills and damp meadows where autumn fogs clung long after the sun had risen elsewhere. It was not a village so much as a name given to a scatter of houses, barns, and fields belonging to one of Lombardy's oldest families, the Taverna, whose estates and influence reached into the very heart of Milan's governing councils.

It was to this obscure locality that Gian Paolo Osio retreated when Monza became too dangerous even for him.

The Taverna villa was no great palazzo, but a solid country house built around a small courtyard, its walls streaked with age and ivy. Behind it, vineyards marched up a low slope, their leaves turned to rust and gold. In front, a stand of poplars shielded the approach from the road, their pale trunks rising like a screen between the house and the world.

Within, in a room whose shuttered windows admitted more damp than light, Gian Paolo sat on a carved chest and listened to the muffled sounds of country life—the creak of a cart, the distant bark of a dog, the clatter of pails in the courtyard below.

He had been there for days. Weeks, perhaps. Time blurred when one could not move freely.

At first, the secrecy had seemed almost amusing, a new game in a life built on defiance. Count Lodovico Taverna, senator and counselor of state, had received him with cautious friendship, his manner that of a man who found himself unexpectedly harboring a wolf in his dovecote.

"For a little while," Taverna had said, closing the door of the small upper chamber they assigned him. "Until tempers cool. You understand, Gian Paolo, that in this I risk no small thing."

"You risk nothing that your name cannot cover," Gian Paolo had replied, smiling with the charm that had seduced nuns and nobles alike. "Fuentes is not fool enough to clash with a Taverna over an old friend seeking a few days' shelter."

But as October wore on, it became clear that the Count of Fuentes was precisely that fool, or rather, that he was determined enough to ignore even the usual restraints of prudence when his pride was engaged.

News filtered in with the servants and the messengers who came and went under various pretexts. Captain Niguarda's patrols had not slackened. In Monza, the people still spoke Rainerio's name with anger and fear, their eyes turning always to the Osio house when the murder was mentioned. In Milan, tongues wagged in the palace corridors; everyone knew that the Governor had made Osio's capture a matter of personal honor.

"He will not let it go," Lodovico Taverna said one damp evening, standing by the small hearth that struggled to warm Gian Paolo's hiding place. The senator's face, lean and worn from years of public service, was drawn with a fatigue that was not only physical. "Every day there are new orders, new riders sent out. Fuentes wishes to show that no one can defy his jails and walk away unpunished."

Gian Paolo shrugged, though the knot in his stomach tightened.

"He blustered when I escaped Pavia," he said. "He blustered when I claimed asylum. Governors come and go. Their wrath dies with their term. When he is recalled to Spain, he will have other matters to fret over than one gentleman's indiscretions in a provincial town."

"You do not understand," Taverna said quietly. "This is no longer about a provincial town. It is about who commands in Milan. Fuentes took you once under his authority and you slipped through his fingers. Now you have killed again. The people cry for justice. If he cannot produce you, it will be said that not even the Governor's prisons can hold a noble criminal, that friends and relatives may always shield him. He cannot allow that."

"Then he should have kept a better watch on his keys," Gian Paolo replied, but there was less bite in the jest than there might once have been.

Taverna studied him, his dark eyes thoughtful. "Cross the Adda," he said at last. "Go into Venetian territory. You have friends there. Gold can buy more protection in the Serenissima than my name can buy here. Stay until this storm has passed."

"And leave Virginia?" The answer was immediate, almost automatic. "Leave her to bear the weight alone? You know as well as I do that if Fuentes cannot hang me, he will be content to see a nun walled up in my place. He is already meddling where he should not, writing to Rome, I am told, over the Cardinal's head. Do you think he will hesitate to make an example of Santa Margherita if he cannot lay hands on me?"

Taverna's mouth tightened. "Your concern for Sister Virginia is touching. It comes twenty years late."

Gian Paolo's eyes flashed. For an instant, the veneer of the polished cavalier cracked, and the raw, dangerous man beneath showed through.

"She is my affair," he said. "Not Fuentes's. Not Borromeo's. Not even yours."

"And your affair," Taverna replied evenly, "has become a matter of state. Do not mistake me, Gian Paolo. I have no love for Fuentes. He struts about as though Milan were his personal farm. But I will not have my house pulled down around my ears for your sake. I have sons. I have estates. I sit on the Council by His Majesty's favor. I cannot shelter the man the Governor has sworn to take, not when the *birri* are already sniffing in these hills."

Gian Paolo looked away, toward the shuttered window where a thin line of gray marked the meeting of wood and stone. Beyond it, the fields of La Canonica lay sodden under a low sky.

"Have they come this far?" he asked, his voice suddenly tired.

"Not yet," Taverna said. "But they will. Fuentes has set the *birri* to combing every village from the walls of Milan to the shores of Como. It is only a matter of time before some overzealous captain decides to prove his loyalty by riding up to my gates with a warrant in his hand. When that day comes, I must be able to look him in the eye and say that you are not here."

"And if you say it now," Gian Paolo murmured, "it will at least be true."

Silence settled between them, thick as the smoke gathering under the low ceiling.

At length, Taverna spoke again. "You cannot stay, my friend. Not here. Not in any house that bears my name. I have already given you more than prudence allows—weeks of shelter, food, safe passage for your messages. My duty to my family and to the Council will not permit more. You must find another hole to crawl into. Or," he hesitated, "you must do what any reasonable man in your place would already have done: cross the Adda and save your neck while you still can."

Gian Paolo rose from the chest in a single, impatient movement, the narrow room suddenly too small to contain his restlessness.

"Reasonable men," he said, "do not bring nuns into their beds. They do not smuggle babies out of convents. They do not shoot apothecaries and blacksmiths. Do not ask me to begin being reasonable now."

He paced the length of the chamber, four strides one way, four strides back, like a caged animal measuring the bars.

"Across the Adda," he said with contempt. "Into the Veneto. To live out my days in some shabby lodging, listening to strangers mispronounce my name while Virginia is questioned, accused, perhaps already confined. No. Better a clean hanging in the piazza than such a lingering cowardice."

"Those are not the only choices," Taverna replied, though his tone suggested he believed they were. "You have always been inventive. Invent something now that does not drag those who help you into ruin."

Gian Paolo stopped. Slowly, almost unwillingly, his mind turned toward the one place in Lombardy where the arm of civil law could not easily reach, where walls and rules and the pride of a noble family might, for a time, provide a shield.

The very place from which all of this had begun.

Santa Margherita.

If he crossed the Adda, he would be safe from Fuentes but lost to Virginia. She would face the Cardinal alone, face whatever inquiries and accusations they brought against her. They would question the nuns. They would uncover Caterina's disappearance. They would find the baby, Alma Francesca, living in his house with his name on the baptismal certificate.

And Virginia, without him there to deflect blame, to bribe witnesses, to threaten enemies into silence, would crumble. She had been a great lady once, imperious and proud. But fear had made her desperate. Isolation had made her fragile. She needed him. She had always needed him.

If he returned to Monza and hid within the convent's walls, he might save himself and her together or destroy them both in a single stroke.

It was madness. It was also, irresistibly, his kind of solution.

He looked back at Taverna, and for an instant there was something almost like gratitude in his eyes, twisted by stubborn pride.

"You have given me much," he said. "More than I deserve. I will not repay you by bringing the Governor's men to your door. I will be gone before dawn."

Taverna inclined his head, accepting both the promise and the necessity. "I will have a horse saddled," he said. "There is a back track that leads toward the Monza road without passing any farmsteads. Take it. Travel by night. And, Giovanni Paolo—"

He waited until the other man met his gaze.

"If there is any path left to you that does not end at the gallows, take it. For your sake, and for hers."

"For hers," Gian Paolo repeated softly, as though testing the weight of the words. "We shall see."

* * *

THAT NIGHT, WHILE the fog rose from the fields of La Canonica and the *birri* slept uneasily in their barracks, Gian Paolo Osio rode out from the Taverna estate by a narrow lane between hedges, his cloak drawn close, his face turned once more toward Monza.

Behind him, the windows of the villa remained dark. Count Lodovico Taverna likely stood for a long time at an upper casement, listening to the diminishing hoofbeats, before turning away with a sigh that would carry the weight of more than one man's sins.

Ahead, beyond the folds of the land and the veil of mist, the walls of Santa Margherita waited, cold, high, and implacable as judgment.

Within those walls, Virginia slept, or lay awake, listening to the silence that had replaced the familiar sound of his footsteps in the garden below.

She did not yet know he was coming. But she would. And when he arrived, when he begged admission one final time, she would face the choice that had haunted her since that first night ten years ago when she had let him through the garden door.

Send him away, and live. Or let him in and die.

In the end, Virginia had never been able to send him away.

* * *

End of October

THE LETTER ARRIVED at midday, carried by a peasant boy who thrust it into the portress's hand and vanished before she could ask his name. It was addressed not to the Prioress, but to Sister Virginia Maria, and bore no seal, only a smudge of damp earth near the wax seal.

In the privacy of her cell, Virginia broke it open. The handwriting was hurried, the ink blotted as if the writer had been glancing over his shoulder with every stroke.

> *They are close. I have nowhere else. Tonight, at the garden wall, when the bell tolls for Compline. For the love of God, do not turn me away.*

There was no signature, but none was needed.

Virginia sat for a long time with the scrap of paper in her hand, listening to the rain drum against the shuttered window. She should burn it. She should go to the Prioress, to the confessor, to the captain of the guard. She should bar the doors and double the watch. Every instinct of self-preservation told her that to open the gate now was to invite destruction.

Gian Paolo was a drowning man, and he was reaching for her hand not to save himself, but to pull her down with him.

"He will be the ruin of us all," she had told Ottavia only yesterday. And it was true. Rainerio was dead because of him. Molteno was dead. Caterina was dead. The blacksmith Ferrari was dead. The list of ghosts stood between them like a wall higher than any stone barrier.

And yet.

She remembered him as he had been in the beginning—arrogant, yes, but alive with a fire that had warmed her cold existence. She remembered the way he had looked at her when no one else dared meet her eyes. She remembered the child they had made together, the little girl whose face she saw only in stolen moments.

If she turned him away, Fuentes would take him. There would be a trial, a scaffold, a crowd cheering as the axe fell. And she would be left alone in the silence he left behind.

"Damn you," she whispered, the tears hot and sudden in her eyes. "Damn you for making me choose."

She stood and held the corner of the letter to the flame of her candle, watching the paper curl and blacken, the words turning to ash until only the memory remained.

Then she went to find Ottavia.

"Tonight," Virginia said. "At Compline. He will come to the place where the ivy grows thickest. You must be there to let him in."

Ottavia's face went pale. "Virginia, if we are caught—"

"We are already caught," Virginia said flatly. "We have been caught for many years. This changes nothing except that now he will be inside instead of out."

* * *

THE MOON WAS a sliver above the Lambro when Gian Paolo came back to the wall.

He did not come as the lover who had once tossed fruit to a girl in the chicken yard, nor as the conqueror who had slipped through the church doors with a key and a smile. He came as a fugitive, mud-spattered and smelling of wet autumn fields, his cloak heavy with damp and his face drawn by sleeplessness.

He found the spot at the garden wall they had used in the old days, where the ivy grew thickest, and waited. He did not have to wait long.

A soft scrape of stone against stone. A dark shape moving in the shadows. Then Ottavia's low, familiar voice.

"Quickly," she hissed. "Before the patrol passes."

He scrambled up, his boots finding the holds his body remembered. When he dropped into the garden, the silence of the convent seemed to press against his ears like water.

* * *

IT WAS ALL Hallows' Eve. In the church, the nuns would soon be chanting the Office of the Dead, their voices rising to pray for souls in purgatory. Gian Paolo wondered, with a flash of his old cynicism, if anyone was praying for the souls still trapped on this side of the grave.

"She is waiting," Ottavia whispered, her face pale as a spirit in the darkness. "In her cell. But be warned, Gian Paolo, this is not a welcome."

"I did not expect a welcome," he said, his voice roughened by the night air. "Only a refuge."

He followed her through the shadows, slipping through the door she held open with a shaking hand. The familiar smell of the convent, wax, incense, and cold stone, washed over him, bringing a flood of memories both sweet and sickly. He had owned this place once. He had walked these corridors as a secret king. Now he crept through them like a thief.

Ottavia stopped in front of Virginia's door and waited in the corridor.

Virginia was standing by the narrow bed, wrapped in a dark shawl over her habit, her face stripped of all pretense. When she saw him, she did not move to embrace him. Her eyes, dark and hollowed by strain, took in the mud on his boots, the exhaustion in his shoulders, the desperation that clung to him like a second skin.

"You came back," she said. It was not a question.

"I could not cross the Adda," Gian Paolo said. He leaned against the doorframe, suddenly too weary to stand upright. "I rode as far as the bridge. I saw the Venetian guards on the other side. I had gold in my purse and a horse under me. One hour, and I could have been beyond Fuentes' reach forever."

"And yet you are here."

"I could not leave you."

He took a step toward her, but she raised a hand, a small, sharp gesture that stopped him.

"Do not," she said. "Do not speak to me of love tonight. Not when the birri are hunting you through every village in Lombardy. Not when Fuentes is writing to the Pope to demand our destruction."

"I know," he said. "I know it all. Taverna told me. The Governor has made this a personal vendetta. He will not stop until he has my head on a pike and you in a dungeon."

"And so, you lure him here," Virginia said bitterly. "To the one place he cannot enter without the Church's permission. You think to hide behind my skirts again?"

"I think to save us both," Gian Paolo said. "Or to die together if it comes to that. But I will not die alone in a ditch in the Veneto while you face them here."

He moved closer, ignoring her hand, until he stood close enough to see the fine lines of tension around her mouth, the pulse beating in her throat.

"There is no other place, Virginia," he said, his voice dropping to a whisper. "Taverna turned me out. His fear for his position outweighed his friendship. My own house is watched. The woods are full of Fuentes' men. If you turn me away tonight, you send me to the executioner."

She looked at him for a long moment. He saw the conflict warring in her face—the anger at his recklessness, the fear of discovery, and beneath it all, the terrifying, unbreakable bond that had held them together through murder and madness.

She could not let him die. He knew it, and she knew it. It was their damnation and their only remaining truth.

"You may stay," she said at last, the words falling like stones. "We will hide you here in my room. I will stay here too. We'll say I'm ill, fainting spells, fever. It will buy us time."

Gian Paolo let out a breath he hadn't realized he was holding. "Virginia..."

"But on one condition," she cut in, her voice hard as flint.

She stepped back, putting space between them, drawing the shawl tighter around her shoulders as if to armor herself against him.

"You are here for sanctuary, Gian Paolo. Nothing else. You are here because I will not have your blood on my hands. But there will be no..." She hesitated, searching for words that would not sound like betrayal. "There will be no touching. No nights together in my bed. No pretense that we are lovers stealing moments in the dark. That is finished."

He looked at her, stung. "Finished?"

"We are drowning," she said, her voice shaking with sudden intensity. "Can you not feel it? The water is over our heads. If we are to survive this, if God is to grant us even a sliver of mercy, we must stop adding to the weight of our sins. You may hide here to save your life. But you must promise me, swear to me, that you will not touch me again."

Gian Paolo looked at her face in the dim light, at the crucifix on the wall behind her, at the woman who stood before him like a stranger. He remembered the nights of passion, the frantic, desperate couplings that had been their defiance against the world. He remembered the feel of her skin, the scent of her hair, the way she had once whispered that she would burn in hell for him.

Now she offered him life but stripped of the desire that had made it worth living.

"I swear," he said hoarsely. "If that is the price, I swear it."

Virginia nodded, her eyes closing for a moment as if in prayer or pain.

Virginia opened the door where Ottavia waited in the corridor and invited her back inside. "Gian Paolo will hide in my cell. For if they find him now, there will be no mercy for either of us."

"You'll sleep there," Virginia whispered, pointing to the floor beside the bed. "I will lay out blankets. Sister Ottavia will also stay here, as I will feign illness and she will tend to me. Benedetta will remain in her cell."

Gian Paolo looked at the cramped space that would be his prison. No chimney flue to hide in. No secret passage. Just this stifling cell, shared with two women, one of whom he had sworn not to touch.

"How long?" he asked.

Ottavia's eyes were wide with fear. "As long as it takes. As long as we can keep the lie alive."

Ottavia left to retrieve more blankets, and Gian Paolo sank onto a chair, his sword and doublet stripped away, reduced from nobleman to fugitive.

He had sworn. He had promised.

But as he sat in the dim candlelight, waiting for Ottavia to rejoin them, he knew with terrible certainty that the fire between them had never been ash. Only embers buried under lies and good intentions, waiting for the darkness to breathe them back to life.

* * *

The 1st of November

THE MORNING AFTER All Hallows' Eve broke gray and sullen, the light creeping reluctantly into the convent of Santa Margherita. Sister Virginia Maria did not appear for Prime, nor for Terce. By midday, the silence radiating from the upper corridor had thickened into a rumor: the Lady was ill.

"A fever," Sister Ottavia whispered to those who inquired, her face pale with anxiety as she blocked the door to her cell. "And fainting spells. I am tending to her in my room. She must not be disturbed."

Behind the bolted door of that small, stifling cell, the air was heavy with the scent of woodsmoke, and the heat of three bodies pressed too close. The room, scarcely ten paces across, had become a prison of their own making. There was but a narrow bed, a wooden chest, and a crucifix that stared down from the wall with an accusation they could not escape. Two pallets on the floor.

For eight days, this cell was their entire world.

* * *

THE ARRANGEMENT WAS a study in claustrophobia and degradation. On the far side of the room, stripped of his sword and silk doublet, Gian Paolo Osio lay on a pallet of rough blankets, curling into the smallest possible shape, a nobleman reduced to a fugitive, pacing the few steps allowed him like a wolf in a cage. Ottavia slept on a pallet near the door.

By day, the shutters remained closed, admitting only slivers of dusty light. They spoke in whispers. Virginia sat on the edge of the bed, her rosary passing through her fingers without prayer. Gian Paolo watched her, his eyes dark with a hunger that was no longer just desire, but a desperate, devouring need for reassurance that he was still alive.

And at night, the silence deepened until it felt like a physical weight.

Virginia had sworn to God, and to herself, that there would be no sin this time. She had demanded his chastity as the price of his life. But in that heated, airless room, with the executioner waiting outside the walls and nothing but the dark to hide them, the promise crumbled into dust.

It happened on the third night. Virginia lay on the narrow bed, rigid with sleeplessness, staring into the blackness. She heard the rustle of blankets, the soft pad of feet on stone.

"Virginia," he whispered.

"No," she breathed, but the word had no anchor.

He climbed into the bed beside her, his weight dipping the mattress, his warmth a sudden, shocking intrusion in the cold cell. And she did not push him away. In the face of death, the old habits of the flesh were the only comfort left to them.

Ottavia, lying on her pallet a few feet away, turned her back to them. She pulled the rough wool of her blanket over her ears and squeezed her eyes shut, praying for deafness, for blindness, for the mercy of forgetting what she could not help but hear, the stifled gasps, the rustle of linens, the sounds of a love that had become indistinguishable from despair.

For four nights they clung to each other in that narrow bed while the convent slept around them, and Ottavia lay in the shadows, a silent, weeping witness to their damnation.

* * *

ON THE NINTH day, the danger became a pressure they could no longer ignore.

"People are talking," Ottavia hissed, slipping into the room with a basket of bread hidden under her apron. Her eyes were wide with panic. "Sister Febronia asked why I needed so much water. Sister Stefana stopped outside the door and listened. I recognized her worn shoes visible beneath the door."

Virginia sat up, pushing the tangled hair from her face. The room felt suddenly smaller, the walls closing in like the sides of a grave.

"He cannot stay here," she said, her voice sharp with fear. "If they force this door, there is nowhere to hide. We are trapped."

"Back to yours and Benedetta's cell then. The hole in the wall," Gian Paolo said, his voice rough with disuse.

The move required a new layer of blasphemy. Waiting until the corridor was empty, Gian Paolo stripped off his shirt and pulled on a spare habit belonging to

Benedetta. The black wool strained across his shoulders. He draped a white cloth over his head, hiding his beard and the hard planes of his face.

He stepped into the hallway, a tall, grotesque parody of a nun, a ghost in holy vestments, and hurried the few yards to Benedetta's cell.

There, the true hiding place awaited.

Behind a heavy oak chest beneath the window, a panel in the wall had been loosened years ago. It opened into the dark, soot-stained throat of an old chimney flue. It was a vertical coffin, black as pitch, where a man could stand upright and vanish into the masonry of the convent itself.

This became his new existence. By day, he crouched in Benedetta's room or stood in the flue, breathing the stale air of the chimney. By night, he sometimes returned to Virginia's cell, gliding through the corridor in his disguise, a phantom passing beneath the sleeping eyes of the sisters.

* * *

BUT A SECRET shared by four is a vessel with too many cracks.

The routine of the convent began to warp around the intruder. Ottavia, Benedetta, Candida, and Silvia became servants to the ghost. They were seen hurrying up the stairs with platters of roast meat and heavy soups, fare far too rich for sick nuns. They covered the dishes with cloths, their eyes darting nervously as they passed the others in the cloister.

"For Sister Virginia," they mumbled when stopped. "She needs her strength."

But the nuns saw the trembling hands. They saw the way the doors were unlocked, opened, and bolted again in the space of a heartbeat.

And they saw the smoke.

Fires burned in the grates of Ottavia's and Benedetta's room all day long, sending plumes of gray into the autumn sky from cells that should have been left cold for most of the day. Wood disappeared from the stores. Buckets of water were hauled up the stairs, slopping onto the stones.

"Who is eating all that food?" Sister Febronia murmured to the Prioress one morning as they watched Benedetta hurry past.

"Sister Virginia and Sister Ottavia are ill," came the reply.

"Illness does not consume firewood like a furnace," Febronia muttered, her gaze fixed on the closed door.

The whispers grew louder, seeping through the walls like damp.

One morning, Sisters Stefana, Marina, and Rosanna walked down the corridor together. As they passed Ottavia's room, the door, which had been standing slightly ajar, suddenly clicked shut. The sound was sharp, deliberate.

The three nuns froze. They looked at one another, the silence of the corridor screaming the name they were all thinking.

"Did you see that?" Marina whispered.

"Someone pushed it," Rosanna said, her voice trembling. "From the inside."

"But Ottavia is at Mass."

"And Sister Virginia is supposed to be too weak to lift her head," Stefana murmured, her eyes fixed on the bolt. "Yet someone in there moved quickly enough."

They stared at the wood, and the ghost of Monza took shape in their minds. Not a spirit, but a man of flesh and blood, breathing the same air they breathed.

* * *

THE BREAKING POINT came with a rumor from the market, carried into the convent like a contagion.

Sister Dionisia, fresh from the city and trembling with excitement, cornered Ottavia by the well.

"They say," she whispered, leaning close, "that the Governor knows. They say he is sending the executioner with soldiers to tear the convent apart stone by stone."

Ottavia turned a brilliant, blotchy red. The water jug slipped from her fingers and shattered on the stones. She turned and ran, sobbing, to Virginia.

Virginia's reaction was immediate. She did not cower. She did not hide. She attacked.

She stormed out of her seclusion, her 'illness' forgotten, her face a mask of imperious, terrifying fury. She seized Dionisia by the wrist and dragged her through the corridors, her grip like iron.

"You spread lies!" Virginia shouted, throwing open the door to Ottavia's room. "You poison this house with your filth! Look! Is he here?"

She dragged the weeping nun to Benedetta's and Ottavia's room. "Look! Is he under the bed? Is he in the chest?"

Dionisia shook her head, tears streaming down her face. The room was empty. She did not know, could not know, that behind the chest, in the dark shaft of the chimney, Gian Paolo Osio stood rigid, holding his breath as the woman he loved screamed lies to save his life.

But even Virginia's fury could not silence the evidence.

Sister Stefana found the ladder in Ottavia's room, the tall organ ladder that Ottavia used for her duties as the convent's organist. But it was not in its usual place near the organ loft. It was hidden, leaning against the wall where it had no business being.

Why would it be there? Unless it was meant to help someone climb to the attic if soldiers came searching?

She reported it to the Prioress. Mother Angela, emboldened by the growing scandal, went to Virginia's room to confront her.

"The ladder, Sister Virginia," Angela said, her voice trembling but persistent. "Sister Ottavia's organ ladder. Why is it hidden in her cell and not where it belongs? Is he using it to reach the attic?"

"He is nowhere!" Virginia screamed, her eyes blazing. "The ladder is there because Ottavia uses it for maintaining the organ! How dare you accuse me? How dare you spy on me? I will write to my brother! I will have you all punished!"

She bullied. She threatened. She invoked the de Leyva name like a weapon, bludgeoning them with her family's power. She forced the Prioress to search the rooms, pulling open chests and cupboards with violent gestures, daring the older woman to find the phantom.

Mother Angela looked, but not look closely enough. She did not think of pushing aside the heavy chest in Benedetta's room or peer up into the dark chimney shaft. She was afraid. Afraid of Virginia's rage, afraid of what she might find, afraid of bringing down the wrath of the de Leyva family. She retreated, apologizing, but her eyes remained cold and knowing.

Virginia slammed the door and leaned against it, her chest heaving, her face slick with sweat.

She had won again. She had terrified them into silence.

But as she looked at Gian Paolo, who emerged from the chimney covered in soot and dust, his face a mask of exhaustion, she saw the truth in his eyes. If soldiers came, the organ ladder would be his escape route, from the hiding place to Ottavia's room, then up to the attic where he might flee across the rooftops.

But that ladder, sitting where it shouldn't be, had nearly betrayed them all.

The walls were not just closing in. They were crumbling.

* * *

The 11th of November

IN THE SOLITUDE of her cell, Mother Angela dipped her quill into the inkwell and held it suspended over the parchment.

She had been a nun for forty years, a Prioress for only sixteen months. She had weathered the storms of the de Leyva pride, the petty factions of the cloister, and the slow, corrosive rot of a scandal everyone knew but no one dared name. She had tried to be prudent. She had tried to be kind. She had tried, God help her, to look the other way in the hope that the madness would burn itself out.

But looking the other way had only allowed the fire to spread until it threatened to consume the entire house of Santa Margherita.

She looked at the crucifix on her wall, seeking some sign of reprieve, but the painted eyes of Christ remained closed. There would be no miracle. There would be no quiet resolution. The walls were whispering, the townsfolk were jeering, and a murderer was hiding somewhere in the convent.

The situation had become intolerable.

With a steady hand, she lowered the quill and began to write. It was not a confession, she was too proud for that, but a capitulation. She resigned her office, her authority, and her burden.

She sanded the wet ink, folded the paper, and sealed it with the convent's wax. When she rose from her writing table, she felt lighter, as if a stone had been lifted from her chest, leaving only a hollow space where her duty had been.

It was time for someone else to face the storm.

* * *

MOTHER ANGELA, WHO had trembled before Virginia's rage only days before, did not tremble now.

The resignation of Imbersaga as Prioress had shifted the ground beneath the convent's feet. Authority, however temporary, had fallen into Angela's hands, and with it came the terrifying clarity of survival. She knew what Virginia was capable of. She knew that if Gian Paolo Osio remained within these walls, they were all damned. If not by the Governor's soldiers, then by the Cardinal's wrath.

She did not consult the Chapter. She did not call for a vote.

Instead, she called for the convent's most trusted messenger, a lay brother who asked no questions. She handed him a letter addressed not to the Governor, nor to the family de Leyva, but to the Archiepiscopal Palace in Milan.

It contained only a few lines, but they were enough to shatter the peace of Monza forever.

> *He is here. The man Osio is hidden within the convent of Santa Margherita. Make haste, Your Eminence, for we can no longer answer for the safety of this house.*

* * *

IN MILAN, THE letter was carried through the marble corridors of the palace to the private study of Cardinal Federigo Borromeo.

The Cardinal read it standing by the window, the gray light of November falling across the page. He did not show anger. He did not show surprise. His face, pale and ascetic, remained as unreadable as a statue's. But his fingers tightened slightly on the paper.

He had waited. He had prayed. He had hoped that the Lady of Monza would find her own way back to the light, or at least that the scandal would be contained by the heightening of the walls he had ordered. He had underestimated the depths of human folly.

He turned to his secretary, who stood waiting in the shadows.

"It is finished," Borromeo said softly.

But it was not as simple as sending a guard to drag a criminal from his hole. Virginia Maria de Leyva was not merely a nun; she was the Lady of Monza, the daughter of Spain, a woman whose veins ran with the blood of princes. To seize her by force, to violate the sanctity of the cloister with armed men, would be to provoke a crisis that could tear the delicate fabric of Lombardy's peace. The de Leyva family would be outraged. The Spanish Governor would claim jurisdiction.

It required a surgical touch.

"We must verify," the Cardinal said, sitting at his writing table. "And we must prepare."

For four days, the inquiry moved with silent, terrifying speed. Borromeo did not strike blindly. He sent agents, discreet priests, men who knew the lay of Monza, to confirm the rumors. He studied the layout of the convent. He consulted the canon law. He weighed the political cost against moral necessity.

The conclusion was inescapable: The infection could not be cured while the patient remained in the house.

A carriage was prepared, unmarked, inconspicuous, but built for speed. Orders were drafted, sealed, and signed with the heavy ring of the archbishop. It was a plan of extraction, cold and precise. There would be no negotiation. There would be no time for goodbyes.

* * *

The 15th of November

THAT MORNING, A black carriage rolled through the gates of Monza, its arrival marking the end of an era. Bypassing the Governor's palace, it rumbled directly over the wet cobblestones to the convent of Santa Margherita, its iron-rimmed wheels sounding against the stones like the slow, rhythmic tolling of a funeral bell.

Inside the convent, in the stifling confinement of Benedetta's cell, Virginia sat on the edge of the chest that concealed her lover, while Gian Paolo stood entombed in the flue, silent as the masonry itself. They had existed this way for days, caught in a rhythm of terror, their hearts beating in time with the footsteps in the corridor, listening for the sound that would signal the end.

When the bell at the main gate finally rang, not the polite chime of a visitor, but the insistent, authoritative pealing of the state, Virginia stood up.

"Who is it?" Gian Paolo's voice came muffled from behind the wall, thick with the dust of his hiding place.

"I do not know," she whispered, though the cold knot in her stomach suggested otherwise.

The heavy, purposeful tread that echoed in the corridor moments later belonged to no nun on her daily rounds. The knock was sharp, and when the door opened, it revealed Mother Angela flanked by two older sisters whose faces were set like flint.

"Sister Virginia," Angela said, her voice carrying a new, strange weight. "You are summoned."

"Summoned?" Virginia smoothed her habit, her chin lifting in the old, instinctive gesture of defiance that had cowed this woman only days before. "By whom? I do not answer to summons."

"You are summoned by His Eminence, the Cardinal Archbishop," Angela replied, stepping aside to reveal the empty corridor. "His Vicar General, Gerolamo Saraceno, awaits you in the parlatory. You are to bring nothing."

Virginia looked at her, then cast a fleeting glance at the closed panel behind the chest, and finally at the room that had been both her prison and her sanctuary.

In that single, suspended heartbeat, the fortress of her name and the illusion of her untouchability evaporated like mist. They had not come for Gian Paolo; they had come for her. And if she refused, if she made a scene here in the corridor, they would search the room. They would find him.

To go was to lose everything she possessed. To stay was to condemn him to death.

"Very well," she said, her voice steady with a terrifying calm. "I will come."

She did not look back at the chest, for she could not afford the weakness of a goodbye. Sweeping past Angela with her head high, her black veil trailing like smoke, she descended to the parlatory where Vicar General Gerolamo Saraceno stood waiting. He offered no ring to be kissed, nor did he bow; he simply pointed to the open door where the carriage waited in the falling rain.

"Sister Virginia Maria," he said, reciting the formula drafted with such agonizing care in Milan. "By order of His Eminence, you are to be transferred this day to the convent of Saint Ulderico at the Bocchetto in Milan. You will accompany us immediately."

"And if I refuse?"

"There is no refusal," Saraceno answered softly. "The order is absolute."

She stepped out into the gray wash of the November rain, where the cobblestones gleamed like slick oil under the leaden sky. The carriage door stood open, a dark maw waiting to swallow her, and beyond the gate, she saw the glint of armor, a cavalry squad waiting in the shadows to ensure the prisoner did not escape.

And then, reality broke her.

The sight of the soldiers, the finality of the carriage, the crushing realization that she was being stripped of her power, her home, and her lover in a single stroke was too much for her sanity to bear. The calm facade shattered into a thousand pieces.

She did not step into the carriage. She screamed.

It was a sound that tore through the quiet morning, a cry of pure, distilled rage that belonged to a maenad rather than a nun. She shoved the Vicar aside and turned on the matrons who reached for her, her hands clawing at the air, her eyes wild with panic.

"You will not take me!" she shrieked, her voice cracking. "I am the Lady of Monza! I command here!"

In the ensuing chaos, with rain slicking the stones and men shouting orders, she lunged toward one of the escorting soldiers. Before the man could react, her hand, a hand that had known only rosaries and silk, snatched the hilt of his sword.

The steel hissed as she drew it, a flash of lightning in the gloom. She brandished the weapon, standing alone in the rain, a tragic, terrifying figure in black wool cutting the air between herself and her jailers.

"Back!" she screamed, swinging the heavy blade with the strength of madness. "I will kill you! I will kill anyone who touches me!"

The rebellion was brief. The soldiers, recovering from their shock, closed in and wrestled the sword from her grip. They seized her arms, forcing her toward the carriage as she kicked and cursed them, raging against the inexorable destiny that had finally caught her. The door slammed shut, the lock clicked, and the driver cracked his whip. As the wheels began to turn, the noise drowned out her cries, carrying the Lady of Monza away from her city, away from her lover, and into the abyss.

* * *

INSIDE THE CONVENT, hidden in the soot-blackened darkness of the chimney, Gian Paolo Osio heard it all.

He heard the scream that curdled the blood. He heard the clash of steel. He heard the woman who had sacrificed her soul for him fighting a war against the entire world, armed with nothing but a stolen sword and her own despair.

And he did nothing.

Paralyzed by abject terror, stripped of his arrogance and his silks, he stood shivering in the dark. He had no weapons; his harquebuses lay useless in his home. He had no clothes but the grotesque parody of a nun's habit. He pressed his forehead against the cold stone, listening to the struggle, a coward witnessing the destruction of a queen.

Inside the cell, pressed against the cold stone of the chimney, Gian Paolo heard the wheels fade into the November rain. He heard the nuns returning to their cells, their whispers like the rustling of black wings. He heard the bell toll for None, and still he did not move.

For six hours, a dead silence reclaimed the room. He would not touch the bread Benedetta had left him, nor would he drink. He simply stood in the soot-blackened void, shivering as the adrenaline curdled into hollow, aching shock. The air tasted of stale ash and the ghost of old fires, but he could not bring himself to step into the light.

Finally, as the gray light of the window deepened into the opaque black of night, the animal instinct for survival clawed its way to the surface.

He moved to the window. Below, the garden was a pool of ink, the rain having left the earth smelling of wet rot and secrets. It offered a path to freedom.

He slipped out of the cell and descended the main stairs, his boots making no sound on the stone. He stepped into the courtyard and found the gardener's ladder leaning against the pergola near the students' dormitory, its rungs slick with moisture. Heaving its weight against his shoulder, he carried it to the high perimeter wall and propped it against the stone.

Benedetta was there, a shadow detaching itself from the darkness of the colonnade. She said nothing, her face a pale blur in the gloom, arriving just in time to see his silhouette pause at the crest of the wall.

He did not look back. He climbed the ladder and leaped over the wall.

The thud of his landing on the road of the Porta dei Gradi was swallowed by the wind. He avoided his own house, knowing it would be watched by the Cardinal's spies. Instead, he melted into the night, a fugitive in the town he had once owned, vanishing like smoke into the labyrinth of streets.

* * *

INSIDE SANTA MARGHERITA, the desperate housekeeping of conspiracy began.

Ottavia and Benedetta rushed back to their cell. The room was empty, but it was full of ghosts, and evidence.

Ottavia fell to her knees and dragged a heavy object from beneath her bed: the wooden organ ladder they had stolen from the loft weeks ago. It was the tool Gian Paolo had used to climb into the attic, to access the high flue of the chimney. It had been their secret bridge, but now, in the cold light of his absence, it was a screaming accusation.

A ladder in a nun's cell was a confession in pine and iron. If the Cardinal's men searched the room and found it, they would know exactly how the 'ghost' had moved through the walls.

"It cannot stay," Benedetta hissed.

Trembling so violently she could barely grip the wood, Ottavia helped Benedetta brace the ladder against the stone floor. They worked in a frenzy of destruction, stomping on the rungs, snapping the sturdy wood like dry bones. The sound of splintering timber seemed deafening in the silent convent, a series of gunshots they prayed no one else heard.

Gathering the jagged shards, they carried them to the privy. One by one, they dropped the pieces down the shaft, watching the evidence vanish into the filth below, swallowed by the earth.

Then, Benedetta went to the hiding place in her room. Her hands, gray with dust and scraped raw, mixed a slurry of mortar. Scavenging stones from the porch, she began to seal the opening of the chimney. She placed the bricks one by one, the wet slap of plaster the only sound in the room.

As the mortar dried, sealing the flue and the black secret within it, they allowed themselves a dangerous, fragile illusion.

He is gone, they told themselves, the thought a prayer against the dark. She is gone. The affair is over. We will escape punishment.

* * *

BUT THE CARDINAL'S justice was not a storm that passed; it was a tide that rose.

In Milan, the question was whispered in the palaces: Why had the Cardinal not seized the man? Why, if Virginia had brandished a sword, had the soldiers not searched the convent and dragged him out?

This apparent oversight was neither incompetence nor mercy. The convent held the ancient right of sanctuary. Not even a Cardinal's vicar could violate it without papal dispensation. Virginia, as a professed nun, belonged to the Church and could be moved by her superiors. But Gian Paolo, the layman and murderer, was ironically protected by the very holy ground he had defiled. To seize him from consecrated space would require weeks of petitions to Rome, legal arguments, and risk of scandal that could ignite conflict between Church and Crown.

By then, he would be long gone.

But now, outside the walls, he was fair game.

The Cardinal issued precise orders: seize the perpetrator. The charges were multiplying. Violation of the cloister, defloration, homicide. The horror of the crime was finally being revealed in the clear light of day.

But the bird had flown. Gian Paolo's house was found closed and empty. The Canonica was barred to him. Overcome by terror, he fled to a deserted property near Velate, hiding in the woods like a hunted animal, trembling at the sound of every breaking twig.

* * *

IN MILAN, CONFINED within the alien walls of the convent of the Bocchetto, Virginia Maria de Leyva descended into a personal hell.

She was a prisoner, banished, reviled, and desperate. The rage that had fueled her final stand at the carriage had not abated; it had merely turned inward, consuming her.

She became almost more maenad than woman. She refused all food, determined to starve herself into oblivion. When that proved too slow, she hurled herself headfirst against the heavy oak door of her cell, trying to crack her skull, trying to smash the vessel of her own life to escape the shame.

They restrained her. They watched her day and night. They kept her alive for a fate she feared more than death.

The Cardinal did not wait. On the 27th of November, just twelve days after her arrest, the proceedings began. The trial did not open in a courtroom, but in the parlatory of the Convent of Santa Margherita in Monza, the very room where she had once reigned supreme.

The silence was over. The judgment had begun.

* * *

The 28th of November

THE MESSENGER ARRIVED at the main gates just as November dusk was settling over Monza. Benedetta spotted him from the corridor window, a man dressed as a farmer, nondescript and forgettable, standing a few paces from the iron gates, his cap in his weathered hands.

His distance from the gates meant he could not seek entry, which meant whatever he carried was too dangerous to pass through normal channels. Benedetta moved with deliberate unhurried steps through the corridors past the portress's office. The portress was occupied with some charitable distribution and barely glanced up as Benedetta slipped past toward the iron gates.

The farmer stood just beyond the bars. His eyes did not meet hers directly, but she saw his jaw tighten slightly in recognition.

"I have been sent with a message." He spoke quietly, barely above the wind's rustle. "You know the hand it comes from?"

Benedetta nodded. She reached toward the grille, and the man extended a folded scrap of parchment through the bars. The transaction took less than a breath. The note passed from his weathered fingers to hers, and she drew it back, tucking it immediately beneath her scapular.

"Tomorrow evening. Same hour. Same place." His voice was barely more than a whisper. "If there is an answer to send, bring it to me then."

He turned and shuffled back toward the street, melting into the purple shadows of November evening.

Benedetta did not read the message until she reached her cell. By then, evening bells had begun to toll, and the convent was settling into the transitional time between offices when the corridors were relatively empty. She unfolded the parchment with fingers that wanted to tremble but which she forced to steadiness.

The handwriting was Gian Paolo's. She would have recognized it anywhere:

> *They have her at a convent called Bocchetto, north of Milan. The Cardinal's men guard her. But she is alive, for now. I needed you to know. Virginia is alive.*

Benedetta sank onto her narrow cot. Virginia alive. The knowledge brought not relief but crushing weight. Alive meant interrogation was coming. Alive meant Virginia would eventually be forced to choose between protecting herself or protecting them all.

The message continued:

> *Everything has changed. The authorities are moving more aggressively. The servants have broken. Domenico testified to Senator Truffi. Isabetta confirmed his story. Even Susanna is being questioned. They're telling everything. It is only a matter of days before formal charges are filed and interrogations begin for you and the others.*

Benedetta knew this already. She had heard the whispers, had seen the shift in how sisters regarded her—the mixture of pity and fear and the careful distance that people maintained from those marked for destruction.

The final section made her throat constrict:

> *I can arrange escape. A safe convent in Bergamo, or another place of refuge. But I need to act before the net tightens further. Ottavia, speak to her. Persuade her. Then come to the garden wall at four hours past sundown, Thursday evening. Bring her. I will have the wall opened and will be waiting.*

The final lines:

> *Return your answer tomorrow evening. Same man. Same hour. Same place at the gate. One word is enough: yes or no. The Madonna will not protect you if you stay. Only distance will. Only flight.*

Benedetta burned the parchment in the candle flame, watching the edges blacken and curl, watching the words transform to ash that drifted to the cold stone floor. She moved to her small writing table and pulled out parchment and ink. Her hands were steady as she wrote the small decisive strokes:

Yes.

That was all. One word. But it transformed everything.

Now she needed to find Ottavia.

* * *

THE DORMITORY CORRIDOR was dim, lit only by a single candle burning in a wall sconce. Benedetta found Ottavia where she expected, in the cell Candida and Degnamerita shared, where Silvia also slept when she grew afraid of her own solitude.

Benedetta knocked softly. Three quick taps. Movement stilled. Then Silvia appeared at the door, her face pale in the candlelight, her eyes wide and wary.

"Sister Benedetta?"

"I need to speak with Sister Ottavia. Privately. In the corridor."

Ottavia rose slowly from the edge of Candida's cot, her bare feet touching the cold stone floor. She padded to the doorway, pulling her shift more tightly around herself against the November chill.

"What is it?" Her voice came out small, frightened.

Benedetta stepped back into the corridor, drawing Ottavia with her, far enough from the door that the others could not easily overhear.

"I need to speak with you about leaving."

"Leaving?" Ottavia's face went pale. "The convent?"

"Listen to me." Benedetta leaned closer, her mouth nearly touching Ottavia's ear. "Everything has changed. The authorities are accelerating their questioning. Sisters are beginning to admit things they swore under oath to deny. The petition is becoming a noose around our necks rather than a shield."

Ottavia began to shake her head, that small repetitive motion that suggested disbelief or denial or panic. "I cannot leave. I cannot break my vows. Where would I go?"

"Gian Paolo has sent word." Benedetta gripped Ottavia's arm, feeling the cold flesh beneath the thin shift. "He can arrange sanctuary. A convent in Bergamo where your name means nothing, where the scandal of Santa Margherita has not yet spread. But we must decide soon. If we do not commit, the opportunity will close."

"What about Sister Virginia?"

"She is already imprisoned. Separated from us. Cut off from any way to help herself, let alone to help us." Benedetta drew on every persuasion tactic she had learned over decades. "You understand what interrogation means? What their methods are? They will ask you about everything—the keys, Gian Paolo's visits, the nights you helped him gain access to Virginia's cell. They will ask about Caterina. And you will be alone when they ask, with no allies, no way to manage what you reveal."

Ottavia's jaw tightened at Caterina's name. "They cannot prove anything."

"They do not need proof. They have testimony from servants. They have information that Domenico provided. They have sisters who are already beginning to hedge their earlier statements."

Benedetta pressed on. "We are in danger if we remain. Authorities may decide that we are culpable not only through knowledge but through active participation. The only safety is distance."

Ottavia pressed her hands to her face, and Benedetta saw the moment her resistance fractured entirely.

"When?" Ottavia's voice was muffled behind her palms. "If I were to... when?"

"Tomorrow night. Four hours past sundown. At the garden wall near the wagon gate." Benedetta gentled her voice, made it sound like comfort rather than command. "We meet him. You will have time to think about this. But when the moment comes, if you decide to come, be ready."

Ottavia lowered her hands. Her eyes were wet, but her expression had hardened into something approaching resolution.

"I will think about it." She wrapped her arms around herself. "But I am afraid."

"Fear is wisdom." Benedetta touched her shoulder briefly. "Now go back inside before Silvia grows suspicious. We will not speak about this again until Thursday night. If you decide against it, simply stay in your cell. I will understand."

But they both knew she would not stay. The seed had been planted. The terror had taken root.

Ottavia nodded and turned back toward the cell door. She paused at the threshold, looking back over her shoulder.

"If this is wrong—if God judges us for this—"

"God will judge us either way," Benedetta said quietly. "At least this way we will be alive to receive His judgment."

* * *

THE REST OF the day moved with the slow inevitability of a cart rolling downhill toward a cliff edge. Benedetta watched Ottavia unravel.

Ottavia appeared in the refectory with circles beneath her eyes dark as bruises. Her hands trembled when she reached for bread at the midday meal. She dropped her prayer book twice during None.

By the evening, when Benedetta delivered her written answer to the farmer at the gate, she passed Ottavia in the corridor and saw the decision already made in her face—a hollow, hunted expression that spoke of hours spent staring into darkness, weighing damnation against imprisonment, choosing between terrors.

The day crawled. Benedetta moved through the convent's routines with exacting normalcy, aware that any visible anxiety might trigger notice. By the time dusk began to settle over Monza, the weight of what was about to happen had compressed itself into a single point of certainty behind her sternum. There was no possibility of retreat now.

* * *

The 29th and 30th of November

WHEN THE FINAL bells tolled and silence settled over Santa Margherita, Benedetta lay in her cell fully clothed beneath her blanket, watching the darkness through the high window. The November night was moonless and cold, the wind carrying the metallic smell of approaching frost.

At the hour she had calculated, four hours past sundown by the convent bells, Benedetta rose and moved through the darkened corridors. She knew exactly which floorboards creaked, which corners held watching sisters, which doors opened without sound.

Ottavia was waiting in the courtyard shadows, dressed in the warmest clothes she possessed, her breath small clouds of white in the cold. They did not speak. They moved together toward the garden, toward the section of wall near the wagon gate.

As they approached, Benedetta heard it, the soft sound of tapping on stone, rhythmic and deliberate. Gian Paolo on the other side, signaling that he was ready.

He appeared as they approached, his silhouette dark against the starless sky. He had already been working on the wall for hours. She could see the section he had selected, a place where the mortar had already begun to weaken.

He gestured for them to stay back and pressed a dagger into Benedetta's hand through the gap. "This will loosen the mortar. Help me widen the opening." He kept his voice low, barely more than a whisper.

Benedetta moved to the wall and began working the blade between the stones, feeling the accumulated calcification of centuries begin to give way. Gian Paolo worked from the other side, the two of them creating a rhythm—dig, scrape, pull, repeat.

The night air carried the smell of dust and damp earth disturbed. Benedetta's hands grew cold, then numb, then began to hurt. Beside her, Ottavia stood with her arms wrapped around herself, watching the darkened courtyard as if expecting sisters to appear at any moment.

It took perhaps an hour to widen the opening sufficiently. When Gian Paolo finally pulled away from the other side, breathing heavily, there was a gap in the wall large enough for a person to squeeze through.

He went through the gap first, then crouched, his face barely visible in the darkness. "It is done. Tomorrow at dawn they will discover you are missing. By then you will be far beyond the walls. I have horses and men waiting just beyond Monza's gates."

Benedetta felt the reality of it crash down upon her. They were actually doing this.

"Go," Benedetta whispered to Ottavia. "Get through and wait on the other side."

Ottavia moved to the gap and began to squeeze herself through, her habit catching on rough stone, the passage so tight that for a moment she seemed stuck entirely. Then she was through, falling slightly as she landed on the other side, Gian Paolo catching her arm to steady her.

Benedetta turned back toward the darkened convent. She could see the chapel dome silhouetted against slightly lighter sky, could see the cells where sisters were sleeping. She thought of Virginia, imprisoned somewhere north of Milan, facing interrogation without any of them to witness or support or share the burden of confession.

But Virginia had made her choices years ago. They all had. Benedetta had simply accepted the final consequence of hers.

She turned to the wall, gripped the edge of the opening, and began to pull herself through into darkness and whatever came next.

Behind her, the convent bells stood silent, marking time in a way that no longer included her.

* * *

THE NIGHT AIR outside the convent wall was absolute and immediate. Ottavia felt it like water closing over her head, the shock of November wind against her face, the smell of damp earth and woodsmoke instead of incense and candlewax, the sudden awareness that she had committed an act that could not be undone.

Behind her, fabric scraped against stone as Benedetta emerged through the opening.

The night was moonless. The stars were distant and frigid. Somewhere in the distance the Lambro River murmured like distant prayer.

"We follow the town wall." Gian Paolo's voice was low and urgent. "Stay close. Keep silent. If we are stopped before we clear Monza's gates, everything is lost."

He moved ahead, and Ottavia followed because there was nothing else to do now. Benedetta moved beside her, close enough that their habits brushed together with each step, the fabric whispering conspiracy.

They walked along the inside of the town wall, following its curve through shadows so deep that Ottavia could barely see Gian Paolo's silhouette ahead.

Once, she stumbled, and Benedetta's hand shot out to steady her, the grip hard enough to leave marks.

They reached a section where the city wall had crumbled, a breach Gian Paolo called Carrobiolo. Near the gap, a small wooden gate stood set into the stonework, little more than a farmers' entrance. Gian Paolo opened it with a key he produced from beneath his cloak, the lock turning with a sound that seemed impossibly loud.

He always had what he needed—keys, daggers, and ways through locked doors. Ottavia wondered how many other gates he had opened in darkness, how many other escapes he had planned and executed.

Then they were truly outside, beyond the town walls, beyond the protection of anything familiar, beyond the boundary of everything Ottavia had ever known.

Ottavia's mind had gone quiet in the way that minds do when catastrophe becomes inevitable. She walked because Benedetta was walking. She followed because Gian Paolo was leading.

The road curved alongside the Lambro, sometimes near enough that she could hear the water moving through reeds. After what felt like hours but was probably less, they reached a church standing alone on the road, its façade pale against the darker sky. Santa Maria delle Grazie, the church where townspeople came to ask the Madonna for mercy.

Ottavia stopped walking.

"We must pray." Her voice came out stronger than she expected, the first words she had spoken since leaving the convent. "We cannot continue without asking the Madonna's protection."

Gian Paolo turned back, his expression unreadable in the darkness. "We do not have time."

"We are nuns." Ottavia moved toward the church door before he could finish. "We have broken our vows. We have committed mortal sin. If we do not ask for mercy now, we will be damned forever."

Benedetta made a small sound that might have been protest or agreement. Gian Paolo stood silent for a long moment, then inclined his head.

"Be quick."

Ottavia knelt on the stone before the church door, feeling the November chill seep through her habit into her bones. Benedetta knelt beside her, and even Gian Paolo lowered himself to one knee.

"*Salve Regina, Mater misericordiae...*" Ottavia began, and the words came without thought, carved into memory by decades of repetition. *Hail Holy Queen, Mother of Mercy, our life, our sweetness, and our hope.* They said it seven times, the traditional petition for urgent need, for desperate circumstances, for souls balanced on the knife-edge between salvation and damnation.

By the seventh repetition, Ottavia's voice had begun to break. The Madonna would not protect them. The Madonna could not protect what they had already chosen. But she said the words anyway, because saying them was all she had left.

When they rose, Gian Paolo led them back onto the road, crossing the bridge over the Lambro near the church, the water black and swift beneath. On the other side, the road divided into three paths.

"Where do they lead?" Ottavia asked.

Gian Paolo gestured toward the leftmost path. "That road goes to La Santa." He indicated the middle path. "That one leads to Velate."

"I will not go on public roads." Ottavia heard the firmness in her own voice. "If we are seen, if we are recognized—"

"Then we take the third path." Gian Paolo moved toward the rightmost road, narrower and less traveled. "It is more secluded. It follows the Lambro away from the main routes."

They walked in single file, Ottavia in the middle between Benedetta and Gian Paolo, the river's sound growing louder. The night was beginning to thin toward dawn, the darkness becoming slightly less absolute, the stars fading.

Ottavia's exhaustion was complete now, a weight that pressed down on her shoulders. Her mind had begun to drift. She thought of Virginia, imprisoned somewhere north of Milan. She thought of the convent waking to discover two sisters missing. She thought of God watching from His throne, seeing everything, judging everything.

The path narrowed further. Gian Paolo slowed, turning back to face them. They had reached a place where the river ran close to the road, the bank steep and slick with mud and dead leaves.

"We should rest." His voice was different now, harder somehow. "The road ahead is difficult."

Ottavia moved toward the bank, thinking to sit for a moment. Gian Paolo's hand closed around her arm, gentle at first, almost careful.

Then he pushed.

The world tilted sideways. Ottavia felt herself falling, felt the ground disappear beneath her feet, felt the horrible moment of suspension before the icy water swallowed her whole.

The Lambro closed over her head with shocking force. The current was stronger than she had imagined, pulling at her habit, dragging her sideways and down. She broke the surface gasping, her mouth filling with water that tasted of mud and winter and death.

"Santa Maria di Loreto!" The prayer tore out of her throat as a scream. "*Aiutami*! Help me! Benedetta, help me!"

She thrashed toward the bank, managed to grab hold of something—a root, a stone—and pulled herself partially out of the water. Her vision was blurred, her lungs burning. Gian Paolo stood on the bank above her, reaching down as if to help.

Then the gun appeared in his hand.

He pulled it from beneath his cloak with practiced ease, the metal dark against the slightly lighter sky. He reversed it, gripping the barrel, raising the wooden stock like a club.

"Ah, Signor Gian Paolo," the words came out broken, disbelieving. "To do this to me? But the Madonna will help me. She will see that I have justice."

The first blow caught her on the side of the head. Pain exploded through her skull, white and absolute. She tried to raise her hand to shield herself and felt the stock connect with her fingers, felt bone crack beneath the impact.

He hit her again. And again. Ottavia pressed her face against the riverbank, tasting mud and blood, feeling the blows rain down on her skull like judgment, like God's own wrath made flesh and wood and violence.

She stopped screaming. Stopped moving. Let her body go limp against the bank, hoping he would think her dead, hoping he would stop.

The blows stopped.

Ottavia kept her eyes closed, her face pressed into the damp earth, breathing as shallowly as she could manage. Voices drifted above her—Benedetta's, raised in protest or fear, then Gian Paolo's response, words she could not make out through the ringing in her ears.

Then the current took her.

She felt herself pulled away from the bank, felt the water close over her again, felt the river claim her with the same indifferent force that had claimed fallen leaves and broken branches.

"Madonna, do not let me die in this sin." She formed the words without sound. "Give me time to confess. Give me time to make it right."

The river carried her downstream. Sometimes she broke the surface and gasped for air. Sometimes she went under and thought she would not rise again. The current swept her toward something ahead. A dam, she realized, where the river divided itself around a mill, the water churning white against stones.

She reached out blindly, and her hand found something solid—a rock, a piece of wood wedged against the dam—and she pulled herself toward it with the last strength she possessed. Somehow, she climbed out of the water, collapsing onto a narrow strip of mud and stone where the current eddied.

Ottavia lay gasping in the approaching dawn, her head screaming pain, her hand shattered, her habit soaked and heavy as iron. Blood ran down her face and mixed with river water. Above her, the sky was beginning to lighten toward gray.

She had been betrayed. She had been murdered, or nearly so. She had trusted and followed, and this was what following led to—frozen mud, broken bones, and the slow creep of dawn revealing the magnitude of her own foolishness.

Somewhere upstream, Benedetta and Gian Paolo had vanished into darkness. Whether Benedetta had tried to stop him or had helped him or had simply watched, Ottavia did not know. Perhaps she would never know.

She closed her eyes and waited for someone to find her, or for death to find her first.

Either way, it was out of her hands now.

* * *

BENEDETTA WALKED. ONE foot in front of the other. The November darkness pressed against her face like wet wool. Beside her, Gian Paolo moved with the same steady pace he had maintained since they left Ottavia bleeding in the Lambro, as if nothing had happened.

Her hands would not stop shaking.

She folded them inside her sleeves, but the trembling spread up her arms, into her shoulders, until her entire body vibrated with it. Her shoes were soaked through from crossing the river, and the November wind cut through her wet habit like knives.

But the shaking had nothing to do with temperature.

She called for you. She screamed your name.

Ottavia's voice, high and desperate, crying *"Santa Maria di Loreto, aiutami! Help me! Benedetta, help me!"* while Gian Paolo brought the gun's wooden stock down again and again, the sound of it hitting skull and bone making a dull, wet percussion that Benedetta would hear for the rest of her life.

And she had done nothing.

She had stepped back. Turned away. Let it happen.

The path narrowed. Gian Paolo led them away from the Lambro, onto smaller roads that wound through fields and farmland. Distant shapes of houses stood dark against the sky. No lights in windows, just the silent bulk of structures where people slept and knew nothing of what had happened tonight.

"How much farther?" Her voice came out thin, cracked.

"Not far."

Benedetta's mind had gone strange. Detached. She watched herself walk as if from a great distance, as if she were floating somewhere above her own body observing a woman in a soaked habit following a murderer through the dark.

Time became meaningless. They might have walked for an hour or three hours. Benedetta's exhaustion was so complete that her body moved automatically. Her feet found the ground. Her lungs pulled in air. Her heart continued its frantic hammering.

Ahead, the outline of a building emerged from darkness. Large. Standing alone in open country, surrounded by a low wall enclosing a courtyard. No lights. No signs of habitation.

Gian Paolo crossed the courtyard without hesitation and stopped at a heavy wooden door. It opened.

Unlocked. Waiting for them.

He had planned this. Arranged it. Which meant he had known, when he convinced her to escape, that it would end with Ottavia dead and Benedetta brought here.

She followed him inside because there was nowhere else to go.

The interior smelled of damp stone and old smoke. Gian Paolo moved through the space with familiarity, navigating darkness as if he carried a map in his head. They reached a place where the floor dropped away. A ladder descended into deeper darkness below.

"Down." Gian Paolo gestured toward the opening.

Benedetta's legs refused to move. Every instinct screamed at her to run. But where would she go? She had no idea where she was, no strength left to go more than a few steps before collapsing.

She climbed down.

The ladder rungs were rough wood that bit into her palms. When she reached the bottom, the space felt close and airless, a cellar or storage room, windowless, smelling of earth and stone.

Gian Paolo descended after her. In the absolute darkness, she heard him move around the small space.

"You will stay here." His voice came from somewhere to her left. "Do not leave. Do not make noise. I will return with food."

"How long?"

"An hour. Perhaps two. We must be careful. They will be searching."

The ladder creaked as he climbed back up. His footsteps crossed the floor above her head. The door opened, admitting a brief breath of less-stale air, then closed.

Silence.

Benedetta stood in absolute darkness, her eyes straining to see anything. Nothing. Just blackness so complete it felt solid.

Her legs gave out. She collapsed onto what felt like pieces of sawn wood stacked in the corner, drew her knees up to her chest, wrapped her arms around herself.

And sat.

* * *

TIME PASSED. SHE had no way to measure it. No bells to mark the hours. No change in light to indicate dawn approaching. Just the eternal darkness and her own thoughts circling endlessly around the same images.

Ottavia's face, twisted with terror.

The gun stock rising and falling.

The sound of impact, wet, heavy, final.

Benedetta's own voice, weak and useless: *"Don't do those things."*

As if words could stop what was already happening. As if protest without action meant anything at all.

She tried to pray but the words disintegrated before they could form. What prayer could a murderer say? What forgiveness existed for standing by while someone begged for help and doing nothing?

At some point, she heard footsteps above. The ladder creaked.

Gian Paolo appeared carrying bread, cheese, grapes, and a flask of wine. He set them on the earthen floor near her feet.

"Eat."

Benedetta stared at the food. Her stomach was hollow, aching, but the thought of eating made her throat close.

"You must eat." His tone hardened. "You will need strength to travel. Later, we leave for Bergamo. The convent."

Lies. She heard them clearly now. There would be no convent in Bergamo. Just more walking, more darkness, more waiting for the moment when he decided she had become as inconvenient as Ottavia.

When he left, Benedetta looked at the wine flask for a long time. She thought about poison. About how easy it would be. She set the flask aside untouched.

The bread she ate in small, dry bites. The cheese she saved. The grapes she left where they lay.

The day stretched endlessly. Benedetta dozed fitfully, jerking awake at every sound. Fear kept her from true sleep.

When Gian Paolo returned, the quality of darkness had changed slightly.

"We must leave now." His voice was tight, urgent. "It is not safe to stay."

Benedetta stood on legs that barely supported her weight. "Where are we going?"

"To a gentlewoman's house. From there, arrangements for Bergamo."

She climbed the ladder behind him, breathing air that felt marginally less suffocating.

They left the house and moved onto narrow paths through countryside. The moon was up now, casting enough light to see shapes but not details. Benedetta's exhaustion was absolute.

She barely noticed when they turned off the road toward a grove of trees.

"My brother built a cistern here," Gian Paolo said conversationally. "For irrigation."

Benedetta saw the stone rim rising from the ground ahead. Circular. About as wide as a man lying down. No bucket. No rope.

Every nerve in her body ignited with warning.

"Come look." Gian Paolo gestured toward it casually.

She approached slowly, muscles coiled to run. When she reached the rim, she peered down into blackness deeper than any she had yet encountered.

She picked up a stone and dropped it in. Silence. Then, far below, the clatter of stone hitting stone—not water, but rock and debris.

"This is not a cistern."

She turned to run.

He was faster.

His hand closed on her arm, spinning her around. She wrenched sideways, trying to break free, but his grip was iron. Her feet scrabbled on loose earth, finding no purchase. They struggled at the rim, her breath coming in gasps.

"You must not!" Her voice broke.

"I will throw you in." His tone was calm, almost conversational. "Or I will stab you first if you prefer."

He dragged her back toward the opening. Benedetta fought with everything left in her, kicking, clawing, trying to scream. He shoved her hard.

The ground disappeared.

She fell through darkness, the cold air rushing past. Her habit billowed around her. Time stretched—one heartbeat, two—then impact.

Her left side hit stone with crushing force. Something inside cracked. Pain exploded through her ribs, her hip, radiating outward in waves. The air punched from her lungs. She couldn't breathe, couldn't move, couldn't do anything except exist in the center of agony.

She lay at the bottom of the well, trying to pull in air through broken ribs. Each breath was a knife twisting. Above, she could see the circle of slightly lighter sky framed by the stone rim. Then a shape moved across it. Gian Paolo's silhouette, looking down.

Something fell.

The rock hit her right knee with a sound like wood splitting. New pain layered over the old. Benedetta screamed, a raw, animal sound torn from her throat. The world went gray at the edges.

His footsteps receded above. Silence descended.

Benedetta lay gasping in shallow sips of air, each breath an act of will. Moving was impossible. Her left side felt crushed, ribs grinding against each other. Her right knee throbbed with a deep, nauseating ache.

Slowly, her eyes adjusted to the darkness. The well was wide, ten feet across perhaps, and very deep. The bottom was littered with stones and debris. Bones. She could see them now, pale shapes scattered among the rocks.

One shape, half-buried in rubble, looked wrong. Too round.

A skull. Tiny. Human.

Horror rose in Benedetta's throat like bile. She understood where she was now. Not a cistern, but a place where Gian Paolo put things he wanted to disappear forever. Evidence. Bodies. People who knew too much or became inconvenient.

Caterina.

The thought arrived with absolute certainty. This must be where Caterina had ended. And this was where Benedetta would end too.

Unless someone found her.

She wedged herself partway under a large rock that jutted from the wall, positioning it to protect her head. If Gian Paolo returned and heard her breathing, she didn't want to make an easy target.

She did not call for help. Not at night. Better to wait for daylight. Better to hope someone else might pass close enough to hear.

* * *

DAWN CAME EVENTUALLY, gray light filtering down from above. Benedetta examined her prison with growing horror.

The bones were everywhere. Adult bones mixed with smaller ones. Cloth remnants, rotted beyond recognition. And there, half-buried in rubble, a skull too small to be anything but a child's. More than one, she realized. Several small skulls, scattered among the larger remains.

How many people had Gian Paolo thrown down here?

She began to cry then, not from pain though the pain was constant, but from the sheer magnitude of what he had done.

When midmorning came, she heard voices above. Men's voices, distant but approaching.

Benedetta gathered all her strength and screamed.

"Help me! I am in this well!"

The voices stopped. Then came closer, urgent now, calling to each other.

"Santa Maria, there is someone down there!"

"Get a rope! Quickly!"

They pulled her out with rope, one man climbing down to secure it around her waist while others hauled from above. The pain of being moved was excruciating. Every jolt sent fresh agony through her crushed ribs and shattered knee.

At the top, they laid her on grass. Men crowded around—villagers from Velate who had been walking to church for Mass and heard her cries.

"I am Sister Benedetta," she gasped. "From the Convent of Santa Margherita in Monza. I was thrown in by Gian Paolo Osio."

The men exchanged glances. One, Alberici, the most prominent man in the village, nodded grimly.

"We must take you to my house. And send word to the authorities immediately."

They carried her as gently as they could, but every movement was agony. Benedetta closed her eyes and focused on breathing, on staying conscious, on holding onto the one thing that mattered now.

She would testify. She would speak. She would tell everything.

The only weapon she had left against Gian Paolo was her voice. The only justice that might come for Ottavia, for Caterina, for all of them, was the truth spoken aloud in a court where it could be recorded.

She would condemn herself in the speaking. Would expose her own complicity, her own sins, her own guilt. There would be no mercy for her.

But there would be truth. And truth, at least, would not die in a well.

* * *

AT ALBERICI'S HOUSE, they laid her on a bed and sent for help. The pain was so intense that Benedetta drifted in and out of consciousness.

When the vicar arrived, Saraceno, with his notaries and ecclesiastical authority, Benedetta forced herself to focus. This was the moment that mattered.

She told him everything. The escape from the convent. The walk to the river. Ottavia thrown in. Gian Paolo beating her with the gun. The house where Benedetta had been locked in the cellar. The well. The bones at the bottom.

She spoke until her voice gave out, until the surgeon arrived and made her stop. Broken ribs. Shattered knee. Severe bruising. She would live, he said, but she would not walk properly again.

Benedetta didn't care about walking. She cared about testimony. About evidence. About making sure that when she was gone, the record would remain. The words would persist. The truth would be known.

That evening, they transported her to the Convent of Sant'Orsola in Monza. In a carriage, with the vicar and dean accompanying her, guards riding alongside.

At Sant'Orsola, the sisters undressed her and put her to bed in an upper room. The surgeon examined her again, recorded her injuries in the official documents. Then he left, and Benedetta lay alone in the darkness.

It was over. The running, the hiding, the desperate hope that somehow she could escape the consequences of everything she had done. Over. Now there was only the reckoning.

She closed her eyes and waited for morning, when they would question her again. When she would have to speak the worst parts. The parts about Virginia and Gian Paolo. About the years of complicity. About Caterina's murder and her own silence.

The truth would destroy them all. But it was the only thing left worth saving.

* * *

The 1st of December

THE KNOCKING WOKE Mother Angela from shallow sleep. She had been dozing in her chair, exhausted from overseeing the past days of fear and whispered rumors that moved through Santa Margherita like fever. Ever since Virginia had been taken away, the convent had become unstable. Fractured.

"Mother Prioress." The portress's voice came through her door, urgent and breathless. "Someone is at the door with urgent news. A notary from the vicar's office. He says a wounded nun was found near the Grazie church this morning."

The words made no sense. Angela stood, smoothing her habit automatically. A wounded nun? From where?

"The vicar has gone to the Grazie to investigate," the portress continued. "But he sent his notary here to inquire if any of our sisters are missing."

Missing.

The word landed on Angela's chest like a stone. She thought immediately of Benedetta and Ottavia, Virginia's closest companions. The ones who had been restless and fearful ever since the Cardinal's men had come.

"Show him to the parlatory," Angela said, her voice sharper than intended. "Wake Sister Imbersaga and tell her to meet me there immediately."

The notary waited in the parlatory, standing rather than sitting, a deliberate posture that communicated urgency and authority. His name was Marengo, and he came with two armed guards who stood flanking the door.

"Mother Prioress." Marengo bowed slightly but did not smile. "The vicar requires an immediate accounting of all sisters in this convent. Every professed nun, every novice, every lay sister. I need names and locations."

"Has someone been hurt?" Angela asked.

"A wounded nun was discovered at dawn by the Lambro River, near the church of Santa Maria delle Grazie. She was brought to the Grazie convent for shelter. The vicar is there now, tending to her." Marengo paused. "She claims to be from Santa Margherita."

The room tilted. Angela gripped the edge of the table. "Who?"

"She has not yet given her name. She is gravely injured and barely conscious. Which is why the vicar sent me here, to determine if any of your sisters are absent."

Imbersaga arrived, her face drawn and her wimple slightly askew from hasty dressing. She took one look at the guards and her expression hardened.

"We will check the cells," Angela said. "Every sister should be in her room or preparing for Lauds."

They moved through the dormitory wing in procession—Angela, Imbersaga, the notary, and the guards. Other sisters appeared in doorways, their faces frightened and curious. Angela wanted to send them back, but she knew it was too late.

Ottavia's cell was first.

Angela opened the door, already knowing what she would find. The small room was empty. The narrow beds made with precise corners. Everything neat, orderly, unremarkable.

Except Ottavia and Benedetta were gone.

"Check their belongings," the notary said.

Imbersaga moved to the first chest and opened it. Her hands stilled. "Ottavia's stockings are missing. And her outdoor shoes."

The notary wrote this down with meticulous care. "Sister Ottavia. Absent. Belongings suggest voluntary departure."

They checked chest. Angela's hands trembled as she raised the lid.

Empty.

"Shoes missing here as well. And her stockings," Imbersaga said, her voice flat.

The notary made another notation. "Sister Benedetta. Also absent. Same pattern."

Angela felt the ground tilt beneath her. Two nuns gone. Both Virginia's closest companions. Both fled in the night with their outdoor shoes.

"How long have they been missing?" Marengo asked.

"I don't know. The last canonical hour was Compline. They should have been in their cells after that. But I didn't check individually."

"Show me the entire convent," Marengo said. "Every room, every passage, every door and window. I want to know how they left."

They searched everywhere. Every corner of Santa Margherita. Nothing. No obvious breach. No sign of forced entry or exit.

Until they reached the garden.

Silvia came running from the winter garden, her face flushed, her breath coming in gasps. "Mother Prioress! The wall, by the wagon gate. Someone broke through!"

They descended into the cold morning. The garden looked ordinary, brown earth, dormant plants, the smell of autumn decay.

Except for the section near the wagon gate.

There, someone had carefully removed stones and mortar from the wall. The opening was perhaps two feet across, large enough for a person to crawl through. Broken masonry lay scattered on the convent side. Fresh scratches marked the stones where tools had worked at the mortar.

"Someone broke in," Angela said, though even as she spoke the words, she knew they weren't true.

"No." Imbersaga's voice was hard as iron. "Look at the stones. Look at the debris. Most of it is on this side. This was opened from inside. They broke out, not in."

Marengo crouched beside the opening. "Recent. Very recent. The mortar dust hasn't even been disturbed by morning dew." He pointed to tracks in the soft earth beyond the wall. "Multiple sets of footprints. At least two people leaving, maybe three."

"Three?" Angela's voice came out sharp with fear.

"Two sets of prints leading away. But someone approached from outside first. Came from that direction, worked at the wall from the other side, then departed with two lighter sets following."

Gian Paolo.

Angela didn't say the name aloud, but it filled her mind with sickening certainty. He had come back. Had broken through the wall. Had convinced or coerced Benedetta and Ottavia to flee with him.

And now one of them was lying wounded at the Grazie, beaten nearly to death.

"I need to speak with every sister who might have seen or heard anything last night," Marengo said. "Starting with those whose cells are nearest to this garden entrance."

"Candida. Silvia. Degnamerita," Imbersaga said, her voice flat, professional.

"Bring them to the parlatory. One at a time." Marengo turned to Angela. "And I need a complete list of all lay workers who have access to the property."

Angela nodded mutely. The Cardinal would hear of this. The diocesan court would descend. Santa Margherita would never recover from this scandal.

"Mother Prioress."

Angela looked up. Imbersaga was pointing down the road that led from town.

Horses. Three riders approaching quickly. As they drew closer, Angela could make out the vicar Saraceno in the lead, his face grim. Behind him rode two more guards.

He dismounted before his horse had fully stopped, striding toward them with barely controlled urgency.

"You've found them missing?" he asked without preamble.

"Sister Ottavia and Sister Benedetta," Angela confirmed. "Gone since sometime after Compline. We found where they escaped." She gestured toward the broken wall.

Saraceno looked at the opening, his expression hardening. Then he turned back to Angela.

"Sister Ottavia is at Sant'Orsola. We moved her from the Grazie for better care."

Relief and horror struck simultaneously. "She's alive?"

"Barely." Saraceno's voice was flat, empty of inflection. "She was found at dawn by the Lambro, half-drowned, beaten nearly to death. Multiple wounds to the head. Her hand broken. She's been conscious enough to speak briefly."

Behind Angela, she heard sisters crying out, gasping, praying.

"Beaten?" she whispered.

"With the butt of harquebus, she tells us. Multiple blows." Saraceno's jaw was tight. "She says Gian Paolo Osio threw her in the Lambro and tried to kill her. She says he beat her while she screamed for help, while she prayed to the Virgin for mercy."

Complete, absolute silence broken only by the wind moving through bare branches.

"And Sister Benedetta?" Imbersaga asked.

"Missing." Saraceno looked at each of them in turn. "Sister Ottavia believes she's dead. Says Osio took her away after the attack. But we have no body, no evidence yet. I've sent men to search the countryside between here and Velate. If she's alive, we'll find her."

Angela's legs gave out. She sat down heavily on the cold ground, heedless of dignity or propriety. Around her, sisters were crying, clutching each other, calling on the saints.

"I need to question everyone," Saraceno was saying. "Everyone who knew Benedetta and Ottavia. Everyone who might have seen or heard anything. This convent is now under full investigation by the Archbishop's court. No one enters or leaves without written permission from Cardinal Borromeo himself."

He turned to Angela, and she saw something almost like pity in his eyes.

"I'm sorry, Mother Prioress. But your house is no longer yours to govern. As of this moment, Santa Margherita is under ecclesiastical sequestration. Sister Imbersaga will assume temporary governance under my direct supervision."

The words should have stung. Her authority stripped, her life's work taken from her hands. But Angela felt only a vast, hollow relief wash through her, leaving her bones light as ash. She had failed. The burden was no longer hers to carry.

"Yes, Your Reverence," she said quietly. "I have already tendered my forthcoming resignation so a new election can be held."

They brought the sisters one by one to the parlatory for questioning.

Candida came first, her round face drawn with fear, her hands twisting in the folds of her habit.

"Do you know why you're here?" Saraceno asked.

"Because of Sister Ottavia and Sister Benedetta. Because they're gone."

"Did you see or hear anything unusual last night? After Compline?"

Candida hesitated. "I heard voices. Late. After the bell for silence. In the corridor near my cell."

"Whose voices?"

"Sister Benedetta's. And Sister Ottavia's. They were arguing in whispers."

"What were they saying?"

"I couldn't make out the words. But Sister Ottavia sounded frightened. Sister Benedetta sounded determined. As if she had already decided something and nothing would change her mind."

Marengo wrote everything down. "And then?"

"Then silence. I thought they had gone back to their cells." Candida's eyes filled with tears. "I should have checked. Should have gotten up and made sure they were safe. But I was afraid."

"Did you see anyone else? Hear anything from outside the convent?"

"No. Just the wind. And later, much later, perhaps two hours before Lauds, I thought I heard footsteps in the garden. But I told myself it was my imagination."

Silvia confirmed similar details when her turn came. She had heard movement in the corridors. Whispered voices that rose and fell. The scrape of something against stone, perhaps the stones being moved in the garden wall.

"I should have raised the alarm," Silvia said, her voice thick with guilt. "But I didn't know what I was hearing. And I was frightened of Sister Benedetta. She had become so hard in recent weeks. So cold."

The pattern emerged slowly, piece by piece. Benedetta had gone to Ottavia's cell sometime after Compline. Had convinced or coerced her to come. They had descended to the garden together. And there, Gian Paolo Osio had been waiting at the wall he had broken through.

When the questioning finally ended, the sun stood high overhead. Saraceno stood, gathering his papers.

"I will return this afternoon to continue the interrogations. Until then, this convent remains under complete restriction. All external doors are to be locked and bolted at all times. No visitors except by my express permission. No messages sent or received without my personal review."

He looked directly at Angela. "Your authority as Prioress is suspended pending Cardinal Borromeo's judgment. Sister Imbersaga will assume all governance duties under my supervision. You will remain available for questioning but will make no decisions regarding convent affairs."

"Yes, Your Reverence."

After Saraceno and his men left, Angela walked back through the convent alone. The familiar corridors felt strange now, as if she were moving through a place she had never truly known.

She stopped at the church and knelt before the altar. The space was empty, cold, the candles unlit. She bowed her head and tried to pray.

But no words came.

She thought of Ottavia, lying broken in some cell at Sant'Orsola, her head wrapped in bandages, her hand shattered. She thought of Benedetta, missing somewhere in the countryside, alive and running, or dead in a ditch, or trapped in some nightmare Angela couldn't imagine.

She thought of Virginia, imprisoned in that convent north of Milan, and wondered if she knew yet what her choices had cost. What her passion had destroyed.

How had it come to this? Angela wondered.

But she knew the answer. They had looked away. Made excuses. Chosen peace over justice, silence over truth. They had known about Virginia and Gian Paolo for years. Had known about the letters, the visits, the corruption spreading through their house.

And they had done nothing.

Because exposing it would have meant scandal. Would have meant the Cardinal's wrath, the loss of dowries, the destruction of Santa Margherita's reputation. So, they had preserved the fiction of propriety while evil flourished in the dark.

Now the reckoning had come.

The church bells rang for Sext, the sound flat and mechanical. Angela remained kneeling, staring at the crucifix above the altar.

Behind her, she heard footsteps. Imbersaga, coming to find her.

"Angela," Imbersaga said softly. "You should rest. There's nothing more you can do today."

"I should have stopped it," Angela said. "Years ago. When it first started. I should have gone to the Cardinal, exposed everything, accepted the consequences."

"We all should have." Imbersaga sat down on the bench beside her. "We all knew. We all chose silence. The guilt belongs to all of us."

They sat together in the cold church, two women who had tried to govern an ungovernable house, who had tried to protect sisters who were already lost.

Outside, the broken wall gaped open, a wound in stone that would never fully heal. A threshold that two women had crossed into darkness, and only one had survived.

And somewhere beyond those walls, Benedetta's fate was still unknown.

* * *

OTTAVIA FLOATED IN and out of consciousness, aware only of fragments—the rough texture of linen against her cheek, the cold that had settled into her bones, the rhythmic throb in her skull that pulsed with each heartbeat like a bell tolling.

Voices murmured above her, distant and distorted.

"Santa Maria," someone whispered. "Look at her head."

Hands touched her, gentle but insistent, peeling away the sodden habit that clung to her skin. The fabric stuck to her wounds, and she cried out weakly as it pulled free, fresh blood seeping warm against the cold air.

"Careful with her hand. The fingers—Mother of God."

Ottavia closed her eyes. Better not to see. Better not to know the full extent of what Gian Paolo had done with that gun.

She had prayed in the river. Prayed as the current carried her downstream, prayed as she wedged herself against the dam, prayed through the long hours of darkness while she waited for dawn or death, whichever came first.

Santa Maria di Loreto, do not let me die in this sin. Allow me time to confess.

The Virgin had heard. Ottavia was alive. But now, lying on this narrow bed with agony radiating from her skull, she wondered if survival was mercy or punishment.

"The barber-surgeon is here."

More footsteps. A man's voice, professional and calm. "Let me see her."

Ottavia forced her eyes open. The face above her was lined and weather worn. Ambrogio Vimercati, the barber-surgeon.

"Sister," he said gently, "I am going to examine your wounds. It will hurt, but I must assess the damage to treat you properly."

"I understand," she whispered.

Vimercati's hands moved with practiced efficiency, probing the injuries on her head. Ottavia felt his fingers part her matted hair, felt the sting of cold air on exposed flesh where scalp had been torn from bone. She heard his sharp intake of breath.

"One wound near the vein toward the forehead," he murmured, and somewhere beside him a notary's quill scratched against parchment, recording each injury as evidence. "Another similar on the opposite side..."

The examination continued, a catalog of violence mapped onto her body. Each touch brought fresh waves of pain, but Ottavia forced herself to remain still. She needed to understand what Gian Paolo had done so she could testify with precision.

"...above the temporal muscle on the left. Another near it, forming a triangle, half a finger long..."

She had raised her hand to shield herself and felt the bones snap like dry kindling beneath the gun butt.

"The scalp is detached from the flesh in several places." Vimercati's voice remained steady. "I will need to make incisions to join some of these wounds, to reduce two or three into one so they may be treated more effectively. The skin is separated from the bone across most of the cranium."

"Will she live?" One of the Sant'Orsola nuns, her voice tight with worry.

"If infection does not set in. But she has lost much blood, and the head wounds... we must wait and pray."

Ottavia felt the first cut. A sharp, clean sensation that was somehow easier to bear than the dull, throbbing agony. She focused on her breathing, counting each inhalation as Vimercati worked with needle and catgut.

One. Two. Three.

She would live. She had to live long enough to tell them everything.

* * *

WHEN VICAR SARACENO entered the room hours later, Ottavia was half-sitting, propped against pillows. Her skull was wrapped in clean linen bandages, and her right hand lay splinted across her lap like a broken bird.

The vicar looked older than she remembered, drawn and tired, his face gray with strain. He carried himself with the authority of the Church behind him, but there was something almost gentle in the way he approached her bed.

"Sister Ottavia." His voice was quiet, respectful of her suffering. "I am Vicar Saraceno of the Archdiocese of Milan. I must ask you some questions, if you are able to answer."

Ottavia nodded carefully, feeling the pull of stitches beneath the bandages. "Yes... Your Reverence."

Behind Saraceno stood his notary, quill ready, parchment laid out. Everything she said would be recorded and would become part of the permanent record.

Ottavia's mind, even clouded with pain, understood what this moment required. Truth, yes, but carefully measured truth. Enough to condemn Gian Paolo who deserved condemnation, but not so much that she destroyed herself in the telling.

She had had two days to think about escape, hadn't she? Two days of mounting terror between the time when Benedetta first whispered in the corridor and the night when they actually fled. Two days to weigh her choices, to make a decision with open eyes.

She could not admit that. Could not let the vicar know she had been complicit from the beginning. That would make her a willing apostate rather than a confused victim swept up in Benedetta's madness.

"Tell me your name," Saraceno said gently. "Your full name, and your father's name."

"Sister..." She paused, gathering strength. "Ottavia Ricci. My father... Agrippa. From Milan. Benedictine nun. Santa Margherita."

The notary's quill scratched steadily across the parchment.

Saraceno settled into a chair beside her bed. "Sister Ottavia, why were you found outside that cloistered convent this morning? How did you come to be at the church of Santa Maria delle Grazie, wounded and alone?"

Here. This was where the lie would begin, or rather, where the truth would be carefully shaped into something that protected her. The words would settle on her tongue like communion wafers that might transform to poison or salvation depending on whether God accepted her offering.

Ottavia took a shallow breath.

"Last night." She chose the words with deliberate care. Last night. Not two nights before when Benedetta first came to her, not the long hours she had spent for two days weighing damnation against imprisonment. Just last night. Simple. Immediate. Sudden. "In the convent. About... six hours past sundown. I didn't want... to go."

"Why not?"

"Uneasy. Since... since Sister Virginia was taken. Couldn't bear. To be alone."

"Where did you go?"

"To the room. Where Sisters Candida... Degnamerita sleep. Sister Silvia... she sleeps there too. I went... to seek company."

Also true. She had gone to that room every night since Virginia's removal. The vicar didn't need to know which night mattered most.

"What happened then?"

"I undressed. To go to bed. Only my shift. Had removed... my stockings. My head veil."

Saraceno leaned forward slightly. "And then?"

This was the critical moment. The lie that would protect her from charges of premeditation.

"Benedetta came. To the door." Ottavia forced her voice to carry surprise, confusion, as though this had been completely unexpected. Not the culmination of two days of whispered planning, but a sudden shock. "She signed. Gestured for me. To come out. Into the corridor."

Forgive me, she prayed silently. But I must survive this.

"What did she say?"

Ottavia closed her eyes, remembering both conversations—the careful recruitment and the next day's collection. She merged them in her telling, compressed two nights into one.

"She said... 'I want to escape. At all costs. I've made Gian Paolo... come to take me away.'"

The notary's quill scratched across parchment, recording her words as truth.

Ottavia felt a twist of guilt. But survival required this. If she admitted she had known for days, had waited and planned, they would see her as equally guilty as Benedetta.

"What did you say?"

"Told her... madness. Don't do it. But she said... Said I should run with her. Otherwise... otherwise the madness would be only hers."

Also, true. Those words had been spoken on which night hardly mattered now.

"Did she force you to go?"

"No." This required careful navigation. "I followed. To stop her."

Lie, her conscience whispered. You followed because you had already agreed.

But Ottavia pushed the thought away and continued. "She went down. The church stairs. To the garden. I ran after. To restrain..." A wave of nausea rolled through her. She closed her eyes, waiting for it to pass.

"Where was Gian Paolo?" Saraceno prompted gently.

"At the wall. Breaking it. Near the wagon gate. She said, 'Come with me. You'll see. He's already breaking the wall.'"

"And you went?"

Ottavia nodded. "Went down the stairs. Put on my stockings. At the bottom. Then... to the garden."

"What happened at the garden wall?"

"Benedetta told him... Through the hole. 'Ottavia doesn't want to come.' And Gian Paolo... he said... 'Her head is in danger if she doesn't.'"

Her head. The head he had later tried to destroy. The bitter irony brought fresh tears.

"He said other things. Frightening things. They convinced me. Said... said if I was reluctant, he would place me. In a convent. At Bergamo."

She watched Saraceno's face for any sign that he doubted her. But he simply nodded, his expression neutral, professional.

"So, you decided to go?"

"Yes." The admission hurt more than her wounds. "Went to my cell. Finished dressing. Came back. Escaped through... through the hole."

Two days, her conscience whispered. You had two days to refuse.

But that truth would stay buried.

The rest came more easily now—the walk along the town wall, the exit through Carrobiolo gate, the long trek through November darkness. All of this was straightforward fact.

"The Grazie church," Ottavia continued. "We came to it. I persuaded them... to kneel and pray. For the Madonna's mercy. We said... the Salve Regina. Seven times."

"You prayed together?" Saraceno's voice held a note of surprise. "All three of you?"

"Yes. At the main door."

That part had been real. Whatever else she was lying about, the prayers had been sincere. In those moments, kneeling before the church, she had genuinely believed the Virgin would protect them.

What a fool she had been.

She continued—the three roads, her insistence on the secluded path, the return to the Lambro's edge. And then the attack. All of this she told truthfully, her voice breaking as she described the push, the fall, the icy water.

"He pushed me. I was... moving toward the bank. To sit. To rest. His hand... closed on my arm. Then he pushed."

She described the terror of drowning, the desperate grab for the bank, and then the gun butt coming down again and again.

"I said... 'Ah, Signor Gian Paolo. To do this to me?'" The memory of her own disbelief was almost worse than the memory of pain. "I couldn't believe. That he would... I said, 'The Madonna will help me. She will see... that I have justice.'"

The rest came in fragments. The blows raining down, her hand raised and breaking beneath the impact, the moment she went limp hoping he would think her dead. The current taking her downstream. The hours on the bank waiting for dawn.

Through it all, Ottavia was careful. Careful about what she revealed. Careful to portray herself as confused, frightened, swept along rather than complicit. Careful to compress timeline, to eliminate the two days of waiting and choosing.

When she finished, exhausted and shaking, Saraceno sat back. His expression was thoughtful.

"Sister Ottavia," he said slowly, "do you know what happened to Sister Benedetta after she and Gian Paolo left you at the river?"

"No, Your Reverence." Tears slipped down Ottavia's cheeks. "I think. She must be dead."

"She is not dead." Saraceno's tone softened slightly. "She was found this morning in a well near Velate. Alive. She has been brought to this convent and is being treated by the same surgeon who attended you."

The relief that washed through Ottavia was overwhelming and genuine. Benedetta was alive.

But then a flicker of fear cut through the relief. Benedetta was alive and would give her own testimony. Would she tell the same story? Would she compress the timeline from two days into the one the same way? Or would she reveal that there had been earlier conversations, that Ottavia had known for days?

They had not discussed this. Had not coordinated their stories. Each would testify separately, and if their accounts conflicted...

Ottavia forced the fear down. She would face that when it came.

"Your Reverence," Ottavia said, her voice stronger now, "I have more. To tell you. About the convent. About Gian Paolo's. Intrusions. About the things. I have seen. And known. And been part of. But I am. Very tired. And the pain..."

"I understand." Saraceno stood. "Rest now, Sister. I will return when you are stronger, and you can tell me everything then. There is time."

He paused at the threshold. "Sister Ottavia, you have been granted a great mercy today. The Virgin heard your prayers and preserved your life. Use the time you have been given wisely."

After he left, Ottavia lay back against the pillows, her mind racing despite her exhaustion. She had survived the attack. She had survived the testimony. She had told her story in a way that might protect her from the worst charges.

But Benedetta would testify next. And Benedetta knew the truth about the two days of waiting, about Ottavia's complicity from the beginning.

Would she tell it?

Ottavia closed her eyes, feeling the throb of her wounds, the ache in her broken hand, the exhaustion threatening to pull her under.

She had shaped the truth into something that might save her. The rest, judgment, consequence, damnation, belonged to God and to whatever Benedetta would say when her turn came.

For now, she was alive. And survival, at this moment, was enough.

Those lies would be recorded. Would become part of the permanent record. Would be read and studied and judged by people who weren't there, who didn't understand the fear.

She had done what she had to do.

The truth, the full truth, would stay buried in her heart, known only to God.

And if God chose to judge her for the omissions, for the strategic reshaping of events, then she would accept that judgment when it came.

* * *

THE UPPER ROOM at Sant'Orsola smelled of woodsmoke and lavender water, scents the Ursuline sisters used to mask the lingering odors of illness and injury. Benedetta lay propped against thin pillows, her left side a constant fire of pain that flared with every breath. Through the small window, pale December light fell across rough blankets that did nothing to warm her.

Three days since the men of Velate had pulled her from that pit. Three days since darkness and stone and bones gave way to this narrow bed, these whitewashed walls, these sisters who tended her wounds with gentle efficiency and watched her with poorly concealed curiosity.

Ottavia is here. Ottavia is alive.

The sisters had told her that much. Her companion had been found, wounded but breathing, pulled from the Lambro by the grace of God. Ottavia was somewhere in this same convent, being tended by the same sisters.

But they had not been permitted to see each other. Had not been permitted to speak.

The memory of those blows returned unbidden. The wet percussion of the gun stock against Ottavia's skull, her screams for the Madonna's help, Benedetta's own weak protest—*Don't do those things*—as if words could stop what was already happening.

The door opened. Sister Maria, the infirmarian, entered first. Behind her came a figure Benedetta had been dreading since the moment she understood she would survive.

Vicar Gerolamo Saraceno moved into the room with the measured steps of a man accustomed to extracting truth from those who wished to hide it. His pale eyes swept over her—the bandaged knee, the way she held her left arm close against her injured ribs, the bruises that had bloomed purple and yellow across her face.

A notary followed, settling into a chair near the door, his quill already poised above fresh parchment.

"Sister Benedetta." Saraceno's voice carried no warmth, but neither did it hold accusation. Not yet. "I am told you are well enough to speak."

"I can speak, Your Reverence." Her voice emerged rougher than she intended, from the moments she screamed for help in the darkness of the well.

He studied her for a long moment. There was knowledge behind those pale eyes, the careful assessment of a man who had already gathered information from other sources.

She had no way of knowing what he already knew. Could only tell the truth as she had lived it.

Saraceno settled into the chair. The notary's quill scratched across parchment, recording even this, the date, the location, the name of the witness.

"Let us begin," the vicar said. "State your name for the record."

"My name is Benedetta Felicia Homati Vimercati. My father was named Matteo. I am a professed nun in the Convent of Santa Margherita in this town of Monza."

"Tell me how you came to be found in Signor Alberici's house near Velate."

Benedetta closed her eyes briefly, organizing the events in her mind. The truth. Simply, completely, without calculation. After what Gian Paolo had done, she owed him nothing.

"Since there was friendship between Gian Paolo and Sister Virginia," she began, "Gian Paolo sent a man to talk to me. I think it was this past Tuesday, after dinner. The man was dressed as a farmer. I didn't know him."

"What did this man want?"

"I went to the gate, and he told me Gian Paolo wished me to know that Sister Virginia had been taken away from our convent. And he wrote me this in a note, and I knew it was Gian Paolo's handwriting because I was used to it."

Saraceno leaned forward slightly. "What did you do with this note?"

"After I read it, I went to my room. His note had offered to help me escape. He gave me instructions, to meet at the garden wall at about four hours past sundown on Thursday. All I had to do was send my answer."

"And what did you write?"

"One word only." Her voice dropped. "Yes."

"How did you send this message?"

"The man returned the next evening at the same hour. I gave him my answer when he came back to the gate."

"And then?" Saraceno prompted.

Her stomach tightened. She would have to speak of Ottavia now, of how she had recruited her, persuaded her, led her into the trap that had nearly killed them both.

"After this, I told Ottavia all about it, telling her that I wanted to get away, while she didn't know if she would come or not." Benedetta spoke carefully. "I spoke to her about it once or twice, that is, I said that I wanted to go."

"And Sister Ottavia? What was her response?"

"She was uncertain. Afraid. But she agreed to come to the wall with me. To talk to him. To decide."

"Tell me about that night."

The rest came more easily. The garden wall at four hours past sundown, Gian Paolo's signal tapping on the stone, the dagger he pressed through the gap for her to help loosen the mortar. The breach widening. Ottavia squeezing through first, then Benedetta herself.

"We followed the town wall. Stayed close. Kept silent. We came out through a small gate at Carrobiolo, where the wall had crumbled."

She described the walk toward the Grazie church, the November darkness, the sound of the Lambro in the distance. At the church, they had knelt and prayed.

"I persuaded the others to kneel and pray for the Madonna's mercy to accompany us," Benedetta said, her voice catching. "And we did this at the main door and said the Salve Regina seven times."

Seven times. As if repetition could undo what they had already set in motion.

"Then we left, taking a road on the other side of the Lambro, till we reached a place where three roads joined. I asked Gian Paolo where they led. He said one went to La Santa and the other to Velate. I said I didn't want to go on such public roads, and so he took us by the third, and again we came to the Lambro."

She paused. The river.

"When we were a little distance, going along the river," Benedetta said, her voice growing harder, "Gian Paolo threw Ottavia into the Lambro. She had been in the middle, between us."

"Describe exactly what happened."

"Ottavia screamed and I ran and gave my hand to help her, but Gian Paolo took her by the other hand, and with his harquebus he had under his cloak, he hit her many blows on the head." The memory brought tears. "Ottavia was praying for help. I drew away for fear he would hit me too, after he told me to leave Ottavia alone, and I began to cry."

"You tried to help her?"

"I gave my hand. But he told me to leave her alone. And I was afraid. So, I drew away."

The guilt of that moment would stay with Benedetta forever. She had made a choice. Had chosen survival over solidarity.

"Then leaving Ottavia, whom we thought must be dead, we continued along the Lambro."

The testimony continued. The farmhouse where she had spent Friday, the room accessible only by ladder, the bread and cheese and grapes Gian Paolo had brought her.

"I didn't drink the wine for fear it was poisoned, and this was because of what I'd seen him do to Ottavia."

She told of when Gian Paolo had returned and insisted they leave. The walked through darkness to the grove of trees. The cistern that wasn't a cistern.

"I threw in a stone and when I didn't hear it strike bottom, I said, 'This isn't a cistern.' And so, I drew away, but coming close to me, he gave me a push on the back to throw me in, but I didn't fall and fled away."

Her voice steadied as she described the struggle. Gian Paolo chasing her, threatening to stab her, dragging her back to the well's edge and throwing her in.

"In the fall, I hit the stones with my left side, leaving me in the state I am in now. After I had fallen, I heard him throwing down a rock, which hit me on my right knee."

"How long were you in the well?"

"I was there all the rest of that night, all the following day, again the whole night after, until yesterday mid-morning when some men heard me crying for help. They pulled me with a rope, one of them having climbed down, for I was half dead."

"Did you cry for help during the night?"

"I only cried for help in the daytime and not at night, fearing Gian Paolo might come at night and look down, and if he heard me cry out, he would throw other stones at my head to kill me. And so, I kept my head under some large stones that were in that well, which was wide, and besides the stones there were also some bones which one could see very well in the daytime."

"Bones?"

"Bones. And also, I seemed to see something which appeared to be a small baby."

The room went very still. Saraceno and the notary exchanged glances.

"A baby," Saraceno repeated carefully.

"Something that appeared to be a small baby. In the well. With the bones." Benedetta opened her eyes and met the vicar's gaze. "I think you will find, Your Reverence, that Gian Paolo has used that well before."

The questioning continued. Details about Virginia and Gian Paolo's relationship, about his entries into the convent, about the births of Virginia's children. Benedetta answered everything with exhausted honesty, too tired to calculate what should be revealed and what concealed.

When Saraceno finally rose to leave, two hours later, Benedetta's voice was nearly gone, and her ribs were screaming.

"One more question, Sister Benedetta." Saraceno paused at the door. "When you spoke to Sister Ottavia about the escape, once or twice, as you said—what was her response?"

Benedetta frowned. "She didn't know if she would come or not. She was uncertain. Afraid."

"But you had multiple conversations about it? Before Thursday night?"

"Yes, Your Reverence. I spoke to her about it once or twice. That is, I said that I wanted to go and asked if she would come."

Saraceno nodded slowly. "Thank you, Sister. Rest now. I may have more questions later."

After he left, Benedetta lay staring at the ceiling, wondering why that particular detail had seemed so important to him.

* * *

IN THE CORRIDOR outside Benedetta's room, Saraceno paused and turned to his notary.

"Make a note," he said quietly. "Sister Benedetta's testimony states that she spoke to Sister Ottavia about the escape 'once or twice' before the night itself. Sister Ottavia's testimony claims she was approached suddenly on Thursday evening with no prior discussion."

The notary's eyebrows rose. "A contradiction, Your Reverence."

"Indeed." Saraceno began walking toward the stairs. "One of them is lying about the degree of premeditation. The question is which one, and why."

"Does it matter, Your Reverence? Both fled the convent. Both were attacked by Osio. The central facts are the same."

Saraceno considered this. "It matters because it tells us something about these women. Sister Ottavia is protecting herself, minimizing her complicity, presenting herself as swept along rather than a willing participant. Sister Benedetta, on the other hand, seems to be telling the truth without calculation. Too exhausted or too honest to shape her testimony."

"Should we confront Sister Ottavia with the discrepancy?"

Saraceno thought of the woman lying wounded below, the thirteen wounds on her head, the broken hand, the damaged voice.

"Not yet. She is very ill. And truthfully, it may not matter. Both testimonies agree on the essential facts—that Osio lured them from the convent and attempted to kill them. That is what the Cardinal needs for his case."

"And the contradiction?"

"Note it in the record. Let future readers draw their own conclusions about which woman was more honest." Saraceno started down the stairs. "For now, we have a murderer to catch."

But as he descended, his mind kept returning to the discrepancy. Once or twice, Benedetta had said.

And Ottavia had claimed it was all a sudden surprise.

One of them was lying. And given that Ottavia had suffered most from Gian Paolo's violence, Saraceno could understand why she might want to minimize her own culpability.

Still. It was a lie told to a Church official during sworn testimony. A lie that would be preserved in the permanent record.

He wondered if she knew what that meant for her soul.

* * *

THE INTERROGATIONS AT Santa Margherita continued for days. Every nun was questioned, every lay sister, every servant who had access to the convent in the past months.

The story that emerged was damning.

Gian Paolo Osio had been inside the convent not once but numerous times over the years. He had slept in Virginia's cell, had eaten meals prepared by her companions, had walked the corridors in a nun's habit with a cloth covering his head. The entire community had known, or suspected, or chosen not to see.

Caterina's name came up again and again.

The lay sister who had disappeared. Who had been imprisoned for impertinence and then vanished without trace. Who no one had looked for, whose absence no one had questioned.

Saraceno sent men to search Gian Paolo's house on the Agrate road. They found it locked and empty, stripped of valuables, abandoned in haste.

But they searched anyway.

And in the lumber room, beneath layers of old wood and dust and forgotten tools, they found the floor had been disturbed. Recently.

"Dig here," Saraceno ordered.

They brought shovels. Picked away at the packed earth. And three feet down, they struck something that was not earth.

Cloth. Rotted and stained but still recognizable as the rough wool of a lay sister's habit.

But her body was not intact. The searched the entire lumber room as well as the garden and uncovered body parts carefully, reverently. What remained of her, after so long in the ground.

Caterina.

The barber-surgeon examined the bones they had collected. "The skull shows trauma. A blow to the back of the head. Fatal."

Saraceno stood in that dim lumber room, looking down at the remains of a woman who had been murdered, dismembered, and buried like refuse, whose death had been concealed for years while her killer walked free and her body rotted beneath the floorboards of his own house.

"Prepare her for Christian burial," he said quietly.

They brought up the collected bones in a plain wooden coffin. The news spread through the town like wildfire. The missing lay sister found murdered, buried in Gian Paolo Osio's house.

The search for Osio intensified. Riders were sent to every town within fifty miles. His description circulated to every border post, every customs house, every ecclesiastical court in Lombardy.

But Gian Paolo had vanished.

Saraceno returned to Sant'Orsola to question Ottavia again. She was weaker now, her skin gray, her breathing labored. The infection Vimercati had feared was setting in.

"Sister Ottavia," Saraceno said gently. "I need to ask you about Caterina."

Ottavia's eyes closed. When she spoke, her voice was barely a whisper.

"I knew. We all... knew."

"What happened to her?"

"Virginia. And Gian Paolo. They killed her. In the... convent."

"Why did you lie to me?"

Ottavia's face twisted with something that transcended physical pain. Her breath came in ragged gasps.

"Because... If I said... same day. Sudden. Then it was... impulse. Terror." Each word cost her. "But if I said... knew for days. Knew about Caterina. Knew about... the murders. The children. Everything." She opened her eyes, meeting his gaze. "Then I was... complicit. In all of it."

"Why did you lie to me?"

The re-asked question hung in the air between them.

"Fear," Ottavia whispered. "I wanted... to live. Wanted... mercy. Thought if I seemed... victim instead of... accomplice..." She coughed, a wet, rattling sound. "Foolish. God knows. God... always knew."

"Is there more you need to tell me?"

This was her chance. Perhaps her last chance.

"Yes." Her chest heaved with the effort to draw air. "Much more. Things I... held back. Before."

Saraceno leaned forward. "Then tell me now. Let us unburden your conscience before it's too late."

And Ottavia began to talk.

She told him everything. The full truth this time, without evasion or calculation.

She spoke of the night Caterina died. How the lay sister had discovered Virginia's pregnancy, had threatened to expose everything to the superiors. How Virginia had sent for Gian Paolo in a panic.

"He came. Over the wall. Like always. And they... they killed Caterina. In the laundry room."

Ottavia's voice was failing, each word a struggle.

"I watched. From the doorway. Virginia held... a candle. Gian Paolo had... wooden wool winder. Caterina tried. To scream. But he was... so fast."

The memory pulled her under like the Lambro's current. She could see it still, the candlelight flickering on Caterina's face as she realized what was happening, the desperate scrabble of her hands against the wood, the way her body had gone limp after endless, terrible seconds.

"When she was... dead. Gian Paolo said. Had to hide. The body. Virginia said... his house. The lumber room. No one would... look there."

"How did they move her?"

"That night. Benedetta and I... we helped. Wrapped her. In old cloth. Carried her. To the hole. In the wall. Near the garden." Ottavia's breathing grew more labored. "Gian Paolo took her. From there. Buried her. In his own house. Like... garbage."

"And the children Virginia carried?"

"Two before. A girl. Francesca. She lives. With Gian Paolo's. Servants." Ottavia paused, gathering what little strength remained. "Another. Earlier. A boy. Don't know. What happened. Virginia never. Spoke of him."

Saraceno's quill scratched steadily across the parchment, recording every damning word.

"Were there other murders?"

"The apothecary. Rainerio. He knew. About Virginia. And Gian Paolo. He threatened. To tell. To write. To the Cardinal."

She described how Gian Paolo had stood outside the apothecary shop on that October evening, how his man Redhead had fired the harquebus, how Rainerio had screamed and fallen.

"We knew. All of us. Knew Gian Paolo. Had done it. But we said... nothing."

"Why?"

"Fear. Of Virginia. Of Gian Paolo. Of... scandal. If we spoke. The convent would... be destroyed. Our families... disgraced. So, we... chose silence."

Ottavia's eyes filled with tears that tracked down her hollow cheeks.

"And now. Caterina is dead. Rainerio is dead. Benedetta... nearly dead. I am... dying. And it is. All. Our fault."

Saraceno sat back. "Sister Ottavia, do you repent of these sins? Do you ask God's forgiveness for what you have done and failed to do?"

"Yes." The word came out as a sob. "With all. My heart. I repent. I beg. The Madonna's. Mercy. I am. So sorry. So... sorry."

"Then I will send for a priest to hear your full confession and grant you absolution. You have told the truth, finally. That is something."

After he left, Ottavia lay in the silence of her small room, feeling her life ebbing away with each labored breath. She had told everything. Had unburdened her soul at last.

It was too late to save her body. But perhaps, just perhaps, it was not too late to save her soul.

* * *

OVER THE DAYS that followed, Ottavia drifted in and out of consciousness. Sometimes she thought she was back in Santa Margherita, practicing the organ, the music swelling beneath her fingers. Sometimes she was a child again, before the veil, before the prison of enclosure.

Mostly she prayed.

Santa Maria di Loreto, have mercy on me, a sinner.

The priest came. Heard her confession. Gave her the sacrament. His voice was kind as he spoke the words of absolution, and Ottavia wept with relief.

She would die. But she would not die damned.

* * *

ON THE MORNING of December 25th, as the bells of Monza rang for Christmas Mass, Sister Ottavia took her last breath.

She died peacefully, the attending sisters said. Her last words were a prayer of gratitude.

The letter reached Vicar Saraceno later that same day. A messenger from Sant'Orsola, dressed in black, his face solemn, carried a letter sealed with the Prioress's mark.

Saraceno broke the seal in his chambers.

> *My Lord Vicar, I write to inform you that Sister Ottavia Ricci departed this life in the early hours of December 26, fortified by the holy sacraments of the Church and attended by our*

community in vigil. She died peacefully, her last words being gratitude for the unburdening of her conscience. Her body will be interred in our cemetery with all proper rites. May God have mercy on her soul.

Saraceno set down the letter and stared at the wall of his study.

She had died on Christmas day. Had lived just long enough to tell the truth, to make her confession, to receive absolution for the terrible things she had witnessed and enabled.

The irony was not lost on him. Ottavia had shaped her testimony carefully, had lied to protect herself, had compressed the timeline to make herself seem less culpable. But in the end, facing death, she had told everything.

The truth had cost her nothing because she had nothing left to lose.

Saraceno pulled out a fresh sheet of parchment and began to write his report to Cardinal Borromeo. The investigation was yielding results. They had testimony from both surviving nuns. They had found Caterina's body. They had evidence of multiple murders, of sacrilege, of conspiracy.

All they lacked was the man himself.

Gian Paolo Osio remained at large.

* * *

IN A SMALL room above a tavern three days' ride from Monza, Gian Paolo Osio stood at the window and looked out at the winter landscape. Snow had fallen during the night, covering everything in white.

He had been here for two weeks. Hiding. Waiting. Trying to decide what to do next.

The news from Monza reached him in fragments, brought by travelers and merchants who stopped at the tavern below. The vicar was conducting a full investigation. The nuns were testifying. Bodies had been found.

Benedetta had survived.

That knowledge gnawed at him. She had seen everything, knew everything, and now she was alive to tell it all.

And Ottavia. He had heard she was gravely wounded, near death. Perhaps already dead by now.

He felt nothing when he thought of her. She had been a tool, a means to an end, and when she had outlived her usefulness, he had discarded her. It was as simple as that.

Virginia.

Her name was a wound that would not heal. They had taken her to Milan, locked her away in the convent of Santa Valeria. He had no way to reach her, no way to know what she was suffering.

Did she think of him? Did she curse him for bringing her to this?

Or did she still love him, even now?

Gian Paolo turned away from the window. Love. What a useless, destructive thing it had proven to be. It had ruined them both.

He had tried to do what was right, in his own way. Had tried to protect Virginia, to keep Alma safe, to silence those who threatened to expose them. But every solution had created new problems, every murder had required another to cover it up, until the weight of it all had collapsed around them.

He thought of Caterina, her eyes wide with terror as the wool winder crashed her skull. Of Rainerio, bleeding out in his shop while his wife screamed. Of Ottavia, her skull split open, her hand shattered, begging the Madonna for mercy he had refused to give.

The mistakes, he realized, had been strategic ones. He should have left Monza years ago, taken Virginia with him, fled to France or the Empire where the Cardinal's reach could not follow. Should have killed Benedetta too, that night by the river, instead of assuming the well would be enough. Should have been more careful, more thorough, more ruthless.

It had not been the murders themselves that were wrong. It had been the execution of them.

That thought should have troubled him. Once, perhaps, it would have. But he had crossed too many lines, committed too many sins, to feel the weight of conscience anymore. He had become something else. Something harder. Something necessary.

He would survive this. He had money hidden away, contacts in other cities, friends who owed him favors. He would disappear into the vast machinery of Italy's underworld and emerge somewhere else with a new name and a new life.

Virginia would face the Cardinal's justice alone.

The thought brought a flicker of something that might have been guilt. But he pushed it away. She had made her choices, just as he had made his. They had both known the risks.

The difference was that he had been smart enough to run.

Gian Paolo sat down at the small table and pulled out parchment and ink. He would write letters, carefully worded, strategically placed, laying the groundwork for his escape. There were people who would help him, for a price. There were always people willing to help, if the price was right.

The Church might have power. But Gian Paolo had something more valuable.

He had the will to do whatever was necessary to survive.

* * *

IN THE CONVENT of Santa Valeria in Milan, Virginia Maria de Leyva knelt in her cell and stared at the crucifix on the wall.

Two weeks since they had dragged her from Santa Margherita. Two weeks of isolation, of silence, of waiting for judgment that had not yet come.

She had heard nothing from Gian Paolo. No letters, no messages, no sign that he even remembered she existed.

He had abandoned her.

The knowledge settled into her bones like winter cold. She was alone. Truly, completely alone.

The Cardinal's investigators would come eventually. They would question her, accuse her, demand confession. And what would she say?

The truth? That she had loved Gian Paolo with a passion that had consumed everything else? That she had borne his children, had conspired with him, had helped him conceal murders?

Or would she lie? Claim she had been coerced, manipulated, forced against her will?

Virginia closed her eyes. She did not know which path would lead to mercy and which to damnation. She knew only that the life she had lived, the power, the freedom, the love, was over.

From now on, there would be only walls. Only prayers. Only penance.

She thought of Ottavia and Benedetta, fled into the night, and wondered if they had found the freedom she had lost. Or if Gian Paolo had destroyed them too, the way he destroyed everything he touched.

The bells rang for Vespers. Virginia rose mechanically and moved toward the door. Time to go to chapel. Time to pray with women who despised her, watched her, whispered about her.

Time to begin the long, slow punishment that would be the rest of her life.

* * *

THE LUMBER ROOM was long and narrow, tucked into the back corner of Gian Paolo's abandoned house. Saraceno descended the stairs carefully, a torch held high to light the way.

The excavation had been completed. Caterina's bones had been removed, wrapped in fresh linen, prepared for proper burial. But the investigation was not finished.

"Your Reverence," one of the workers called. "There's something else here."

Saraceno moved closer. In the corner of the room, beneath layers of old wood and debris, they had found another disturbance in the earth.

"Dig," Saraceno ordered.

They worked carefully, methodically, removing the dirt handful by handful. And there, perhaps a foot down, they found it.

Cloth. Old, rotted, stained.

And inside the cloth, bones. Small bones.

An infant.

Saraceno stared down at the tiny remains. One of Virginia's children, perhaps. Or another victim, from another time, whose story would never be known.

"Prepare these for burial as well," he said quietly. "And search the rest of the property. I want every room examined, every floor checked. If there are more bodies, I want them found."

They searched for three days. And found nothing else.

Only Caterina. And the infant. Two lives ended and hidden away, as if they had never existed.

Saraceno stood in the empty lumber room after the workers had gone, holding his torch high, looking at the disturbed earth where the bodies had lain.

This was what sin looked like, he thought. Not the passionate drama of the moment—the stolen kiss, the forbidden touch, the surrender to desire. But this. The cold, practical disposal of inconvenient lives. The burial of evidence. The transformation of human beings into problems to be solved and forgotten.

Virginia and Gian Paolo had loved each other. Of that, Saraceno had no doubt. But their love had been built on a foundation of death, and now the foundation was crumbling, revealing the bodies buried beneath.

He climbed the stairs and emerged into the December afternoon. The house would be sealed, held as evidence until the trial concluded. And someday, perhaps, it would be torn down entirely, erased from the landscape like its owner had tried to erase his victims.

But the dead would not be forgotten. Saraceno would see to that.

* * *

THE WELL AT Velate drew Saraceno like a lodestone. He needed to see it for himself, to understand what Benedetta had endured.

He rode out on a cold morning, accompanied by two guards and his notary. The countryside was bleak, stripped bare by winter, the fields empty and the trees skeletal against the gray sky.

They found the well easily. It stood in a grove of bare poplars, its stone rim barely visible above the ground. Someone had laid planks across the opening after Benedetta's rescue.

"Remove the planks," Saraceno ordered.

The guards lifted them away. Saraceno approached the edge and looked down.

Darkness. A throat of stone descending into blackness.

He dropped a pebble and counted. One. Two. Three. Four. Five.

The strike came faint and distant.

"Deep," one of the guards muttered. "How did she survive?"

"By the grace of God," Saraceno said. "And by her own will."

He thought of Benedetta, lying at the bottom of this pit for two days and a night, surrounded by bones and darkness, crying for help only during daylight hours because she feared Gian Paolo would return to finish what he had started.

"I want to go down," Saraceno said.

The guards exchanged glances. "Your Reverence, it's not safe. The walls could be unstable."

"I need to see what she saw. Bring rope."

They secured the rope around his waist and lowered him slowly into the well. The stone walls pressed close, slick with moisture. The light from above faded quickly.

Down. Down. Down.

His feet touched bottom, not water, but stone and earth, his torch casting wild shadows on the curved walls.

And there, scattered across the bottom, were bones.

Human bones. Animal bones. All jumbled together.

Saraceno crouched, examining them carefully. An adult skull, cracked and weathered. Smaller bones that might have belonged to a child or an animal. And there—

A tiny skull. Unmistakably infant.

His hand trembled as he lifted it. So small. So fragile.

This was what Benedetta had seen. This charnel pit where Gian Paolo had disposed of his victims, assuming they would never be found.

How many? Saraceno wondered. How many lives had ended here?

"Your Reverence!" The voice came from above, distant and distorted. "Are you well?"

"Pull me up!" Saraceno called back. "And bring a basket. We're recovering everything."

They worked for hours, bringing up bones piece by piece. The barber-surgeon would examine them, try to determine how many individuals, how long they had been there.

But Saraceno already knew the essential truth.

Gian Paolo Osio had been killing for years. And they had only now discovered the extent of it.

* * *

THE REPORTS WENT to Cardinal Borromeo in a steady stream. Each new discovery, each testimony, each piece of evidence carefully documented and dispatched to Milan.

The Cardinal's response was swift and unequivocal.

> *Proceed with full investigation. Spare no expense. Leave no stone unturned. I want every crime documented, every victim identified, every accomplice named. This sacrilege will not go unpunished.*

The machinery of ecclesiastical justice ground forward, inexorable and thorough.

December wore on. The investigation expanded. More witnesses were called. More secrets exposed.

The convent of Santa Margherita remained under sequestration, the nuns confined to their cells, forbidden to speak to outsiders. Some had known about the murders. Others had simply looked away. All bore the weight of collective guilt.

* * *

BENEDETTA RECOVERED SLOWLY at Sant'Orsola. Her ribs healed. The bruises faded. But the nightmares remained. Dreams of falling, of darkness, of Gian Paolo's face above the well's edge as he prepared to throw her in.

She testified again, providing more details, more names. She told them about Caterina's murder, about the disposal of the body, about Virginia's children and where they might be found.

She held nothing back. What was the point? Ottavia was dead. Virginia was imprisoned. Gian Paolo had tried to kill her and failed.

The truth, at last, was her only weapon.

* * *

IN THE SMALL tavern room three days' ride from Monza, Gian Paolo Osio packed his saddlebags and prepared to disappear.

He had waited too long already. The net was tightening. Soon there would be warrants issued, descriptions circulated, rewards posted. He needed to be gone before that happened.

The money he had hidden would last a year, perhaps two if he was careful. Long enough to establish himself somewhere new. Long enough to become someone else.

He thought one last time of Virginia, locked away in her cell, facing judgment alone.

Then he pushed the thought away.

Survival required focus. Required ruthlessness. Required the ability to cut away everything that might slow him down, including sentiment.

He had loved her once. Perhaps he still did, in his way.

But love was a luxury he could no longer afford.

Gian Paolo settled his cloak around his shoulders and checked that his weapons were secure. The dagger in his boot. The small pistol hidden in his doublet. The coin purse tucked inside his shirt, close to his skin.

He was ready.

The night was dark, moonless, perfect for travel. He would ride north, toward the border, where the Cardinal's authority grew thin and men asked fewer questions.

Somewhere out there was a life he had not yet ruined. A future he had not yet destroyed.

All he had to do was reach it.

Gian Paolo walked down the narrow stairs, through the empty tavern, and out into the stable yard. The cold hit him immediately, sharp and clean, cutting through his cloak.

Above, the sky was a vast blackness. The wind moaned through the bare branches of the trees, a mournful, hungry sound.

He could not go back to Monza. The thought flickered in his mind, a desperate ride, a final moment with Virginia, but he crushed it instantly. The authorities were there. Waiting for him. And so was Benedetta.

And Virginia?

She was truly alone now. The walls of Santa Valeria in Milan had become her prison. She would face the Cardinal's judges by herself, defenseless. They would strip away her name, her pride, her dignity, until nothing remained but the sinner beneath.

He had done this to her.

The realization hit him with the force of a physical blow. He had lost. The game he had played against the Church, against the law, against the very order of the world, was finished.

He reached for his cloak; heavy wool lined with fox fur that was matting and starting to rot at the hem. He checked his boot for his dagger, feeling the cold steel against his calf. He took his purse from the table; it felt terrifyingly light.

He walked out to the stable. The horse was there, a strong roan gelding, its breath steaming in the frigid air as it stamped its hooves on the straw. Gian Paolo pulled himself into the saddle, the leather creaking under his weight.

He turned the horse's head north.

Not toward Venice. Not yet.

He had one card left to play. There was a friend near the border, a man he had known for years, who lived in a fortified villa and laughed at the laws of priests and governors. A man who owed him favors. He would give Gian Paolo shelter. He would help him plan.

It was a gamble. A desperate one. But it was the only card he had left to play.

Gian Paolo dug his spurs into the horse's flanks. The animal leaped forward, iron shoes striking sparks from the frozen stones of the courtyard. He rode out into the darkness, leaving the warmth of the dying fire behind him.

The wind howled, erasing his tracks as fast as he made them, as if the land itself was eager to wash its hands of him.

* * *

THE ROOM AT Santa Valeria smelled of old paper and the damp, stone-cold breath of Milanese winter. It was not a cell, strictly speaking, a small parlor on the ground floor, but the heavy iron grille on the single high window made the distinction irrelevant.

Virginia Maria de Leyva sat on a high-backed wooden chair. Her hands were folded in her lap, fingers laced together so tightly the knuckles were white. She wore the black habit of her order, but her veil was pinned back, leaving her face exposed. She felt naked. For twenty years, she had hidden behind the veil; now, there was nothing between her and the man who held her life in his hands.

Vicar Monsignor Gerolamo Saraceno sat across the narrow table. He was unassuming in appearance, with ink-stained fingers and pale, watery blue eyes that seemed to have catalogued every sin the human heart could devise. He did not look like an inquisitor. He looked like a clerk, a man of ledgers and lists.

That made him terrifying.

He dipped a quill into a small pot of ink. The scratch of the nib against parchment was the only sound in the room, a dry, rasping noise like an insect skittering across dry leaves. It grated on Virginia's nerves, louder than any shout.

"Sister Virginia Maria," Saraceno said, without looking up. His voice was soft, dry as dust. "We are here to establish the truth of the events at Santa Margherita. The accusations are extensive."

He turned a page. The parchment crinkled.

"Violation of the vow of chastity. Conspiracy to commit murder. Violation of sacred enclosure. Sacrilege." He looked up then. "How do you answer?"

Virginia straightened her spine against the hard wood. She was a de Leyva. She was the Lady of Monza. Even here, stripped of her title and her power, she would not cower before a clerk.

"I answer that I am a victim, Monsignor," she said. Her voice was steady, though her heart hammered against her ribs. "Not a criminal."

Saraceno paused. He set the quill down carefully. "A victim? Of whom?"

"Of Gian Paolo Osio." The name tasted like ash. "And of the dark arts he employed to enslave my will."

This was the strategy. The only path left through the fire. She could not deny the acts—the child, the letters, the body in the wall—so she must deny the intent. She must become a puppet, and Osio the puppet master.

"Explain," Saraceno said, leaning back.

"It began years ago," Virginia said, leaning forward into the light. She let her voice tremble, just enough. "He pursued me. I resisted. I prayed, Monsignor. I sought to protect my convent. But he would not be deterred. He used... means."

"What means?"

"Potions," she whispered. "Powders mixed into my food. A magnet he claimed had power over the human heart. He boasted of it. He spoke of consulting with Jews and sorcerers, of casting horoscopes that bound our fates together in the stars."

She saw Saraceno's eyes narrow slightly. Sorcery. It was the one accusation the Church feared more than adultery.

"I felt it happen," she pressed on, her voice rising. "My will... dissolving. I would resolve to bar the door against him, to cry out for help, and then a fog would descend. My limbs would move without my command. My voice would speak words I did not intend. I was a prisoner in my own body, Monsignor. I watched myself sin and could not stop it."

Saraceno watched her. He did not blink. "You are suggesting that for a decade or more you were under a spell? That you bore a child, wrote love letters, and arranged secret meetings, all without your consent?"

"Not without my knowledge. But without my freedom." She pressed a hand to her chest, feeling the frantic beat of her heart. "It was a possession. A devil's work."

Saraceno picked up the quill again. He examined the tip, peeling away a stray fiber.

"We have testimony from others," he said quietly. "Sister Benedetta. Sister Ottavia, may she rest in peace. They speak of passion, Sister. Of jealousy. Of a woman deeply in love who would destroy anything that threatened her happiness. They do not speak of magnets."

"They were deceived!" Virginia cried. "They saw only what Osio wanted them to see. Or perhaps they were bewitched as well. He had power, Monsignor. Terrible power."

"And the murder? The killing of the lay sister, Caterina?"

Virginia flinched. The image rose unbidden—the dull thud of the wool winder, the blood pooling on stone.

"I tried to stop him," she lied. "I begged him to spare her. But he was a madman. He struck her down before I could intervene. And then... then the fear took me. He told me I was complicit. That if I spoke, I would be executed. He used my terror to bind me further."

Saraceno dipped the quill. He began to write. *Scratch-scratch.*

"Magic," he muttered, almost to himself. "It is a convenient defense, Sister. It absolves the sinner of the sin. It makes the will irrelevant."

"It is the truth!"

"Is it?" Saraceno stopped writing. He looked at her, and for a moment, the watery blue eyes hardened into something sharp. "Or is it simply the last refuge of a woman who cannot bear to look at what she has become?"

The question struck her like a slap. Heat flared in her cheeks.

"I am a daughter of the Church," she said, her voice icy. "I have been grievously sinned against. If you seek justice, seek it from the man who used sorcery to corrupt a bride of Christ. Do not blame the victim for the crime."

Saraceno closed the heavy ledger. He stood, gathering his papers with methodical slowness.

"We will investigate your claims, Sister. We will question everyone with knowledge. We will search for evidence of these... arts." He moved to the door, his hand resting on the latch. "But I must warn you. The Holy Office deals harshly with witchcraft. If Osio is a sorcerer, he will burn. But if you are lying... if you are using the Devil's name to mask your own desires..."

He let the silence stretch, heavy and suffocating.

"I am not lying," Virginia whispered.

Saraceno nodded once. It was not a nod of belief. It was a nod of recording.

"We shall see. The truth has a way of surfacing, Sister. Like bones in a river. It always rises eventually."

He stepped out. The door closed. The heavy bolt slid home with the sound of a hammer strike.

Virginia remained in the chair. The room was silent again, save for the wind rattling the grille. She was shaking now, deep tremors that started in her marrow. She had played her card. She had named the Devil as her co-conspirator.

She closed her eyes and prayed that the Devil would play along.

Chapter Fourteen
1608

The 14th of June
Convent of Santa Valeria, Milan

THE CHAMBER BENEATH Santa Valeria had no windows. The only light came from candles mounted in iron sconces on the walls, their flames guttering in drafts that descended from somewhere above, casting shadows that seemed to move of their own accord across stone that had been worn smooth by centuries of suffering.

The air was thick and humid with moisture and something metallic that coated the back of Virginia's throat like a copper coin. Fear had a smell, she had learned. It was acrid, layered upon itself, generations of terror soaked into mortar and stone until the walls themselves seemed to weep it.

The torture chair sat in the center of the chamber. It was a simple wooden construction, heavy oak reinforced with iron bands, but its very ordinariness made it worse. No elaborate mechanism. No theatrical cruelty. Just a chair designed to hold a body still while that body was made to suffer.

The torturer was a functionary. He was neither young nor old, his face unmarked by cruelty or compassion—merely functional. He moved through the chamber with the detached efficiency of a tradesman preparing his tools, positioning implements with the care one might use arranging surgical instruments. A thick rope lay coiled beside the pulley mechanism mounted to the ceiling beam. Beside it, leather straps for binding wrists.

Virginia had seen the strappado described in whispered conversations among nuns who had witnessed Inquisition proceedings. Now she understood why they had fallen silent when pressed for details.

Saraceno stood to the side, watching. His pale eyes tracked every movement with the intensity of a scholar observing an experiment. A physician attended as well. Church law required a witness to ensure the torture did not result in death, only in the shattering of resistance. The physician was young, his face beneath his cap the color of old cheese, his fingers gripping his leather satchel with white-knuckled intensity.

"Sister Virginia," Saraceno said, his voice carrying the same measured tone he had used during the earlier interrogations. It was a voice that suggested he was discussing theology, not what was about to happen to her body. "Your continued insistence that you were bewitched contradicts all evidence. All testimony. Your own letters, written in your hand, expressing desire and intention."

He paused. Let the silence settle.

"Lie after lie, Sister. Layer upon layer of deception. The sorcery. The potions. The magnets that supposedly controlled your will." He stepped closer to the chair where she stood trembling. "But bodies do not lie, Sister. Bodies speak a truth that mouths cannot hide."

The torturer approached. His hands were impersonal as he guided Virginia toward the chair. She tried to resist, but her legs were already weak from the weeks of confinement and fear. She sank into the heavy oak frame, her body finding its shape in a depression made smooth by other bodies, other sufferers.

"Begin," Saraceno said.

The torturer pulled Virginia's arms behind her back with practiced efficiency. The leather straps came first, binding her wrists together so tightly that her hands began to tingle. She could feel the rope being threaded through the bindings, hear the creak of the pulley as he tested the mechanism.

"Your wrists, Sister," the torturer said. It was the first time he had spoken. His voice was quiet, utterly devoid of emotion.

Virginia shook her head. "No. I confess. I confess to everything. The affair. The child. I confess—"

"The cord," he said, as though she had not spoken.

The torturer began to pull. The rope tightened. Virginia felt her arms being drawn upward behind her back, felt the unnatural angle as her shoulders began to bear her weight. Then her feet left the ground.

The pain was immediate and absolute. Her shoulder joints screamed as her full weight hung from arms wrenched behind her back. It was not a sharp pain but a tearing sensation, as though her arms were being slowly pulled from their sockets, as though her shoulders were being systematically destroyed.

"The sorcery, Sister," Saraceno said. "Was it real?"

Virginia's breath came in gasps. The rope continued to pull, lifting her higher. Her toes pointed uselessly toward the stone floor, unable to find purchase, unable to relieve even an ounce of the terrible pressure on her shoulders.

"Yes. Yes, it was real. He used—"

The torturer released the rope.

Virginia plummeted. For one blessed instant, the pressure ceased. Then the rope caught with brutal force, jerking her body to a halt. Her shoulders made a sound, a wet, grinding pop, as the joints partially dislocated. The pain exploded through her entire body, white-hot and consuming.

She screamed.

"Or was it your own will?" Saraceno continued, his voice never changing. "Your own desire? Your own choice?"

"No," Virginia sobbed. "No, please. Stop. Stop."

Again, the rope pulled. Again, she was lifted, arms wrenched behind her, shoulders grinding in their sockets. Again, the drop. Again, the terrible, sickening jerk as the rope caught her weight.

Her vision went gray. The pain had become everything—thought, consciousness, selfhood. There was nothing in the universe but the tearing of her shoulders and the terrible knowledge that it could happen again.

"The truth, Sister."

"Yes!" she shrieked. "Yes. I chose. I chose him. I chose the affair. I chose it all."

The torturer lowered her slightly, allowing her toes to touch the ground. The relief was temporary. Virginia's entire body shook violently. She could feel her shoulders throbbing, swelling, the joints loose and damaged in ways that would never fully heal.

"The murder of Caterina de Meda," Saraceno said. "You claim Osio acted without your knowledge?"

"Yes," Virginia gasped, knowing this was a lie but desperate for him to believe it. "I tried to stop him."

The torturer pulled the rope again.

The second suspension shattered the last defenses of her will. Perhaps it was because she had already suffered once and knew exactly what was coming. Perhaps it was that her body could no longer bear additional trauma. But as she rose again, arms screaming behind her, something in Virginia de Leyva broke that could not be repaired.

She began to confess. The words poured from her like blood from a wound. Unstoppable, flooding, draining.

"I knew," she sobbed. "I knew he was going to kill her. Caterina threatened to expose us. She said she would go to the Cardinal. And I was afraid. I was so afraid of what would happen to me, so I said nothing. I let him kill her. I watched him strike her and I did nothing. I helped bury her body to protect myself. To protect my reputation."

Again, the drop. Again, her shoulders screamed as the rope caught her weight.

"And the child?" Saraceno asked.

"Mine," Virginia screamed. "Mine and Osio's. Alma Francesca. He took her. He took my daughter and I never held her again."

She could not continue. The pain had become everything. It had expanded beyond her body to consume the entire universe. She was nothing but pain. She was nothing but the tearing of her shoulders and the breaking of everything she had built her life to protect.

"Lower her," Saraceno said.

The torturer released the rope. Virginia collapsed onto the stone floor in a heap. As blood rushed back into her damaged shoulders, the sensation was almost as agonizing as the suspension had been, hot needles stabbing through her arms, her whole torso screaming with returning sensation.

She wept. She could do nothing but weep.

"You will sign a full confession," Saraceno said. "Detailing your affair with Gian Paolo Osio. Your willing participation in all acts. Your knowledge of and complicity in the death of Caterina de Meda. Your violation of your sacred vows and your sacred enclosure."

Virginia nodded. She had no strength left to resist; no will remaining to maintain any pretense.

The torturer had to help her stand, had to support her as he guided her toward the writing table positioned in an adjacent chamber. Her arms hung useless at her sides, the shoulders so damaged she could barely lift them.

Over the following hours, Virginia wrote. Her hands shook so badly that the script was barely legible, and each movement of her damaged shoulders sent fresh waves of agony through her body. But she wrote. Word by word, sentence by sentence, the confession poured from her destroyed will.

> *The affair with Gian Paolo Osio. Willing. Consenting. Passionate.*
>
> *The pregnancy and birth. Delivered in secret. The child placed in his custody. My daughter, whom I have rarely seen and rarely been permitted to hold.*

What will they tell Alma Francesca about her mother? That she was a whore. A murderess. A bride of Christ who chose the flesh. The child would grow up knowing her mother's name was synonymous with scandal, that to be the daughter of the Nun of Monza was to carry a stain that could never be washed clean.

> *The murder of Caterina de Meda. She threatened to expose us. Osio struck her down. I watched. I did nothing to stop him. I helped conceal her body. I lied about it to every authority.*

The letters to Father Arrigone. I wrote them in rage to destroy him, knowing the consequences that investigation would bring upon myself.

With each word committed to parchment, something in Virginia's chest that had been clenched for months finally began to release. The lie was ending. The pretense of bewitchment was crumbling into ash.

She was guilty. Absolutely, unambiguously, irredeemably guilty.

When she finished writing, her hands were so damaged she could barely hold the quill. The shoulders were swollen grotesquely, the joints loose and grinding. She knew they might never function properly again. Permanent damage. Permanent reminders of the price of her resistance.

Saraceno read the confession slowly, taking his time, allowing her to sit in silence and understand what she had just done. When he finished, he set the pages aside without comment. He did not smile. He did not congratulate her on her honesty. He simply nodded, as though she had finally confirmed what he had known from the beginning.

"You will return to your cell," he said. "Your case will be presented to the tribunal. Sentencing will be rendered in October."

Virginia was led back through the corridors of Santa Valeria, past cells where other women were imprisoned behind locked doors, past the chapel where evening prayers were being sung by voices untouched by torture. Her damaged arms hung useless at her sides, every movement sending fresh spears of pain through her shoulders.

In her cell, sparse, cold, with a single narrow cot and a bucket for her waste, Virginia lay down and stared at nothing. Her shoulders throbbed with a rhythm that seemed to echo the beating of her own heart. The pain was a constant, present thing, impossible to ignore, impossible to escape.

She had finally told the truth.

And the truth, she understood now, was far more damning than any lie could ever have been. Because the truth meant there was no excuse. No magic. No external force. Only Virginia de Leyva, making choice after choice, choosing passion over piety, choosing her own desires over the safety of innocents, choosing her own reputation over the life of a girl who had threatened to expose her.

In the darkness, she wept. Not for what would be done to her in October. But for what she had revealed herself to be.

A murderer. A deceiver. A woman who had sacrificed everything, including her daughter, to protect her own secret.

And the worst part was knowing that she deserved every moment of suffering that was to come.

* * *

SHE LEARNED OF his escape three days after her confession. Saraceno delivered the news with detachment: Gian Paolo Osio had been sighted in Venice, beyond Milanese jurisdiction, beyond reach. He would be tried and sentenced in absentia. He would never face the noose, never feel the Inquisitor's questions. He was free.

Virginia said nothing. What was there to say? She had destroyed herself protecting a man who had not even bothered to stay and watch her pay for her sins.

* * *

The 18th of October
Archbishop's Palace, Milan

THE ROOM WAS not a court. It was an antechamber to hell, disguised with velvet drapes and the smell of beeswax polish. Virginia stood alone in the center of the floor, her hands clasped before her to hide their trembling. She wore the plain black habit they had given her for this day, no longer the fine pleats of the Lady of Monza, but the rough wool of a sinner brought to account.

Cardinal Federico Borromeo sat behind a table that looked like a barricade. His face was a landscape of sorrow and iron. To his right stood the new prosecutor, Mamurio Lancillotti, who had replaced Saraceno in the spring. He held the parchment that contained her future.

"Virginia Maria de Leyva," the Cardinal began. His voice did not boom; it resonated, low and terrifying, the sound of a stone door sliding shut. "We have heard the testimonies. We have weighed the evidence. We have prayed for guidance."

He paused, and in the silence, Virginia heard the distant tolling of a bell. Midday. In Monza, the sisters would be gathering for Sext. Here, time seemed to have stopped.

"For the crimes of carnal sacrilege," Borromeo continued, his eyes never leaving hers. "For the facilitation of murder. For the corruption of your sisters and the violation of your sacred vows. For the scandal given to the faithful and the injury done to God."

He signaled to Lancillotti. The prosecutor stepped forward and unrolled the parchment. The sound of dry parchment crackling was louder than a scream in the quiet room.

"You are hereby sentenced to be immured within the House of Santa Valeria in Milan," Lancillotti's voice was precise, clinical. "For perpetual imprisonment. So long as you live."

Perpetual. The word hung in the air like a death knell. Not thirteen years. Not any fixed term. Forever. She would die in that cell, walled in like a corpse in a tomb.

"You will be confined to a small cell," Lancillotti read. "The door will be walled up with stone and mortar. A small aperture will remain for food and the sacraments. Another for light and air. You will see no human face. You will hear no human voice. You will speak to no one but your confessor."

Virginia felt the blood drain from her face, leaving her cold and hollow. The cell at Santa Valeria—that house of reformed prostitutes where the Cardinal had hidden her these past weeks. A deliberate humiliation. A Spanish noblewoman imprisoned among common whores.

“And... the others?” she whispered.

Lancillotti looked up. “Sister Benedetta Homati, Sister Candida Colomba, and Sister Silvia, having confessed their roles, are sentenced to perpetual imprisonment in separate cells at Santa Margherita. They will do penance for their sins in isolation, immured as you are.”

He paused, consulting the parchment. “Sister Ottavia Ricci succumbed to her wounds on the eighth day of December in the year of our Lord sixteen hundred and seven. May God have mercy on her soul.”

Virginia closed her eyes. Ottavia, dead. The girl who had carried letters and kept secrets and died in a river because Osio had beaten her skull until it cracked. Benedetta and Candida and Silvia, walled alive into stone tombs. The circle was broken, the conspiracy shattered into solitary shards.

But there was one name left. One question that burned in her throat like acid.

“And Gian Paolo?” she asked, her voice barely audible. “What of Signor Osio?”

The silence that followed was different. It was heavy, final. The Cardinal looked at Lancillotti. Lancillotti looked at the parchment, then back at Virginia.

“Gian Paolo Osio has been tried and sentenced *in absentia*,” he said.

“He escaped?” The word came out strangled.

“He fled to Venice. Then to Spain.” Lancillotti’s voice held no satisfaction, only a flat recitation of facts. “Beyond the reach of Milanese justice. He was sentenced to death by hanging, his body to be dismembered and displayed at the sites of his crimes. But the sentence cannot be executed while he remains in foreign lands.”

Virginia made no sound. The revelation struck her like a physical blow. Escaped. Free. The man who had climbed her garden wall, who had written letters soaked in false piety, who had killed for her and loved her and destroyed her—he was *free*. Living somewhere in Spain under a different name, breathing air, eating food, sleeping in a bed.

While she would be buried alive.

"It is over," Cardinal Borromeo said, not unkindly. "The bond of sin is broken. Now the work of repentance must begin."

He extended the quill. "Sign, Sister. Accept your penance."

Virginia moved forward. Her legs felt like wood. Her damaged shoulders throbbed where the strappado had torn the joints. Her hand, when she took the quill, belonged to a stranger. She looked at the parchment, at the words that walled her in and the words that set her lover free.

She signed her name—*Virginia Maria de Leyva*—and the scratch of the nib was the sound of the last earth falling on a coffin.

"Take her," the Cardinal said. "The cell is ready."

Two guards stepped forward. Virginia did not look at them. She did not look at the Cardinal or the prosecutor. She looked at nothing.

Gian Paolo Osio would live. He would walk under Spanish skies. He would grow old. Perhaps he would marry, sire legitimate children, die peacefully in his bed surrounded by priests murmuring prayers.

And she would rot in a stone box, alone in the dark, until her body was dust.

There was nothing left to see.

Chapter Fifteen
1609

January
The Convent of Santa Valeria, Milan

THE MASON'S HANDS were shaking.

Virginia knelt on the flagstones, watching him fumble with the first brick. He was perhaps fifty, with the broad shoulders and scarred fingers of a man who had worked with stone his entire life, and his hands should have been steady. But they trembled as he spread mortar across the threshold, and when he positioned the brick, it sat crooked. He had to pry it up and start again.

Vicar Monsignor Saraceno stood in the corridor, watching. "Proceed," he said.

The mason did not look up. He reset the brick, tapped it into place with his trowel, and reached for another. His breathing was audible in the silence. Quick and shallow. The breathing of a man trying not to be sick.

Virginia studied his face. He would not meet her eyes. His gaze stayed fixed on the work, on the bricks and mortar and the growing wall, as though she had already ceased to exist. Perhaps for him she had. Perhaps the only way he could do this was to pretend he was building something ordinary. A garden wall. A boundary marker. Anything except what it actually was.

The first row of bricks rose across the threshold.

The cell behind her measured six feet deep, four feet wide. She had already measured it. Had paced it out twice while the guards stood watching, their faces blank. Six feet. Four feet. Barely large enough to lie down. Not large enough to take three full steps in any direction. A straw pallet in the corner. A wooden bucket beside it. High above, a narrow window admitted gray January light that illuminated nothing useful.

Forever in this box.

Perpetual imprisonment, the sentence had said. So long as she lived. No end date. No promise of release. She would die here. The word 'perpetual' had no boundaries, no horizon. It simply stretched forward into darkness until her body gave out and they carried her corpse through whatever door they eventually broke through to retrieve it.

The mason worked the second row. His hands had steadied somewhat, though his face remained pale. He was young enough that he might live to be an old man, might tell his grandchildren someday about the time he walled up a nun alive. Would he tell them the truth? Or would he lie, and say it was just another job, just another wall, nothing that troubled his sleep or haunted his prayers?

The bricks rose past her knees.

Saraceno remained motionless in the corridor, a shadow in black robes, his pale face expressionless. He had been present at her torture seven months ago. Had watched them hoist her by the wrists with the strappado, her shoulders wrenching from their sockets as the rope bit into flesh. Then they had crushed the fingers of her left hand until she confessed the affair, the child, her knowledge of Caterina's murder.

He had shown no emotion then either. Had simply taken notes while she screamed, recording her confessions in his precise handwriting, asking clarifying questions when her answers were ambiguous. A clerk documenting testimony. That was all she had been to him. All she remained.

The wall rose past her waist.

Virginia watched the opening narrow and felt something unexpected. Not terror. Not despair. But a perverse relief that made her want to laugh. It was ending. All of it. The fear and the hiding and the desperate calculations. The performance of grief and innocence. The exhausting labor of being Sister Virginia Maria de Leyva, daughter of Spanish nobility, woman who had committed murder and fornication and every sin the Church could name. That woman was being sealed away. Buried. Erased.

What would be left when the wall was finished? What would exist in this darkness until death came?

She did not know. But God help her, part of her wanted to find out.

The mason paused to wipe sweat from his forehead. His hand left a smear of mortar across his temple. He did not seem to notice. He reached for another brick, positioned it, tapped it level. His movements were becoming more automatic. The body learning what the mind refused to accept.

Past her shoulders now.

Through the shrinking opening, Virginia could see the corridor beyond. Stone walls. Burning candles. Two young priests standing behind Saraceno, their faces carefully blank. One was perhaps twenty-five. The other younger still. They were watching her. Studying her. Memorizing this moment so they could describe it later. The walled-up nun. The woman buried alive. They would dine on this story for years.

She wanted to say something. Wanted to give them something memorable. Some final pronouncement they could repeat to prove they had been present at this extraordinary punishment. But no words came. Her throat was too dry. Her tongue felt thick and foreign in her mouth.

The mason worked another course. The opening was perhaps two feet square now. Just large enough to see faces. Just large enough to remember that human beings still existed beyond this threshold.

Not for long.

He reached into his leather satchel and withdrew something wrapped in cloth. When he unfolded it, Virginia saw a wooden frame perhaps two feet square, its edges fitted with metal rings. He positioned this in the remaining gap, securing it with mortar, working it into the brick until it sat flush. The aperture. Through this opening, food would be passed. Water. Clean garments when her current clothes rotted away. The Host when priests came to administer communion to a woman who had long since stopped believing any of it mattered.

Two feet. Enough to pass a bowl or a bucket. Enough to see faces. Enough to reach through and touch another human hand if anyone dared to offer such a merciful kindness. She doubted anyone would.

Perfect for keeping someone alive while ensuring they remained completely alone.

The mason built two more rows around the frame, sealing it into place. His hands were steady now. He had found his rhythm. Mortar, brick, tap. Mortar, brick, tap. The sound filled the cell, echoing off close walls. It would be the last sound she heard from the living world for how long? Days? Weeks? Months? Years? Decades? She had no way to know. No way to measure the time that stretched ahead until her body failed and she was finally released by death.

Virginia's shoulders ached with a deep, unrelenting pain where the strappado had torn the joints seven months ago. Her left hand throbbed where they had crushed her fingers afterward. The pain was constant now, a dull ache she had learned to ignore. But in this moment, kneeling and watching the world disappear behind brick, the pain seemed to sharpen. Her body's protest. Its insistence that this was wrong, that human beings were not meant to be sealed in stone boxes, that something fundamental was being violated even if she could not name what it was.

Too late for protest. Too late for anything except endurance.

The mason placed the final brick. Positioned it carefully. Tapped it level with three precise strikes of his trowel. The last opening disappeared. The corridor vanished. The light from the high window cut off as the wall completed itself, leaving only the thin shaft that penetrated through that distant opening above.

Gray January daylight now illuminated only the cell itself.

Virginia could see everything. The pallet in the corner. The wooden bucket beside it. The crucifix on the far wall. The stone floor beneath her knees. The walls stretching up toward the window, damp with moisture, their surface rough and scarred. She could see it all with perfect clarity, and the seeing was somehow worse than absolute darkness would have been. She could measure her prison with her eyes. Could count the paces that were all the space she possessed. Could see exactly how small her world had become.

She heard the mason moving beyond the wall. The scrape of his trowel smoothing mortar across the outer surface. The sound was muffled now, distant. Then the sound of tools being gathered. His footsteps retreating down the corridor. The younger priests murmuring something she could not make out. Saraceno's voice, cold and clear: "It is done."

More footsteps. Fainter now. A door opening somewhere distant. Closing. The thud resonating through stone, through her body until she felt it in her chest.

Silence.

Virginia remained kneeling. Her knees were numb from the cold flagstones, but she could not seem to move. Could not seem to do anything except listen to the sound of her own breathing, grotesquely loud in the enclosed space. In. Out. In. Out. The body's stupid insistence on continuing.

She should stand. Should explore the cell while the light remained. The pallet in the corner. The bucket beside it. The walls she could now see pressed close on all sides. But movement required decision, and decision required some sense of purpose, and she had none. No plan. No strategy. Nothing except the next breath and the one after that and the thousand breaths that would follow before anyone opened that aperture to pass food through.

How many years of breathing? How many decades?

The light through the high window was already beginning to fade. Evening approached. In a few hours, real darkness would come. Not the absolute black she had feared, but a dimness that would render the cell nearly invisible. She would spend the night seeing almost nothing. Would only know where the walls were when her hands found them.

How much light would that window admit once full darkness fell? Enough to see shapes? Or would it provide only the knowledge that light existed somewhere beyond her reach?

Virginia became aware of sound. Not from beyond the wall. From inside the cell. A dripping. Slow and irregular. Water seeping through stone somewhere above, falling to the floor in fat drops that echoed strangely in the confined space. Drip. Silence. Drip. Silence. The cell was damp. She had noticed it earlier but had not understood what it meant. She would be wet here. Cold and wet. Her clothes would mildew. Her skin would never fully dry. The damp would sink into her bones and stay there, a permanent chill that no blanket could dispel.

However many years God allowed her to live. All of them cold. All of them damp.

Virginia's knees screamed at her to move. She could not feel her feet. But she stayed kneeling for a long time, staring at the wall that no longer existed as an opening, seeing through it anyway to the corridor beyond, to Saraceno's pale face, to the younger priests who had watched her be sealed alive as though she were some sort of theatrical performance.

Slowly, forcing each movement, Virginia stood. Her knees cracked. Her feet were numb blocks of ice that barely supported her weight. She swayed, dizzy in the dim light, and had to put her hands out to catch herself. Her palms met cold stone. The wall to her left. She pressed against it, feeling the slight dampness, the rough texture of ancient mortar crumbling between dressed stone.

This wall was real. This cell was real. She was sealed inside it, alone, and no amount of wishing would change that fact.

She would die here. Might be decades from now. Might be next year. There was no way to know.

Virginia began to laugh.

It started as a small sound, almost a cough, but grew louder until it filled the cell, bouncing off stone and coming back to her distorted and strange. She laughed until her stomach hurt, until tears ran down her face, until the laughter twisted into something else and she was gasping for air, her chest heaving, her damaged left hand pressed against the wall to keep herself upright.

This was penance. This was justice. This was what she had earned through every choice that brought her here.

And the worst part, the part that made her want to scream or laugh or both, was that some small stubborn piece of her soul refused to regret it. Refused to wish she had chosen differently. Because those years with Gian Paolo, those stolen nights when she had felt alive for the first time since her father abandoned her to convent walls at thirteen, had been worth this. Had been worth everything.

God forgive her. She was irredeemable.

The laughter died. Virginia wiped her face with her sleeve and began moving through the dimming light, hands outstretched, learning the dimensions of her new world. Three steps to the far wall. Two steps to the side wall. The pallet there, exactly where she remembered. She sank onto it, pulled the thin blanket around her shoulders, and lay down on her side.

The straw crackled beneath her. The blanket smelled of mildew. Her breath misted in the cold air. The light through the high window was fading rapidly now, the gray growing dimmer, the cell retreating into shadow.

This was day one.

How many more days would there be? A thousand? Five thousand? Ten thousand? She had no way to count them. No way to mark the passage of time except the slow deterioration of her body, the gradual weakening that would eventually bring the mercy of death.

Virginia closed her eyes and waited for night to teach her what absolute isolation truly meant.

When they finally broke through that wall, whenever that was, however many years from now, they would find bones and rotted cloth. Perhaps a skull grinning in the darkness. The remains of Sister Virginia Maria de Leyva, daughter of Spanish nobility, lover, sinner, woman who had dared to choose passion over obedience.

Let them find her. Let them whisper her name as a warning to other women who might be tempted to step outside the lines drawn for them.

She would be dead by then. Beyond their judgment. Beyond their horror.

Beyond everything.

Epilogue

The 25th of September 1622
Convent of Santa Valeria, Milan

THE DOOR OPENED, and Virginia's first thought was that the light would kill her.

It poured through the threshold like molten silver, hot and weightless, striking her retinas with the force of a physical blow. She flinched, raising a hand that trembled with a fine, constant tremor she could not control. For nearly fourteen years, the only light had been the guttering flame of a tallow candle, rationed to her each evening for an hour of prayer. Now the sun itself assaulted her, needling through corneas that had forgotten how to contract, how to protect.

Her body remembered stone. Her skin, pale as something that had never lived, remembered the exact temperature of the cell walls, the precise texture of the stones that had pressed against her spine when she slept. Her muscles remembered five paces. Her lungs remembered filtered air. Everything else was betrayal.

"Step forward, Sister." The voice came from beyond the light, disembodied, male. The stonemason who had sealed her inside, now returned to release her. "You must cross the threshold yourself."

She tried. Her legs, after nearly fourteen years of walking only the length of her cell, of kneeling on stone, of sleeping on a wooden pallet no wider than her shoulders, refused the command. They spasmed, the muscles firing in the wrong sequence, and she would have fallen if the stonemason hadn't caught her elbow.

His hand on her arm was the first human touch she had felt since 1609. The sensation was obscene. His fingers were warm, calloused, alive. She jerked away, lost her balance, and collapsed against the doorframe. The stone bit into her shoulder where the habit had worn thin, and the pain was shocking—real, external, not the familiar ache of her own body consuming itself.

"Take your time," the stonemason said, but she heard the impatience in his voice. He wanted to be done with this, with her, with the scandal that had required nearly fourteen years of immurement rather than execution.

She forced herself upright, one hand pressed flat against the corridor wall. The stone was different here—smoother, warmer. Her palm recognized the difference instantly, the way a blind woman reads text. This stone had been touched by hundreds of women. Her cell walls had been touched only by her.

The first step was agony. Her knees, which had spent years supporting her weight in genuflection, protested the unfamiliar motion. Her spine, curved permanently forward from praying, from reading, from the sheer weight of stone pressing down on her soul, sent spikes of pain along her nerves. The second step was worse. The third brought nausea so severe she had to stop, breathing through her mouth, tasting the corridor's air, air that carried the scent of other bodies, of cooking food, of incense and lye soap and the living, breathing world she had left behind.

"Sister Virginia." A new voice, female, uncertain. "I am Sister Anna Maria."

She turned toward the sound, and the motion itself was disorienting. In her cell, turning meant facing the crucifix or the wooden bucket or the small shelf that had held her Book of Hours. Here, turning revealed a corridor stretching in both directions, honeycombed with doors, filled with light and sound and smells that made her head swim.

Sister Anna Maria was perhaps thirty, with a round face and hands that plucked at her rosary with the same nervous rhythm Ottavia had once employed. Virginia's breath caught at the similarity.

"Where is Sister Benedetta?" The name emerged as a rasp, her vocal cords protesting the unaccustomed exercise.

Anna Maria's face crumpled into an expression Virginia recognized from confessionals—the particular anguish of bearing news that will break someone already broken. "Sister Benedetta died nine years ago, Sister. In her walled cell at Santa Margherita in Monza, four years after her imprisonment began."

The words struck Virginia's chest with physical force. She gripped the wall, feeling stone warm from the sun where her cell walls had always been cold. Benedetta dead. The woman who had calculated every risk, who had documented their sins with the precision of a notary, who had told Virginia that survival required becoming stone yourself. Benedetta, who had never wept, never prayed, never broke. Dead in 1613, sealed in stone just as Virginia had been, but miles away in Monza, in the convent where this had all begun.

"Did she..." Virginia's voice failed. She tried again. "Did she speak of me?"

Anna Maria shook her head slowly. "She was alone in her cell, Sister. Walled away. But I heard she wrote until the end. Pages and pages. The Prioress burned them after."

Of course. Benedetta would have left documentation. She would have recorded everything—the dates, the times, the precise mechanics of how they had killed Caterina and disposed of her body. She would have written it all down, not as confession but as evidence, proof that she had understood the mathematics of their survival.

And it had all turned to ash.

"What of the others?" Virginia whispered. "Sister Candida. Sister Silvia."

Anna Maria's expression shifted—something that might have been relief. "Released today, Sister. By the same order that freed you. They were walled up at Santa Margherita these many years, too. The Cardinal ordered them freed this morning."

Virginia closed her eyes. Candida and Silvia, alive. Emerging from their own cells in Monza, blinking into the same September sunlight, breathing the same air of reluctant freedom. They had survived. All three of them had survived when Ottavia and Benedetta had not.

But they were in Monza, and Virginia was here in Milan. Separated by distance as they had been separated by stone. She would never see them again. The Church had made certain of that.

Benedetta dead in darkness. Ottavia dead in the first chaos of their arrests. Candida and Silvia released to whatever new prison awaited them in Monza. And

Virginia here, alone in Milan, with no one left who remembered what they had been before the walls closed in.

They moved through corridors memory had rendered larger. The stones of Santa Valeria were the same gray as Santa Margherita, quarried from the same hills above Bergamo, but they wore their age differently. These walls were polished by centuries of hands, smoothed by the passage of women who had walked these paths since the time of Charlemagne. Her rough hem glided over stone worn smooth by the devoted.

The Cardinal's reception room overlooked the cloister garden, where autumn roses bloomed in defiance of the coming winter. Virginia stood before the man who held her future in his ringed hands—Cardinal Borromeo himself, the powerful churchman who had first immured her and now finally ordered her release.

He did not rise. His face carried the polished certainty of those who have never doubted their own righteousness.

"Sister Virginia," he said. "Your sentence is complete. The Church has shown you mercy."

Mercy. The word settled in her chest like a stone. Had she received mercy at thirteen when they forced her into this habit to seize her inheritance? Had she received mercy at thirty-three, when they walled her into darkness rather than burn her as a witch?

"Your family's estates have been confiscated," the Cardinal continued. "The de Leyva name is retired. You will live here at Santa Valeria, under supervision. You may attend Mass with the community. You may walk in the garden for one hour each afternoon."

She understood. Confined first by vows. Then by stone. Now by these careful boundaries, these measured permissions that might be revoked at any moment. Forty-six years old, and every moment of her life had been bargained away, bartered, seized by others' hands.

"My daughter," she whispered, the words emerging against her will.

The Cardinal's face tightened. "She lives. She was raised by Osio's mother, as arranged. She is married now. A respectable woman in Bergamo. She knows nothing of her origins, and it will remain so."

Alma Francesca. The child Virginia had delivered in secret, had held for one hour before they took her away. Old enough now to be married. Living a life built on the lie that her mother had been a saint, not a murderer.

"She is happy," the Cardinal added, as if this were compensation.

Virginia closed her eyes. The darkness behind her lids was familiar, the only place that had never betrayed her. In darkness, she had learned to survive. In darkness, she had become something that could endure stone and silence and the memory of blood.

The Cardinal rose, signaling the interview's end. "You will be assigned duties. Light work, given your condition. The infirmary, perhaps. Sister Anna Maria will show you to your chamber."

He left her then, and she stood alone in the reception room, staring at the autumn roses that bloomed in defiance of coming winter. The sun had moved lower in the sky, casting long shadows across the cloister, and she realized with a start that she had been standing for nearly an hour—longer than she had stood in nearly fourteen years. Her legs trembled. Her vision blurred. But she remained upright, as she had learned to remain upright through decades of impossible endurance.

Anna Maria touched her shoulder. "Sister?"

Virginia turned toward the door, her habit whispering against stone. As she passed the window, she saw her reflection in the glass—gaunt face, white hair cut short as a penitent's, spine curved into a permanent stoop. She looked nothing like the woman who had stood in the scriptorium window twenty-four years ago, watching Gian Paolo stroll through his garden in burgundy silk.

Her chamber was on the ground floor. Four walls and a narrow cot and a crucifix that looked exactly like the one she had stared at for nearly fourteen years. The only difference was the window, which faced the courtyard rather than an interior wall.

She stood at that window as darkness fell, watching the nuns walk their meditations, their habits rustling like leaves, their voices murmuring prayers she had once believed could save her. The bells rang for Compline, and the sound pierced her chest with the same sharpness it had possessed when she was sixteen and new to the convent, when she had believed that God's love would be enough to fill the hollowness her father's ambition had carved in her heart.

She thought of Benedetta, dead nine years in her walled cell at Santa Margherita, her documentation burned.

She thought of Ottavia, dead before the trials even began, her heart broken.

She thought of Candida and Silvia, somewhere in Monza, emerging today from their own stone tombs into whatever new confinement the Church had prepared for them.

She thought of the servants, Domenico and Isabetta, who had carried letters and lies between her world and Gian Paolo's, who had paid with their safety for her sins.

She thought of Caterina, whose blood had brought it all—the walls, the silence, the survival of those who had killed her. Caterina, who had been innocent. Who had been desperate enough to threaten Virginia's secrets. Who had been silenced not with mercy but with the kind of violence that left no room for forgiveness.

She thought of Father Arrigone, sentenced to the galleys and banishment. Had he rowed himself to death in those ships? Had he survived to live out his years in exile? She would never know.

And she thought of Gian Paolo. She had spent nearly fourteen years not knowing what had become of him. Was he alive? Dead? Living under a false name somewhere beyond Milan's reach? She would never know. The Cardinal had told her nothing, and she had not dared to ask. Perhaps he was wealthy, remarried, father to children who bore his name without shame. Perhaps he had been caught, executed, his body left to rot as a warning to others.

She would die without knowing.

The moon rose over Milan, pale and indifferent to all the small cruelties that had been wrought in its light. The convent slept. The nuns dreamed their innocent dreams. And Virginia remained at the window, her forehead pressed against cold glass, watching a world that had moved on without her.

She was forty-six years old. She had been imprisoned for more than two decades—first by vows taken at thirteen, then by stone walls at thirty-three. She would live here, in this convent, until her body finally surrendered to the slow destruction that had begun the day she crossed the threshold of Santa Margherita.

When they buried her in the convent cemetery, beneath a simple stone that bore only her religious name, no one would remember that Virginia de Leyva had ever existed at all. No one would know about the woman who had loved so fiercely that it had poisoned everything it touched. No one would speak of the blood. The lies. The careful calculations of survival that had devoured her from the inside.

She would be forgotten as completely as if she had never lived.

And perhaps, Virginia thought as the moon climbed higher and the bells fell silent, that was mercy after all.

Afterword

The story of Virginia de Leyva—the Nun of Monza—remains one of the most scandalous episodes in Counter-Reformation Italy. While I have endeavored to remain faithful to the documented historical record, the nature of this story required creative interpretation where the archives fall silent. This afterword distinguishes between what we know happened and the choices I made as a novelist.

What Became of Sister Virginia

On October 18, 1608, Sister Virginia Maria de Leyva was sentenced to be walled up alive—*murata viva*—for thirteen years in the monastery of Santa Valeria in Milan. Her cell measured approximately nine feet by four feet, a space barely large enough to lie down. She was forbidden from participating in communal prayers, meals, or any contact with other nuns or the outside world. For more than a decade, she lived in near-total isolation, a punishment designed to break both body and spirit.

Yet what emerged from that tomb was unexpected. When Virginia was released in 1622, Cardinal Borromeo witnessed a transformation that impressed even that stern reformer. Her repentance had taken on what contemporaries described as "an entranced, mystical quality". The woman who had scandalized the Church became a devoted servant of its most marginalized souls.

Virginia spent the remaining twenty-eight years of her life at Santa Valeria, working among the prostitutes and fallen women housed there. She became a kind of spiritual mother to these women, offering them the compassion she herself had been denied. Contemporary accounts describe her in her later years as "old and bent, emaciated and venerable," yet still fiercely proud of her de Leyva blood.

She survived the great plague that devastated Milan and died in 1650 at the age of seventy-four. Whether her transformation was genuine spiritual awakening or the survival strategy of a woman who had learned to adapt to impossible circumstances, we cannot know. Perhaps it was both.

The Fate of Gian Paolo Osio

History is less certain about what became of Gian Paolo Osio. The documented facts end abruptly: he was arrested on Carnival day, February 27, 1607, at the arms fair in Pavia. He was imprisoned in Pavia Castle, from which he subsequently escaped. In 1607, he was sentenced to death in absentia by quartering. His properties in Monza were confiscated and destroyed.

Beyond this point, the historical record fractures into legend and rumor. One popular tradition holds that he sought refuge with Senator Ludovico Taverna in Milan and was murdered in the cellar of Taverna's palazzo (now Palazzo Isimbardi), where his body was allegedly walled up. However, Italian sources describe this as "*una leggenda popolare*"—a popular legend—and note that historical sources "do not agree on the reasons" for his supposed death.

In crafting this novel, I chose to follow the alternative interpretation: that Osio successfully escaped Spanish Milan's jurisdiction and lived out his days as a free man in another territory, likely Venice. This choice reflects both the historical uncertainty and a thematic consideration. A man of Osio's connections, intelligence, and resources would have known that flight, not confrontation, offered his best chance of survival. That the historical record contains no confirmed account of his capture or execution suggests he may well have succeeded.

The popular ghost stories about his spirit haunting Palazzo Isimbardi tell us more about how subsequent generations needed to believe in his punishment than about what actually occurred.

Paolo Arrigone

The priest Paolo Arrigone was interrogated from November 19, 1607, until March 27, 1608. He was subjected to torture, and even his doorman and the doorman's wife were shown the instruments of torture to compel testimony against him. Beyond this, the historical record provides no clear indication of his final sentence or fate. This silence is itself telling—the Church often preferred to handle its own scandals quietly, and a disgraced priest might simply disappear into a distant monastery or prison without further documentation.

Alma Francesca Margherita

Osio legally acknowledged his daughter Alma Francesca Margherita as his illegitimate child in 1605, and she lived with him before his arrest. What became of her after her father's escape remains unknown. In an age when illegitimate daughters of disgraced noblemen had few options, her fate was likely determined by whichever relatives could be persuaded to take responsibility for her—or by the Church institutions that housed inconvenient women.

A Note on Sources and Creative Choices

The trial records, witness testimonies, and ecclesiastical correspondence that documented this scandal have provided the skeleton of this story. Where I have taken creative liberty is in the flesh I have added to those bones: the private conversations, the interior thoughts, the emotional textures of these lives. We know what Virginia and Osio did; we can only imagine why, and how it felt to do it.

I have also made choices about emphasis and interpretation. Some accounts portray Virginia primarily as a victim—forced into the convent, seduced and manipulated by an older man. Others cast her as the primary instigator, a calculating woman who used her noble status to commit crimes with impunity. The truth, as is so often the case, likely lies in the complicated space between. I have tried to portray her as both: a woman denied agency who seized it in the only ways available to her, and who paid a terrible price for that seizure.

What remains undisputed is that this scandal rocked Counter-Reformation Italy, that it exposed the rot beneath the surface of enforced religious vows, and that it raised questions about power, gender, and justice that remain relevant four centuries later.

The house next to Santa Margherita where Osio lived was demolished after his flight. The site became a popular venue for ball games, and according to local tradition, any ball that went over the convent wall was never returned. It's a small detail, but one that captures how communities process scandal—by quite literally making a game of it, while ensuring the walls that should have prevented the transgression remain inviolate.

Sister Virginia's story has inspired plays, films, and novels for centuries, most famously appearing in Alessandro Manzoni's *The Betrothed* as "the Nun of Monza." Each age has found in her something that speaks to its own concerns. For our time, perhaps it is the recognition that even within the most rigid systems of control, human desire and will find ways to assert themselves—and that the price of that assertion is often paid in full.

Calgary, Alberta
February 2026

A Word from the Author

Thank you for journeying with me through Virginia Maria's tumultuous life. Bringing her story from the shadows of history into your hands has been a labor of love that consumed years of research, countless revisions, and an unwavering commitment to honoring the truth of her extraordinary existence.

If this novel moved you—whether it sparked outrage at the injustices Virginia endured, compassion for her impossible choices, or simply kept you turning pages late into the night—I would be deeply grateful if you would consider leaving a review. As an independent historical novelist, reader reviews are the lifeblood of my work. They help other readers discover stories like Virginia's that might otherwise remain forgotten. Each review, no matter how brief, amplifies voices from the past that deserve to be heard and helps me continue unearthing these hidden histories.

Your honest thoughts matter more than you might realize. A few sentences about what resonated with you, which characters captured your imagination, or how this story changed your perspective can make all the difference to both fellow readers searching for their next book and to authors like me who pour our hearts into illuminating these forgotten corners of history. Reviews on Amazon, Goodreads, or wherever you discovered this book help ensure that more stories of remarkable women like Virginia Maria de Leyva find their way into the world.

Thank you for reading, for caring about these historical voices, and for helping keep their stories alive.

With gratitude,

Mirella Patzer

Book Club Questions

1. **Agency and Coercion**: Virginia was forced into the convent at age thirteen by her father. To what extent does this coercion absolve her of responsibility for her later actions? At what point does a victim become an agent of her own choices?

2. **The Price of Silence**: Multiple characters—Ferrari, Roncino, Domenico—knew about crimes but remained silent out of fear or self-preservation. Were their choices to stay silent morally defensible? What would you have done in their positions?

3. **Complicity and Guilt**: Sister Benedetta, Ottavia, Candida, and Silvia all participated in or enabled Virginia's affair and the subsequent murders. How do you apportion guilt among the various accomplices? Are some more culpable than others?

4. **Power and Privilege**: How does Virginia's noble status as a de Leyva shape the story? Would events have unfolded differently if she had been from a common family? How do class and privilege function as both protection and prison in this narrative?

5. **Transformation or Performance**: After her release from immurement, Virginia became a devoted servant to prostitutes and fallen women, living a life of apparent sanctity for twenty-eight years. Do you believe her transformation was genuine spiritual awakening, calculated survival, or something in between? What does it mean to "repent" after such crimes?

6. **The Nature of Love**: Was the relationship between Virginia and Gian Paolo genuine love, obsessive passion, mutual exploitation, or some combination? How did their affair change over the course of the story, particularly as bodies began to accumulate?

7. **Systems of Control**: The novel exposes the consequences of forcing unwilling women into religious life. What does this story reveal about how institutional systems—religious, political, familial—control women's bodies and choices? What parallels, if any, do you see with contemporary issues?

8. **Escalation of Crime**: The story shows how Virginia and Gian Paolo move from a forbidden affair to pregnancy to murder. Trace the escalation of their crimes. At what point could they have stopped? Was there a moment when their doom became inevitable?

9. **Justice and Expediency**: Governor Fuentes knows about Osio's crimes but delays action for political reasons. Captain Niguarda is frustrated by this calculated approach to justice. When, if ever, is it acceptable to compromise justice for political stability? Does the novel suggest that "reasons of State" are ever legitimate?

10. **Victim, Villain, or Both**: By the end of the novel, how do you view Virginia? Has the author successfully portrayed her as a complex figure who is simultaneously victim and perpetrator, or does she lean more heavily toward one characterization? How did your opinion of her change throughout the story?

Bonus Question for Historical Context: Knowing that this story is based on actual events from 1598-1608, what does it reveal about Counter-Reformation Italy? How might this scandal have challenged or reinforced contemporary beliefs about women, religious authority, and social order?

About the Author

Mirella Patzer is a Canadian author who brings the rich tapestry of Italian history to life through compelling historical fiction. Drawing upon her heritage as a first-generation Italian Canadian, she crafts authentic stories that bridge the gap between past and present.

Based in Calgary, Alberta, Mirella has always been captivated by the courage, passion, and resilience of individuals navigating the complexities of their times. Her deep connection to Italian culture, combined with meticulous research, allows her to create immersive worlds where readers can experience the atmosphere and emotions of historical Italy. Her work explores themes of justice, survival, and the enduring power of truth, while celebrating the strength of women who refuse to be silenced.

When not writing, Mirella enjoys researching the hidden stories that continue to inspire her work. She can often be found spending time with her family, cooking, reading, or enjoying a good dose of Netflix.

For more information about Mirella Patzer and her upcoming releases, visit www.mirellapatzer.com or follow her on Facebook, Instagram, TikTok, and Threads

www.ingramcontent.com/pod-product-compliance
Lightning Source LLC
LaVergne TN
LVHW041050080826
845145LV00007B/1522